ELEGY

of a

RIVER
SHAMAN

a novel

FANG QI

看三峽
看長江
看中國

Behold the Three Gorges.

Behold the mighty Yangzi River.

Behold the very crucible of Chinese civilization!

ELEGY

of a

RIVER
SHAMAN

a novel

FANG QI

Translated by Norman Harry Rothschild and Meng Fanjun

MerwinAsia
Portland, Maine

MerwinAsia
59 West St., Unit 3W
Portland, ME 04102
USA

Library of Congress Control Number: 2016952966

Distributed by the University of Hawaii Press

978-1-937385-38-5 (Paperback)
978-1-937385-39-2 (Cloth)

The paper used in this publication meets the minimum requirements
of the American National Standard for Information Services—
Permanence of Paper for Printed Library Materials,
ANSI/NISO Z39 / 48-1992

Author's Introduction by Fang Qi

One day during the decade I spent gathering folklore and shamanic chants in the mountains, I saw jutting out from a cliff a huge stone shaped like a dragon's head with an opened mouth, looking down on the valley and fields below; layers of sedimentary rock made it appear as though the suffering dragon immured in the cliff face were racked in a cangue. A local shaman told me that the gods on high had imprisoned the water dragon in the cliff because the temperamental creature, filled with wild-hearted ambition, had created a great flood, wrecking fields and destroying villages. Many legends swirling about the middle and upper reaches of the Yangzi River involve wicked dragons wreaking havoc, causing destructive floods or disastrous droughts. While the mythological interpretations of this region's karst topography—its gorges, crags, and underground grottoes—do not concern geologists, they were for me a source of tremendous inspiration.

The Three Gorges region, the setting of this novel, is not just the location of my hometown; it is the former homeland of an ancient Asian people, a vast primitive wildlands where civilization improbably sprouted and where human wisdom first was accumulated. Now, several millennia later, even after the industrial tide had swept through the region, an aura of its primitive wildness and mystery remains. Perhaps the internet and science will offer new tools and approaches that make it possible to unravel some of these mysteries.

Contemplating the Yangzi River's boundless vitality, I cannot but sigh with humility, reflecting upon my own fleeting and limited existence.

Legend has it that long ago villagers and creatures fled together from a terrible drought. After who knows how many exhausting days of wandering, they stumbled upon a creek where the water still flowed. Everyone clustered around, parched and eager to drink. Butterflies swarmed, forming a bucket brigade to irrigate the dried-out forest: in pairs, myriad butterflies flew skyward, keeping a regular distance from each other, making sure not a single precious drop of water was lost.

Returning from a tour of inspection, the Celestial Emperor saw mist rising from the forest, taking the shape of a beautiful rainbow. Sighing, he said to the other gods, "Look, the greater creatures are not working together; only the small butterflies cooperate to get the job done." Therefore, he issued an imperial decree, "Whenever butterflies carry water, Heaven shall send down rain." Then and there the wind rose and thunder rumbled, and soon a saturating rain poured down from the heavens. The fields and forests greened, becoming once more lush and luxuriant; the people and animals returned to their homes.

Nowadays some old folk still say that whenever butterflies cluster at a creek's margin to fetch water, timely rains will come to alleviate the drought. Unavoidably, some butterflies will fall to the ground and die, flitting and twitching in final exhausted spasms. This is the epic poetry of the weak. I spent seven years writing this book, seven years flitting between heaven and earth, plagued by anxiety and uneasiness. Opening wide my hidden wings, I join the persevering butterflies in their never-ending struggle to carry healing waters.

Truth is like the sun: if you look directly at its scintillating light, you'll be blinded. Thus, there are those who commit their lives to confronting and earnestly observing the "radiance of the sun," then conveying their impressions and feelings to others. Musicians convey and express these impressions through the medium of notes and rhythm; artists depict them with line and color; and writers render them through narrative and plot.

The first vestiges of human civilization can be traced to the banks of the Three Gorges. One bearing witness to the grandeur, beauty, and raw power of the scorching sun set above the violent roar of rapids churning through the Yangzi's meandering gorges cannot help but be imbued with a sense of awe and wonder.

I offer sincere and gracious thanks to Professors Norman Harry Rothschild and Meng Fanjun for taking on this tremendous challenge and doggedly endeavoring to translate this novel into English. Thanks are also due to Tang Wanghu and Kevin Yan for their ongoing support and promotion.

And, of course, thanks to the shamans and loremasters for their chants and incantations. Without them, there would be no story.

Fang Qi
July 19, 2015

ELEGY

of a

RIVER
SHAMAN

a novel

FANG QI

Prologue

Once again, a banner rose over the village. Xia Qifa thrust his palms aloft, his fingers gathered in a mudra, taking the form of a crouching tiger. Completing the mudra, he forcefully blew the oxhorn. His chants pierced the dense clouds and mists shrouding the Yangzi River—that meandering creature that carved its course through the gorges, exiting at the Gate of the Thunderous One-Footed Dragon, Kuimen—echoing in the halls of the seventy-two temples:

> *O celestial White Tiger,*
> *Gliding across the firmament with your long loping stride,*
> *Covering endless stretches of road.*
> *O gorger on flesh and hide,*
> *Forests splinter and earth sunders in your terrible wake.*

For as long as the elders could recall, the village had been controlled by invisible hands, the evidence of which was that the flag, without wind at dead noon, now moved spontaneously, twisting and fluttering. Faces soaked in perspiration, villagers knelt on the scorched earth, watching and waiting for the tassels on the fringe of the banner to first sway, then twist their way into knots as the banner rose.

Presiding over this grand sacrifice was Xia Qifa, chief *tima*, a shaman revered above all other men in these parts. To welcome his tiger ancestor, the *tima*, crowned with a feathered crest, gyrated as he tinkled his bell, his skirts sweeping the dusty ground.

Five years earlier, when the reaches of the Yangzi River were in the throes of a similar drought, county official Pock-faced Zhang, pistol in hand, stood in Xia Qifa's yard and said politely, "I've heard you possess great magical powers. You have three days to make the dragon king bring rain. If you succeed, you'll be rewarded generously. If you fail, you'll be shot!" With these words, he fired the pistol into a straw effigy of the wicked dragon, making smoke issue from the parched stalks. As cumbersome darkness receded and the first rays of the sun broke forth like so many unleashed arrows, Xia Qifa, thirty-seventh in the family line of *timas*, led his disciples to fashion an earthen altar. To the blowing of horns and beating of drums, the *tima* donned his bird-shaped crest and red skirt, like a phoenix readying for battle. Under the unfurled banner of their tiger ancestor, he led a procession of hundreds on a march to Baizhang Valley to a dark cave of unfathomable depth wherein dwelled the dragon king's third prince, a volatile creature who capriciously swallowed rivers and roiled oceans. When the mercurial dragon tired of this sport, he disgorged the waters into the cave bottom, creating the underground river that flowed all the way to the Eastern Sea.

At the mouth of the cave, gazing amid the rising incense smoke at the whirling currents, an anxious Xia Qifa burned sacrificial paper. Beside him, disciples fired their guns into the maw of the cave, the reports giving off a terrifying echo.

It was the *tima*'s duty to subdue the wicked dragon. Once upon a time, a figure clad in golden armor appeared to his first Xia ancestor in a dream, announcing, "I, the Immortal Tiger, have come to transmit to you the mystical arts of the *tima*." Thus, the ancestors of the Xia family were taught how to exorcise demons and defeat dragons. Generation after generation of Xia shamans, sometimes in triumph, sometimes in defeat, waged battles against the dragon prince. These victories and failures were faithfully recorded in local annals: so it was known that the first Xia ancestor had perished in mortal combat with the dragon. In this fiercest of battles, as passed down in local lore, two straw sandals outside the cave rose from the ground, attacking one another like fighting cocks! The disciple assigned to beat the drum was so dumbfounded that he forgot his duty. Just at that instant the *tima*, exhausted yet victorious, emerged from the cave dragging the wicked dragon by the beast's horns. The sudden cessation of the drumbeat enabled the crafty creature to shake free and surge back into the cave. Then, with a terrible explosion, a mighty gust of thick smoke and flame erupted from the mouth of the cave, incinerating the first ancestor, leaving behind only a hero's name.

During that unforgettable summer of 1929, Xia Qifa approached the vast mouth of the cave, hiking his worn skirt up to his knees; like his first ancestor he removed his straw sandals. Grasping a charm in one hand and holding aloft his sword in the other, his face a mask of otherworldly isolation, he waded through the churning torrent into the cavernous darkness. People waited outside, as the cave exhaled a violent wind. They heard an ear-splitting cacophony, like the clamor of two armies of ten thousand engaged in battle. At the height of the fury, the nervous throng faintly glimpsed a huge tiger paw within the cave. Knowing this to be the supernatural form of Xia Qifa, some dared hope he might overcome his foe. The battle raged on; then, lo and behold, a heavy mass of cloud floated across the baking firmament. The skies sundered, bringing a sudden thunderstorm. O splendid *tima*! The ox-skin drums of the shaman's disciples below kept time with the thunder booming above, and the world was saturated in a salubrious downpour. Garments tattered beyond recognition but wearing an expression of utter serenity, Xia Qifa strode out of the cave. Naturally, this hard-fought victory over the dragon brought him great fame.

And yet five years later, the calamity-bringing dragon sought to swallow the river once again, prompting Xia Qifa to don his shamans' robes and straw rain poncho to fight the wicked creature a second time. Swaying like a serpent, flitting like a bird, bowl of water in hand, he moved forward.

Floating in the war-stricken wilderness, strains of an ancient ode hung in the air:

> O Great King Immortal Tiger,
> I humbly follow your path
> As you rage ever forward.
> If you walk the path to drought, I follow,
> If you find a road to water, I follow.

In the aftermath of the flood, Bodhisattva-King Yu the Great had used the same strange swaying gait to beg the intercession of spirits to help vanquish the dragon and quell the deluge. So now under the yellow banner of his ancestors, Xia Qifa, thirty-seventh *tima* in the illustrious Xia line, gracefully staggered, following the cryptic divine paces, shaking his bronze bell to summon the Immortal Tiger. On this day, however, the banner hung motionless.

Sweat coursing down, Xia Qifa realized this was the most formidable test he had confronted. He looked closer at the pottery bowl in one hand, carefully scrutinizing the water. Gloomily, the befuddled shaman murmured, "The hidden river . . ." Why, with the same movements and paces, the same prayers and spells, could he not call forth that set of hands to release the winds and unfurl the flag? After repeatedly consulting the trigrams of the *Book of Changes*, the shaman darkly pronounced, "The dragon prince has claimed that swallowing the river is not a crime. He's filed a lawsuit in the Celestial Court against the Immortal Tiger." Puzzled and weary, the pale *tima* choked out the following words, "Matters in the Heavenly Court can drag on for decades—a day up in the heavens is a year down on earth. We mortals can't wait for our Tiger ancestor to resolve his lawsuit. We need to move now and find a new place to settle. Shoulder your carrying poles and gather your belongings . . ." Though over the centuries the Tribe of the Tiger had moved countless times, this was the first time that the men and women of the village had relocated.

Those who trusted the *tima* gathered all they could carry and left; those who couldn't bear to pull up stakes remained to face whatever came. Cloth parcels fastened to their waists, a hungry exodus followed the shaman.

Rifle slung over his shoulder and straw sandals on his feet, Li Diezhu led his family, following the refugees eastward along the dried-out bed of the Guandu River. Xia Qifa, ancestral Tiger staff in hand, the mystical instruments of generations of shamans bundled in a rucksack, moved solemnly ahead of the miserable villagers. A melancholy chant slowly flowed from his lips—

> *Father-in-law takes to the road,*
> *Mother-in-law takes to the road.*
> *The sun rises, off we go.*
> *The suns sets, we rest our weary feet.*
> *Walking trails where the deer run.*
> *Passing places where the monkeys jump.*
> *Climbing cliffs where the mountain men walk,*
> *Wandering shores where the crabs crawl.*

In 1934, 3,936 years after Yu the Great quelled the flood dragon and came to rule China, the region was so severely drought-stricken that the land burned, crops died, and wells dried up. The sun hung in the sky, a relentless blazing fireball that left people squinting and dizzy. Observing bamboo trigrams to seek the guidance of the spirits, the last *tima* of the Three Gorges region of the Yangzi River worried day and night over the starving refugees in his charge. Guided by birdsong and the coloration of river shrimp, the weary, tattered band moved toward the sunrise. To the accompaniment of the homespun chants from the village they had left behind, they clambered over Nanmuya Hill, passing through Azure Dragon Hamlet, Shi Family Embankment, and other villages. So they drifted, dancing in the breeze like a handful of windsown seeds, borne on a faraway journey to they knew not where.

Part I

Chapter One

I

Standing atop the ridge, Li Diezhu craned his neck and howled, *"Waoooh!... Waoooh!... Waooo!... Waoooooooh!"* The howling echoed in the mountains and valleys before dying in faraway skies. Soon, the faint chants of the mountainfolk resounded from distant ridges:

> *Woe, wei-ya!*
> *Moving mountains is our plight in this bitter life.*
> *Woe, wei-ya!*
> *Yet we never lose heart and abandon ourselves to strife.*
> *Woe, wei-ya!*

Following footpaths of tigers, generation upon generation of mountainfolk made a living entering the dense forest, seeking precious goldthread rhizome. Here and there, one might run across a ramshackle lean-to, an enclosure for cultivating the wild rhizomes. Li Diezhu cut down trees, put up a low wooden shed, and fenced in a patch, perhaps fifty feet by seventy, to grow goldthread. At daybreak, he squatted on his plot, clearing the grass. Goldthread, folks said, possessed powerful curative properties and was far more valuable than rice. According to the Gazetteer of Fengjie, long ago two mountainfolk drank essence of goldthread daily: one ascended to heaven as an immortal, and the other cultivated internal alchemy as a Daoist and lived more than a hundred years. Wealthy chief of the tenth ward, Qin Zhanyun, who had lived for more than thirty years on a rich plot overlooking Inkblack Creek, boasted that while some may have drowned or perished in accidents, not a single soul under his magistracy had ever died of disease. Such was the potency of goldthread.

People of the region grew potatoes and corn along the margins of the primeval forest. Soil was so rich that with neither irrigation nor fertilization crops ripened of themselves. On a ridge not far from the Li family's hut, Li Diezhu cleared the land to farm potatoes.

Harvest was coming. Farmers united to drive off the wild beasts that destroyed their crops. By day, their blood-curdling howls frightened the creatures away; by night, they lit torches and defended their crops. Li Diezhu put up a birds' nest-like tree stand overlooking his field and jealously guarded his potatoes day and night.

At noon one day, after swallowing several mouthfuls of corn liquor, he responded to the ululations of fellow mountain farmers near and far, loosing a deafening yowl. Li Diezhu listened to the echoes from fellow farmers, then, exhausted by his long vigil, settled in his lean-to and slept. The alarm bark of his hunting dog cut through the webs of sleep. He burst forth to find his entire field a tumultuous mess of upturned earth: rapacious wild boars had devoured every last potato, leaving only trampled plants and leaves. Cudgeling his head in sorrow and fury, he roared like a wounded tiger. The *"Aooooow!... Aoooww!"* of his impotent fury echoed mockingly off the mountains. All his bitter toil had come to naught. Alternating between despondency and rage, grinding his teeth, Li Diezhu trod slowly homeward, pondering what to say to his family.

Lo and behold, a pack of wild boars crashed out of the underbrush and made straight for him. Leading a motley pack of two-dozen wild hogs, a massive boar, a monster staunch as a bullock, with bristles upright, sharp-tipped ears, red brows, green eyes, and a protruding jaw, bore down on Li Diezhu!

Recklessly, with a snort and a squeal for a battle cry, the lead boar surged forward, his dagger-like tusks poised to gore, skin so thick and hard that even a leopard would hesitate to confront him. With a steep escarpment to the right and a deep valley to the left, Li Diezhu had no time to escape and no place to hide. With blood-shot eyes, he fired a single shot from his homemade rifle at the oncoming boar. However, the gunpowder must have been too damp: nothing happened. Panic-stricken, feeling as though his soul had fled his body, he thumped his gunstock on the ground, screaming frantically. The impact prompted the gun to fire skyward. Spooked, the great bristled creature, now almost on top of Li Diezhu, lost his bearings, and, staggering, flung itself into the deep gorge. The other boars, thinking this the best way to survive, followed their leader, one after another plunging down the escarpment. Sodden with rivulets of sweat, Li Diezhu slumped to the ground, only regaining his wits and rising a full hour later. Surveying the surrounding mountains, he sank back to his knees, kowtowing three times in each of the four directions.

Midnight in the deserted, pitch-dark heart of the mountains witnessed Li Diezhu and wife Tao Jiuxiang, clad in sackcloth, heads swathed in blue turbans, piety etched on their faces, burning incense, lighting candles, and offering buckwheat bread to the gods—the mountain gods, the tree deities, the hunting gods, the Earth god, the White Tiger, and others—thanking them for their generous blessings that had enabled Li Diezhu to survive.

Early the following morning, Li Diezhu, armed with gun, machete, and axe, led his wife and Mawu, his eldest son, to the bottom of the valley. A heap of dead wild boars lay jackstrawed at the bottom of the escarpment. Li Diezhu ran to and fro, cutting tree branches as poles and vines for ropes to fashion a litter. With the litter, Mawu and Tao Jiuxiang carried one of the boars up from the valley, while he carried a second in his woven bamboo back-basket. It was slow, arduous work. After two exhausting days, seven dead boars remained.

Running to the homesteads of mountain neighbors, Tao Jiuxiang called out, "Sun Fuwa, come to the bottom of the crag and fetch one of the wild pigs my man killed! Hurry! . . . Second Lady Zhou, come to the cliff's foot and fetch the wild pigs my man killed! Take as many home as you can carry!" While Tao Jiuxiang couldn't see the homes of her three or four neighbors scattered through the mountains, they responded to her resonant voice. With the lead boar's bristles, Li Diezhu painted blood on his gunstock. He thrust his gun skyward, throwing his head back and roaring exultantly, "Ahhh—waaoooh!" His stentorian roar echoed in waves, moving through the mountains and valleys.

In these remote thickly forested mountains where beasts were many and people few, the only rival to a tiger was a large mature wild boar. After Li Diezhu's improbable triumph over the strapping boar and the pack of wild hogs, mountainfolk near and far came to believe that he possessed the blessings and protection of the White Tiger Immortal.

Many legends swirled around this White Tiger. In most stories, Mengyi, a female *tima*, her body and spirit responding to a white light emanating from the heavens, birthed a baby boy at the Hour of the Tiger, on the Day of Tiger, in the Month of the Tiger, of the Year of the Tiger. The child, named Wuxiang, grew to be fierce and imposing, brave and heroic. Possessing the unique abilities to craft boats without equal and throw his sword with peerless accuracy to kill enemies, he led his tribes out of the Zhongli Mountains, carving out a kingdom in a great valley several hundred miles long, fertile land rich with salt, taking the title Emperor Xiang the Great. After his death, his soul, suffused with boundless martial force and murderous energy, transformed into a white tiger, ascending the heavens as the Celestial White Tiger Emperor. Ever since, descendants of the Tribe of the Tiger reverently worshiped him, for countless generations burning incense and offering blood sacrifices that they might prosper and reproduce.

Li Diezhu's fame spread like wildfire. Local lore held that the earliest ancestor of the Li family was a tiger! Tao Jiuxiang heard another legend, one that told of a long-ago dynasty in which a marauding army slaughtered everyone in the tribe except a lone herder girl, who vowed to marry whoever could protect her herd of goats from wolves. Instantly, as though from the mountain mist, a white tiger materialized and drove the wolves away. When the girl shepherded her goats back into the sheltering cave for the night, the white tiger turned into a handsome young man. He married her, and she bore seven sons and seven daughters. Thus, once again the tribe of the Tiger repopulated and prospered.

Another peculiar local tale from yore told of a bastard child born to a Li family girl and her clandestine lover that had been abandoned under the vines and creepers of an old tall tree. When a farmer went into the mountains to gather medicinal herbs, he saw a tigress sleeping in a clump of grass, a naked baby seated between her forepaws. Alarmed, the farmer reported to the village head. Shouting and beating drums, villagers swarmed to the spot. Irritated by the clamor, the tigress retreated, tenderly glancing back at the baby as she left. Strangely the baby, breast-fed by the tigress, was not fierce and wild in the least. Later, he even became the assistant head of the village. Although these legends were not completely believable, the aroma of wild boar meat permeating the house aroused in Tao Jiuxiang a deep admiration for her Li family husband.

Once, overwhelmed by her husband's relentless lovemaking, Tao Jiuxiang had breathlessly asked, "You're so goddamned fierce! Are you the reincarnation of a spirit tiger?"

With a coarse, earthy pant, still firmly cupping her hips as he gazed down at his wife, Li Diezhu answered, "A spirit tiger would take you from behind. But I'm just here goin' at you from the front, so I'm only a man!"

II

From a bird's-eye view, the mountains wound their way for more than a thousand miles through Hunan, Hubei, and Guizhou. In ancient times, the mountain chain formed the boundary of the Ba State. The distinctive landscape bore many mysterious place names—Country of Shamanscript, Commandery of the Night Gentleman, Spring of the Martial Tomb, Plains of the Divine Farmer.

Pacing steadfastly, robust Li Diezhu walked through the thick forest, toting a carrying pole, gun at his side, mountain dog trotting at his heels. Of medium stature, he was dressed in a short gown. His trousers legs were rolled up to reveal sturdy calves matted with black, curly hair. The ten wild boars his family had carried home were cut into hundreds of pieces, smeared with salt and ash before the thick dark meat was suspended from roof joists. Although his crops had been ruined, the unexpected harvest of wild hogs had filled his cooking pots. One early morning, Li Diezhu carried two well-cured hams to ward chief Qin over at Inkblack Creek. After all without Qin Zhanyun how could his family have enjoyed the bounty?

Half a year earlier, on a noonday after the morn's white fog had risen, as Li Diezhu used a final swatch of straw to finish covering the roof of his hut a series of dog barks announced a stocky man in black cotton gown emerging from the woods, a white kerchief wrapped round his head, a handmade rifle on his shoulder. Nose in the air, the man called out, "Where are you from?"

Li Diezhu answered, "Greenstone Hamlet. My hometown was drought-stricken so I'm putting down stakes here."

With a dignified air, the man remarked, "This is the tenth ward of

Huangshui. I'm the chief administrator of this ward!"

Li Diezhu jumped down to the ground from the roof, wiping sweat from his brow. With a humble smile he asked, "What is your honorable surname?"

"I'm Qin. If you want to live here, the government requires that you come to my home and register."

"Okay, okay, ward chief, I'll come register." Gulping down a bowl of water, Li Diezhu picked up his hunting gun and headed off with the ward chief.

"You've made a good choice—your land is elevated and sheltered from the wind," Qin remarked approvingly as they walked through the woods. He pointed out a place called Lihaku in the local tongue, meaning "Land of the Tigers" in Mandarin. Ringed by nine ridges, next to Inkblack Creek, the place was set to the northeast of Huangshui. Over the past several centuries, waves of people had moved into the region, slashing-and-burning primeval forest to open up fields, setting up rough, low-roofed sheltering huts with tree trunks, growing goldthread in the fertile land to sell. Some mountain households were rather wealthy.

Contentedly, Li Diezhu mused that he had found a good nest in which to settle his family.

After thanking Qin for his kindness, Li Diezhu cheerfully headed homeward through the thick forest with his mountain dog at his heels. The afternoon sun careered ever westward, dyeing the sky with a brilliant salmon glow. With an empty basket and a hunting gun on his back, buoyant Li Diezhu chanted a lilting folk song to express the pleasure bursting from his breast:

> *My lover's on the east slope and I'm out on the west,*
> *But the ridges they won't keep me from the girl I love the best.*

As he drawled the ending, the strains of his song cut through the ethers of early evening like a knife, prompting in response a chorus of howls from wild beasts. The mountains and forests pulsed with vitality. His heart was full of warmth, like a well-toasted, fragrant potato.

As he headed homeward, layers of mist blanketed the mountains; the thick forest exhaled its earthy verdure. Excitedly, the hound sniffed here and there, and then suddenly held in its mouth a wet pig bladder pawed from the decayed leaves. Li Diezhu stopped singing, took it and felt it: the bladder was filled with bullets, like the kernels of so many peanuts. Qin had told him that when bandits looted Fengjie, the county seat, earlier that year, General Yang Sen had driven them away. Some bandits had broken free and fought a skirmish at Lihaku against the Huangshui Militia. Corpses of fallen bandits were buried in the valley. Exuberant with the windfall, Li Diezhu picked out a pair of bullets, popping one into his gun. "Peng!" Then another, "Peng!" A pair of crisp reports from his handcrafted rifle resounded. Before the second gunshot's resonant echo had died, however, a savage "Wa-oooough!" sounded from the foot the mountain.

Terror-stricken, Li Diezhu shimmied up a tall tree. Through its thick branches, he looked down the mountain slope in the direction of the bloodcurdling howl. Behold! Partly screened by a massive rock, a huge broad-shouldered tiger, yellow-orange with vivid black stripes hid amid the coriaria, the horse mulberry shrubs. Only after a long wait did the tiger finally stalk off. Weak-kneed, Li Diezhu nearly crumpled as he jumped down to the ground. He staggered to his hunting dog and scooped up the animal, which had stood rooted in paralytic horror. In a lightheaded, vertiginous stupor, he headed homeward, constantly feeling the tiger's lurking presence in the pitch-dark night.

After she heard the tiger howl, Tao Jiuxiang climbed the mountain ridge several times to watch for her husband. Finally, she relaxed when she saw him coming from afar. Breathlessly, he called out, "A tiger, a kingly tiger!"

"You saw it?" Tao Jiuxiang blurted.

"Yes…near the valley's mouth…at the bottom of the steep cliff," Li Diezhu stammered, still lost in horror. Setting his dog down, he rushed into the hut, took the liquor bottle from the wall, and swallowed a big mouthful.

"Don't go back," warned Tao Jiuxiang, taking a bone from the cooking pot to calm the dog. Full-figured and solid, dressed in a patched, low-collared gown, with short, wide sleeves, she looked like an ear of ripened corn in the autumn, ready for husking. She glanced curiously at the pig bladder Li Diezhu had brought back.

Wiping sweat from his brow, Li Diezhu took a handful of dark-brown "peanut kernels" in one of his palms and saying tenderly, "See what I picked."

Furrowing her brow, Tao Jiuxiang pursed her moist lips and asked, "What are they?"

"Bullets," said Li Diezhu, supping another mouthful of liquor, wiping his mouth with relish.

Tao Jiuxiang took one of the peanuts and bit down on it. Astonished, she exclaimed, "It's soft, like a bean of gold!"

Li Diezhu bit another bean. "Oh, no!" he roared in a low, excited voice. Turning, he burst out the door, nearly knocking Tao Jiuxiang to the ground.

Staggering to the table, she held up the pig bladder and cried out in an agony of joy, "These aren't bullets, they're gold nuggets!"

Seething with regret, Li Diezhu dashed back to where he had fired his gun to look for the two gold beans he had shot as bullets. For better than an hour, he searched the dense undergrowth, but tramping through the vast sea of woods merely left him covered with thorns and decayed leaves. Dejectedly, head down, his two eyes swept the ground.

Instinctively, he turned to see the huge yellow-orange mottled tiger, moving swiftly toward him, its tail tracing the ground. Soundlessly, as though treading on cloud, the tiger closed in, its fierce eyes riveted on its human quarry, its terrible mouth agape beneath long whiskers. Li Diezhu was paralyzed, his legs trembling with horror, his mind utterly blank. Finally, stilling his violently beating heart, he prayed silently: "Dear tiger, great spirit beast, please leave me in peace. Good ancestor, please go away."

Ears erect, the tiger stopped, glaring at him from a few feet away. Cowed by the creature's fierce majesty, Li Diezhu bowed his head, not daring to breathe. He regretted that in his haste he had brought neither carrying pole nor rifle. Finally, awakening from the dreamlike shock, he recalled that shaman Xia Qifa had once told him the longest whiskers on the tiger's maw possessed a divine sensitivity enabling the creature to see a person's true essence. If the whiskers sensed the aspect of a pig or goat, the tiger would attack; if the whiskers sensed a human it would not. He also recalled the proverb, "A serpent attacks if riled or provoked, but a tiger attacks for revenge." He also remembered Xia Qifa's instruction that when one meets a tiger, he should walk sideways. With trepidation, he edged sideward toward the slope. After a dozen paces or so, he risked a glance back in the direction of the tiger and saw that it had vanished into the underbrush, parting branches that still swayed as though blown by a fierce wind.

"I'm sorry, good ancestor, it's my fault! My forefather, please oh please don't be angry . . . don't be angry," murmured Li Diezhu once he came to himself, once his soul, cast adrift by fear, had rejoined his body. Repeatedly, he slapped himself in his face so fiercely that alternating strips of gold and bands of darkness dazzled his eyes.

III

The five members of the Li family were wild with joy at their unexpected wealth.

Clasping the bag of gold beans in her arms all night long, Tao Jiuxiang cheerfully asked her husband and three sons, "Is this a dream?"

Excitedly, Mawu, the eldest son, shouted, "This is no dream, Ma. How are we going to spend the gold?"

Mahe, the youngest, cried, "Let's go to Huangshui market to buy a mule, a horse, and some rice."

"And sugar and rice cakes," added Mawu.

Li Diezhu grinned, "You greedy eaters!"

Masui, the middle son, ventured, "Maybe we can go to school now!"

All the cagey merchants on Huangshui's old market street, which was chock full of rice dealers, cigarette vendors, opium dealers, cloth traders, silversmiths, and barbers, got tidings of Li Diezhu's golden windfall and swarmed to do business. "I just picked up one tiny nugget, so I need to be thrifty," Li Diezhu laughed, lying as he tried to figure out how to spend his gold.

Masui, his sharp-minded second son, sorely wished to learn to read and write characters. Masui was at once clever and foolish. At six, he had contracted monkeypox, which left scores of pockmarks on his face. One day, a pack of monkeys had gathered in the bamboo grove next to the family's cabin to eat the bamboo shoots. Barking wildly, the hunting dog tore after the monkeys. A ferocious monkey seized the hound by the ears, fiercely slapping and rending the yelping animal. Scared, Masui called for his parents. Mawu and Mahe burst out of the house with rifles, dispersing the pack of naughty monkeys with a couple of shots. When one monkey stopped running, the lead monkey, knowing it was wounded, carried it off on his back. Curious, Masui followed the monkeys up the forested ridge and spied on them. The monkeys dug a hole and buried their fallen comrade. Surrounding the dead monkey, they wept and howled. After a while, they dug up the dead monkey and fondled it. The pack then repeated their rite: digging, burying, exhuming, collectively fondling, and re-burying. Moved to tears, Masui cried aloud. Abruptly, the monkeys surged toward him with wild howls, knocking him down, scratching and dragging him. Hearing his brother's screams, Mawu charged into the forest and shot at the monkeys, driving them away.

Tao Jiuxiang pounded mountain herbs into a plaster and daubed it on the wounds of her stupid son. Fever-wracked and in agony, Masui wailed as the grieving monkeys continued their howling lament on the slope. All night, man and simian carried on their symphony of grief, long and short, high and low lugubrious howls of monkeys echoed in the mountains, answering Masui's piteous sobs that filled the cabin. Seething as he listened to this strange concert, it seemed to Li Diezhu that as wild beasts dominated these mountains he'd best send his sons to school in Huangshui to learn the *Thousand Character Classic* and the basics.

So it was that one snowy winter morning, Li Diezhu and his three sons pulled on their new straw sandals and set out, food and clothing on their backs, for Master Wang's private academy.

Mawu distractedly asked, "New Year's is almost here: why don't we just wait and start school next year?"

Li Diezhu retorted, "Unless you start learning how to pay proper respect to a teacher, you guys will become a bunch of ignorant monkeys. Besides, it's quite a while till New Year."

Mahe asked, "If we're all off at school, who'll accompany you and Ma at night?"

"I'll get a couple more dogs," Li Diezhu answered.

Despite these words, when he returned from Huangshui, Li Diezhu felt very lonely. Lying sleeplessly in bed next to Tao Jiuxiang, he tossed and turned. While he vaguely felt the presence of some untrammeled mysterious force challenging him and his family, Li Diezhu stubbornly clung to his wild-hearted ambitions for a splendid future. Wide-awake in the long hours before dawn, he mulled over two questions: Where would he buy a parcel of land? And from whom would he buy it?

The misty veil of snow that fell through the night stopped at dawn. Li Diezhu, fragrant newly purchased tobacco leaves in the bamboo basket strapped to his back, set out to ask ward chief Qin, who seemed to know just about everything about land around Qin's house on the bamboo-shaded plain of Inkblack Creek. Locals called the creek, which roared with turbulent currents, Arrow Bamboo Gulch. Leaves playfully floated in the sky, dancing in the magnificent winter sun.

"Ward chief Qin!" Li Diezhu called toward the plank-sheathed cabin half-hidden in the thick branches of the surrounding undergrowth.

An embankment screened the front of the Qin's homestead. Roiling creek waters rushed against the cliff, then tumbled into the valley. With a single misstep one might slip and plunge to the gully's bottom. Fortunately, a thick cluster of bamboo shielded the Qin family from this precipitous edge. Four boys of various age and height, ranging from five or six to thirteen or fourteen, played wildly, tearing around the yard as they flailed at one another with bamboo staves. The youngest, chunky as a piglet, cheerfully imitated his brothers, plodding here and there, slit-cloth trousers dragging around his ankles and huge belly exposed.

Seeing Li Diezhu, the eldest boy, wet with sweat, approached. He extended a staff, saying, "Uncle, let's have a battle with bamboo staves. Go all out, and don't stop till I say."

Li Diezhu had played such games with his sons before. He gripped the bamboo pole with his large hands, strong from tilling earth and chopping kindling. "Go!" he cried, and began attacking. However, the boy proved surprisingly agile, deftly parrying Li Diezhu's every blow.

"Away with you, Liebao!" shouted Qin, emerging from his house. With an approving glance toward the boy, Li Diezhu dropped the pole.

"He only likes martial arts," remarked Qin, turning to his eldest son. "Next year I'm sending you off to school so you can study the *Thousand Character Classic* and learn to write and read."

Li Diezhu guffawed, "My rascals just started school the day before yesterday. They'll be classmates."

"Just as long as they can learn some math, and don't turn out to be wastrels and idiots," Qin replied. "So, I heard you found some gold nuggets. Tell me the truth... how many did you find?"

Brushing caked mud from his trousers, Li Diezhu lied, "Not many... just a scanty few so that I can buy a meager patch of land."

"You heard of a Mr. Xiang from Peartree Moor? Yesterday, he sent a message asking if I wanted to buy land. As you know, it's going to be tough for me to buy more land—I'm sending Liebao off to school and planning to build two new courtyards so my wife has a little more space. It's a great opportunity, but I don't have the means. You'd better buy Xiang's land with your gold. Otherwise, lend it to me. Don't just leave it to gather dust."

Liebao, Qin's eldest son, had just been engaged to the daughter of Jin Shaosan, a wealthy man from Peppercorn Bend. Li Diezhu knew Xiang Jintang was the mayor of Peartree Moor in Enshi County. For generations, dating back to the late Qing dynasty when an ancestor had passed the military examination and entered imperial service, the Xiang family had enjoyed local prestige. Qin's eldest daughter, Li Diezhu recalled, had married one of Xiang's nephews. Curious, he blinked his eyes, and asked, "Xiang doesn't need money. So why does he want to sell land?"

"Bandits robbed the Xiangs," explained Qin's capable wife, a tall, thin woman, her head swathed in a black scarf. Hospitably, she placed a cup of tea in front of their guest.

"Late last year when bandits passed through Lihaku," Qin continued, "the damned devils cut down Captain Huang's underlings. Afterward, leaving several of their dead behind, they fled toward Enshi County. At Peppercorn Bend, the bandits fought Xiang's men. Many on both sides were killed or wounded. Guess he feels his land in Lihaku is too remote and he wants to consolidate his property."

Li Diezhu took the broad tobacco leaves from his basket and placed them neatly on the table, saying with a smile, "On your advice, I'll buy the land. Since the land's so far from their place, it'll be a lot of trouble for the Xiangs; but since its right near mine, it'll be easy for us to take care of. Please do me a favor and help persuade the Xiangs to sell the land to me."

"Okay, okay, okay . . . you are just fortune's favored. If I don't help you out, who will? I'll convey your intentions to Old Xiang," Qin answered amiably.

IV

So it was that in the winter of 1935, Li Diezhu, with the help of his miraculous windfall and ward chief Qin Zhanyun, negotiated the purchase of a large plot of land from rich landlord Xiang Jintang of Enshi County, an acre of prime flatland plains and half an acre on the mountain slopes. This made Li Diezhu a wealthier landholder than the ward headman.

The goldthread seedlings grew into thick, green shoots. Rain, sunlight, and moonrays seeped through the dense overhead tangle of branches and leaves, intermingling in perfect balance to anoint and enrich the ever-growing goldthread. When the clouds and mist cleared, Li Diezhu, standing in front his hut, could see the valley through which Inkblack Creek ran, faint and majestic in the distance. The setting evening sun behind the mountains left a golden magnificence melting in the sky that he imagined resembled the radiance of the imperial palace. For centuries, this divine brilliance of the sunshine above coupled with the mysterious potency of the goldthread at their feet gave the rugged mountainfolk a sense of pride that they were connected to something regal and powerful.

In the early spring, icicles hanging under the eaves and on the branches began to melt. Throughout the mountains, crystal water droplets adhered to pine needles, scintillating as diamonds in the sunlight. Exhaling, forests and mountains murmured goodbye to the cold desolation of winter. Li Diezhu was so intoxicated by the new season that he worked diligently day and night with Tao Jiuxiang putting up a new shed and planting goldthread rhizomes. After a month of nonstop toil, they finally finished spring planting and relaxed one evening in their old cabin with wine and a few meat dishes, dwelling cheerfully on future plans.

Ma San, the medicine dealer, suddenly appeared at their door.

"Come on in for a drink," called Li Diezhu.

"I've got something to discuss with you," said Ma San directly, setting down hoe and basket, taking a seat behind the steaming pottery jar of liquor.

"What is it?" asked Li Diezhu, grinning.

"Since you found those gold nuggets, why not buy some land? The terrain of Gengguping is like a rhinoceros: my plot of land is right on the buttock. And people say rhinos shit gold bricks . . . it must be fate. So, you interested?"

Puzzled, Li Diezhu asked, "Why do you want to sell good land?"

Emptying the cup of liquor Tao Jiuxiang had set before him, Ma replied, "I want to move to Peppercorn Bend, so just name your price."

Peppercorn Bend was a cluster of narrow alluvial plains between Huangshui and the primeval forest. Li Diezhu knew Ma San, grown rich from collecting herbs and peddling remedies, wanted land along these fertile plains. Without hesitation, he rejoined, "I'll check it out tomorrow morning. The slightest nudge from a wild boar would knock down this old ramshackle hut." Ever since he had seen the Qins' plank-sheathed post-and-beam house,

Li Diezhu had been tormented by envy, and had looked for a suitable place to build a fine home just as spacious and grand as the Qins.

The traveling apothecary stayed the night at the cabin. As planned, the following morning, Li Diezhu went with Ma San to look at the land.

The buttock of the rhino that was Gengguping was six or seven miles from the cabin, roughly the same distance as the jaunt from Peppercorn Bend to Azure Dragon Daoist Temple, secreted in the mountains. The three sites formed a triangle. Nearing the crest of a mountain as they walked, wet with sweat, the two came across a dilapidated hut. Ma San said, "Here it is. This hut is smack dab on the fecund asshole of the rhinoceros." Several years ago, he told Li Diezhu that he had purchased the plot from a goldthread farmer. Over the years, around the hut he had broken sod and opened up several plots of farmland. As the sun set behind the hut, the roseate sky clearly silhouetted the surrounding mountains. From his lofty vantage, forests joined endless forests, mountains merged with boundless mountains, all bathed in the gloaming's last red rays. Wild with excitement, he threw back his head and howled in delight, "Isn't this place wonderful!?"

The wilderness echoed, "Isn't this place wonderful!?"

Taken aback, he paused for a moment, before howling, "Isn't this place booming!?"

The mountains echoed, "Isn't this place booming!?"

He thundered, "Good!"

"Good!" resounded the hills and valleys.

Li Diezhu loved the plot of land at first sight. On the spot, he promised to pay two gold beans for the deed.

He wasted no time. During late spring and early summer, a dozen workers set out to build a new house on the mountainslope. Under the selfsame warm vernal sun that legendary master craftsman Lu Ban had worked several millennia earlier, bossman Li Diezhu oversaw a spirited crew sawing joists and beams, erecting the new post-and-beam house that grew by the day! A lively expression on his creased face, half-chanting and half-talking, foreman Zhu Shun spun a rhythmic song as he toiled:

> *Oh carpenter king, where are you living now?*
> *You live on Black Dragon Mountain, grew up on the dragon's brow.*

Who is it that gave you life? And who has helped you grow?
Nurtured by the sweet dew, your life from Earth God below.
Where you were born branches interlock and leaves they intermesh;
Wayfarers dared not harm you and crows they dared not rest.
Axe in hand, God-like carpenter Lu Ban stands by your side;
Hewing joist, rafter, then purlin, deft of hand, with pride.
Sunrise to sunset with tools he carves so straight and plumb,
Till rising from sweat and nothing a magnificent house comes.

For half a year, from chopping down the first straight-grained tree to laying the final rafter, Zhu Shun chanted without cease, forgetting his exhaustion. Sometimes workmen chimed in, as this ditty—prayer, chant, and workers' anthem rolled into one—was widely sung by builders throughout the mountains.

Hearing this tireless chant day after day as his house rose on the rhino's buttock, Li Diezhu sometimes laughed aloud in delight.

V

Built to Zhu Shun's cheerful rhythmic songs, the stout wooden house stood proudly near the crest of the mountain, oriented in the cardinal directions, with railed external corridors and more than twenty rooms. Based on strict scholarly principles, flanking the A-frame main gate, two smaller gates were built for Tao Jiuxiang and her future daughters-in-law to go in or out during menstruation. Ebullient with joy, Li Diezhu sent for Mawu, Masui, and Mahe to help move. As soon as the first orange and salmon of the pre-dawn brought faint light to the dark forest, the Li family busied themselves with the move.

"What a perfect, clear morning," shouted Li Diezhu passionately, looking at his new house built atop the sun-gilded egg-shaped hill. He chanted aloud:

Cleansing our hands, dong dong qiang,
Burning the incense, dong dong qiang,
Kneeling with reverence, dong dong qiang,
Worshiping the family gods, dong dong qiang.

Lost in excitement, Li Diezhu held aloft a lit incense burner, walking as he chanted. Eldest son Mawu held the memorial spirit tablet of their ancestors; Masui, his second son, a torch of tree bark; Mahe, the youngest, a pot; and Tao Jiuxiang, candles and ceremonial paper. Dancing as they filed into their new house, all followed Li Diezhu's lead. Only once the spirit tablet of their ancestors was set respectfully before the family altar did everyone busy themselves with more mundane matters, moving in household utensils—pots, bowls, plates, and basins.

Most people in the mountains around Huangshui made a living as goldthread and opium farmers, or as bandits. Li Diezhu, however, had become wealthy by sheer luck. Availing himself of his good fortune, he created an orchard on his new plot, digging up seedlings and transplanting walnut, ginkgo, water bamboo, red fir, pear, and peach. Tao Jiuxiang raised several hunting dogs as well as a pig and a horse. To keep out predatory wild beasts, clever Zhu Shun built a tall stone wall ringing the house, reinforced with thick wooden planks. In the sheltered yard, under the loving ministrations of Tao Jiuxiang, the animals led contented lives, growing plump and robust, looking like prize stock.

Behind the house, husband and wife grew a small patch of opium poppies as medicine for livestock or family members. Rain or shine, everything went perfectly for the Li family: the mountain air seemed to carry a hint of the divine, its salubrious ethers so fresh and nourishing that it seemed to possess some sort of rich, heavenly ferment. As sunlight saturated the fields, stalks of corn grew taller by the day.

That was the happiest period in the checkered Li family history. Cattle and goats reproduced thick and fast. In Huangshui's market, Li Diezhu swapped four piglets and a colt for a calf. Frugal, cheerful, and possessed of a boundless energy, Tao Jiuxiang rose with the sun each morning and worked unstintingly all day until the last light of the evening, never asking for help. Likewise, from the moment the first warblings of forest birds and the first light of dawn cut through the darkness, Li Diezhu, his body quivering with energy like some ebullient chthonian deity, burst outside inhaling the earthy fragrance and squatted in the fields weeding, moving from one plot to the next, never showing the slightest hint of exhaustion.

One noon, as the golden sunshine thrust through the clouds suffusing the fields with its enriching warmth, Tao Jiuxiang, wearing a broad-brimmed bamboo hat, five sturdy mountain dogs at her heels, carried a basket of cooked potato, cured pork, and salted vegetables to Li Diezhu. While he could endure hunger, Li Diezhu had a prodigious appetite: he wolfed down almost everything. For a moment he stood happily, sated with food and water, his low-riding pants dangling down. There was not another soul around. Exulting in fullness of life, Li Diezhu loosened his trousers, pouncing on Tao Jiuxiang and pushing his wife down to the ground.

She resisted, trying to fend him off with hands and knees, cursing, "You beast!"

"Haven't you heard that plowing the fields and planting seeds in the soil brings a bountiful harvest!" cried Li Diezhu with delight.

Angrily lashing out, Tao Jiuxiang spat, "Shameless!"

"C'mon, let yourself go!" Li Diezhu roared, pressing his wife to the ground, as he ground himself into her. "Abandon yourself to it. Be wild, be unrestrained!"

At once abashed and angry, Tao Jiuxiang realized that she couldn't push her husband away. And, after all, she had heard that the sex in the fields at beginning of spring gave rise to a good harvest. So, half-believing and half-skeptical, she abandoned herself to a bout of wild lovemaking on the sward as the five mountain hounds circled them, eyes wide open, sniffing curiously.

"Do you really think it works?" Tao Jiuxiang asked, rising from the ground and smoothing her trousers.

Li Diezhu eyed his wife—a pretty woman with a broad forehead, a well-formed nose, and expressive clear eyes under her charming black brows, and provocatively answered, "It would work even better if you unbound your hair and ran around our fields naked."

Tao Jiuxiang retorted, "Okay! You go first, and I'll follow behind your bare ass."

Gazing heavenward, Li Diezhu giggled, "A woman's hips are the source of magic power, not a man's."

"Not a woman," said Tao Jiuxiang, gathering the bowls and chopsticks. "A witch."

"As long as it brings an abundant harvest, it doesn't matter if you act the witch once in a while." Li Diezhu carelessly teased, gazing at his wife.

"So you want me to be a witch-woman, you bastard? Witch-women marry snakes: you want me to marry a serpent?" Tao Jiuxiang spat at her husband and stormed off, leaving him with the five dogs.

The sun sank behind a curtain of darkness. Contentedly, Li Diezhu hummed a ditty as he headed homeward. He passed through a grove of stalwart ancient trees, their lush green canopy more vital than the saplings in his freshly planted orchard. Though he was not much of a singer, even an immortal would have envied his buoyant spirits as he belted out his jaunty tune:

> *The sun has set,*
> *And the mountains are cooling.*
> *Ah—ho—yah—ho—ho—*
> *Look, oh, look my way;*
> *My love is looking for me—yah,*
> *Happily awaiting my return, yah.*
> *Ah—ho—yah—ho—ho—*
> *Ah-ha—a-ha-ah,*
> *Sharing the hearth, way-a-yi,*
> *I'm marrying you, a-ha.*
> *Ah—a-ha—hey—ah,*
> *Ah—ho—yah—ho—ho . . .*

When he returned, Tao Jiuxiang set out rice and several steaming hot dishes for the two of them. After the meal, as Li Diezhu smoked, she washed the pots and bowls, cleaned her face and feet, tended the fire, and blew the lamp out. The two of them then clambered into the wooden-framed bed. Every night, Li Diezhu hung a pair of bottles of strong corn liquor above the bed. In these mountains, haunted by wild creatures, during the endless pitch-black nights there was no light except starlight, no clear delineation between heaven and earth. So he drank to the intermittent rhythmic trilling of insects: in the first half of the night, he guzzled down the bottle to the left of the pillow; during the second half, the one on the right. In this desolate primitive wilderness, husband and wife nightly waged fierce sexual battles.

Chapter Two

I

Graduating after three years, filled with boundless optimism about the future, Mawu, Masui, and Mahe proudly strode back to Gengguping from the private school, each shouldering a blue parcel containing a coarse-edged copybook filled with characters. Nineteen-year-old firstborn Mawu—broad-faced, thick-browed, and sunburned—was especially buoyant, sporting a wispy moustache on his upper lip and a protruding Adam's apple, the surging vitality of his ancestors bursting from his being.

As the cheerful trio of Li tiger cubs headed homeward, moving from cleared fields through a swath of primeval forest, sunlight filtering through the leaves and illumining the path before them, the mountainfolk moved in the opposite direction, shouldering huge sheaves of long, broad-leaved corn stalks. In the rays of the setting sun, each bundle looked like a golden hillock moving rhythmically. Bleating endlessly, herds of goats followed.

Tao Jiuxiang had prepared a celebratory dinner for her graduates, but upon their arrival the three brothers asked for neither food nor drink; rather they stood upright before the memorial tablets of their ancestors, each in turn reverently reciting a section of the *Thousand-Character Classic*. An elated Li Diezhu then proudly presided over dinner. The entire afternoon, wetting his fingers as he leafed through his sons' coarse-edged notebooks, Li Diezhu scrutinized each and every character. Finally, he rose and dashed out of the gate, unleashing a howl of delight that echoed in the green mountains: "All my sons are literate now! *Loooough!*"

With the sons' return, productivity soared. While the crops grew prolifically in the fields where Li Diezhu and Tao Jiuxiang had coupled, so, too, luxuriant weeds grew thick and fast. They needed to pull these weeds before they overwhelmed and strangled the young seedlings. Flashing his wife a complicit grin, Li Diezhu headed to the plot with his three sons. Bent over or kneeling, they worked from daybreak to sunset, pulling lush clumps and tufts of grass up by the roots, shaking the mud off, and tossing them to the margin of the field. After several days of hard work, they were dog-tired. Cunningly slinking off to a nearby slope, Masui and Mahe lazily lay down for a nap while their elder brother continued to toil with their father.

Backs aching and trunks sore, Li Diezhu and Mawu trudged to the margin of the field, where Mawu cast aside a clot of weeds. Vigorously he roared, "Ahhh! Hallo—!" His roar scared off both the wild hares on the ground and the scudding clouds in the sky. With great pride Li Diezhu watched his eldest son, who, sturdy and handsome, was a full head taller than he. Thinking of a tale handed down from his ancestors, he couldn't refrain from taking a step toward Mawu, nodding with a smile, and beginning:

"Long ago there lived a forefather of our family who was very handsome in his youth. Each time he returned home, he found a steaming, fragrant dish of mutton prepared for him. One day, he saw from afar a tigress holding a goat in her mouth. After bowing several times in front of the Earth God Temple, the tigress rolled over and over on the ground before removing her skin. Then and there, in place of the tigress appeared a beautiful girl."

Eyes flashing a golden light, Mawu blinked in wonder. Pleased, Li Diezhu took his pipe from his waist belt, continuing cheerfully, "The girl skinned the goat, cut it up and prepared it. Having fallen for the lovely girl, he secretly hid the tigress skin she had shed. Without her pelt, the girl could not turn back into a tigress, and had no choice but to marry our forefather and birth children with him." Mawu gasped, mouth agape, dumbfounded. "Years passed, and one day the tigress said to her grown son, 'I've been married to your father for decades and now I even have grandsons, yet I've never gone back to see my parents, nor have I gone on a single outing. Get me my skin. I want to visit my parents.'"

Sitting on the ridge, Li Diezhu paused and deliberately packed his pipe with tobacco before continuing, "The son didn't want to let his mother leave, but our forefather said, 'Your mother has lived with me for thirty years without going to see her parents. Now she's old, so let her go.' "

Lighting his pipe with his flint, Li Diezhu continued, "So the son gave his mother the tiger skin which had been hidden under the floorboards in a corner of the house. When his mother left, he followed. The moment she stepped out of the gate, she turned into a tigress. Seeing a neighbor's five-year-old child, she pounced. 'No!' cried the son, 'Mama, Mama, don't do it!'"

Li Diezhu put his pipe into his mouth, puffed twice, and kept on with relish, "Seeing her son, the tigress abandoned her prey and plunged into the forest, disappearing from their lives forever. Anxiously, her son pleaded with hunters, 'If you see a lame tigress, please let me know. Don't kill her. That's my mother!'"

Mawu shuddered as his father took a couple of casual draws on the pipe. Deliberately, after a dramatic pause, Li Diezhu finished, "The tigress was killed after all. Her son carried her back home, hired a *tima* to clear the path to the spirit realm, and then buried his mother in a coffin."

Hair standing on end, soul aquiver, Mawu found himself lost in the legend. From childhood, he had heard countless such family legends, but he never took them seriously. Now having reached marriageable age he wondered, blushing at the thought, if he, too, living in these lonely mountains, would marry a tigress.

"If they hadn't given her the tigress skin, she never would have left!" Masui interrupted, appearing suddenly. He was nearly as tall as Tao Jiuxiang.

"Bugger off!" huffed Li Diezhu, with a sidelong glare. "Lazy swine!"

"I was betting with Mahe. Which came first, the goldthread rhizome or its seed?" Masui replied, with an aggrieved tone.

Li Diezhu frowned at his pock-faced second son, asking, "So, what's your answer?"

"I said the seed came first," replied Masui, looking at his father and scratching his head, "What do you think, Pa?"

"It's obvious. What a waste of breath! How could goldthread grow without a seed?" Li Diezhu spat angrily.

"But Mahe said the goldthread rhizome came first. He said, 'how could the seed come into being without the root?'" Masui said earnestly.

Confused, Li Diezhu stammered, "Damn it, the two of you fools were laying about debating which came first the chicken or the egg while we're busting our asses working. Careful or I'll give you a good smacking!"

Masui ran away, disappointed.

Timid but thoughtful, Masui was always rife with fanciful questions. His calligraphy was far better than his elder brother's, and Master Wang, head of the private academy, adored him. It might be better, Li Diezhu mused, once the goldthread was sold, to ask Wang to help send Masui and Mahe to a new-style school in Chongqing, leaving Mawu at home to help out. After all, he had heard Mr. Wang's two sons were enjoying the new modern schools in Chongqing. And educated folk were clever and cunning.

With this thought, he turned to Mawu and with a giggle, and murmured tenderly, "Once we sell the goldthread and make a pile of money, we'll find you a fairy maiden wife to cook meals and wash clothes, to do housework and birth some little ones. Then these mountains will be alive with excitement!"

Initially, Mawu was struck dumb by this prospect. Then slowly his lips parted and he grinned from ear to ear like an idiot.

II

Crouched next to the damp shed, Li Diezhu and Mawu gazed up at the verdant surrounding mountains, each anticipating a bright future. Hillocks of weeds and grass were piled along the margin of the field.

Gradually, the goldthread seedlings turned dark green. At harvest time, using a three-tined iron claw, Li Diezhu and his sons dug out the rhizomes one by one, cutting away the tendrils and wisps, fanning them out on the bricks of the stove to bake ten times, sun-drying them on the courtyard embankment ten times, and, finally, vigorously shaking the rhizomes in a bamboo basket to winnow away stray chaff and root hairs.

A small village of one hundred households, Huangshui was composed of fifty-odd cabins and sheds lining two streets: the two-hundred-yard-long earth-packed main road and a sixty-yard dead-end lane. Yet this small town was located along the main road connecting the city of Chongqing to Hubei Province. Each year Huangshui exported roughly three thousand hundred-pound bundles of goldthread, sold along with timber, herbal medicine, opium, and mountain handicrafts to a swarm of buyers from Chongqing and Hubei. Some merchants came and went, while others stayed year round. The long-established goldthread market was located at one end of the main street. In the distinctive calligraphy of Master Cui, a local gentleman who had passed the imperial examinations three decades earlier before the fall of the Qing dynasty, the graven, weather-ravaged sign for the market advertised:

> *A wonderful herbal medicine,*
> *Goldthread can match cinnabar;*
> *Dispelling inauspicious and wicked spirits,*
> *It provides lasting numinous power.*
> *A dragon majestically traverses the heavens,*
> *A fast team of horses churns across the earth,*
> *A swan soars with consummate grace,*
> *Just so this rhizome brings fortune and wealth.*

Crammed with people, the market exhaled choking odors of sweat, tobacco, mud, and silver coins. Leading several hired hands toting huge baskets of dried goldthread rhizomes, Li Diezhu excitedly shouldered his way through the throngs. Excitedly, he dumped the rhizomes into an impressive heap, then, burning with impatience but feigning calmness, he waited expectantly for the milling buyers.

Merchants swarmed, haggling by flashing quick finger gestures partly hidden by sleeves, visible to Li Diezhu but hidden from their competitors. While he knew of this bargaining style, this was the first time he had experienced it himself. Focused, his eyes beamed with a cheerful cunning, his face a mixture of pride and anxiety. In the end, he sold the goldthread for the top market price, earning three hundred and forty silver dollars per basket. His assistants shared looks of astonishment.

This sudden bonanza spurred the family at Gengguping into a frenzy of action. Driven by dreams of prosperity, from morning to night Mawu tirelessly dug up more goldthread. Tao Jiuxiang kept the *kang* stove-bed fired, drying the precious stems. Li Diezhu watched the road, waiting for his assistants. No one had expected it was so easy to make money: a basket of goldthread could be traded for half a basket of silver dollars! When they finally had sold all the goldthread, they accumulated such a dizzying fortune that silver dollars piled high and far spilled off the edges of the family's two tables.

At that time, before people grew goldthread on a large scale, Li Diezhu became the largest grower in the region. With great pleasure, he used his fortune to purchase half a barren mountain from Xiang Jintang of Enshi. As these hinterlands on the nebulous boundary between Enshi and Gengguping were too far away and inconvenient for Xiang Jintang, he quickly concluded a contract with Li Diezhu.

It was good to have a literate son: Watching Mawu sign the contract and then carve "Property of the Li Family" into the big camphor tree on the margin of their land, an incomparable pride filled Li Diezhu. Stepping back to appreciate his inscription, Mawu set a leaf between his lips and blew a piercing whistle like the call of a mate-seeking bird, a whistle so keen the sharp-edged leaf bit into his lower lip and drew blood. Recalling the promise he had made to his son on the field's margin, Li Diezhu smiled.

In Huangshui, there were different kinds of marriage ceremony. Coarse, wild men dragged brides home by force; the more civilized sought the assistance of a matchmaker and held a marriage ceremony; and the half-wild, half-civilized compromised, simply lighting firecrackers to stake their claim. Twenty years ago Li Diezhu had seized Tao Jiuxiang by force, swaddling her in a quilt, hefting her over his shoulder and carrying her off. But Mawu had enjoyed two years of private school education, and Li Diezhu wanted him to marry a wife according to the more civil wedding customs of the rich.

After spring plowing, he sent Masui and Mahe back to Fengjie City, the county seat, for further schooling. Bringing her honeyed tongue and goading words to the gate of the Li household, the matchmaker Third Auntie Zhang, a portly middle-aged woman, rode a mule, her large feet jouncing up and down as it sauntered along the mountain trail to Gengguping. The rhino's rump was a vision of spring beauty, an endless efflorescence of colorful flowers stretching from ground to sky, a vivid, multihued splendor matched only by the bright, embroidered silk shoes this woman carried bundled in a brown parcel. Excited to a fevered pitch, Mawu wrestled affectionately with one of the mountain hounds, rolling over and over on the ground. From the time he had watched roosters coupling with hens and dogs topping bitches as a young boy, he yearned for his own wedding day.

Passing a tobacco pipe to Third Auntie Zhang, Li Diezhu flattered, "The meadow lark has warbled all morning to herald the arrival of our honored guest." He cut a fine figure, having changed his workclothes for a gown fashioned of fine foreign cloth. He had replaced his usual gunpowder horn with a splendid three-foot bamboo pipe that ended with a generous brass bowl carved like the gaping maw of a tiger.

Entering the room with a piping hot dish, Tao Jiuxiang politely offered it to the guest, smiling, "Third Auntie, try these rice-fried eggs."

"We don't have fare worthy of you," Li Diezhu casually remarked, before cutting straight to the point, "Third Auntie, what family around here has a fitting nubile girl? Can we trouble you to help hunt for a suitable betrothal for Mawu, my eldest?"

Knitting her fine, high-arching brows, the matchmaker authoritatively responded, "Just as there can be no rain without clouds, so no match can be concluded without a matchmaker. So our ancestors have decreed. Nowadays, young lovers get engaged after lighting firecrackers and serenading each other with a couple of nights of love songs. Pah!" She spat scornfully, "What kind of half-assed pig's head of a custom is that?"

"True, so true," agreed Li Diezhu, "How could young lovers figure things out for themselves?"

Third Auntie ruminated for while before saying, "I'm afraid to say there aren't any good matches around Huangshui: The girls from wealthy families are all married; while none of the daughters from common families are suitable. How about going to Enshi and asking for the hand of Xiang Jintang's youngest daughter?"

Although bandits had plundered the family, the Xiangs had been wealthy for generations. Furthermore, Xiang Jintang's son-in-law was a commandant under Yang Sen, a warlord in Sichuan Province. Fearing the Xiang family would look down on them, Tao Jiuxiang felt the match was fanciful and ill-suited. On the other hand, as soon as he heard the suggestion Li Diezhu's eyes lit up: folks said that Xiang Jintang and his son had both passed the imperial military examination, and that two hundred soldiers guarded their compound. Such a marital alliance would afford great safety and security. Even if the odds were slim, it was worth a try. Without hesitation, he said to Third Auntie, "Okay! Let's go for it."

III

Toting a smoked ham, curly tail still attached, the matchmaker arduously picked her way along the rugged path through the dark, deep vale of Inkblack Creek, the sole route connecting Huangshui to Enshi. Engulfed by the canopy of the primeval forest, burbling torrents of the stream ran around huge blocks of stone. Nervously, she trod the precarious plank road cut into the cliff face. The narrow path allowed only foot traffic: there was no room for her mule. She paused, fearing greedy demons, coveting the fragrant haunch, would descend upon her. She took off her homemade knickers and hung them on one end of her carrying pole. Everyone knew demons were afraid of such things. Looking up at the neatly carved caves cut into the cliff face, she lit her tobacco pipe, puffing contentedly as she walked.

Locals called these the "Caves of the Immortals." They contained rectangular coffins that over countless centuries had blended in with the mountainscape, turning the same metallic gray as the cliff face. Myths and legends related to the caves proliferated. Historical evidence had proved that the Ba people used these caves as tombs, placing the coffins in with ropes. Though they no longer followed this funerary practice, mountainfolk in nearby valleys called themselves descendants of the Ba. Even so, not a one of them knew how their ancestors had managed to hoist the huge coffins into the cliff caves.

As far as the eye could see, the creek rushed on. A kite circled in the narrow strip of sky above the fast-moving waters. Bold as a heroine, Third Auntie Zhang put on her knickers again before reaching the gate of the grand Xiang compound in Enshi, carrying with her not only the ham but Mawu's dreams for marriage. She knew very well that soldiers from Xiang's private militia were stationed in the entry courtyard. Carrying pole on her shoulder, she sang aloud:

> *A new house foundation, plumb and square,*
> *Four walls carry earth and stone from everywhere;*
> *Like the rumble of thunder heard world round,*
> *Praise for the clever girl's beauty and talent resounds.*

Hearing her song, a senior laborer emerged from the gate, sizing her up. As soon as he came out, the matchmaker, soaked in perspiration from her journey, resumed her song:

> *As the bean flowers large and round,*
> *So the piglet grows fast and sound;*
> *The girl eighteen, the lad nineteen,*
> *A good match made, harvester's dream.*

Understanding at once that she was a matchmaker, the gatekeeper led Third Auntie Zhang through the main entrance, a secondary gate, and into the hall of the inner courtyard. Xiang Jintang, attired in a silken gown, entered and addressed her, "Where are you from?" he asked, gesturing for her to take a seat. A servant poured her a cup of Laoyin tea.

"My name is Zhang, and I come from Huangshui." She introduced herself in a manner befitting her position. Her ruddy unkemptness and evident fatigue testified to the hardy woman's grueling journey along the mountain paths in the name of nuptial love.

"Tough journey?" mused the impeccably groomed Xiang Jintang, looking askance at the disheveled matchmaker.

"I can climb any high mountain on foot, and cross any river by boat, clambering over peaks like a sure-footed ox, traversing plains like a round-hoofed horse.

> *Having a rising son-in-law, like a lotus that adorns,*
> *Can complete the luster of your family so highborn,"*

returned Third Auntie with a flourish of ready flattery, skillfully mingling prose and verse. She added, "My honorable patron Li Diezhu has a son worthy of a fine marriage who seeks an everlasting union, no matter the distance of the prospective bride."

"Li Diezhu?" replied Xiang Jintang scornfully, "I've just spared him a hill. Now he covets my daughter as a wife for his eldest son?"

"His eldest son Mawu is literate, capable of reading essays and writing characters; in appearance, he is most handsome, one in a thousand," gushed the matchmaker. "Li admires both your kindness and strictness in household management. Although his family is less wealthy than yours, he enjoys the blessings and protection of his ancestors—at every turn meeting with good fortune and accumulating prosperity. They have enough cured pork hanging from the rafters and millet wine stored in jars to eat and drink for more than three years."

Xiang Jintang chuckled, saying, "Li Diezhu, ah, Li Diezhu." The proud scion of three generations of officials who had passed the military examination, he took a sip of tea and said conceitedly, "He reeks of the cornfield. Just because it is up in the heavens doesn't make a star brilliant and lofty. An ox or a horse is inferior by nature: a proud ox will clash until his horns break, and a proud-spirited horse will buck until its back breaks." Humming a cheerful ditty as he rose, he politely asked the servant girl to accommodate the matchmaker and see her off the following morning after breakfast.

Xiang's humming and casual dismissal brought Third Auntie back to her senses. "Thank you much, good Master," she mumbled, though beneath her ingratiating smile and expression of gratitude she felt despondent and humiliated.

"What a benevolent and merciful Master," remarked the servant girl. With a single deft stroke, she cut the tail off the smoked haunch and placed the ham back in the matchmaker's basket. She led Third Auntie Zhang to the guesthouse, saying, "Food and lodging is free. When you hear the gong, just come to the kitchen for supper and breakfast."

"Okay, Okay!" said Zhang, smiling, seeing the servant girl out, her mounting fury gathering like fast-moving dark clouds. So despite her tribulations, filthy rich Master Xiang had ruined her long-considered designs with a single stroke!

> *Planting tobacco with fine manure not a single leaf's yellow;*
> *But without a mate to match him, the son of Li's a lonely fellow.*

Such rhythmic musings hammered her aching heart. She had never expected things would turn out so badly. Quietly setting down her basket, she sat down on the bed, tormented by a biting shame.

As soon as the trumpet blew reveille the next morning, she set aside her pride and went to the kitchen for two corn cakes. Leaving the gate of the conceited Xiangs, she returned homeward in a huff, the tailless pig leg more cumbersome with each step. In half a lifetime of matchmaking, this was the first time the family of a prospective bride had refused the betrothal gift. Xiang had not only refused the gift, but had severed the tail! How shameful!

Zigzagging forward, the road cut into the cliff. She put down her basket next to a large withered branch. Undoing her pipe from her waist belt, Third Auntie sat on the basket. She lit her pipe and took several fierce puffs before tapping out the bowl against the branch. Suddenly, the brown "branch" reared up and, torqueing its body, twisted around and shot along the cliff face. Recoiling a good ten feet, Third Auntie tumbled backward. Alas, it was a "flying javelin snake." Camouflaged like a tree branch, nobody knew the position of the snake's eyes, ears, nose, or mouth. Slowly, Third Auntie calmed down after the shock. Finally, wiping away the cold sweat from her brow with a sigh of irritation, she hoisted her basket and left.

Though spring sunlight seeped into the deep gorge shedding light on the steep cliff and the road cut under her feet, the matchmaker was sunk in bitter gloom as she trudged forward. Despite her anger, afraid the "flying javelin snake" might return, she cast a wary gaze toward the steep, forested slope. Suddenly, her face contorted in fear: a dhole wild dog, pursued by an ambling white-breasted moon bear, ran through the woods. The black bear loped forward in a queer fashion. At second glance, she saw a second dhole latched to the moon bear's back. Bigger than a dog, the dhole was tinged yellow, with sharp, powerful forepaws. Thirty or forty fellow dhole trailed.

So the dhole leisurely leading the moon bear on was just bait, a go-between! With a sudden thrust and a jerk, the dhole on the moon bear's back plunged its forepaw deep into the asshole of the larger creature and extracted a winding length of intestine, seizing it between its sharp teeth. In a frenzy of pain, the tormented bear dashed to and fro, then tumbled in agony down the steep slope. As Third Auntie watched in rapt paralysis from her vantage on the cliff-face road, the pack of dhole descended on the injured bear.

Moving fast as lightning, with its long, pointed muzzle and horsetail, the dhole was the most bloodthirsty predator in the forest, its razor-sharp two-inch claws perfect for tearing asunder the assholes of prey. Even a leopard, encountering a pack of dhole, would alertly back into a corner to protect its backside. The pack would devour the poor moon bear in a trice, leaving only the head and gray piles of scat clotted with black hair here and there in the mountain forest. Eyeing the terrible scene, the matchmaker initially sunk deeper into her haze of despondency. Yet the sturdy woman discovered in the violent episode a certain cathartic inspiration: She, too, would claw back her honor like the fierce dhole.

IV

Around the mountaintops, bright-colored clouds danced, yet at the foot of the mountain all appeared somber and dark. No human speech was heard from the Li ranch, only the howling of monkeys from the surrounding forests. Where on earth could they find Mawu's future wife?

When the shamed Third Auntie Zhang returned to Gengguping, beating her chest in indignation, a cloud of gloom enveloped the Li family. Furious and embarrassed, Li Diezhu seethed at Xiang Jintang's indecorous, mean-spirited rejection. If Xiang didn't want to betroth his daughter that was one thing, but to hum those hurtful ditties was excessive! Anyhow, given his family's wealth, Li Diezhu felt that to be disparaged as "reeking of the cornfield" was disgraceful. With the same determination as the matchmaker, he vowed to reclaim his dignity with a good match.

At daybreak several months later Mawu rose and resolutely set out, riding to Huangshui. After buying a string of firecrackers, he passed purposefully before the Jin family home where he saw a woman and a beautiful young girl, each carrying a wicker pan of sliced potatoes, sauntering into the courtyard to bask in the sun. He guessed that the woman must be Jin Shaosan's wife and the girl his daughter, a famed local beauty. At once, he called out with a blushing face, "Mrs. Jin, your daughter is now engaged!" Then and there, right in front of the two surprised women, before either could respond, he lit a string of firecrackers he had hung from a tree branch.

All this stemmed from the unexpected death of Liebao, the ward chief's eldest son. One day shortly after Third Auntie returned defeated, a disturbance shook the forested slope as downtrodden Li Diezhu and Mawu weeded the fields. Fetching his shotgun, ever close at hand, Li Diezhu beheld a ravening pack of dhole, savage mountain dogs, besetting a black wild ox. In an effort to disperse the pack, father and son loosed a series of yells. Unfazed, the dhole pressed their attack. One crawled up the back of the ox and scratched out an eye. Li Diezhu fired, a fine mist of gunpowder blackening his face. Finally, the dholes scattered.

Bellowing in pain and rage, the frenzied ox crashed through the underbrush, Li Diezhu and Mawu on its heels. With only a single hunting gun, they dared not fire again for fear that if they missed the wild ox would round on them.

"Ho, everyone! We need reinforcements!" shouted Mawu. The mountains winds whistled through the forest. After a while, he blew a blast on his oxhorn, sending a low, resonant echo through the mountains.

Dusk descended. Several farmers, including Liebao and his younger brother Liexiong, flintlock rifles in hand, rushed through the woods toward the sound, racing after the baying hounds—the white bitch capering up scarps like a mountain goat, the heavy black hound ambling like a bear, the brindle leaping gullies like a magpie taking flight, the roan surging forward like a badger, the gray hound at the fore like a ramping tiger.

The hunting dogs barked fiercely at the wild ox, a staunch three-year old male separated from its herd by the dhole pack. Known for their prodigious appetites, wild oxen roamed in herds over a vast territory, ever seeking food. But no one had seen a wild ox around Huangshui for years; most folks figured they were extinct. First coursed by the relentless dhole pack and now by the determined mountainfolk, the unfortunate creature wearied. Guns in hand, dogs excitedly running ahead, they drove the wild ox into the turbulent currents of the river. Losing its footing, the ox staggered and tumbled over and over along the riverbed, swept along by the torrent.

Mawu was in close pursuit. Not far behind, the two Qins tore along, whooping with wild fervor. Liebao had gone to Huangshui to attend Master Wang's private school a half-year after the Lis; he had returned to the Qin's homestead only six months earlier. A green hunter, he had never encountered such large quarry. When mountain men hunted wild boar, deer, or badgers, they coursed their prey doggedly, with a nimble recklessness. Unfortunate Qin Liebao, however, stumbled and fell head-over-heels into the ravine. Breathless, Liexiong called, "Brother!" To reach his Liebao, he dragged a small fallen trunk to the escarpment. Under the sunless forest canopy, though, the rotted trunk proved too punky; with a hollow cracking sound, it split and Liexiong tumbled between splintering branches into the gorge below.

Wounded and exhausted, more dead than alive, the wild ox drifted with the powerful current until it lodged against a boulder. Li Diezhu, Mawu, ward chief Qin, and several other mountainfolk forded the shallow, strong waters, approaching the beast. While Lie Diezhu had killed water buffalo, he had never killed a wild ox. Guessing that other than the thicker hide of the powerful ox the creatures were built in similar fashion, he figured he just needed to use a little more force. Therefore, taking an axe from a farmer, he put all his strength into a mighty blow targeting the one-inch gap between vertebrae on the back of its thick, muscled neck. The axe cut cleanly through. The creature's four hooves twitched in a series of violent spasms before the ox slumped lifeless in the shallows.

Binding the four hooves with bamboo-strip ropes, the men thrust a sword between the collarbone and ribs of the ox, making a hole for the icy brook water to chill the chest cavity. Then, with great effort, they dragged the ox to the boulder-strewn riverbank, before hurriedly dressing and cutting it into pieces.

Li Diezhu counted those present. Each piece of meat was wrapped in palm fronds so nobody could tell which portions were choicest. Then, leaving the coagulated blood and innards to the dogs, each hunter took a palm-bound parcel.

Only then did Qin notice the absence of his two sons, Liebao and Liexiong. He raised his voice and called out into the pitch darkness, but there was no response. Stricken by dread, he backtracked, torch in hand.

Mawu wondered, "Could they have fallen down a cliff?" Passing his bundle of meat to Li Diezhu to bring home, Mawu and several others, torches held aloft, bound at their waists by a bamboo-strip rope, rappelled down to the bottom of the gorge next to the quick-rushing waters, seeking the lost brothers. After searching for a spell, they came across Liebao and Liexiong sprawled in a clump of bushes, one unconscious and the other groaning sadly. The torchlight illumined two pools of blood.

In the end, man's destiny is little different from that of animals. Casting himself on the bodies, Qin howled in distress. As the mountainfolk bore his beloved sons back to the Qin ranch, he wept in grief.

Poor Liebao's skull had been smashed to pieces on a limestone protrusion. Wet with blood, Liexiong had suffered a broken leg.

Mawu returned home. "Did you find them?" Li Diezhu asked.

"Liebao fell to his death and Liexiong broke his leg." Shocked by the death of his peer, Mawu's face convulsed in horror.

"Such a pity," Li Diezhu remarked sadly, mouth agape. He recalled when he and Liebao had sparred with bamboo poles.

Struck dumb, Tao Jiuxiang stared blankly. Could it be true? The sturdy young pup was no more. The painstaking years of schooling, taxing mind and spirit, all for naught! Gasping at the thought, she murmured sadly, "All that education gone to waste: he would have been better off marrying earlier and leaving behind a seed."

Mawu raised his head and looked at his father, and the latter met his gaze. Both were thinking the same thing: now no one was betrothed to Miss Jin, the eldest daughter of Jin Shaosan, a wealthy villager from Peppercorn Bend.

It was said that Jin was a beauty, lovely enough to inflame men in this world and goad spirits from the next. One day, Zhou Taiwang's wife saw the girl and returned home to tell her husband that a fairy maiden had been born to the Jins. A hired laborer for the Qins, Zhou Taiwang told Liebao and Liexiong dirty stories. Just starting to have some notion of love and sex, Liebao couldn't stand the titillation and deep into the night, hugging his pillow beneath his body, vented his ardor. The next day, he marched ten miles along mountain roads to Peppercorn Bend, his little fourteen year-old rooster, his cock, standing erect the entire way, his younger brother Liexiong in tow. Reaching the gates of the Jin household, they lit string after deafening string of firecrackers. According to local custom, this marked their engagement. After that, ward chief Qin asked Zhou Taiwang's wife to visit the Jins to ask the girl's birthdate and formalize the betrothal. The wedding to welcome her to the Qin household had been planned for the coming fall.

But the sweet girl had become a widow before marriage!

Heedless of reason, racked by desire, Mawu conceived a searing passion for Jin that diminished his sorrow for Liebao's untimely death. The fundamentals of modern education he had gleaned in the private school led him to think independently about marriage. Liebao had publicly declared his engagement to Miss Jin by lighting firecrackers at the family's gate, but now he was dead. When a hawk drops a choice piece of meat, if one wolf doesn't seize it another hound will. Mawu gathered his wits and said to his father, "I hear Liebao's betrothed Jin was lovely enough to inflame men in this world and goad spirits in the next."

On the streets of Huangshui Li Diezhu had seen Jin Shaosan, clad in a collarless blue shirt and sporting a melon-skin skullcap all year round. Ever smiling, like the Buddha in the earth temple, Jin Shaosan had an A-shaped moustache, like the character eight [八]. Folks called him Cheerful Jin. Jin's family was wealthy, on top of which his daughter was gorgeous. At his son's remark, Li Diezhu emptied his smoking pipe and, with the same lack of compunction as his son, nodded, "Everybody says she's a beauty. Now, let's get Third Auntie to persuade the Jins to let her remarry."

The more he mulled it over, the more Mawu thirsted for the match. Finally he burst from the house, saying, "I'd better claim her by lighting a string of firecrackers before some other guy does!"

Chapter Three

I

Though after Liebao's death the Jins heard no further tidings from the Qins, when handsome Mawu lit firecrackers signaling his intent to marry Jin, Old Mother Jin felt misgivings.

In the bloom of youth, Mawu sported the same smart, mid-length hairstyle as in his school days. With his slightly sun-browned complexion, thick brows, and high nose, he was the most dashing young man Huangshui had ever seen. Together with Sun Fu, one of the Lis' newly hired day laborers, Mawu was searching for "breaking snakes," as locals called glass lizards. Roughly a foot long, when "breaking snakes" fell from trees, they shattered into several pieces. Miraculously, within ten minutes, the fragments sutured together and the snake would slither away intact. Local apothecaries used the "breaking snake" to mend broken bones. Regretting the accident that had befallen Liexiong, Mawu hoped to use this divine medicine to heal his neighbor's fractured leg.

After wandering up slopes and down gullies the entire day, sharp-eyed Sun Fu glimpsed a small, black-backed snake sunning itself on a large rock. "There it is!" he exclaimed, raking the snake down from the rock with a horse mulberry branch. Then and there, the snake broke into four writhing segments, its tail longer and the other three shorter. As the fragments thrashed about, the head slid into the deep grass. With bated breath the duo watched as, after a spell, the head-end slowly emerged from the undergrowth and timidly approached another segment. When the two broken ends came into contact, after several trembling spasms, the parts joined together! Soon all four parts fused together and the snake was whole again.

"That's it!" said Sun Fu, lifting the snake into a bamboo cage with the mulberry branch. Mawu rushed the bamboo cage to the Qins. As the lizard was neither poisonous nor aggressive, Qin simply placed it in a wine vat by hand. In return, he gifted Mawu a handful of tobacco leaves.

When Li Diezhu heard Sun Fu had caught a breaking snake, he was greatly relieved. At once he sent Third Auntie Zhang to the Jins to exchange betrothal horoscopes—recording year, month, day, and hour of birth—for marital compatibility. However, Jin Shaosan told her that the Qins had never returned his daughter's horoscope.

"Liebao is no more," oily Third Auntie responded, nimbly wagging her silver tongue. "Besides, the government recently issued a law prohibiting a widow from remarrying her deceased husband's brother. It doesn't matter whether her horoscope is returned or not."

"Who listens to the government?" Jin Shaosan replied anxiously.

"Think of how well Mawu matches your daughter!" exulted Third Auntie. "In property and wealth, no household in the tenth ward surpasses the Lis. Liexiong is too young to marry your daughter—it'd be like raising a child-husband. And if your daughter waits a couple of years, she'll be too old to marry. Why not give her betrothal horoscope to the Li family? An *yin-yang* diviner can gauge her compatibility with Mawu. Who knows, this might be the perfect match destined by Heaven. If you miss out, you'll regret it."

Jin Shaosan and his wife mulled it over and over before reluctantly giving Third Auntie their daughter's horoscope card.

The hard-won horoscope in hand, a satisfied Third Auntie Zhang returned to Gengguping. However, she shook her head, sighing as she addressed father and son, "Ah, this is going to be hard to pull off. The Qins want their second son to marry Jin."

At these words, sweat beaded on Mawu's brow. Rife with restless primal energy, the mountain air was so pregnant with moisture that the slightest touch brought about a rain of water droplets. Clouds enveloped the yard, and wild vines and creepers climbed the ancient trees. Clinging to the trunks, flourishing in the dampness and decay, fungi grew thick and fast. Each night, each endless forest night, surrounded by this generative force, this sensual symphony, Mawu listened in an agony of desire to the whistling of the wind through the groaning trees, the howling of wolves, and the buzzing of cicadas. As the calluses on his feet thickened during his five years of forest life, so too, day by day, month by month, year by year, grew the meaty organ between his legs. Now, no matter whether he lay or stood, that creature swelled and grew turgid. How he thirsted in anticipation for the fairy maiden his father had promised!

Li Diezhu sank into a state of vexation. Over the past five years, his wild-hearted ambitions had grown apace with the rapid expansion of the family enterprise. However, now he was mired in a prickly situation, an impasse, unsure of how to handle his relationship with the Qins and Mawu's prospective marriage. Humbly, he consulted Third Auntie Zhang.

The matchmaker remarked, "An ox should graze good grassland, and a daughter should be married to a good husband." Thoughtfully, she continued, "Liexiong is lame and too young for marriage. Of course the Jins favor Mawu. The Qins are grief-stricken with Liebao's death and Liexiong's injury, so this year they won't concern themselves with a happy matter like marriage. Just wait. Sooner of later Jin Shaosan will come to you." Though father and son felt uneasy and burned with impatience, the matchmaker's words sounded so reasonable that they agreed to wait.

Like flowing water, days and weeks passed. Jin Shaosan and his wife hemmed and hawed, not knowing what to do. Finally one day, riding a pony, Liexiong called on them. Since he had recovered, ward chief Qin had hired an instructor from Enshi to teach his son reading and stick fighting. The master also taught Qin's third and fourth sons, Lieniu and Longping. This way, the ward headman felt, the three brothers might make their way in the world without being bullied.

Though Liexiong was lame in one leg, he rode well enough. When he ventured out to the bustling market in Huangshui for the first time since his convalescence, he took the occasion to drop in on the Jins and see his future wife. It still needled him to recall that last time when he had lit firecrackers with Liebao to stake his brother's engagement claim, they had run away too hastily to get a good look at her.

Jin Shaosan's wife was chopping kindling for dinner when the barking of the dog startled her. Seeing thirteen-year old Liexiong stumping over the embankment toward the gate, she frowned, entered the house, and said to her daughter, Miss Jin, who was doing embroidery at the window, "I'm afraid the second son of the Qins has come."

Alarmed, like a mouse fleeing a cat, Miss Jin hurriedly slammed the door and hid herself in the inner recesses of the house.

Liexiong knocked. As Jin Shaosan had gone out to work in his fields early in the morning, Mother Jin nervously opened the door, unsure how to handle the situation in her husband's absence. Bowing respectfully, Liexiong called out, "Auntie, I am Liebao's younger brother Liexiong. I've come to Huangshui for fun, and figured I'd stop by to see you and Uncle Jin." With these words, he laid a wild hare he had shot on the floor.

A clumsy hostess, Mother Jin served the young fellow tea and sat with him awkwardly for a spell, trying to guess his intentions. Looking around, Liexiong failed to spot Miss Jin. Disappointed, he stood up shortly and took leave, "Auntie, I have to go, but I'll visit again in a couple of days." He turned and stumbled out the door.

The moment Mother Jin shut the door behind the unexpected visitor, Miss Jin ran out of her room and peered curiously through the crack in the door. Though she didn't want Qin Liexiong to see her, she wanted to get a peek at him.

However, hearing a noise behind him, Liexiong whirled and pushed the upper half-door violently inward leaving him face-to-face with startled Miss Jin. Her brows rose in shock, her pert black lashes set above her wide, lovely shimmering eyes. Letting out a cry, she spun away and retreated to her room, her wonderful braid dancing behind her, and began sobbing.

Liexiong hurriedly apologized for his intrusion. Though annoyed, there was nothing Mother Jin could do.

Recalling Liexiong's leering smile, Jin seethed with humiliated rage, feeling severely insulted. Liexiong was four years her junior, three inches shorter than her, and lame to boot. Better to die alone than marry such a man.

As Liexiong, satisfied, left, Mother Jin accompanied her weeping daughter. She suddenly thought of Mawu, who had lit firecrackers to announce his intention to marry Miss Jin and had his horoscope delivered. Why hadn't they heard further tidings from the Lis over the months? According to his horoscope Li Mawu was nineteen years old, an age at which a young man would be eager for marriage. The fierce wind roared in the mountains, howling forth the distress and agitation of the Jin family.

When Jin Shaosan returned from the fields he told his flushed and weeping daughter, "Since Li Mawu has lit firecrackers and delivered his horoscope, he'll come to claim you sooner or later. I'll go discuss the matter with them."

II

It was the tenth lunar month. As the grass turned yellow and falling leaves danced capriciously in the breeze, a listless mountain spirit dozed off in a crevice of rock. On this bleak autumn afternoon at Huangshui's finest inn, anxious Jin Shaosan called for tea and set places, readying a banquet for several special guests. Fearing disaster, he had decided with no little trepidation to follow Third Auntie's suggestion to spend some money to invite a respected local gentleman, Wang Binquan, to mediate between the Lis and the Qins and settle the matter once and for all.

On horseback, the fathers and sons of the two families rode along the cold and cheerless street. Since each father had learned about his son's desire to take Jin in marriage, Li Diezhu and Qin Zhanyun had taken pains to avoid meeting one another. Now, solemnly approaching the inn, the two men exchanged an awkward greeting.

All those present were fellow townsmen and neighbors. In the final decade of the Qing dynasty, the mediator Wang Binquan had earned a position as a state scholar at the Imperial University. Later, he was appointed commander of the local army in Huangshui but, unable to get along with the greedy officials and corrupt bureaucrats staffing the ranks, he was dismissed for his unbending righteousness. Filled with indignation, Wang returned home and set up a private academy, where, with two assistants, he had educated local children for the past thirty years, including the sons of the Qins and Lis. Far and wide in greater Huangshui, all praised his lofty reputation and impeccable character.

Stroking his white beard, the mediator began straightaway, quoting the classics: "As Confucius says, 'All men greatly desire food, drink, and nuptial union.' And in the *Book of Poetry* it is written that 'The modest, virtuous beauty makes a perfect match for a true gentleman.' Yet though the conjoining of man and woman is a natural principle of heaven and earth, it must be undertaken with proper decorum."

Bowing and nodding repeatedly in assent, Jin Shaosan murmured, "Yes.

So true, so true."

Master Wang wore a round cap and a long gown. Shaking his head, he criticized the backward customs in the mountain regions, "Nowadays, even in provincial cities young people freely choose their marriage partners. But here in Huangshui, people still light firecrackers, kidnap brides, and marry their own cousins! All our folk, man and woman, old and young, are wonderful singers and dancers—wandering the hills and valleys singing ululating love songs. And we wonder why others call us 'savage!'"

Grinning sheepishly, Li Diezhu and ward chief Qin jointly acknowledged, "Yeah, no doubt, we mountain folk are a savage lot."

Master Wang corrected them, "That's because in these changing times we are tucked away in the remote mountains clinging to backward, primitive customs, and so a man still tends to seize a wife by force. It's shameful, but we regard it as glorious!"

Continuing to bow and nod, Jin Shaosan agreed yet again, "Yes. So true, so true."

Sprinkling his suasions with quotes from the *Book of Poetry* and the *Analects* of Confucius as he presided, Master Wang sought to convince Li Diezhu and Qin Zhanyun to have their sons relinquish their respective firecracker claims to Jin, and to seek a new engagement based on equality and freedom.

"Sir, how do you think we should resolve this matter?" Qin asked anxiously.

Mr. Wang, fingering his white mustaches, answered, "First of all, let's get one thing straight: Are both families willing to take Miss Jin as a daughter-in-law?"

"Yes!" replied Li Diezhu and ward headman Qin simultaneously, facing each other across the banquet table.

"Is the daughter of the family Jin willing to marry into either the Li or the Qin family?" asked Master Wang.

"I have only one daughter. How can she be daughter-in-law to both?" gasped Jin Shaosan.

"Then let your honorable daughter choose," the arbiter smiled.

Nervously, the two fathers of the prospective grooms stared at each other. Jin Shaosan glanced at Mawu, seated next to him. Around his high-bridged nose, Mawu's swarthy complexion took on an anxious glow. Glancing at Liexiong behind him, Jin Shaosan saw that the agitated little fellow was fidgeting with his nose, fervent eyes aflame with expectation. Flushing with embarrassment, Jin Shaosan stammered, "Both are fellow villagefolk and neighbors. How could I . . ."

As other patrons of the inn drifted over to see what the hubbub was about, ringing the table, the tension grew: the situation had reached an impasse. Irritated, Master Wang snapped, "Is this really that hard? You summoned me to act as arbiter in this dispute, then vacillate like this. How am I to act as a mediator? I cannot keep this company!" With these words, he sprang to his feet to leave.

"Please don't go, sir!" begged Jin Shaosan, with an obsequious tug at one of Master Wang's sleeves. "Please be seated, and let me think it over."

"Let the spirits decide!" blurted one of the onlookers.

"Yeah!" chimed in a cacophony of other impatient villagers, seeing rattled Jin Shaosan hemming and hawing. "Better let the spirits decide."

"The spirits decide?" Jin Shaosan mopped sweat from his forehead. "Uh . . . um, so be it. Let the spirits decide!"

"How?" Master Wang asked thoughtfully.

"The two young men can play the grass game," Jin Shaosan answered, regaining his wits. "The winner shall marry my daughter."

"Do you both agree?" Master Wang asked Li Diezhu and ward chief Qin.

"All right," said Li Diezhu.

"Win or lose, it's Heaven's will. This way we can maintain harmony," Qin consented.

With a bitter smile, Master Wang shook his head, saying, "Will someone kindly help pick some stalks of grass?"

"I'll go!" volunteered a villager named Shi Eryang. He dashed out the door and a moment later returned with a handful of half-withered grass.

"Li Mawu," called Mr. Wang, "Choose a stalk."

From the tightly bunched bundle Mawu chose a princely stalk, strong yet pliant, and set it on the table.

"Qin Liexiong," said Mr. Wang. "Your turn."

As more onlookers clustered around the table, Liexiong eagerly picked a stalk of his liking.

"Once for all, or best two of three?" asked Mr. Wang.

"Once for all!" cried Mawu and Liexiong in unison, without hesitation.

Every boy in Huangshui knew how to play the grass game. Riveted, the two fathers watched their sons knot their stalks together then seal the rite of competition with a mysterious exhalation, a holdover from earlier traditions of grass divination. Facing each other, Mawu and Liexiong each held an end of the interlaced stalks. Simultaneously, they chanted, "One . . . two . . . three," then forcefully pulled back. Then and there, the interlaced stalks separated. The straw in Liexiong's hand was broken, while Mawu's princely stalk remained undamaged.

Li Diezhu looked at his son with pride, though an odd disquiet rumbled within, reverberating in his chest.

"As we agreed, the competition was one match, winner take all," Master Wang said authoritatively. "Li Mawu is the winner. Thus, freely and on equal terms, Miss Jin shall be engaged to Li Mawu. This marks progress for our town of Huangshui: the backward practice of engagement by force has been avoided. Let me suggest that Jin Shaosan play host and entertain all present with a round of liquor."

"Certainly!" said Jin Shaosan, greatly relieved. He called out to the inn's attendants, "Come and serve liquor. Bring the wine! It's on me."

"Once more," cried the aggrieved Liexiong. "Best two out of three."

The surrounding villagers exploded with laughter. Squeezing to the front of the crowd, Shi Eryang gloated, "Guess you shouldn't have let the spirits decide."

"Offer congratulations to your elder brother Mawu," instructed ward chief Qin angrily. Magnanimously, he led the crestfallen young man before his rival.

When distraught Liexiong thought of Jin's lovely melonseed-shaped face, her rosy cheeks, her thick lashes set above lovely dark eyes, her exquisite mouth, and her and pert nose, tears welled in his eyes. He said to Mawu, "Now, Miss Jin is yours."

Li Diezhu was not the only one who felt the rumbling. Coming from the eastern skies, the droning hum grew ever clearer. Now Master Wang and others heard it, too.

"Listen. Listen!" said Master Wang. Knitting his brow, his relief quickly turned to puzzlement, "How is it that gunfire is sounding in the heavens?"

III

Tucked among interconnected valleys and chains of mountains, high in the east and low in the west, Huangshui was situated along the many branches of Inkblack Creek. Fecund alluvial plains that locals called *caoba*, "grassy carses," stretched along the banks. Of these rich fields, villagers said, "A bowl of mud on the *caoba* is worth a bowl of rice." The Jins were petty landlords who owned one of these fertile sections of riverbank.

With silver and some land of his own, Li Diezhu, still stinging from Xiang Jintang's sarcastic jibe about "reeking of corn" and burning to prove himself, managed to acquire ten additional prime acres of *caoba* along Peppercorn Bend. Possession of this lush alluvial belt not only salvaged family dignity, but promised to provide prolific harvests of rice and corn for decades to come.

Mawu's engagement to Jin put father and son in high spirits. Li Diezhu told the Jins that the wedding ceremony would take place in the last month of the lunar year. Returning to Gengguping, the entire family was abuzz, busily and excitedly preparing for the wedding.

"We must invite Xia Qifa, the *tima*, to our home. Without him, our family would be living destitute on the banks of the Greenstone River!" As the wedding day drew near, Li Diezhu selected a haunch of cured meat hanging from a rafter, placing it along with half a sack of rice into a back-basket, and sent Sun Fu, his hired laborer, to call on Xia Qifa in Dragon Decapitating Gorge.

Sun Fu peered into the back-basket. Apprehensively, he shook his head and said, "Master, a ghost will seize the cured meat. I don't dare to head through the forest toting that haunch on my back."

Standing to one side, Tao Jiuxiang responded pensively, "Bind a couple of swords to it, and no ghost will dare to touch the meat."

Still partly incredulous, Sun Fu said, "Mistress, don't fool with me."

Tao Jiuxiang said seriously, "No one's fooling you. Just think about it. No mountain ghost would touch something to which a shaman had bound a sword."

Finding her logic sound, Sun Fu promptly found four daggers of various lengths. He fixed them to his back-basket so they pointed upward like oxhorns, their sharp blades glinting in the sun. In this terrifying manner, he marched toward Dragon Decapitating Gorge.

Six days later, clad in a patched cotton gown, his five-foot staff in hand, Xia Qifa arrived at Gengguping, trudging through ankle-deep snow with his twelve-year-old son Xia Liangxian and Sun Fu in tow.

On this sunny winter day, light clouds scudded past as tree branches layered with ice creaked and cracked in the cold wind. Xia Qifa could speak to birds. A pair of birds began to follow him, flying back and forth, from time to time perching on his shoulders, twittering and chirping. He paused in surprise, then broke off pieces of potato cake to feed them. Putting his numb, cold-reddened fingers into his mouth, he mimicked a lilting bird call, "*Ji-jiu-jiu! Ji-jiu-jiu! Jiu!*" Knowing they had met with a kindred spirit, the birds flitted cheerfully just above his head, twittering, "*Zhi-cha-cha . . . zhi-cha-cha.*" As they crossed the plains of Lihaku, they heard a small brook gurgling, though they could see no water. Frost crusted the ancient trees on both side of the creek, while ice coated bushes and grass—a world of jade trees and crystal flowers! Strangely, the grounds around the hidden brook were unfrozen; among the clustered dead leaves at the creek's margin grew snow-capped wild fruit and mushrooms. Xia Qifa exclaimed, "I've got it! So that's what you wanted to tell me!"

Curiously, Xia Liangxian asked, "Dad, what did the birds say?"

White steam issuing from his mouth, his eyes bright, Xia Qifa answered,

"They are singing,"

> We step here and there, curling our toes, we step there and here;
> Curling our toes, we step here and there;
> Toes move back and forth, claws clench into a ball;
> We step here and there, step and step.
> Glance at the sky, the sky narrows,
> Glance at the earth, the earth narrows, too.

He followed these words with a series of rhythmic, lilting twitters and chirps that drew more birds, flitting high and low, back and forth, as they circled the *tima*.

With dawning understanding, Xia Liangxian pointed to the creek, saying excitedly, "They are twittering about the hidden river!"

In straw sandals bound with palm leaves, Xia Qifa moved gingerly, drifting like an immortal. He nodded cheerfully, "Your uncle Li is a lucky fellow. With no work, he gets something for nothing."

In the afternoon, treading lightly after Sun Fu, father and son entered the main gate of the Li household. Xia Qifa's eyes beamed like torchlight. Paying no attention to the coarse-hewn beams of the house, he caught sight of Tao Jiuxiang, a thick cobblestone pestle in hand, pounding tealeaves in a tapered stone mortar out in the yard. With an intimate air, the *tima* bantered, "Mistress, you are pounding too hard. I don't care if the mortar breaks, but take it easy on the pestle."

Nonplussed by Xia Qifa's suggestive, ribald greeting, Tao Jiuxiang flushed and cursed in the local dialect, "During these last few years that we haven't seen you the *tima*'s changed into a lecherous insect-spirit and sparrow demon!" Beset with conflicting emotions, she wiped her eyes with her sleeve.

"The *tima*'s here!" thundered Li Diezhu. He rushed into the yard and clasped Xia Qifa in a hearty embrace. Together, they entered the house. Turning round, Li Diezhu roared, "Boys, hurry up and greet Uncle Xia! He's the one who directed us to this land of luck and bounty."

Just back home from the county school in Fengjie for vacation, Mahe and Masui were behind the house taking turns lifting and shaking one end of a large, heavy bamboo winnowing pan filled with goldthread rhizomes to shake loose tendrils and dirt, staunch Mawu holding the other side. Hearing the shouts of their parents, they set it down and headed inside.

"You've been gone a while. Did you have trouble finding him?" Tao Jiuxiang asked Sun Fu in the kitchen, adding boiling water to a bowl of seasoned flour mush.

Sun Fu said, "It's easy to find *Tima* Xia. He was out helping a couple birth a son. I waited two days before he got back home. As soon as he heard your invitation, we took off right away."

The Li family entertained the *tima* with their finest fare. Regrettably, the shaman abstained from alcohol. At the dining table, Tao Jiuxiang looked at handsome Xia Liangxian and remarked with doting affection, "Liangxian has grown into a dashing young man. Where can you hunt up a beauty who's a worthy match?"

"This coming spring I'm sending him to Master Wang's private academy to learn a little 'Confucius says'—teach the boy to have a nimble mind," said Xia Qifa. Xia Liangxian had been born when the shaman was forty. With a blade-straight brow set above sparkling eyes and a high nose, he had grown into a singularly handsome youth. The trio of Li sons cast curious glances at their younger guest. But it was pockmarked Masui's lingering gaze, mingling envy and curiosity, that caused Liangxian to flush with childish nervousness.

"What about your daughter Yinmei? How old is she?" asked a drunken Li

Diezhu, thinking of the infant girl clambering along the back of Xia Qifa's wife like a doe hare's little kit.

"Lo! We've fed her for nine years," laughed Xia Qifa.

"Why not engage Yinmei to Mahe later? I'll stage a wedding even grander and more extravagant than this one." With boisterous cheer, Li Diezhu approached his old friend, courting Yinmei for his youngest son.

"Mahe has been educated in a modern school. How could he fancy Yinmei?" As he spoke, the *tima* looked appraisingly at Li Diezhu's youngest son.

"Masui is bright, but his face is pocked. The match wouldn't be fair to Yinmei. Now Mahe—he's perfectly sound, not a flaw or scar on his entire body. Their ages are well suited, too. Let's make an oral engagement, a gentlemen's agreement!" Li Diezhu lowered his voice, afraid his middle son Masui would be hurt at these words, then, his voice rising with emotion, he called out, "*Tima*, since you have led us to a good place to put down stakes, I'll give you a good fellow for a son-in-law."

"We know each other inside-out, why not set an engagement?" Xia Qifa declared briskly, his smile receding.

IV

Years earlier, when the *tima* led the overland diaspora from their former drought-stricken village, the five members of the Li family followed, saying countless goodbyes to other former neighbors who settled along the way. One evening, as the roseate evening clouds burned grandly on the horizon, they had just entered a gulch thick with speargrass when the *tima*, at the head of the tattered émigrés, stopped suddenly, gesturing for a pause. Obediently, the throngs halted. From behind a horse mulberry came a loud growl. The *tima* threw a stone toward the tree. Chilling the hearts of the villagers, the thrum, full of warning and menace, grew in volume.

"What's that?" Tao Jiuxiang asked nervously.

"A wild boar," said Li Diezhu.

Signaling, Xia Qifa said in a low voice, "Go! Go sideways!" He ordered Li Diezhu and the other émigrés into the concealment of the woods, then followed.

It grew silent.

Straw pricking his feet, Li Diezhu peered beyond the *tima* to see branches swiftly parted as if by a gust of wind. Suddenly, a guttural roar exploded, plunging the tattered throngs into muscle-clenching terror.

"Ah—Woooo!"

"A tiger? A striped tiger?" quaked Tao Jiuxiang, her soul sundered.

"Hurry!" exclaimed Li Diezhu, his heart racing madly.

As it moved away, the huge creature let loose another roar, lethargic and careless, but majestic. Walking past Li Diezhu and the frightened villagers, Xia Qifa said casually, "The tiger could have attacked if he had wanted to. Its paw-print was more than six inches long."

Calmly, the *tima* led the wanderers in another direction. After the time it takes to smoke several pipe bowls, they found themselves on a mountainslope covered with speargrass and horse mulberry scrubs. Opposite rose a steep cliff from which an ugly dragon's head protruded, fiercely gazing down at the valley below, its terrible mouth agape. A thick fir tree grew from the dragon's brow, as if it were the creature's horn.

Xia Qifa sized up the dragon for a moment, then remarked, "The wicked monster! When it violated the rules of heaven, causing floods and pulverizing mountains, Yu the Great, the flood queller who founded the Xia dynasty of old, captured and shackled this creature. He bound the dragon so firmly it couldn't move its claws. Look, all the other mountains are thickly forested; this peak alone is bare."

"Dragons often wreak havoc!" Li Diezhu said, looking round with amazement.

"A male dragon has two horns, and a female none. A one-horned dragon like this is called a *jiao*, a water dragon." Eyes aflame, Xia Qifa looked up at the dragon immured in the cliff, only its head sticking out. He added, "Each year the spawn of water dragons fall from the heavens. Any creature—whether man, pheasant, or cricket—eating the spawn, will itself turn into a *jiao*. When a *jiao* comes into being, the creature awakens to its might and causes catastrophic damage, inundating valleys and crushing mountains to rubble, leaving destruction in its wake. Yu the Great brought this water dragon under control with his golden lightning hooks."

Filled with mingled loathing and pity, Li Diezhu's eyes ran up the speargrass clustered along the stone crevices leading up the steep cliff-face until they finally reached the water dragon. After a long while he asked the *tima*, "Which is fiercer, a dragon or a tiger?"

"Both are kingly celestial beasts, numbering among the twelve creatures of the zodiac. As close supporters of Yu the Great, both were assigned to guard his domain. This one-horned dragon, however, was punished because it committed a crime as it moved toward the sea," an animated Xia Qifa explained.

A woodcutter emerged from a mulberry grove, beholding the wanderers in surprise. Unkempt Li Diezhu approached him, loudly inquiring, "Hey brother, what's this place called?"

In the local dialect, the rustic replied, "Dragon Decapitating Gorge, it's on the border between Huangshui and Greenstone."

Encircled by serene mountains, Xia Qifa listened attentively and looked around. The divine rite had foretold that their destination would be near a river with invisible water. For several moments he vacillated, uncertain—gazing upward at the stone water dragon's head jutting from the cliff. Infused with a sudden energy that set his spirit atremble, the *tima* set down his bamboo basket, raised the lower part of his long gown, knelt, and said with sparkling eyes, "This is it! This is the where we put down roots!"

Raising his brows, Li Diezhu mused, "I wonder if there is a spring, a stream, or a river around here?"

"With a dragon's head above us, how can we worry about a lack of water?" Running fingers through his matted rat's nest of a beard, Xia Qifa pointed to the ground beneath his feet, "Enclose this with stones, and it will become a paddy field."

While Li Diezhu trusted Xia Qifa's wisdom, he worried that the valley might be an inauspicious site to settle. How could the flood-bringing dragon, so long immured in the cliff as punishment for its wickedness, not seethe with resentment? Maybe the *tima*, a veritable demigod, was unafraid to have a dragon for a neighbor, but ordinary folk were different! In a low murmur he said to his wife, "Our children are springing up as quickly as bamboo shoots, but this place is too small for so many people. It won't be hard to find another site nearby with a spring or a stream." With these words, he lowered his gun and fired. Mawu dashed into a thicket and returned with a wild goat, limp in his hands.

"Seedlings grow into a forest. You may do well to delve deeper into these woods. The goldthread growing along the banks of the Yangzi originally came from this region. It is a site that may bring us great fortune." Raising his head, the *tima* gazed toward the dense forest, his expressive eyes brimming with excitement. Quickly, he walked to a nearby stubby, broad-leafed hardwood, broke off a branch, and, passing it to Li Diezhu, said, "Carry a sturdy branch like this with you, for this kind of *beijue* tree was named by the Bodhisattva King Yu the Great. Tigers fear it. One stroke and their hairs turn backward—can't raise their hackles!"

Li Diezhu well knew that after King Yu had quelled the great flood, the heroic savior had fixed names upon all the birds, beasts, insects, and fishes; the mountains, rivers, grasses, and trees. Delighted, he took the branch from the shaman.

That evening, the two families shared a delicious feast of roast wild goat. Xia Qifa taught Li Diezhu several series of hand gestures and finger movements, secret mudras of the Ancestor and Ancestress. Before ghosts could be exorcised or demons expelled these two venerable deities had to be summoned. In making virtually any spirit or demon submit, the mudra of the Ancestress was particularly effective. Though most often women employed the mudra of the Ancestress, the female *yin* principle was strong in the moist umbrage of the forest, so Xia Qifa taught it to Li Diezhu that he might better protect himself.

The following day, tiger-warding branch in hand, Li Diezhu led his family into the heart of the primeval forest. Two sunsets later, they cheerfully settled in the green woods, among red wildflowers. Next to a huge rock on the south exposure of a mountain, Li Diezhu cleared the ground with his brush-axe, while Tao Jiuxiang knocked down wild fruit with a stick, gathering them into a pile for her family. Exhausted from the journey, their three sons—the eldest sixteen, the second fourteen, and the youngest thirteen—sprawled on the ground eating wild oranges and grapes. As dusk turned to night, only vague outlines of mountains and forests remained visible. Li Diezhu kindled dry straw with his flint, immediately tossing it onto a pile of dry horse mulberry and pine branches. In the gusting night wind, the pile burned fiercely. Legend told that horse mulberry trees used to be so high they reached the heavens, allowing people to climb up and reach the sky. Later, however, a divinity cursed the mulberry, causing the trees to grow so stunted and gnarled that they were good only for firewood. For generations, people of the region had used this quick-kindling wood for cooking fires. Tao Jiuxiang attentively turned a wild hare Li Diezhu had shot on a spit; its aromatic smoke rose, portending a delectable meal. Drawn by the firelight, a tiger-striped monarch butterfly the size of human palm flitted over, circling Li Diezhu and Tao Jiuxiang. Li Diezhu waved his arms to drive it away. The monarch glided off gracefully but returned a moment later, flitting to and fro. Tao Jiuxiang gazed at it for a moment, held out an ash-stained palm, and intoned quietly, "Butterfly oh butterfly, if you come from my ancestors please come down and land on the back of my hand."

Unbelievably, the tiger-patterned butterfly alit on her palm. As Li Diezhu, amazed, gazed fixedly at his wife's extended hand, a strand of doubt welled up. He echoed Tao Jiuxiang's prayer, "Butterfly, if you've truly come from the spirits, please land on the back of my hand." With these words, he deliberately turned over his palm. The butterfly, however, merely moved its delicate legs, twitched its wings, and soared into the night. "What a fool I am!" Li Diezhu groaned, repentant, slapping himself on the thigh, his eyes opened wide. "You proved your presence, yet I still wanted you to prove it again. How utterly stupid!"

This unforgettable night was stored in family memory, from the miraculous butterfly to the mouth-watering fragrance wafting from the fat hare spitted above the fire, its drippings crackling. Unchanged from antediluvian times, wood, fire, earth, wind, and water surrounded the family. Li Diezhu burned another small pile of wood to heat the narrow strip of ground, quickly clearing the ashes to allow his wife and sons to rest in comfortable warmth. Shotgun in hand at the fireside, he sleeplessly stood guard. At dawn, he began to hew a tree trunk into a beam with his brush axe. Tao Jiuxiang and their trio of unkempt sons ran back and forth, helping move building materials. Like a colony of ants making a nest, inspired by their flitting ancestral spirit, they built a primitive shanty on the very spot.

V

Now, decked in green and red ribbons, the Lis' new, splendid estate on the rhino's rump of Gengguping had taken on a festive air for Mawu's wedding. The dry winter winds blew with a piercing chill; a layer of snow coated the surrounding valleys. The wedding sedan from Peppercorn Bend bearing the seal of the Li family had embarked. Jin Shaosan hired master-craftsman Zhu Shun as the wedding escort, charging him with organizing and transporting the bride's sizeable trousseau. Rhythmically swaying as they carried the sedan chair, carriers marched toward Gengguping, followed by a cluster of porters. In their wake trumpets, drums, and gongs played a repetitive bittersweet ditty:

> *Aha, aha, ahee,*
> *Get a wife to boil the tea!*

As Jin was a widow-fiancée—her first husband had died before marriage—according to custom she should have been transported in a black sedan chair. However, smitten with his lovely bride-to-be, Mawu insisted on a red sedan chair. The eighth day of the new lunar year saw the arrival of seventeen-year-old Jin wearing an elegant red "dew gauze" wedding dress. A red silken kerchief covered her head, its four corners fixed to copper coins, hanging plumb; beneath, a silver necklace encircled her neck and silver bracelets engirded her wrists. When she had departed, a cousin carried her from the family hall to the sedan chair, for if her wedding shoes so much as touched the earth, it would bring about a decline in the family fortune.

Surrounded by a boisterous entourage, the bridal sedan chair reached Gengguping. Although outside it was bone-chillingly cold, as the sedan chair entered the Li estate Jin felt as though her heart were buoyed by a warm spring breeze. Her cheeks were flushed with eagerness, and the intoxicating radiance in her eyes illumined the primeval forest. As Third Auntie Zhang plucked a downy hair from her forehead, Jin felt a tingly itch. Her hands and mouth working with nimble rhythm, like a skilled cotton weaver, Third Auntie cleared Jin's forehead of these fine hairs. Then she set to work shaping Jin's brows, tidily arching them before lining them with a mixture of tung-oil and the ash of bamboo shoots. After these ministrations, Jin appeared breathtakingly rosy-cheeked and radiant.

"Here they come!" clamored Masui, tearing into the yard trailed by younger brother Mahe. Sporting their school uniforms, the two brothers appeared as cosmopolitan and modish as bridegroom Mawu looked dashing. The gabbling throng of neighbors and friends immediately quieted. With a smile, Xia Qifa, seated at a square table laid with incense, candles, wine bowls, and fruit, awaited the arrival of the sedan chair.

When the bearers set the sedan chair down, the *tima* bowed and chanted cheerfully:

Let the now bride's family go back,
And the groom's family come forth.
The Immortal White Tiger has come,
Driving off all malevolent spirits.

As he sang, he picked up a rooster, long since at the ready for the ceremony, tore its cockscomb and let its blood drip into the wine bowl. After that he threw the cock behind the sedan chair and sprinkled the vehicle with a rain of blood-wine. With this libation, the inauspicious ethers from the bride's family were dispelled, leaving only pure air to accompany the bride as she crossed the threshold to join the Li family.

In the most elaborate wedding ceremony the region had ever witnessed, onlookers clustered in the courtyard. In the gateway of the ancestral hall, Xia Qifa and Zhu Shun drew a crowd as they matched wits, engaging in clever badinage, parrying folksy wisdom and anecdotes of the ancestors.

"As I am unlearned and untalented, I wish to seek knowledge from you," Zhu Shun addressed the *tima* with stylized humility. He was attired nattily in a long gown, cutting an elegant and modest scholarly figure. "Who invented marriage? Which emperor promoted planting and harvest of the five grains? And under which ruler was clothing created?"

"I'm but a mulish fool, a beggar's empty basket," Xia Qifa simpered, before responding with the tone of a sage, "The union of man and woman began in the reign of Emperor Fuxi. Under Divine Farmer Shennong men began planting the five grains. And under the Yellow Emperor, men began weaving clothes. Please correct me if I am mistaken."

"From her earliest years, the bride has received little instruction and is therefore spoiled and lazy," tactfully Zhu Shun shifted topics, delivering obligatory prepared remarks. "If she annoys her parents-in-law or relatives with coarse or inappropriate talk, please be tolerant."

"The parents-in-law will treat her as their own daughter, and she will be well-treated by other family members," Xia Qifa reassured crisply, adding in a poetic flourish, "When diligently husband tills and assiduously wife weaves, the couple many springs and winters in love and kindness lives."

After a few rounds of repartee, each found the other a good match. Thus Xia Qifa and Zhu Shun paid respects and bowed to each other before heading into the ancestral hall together, bowing three times before the votive niche.

With their departure, the limelight shifted to the bride and groom.

Li Diezhu invited Master Wang Binquan, head of the private academy, to preside over the ceremony. In the spirit of etiquette, ward headman Qin Zhanyun had been invited and had come. Wearing red flowers on their chests, the newlyweds came forward and served the ward headman tea; in return, he graciously gifted each of them a little red parcel of money.

The wedding feast began with an intoxicating air of good cheer. But in the midst of the festivities, Qin Zhanyun, foremost authority in this ward of Huangshui, announced a piece of sobering news: "The Japanese devils have attacked Hubei Province. A government order has come to the township demanding that we take a levy of grain and contribute men for soldiers in the War of Resistance against Japan."

"Japanese devils?" asked Li Diezhu curiously.

"Raiders from Japan, robbers seeking to seize our land and wealth," Master Wang sighed. "Battles have been waged against them in Beijing, Nanjing, and now in Hubei."

Xia Qifa asked, "How far away is Japan?"

Masui said, "Where the Yangzi River and the land end, if one sailed eastward with a tailwind for a day and a night he'd reach Japan: we live in the mountains, they live on the sea."

"Don't we have to cross over mountain ridges to get there?" Li Diezhu asked skeptically.

"No mountain ridges," Masui replied.

"One can go there by ship," Xia Qifa asserted. "King Yu the Great connected all the waterways of the world into a network of rivers that allow us to go anywhere by boat, even the edge of the world."

"Our teacher told us Japanese place names have a fell and noxious air: evil-sounding names like Devil Hill, Ghostlake, Demonfield, Demonspirit, Demonking, or Demon City. They're not a good people," chimed in Mahe from another table.

Zhu Shun shuddered, saying, "The plague spirits have been unleashed."

"Therefore, we must fight back! Who wants to sign up? Anyone eighteen or older can enroll," the ward chief ardently offered.

Li Diezhu mulled that Mawu was just starting a family with his wife, while Masui was not soldier material. Still thinking, he looked at the newlyweds clad in cheerful red wedding attire, and said, "I'd join the army eagerly if the battlefield were in Huangshui . . . it'd be just like going to hunt leopards. But Hubei's so far it's troublesome. So let me donate fifty stone of grain!"

"That counts. How about you, Donghe? Will one of your brothers enlist?" Qin asked, peering at Wang Donghe, a tall, sturdy hunter.

"Who's afraid of battle? I just don't dare leave my wife for too long," answered Wang Donghe.

"I want to join the army," Sun Fu's youngest brother bravely volunteered.

"You'll never worry about food, drink, or pay in the army. And once you win merit on the battlefield, you can head home, buy some land, and take a wife," encouraged the ward headman.

"And when you have children, they can attend my school free of charge," added Master Wang.

"Thank you, Master Wang," chuckled Sun Fu and his brother.

"Mawu, my lad," came a shout from another table. Ma San, the medicine dealer, teased, "You take care of your health! Don't get so wrapped up indulging in pleasure with your new bride that you collapse of exhaustion." The house exploded with riotous laughter.

Flushed with immeasurable joy, Mawu beamed, "Uncles and aunts, please enjoy yourselves to your heart's content. By your leave, I'll join you again tomorrow."

VI

All in red silk, Jin sat motionless on the wedding bed. She seethed with uneasiness within, as though a multitude of wild hares were dashing madly about.

Mawu returned to the wedding chamber, intoxicated with content, his entire face lit up with a foolish smile. He looked Jin up and down before asking, "Was the bridal sedan chair comfortable? It must have felt like you were roaming on clouds."

Jin lowered her head, giggling lightly. Emboldened by her musical laugh, Mawu reached out and pulled off her red veil. Even with her head down and her jaw quivering timidly, Jin's gentle voluptuousness suffused the entire wedding chamber.

Overwrought with emotion, Mawu's heart melted. Pulling his new bride to his bosom, he blew out the red candle. His incandescent desire nearly lit up the darkness. Feeling it all unbearably awkward, Jin suddenly recalled that her mother had repeatedly told her not to laugh at this pivotal moment, otherwise her firstborn would be a daughter. "Oh!" She exclaimed breathlessly, trembling with nerves. "Damn it!" She found herself naked, Mawu having stripped off her wedding clothes piece by piece. Mawu's entire body, above and below, was afire, trembling with eagerness. However, his repeated efforts proved futile. Finally, abashed and flustered, he rose from the bed, saying, "I can't see a thing. I'm going to light the candle." Watching naked Mawu return to the wedding bed and bore under the covers, Jin was consumed with shame. And then in a tumultuous instant, a part of her sealed off for seventeen years was torn open, a piquant prick of pain followed by a hot eruption of intense pleasure. Relief flooded over Mawu, who felt happy as a king, swollen with perfect contentment like the full harvest moon.

The wedding ceremony was over, but Li Diezhu insisted that Xia Qifa stay for another few days. He showed him his newly purchased fields, hoping to lay a foundation for the prospective marriage of his youngest son Mahe to the *tima*'s daughter.

Finding it difficult to turn down such an earnest, warmhearted offer, Xia Qifa remained. Together the two friends wended through the mountains for half a day till they reached Peppercorn Bend. From time to time snowflakes drifted down from the heavens, flashing a silvery light.

The fields along both sides of the river valley had lain fallow during the winter, awaiting the spring plowing that would break up the soil. Along the embankments they watched a gathering of tenant farmers, clad in broad-brimmed hats and long straw ponchos, who had formed a line and, like fishermen dragging a net to catch fish, were clearing withered grass and roots as they moved across the field. With a flat drum fastened to his waist and a gong in one hand, the head worker sang as they moved in unison. Rhythmically he beat the drum and struck the gong, the others keeping cadence as they intoned a primitive work chant:

> *Pulling weeds, pulling weeds, Ah-oh ha, Ah-oh hey,*
> *This side, that side, Ah-oh ha, Ah-oh hey.*
> *Weeding one field after another,*
> *Weeding one field after another,*

Yo-ho . . . yo-ho.
The sun . . . is setting,
Hey-oh, Hey-oh, Ah-oh-hey.
The skies . . . they darken, yo.
City gates . . . they close, lo.
Main door . . . its bolted, yo.
Homeward we go, lads, lo.
Darkness has arisen, yo.
Tomorrow we toil again, lo.

Between songs, they joked around in a spirit of ribald camaraderie, cursing in turn their landlord and their lazy mates. Far from being annoyed, Li Diezhu laughed along with them. He picked out several copper coins to reward the head worker.

Approaching Li Diezhu, his fellow émigré, Xia Qifa squawked in a bird-like trill, "This is a good place. The small, hidden river nearby on the plains of Lihaku, covered with leaves, once connected with a great ancient waterway by which people could reach the Qing River and Zhongli Mountain in Hubei. Swift as an arrow the ship would sail: it would take only ten days. Our clan's god and ancestors were all fond of this place."

Skeptical, Li Diezhu asked, "Could we really travel by boat from a branch of Inkblack Creek to the Qing River in ten days?"

Xia Qifa said, "Our ancestors possessed Yu the Great's *River Chart*, mapping all rivers of the Nine Provinces, great and small. With this map, we knew the quickest course by waterway to reach any place. Sadly, the map was lost, and now many waterways are unfit for travel by boat. No longer can we reach the edge of the world. Now from these mountains there are only two paths to reach the Qing River: one along the creek, and the other clambering over the mountain ridges. The creek is too steep and narrow; you can make it traveling the plank paths over mountain peaks and ridges, but it's a long journey."

"How I wish we could still go by ship!" uttered Li Diezhu regretfully.

Xia Qifa narrowed his eyes, his guttural hum swelling into a dreamlike chant:

Through turbulent channels the vessel floats,
Rapids pound the sampan, froth leaps the gunwale.

Jagged rocks bite the planks of the flat-bottomed boat.
Lo! The haulers tow the sampan,
Fighting forward, noses touching the cliff;
As the man poling the vessel
lowers himself to the bottom of the skiff.
We've passed countless mountains and crags,
And crossed endless lakes and rivers;
With the last ounce of strength and drop of sweat,
To Inkblack Creek our destination we get.
Looking upward we can't see the skies,
Heavens hidden by the thick overgrowth along the banks;
Looking downward, the waters vanish 'neath these shrubby eaves,
The river covered by a floating canopy of leaves.

"If we hadn't lost Yu the Great's map, we could sail to the sea." Xia Qifa said.

Covered by a layer of fallen leaves, the invisible river was a little more than half a mile from Lihaku, merging with Inkblack Creek at the foot of a cliff near the Qins' ranch. Originating in the mountains of Huangshui, Inkblack Creek meandered through the vast primeval forest, flowing south to north. Its banks were clustered with luxuriant growths of waterweeds and reeds. At mysterious Lihaku, however, the creek plunged down a steep declivity, becoming ever wilder and more turbulent as it rushed unbridled through the long, narrow gorge, then circled back toward Enshi in Hubei, before emptying into the Yangzi River in Wanxian County. According to the *tima*, poling sampans and punting sculls, their forefathers had come from afar, following the ancient network of waterways to this very spot. Here they settled, cutting timber to build houses, netting fish in the rivers, hunting pheasants in the mountains, listening to the birds sing, and watching beasts run. While Li Diezhu knew nothing of geomancy, he trusted the shaman's wisdom. Thus, he was delighted that he had put down roots in this auspicious place and found a wife for his eldest son.

Two days later, son in tow, a contented Xia Qifa said his goodbyes and departed, weaving his cryptic singsong chant as he went.

Chapter Four

I

Masui and his brother Mahe returned to school in Fengjie City. Occasionally, gunfire echoed in the distant skies. Carrying several pairs of straw sandals, a belt-bag sewn by his mother fastened to his waist containing money for supplies, the third son of the Sun family headed to Huangshui to enlist in the army. As the silent fog encompassed the mountains, the war still seemed far away.

Humming a merry tune, Li Diezhu often wandered the ridges, his trousers scrolled up above his calves, hands locked behind his back as he walked, bamboo pipe between his fingers. Gengguping was more savage than the villages in the surrounding valleys. Radiant with delight, he mused that his firstborn Mawu, with his rudimentary education, was well set up to lead a decent, prosperous life. He had decided to divide the family holdings, placing the fields he now owned at Peppercorn Bend under the supervision of the newlyweds, also giving them the attached half-barren mountain slope to bring under cultivation.

With this newfound independence, the Mawu and Jin should been happier than immortals. However, worried about the attendant troubles of living apart from the larger family, both felt ill at ease.

With her pretty face and slender figure, Jin was so small and tender, so soft and pliant, that when Mawu locked her in a bear hug she seemed to be a lovely little perfume-bathed loach. Intoxicated by tender love, mind and body consumed by a seemingly unquenchable conflagration of lust, Mawu was utterly distracted, his three ethereal spirits drifting aimlessly above and six corporeal souls roaming listlessly below. Though he sought to control his desire, it had its own terrible momentum: with a simple nudge or gesture it would awaken once again, redoubling in intensity. Mawu had no choice but to abandon himself to the ecstatic throes of new conjugal love.

All night long the floorboards of the wedding chamber creaked and groaned, but Mawu showed no sign of exhaustion. His face glowed with a radiant sheen of happiness. Half a month passed. Tao Jiuxiang knit her brows. When Jin had left the room, she looking into Mawu's eyes searchingly and said, "Oh, my son. Your eyes are circled in black. Go over to the table and eat those rice-starch eggs. If you keep growing thinner, I'll have you two live separately like a lonely tiger and tigress!"

These words frightened Mawu. Restless, seeking a change of pace, he set out with Jin to visit her parents. Several days later, they returned from Peppercorn Bend bearing alarming news. Entering the gate, Mawu called, "Pa! Bandits ransacked Xiedong Township. A bunch of people were killed!"

Xiedong bordered Huangshui. Calling themselves incarnations of the White Tiger, these bandits had ravaged these parts for generations. When they struck, local annalists recorded that the "the scourge of the tiger had entered the villages, causing chaos and disrupting the lives of the people."

Puffing on his pipe as he hunkered down beside the gate, Li Diezhu furrowed his brow and nervously asked, "Didn't General Yang Sen drive the bandits back to Enshi a couple of years back?"

"They're back!" said Mawu bluntly, "Causing havoc in Xiedong. They make everyone over eighteen pay, otherwise they seize their cattle and property. A bamboo craftsman named Liang claims to be possessed by a divine spirit, blessed by gods on high, and protected by heavenly soldiers and generals. He calls himself Tiger Incarnate Bodhisattva Liang. To make people believe, he wrapped his hand in boxthorn bark, plunged it into boiling vegetable oil, and showed it the people, proclaiming that when spirit soldiers emerged from the netherworld only the faithful would avoid slaughter."

Taken aback, Li Diezhu asked, "Was he burned?"

"Not at all," cried Mawu excitedly, his eyes glistening with admiration. "He claims he's going to butcher the local militia, seize tax levies, and plunder the wealthy."

Li Diezhu interrupted him, "He's got the gall to call himself the Immortal Tiger Incarnate?"

Gulping down a mouthful of water, Mawu wiped his lips with one hand, before hastily explaining, "He's built up a congregation of supporters who treat him like a living god, burning incense, and singing:

> *The wind it whistles and fades,*
> *From the heavens come myriad blades.*
> *The immortal tiger is here!*
> *Little lambkins hide in fear.*

Two nights ago, Liang led a dozen men armed with machetes with white tassels to attack the militia barracks in Xiedong. They killed the sentry and stormed the barracks, hewing down every militiaman they met."

From time to time, whipped into a devotional frenzy by one charismatic mystic or another, mountainfolk in the region rose up in the name of the Immortal Tiger, binding tiger talismans to their waists, and recklessly sallying into battle, always advancing and never retreating. Ward headman Qin had previously told Li Diezhu that according to local records, over the centuries plagues of rabble-rousing bandits periodically ran riot, stirring up trouble. These uprisings were difficult to quell.

Mawu went on: "The militia in the barracks were sleeping and had no idea what was going on. In the chaos, more than twenty were killed. Liang burned the barracks to the ground and carried off scores of guns. Now the whole town's plunged into terror; the rich especially fear being robbed."

"What happened to the head militia officer?" Li Diezhu asked nervously.

"I heard he'd escaped and fled to the county seat." From his back-basket, Mawu removed a sheaf of dried tobacco leaves Jin Shaosan had given them as a gift for Li Diezhu. Then he broached the suggestion he had mulled over along the road, "Pa, Xiedong isn't far from Huangshui. Let's build a stone tower. If bandits come, we can hole up in there. And in times of peace, Jin and I will use it as our house."

Rising deliberately to his feet, Li Diezhu glanced at his eldest son and nodded his assent, "All right, on the condition that you contribute some of the money." From what he had heard, bandits were a motley crew of dirt-poor migrants, deserters, mercenaries, and starvelings. In the name of gods or ghosts, they plundered the rich to give to the poor; other times, they simply butchered the innocent. With the bandits running wild in Xiedong, how long could Huangshui remain tranquil? And though he had done no evil, his meteoric rise to prosperity had stirred up the mountainfolk, near and far. Building a stone block-tower to defend the family would be a sound idea.

Mawu said, "I'll cover half the expenses."

Immediately, Li Diezhu sent his firstborn to Huangshui, seeking master builder Zhu Shun to build a staunch stone tower.

Followed by seven or eight workers, Zhu Shun returned to Gengguping. He spent an entire day surveying the grounds. Finally, he stopped before a massive boulder a hundred yards from the household. Burning a long stick of incense he solemnly prayed,

> *Mighty deity power vast,*
> *Sage virtue brilliant to the last;*
> *Please hear your disciple's earnest plea,*
> *Let the obdurate earth yield to me.*
> *My hand grasps this hammer with all its might;*
> *Please let me raise a stone tower on this site."*

With these words, he bowed three times before the boulder and the construction of the tower commenced.

High as a three-storey building, set against the blue sky atop the boulder and an outcropping of rock, the stone tower was completed in the fall. From atop the tower one could see far in every direction. Logs and stones were stockpiled as weapons to rain down on attackers. Hurled from high above, even an egg-sized stone could pack a devastating wallop. Clad in a sheet of iron, the stone tower's door was three or four inches thick. Inside, the floors were thick planks. On the walls there were loopholes on every side for watching or firing rifles.

From the tower a steep, long stair, cut into the natural stone, wound its way back to the yard. On three sides, dense trees and thorny underbrush surrounded the fortification. Concealed amid the brambles was a cave, where one might hide in an emergency.

"Master, I guarantee this tower is impregnable," Zhu Shun proudly told Li Diezhu. "As long as you keep vigilant watch day and night, no one, neither heavenly soldier nor demon warrior, can breach this tower."

As a single cumbersome mass of cloud drifted across the blue sky, scattering the autumn sunlight, Li Diezhu gazed up at the tower for a long moment, before exhaling an approving sigh, "We're safe unless someone can change into a bird and fly in or turn into a snake and slither in!"

The Lis were delighted with the block-tower. Minds at ease, they carried their silver dollars from selling goldthread and other treasures to the tower for safekeeping.

II

In the final month of the lunar calendar the school had winter vacation. A series of government reforms were announced in Huangshui. But around Gengguping the only thing anyone worried about was news of the bandits. Word had it that they tended to plunder around Spring Festival, before and after the New Year. To protect against a sneak attack, Li Diezhu moved his entire family into the tower.

Around the stone fireplace everyone drank corn liquor; flushed with drink, they showed no sign of stopping. Mawu placed a second earthenware jar of liquor on the table for his father. Narrowing his eyes, Li Diezhu tilted his bamboo pipe upside-down in the jar, sucking in a deep draught; other family members followed suit, one after another. Masui narrowed his eyes, breathed gently, and drew slowly on the pipe, his pockmarks reddening. Mahe sucked with abandon, devouring the sweet liquor like a fish, his face swollen red with the rush of blood.

Apart from fermented corn, Tao Jiuxiang put jujubes and other wild fruit into the earthenware jars before burying them in the fall. Thus, the wine possessed a distinctive sweet tang. Ruddy and vital, the cheerful faces of the family members glowed in the dim light of a tung-oil lamp.

Hale and hearty as ever, Li Diezhu was a good drinker. Looking at the pockmarked face of his second son Masui, he promised, "Masui, I'll find a wife for you in the new year." He dared not mention that Mahe was already engaged to Xia Yinmei, fearing that it might wound Masui's pride.

"Pa," said Masui, "I'm too young to get married. Let's worry about it once I grow up."

"An engagement needs to be planned ahead of time," said Tao Jiuxiang, taking a mouthful of the sweet liquor, flashing a reproachful smile at her middle son, "How are you going to find a suitable young woman on the spur of the moment?"

Responding with a noncommittal grin, Li Diezhu reckoned he ought to relate to Masui the story of the tigress wife that he had told Mawu. Far into the night, bamboo pipe in hand and deep satisfaction in his heart, he supped the wonderful homemade liquor and mulled his good fortune. With his acquisition of the new fields along the river at Peppercorn Bend he had gained a degree of local celebrity. In this pleasing reverie, he absently took one mouthful after another, until only with the assistance of Tao Jiuxiang was he able to stagger back to the bedroom, dragging his long tobacco pipe behind him.

Having put her thoroughly inebriated husband to bed, Tao Jiuxiang returned to her sons and daughter-in-law, who were sitting around the fireplace, chatting as they peeled and ate wild chestnuts. All year long, the barren field on the mountain slope allotted to the young couple had remained untouched. Slack-limbed from dawn to dusk, Mawu stuck close to Jin, who for her part cheerfully and shamelessly basked in her husband's adoration. How Tao Jiuxiang yearned to extinguish the spark of lust! With a long-brewing but impulsive indignation, goaded by the corn liquor, she rounded on Mawu and Jin, shouting, "The ancestors on earth and the Duke of Thunder on High set down a golden rule: one must work hard! Not only in bed, but in the fields. If you neglect one, it will bring about the ruin of the family, understand?"

A seductive fragrance arose from the wild chestnuts roasting on the open fire. At Tao Jiuxiang's words, Jin's cheeks blushed as hot as the wood burning in the fireplace. Mawu turned over a log forcefully, causing sparks to rise into a frenetic dance, as if he wanted to burn the block-tower to the ground.

Spring Festival passed safe and sound as the New Year dawned. Masui and Mahe returned to school. Li Diezhu and Tao Jiuxiang moved back to their homestead. Goldthread sold so well that Mawu finally suppressed his lust and got to work. Together with the family's tenant farmers, they worked the rice fields, and began to cultivate their fallow field on the mountain slope. He grew goldthread on the northern slope, and planted corn and potatoes on the sunny southern exposure.

The shadowy northern slope of the mountain was patched with tiny overgrown parcels where farmers had grown goldthread hundreds of years ago. Mawu and the tenants reopened the fallow land, reclaiming several acres and setting up goldthread-growing lean-tos. Here and there pheasants and wild hares hurried across the fields, glancing curiously at the farmers.

A thick layer of fallen leaves matted the ground, giving off the sweet reek of mildewed ferment. One crossing these leaf-covered fields left no footprint. Caves dotted the crags above, the lairs of wild beasts; wild boars and muntjac deer bedded in forest glens. In their comings and goings men and creatures usually coexisted in peace, like well water and river water. From time to time, crashing sounds echoed through the forest as the fat, clumsy moon bears who had clambered up mossy trunks tumbled noisily down to the ground. The foolish bears fell several times a day, never appearing the worse for it. Some said this helped toughen up the bears for winter.

One day, accompanied by several policemen, Huang Tianliang, captain of the Huangshui Militia, went into the mountains on an inspection. Pleased by the scenery, he hailed the small group of young men hard at work in the fields, "Hey, what's not to love about gardening a plot encircled by these wonderful mountains?"

Startled by the strange voice, wild hares and pheasants ran into the woods. Mawu rose and respectfully greeted him, "Hi, Captain Huang."

Captain Huang, a felt hat perched on his head, looked Mawu up and down. The strapping young man wore no head kerchief, his mid-length hair was well-cropped; his ruddy face was sun-browned, two thick brows set on a square forehead, and his eyes beamed with tiger-like vitality. Seeing that Mawu looked like Li Diezhu, the locally renowned goldthread grower, Huang asked, "Say, are you Li Diezhu's eldest?"

"Yes, I'm Li Mawu."

"A wealthy family like yours," Captain Huang said, groping for something in his leather satchel, "should be careful. The bandits under bamboo-craftsman Liang ran riot in Xiedong. They're targeting rich households, violently plundering wealth and property."

Mawu replied, "Thanks, Captain. But we're not afraid. We built a stone tower."

"Great. Prepare rifles and gunpowder. Give those wretched brigands something to fear!" Captain Huang took a red certificate from his leather satchel and handed it to Mawu in a formal manner. "As your family has donated grain twice, the county government would like to present this certificate in appreciation on behalf of Generalissimo Chiang Kai-shek. Give it to your father when you get home."

Mawu unfurled the certificate and saw the four characters "Generous Donor of Crops," next to the official seal of the Fengjie county government. He said in a hurry, "Thank the mayor of Huangshui, and thank you, sir. It's our family's duty." Filtering through the dense branches and leaves, sunlight played on his well-built frame.

Captain Huang sized him up again and asked, "So what would a rugged fellow like you think about joining me?"

"Sure! Absolutely!" said Mawu cheerfully. "I'd love to serve under you, riding horses with the troops and eating in the mess hall!"

Staring at him, Captain Huang remarked, "I wonder if your father will be willing."

Mawu said eagerly, "He will! I have two younger brothers."

The Captain burst into laughter, "You Lis are no fools. Do a good deed by fixing the horse trail that cuts through the mountains. It will make it easier for your family to collect rent. When you're done, come to Huangshui and find me."

Mawu was just as hardworking, shrewd, and capable as his father. As Jin's belly swelled with child, his fiery lust finally abated. He began to yearn for excitement and adventure in Huangshui. He hired several mountainfolk to help hack through briars and cut down thorny thickets, clearing a shortcut from Gengguping to Peppercorn Bend. Although Captain Huang had requested that they mend the road, Li Diezhu was well aware that the Li family would benefit most. Furthermore, he wanted the family to be better armed, and so he agreed to let Mawu join the Huangshui Militia. He even contributed funds to help repair the trail; when it was finished, one could ride straight from their home to Peppercorn Bend without spending hours cutting a swath with a machete.

Traveling this freshly widened trail, Li Diezhu accompanied Mawu to the Huangshui Militia barracks.

III

Huangshui was composed of eleven wards, which were subdivided into 120 tithings. Overall, roughly a thousand households were scattered in the 80 square miles of mountains and valleys that made up the rural district. During her second summer at Gengguping, Jin birthed a baby daughter, Yongyu. Under the patronage of Captain Huang, Mawu was appointed squadron leader, placed in charge of a militia detachment of twenty riflemen responsible for the security of the hundred-odd households in the tenth and eleventh wards.

The two wards in Mawu's charge were remote and sparsely populated. Once a month they made their rounds, clambering up steep slopes and over mountains on an arduous ten-day inspection. Mulling over the difficulty in covering such a large region, Mawu hit upon a good idea: he set up a duty post in each ward, assigning a detail of militiamen to keep guard. The tenth ward's duty post was his family's stone tower. Throwing himself wholeheartedly into his new role, he strutted proudly along the streets of Huangshui, past merchants selling seeds and fruit, clothing and hardware, pleased to hear them greet him as "Sergeant Li" as he made the rounds with several militiamen. Only occasionally did he ride back to Gengguping or inspect the more remote areas.

With a detachment of eight men keeping watch on the family's stone tower day and night, Mawu's mind was at ease. Family and ward were both secure. From the panoramic vantage of the watchtower, any passing stranger would draw the attention of the alert men on duty. From time to time silver pheasants, bamboo partridge, and wild chickens burst out of the bosky coverage.

In the days of their destitute migration, Li Diezhu had never imagined, even in his wildest dreams, that the family might come to possess such bounty and that he might proudly watch such a splendid and promising future unfold before his eldest son. Unfortunately, however, since duty bound Mawu to the barracks in the Huangshui station, Li Diezhu was left busier and busier tending to farmwork. Suddenly, he had an idea. He asked Mawu to send for Masui, with a message telling his middle son to return to Gengguping to take over work on the farm.

So it was that Masui, at nineteen years of age, returned from Fengjie City. Carrying a wicker suitcase, wreathed in youthful energy, he came back to Gengguping clad in an imported cloth school uniform, the pockmarks on his face clearer and larger than ever. Delighted, Li Diezhu welcomed Masui home with a feast, inviting Mawu and Jin to share in the festivities.

Supping on Tao Jiuxiang's sweet fermented corn liquor amid the aroma of cured meat, Masui animatedly exclaimed, "I saw a Japanese plane shot down."

"Where?" asked Mawu, surprised.

"On the outskirts of the city," Masui replied excitedly, putting down his liquor. "I had just left Fengjie City when I heard the guns. Two fighter planes, coming from Chongqing, were locked in a dogfight. Tons of people were watching. Suddenly, the Japanese plane careened into a tree halfway up a nearby mountain and exploded."

"Did you see it clearly? A Japanese fighter?" pursued Mawu eagerly.

"The smoke was thick, but the fighter was close by. I saw the red solar disc clearly. It caused a sensation in Fengjie."

"What about the pilots?" asked Mawu.

"They were scorched. I rushed over with others for a look and saw one man more dead than alive, crawling from the wreckage with severe wounds, blisters covering his face." Masui said proudly, "We took his pistol, then searched him—found a map and an amulet."

"Was the map the River Chart of the Nine Provinces?" asked Li Diezhu, snatching a piece of vinegar-fried pork.

"What's the River Chart?" asked Masui, puzzled.

"A map drawn by King Yu the Great, with all the waterways of China, great and small," Li Diezhu told them.

Masui said scornfully, "How closed-off and backward Gengguping is! Dad, the Japanese devil's chart was a military map. He said something, but I didn't understand a word."

Rapt, Tao Jiuxiang, Mawu, Jin, and Sun Fu gazed at Masui without moving their chopsticks.

"What happened to the wounded pilot?" Mawu asked.

Masui took a bite of cured pork sautéed with pepper, and answered, "Died. He died before the county officials arrived. Funny thing, his amulet was just like the ones Xia Qifa makes, exact same as the *tima's*. We gave it to the county government."

"Devil soldier! Even a protective amulet couldn't save him!" Li Diezhu spat. Wearing a white silk turban, a blue waistcoat, and deerskin trousers, he squatted on a broad armchair in the center of the room, adding with a smile, "You've been at school for two years now, and have gathered several basketsful of knowledge. It will come in handy here at home. Now that Mawu is a militia sergeant, he's too busy to attend to everyday chores round here. Therefore, you'd better come home and take charge."

Masui had expected something like this, but hearing his father's request that he quit schooling and return home made him shudder inwardly. Though deeply upset, he said nothing.

Li Diezhu put down his chopsticks, filled his pipe with a plug of rolled artemisia, lit it, and took several puffs. Strands of fragrant smoke wafted upward, filling the room. Contentedly, he said, "A couple days ago, Third Auntie Zhang introduced a would-be wife for you; me and your mother were both satisfied. Since you're back home, you ought to go visit the girl, and confirm the engagement to make sure everything's all right." Feeling it odd that Masui had taken on a melancholy aspect at these tidings, he asked, "Aren't you happy about this?"

"Dad, I don't want to get married. I want to go to school in Chongqing and take part in the anti-Japanese movement to help save the nation."

What sort of young fellow would rather write and count than farm and hunt! Li Diezhu snorted in disgust, "To Chongqing? I think not. You've already gained more than enough knowledge! Besides, the Zhous just sent their second son to the front, and the Li family sent a nephew; so we don't need you to go fight against the Japanese devils."

"I'm not fighting, I want to do ancillary work," Masui explained anxiously, alarmed by his parents' arrangements. Several years of civility and education in Fengjie City had instilled in Masui an idealistic vision of love and of a bright future, a vision in which marriage to an illiterate mountain girl had no place.

"The girl's name is Zhou. She's a proper and attractive young woman, with a face rounder than Jin's," Tao Jiuxiang chimed in, puzzled at her middle son's reluctance. "The Zhous aren't well off financially, but their two daughters are fine. You'll marry the elder, and Qin Liexiong the younger. Afterward, our Li family and the Qins will be relatives. Works out well for everyone involved."

After his fall and injury, Liexiong had ceased growing, earning him the nickname "Short-an-Inch." Yet the resourceful youth was strong-willed and clever; for several years he trained diligently with a master of martial arts, until with his bare hands he could fight off several opponents at once.

Mawu drained his liquor bowl, and said to his younger brother, "Liexiong's seventeen, two years younger than you. It would be perfect if you two married the sisters and became brothers-in-law."

Masui murmured with disgust, "Why would it be perfect? Because he's a cripple, and I'm pockmarked?"

Annoyed, Mawu explained, "What I mean is that you two are of similar age and have clever minds." Since his marriage to Jin, he felt somewhat bad for Liexiong. Thus, he prodded Masui to accept an engagement with the elder Zhou daughter.

"And our families are similar in wealth." Tao Jiuxiang added seriously.

"Don't make a fuss about nothing," Li Diezhu warned, furrowing his brow.

IV

Third Auntie Zhang was so quick-witted and sharp that she could virtually read minds. Yet in vain she exhausted every means at her disposal to induce Masui to visit the girl. Masui, however, could not resist the persuasion of his elder brother, Mawu. Finally he shed his school uniform, donning in its place a tenant farmer's clothes and a broad-brimmed, conical bamboo paddy hat that half-covered his face. Following Third Auntie's husband, he reached the Zhous' homestead and sat waiting under a big banyan tree near the wooden outbuildings.

After a long wait, they finally saw two girls coming, one tall and the other shorter, each with a basket of pungent fishwort grass hanging from her arm. Masui gaze was drawn to the taller girl. She had a well-proportioned figure and a fine complexion; a long, glossy black braid hung down beyond her kerchief; her round face was like a silver disc, set with a pair of flashing dark eyes. He turned to the shorter one. She had a fair complexion, red lips and a sharp lower jaw; a silvery sash was fastened round her slender waist. The giddy fragrance of wildflowers filled the air; Masui found himself standing on ground carpeted with an array of tiny flowers—yellow, white, and purple. "Oh!" cried Third Auntie's husband, "It's the two beauties."

Seeing the two sisters ascending the slope, Masui scurried up the banyan tree. Suddenly, a dolorous whistle pierced the air, followed by a man's voice belting out a mountain song of courtship:

> *I saw you across the river, sweet red peony,*
> *Beautiful flower, hang a lantern for me.*
> *But as the peony fears a sudden shower,*
> *The lantern's afraid of a whirlwind's power.*

To Masui's surprise, the taller girl responded:

> *When the great river's waters swell the little river flows,*
> *Two turtle doves float side by side, pressed close,*
> *Paired, drifting turtle doves fear not death;*
> *Coupled lovers, stride for stride, breath for breath.*

Hidden in the dense branches, Masui whistled. Impulsively, Third Auntie's husband warned her with a song:

> *Little sister, you look fine with a single flower,*
> *But a headdress of floral sprays can overpower.*
> *One good lover great contentment brings,*
> *Two lovers invite enmity's barbs and stings.*

Abruptly, the songs on the slope stopped.

Burning with rage and humiliation, Masui climbed down and ran home. Taking off the farmer's clothing, he flung himself on his bed, cupping his face in his hands.

"What's wrong?" Tao Jiuxiang asked, alarmed.

With one hand, Masui wiped away tears.

"What on earth's the matter?" asked Tao Jiuxiang, her eyes widening.

"I just heard her sing a shameless courtship duet with another man!" Masui huffed.

Tao Jiuxiang frowned, "Now that she's engaged, she needs to know how things stand. I'll send Third Auntie to talk to her mother!"

"I don't want to marry her!" Masui cried out in anger.

Tao Jiuxiang gazed at her son and said, "You asked Mawu to post a letter for you. He read me the letter. 'Knowing you're so far away, I feel my heart floating on the winds.' What kind of muddled swamp is this? You don't want to get married, but you want to be an idler fooling around in Fengjie City?"

"You . . . how dare you open my letter!" Masui choked, pale and trembling with fury. He had sent the letter to a female classmate of his. As he was an excellent student and kept his distance from the lovely girls at his modern co-ed schools, the teacher trusted him to tutor one of his female classmates. The two had hit it off. Masui had planned to start a new life of work and study in Chongqing with the girl, never expecting that his letter would be opened and read by his mother and brother. What a backward hometown! How uncouth his mother and brother were!

"Listen!" Tao Jiuxiang declared, knitting her brows. "Your engagement to the elder daughter of the Zhous is already fixed. Think about it from the family's vantage. I'll ask her parents to keep her in decent behavior. The day before yesterday, the Zhous sent a message urging us to hold the wedding at an earlier date."

Flushing, Masui briefly protested Huangshui's backwardness and wildness, before sinking into a despondent state of gloom and tears.

Masui was not the only soul in those mountains mired in dejection.

The Zhous lived in a mountain hollow near Inkblack Creek, where for many years they had served as tenants of the Qin family. At sixteen, Elder Sister Zhou, Damei, was like a tender ear of sweet corn, irresistibly attractive to young fellows.

Jiang Ermao, a collector of herbal medicine, was smitten at first sight, buzzing around her at every opportunity. After drawing her attention with a piercing leaf whistle, he drawled out a ribald mountain song:

> *O fair lady, tender skin so white,*
> *Dancing like a blacksnake's tail, braid dark as night;*
> *Like a pliant osier swaying in the wind,*
> *One glance and I can't get you out of my mind.*

Shortly after the swarthy-faced young man came to the mountains, he set up a cabin at the foot of a cliff three miles from the Zhou homestead. Hearing Jiang Ermao's song as she gathered wild onions with her younger sister, Damei lifted her head and responded:

> *Lightning flashes when rains fall and thunder rolls.*
> *A wild silver carp can swim in the grass carp's pool,*
> *But won't share fishmeal in the water's cool:*
> *A mountain girl who marries a pauper is an arrant fool.*

Tall and sturdy, eyes clear and bright as the creek's water, Jiang Ermao responded with a song as doleful as the cumbersome mountain fog:

> *True, I'm a valley sparrow in these mountain peaks,*
> *Flitting hither and thither, no place to roost.*
> *Seeking a girl who loves me best,*
> *I'll supply the straw to make a warm nest!*

How could a beggar expect a royal banquet? Had he no sense of shame! Carrying her basket, Damei promptly replied:

> *Don't be crazy in your frivolous love so false;*
> *There you are, poorer than a temple mouse!*
> *Not half a bowl of rice can your cabin claim;*
> *Not half a string of cash left to your name.*

She sought to quash her suitor's amorous hopes, bluntly telling him that she wanted to marry into a wealthy family. Hoping to secure a good marriage for their daughter into the Li family, her parents had worked hard to curry the favor of matchmaker Third Auntie Zhang. Her wedding trousseaux—homespun sheets, curtains, and the like—were already prepared.

Jiang Ermao sang once more, his ardor dampened:

> *The duck's bill is round and the chicken's beak sharp,*
> *You speak with a honeyed tongue, I speak from the heart.*
> *You just see me as poor Huangshui trash,*
> *I sought your love and you choose cash.*

On this cruel evening, sharp pangs of unfulfilled love rent the tranquility of the forest.

V

While the head of the Zhou family was a straightforward fellow, his wife was incomparably more clever and perceptive. Feeling something amiss, she summoned her younger daughter, Ermei, and asked, "Why aren't you gathering firewood with your sister?"

Ermei answered, "As a fellow often sings to her, she asked me stay home and embroider."

"What's he like?" asked her mother.

"Tall and swarthy, with a square face . . . he carries a sheepskin pouch."

At this, the mother figured it must Jiang Ermao, the herbalist, that gatherer of wild orchids! Several families of Jiangs lived in Peppercorn Bend as tenants of Li Diezhu, but Jiang Ermao lived alone, collecting wild medicinal herbs and roots. Gazing toward the forest behind her house, her brows knit into a tight knot.

At that very moment, Damei, tired from collecting firewood on the slopes, sat down to rest, reclining against the bundle of wood. Drowsing in the warm sunshine, she drifted off in an afternoon nap. Jiang Ermao emerged from the woods, basket on back and trowel in hand. He couldn't believe his eyes when he saw the lovely Damei dozing atop her bundled firewood, her eyes lightly closed, her fair complexion slightly sun-browned, her breasts swelling like two freshly steamed rice buns. Sweet mother! Carefully, so as not to wake her from her reverie, he pressed closer. Then, blood roiling, he looked around, and, casting basket and trowel aside, he pounced upon Damei and seized her in an ardent embrace.

"Have I hurt you, dear sister?" asked Jiang Ermao, his eyes dancing

Damei awoke with a start, crying out in shame and anger, "Why, you!" Her breasts heaved like a pair of wild hares struggling in a hunter's game bag.

"I'm sorry . . . so sorry . . . sorry," Jiang Ermao rattled off a chain of meaningless apologies, his palms cupping her breasts, his eyes blazing with desire.

Releasing the rope binding the kindling, Damei freed her hand to push him away, yet found that she was caught still more tightly. His hot breath tickling her cheeks, she heard his singsong whisper, "I want to be your man."

Not a soul was in sight. Reclining against the firewood bundle, Damei felt her whole body soften and go slack.

Seeing Damei neither resist nor protest, Jiang Ermao snaked one of his hands into her crotch, kneading as he whispered shamelessly, "Why, it's wet with dew!"

Swooning, Damei collapsed against her firewood.

A bit abashed, Jiang Ermao stammered, "I have a cock without a roost, and you a roost without a cock. I want your roost for my cock."

At that instant, a gust of wind carried the piercing yell of Mother Zhou, "Damei!" Jiang Ermao stood up in alarm. Damei wanted to stand, too, but the cumbersome bundle of firewood was too heavy. Jiang Ermao unburdened her, saying, "I'll carry it back to your house."

Guiltily, Damei struggled to her feet. "No! My mother will scold me if she sees us together."

Gently, Jiang Ermao fixed the bundle on Damei's back, saying with distressed sweetness, "I'll cut firewood and pick mushrooms for you every day, and leave them near your house." His eyes followed her as she disappeared down the slope.

"Damned girl! What took so long? From now on just gather the firewood and hurry home. No dilly-dallying and talking with strangers," Mother Zhou cursed angrily as Damei trundled into the yard, the bundle of firewood on her back. Damei realized that her sister had sold her out, revealing her secret, but she merely stacked the firewood neatly and said nothing.

The Zhou family's firewood was stacked high, more mushrooms were gathered than they might possibly eat, but Damei was restless as an unbridled filly, prone to run wild on the mountain slopes and in the valleys for the better part of the day. All evening and well into the night, Mother Zhou tore into Damei, scolding her for her waywardness. Immediately, she sent her husband bearing notes to the Lis and Qins, urging them to set wedding dates as soon as possible.

One day shortly thereafter, Damei carried her washbasin to Inkblack Creek to bleach the hempen mosquito netting for her wedding curtains, scrubbing the yellowish curtains until her hands were red and swollen from the icy waters. Yet, distracted by her turbulent emotions—the imminent wedding and the tangled prospects of her future—she felt nothing at all. The visage of tall, handsome Jiang Ermao seemed to ever flash before her eyes, obscuring the pockmarked face of Li Masui.

As if on cue, a familiar leaf whistle sounded from the opposite bank. The keen beauty and sadness in Jiang Ermao's achingly plaintive notes sounded like the warbling of a mountain oriole in mating season. Intoxicated with the sweet melancholy of his melodic trill, her features softened, taking on a tender aspect.

His entire being borne by amorous buoyance, Jiang Ermao emerged from the underbrush. He blew his leaf whistle and sang a sultry song that set Damei atremble; she felt his rhythmic tune and lyrics seeping into her lovesick mind, into her sinews, into her heart.

> *One plate, two plates, yours and mine;*
> *One fishing net, two nets intertwined.*
> *Boar and sow cavort, biting with playful nips,*
> *Man and woman merge, joined at the hip.*
> *I'm by the riverside cutting wood,*
> *You're washing sheets, so lovely and good;*

How I want lock you in tender embrace,
Mouth to mouth, face to face!

Damei blushed, reddening to her ears. And though her heart had already flown to the opposite bank, she lowered her head and sang:

I'm a poison mountain-grown scrub coriaria, see?
From antiquity, none have dared touch me.
If you don't believe me, brother, come and try,
You're sure to be turned back in misery.

With a wan smile, Jiang Ermao answered her scornful retort:

Poison mountain coriaria yonder, you I see,
Who else could covet you more than me?
Now I've come, a rugged mountain fellow,
Here to dig you up with my trowel.

Though Damei wanted to laugh, she rebuked him firmly, "Don't talk nonsense— I can't marry you!"

Gloomily, Jiang Ermao let loose one last plaintive leaf whistle, and sang:

Washing wedding curtains on the river's edge,
Sweet sister pounds them in a daze.
But as you thump endlessly on the rocky ledge,
Elsewhere drifts your heart and gaze.

Relentless! This Jiang Ermao was so thick-skinned that three blows with an axe couldn't break his flesh! His cloying love was maddening!

Damei lowered her head and thought about Li Masui, her would-be husband, the second son of the Li family who had been educated at a modern school. Could a modern gentleman like Masui really love a mountain girl like her? A modern education was of no use in these mountains! She had heard that Masui had a pockmarked face, and people said nine of ten pockmarked men were eccentric. For all of these reasons she was apprehensive about marrying into the Li family. Though Jiang Ermao was not wealthy, he lived comfortably by hunting and gathering medicinal herbs. She would lack for nothing. Furthermore, she possessed the same family status as the agreeable and good-natured fellow, so he wouldn't look down on her. She felt confident she could live happily with such a husband. With this thought, she set down her pounding stick. Whistling back across the river, she sang in a long, slow drawl:

> *The wind so crisp, the sun so bright,*
> *Tang of ginger pairs with hot peppers' bite.*
> *Crisp wind augurs a clear, fine day,*
> *Come back, my love, and take me away.*

VI

Grasping the intimations behind Damei's song, Jiang Ermao felt a great stone had been lifted from his heart. Immediately, he began to plot how he might take Damei away. But just days after he had finally won over his lover by the riverside, he heard that the Lis had asked for Damei's horoscope, meaning the wedding was imminent. With these tidings, his worry took on a new urgency. Jiang Ermao was not afraid of a battalion of militia; he only feared that Damei would lose her nerve and not keep her promise. The first time Masui had deliberately humiliated Damei by whistling from the tree. Now once again his rival had blocked his path. An umbra of hatred for his rival, a young man he had never met, clouded Jiang Ermao's bright eyes.

Time flew past, and the wedding drew closer with each passing day. Whether Masui liked it or not, the three families milled with excitement.

Seething with anxiety, Damei was kept locked in her chamber, embroidering all day under her mother's watchful eye.

At the Zhous' request, the wedding date was moved forward a month, and so it was that mere days later a red sedan chair followed by a musical troupe performing merry tunes entered the Zhou courtyard. Mother Zhou, anticipating trouble and wanting to save face, had urged the Lis to send a detachment of six militiamen for protection and to help create a festive ambience for the wedding procession.

"Sister, how proud you must be! Your wedding sedan has a militia escort!" whispered clueless Ermei. Knowing now there was no chance she would be with Jiang Ermao, Damei covered her face in a kerchief and sobbed.

Having succeeded in marrying her daughters into two of the wealthiest families in Huangshui, Mother Zhou was proud as a queen. Although one son-in-law was pockmarked and the other was lame, both were very creditable matches that stood the Zhou family in good stead. The matches were advantageous to all involved: not only did they allow the Zhous to enter the circle of Huangshui's elite, it also bound the Lis and Qins, two of the most eminent families in the tenth ward, together in kinship. Such a pair of marriages was sure to excite envy and admiration throughout the mountains!

As the matchmaker who had brokered both unions, Third Auntie Zhang beamed. Relentlessly busy, she attended to matters at the Zhou household. On the wedding morn, she neatly shaped Damei's long braid into a round bun and covered her head with a big red handkerchief. At that moment, Damei, seated on the bed, burst into a bitter and indignant verse, echoing a song that countless heartbroken brides in those mountain regions had sung for centuries:

> *Wicked dog matchmaker, eating from both sides of the plate;*
> *Lures bird from tree, and monkey from mountainscape.*
> *Tricks my father into the engagement,*
> *Cheats my mother into this dreadful arrangement.*
> *Curse you, matchmaker, may your only son*
> *Lie dead in yonder bean field—leaving you none.*
> *Then wicked matchmaker you'll have no posterity,*
> *Your family line severed for eternity.*
> *May you fall off a high cliff into a stony river,*
> *Smashed into pieces, broken limbs all aquiver.*
> *May you be plunged into a hell of endless strife*
> *Or suffer rebirth as a corpulent boar's wife.*

Thick-skinned Third Auntie was used to this sort of abuse and, feeling neither shame nor sadness, simply took it in stride. Wracked with despair, Damei's song grew ever more heartrending:

> *So heartless, my dear, helping others with no regrets,*
> *You carry me to cast me in a fiery pit.*
> *Better abandon me on the desolate hill,*
> *And let me become a lonely quail;*
> *Then, rather than suffer, languish, and sigh,*
> *I might soar into the boundless sky.*
> *Or carry me and in a plumbless pool throw me,*
> *That I might, a little fish, swim to the faraway sea!*

As the eldest son in the family, Zhou Taiwang was responsible for seeing off his sisters. He had asked Mawu to send a complement of militia, in uniform with guns, to escort the wedding sedan. So, Mawu dispatched a half-dozen off-duty militiamen as an honor guard for the procession. Taiwang carried his weeping sister Damei to her sedan on his back. With a red kerchief covering her head and tears coursing down her cheeks, she clambered into the sedan chamber.

As the procession neared Gangou Bridge, however, Damei heard a familiar leaf whistle and a mellifluous tune:

> *Dearest, don't leave me, let us not be parted,*
> *Dearest O dearest, don't be so cruel-hearted.*

As a warning, Mawu raised his gun and fired two shots skyward.

Hearing the hubbub outside, Damei nervously and tenderly rent her breast. Soon, though, everything calmed, and the sedan continued its inexorable course. Tears flooded Damei's cheeks.

Masui could do nothing to cast off his fate. Like Mawu years before, a red flower was pinned on his chest. He and the bride, her face covered with the red kerchief, conducted the wedding rites: they greeted the guests with tea; paid respects to heaven, earth, and the ancestors; and finally entered their wedding chamber together.

Mahe had returned for the wedding. With mingling sympathy and envy, he watched his brother Masui become the bridegroom and marry an unknown mountain girl; he saw ward chief Qin and his stumpy son Liexiong, soon to marry Ermei and become a brother-in-law, offer congratulations; he observed his parents' solicitude and smile toward Third Auntie, treating the matchmaker as if she were an honored family member.

Though Mahe was several years younger, he was already as tall as Masui. A handsome young man, his hair was cropped close behind the ears, in the smart-looking modern style that students wore. Tao Jiuxiang secretly told him that he was engaged to Yinmei, Xia Qifa's daughter. Thinking him too young, they hadn't revealed this to him earlier. There was no rush: Now that Masui was married, they would wait a few years. Mahe flushed red, sadly musing that he had forgotten what Yinmei looked like. Whenever Xia Qifa visited, he brought only his son Liangxian. This time was no exception. Filled with eager curiosity, he wondered if Xia Yinmei looked like either of the two

Zhou sisters.

Amid these reflections, Mahe looked for the *tima* and his son, finding them with his parents, thanking the matchmaker. At their behest, Third Auntie was seated in the place of honor on the northern side of the large square table in the main hall, with the newlyweds on the southern side. Tao Jiuxiang carried a pig's head, its mouth covered with red paper, and placed it on the table, chanting in a singsong tone,

> *Look at this high table with four corners,*
> *A pig's head at the center of the four quarters.*

She turned, cheerfully looking at Third Auntie Zhang and continuing,

> *From this table large and square,*
> *Please take this gift in a basket with care.*

She placed two parcels of sugar to the left of the pig's head and two bottles of wine to the right, urging, "Good matchmaker, please accept these gifts—two bottles of wine and two packages of sugar—along with the pig's head. The sugar will give you health and longevity." Wreathed in smiles, friends and relatives from the bride's party looked on. Third Auntie replied confidently, "I deserve the pig's head, as I've worked hard to bring the new couple together; if I take the sugar and wine, too, the couple will live to ninety-nine years of age, until the husband is a white-haired old man and the wife a venerable toothless old matron!" With this declaration, she said her final good-byes, casually packing the pig's head, sugar, and wine bottles in her basket, then bending to slip the basket over her shoulders. At the very moment, however, the Zhou family's relatives and friends swarmed her, wildly throwing ashes and peanut shells in her direction. Anticipating this, the matchmaker took a ready pouch of sawdust from her pocket, launching a counterattack of her own, and then ran for dear life, dashing madly out the gate like a wild hare, her basket falling off in the ruckus.

"Go, go, bring Third Auntie her basket!" Tao Jiuxiang urged, frantically nudging Masui. Mahe giggled, watching his brother sling the basket over his shoulder and awkwardly clamber after Third Auntie. By the time Masui caught up with the big-footed matchmaker, he was soaked with sweat.

Chapter Five

I

Rolling clouds and mist shrouded the primeval forest and towering mountains.

The newlyweds had adjourned to the nuptial chamber upstairs. For the whole afternoon, the Zhou family and their relatives, the Lis, Mawu's militiamen, and various friends and neighbors drank tea and chatted, paying them little heed.

In the afternoon, Ermei went upstairs to the wedding chamber to see Damei and found her older sister napping. Knowing that Damei was exhausted, she quietly left her to sleep. When she returned for a second time after dinner, however, Ermei was astonished to find that Damei had vanished. Ermei asked her brother Zhou Taiwang, but he knew nothing. Tao Jiuxiang and Jin hunted up and down for the bride, but discovered no trace. What a shame! Tearful and speechless Masui sat down beside Mahe in front of the fire. Zhou Taiwang consoled, "Don't worry, brother. Damei's probably just a little shy and hid herself. She'll probably come out in a little while."

Li Diezhu tried desperately to control himself. For a bride to run away on her wedding day was utterly outrageous! Deeply embarrassed, Zhou Taiwang stamped his feet and cursed, "Damn! When I find her, I'll be damned if I don't break both of her legs." But another hour passed and long past midnight Damei was still missing.

The wife of Sun Fu, Li Diezhu's tenant farmer, surreptitiously whispered to Tao Jiuxiang that she had poked a hole in the paper panel of the window to peek in on the newlyweds. In the moonlight the bride had been lying on the nuptial bed behind the gauze drapes, while Masui had spread out a quilt and reclined on the floor.

The happy occasion had become a fiasco! Tao Jiuxiang stalked resolutely into the wedding chamber, peeled back the quilting and inspected the sheets. She found nothing at all: they were clean as a blank sheet of paper. She stared at Masui, sternly asking, "What did you do last night?"

Masui answered, "She was in bed, agitated . . . she didn't let me touch her. She said a young guy in white was calling to her, asking her to giggle. I warned her not to laugh or else she'd meet with misfortune. She said the young man was breathing toward her, then she couldn't control herself and burst out laughing."

By the ancestors! thought an exasperated Tao Jiuxiang. These two sons of hers both had issues in the nuptial chamber! Mawu and Jin had only just settled down, and now this new couple had begun to kick up a fuss. Gravely, she urged Xia Qifa to figure out what sort of devilry had overtaken her daughter-in-law.

Xia Qifa could make the blind see and the bald grow hair. After performing several divinations with the trigrams, he determined that the missing bride was to the northeast, hidden not in a mountain cave but in the hollow cavity of a huge tree.

In their anxiety, Tao Jiuxiang and Li Diezhu both turned a stony gray. Such queer things had happened before. In these mountains, it was said that introverted girls caught up in romantic fancy sometimes wept leaves rather than tears. Now on her wedding day, Damei had concealed herself in a tree hollow! Unless the *tima* got to her immediately, it could mean madness or death! A lecherous tree spirit might wive her!

It was not a tree spirit but Jiang Ermao that most worried Zhou Taiwang. From the moment the wedding date was set, their parents had locked Damei in her room, kept under watch day and night, and left to her embroidery. Zhou Taiwang had been one of the Qins' hired laborers, but because of their new marriage ties to the Lis and Qins, he was allowed to enroll as a militiaman in Huangshui. Shortly after he enlisted, Mawu sent him home to help out in the weeks leading up to the wedding. Every day, he had carried firewood and shepherded goats for his parents. Before he carried her to the wedding sedan, he hadn't even seen Damei set foot outside, let alone meet with Jiang Ermao. It seemed highly unlikely the two had plotted to elope, but Damei had to be located immediately.

The previous afternoon, Ermei had seen her sister reclining on the wedding quilts, head-down and dozing. But when she checked back around sunset, Damei was gone. In the dense night fog, Damei could not have run far. When cocks crowed for the third time in the early morn, Mawu dispatched several militiamen to scour the nearby mountain slopes.

After the search began, Tao Jiuxiang asked Li Diezhu and Xia Qifa to lie down and rest, while she and Jin put aside the wedding gifts and swept up the detritus of firecracker casings and peanut shells. Afterward, they lit the stove for breakfast. The cooking smoke rose from the yard, intermingling with the mist and floating into the labyrinthine primeval forest.

Eighteen-month-old Yongyu awakened, sensing something awry. Stricken by an unfamiliar feeling of desolation, she squalled lustily and pedaled her long legs. Jin held up Yongyu for a piss, then brought her over to the warmth of the fireplace and fed her porridge. At this instant, however, Mahe surged in, frantically calling, "Ma, sister-in-law's been found in a hollowed-out old tree near Gangou Bridge!"

"Was anyone else with her?" Tao Jiuxiang's voice quavered. She felt the flesh crawl on her back.

Mahe frowned, answering, "No."

Long ago, mountainfolk set up Gangou Bridge using two massive tree trunks to span a deep gulch. It was the only route connecting Gengguping to Inkblack Creek. Hundreds of ancient trees grew on the slope approaching the bridge, many with large hollows in their wide trunks. In some of these dark and moist tree holes, passing herb collectors had laid down a matting of straw, making the space tidy and dry. Each year when chestnuts fell on these slopes, the elders forbid others to gather them, fearing the wrath of the possessive Tree Spirit. Indeed, few people even spoke of the nuts, fearing casual mention might cause them or their children to fall ill.

A clamor of stamping was heard from outside. "Here they come!" Mahe called. Tao Jiuxiang doused the fire-pit with cold water before heading out. Exhausted, Mawu and his soldiers entered the house, followed by Damei. Mawu had searched several tree holes before locating Zhou Damei curled up in a hollow, shoeless and disheveled, singing and giggling queerly.

Unkempt, her face smudged with dirt, the bride suddenly broke away from the militiamen, dashed forward, and tore down the wedding couplets flanking the doorway. Ermei let out a dismayed cry that brought in a throng of Zhou relatives, who sought to restrain Damei. The bride, however, ran riot, crying and screaming, wildly lashing out at anyone and anything within reach. Paralyzed with fear and confusion, Masui stood helpless. Finally the militiamen entered the ruckus, dragging the bride out into the yard and forcefully sitting her down in a chair.

Awakened by the brouhaha, bleary-eyed Li Diezhu emerged from the bedroom to see the bride, her red wedding dress torn to ribbons, clumsily fixing her hair. Sternly, he roared, "What's going on here?"

Scared out of her wits, Ermei said, "When my sister's sedan passed that thicket yesterday, I felt a sudden cold draft of wind and shuddered. I'm afraid we've offended the Tree Spirit."

Majestic and imposing, one tall hardwood towered above all others on the slope near Gangou Bridge. When mountainfolk gathered kindling, they gave the tree a wide berth. When the search embarked that morning, Masui thought of that very place. Sure enough, the bride was found curled up in the hollow of the tree, barefoot and disheveled, like a mountain sprite. Rocking back and forth as she swayed her hands and kicked her feet, she put a leaf in her mouth and whistled, then chanted like an idiot,

> *The moon it rises like a radish drying screen,*
> *Mother and Father, you treat me so mean.*
> *Now I shan't heed you, Dad and Mum,*
> *But, you, my dearest, hither to me come!*

Nobody knew whether she was singing to the Tree Spirit or to her mortal lover.

Damei's brain was addled! Stamping his foot, Zhou Taiwang sighed, "I didn't want to provoke that spirit, so yesterday as the sedan passed Gangou Bridge and approached the tree I specially ordered the troupe to stop with the music and firecrackers. But it still turned out disastrously."

One of the Zhou aunts grumbled, "Poor niece, what an unlucky creature!"

Seeing Damei's dirty bare feet, Jin went upstairs and returned with her silk embroidered shoes, coaxing Damei in a saccharine tone, "Dear sister-in-law, please put on my shoes."

Damei took a look at Jin, and accepted the shoes.

Realizing his bride had not eaten anything on the wedding day, Masui worriedly said, "Go into the other room and get something to eat."

At this, Damei, her eyes bloodshot, swerved and rushed at Tao Jiuxiang.

"Halt!" commanded Xia Qifa, walking out of the house. To everyone's surprise the stark raving mad bride obeyed, stopping in mid-step. "Sit!" shouted the *tima*, pointing at a chair. Damei seated herself at once in the vacant chair.

After a glance at the bride, Xia Qifa turned to the onlookers and sighed, "Seeing the resplendent red wedding sedan, the Tree Spirit was so possessed with envy and admiration that he wanted to carry off the bride himself."

Tao Jiuxiang secretly dragged Mawu aside and asked, "Was anybody else hiding nearby?"

Mawu replied, "Not a soul. Twenty-odd people with dogs and torches searched high and low. We didn't find a thing."

"Was she ill before the wedding?" Jin wondered aloud.

Turning to Zhou Taiwang, Li Diezhu gruffly queried, "Well, was she *ever* sick like this before?"

In spite of Li Diezhu's flat tone, Zhou Taiwang felt apprehensive. His response was sincere, "Oh, no! She's not sick at all . . . probably just overwrought."

"Exhaustion weakens the body and mind, leaving one vulnerable to evil spirits," Li Diezhu said, nodding. "We'll let *Tima* Xia deal with her after breakfast."

II

Plunged deep in misery over his unhinged bride, Masui lost his appetite. Tearful and distracted he turned to Xia Liangxian, and murmured, "Brother, a handsome fellow like you needs to find a good wife. Don't end up like me." Only fourteen, the *tima*'s shy young son flushed red at the very mention of marriage.

Tao Jiuxiang found two kerchiefs, and with the help of several Zhou kinsmen, bound Damei to the chair. The girl resisted, scratching and clawing, struggling and crying. Soon, however, she lapsed into a listless daze, her head lolled to one side, and she stared vacantly. Nobody knew whether she had slept at all the previous night in the tree hollow.

To keep them quiet, Xia Qifa bound the dogs' mouths and fowl's beaks. The shaman donned his ceremonial robes and his eight-cornered, feathered headdress painted with the immortals, then burned incense to invite the spirits.

Masui and Mahe assisted Xia Liangxian with minor preparations. The strange, sweet reek of incense filled the room. Following Xia Qifa's instructions, Sun Fu placed eight old plowshares into the stove. Li Diezhu tended the stove, from time to time adding kindling and turning them over. He had seen the shaman cure the mad, and knew the plowshares needed to be red-hot to be effective. Xia Liangxian looked and, finding the plowshares already glowing with heat, added several pieces of firewood.

People milled about in shock and sorrow, waiting.

Firecrackers sounded, leaving a lingering odor of saltpeter in the air. Mawu sent one of his men to fetch Zhou Taiwang to accompany his sister Damei. Mawu regretted that he had given Masui's letter to his mother. Had he known beforehand Masui and Damei were so ill-suited, he would have let his brother go off to Chongqing to be with that classmate of his.

Setting his staff beside the table, Xia Qifa used an ancient set of bamboo slips marked with trigram patterns to commune with the spirits. Attentively, Xia Liangxian watched the rhythmic movements of his father's hands as the slips, passed down for hundreds of years, fluttered to the ground. Xia Qifa squatted down to read them; then he jumped up and blew several sonorous blasts on his ox horn.

Immortals and spirits in the region were all familiar with Xia Qifa. When they heard the summons of the *tima*, they came into his presence, assembling in majestic fashion.

Li Diezhu stoked the fire beneath the plowshares with two more pieces of wood. Xia Qifa opened his deerskin bag, removed a cluster of grasses and roots, and asked Li Diezhu to boil them in a pot.

Roused by the firecrackers and the ox horn, the bride began to cry and struggle. Breathless and panting, Zhou Taiwang arrived, followed closely by several mountainfolk who had been gathering medicinal herbs and cutting wood nearby when they heard the oxhorn. They threw down their baskets and rushed headlong toward the sound, in their haste nearly tumbling down a steep escarpment. The three entered the courtyard to see Xia Qifa chanting over a bowl of water. One of his hands formed a series of mudras, his deft fingers, supple and seemingly boneless, moving and taking on new shapes so rapidly that even the keen-eyed Zhou Taiwang could not keep up. The *tima* inhaled a mouthful of water from the bowl and spurted it onto his hands to cleanse them; then with tongs he removed the red-hot plowshares from the stove, brushing off the ashes. With his bare hands he carried six of the plowshares two at a time to the open courtyard, where he arrayed them in the shape of a hexagonal plum blossom. On his final trip, he laid a seventh plowshare in the center of the hexagon.

To conquer the searing and sharp angular metal in the presence of the hosts of spirits and ghosts, to show them his power, the shaman poured tung oil, sizzling and crackling, onto the plowshares, prompting flames to leap high, turning the open courtyard into a sea of fire. Xia Qifa took off his straw sandals, fastened the eight pleats of his robes round his waist, and oiled the bottoms of his feet. After that, he held the *tima* staff in both hands, and, lo, easily stepped onto the burning plowshares! Slowly, in a queer dance, like a willow osier swaying in the breeze, he followed the ambling gait of Bodhisattva-King Yu the Great, moving from one plowshare to the next in uneven steps.

Off to the side, Xia Liangxian rhythmically struck a gong, his bright eyes following every movement. He knew that his father possessed tremendous magical powers, enabling him to see and commune with all nature of spirits, demons, ghosts, and ancestors. At the moment, it was no mere man dancing in the fire—it was a spirit! And he was in the company of other gods, dancing with the Three Sovereigns: creator Fuxi, Divine Farmer Shennong, and Suiren, the discoverer of fire. It seemed to the youth miraculous and delightful that only his father could see these deities. He longed to learn, but his father had not yet taught him the inner workings of the shamanic arts. Only once his father passed on the basic principles could he become a formal disciple. A disciple had to abide by many regulations. During the course of a year, there were very few days when the apprentice might learn and practice his arts. If a disciple practiced at other times, an evil fate would befall him. Admiringly watching the awestruck expressions of the throngs, he wondered if he would ever command the same power. Though his father had emphasized that he should brook no distractions during a rite, he could not help shooting a glance toward Mawu and Jin. Then, regaining his focus, he concentrated on striking the gong.

Incandescent flames and showers of sparks rose from the plowshares like streamers. Full of elasticity, Xia Qifa's thin legs moved rhythmically and easily as he stepped from plowshare to plowshare. In this numinous space outside of time, gods, spirits, and ghosts congregated, capriciously making merry with the *tima*, helping him give full play to his talents.

Mahe was dumbfounded. He heard two awestruck woodcutters talking admiringly:

"The wilder the flames, the more blithely the *tima* dances."

"He's more powerful than *Tima* Wu!"

The rite whipped the raving bride, Damei, into a frenzy of agitation. Eyes blazing, she cried out wildly. Had she not been bound to the chair, Damei doubtless would have leapt into the fire, vying with the *tima* for the attention of the spirits!

After a while, when the sparks had faded and the flames dwindled, Xia Qifa nimbly stepped away from the plowshares. Though he had danced on red-hot metal, the shaman appeared wholly unscathed! He sent Tao Jiuxiang to fetch the herbal decoction that he had boiled.

Xia Liangxian, too, carried over a bowl of mixed liquor and pine resin. The *tima* took a mouthful and held up a plowshare, still searing hot. He moved in front of Zhou Damei, who cried and giggled madly, her eyes rolling back into her head. As the *tima* spurted the liquid onto the plowshare, tongues of red flame erupted toward Damei with a sizzle of white smoke. The fragrance of pine enveloped her.

Zhou Taiwang's heart was in his throat. His sister convulsed and twitched, screaming and thrashing, shedding a cascade of tears; rivers of drool pooled at her feet, before she finally lapsed into unconsciousness!

Later a woodcutter claimed that he had seen a golden weasel dash out the gate from behind a kindling pile. People believed the weasel to be the incarnation of the Tree Spirit. Pity that the *tima* was engaged in the ceremony and couldn't chase it! But Xia Qifa had to devote his full attention to the exorcism. At a hand signal, Liangxian handed his father the bowl that he had incanted earlier. He dipped a hand into the holy water, then moved to a wooden basin Li Diezhu had carried over, scooping out a handful of grasses and roots. Picking up the basin, he threw the steaming herbal decoction right in Damei's face.

Shocked into consciousness, the runaway bride cried, "Oh, Mother! It's so hot."

Xia Qifa said, "Untie her. It's over."

The congregated mountainfolk were skeptical. Even Tao Jiuxiang hesitated.

The *tima* put the tip of a plowshare into the bowl, prompting the water to boil fiercely and give off puffs of white steam. He removed the plowshare, shook the bowl, and told Damei to drink it before it grew cold.

Bewildered, the mad bride looked at the throng of onlookers, then, knitting her brows, lowered her gaze.

Tao Jiuxiang signaled Jin to untie the bindings. "Daughter-in-law," said she, "The *tima* is treating your illness. Drink the water. Endure it!" With these words, the mother-in-law poured the entire bowl down the throat of the exhausted bride.

Unable to keep down the liquid, Damei disgorged a pile of bilious filth.

Hurriedly, Li Diezhu ushered the onlookers into the house for a rest. Tao Jiuxiang ran back and forth like a weaving shuttle. With Jin's help, she got Damei into the rear courtyard, where they prepared a bath for her in the various basins, large and small.

"Boil rice and prepare pork dishes! Today the host will entertain us!" bellowed the *tima* with a smile.

III

Seven or eight meat dishes were stewed, fried, roasted, or boiled. After Damei had been scrubbed clean, she put on a new dress, devoured her dinner, then squatted before the stove to boil water with her head lowered.

Tao Jiuxiang asked, "Is anything wrong, daughter-in-law?"

Damei answered meekly, "Mother, I'm dizzy."

Exasperated, Tao Jiuxiang insinuatingly rejoined, "If you have a bed but don't sleep in it, who wouldn't feel dizzy?"

Right cheek cupped in one hand, Damei said nothing.

"Go up to your room to sleep," said Tao Jiuxiang, adding, "in the bed!"

Embarrassed, Damei trudged upstairs.

Seeing Masui in low spirits, Xia Qifa took a bowl of water once more and uttered an incantation over it. He dipped his hands into the bowl, and then removed the eighth and final plowshare from the stove. He held the plowshare with one hand, rubbing it with the other. Putting the plowshare aside, he repeatedly pressed his searing hands to Masui's forehead to expel baleful spirits. Slowly, some of the luster returned to Masui's eyes.

Wide-eyed, Mahe asked, "Uncle Xia, Why aren't you afraid of fire?"

Xia Qifa said, "Fire comes from thunder and lightning, from dried bones and forest groves. When our ancestors were primitive and wild, fire was everywhere. Because they couldn't avoid the fire, they learned to love it and tame it, and in the process came to apprehend many of its mysteries."

Curious, Mahe pursued, "What kind of mysteries, Uncle Xia? Please tell me."

Xia Qifa laughed, "That would be a long story. Suffice it to say, that if you dance like this, you can commune with heaven and the netherrealms." So saying, he went through a series of motions with his hands.

Reaching out as if to grasp the patterns the shaman had described in the air, Mahe asked curiously, "Are those mudras?"

"Clever boy! It was indeed a mudra. If I drew it on paper it would be a magical charm capable of controlling dragons and summoning tigers. Back when Yu the Great used fire to sunder rock and create Kuimen, the Gate of the Thunderous One-Footed Dragon, guiding the waters to the Eastern Sea, this is the technique that he used."

"King Yu was amazing!" exclaimed Masui.

"He understood the mysterious script written into the patterns of heaven and earth, so that within the eight regions of the four directions, under the vast canopy of the twenty-eight constellations, neither god nor demon dared disobey him," Xia Qifa said reverently.

"That year of the drought when we moved, why didn't you summon our ancestral Tiger to help?" Masui cautiously inquired.

"That wicked dragon was pressing a lawsuit against our Tiger ancestor; King Yu the Great was judge. Therefore, the Tiger couldn't come. As mortal beings, we couldn't await the outcome. We needed another place to settle."

"What does the mysterious script of heaven and earth look like, Uncle Xia? Please write some of the characters for us." Mahe implored, full of interest.

"Many of them have been lost. When your sister-in-law needed it, I drew one for her. The script reveals the truth of the ebb and flow of sun and moon, stars and constellations, seasons and climates, even the flowering and decay of plants and trees. I can't just casually jot them down." Xia Qifa answered with a smile.

It suddenly dawned on Mahe how quickly Xia Qifa had written the esoteric characters in the air. What a pity those characters had been dispersed by the winds and those on paper burned to ashes, leaving no trace! Resting his chin on interlaced fingers, Mahe asked, "What's Yu the Great like, Uncle Xia."

Xia Qifa explained patiently, "Disheveled and tattered, he wore a woven straw raincape and a bamboo hat, tirelessly seeking out and defeating wicked spirits and chopping the heads off water dragons as he redirected the floodwaters from the rivers of the Nine Provinces into the sea."

Masui asked, "Why did he direct the floodwaters into the sea?"

His eyes suffused with reverence, Xia Qifa responded, "He undertook this arduous task so that the common people did not become fodder for fish and shrimp. He did it to dredge the watercourses. He did it to fulfill the sacred charge of gods and men to reach the edge of the world."

Mahe recalled that in the *Classic of Mountains and Seas*, one of the earliest canonical texts, Gun, King Yu's father, had vainly tried to build dikes and embankments to contain the floodwaters. When this method failed, the Heavenly Emperor executed him. Puzzled, he knit his brows and asked, "Didn't Yu the Great hate the Heavenly Emperor for killing his father Gun?"

Xia Qifa replied seriously, "Not at all. Gun and Yu were not ordinary beings. Their love was a greater love, extending to all people under heaven. That is why spirits and ghosts alike all revere them."

As they chatted, Tao Jiuxiang, Jin, and Sun Fu went to and fro, busily preparing a feast. Delighted and relieved, Li Diezhu cheerfully invited the two woodcutters and the militiamen on duty to the tower to partake. Happy that his sister-in-law had recovered, Mawu ordered his underlings, clad in identical gray uniforms, to offer individual toasts to Xia Qifa. The *tima* didn't drink wine at all, and respectfully presented the wine in his cup as a libation to the spirits.

Zhou Taiwang, too, was delighted that his sister seemed normal. The rebellious light in her eyes had dimmed. After all, the road to happiness is never smooth. Anxiety subsiding, his heart descended from his throat back into its usual position in his chest. Flooded with relief, he held up his wine cup, smiling ear to ear. He drank until, flushed hot with inebriation, oily sweat coursed from his rough pores.

After dinner, Xia Qifa burned a large stack of paper money for the spirits and ghosts, respectfully seeing them off one by one as they headed to their various destinations in heaven, on earth, or in the netherworld.

As moon and stars sank westward and dawn broke, the peaks, long inundated by darkness, came into ever-clearer resolution. Tao Jiuxiang rose early, listening for any sound from upstairs as she cooked breakfast. In the growing light of morning, Damei descended the stairs, her head lowered. Tao Jiuxiang gazed at her daughter-in-law for a moment, then ventured, "Are you still dizzy?"

Damei murmured, "No, Ma. I'm not dizzy now. I'll go out and graze the ox." At this, she headed out to pasture and led the black ox to the slope to crop grass.

Seeing this change in Damei, Tao Jiuxiang felt that her daughter-in-law was healthy and sound. Thank the ancestors! Now everything could return to normalcy. She mused that although pockfaced Masui was not good-looking, according to the lore of the elders all those pocks meant a passel of sons. She wondered when her daughter-in-law would bear her first child.

As Ermei's marriage to Qin Liexiong was imminent, she and brother Zhou Taiwang eagerly headed home right after breakfast. Xia Qifa, together with his son, also readied themselves to take their leave. Hurriedly, Li Diezhu placed three silver dollars into the pockets of Xia Qifa's robes.

"How generous you are! A rooster would be enough." Pleased, Xia Qifa put the silver dollars back on the table and began gathering his instruments. Li Diezhu urged him to stay longer, but it was in vain. "I'm afraid someone is waiting for me at my home," he explained, determined to leave with his handsome son. Tao Jiuxiang picked up the back-basket containing the *tima*'s tools, instructing Sun Fu to lead over a horse to carry the heavy back-basket and a second basket of salt and rice.

Xia Qifa, however, grabbed the straps of his basket, warning, "Never place this basket on a horse's back! It would make the creature buck wildly in terror."

Only then did Tao Jiuxiang realize that Xia Qifa's sword and copper bell, his oxhorn and his tallies, had been smeared with cock's blood and incanted, and therefore possessed great ritual power. So she cried, "Then let Sun Fu carry them for you." She turned to Mawu, shouting, "Quick, go and catch a cock!"

Mawu caught their big red cock and put it in a bamboo cage. He was about to fasten the cage to the flanks of the horse when the Xia Qifa signaled to stop him, saying, "Just let him go. He knows the path to my home."

Amid the surprised gazes of the Lis and the remaining guests, the big cock strutted majestically out the gate, following the *tima*'s ancestral staff without a backward glance at his mates scratching and pecking for insects in the bamboo grove.

As they departed, a chorus of birds of every feather erupted, chirping and chortling. With a sense of awe, the eyes of all followed the *tima*, Xia Qifa, until he disappeared into the forest.

Chapter Six

I

One night, after several days of over-exertion, Sun Fu was in pain and knocked at the door of Masui's chamber, crying, "Second Master, please lend me a silver dollar to scrape off the sunburn on my back and shoulders."

He called several times, but got no response. However, the door of Mahe's room was ajar. But Mahe had already gone back to school in Fengjie, so who could be in the room now? Scared, Sun Fu stared toward the open door. A moment later, Masui poked his head out, rubbing his eyes and peevishly grumbling, "Why bother me at this late hour?"

"My sunburn is agonizing," replied Sun Fu. "Why are you in this room?"

"Come in." Without replying, Masui retreated to put on his clothes.

Sun Fu entered the room, looking round, but saw nobody else. Straightaway, he took some *tung* oil from the lamp, lay prone on the bed, and asked Masui to scrape his back with the silver dollar.

Taking a silver dollar from a drawer, Masui dipped it in the tung oil and started noisily scraping Sun Fu's back.

"Oooh, a bit more gently! Why are you in here?" Sun Fu asked, curiously canting his head to one side.

"None of your business. That's it, I quit scraping!" Masui, annoyed, slammed down the silver dollar.

"Okay, Okay! It's none of my business. Second master, please keep scraping till dark prints appear where the poison's come to the surface." Sun Fu begged earnestly. Masui kept scraping till Sun Fu finally felt better. Then the tenant put his clothes back on and thanked Masui graciously. The next day, however, the loose-tongued ingrate let out the secret.

What on earth had happened to the star-crossed couple now? All the pains taken to set the newlyweds' life onto the right track proved for naught: Obstinate Masui had been sleeping in Mahe's bedroom every night!

Tao Jiuxiang's brow, relaxed after Damei's recovery, immediately knit and tensed again. She called Masui and got straight to the point, inquiring why he wasn't sleeping with his wife? Infuriated at loose-lipped Sun Fu, he bluntly told his mother that he didn't want to! He simply wanted to go back to school! Fate was unfair. Although his wife had returned to her senses, knowing how to tend to her husband, it made him sick with disgrace that she had sung lascivious songs and spent the night in the tree hollow. People were gossiping; tongues were wagging. Some said the old tree lusted after the beautiful bride. Others maintained that she wanted to marry Jiang Ermao, who had joined the bandits under bamboo craftsman Liang. Tormented by Damei's lovers from two worlds, Masui felt utterly miserable. Pockfaced though he was, he was beloved by teachers and classmates in Fengjie City for his hard work and intelligence. Why should he have to endure such humiliation? Why incur the wrath of Jiang Ermao and his bandit mates over some illiterate madwoman? He figured if he didn't live with her as husband and wife, he need not fear her lover's vengeance.

While the militia on duty in the stone tower gossiped about the madness of Damei and Jiang Ermao's joining the brigands, they remained tactfully quiet around Mawu and Tao Jiuxiang. They speculated that Jiang Ermao had not known his lover would flee from her wedding chamber, thus he failed to meet her at the old tree. Now that the wood had already become a boat, they figured Jiang must be seething with regret. As a precaution, Tao Jiuxiang told the militiamen to stockpile logs and stones atop of the tower to rebuff the devil bandits.

She scolded Masui, "Marriage is predestined. Even if the sky is falling, a man has to get married and embark on a career. It's time to show that you've got the mettle!"

Masui grew silent.

Tao Jiuxiang felt an agonized empathy for her second son. To save the marriage from becoming untracked, she asked Jin to help guide Damei out of her misery.

Accepting her mother-in-law's decree, Jin sat before the fireplace with Yongyu on her lap, chatting with Damei as she shucked corn. "Sister-in-law, do you think I care about you?"

Damei, her jaw resting on her right hand, answered, "You are kind to me as my true sister."

Ermei was to marry Qin Liexiong the next day, offering Jin a good occasion to ask Damei about Masui. She whispered, "Then tell me the truth so that I won't be unnecessarily anxious about you. Are you unhappy with Masui?"

Damei lowered her head, and then shook it.

Jin blinked her beautiful eyes, sighing, "A man is like a stove. A woman needs to learn to tend him, dampening the fire if it burns too hot and stoking the flames if the fire is guttering. A wife must serve her husband until she enters the earth and becomes a spirit, otherwise she won't enjoy a prosperous life. Masui is a slow-burner, a literate man with a deliberate, refined character. So you need to take pains at first to kindle and stir up his love. Our mother-in-law is craving another grandchild soon!"

Once Jin departed, Damei bathed herself and put on her new imported cotton dress, a gift from her parents-in-law. After supper, she washed the dishes, combed her hair in a modish style, and adjusted the lamp to brighten the room. With a gentle whisper she summoned Masui and asked about Fengjie City.

His pocked face inexpressive, Masui said woodenly, "It's different! In the city, men and women can love whom they choose. Even once they're married, if they find they're incompatible they can get divorced. Then they can remarry."

She didn't know how to answer. How true the saying, "Of ten pockfaced men, nine are eccentric"! Just because Masui had a few years of schooling, he held up city customs to mockingly trample all over the ways of the mountainfolk! Now that she had married Masui, Damei mused, how could Jiang Ermao possibly still want her?

"You needn't hide anything from me. I've heard you two singing courtship songs." Looking at the fine hair behind her ears, Masui said clearly and thoughtfully, "I don't want to be hard on you. I have a lover in Fengjie City, too—a fellow student. Both you and I are victims of a backward system. We should get a divorce."

Thunderstruck, Damei sat on the edge of the bed, gazing wordlessly at the lamp.

Not knowing if she had understood, Masui continued, "According to government law, a rural couple can get a divorce if they can't live together happily. I know you have a lover; once we divorce you can marry him. What do you think?"

Damei looked up vacantly, tears pooling in her eyes. A chill night wind blew into the room, as if to accent the air of melancholy and misery.

Time ground to a halt. Amid the nocturnal chorus of insects, Damei dropped her head and began undressing. As Masui watched her, the image of a grubby tree sprite, chanting and laughing, floated into his mind. Lowering his gaze, he left the room and collapsed into a dead sleep on Mahe's bed.

From the corridor, Tao Jiuxiang had listened to all that transpired in the wedding chamber. Dismayed, she mused that Masui had as many off-kilter ideas as he had pocks on his face! Disconsolate, she lay beside Li Diezhu in the dead of night, turning the matter over in her mind before finally sinking into a fitful sleep.

II

A faint salmon light pierced the dark blue sky in the east. After another sleepless night, Damei, her bleary eyes swollen and her head aching as though riven by an axe, rose and prepared corn fritters for breakfast. Her listless eyes swept around the breakfast table, coming to rest on her pockfaced husband. This morn, the neighbors and folks who had recently gathered at the Li homestead for Damei and Masui's wedding would congregate at the Qins to drink and celebrate again. At the second cockcrow, Li Diezhu, together with Mawu and Masui, followed by Sun Fu, his wife, and three militiamen, set off for the wedding ceremony. Damei wanted to go to her sister's wedding, but Masui hadn't saddled her a horse.

Tao Jiuxiang had decided that Damei would remain. Given her daughter-in-law's volatile temperament, she feared a mishap en route. Moreover, Jin was unwilling to see Qin Liexiong. Thus, Tao Jiuxiang had determined it would be best to stay home with her two daughters-in-law. To keep them safe, Mawu left two militiamen to look after the house.

Several fields needed weeding. Young laborers whose homes were far away sometimes ate and spent the night at the Li's household, so the family needed abundant stores of food. After breakfast, the two militiamen, toting a lunch basket of buckwheat cakes, drove ten-odd cattle and sheep to graze the slopes. After washing the dishes with a lowered head, Damei set a large bowl of corn kernels and a wooden basin of buckwheat on a bench. Jin took the millstone from beneath the eaves and cleaned it. Then the two young women worked in tandem, Damei turning the millstone round and round while ladle by ladle Jin poured kernels of corn through the eye of the millstone. To flavor the rice, Tao Jiuxiang would add cornmeal, buckwheat flour, or slices of potato.

With a grinding sound, the heavy millstone turned, golden cornmeal spilling from the side crevices like fine sand. Jin used a bamboo brush to sweep the flour into a stone tub beneath the millstone. Several hens rushing to peck at the cornmeal were driven away by a barking dog, which Tao Jiuxiang rewarded with a bone.

Toddling over with a pear in her hand, Yongyu grasped a handful of corn kernels and scattered them for the hens. Tao Jiuxiang picked her up and carried her back to the bench, before heading to the backyard to make pickled cabbage. She poured two pounds of salt in a large basin of cabbage, rubbing and twisting it into the leaves as though she were washing clothes. The following spring, the brined vegetables would be ready to eat. Mulling the recent weeks, she sighed as she twisted and rubbed, singing,

> We look around for the highest mount,
> Never knowing we're on the summit.
> We awaken at cock's crow, at the break of dawn;
> Till the dead of night, third watch, still we labor on.

Grinding away at the millstone, Damei's arms ached. Jin, with Yongyu on her back, wanted to switch jobs with weary Damei. During a pause, they caught snatches of their mother-in-law's ditty. Just as Jin pricked up her ears to listen, Tao Jiuxiang stopped.

The millstone turned round and round. Wearing a faint smile and raising her eyebrows, Jin asked, "What's our mother-in-law singing?"

Listlessly, Damei replied, "No idea."

Jin said shyly, "It's related to 'labor' in the 'dead of night'. Get it?"

Damei exhaled the same two dry words, "No idea."

Jin's smile receded. Sincerely, she said, "Didn't you think the advice I gave you yesterday was reasonable?"

Damei looked down at the turning millstone, tongue-tied.

Jin furrowed her brow. She knew Damei was hiding something, and wanted to unburden her through talking, but her sister-in-law acted in such a peculiar manner she felt there was nothing she could do.

By early afternoon, they had finished grinding all the corn and buckwheat. Tao Jiuxiang carried in a hot meal. Like other mountainfolk, the Lis had eaten two meals a day, but once they got wealthy they began to take three meals a day like people in Huangshui. Because they were busy in the fields all day, lunch tended to be the simplest meal. The three women sat together at the dining table. Damei ate slowly. Tao Jiuxiang said, "You'd better eat more—take care of your health. Once you're with child, you can go see your sister. Masui will go with you. He'll ride a horse, and you'll be carried in a sedan chair."

Damei stared vacantly at her bowl.

Jin served Damei a piece of tofu with her chopsticks, then turned to ask Tao Jiuxiang naughtily, "Ma, what was that you were singing just now?"

Tao Jiuxiang said sternly, "A song handed down from the ancestors: from this peak we look longingly to that mountain crest, from that crest we look covetously to this peak, yet the truth is that we've been standing on the summit all along."

Speechless, Damei lowered her head and poked at her bowl.

A series of squeals and grunts issued from the pregnant black sow in the pigpen. Her forelegs atop the enclosure's fence, the creature was demanding her lunch. An iron pot was filled with cooking water, sweet potato vine, rice chaff, rotted vegetables, and other scraps for the sow. They fed her twice a day, and while ordinarily it wouldn't matter if her supper came an hour late, the sow was nearly in labor and thus quick to hunger. Hurriedly, Tao Jiuxiang shoveled down the remainder of her lunch and shuffled off to pour the sow's feed into the big wooden basin in the pigpen.

As Jin fed porridge to Yongyu, Damei washed the dishes. Jin knew she was unhappy, and gently suggested, "As there's nothing to do this afternoon, you ought to rest up. When Masui comes back tonight, receive him in a warm, intimate fashion. Don't make our mother-in-law worry. Sooner or later Masui will bring you over to visit your sister and her new husband." So saying, Jin carried Yongyu off to a bed in a side chamber and lay beside her daughter, covering them both with a quilt. Before long, mother and daughter were asleep.

An ashen pallor darkened Damei's cheeks. She returned to her chamber and lay down, eyes wide open. After a while, she rose tearfully, opened her dowry chest, and removed a long silken ribbon. She fastened a wooden comb on one end, stepped on a bench, then threw the comb over a rafter. Both ends of the ribbon in hand, she untied the comb and set it on the table. All the while she thought of Jiang Ermao's charming songs and doleful leaf whistle. Choking on something sour and hot in the back of her throat, she wiped her eyes with her sleeve for one last time, then tied the two ends of the ribbon together, pushed her neck through the loop, and kicked away the bench beneath her feet. As the noose tightened around her neck and she departed the world, final thoughts of humiliation, anguish, and despair, mingled with tender musings of her lover, raced through Damei's mind.

When Jin awakened, she saw Tao Jiuxiang returning from the mountain slope, a large bundle of sweet potato vines and ragweed slung over her shoulder. Bustling, she hurried to help her mother-in-law.

After washing the mud from her hands and the sickle, Tao Jiuxiang sat before the fireplace, resting her head in her hands. The rhythmic, repetitive cadence of her daughter-in-law mincing the greens into pig fodder with the foot-long iron cleaver lulled her into a sound sleep.

When Jin finished cutting, Tao Jiuxiang woke up and put up a steamer of corn cakes for supper. She took Yongyu from the side chamber, leading her by the hand and teaching her to walk for a few moments, then said, "Let's go see your auntie," and headed upstairs with her granddaughter.

Jin put the chopped fodder into the big pot and, adding water and rice chaff, boiled tasty fare for the sow. Then, surprised that with the sun sinking behind the horizon Damei still hadn't come down, she fixed rice and buckwheat noodles for dinner. Hearing Tao Jiuxiang's piercing screech, her heart leapt from her chest. Fearing that Damei had gone mad again, she dropped the spatula and rushed upstairs.

Yongyu was sitting outside the chamber in the corridor. She rose to her feet and stumbled forward, her two little hands waving about. Jin strode past her and into the chamber, where she was struck dumb by the sight of Damei dangling from the rafter, her eyes protruding, mouth agape, and tongue lolling against her cheek. Having climbed up on the bench, Tao Jiuxiang was struggling to get Damei down.

"Damn!" cried Jin, her voice quavering. She hustled over to help Tao Jiuxiang lower Damei's still-warm corpse.

"Her body's still warm," said Tao Jiuxiang regretfully, looking at the hideous expression of fury frozen on Damei's ashen face. "I wish we'd come earlier."

III

Jin flew down the external stone steps carrying Yongyu. One of the militiamen, Cui Four, gawked in surprise from the tower, wondering what had sent her scurrying so frantically. Jin glanced up at him, yelling in alarm, "Send two men, come quick! Zhou Damei's hung herself!"

Momentarily dumbstruck, Cui Four gathered his wits and dragged Lidu over to the house, his gun hanging from his back. Halfway, they met Jin who passed Yongyu to Cui Four, calling sharply, "Find someone to take care of her." Cui Four handed Yongyu over to Ran, the cookwoman, then dashed back toward the yard.

Jin lit a *tung*-oil lamp, leading the militiamen upstairs. Zhou Damei had been laid on her bed. Beholding her grotesque frozen face, the two militiamen could hardly believe their eyes.

"Oh, daughter-in-law, we haven't wronged you!" Tao Jiuxiang gasped, anxious tears coursing down her cheeks. She covered Damei's face with a piece of straw mat.

Two other militiamen who had driven the cattle and sheep back from the slope arrived to find everyone congregated in Damei's chamber. Going downstairs, the growing crowd gathered round the fireplace, astonished and horrified. How gruesomely tragic the short and unhappy course of her life at Gengguping!

Tao Jiuxiang said faintly, "Send for Masui to come back."

Tearfully, Jin added, "Mawu said he'd be back after supper if it wasn't foggy. The waxing moon is round tonight, so they're surely heading back."

Tao Jiuxiang sighed, "We have to tell the Zhous."

Dejected, Jin responded, "But they're in the middle of a wedding, a joyful event..."

Wiping tears from her cheeks with her sleeve, the perplexed Tao Jiuxiang helplessly uttered, "What else can we do? She was unwilling to wive our Li family."

Lidu muttered, "I'm afraid that Tree Spirit has snatched her soul."

Cui Four added, "That old tree is haunted. When we crossed the bridge near the tree on the wedding day, we heard singing, so Captain Li fired two shots. When we found the bride, she was mumbling some weird song and that old tree whistled airy laughter in response. It's like bride and tree had some strange bond."

Lidu said, "I heard her singing, too. It went something like,

> *I'll sing you a ditty, tree spirit;*
> *Tell me if you are animate.*
> *If you are, you I'll marry;*
> *If you're not, I'll not tarry.*

Terror-stricken Cui Four sputtered, "I-I-I was too far away to hear clearly."

Eyes shining, Lidu asserted, "That's what I heard."

Aggrieved, Tao Jiuxiang ordered, "Go tell the Zhous."

Cui Four said to Lidu, "You can go. You're sure to meet Captain Li on the road."

Fearing the horse would crop poisonous grasses in the darkness, Tao Jiuxiang brought a basketful of grass. Telling Lidu to lead the horse over, she tied four long knives of different lengths on the edges of the backbasket, then gave him several freshly-steamed buckwheat cakes.

Though Lidu was afraid of the darkness, the sharp knives and his rifle buttressed his courage. Torch aloft, he rode toward Inkblack Creek, a hunting dog following. Though the primeval forest was so dense that only threads of moonlight filtered through, Lidu's eyes grew accustomed to the darkness. After covering more than half the route to the Qins, he heard the horse bells ahead. When the dog wagged its tail and bolted forward, Lidu knew it was the party from Gengguping. Sure enough, shortly Li Diezhu, Mawu, Masui, Sun Fu and his wife, and three other militiamen came trotting along. Hearing the familiar bark of one of their dogs and seeing the torch as he rode in the front, Mawu knew that something was awry. Alarmed, he asked, "What's wrong?"

"Captain Li! Master Li! Second Elder Brother Li!" called out Lidu anxiously, "The old tree spirit hasn't released his hold on Zhou Damei. He's taken her soul!"

Thinking Damei had lapsed back into madness, Mawu frowned, "Did she run off again?"

Lidu mumbled, "Hung herself . . . the Mistress sent me to tell the Zhous."

These words struck the father and two sons like a bolt from the blue, jarring them from inebriated cheer to grim sobriety. Terrified, Masui asked, "But why?"

"I have no idea," said Lidu. Making way for Mawu and the others, he dismounted and led his horse to a tree, set down the back-basket, its four mounted knives pointing skyward, and took several handfuls of grass to feed the creature.

Sun Fu's wife sighed, "I'm afraid it's that tree spirit. Once when I passed that tree, it whispered to me in a man's voice. I was so scared, I burst into a cold sweat."

Urgently, the group pressed forward, rushing back to Gengguping.

Puffing his pipe fiercely from atop his horse, Li Diezhu turned to Masui and asked suddenly, "Had you two been quarreling?"

Masui answered tremulously, "No. We never quarreled once!" Any trace of the urbane aplomb that he had possessed when he returned from Fengjie City was long gone. Like a cumbersome dark cloud, vexation weighed on his heart. His brooding pocked face took on a darker aspect in the grim dampness of the nighttime forest.

What an unexpected disaster! Li Diezhu had been proud of bookish Masui, but now misfortune had stricken his middle son. For the first time, he felt tired of the forest, haunted by ghosts and spirits, its endless creepers and trees, its tendrils of hanging vine and clustered underbrush, ever closing in on him.

As the party crossed over the bridge spanning the gulch, gathering clouds blotted out the faint moon. Holding torches aloft in the inky darkness, they moved through the dense forest toward Gengguping like a luminous procession of wandering spirits.

Back at the Li homestead, a riot of nightsounds, buzzing insects and birdcalls, pierced the cumbersome darkness. Cui Four and two other militiamen hastily wolfed down a meal, then, at Tao Jiuxiang's direction, sawed timbers in the corner of the yard into lengths of board to fashion a coffin.

A fierce wind rattled the doors and windows. Tremors of rumbling thunder shook the house and intermittent streaks of lightning lit up the darkness. Several times the main gate to the courtyard was almost jarred open.

Amidst the storm, the five people in the house grew pale with terror. Raising her head, Tao Jiuxiang quailed, "My daughter-in-law, we'll read more prayers for you and burn more paper offerings. Please don't harm us! Please don't blame us!"

Again, the main gate clattered. Cui Four and the other militiamen timidly ventured out, asking, "Who is it?"

From the darkness, Mawu's voice sounded, "Open the door!"

Relieved, Cui Four unbolted the gate.

A chill rain fell, accompanying the rumbling thunder and streaks of lightning, soaking everyone to the bone. Li Diezhu and his two sons, Sun Fu and his wife, and the three militiamen rushed into the yard.

"What's going on here?" demanded Li Diezhu.

At the sight of her husband and two sons, Tao Jiuxiang burst into tears, howling, "The corpse is upstairs!"

The rain pounded down. Masui dashed upstairs three steps at a time, with Li Diezhu, Mawu, Sun Fu, and the militiamen on his heels.

Zhou Damei's corpse was in rigor-mortise.

An arc of lightning cut through the night sky, outlining the room in spectral blue.

"Captain Li," cried terrified Sun Fu, "We . . . we . . . we'd better call the Daoist master from Azure Dragon Temple to perform an exorcism."

Without answering, Mawu dragged his father and brother back downstairs.

IV

Ominous clouds shrouded the mountains and valleys.

Wiping away tears, Tao Jiuxiang accusingly asked pallid Masui, "Did you two fight?"

Vacantly, Masui replied, "No. I didn't touch her, and we never quarreled." He dared not mention that he had broached divorce with his wife the previous evening.

Rains cascaded down, soon filling the basins and stone troughs in the courtyard.

"The dead don't come back," said Mawu severely, adding, "Pa, Sister-in-law died an ill-omened death, so we'd better invite Daoists to perform her final rites."

According to the inscription on the stele set before Azure Dragon Temple, long ago men and spirits had commingled, fiends and sprites of every description occupying the mountains of the region. Therefore, the Daoists set up an altar to expel the demons and sweep away the ghosts, allowing men to live in brightness and banishing ghosts and demons to the nether realms. When a person was possessed, folks in Huangshui called upon the *tima* to exorcise the spirit, but for funerary rites families who could afford it invited the Daoists of Azure Dragon Temple. However, whereas you could pay a shaman with a rooster or paper money, the Daoists insisted on silver.

Forceful streaks of lightning rent the skies, shedding a hauntingly beautiful blue light over the pigpen and beyond to the alluring bloom of wild poppies, the bamboo groves, the forests, and the mountains.

"Right," replied Li Diezhu, his face dark and tense. "Go to Azure Dragon Temple . . . quick!"

"Take my horse," Mawu urged Cui Four.

"Keep your lips sealed," Tao Jiuxiang hastily added. "It is a law handed down from the ancestors: family disgrace should not be made public, never openly air the family's dirty laundry."

So at chanticleer's first crow, Cui Four set off on horseback. That evening, he returned with ten Daoists, all clad in black gowns, led by Master Wang, who's family had presided over Azure Dragon Temple for thirteen generations. In orderly fashion, his disciples set up an altar, around which they planted a series of banners, then hung pictures of the seventy-two Daoist gods on the walls and spread diagrams of the twenty-eight constellations on the ground.

When Zhou Ermei saw her elder sister Damei go mad, she swore to her parents that her wedding would go smoothly: there would be no running away or eloping. At Ermei's wedding ceremony, her elder brother Zhou Taiwang, one of the militiamen under Li Mawu's command, had got thoroughly soused, so inebriated he didn't know if he was coming or going. He was contented that, through these marriages—one with the Li family on the first of the month, the second to the Qins in mid-month—he had secured relations with two of the most important families in the region; with these connections, he'd be carrying a full sack of rice rather than a pocketful of chaff. Lost in a sound drunken sleep, snoring thunderously amid fantastic dreams, it was impossible to pinch him awake. Lidu was terrified that Zhou Taiwang would suffocate and that with all the pinch marks on the body he'd get blamed for murder.

Only when Zhou Taiwang finally rose the following day were they able to reveal to him—quietly, so the Qin family wouldn't get wind of the matter—the tragic news of Damei's death. Zhou Taiwang kept stamping his feet in anguish, feeling that his six spirits had lost their mooring. Masui told folks at the Qins' that as Damei had just recovered from her madness, they hadn't brought her to the wedding for fear she might relapse, promising that sometime soon he would accompany his wife to congratulate her sister Ermei and her new husband. Yet despite these precautions, Damei could not avoid catastrophe! Damei was so strong-willed that even after marrying into a rich family she had committed suicide. What an ill-fated creature!

The Qin household was alive with with laughter. Zhou Taiwang sent a kinsman home to report the grim tidings about Damei, offered congratulations to Qin Liexiong and Ermei, then hastily departed with Lidu. At dusk, the two reached Gengguping.

An encompassing despair gripped Zhou Taiwang: after all, it was he who had piggybacked Damei from the threshold of the house to the wedding sedan. He wandered upstairs, and stood before his sister's nuptial bed for a spell; then he headed back down to listen to Tao Jiuxiang's account of the unfortunate event. Tearfully, he asked, "Aunt, did you criticize her or blame her for anything?"

Tao Jiuxiang wiped her tears with a sleeve. The old saying, "A girl of eighteen commits suicide: fertile soil, abandoned land," flashed through her mind. Miserably and uneasily, she replied, "First, take a look at Jin, who, despite the complicated wedding negotiations, I treat as my own daughter. How much more so with your sister Damei? For better or worse, Masui was a modern student in Fengjie City, and we had him quit schooling for the sole sake of marrying Damei. How could you think we might ill-treat Damei, my newlywed daughter-in-law?"

Unblinkingly, Li Diezhu stared at Zhou Taiwang, asking, "Then why did she go mad and hang herself?"

Zhou Taiwang grumbled, "Oh, how cruelly the spirits toyed with and tormented that unfortunate creature!"

Grimly, Li Diezhu asked, "Tell the truth. Had Damei shown any signs of madness before the marriage?"

Bitterly, Zhou Taiwang responded, "No."

Deeply disgruntled at having such a daughter-in-law, Li Diezhu gazed fixedly at Zhou Taiwang. The young man's face, however, was cloaked in cumbersome sorrow.

Beneath the watery moonlight, Daoist Master Wang held paired Big Dipper swords aloft—one male, the other female—moving through the firmament in a series of positions and poses as he paced the Dipper. In this manner, he might ascend the heavens and ask the deity of the Eastern Marchmount, Mount Tai, to issue an edict to open the gate of the netherworld and release Damei's corporeal soul. Master Wang thrust his paired blades, numinous weapons capable of summoning and banishing spirits and ghosts, deep into the earth. Meanwhile, his disciples banged on gongs and blew trumpets. Then, in turn, they danced around the four corners of the yard, finally coming to a stop in front of the altar. As the yellow candlelight grew ever smaller, until it was no more than a guttering greenish spark engulfed by the surrounding darkness, Masui's unease grew into a consuming, ghastly horror.

The sky was like a dark-blue curtain, as, to the lugubrious airs of the horns, Daoist Master Wang moved from the heavens to the underworld, his fingers forming four or five mudras in succession as he murmured a prayer to placate and cure Zhou Damei's ghost: "Let the filth of a thousand lifetimes be dispersed like fallen dust; may countless epochs of entangling calamities be lifted from your eternal soul, that you might forever break away from the dark hell and find solace in bright heaven." With greater literary aplomb than the *tima*, Xia Qifa, Master Wang recited the incantations to entice the aggrieved, angry ghost of Zhou Damei to follow the bright path to paradise. As he incanted, his disciples continually burned the amulets and banners into ashes.

The exorcism lasted five days. Li Diezhu paid the Daoists six silver dollars. To assuage the old tree spirit, a gravesite was chosen not far from the tree on the ridge near Gangou Bridge, that Damei might be wed to the amorous deity in the afterlife. Five days later, her coffin was buried. Amidst fierce bursts of firecrackers, the leaves of the vigorous, moss-covered tree became tinged with the first red of autumn.

The bride had committed suicide. The Li and Zhou families each feared the other family blamed them for Damei's death. Wretched Masui, wracked by sadness and fear, never again mentioned returning to school. Even if he did, he mused, he wasn't the same person he had been six months earlier. Inundated with sorrow, his insides twisted in a hundred knots, an idea suddenly struck him: why not enlist in the army and leave Gengguping and the primeval forest far behind? Just at the very moment, however, a letter from Mahe arrived from Fengjie City: the moment he had returned to school, not wishing to be pushed into a hasty marriage like Masui, he had enlisted in the army. He wanted to go to the front to fight the Japanese devils. He begged his parents and brothers to forgive him.

So furious that the sinews in his arms bulged to the breaking point and the veins in his neck stood out, Li Diezhu slammed his pipe down so violently that he made a divot in the floor. With the tragic end of Masui's marriage, he had figured that after a period of mourning he would announce the happy betrothal of eighteen-year-old Mahe to Xia Yinmei, who at thirteen was a perfect match. But now, without so much as a by-your-leave, the little devil had run off and joined the army, ruining all of his carefully-laid plans! From childhood, Mahe was the most mischievous and headstrong, the most playful and adventurous, of the brothers. One afternoon, around the time the first peach fuzz appeared on his chin, while delivering lunch to Li Diezhu in a distant field, Mahe had noticed a wild boars' den tucked in a dense bamboo grove. Ax in hand, he had recklessly trampled through the nest, terrifying and scattering the brood of piglets. Lucky for him, the adult boar and sow were gone; otherwise, who knows how things might have turned out? Several times, to no avail, Li Diezhu had warned Mahe of the ferocity of wild boars. Alas, he thought, may the Ancestors bless their wayward scion!

Tao Jiuxiang was even more infuriated and broken-hearted. For the past two years, not a word had come from the third son of the Sun family who had joined the army—only the heavens knew if he was alive or dead. Who knew when or if Mahe would return? If she had known Mahe's intentions, at least she could have gone to the *tima* Xia Qifa for a protective amulet!

In low spirits, Masui dared not mention that he, too, wanted to join the army. He had lost all zest for life. This, he thought, is fate! If only, like Mahe, he had never returned to Gengguping, then he wouldn't have met with this succession of frustrations and failures.

Tao Jiuxiang seemed to read Masui's mind, and warned him, "You'd better stay here. Where the grunts and squeals of wild boars drown out the voices of men, how can I live without a son?" Though the Japanese devils certainly deserved death, the hungry wild beasts that prowled around Gengguping— boars, bears, and panthers—seemed a more immediate threat.

Chapter Seven

I

Mawu was truly a fortunate man: widely respected when he was out and about, and enjoying the lavish attentions of his beautiful, gentle wife Jin when he returned home! Dependent and submissive, she would curl up like a cat in his bosom. What fellow wouldn't be delighted with such a wife?

People in the mountains of remote, sparsely populated Huangshui hollered to one another to communicate, relied on shank's mare for communication, and depended on dogs for security. When the bandit Liang, the bamboo strip craftsman, ran riot in Xiedong, local militias, fearing the unruly nature of the mountainfolk, urgently recruited new members. Mawu was in charge of the tenth and eleventh wards, which were located in the mountains around Huangshui. His primary responsibilities were upholding routine security and collecting taxes, in money and rice, from the local populace.

The mountain fog gathered and dispersed, the solar orb rose and set, and soon Spring Festival was right around the corner again. As usual, Mawu tightened security; as folk say, preparedness prevents disaster. By way of precaution, hoping to pass another peaceful Spring Festival, he moved the rest of the family into the stone tower.

At dusk, everyone gathered round the stove for supper, the room lit by an overhanging *tung* oil lamp. Over the six months since Zhou Damei's suicide, Li Diezhu had been in low spirits. In addition, goldthread prices had fallen precipitously and news had arrived that the Japanese airforce had cut off eastward water routes along the Yangzi. These tidings stirred his anxiety about Mahe. As soon as he emptied one bowl of wine, he poured another. At the end of the evening, Tao Jiuxiang helped him stagger to his bedroom.

The night wind cutting through the gorges was bone-piercingly cold. The timeless and endless sounds of mountain creatures rent the curtain of darkness: insects, birds, and beasts went on mating, feeding, and waging their unending struggle to survive.

Mawu let most of his militiamen head home for Spring Festival, but kept five crack troops to guard the tower. After Zhou Damei's death, when her brother Zhou Taiwang had requested to leave his detail and join Qin Liexiong's detachment in exchange for one of Qin's troops, Mawu had readily agreed. It was natural, Mawu figured, that Zhou would want to take care of the Qin family and his other sister.

Ordinarily, nothing is softer than the moonlight above. On this night, however, the thinnest crescent of white moon rose silently, like a scimitar, hard and cutting as a blade. It was the sort of moment youthful lovers would choose to express their emotions in song. Missing their paramours, several militiamen blew desolate strains on their flutes. To the accompaniment of their pleasant tune, a scudding cloud veiled the moon, enveloping the mountains in total darkness.

One of the militiamen, Cui Four, headed into the kitchen to flirt with Ran, the Li family's kitchen maid, who was pounding rice starch. Upstairs, little Yongyu was sound asleep. In the darkness, Jin softly coiled herself against Mawu, her cheek pressed to his familiar chest, lightly running her fingers through some new-grown hairs on his abdomen. She loosened her hair so that a little bundle gently brushed Mawu's neck. He had been on the verge of drifting into a drunken sleep, but her titillating locks roused him, goading him to an uncontrollable pitch of desire. He wrapped Jin's supple body in a strong embrace, gritting his teeth and panting like an ox as they lost themselves in wild coupling that made the wooden floors tremble beneath them. They kept on and on, nearly killing themselves in their unbridled enjoyment of that most primitive and ancient of human pleasures.

"You should give birth to a son this time!" said Mawu.

"Remember that first time you lifted my wedding veil," said Jin abashedly. "You made me laugh."

"This time," whispered Mawu, with a forceful thrust, "I'll make you cry with ecstasy!"

In the vast, wild forests, boundless pulsating vitality went hand-in-hand with an unfathomable murderous energy. All of a sudden, torchlight and shouting erupted outside. In an instant, Mawu plunged from the heights of pleasure to the depths of alarm. Jumping up, he cried out, "It's a sneak attack!" Throwing on clothing, he asked Jin, who was atremble with fear, to fetch his pistol from under the pillow.

Waiting in ambush, the bandits had concealed themselves in a little grove close to the tower. Hearing gunfire close by, Mawu ordered his men to counterattack by dropping stones and logs on the bandits. As no bandits were near the tower, this tactic proved wholly ineffective. Countering, the brigands drove a flock of a dozen goats toward the tower, smoking incense sticks lashed to their horns and strings of bursting firecrackers dangling from on their tails. Simultaneously, they beat drums, fired their guns, and shouted wildly; amid the noise and chaos, the ground trembled.

"O Tiger spirit!" exclaimed Tao Jiuxiang, shaking Li Diezhu from his drunken sleep and hurriedly dressing herself. It was the raucous chorus of "Kill! Kill!" issuing from the bandits without rather than Tao Jiuxiang that roused Li Diezhu from his stupor. Suddenly wide-awake, he leapt from bed. By this time, the stones and logs were exhausted, and the bandits launched a fierce assault. Peering out the observation slits, he saw scores of yellow banners featuring the character "Divine" and dozens of bandits, yellow turbans wrapped round their heads and swords strapped to their backs, charging toward the block tower with reckless abandon.

"Damned divine brigands!" shouted Li Diezhu hoarsely, his brow wet with fear.

Heedless of the gunfire from the tower, the bandits surged forward yelling "Kill! Kill!" as they relentlessly charged, three-foot swords in hand. Li Diezhu fired his gun through the sentry slit, shuddering as he thought: Accursed dog-mother brigands! Who could resist them? With his own eyes amid the smoky chaos he had seen bamboo-weaver Liang stop logs and stones mid-flight simply by pointing at them.

Mawu and several men guarded at the gate, concentrating their fire on the bandits. But when their bullets went astray, inexplicably missing their marks, these stouthearted militiamen quailed and fled into the tower, barring the gate behind them. With blood-curdling cries, several fierce brigands leapt to grasp the latticework, a full fifteen feet off the ground, pulling themselves up and pushing at the lowermost barred windows. Others, seemingly unfazed by the hail of bullets, furiously rammed the reinforced tower gate. The militiamen were scared to death, but held the gate fast. One bandit forced his hand into the crevice between the gate doors, and Mawu shot it with a pistol; when blood spattered the door, he was heartened.

The bandits outside rallied with greater fury, launching an all-out attack, shielding themselves from attacks with wet quilts thrown over their heads. Clad in yellow, a bannerman marshaled the brigands from a nearby bluff, waving his triangular flag to direct his comrades.

The frightened family fled from the back gate. Jin, her hair loose, stumbled after the others, two-year-old Yongyu in her arms. Terrified Yongyu wailed loudly, inconsolable. As he ran, Li Diezhu yelled, "Set her down!"

"Dad!" Jin imploringly looked from person to person. Tao Jiuxiang reached out and took Yongyu in her embrace, but the child kept shrieking.

"Put her down!" Li Diezhu ordered again. Jin had never imagined that her father-in-law would heartlessly abandon his own flesh-and-blood granddaughter in a time of peril. Maybe it was true: Li Diezhu was born of a tigress rather than a woman. Tears coursed down Jin's face.

Quickly, they moved into the bosky undergrowth, leaving the child behind. Concealed, they had a clear vantage of the outside. Yongyu's ear-splitting wails covered some of the bandits' shouts. Several times, Jin tried to rush out and rescue her daughter, but Tao Jiuxiang restrained her. Sweat and tears of desperate grief scarred Jin's beautiful face as she gazed hopelessly out at little Yongyu.

II

Amid the chaos, the bandits seized the stone tower. Under the moonlight, they rammed through the bulwark, swarmed in, and killed two militiamen. As Yongyu howled relentlessly, Mawu knelt begging for mercy. The leader of the brigands ordered his men to bind Mawu and the three surviving militiamen. The bandits searched every corner of the house, turning trunks inside-out and cabinets upside-down, plundering money, valuables, and guns, but they didn't harm Yongyu, who was left wailing on a bed. Tirelessly, they moved to and fro, gathering the Li family's heirlooms and stores. Finally, they bound Mawu to the stout banister of the stairway, his head covered in a piece of cloth. The leader barked harshly at the trio of remaining militiamen, "A treasure for a treasure: Within ten days, the Lis must bring a ransom of two thousand silver dollars to the huge sour fig tree behind Azure Dragon Temple—or else." With that, they carried Mawu away.

After the bandits left, Li Diezhu and others emerged from the copse. The air was filled with the choking reek of blood and gunpowder. Outside the tower was a scene of carnage: the bodies of two militiamen and more than a dozen scattered corpses of goats were strewn on the ground. Inside was a dreadful mess: the precious items, gold and silver, anything elegant and fine, had been stripped bare. The surviving militiamen laid out their comrades on bamboo mats, covered them with grass paper, and lit slow-burning candles. With an expression of astonishment and grief, beholding the corpse-strewn, blood-soaked land and the upward-curving horn of a dead ram, Li Diezhu murmured, "Those weren't men—they were spirit soldiers from hell!"

Stained with dirt from head to toe, Jin held Yongyu tightly in her arms, weeping disconsolately as she nursed the toddler, her quilted cotton overcoat wet with tears. Dumbly, Masui trembled in horror. Tao Jiuxiang alternately cried and cursed, "May the family lines of those god-damned bandits be severed at the root! May the lot of those vile bastards die horrible deaths!"

Under the sinking hooked moon, Sun Fu worked tirelessly dressing the goats littering the grounds, preserving the meat in a big crock with salt, which he buried underground.

Everything about the bandits' well-coordinated attack bespoke careful orchestration. One thing was clear: for the brigands to be so well informed, so familiar with the layout and defenses, someone must have told bamboo craftsman Liang everything about the tower. But who? It couldn't be Jiang Ermao: he knew nothing about the tower. Jiang couldn't know anything about the design unless Zhou Taiwang had colluded with him. Li Diezhu couldn't figure it out. Fearing the bandits would kill their hostage Mawu, he didn't dare report the attack and kidnapping to the authorities. Stricken by a combination of burning anxiety for his son and a chill caught hiding in the cave, stalwart Li Diezhu fell ill for the first time.

Learning of the attack, Jin Shaosan came to visit. When he saw the bullet holes scarring the wood and stone of the tower, his face turned an earthen hue.

After Tao Jiuxiang finished relating the entire story, her animated account punctuated by tears and curses, Jin Shaosan was overwhelmed with chagrin. Outraged, he slapped his thigh, exclaiming, "I've got it! Three days ago, a man claiming to be an agent for a trader came purchased more than a dozen of my goats. He paid a high price. I never expected he'd use the flock in the attack on your home!"

"Did you recognize him?" asked Li Diezhu straightaway, gazing at his in-law. Almost overnight, this vigorous and rough-and-tumble man had become a haggard and aged creature.

At his words, Jin stopped sobbing, repeating, "Did you know the man, Daddy?"

"No, I didn't," replied Jin Shaosan, with a long face.

Tao Jiuxiang gnashed, "Obviously it was Damei's wicked paramour who led the bandits to our home! But the urgent problem now is how to save Mawu."

"So how much are they trying to extort?" asked Jin Shaosan uneasily.

Tao Jiuxiang answered, "Two thousand silver dollars. You'd better do us a favor as an in-law and buy back the goldthread lands on the slopes. Land is all we've got left: those brigands stripped us bare!"

Jin Shaosan hesitated, "Why not borrow some money to get through this crisis?"

Leaning close to the stove, Li Diezhu sighed anxiously, "To tell the truth, even if someone could afford to lend me that kind of money, given the price of goldthread this year I could hardly pay the debt off in five or even eight years."

Wiping her tears, Jin said, "Dad, blood is thicker than water. Please purchase some of our land; once we recover, we'll buy it back."

Jin Shaosan moaned, "But others will blame me for taking advantage of my own kinsmen in a time of crisis."

Li Diezhu coughed twice, and said cool-headedly, "In Huangshui, there's nothing more valuable than goldthread; and there's no better man than you, my good relative-by-marriage. Please don't refuse any longer!"

Frowning, Jin Shaosan murmured bitterly, "Goldthread prices are plummeting. It won't sell until those Japanese devils have been defeated."

Tao Jiuxiang said, "Mawu says we'll triumph this year; sooner or later, the price will rise."

Li Diezhu said, "Come on, let's go survey the land. I'll sell you the goldthread slopes at a rice field price. Someday it will be the worth a fortune, like shaking a money-tree."

"Let me mull it over," Jin Shaosan said reluctantly.

After Jin Shaosan left, Tao Jiuxiang asked Masui to draw up a contract: Jin offered the rhizome slopes allocated to her and Mawu after the wedding, and Li Diezhu put up five prime acres of alluvial rice fields along Peppercorn Bend. Selling his hard-won property left Li Diezhu with a splitting headache. Masui was in such lackluster spirits that his whole being seemed slack.

One newlywed bride was dead, one son was kidnapped, and the father and youngest son had sunken into a torpor. When roving gangs of monkeys devoured bamboo shoots from the grove in front of the house, no one bothered to shout at them or drive them away. Opium was the only thing that afforded Li Diezhu, heartsick and physically ill, any measure of relief. When Masui called out from his room, "I want some, too!" Tao Jiuxiang ignored him. Anxious about Mawu, she entrusted Masui and Jin with the sale of the property. She sent Sun Fu to invite Xia Qifa, with the instructions, "Quick, invite the *tima* to our home to fashion a protective amulet."

Once again, Sun Fu headed to the Dragon Decapitating Gorge, carrying on his back the basket with four sharp swords of different lengths lashed to it. Several militiamen were also dispatched to invite ten mountainfolk to act as guarantors before Yama, the King of Hell, and pray for Mawu's safe deliverance. Fraught with worries, the Lis burned endless incense as they awaited the *tima*'s response, Jin Shaosan's silver, and the coming of their neighbors.

Several days after Jin Shaosan returned to Peppercorn Bend, word arrived that he had agreed to purchase Mawu's land. Though pained by the sale, Tao Jiuxiang was greatly relieved. At least, she comforted herself, they had sold it to a relative and not an outsider!

III

One after another, the guarantors arrived at Gengguping. Along with his son, Xia Liangxian, and two disciples, Xia Qifa arrived under a cloak of moon and stars. Perched atop the shaman's ancestral staff was a handsome rooster, still as a statue. When night fell, the uproar died away, and a ponderous calm enveloped the settlement in the woods. Ward chief Qin and his son Liexiong, Zhou Taiwang, and several other relatives and neighbors took their seats at two rectangular tables. Tao Jiuxiang and Sun Fu served dinner, bringing out a succession of dishes. Li Diezhu kept puzzling over why, when he had done no evil, his family had been stricken by this series of unfortunate events over the past two years?

Once again, Xia Qifa sounded his curved oxhorn in the Li family courtyard. Rolling up his sleeves and trouser legs, straw sandals on his feet, Xia Qifa rang a copper bell with one hand while waving a sword with the other. Each graceful flourish of the blade toward the gate marked an invitation to a god or spirit. Graven on the arrow-shaped tip of his sword were the two characters *life* and *death*. A big iron ring was set on the end of the pommel, interlinked with several smaller rings. With every movement of the *tima*, otherworldly sounds issued from the bells and rings. Next, to the backbeat of drum and gong, Xia Qifa sat upright at a table. With paper streamers waving behind his head and a curtain shrouding everything except his face, he assumed the majestic part of Yama, King of Hell. Staring at the straw effigy of Mawu placed at the main gate, the gate to the netherworld, Xia Qifa held the register of souls in hand and inquired loudly of the first guarantor, "Who are you?"

"I am Qin Liexiong." Although he had wept bitterly under an incense table the night Mawu wed Jin, today he had set aside past jealousy to pray for Mawu's deliverance.

The King of Hell asked, "Guarantor for whom?"

"For Li Mawu," the young man Qin replied.

Yama continued, "And what is that you wish to guarantee?"

"That he averts death and lives; that he avoids disaster and finds safety," answered Qin Liexiong, gazing at the polished black divinatory bamboo trigrams arrayed before the *tima*.

Yama cast the trigrams twice, and both readings proved inauspicious. He sentenced the hot-blooded cripple to drink six cups of wine; with each successive cup, Liexiong's face and ears blushed a deeper shade of red. Anxiety clouded his father's face; and Li Diezhu and Tao Jiuxiang were seized with alarm. Puzzlement reflected in his eyes, the "King of Hell," asked bluntly, "Are you truly a sincere and good man?"

Kneeling on the ground, quavering, Qin Liexiong answered, "I'm really a sincere and good man." Having completed his training in the martial arts, Liexiong was far more agile than most. Like Mawu, he led a militia division under Captain Huang. Tranquilly married to the younger Zhou sister, he enjoyed racing his horse along the streets of Huangshui.

Confused and expectant, all eyes were riveted on the nimble hands of Xia Qifa, the disguised Yama. He cast the trigrams for a third time, and finally obtained an auspicious reading. Relief swept over the room. Qin Liexiong, staggering under the effects of the alcohol, hurriedly drank four more cups to redeem Mawu's soul, before slumping down at the table. Thoroughly inebriated, his reddened eyes scanned the room for any trace of Jin.

With a profound sense of gratitude, Li Diezhu sat to one side, watching his friends and neighbors come before Yama to guarantee the deliverance of his eldest son. Soon, Zhou Taiwang came before Yama to act as guarantor. When the King of Hell asked, "Who are you?" the pale young man grumbled, "I'm Captain Huang Tianliang."

From behind the proceedings, a voice roared, "What kind of backbiting devil dares use my horoscope and name?" In the flesh, militia Captain Huang Tianliang stood glowering in the doorway.

All eyes were fixed on the unfolding spectacle. Overwhelmed with shame and horror, Zhou Taiwang cowered, trembling, his shoulders contracting. He had feared that a soul so ordinary as his own couldn't bear the stern countenance and trial of Yama. Therefore, he had used the captain's name, little imagining that at that very moment Captain Huang would appear and furiously curse, "Why the hell do you vainly abuse my name?"

Tao Jiuxiang stepped forward, trying to keep calm, and saying, "Our family was robbed by the brigands. If you don't protect us, who will?"

"I will, but first serve me wine and food!" replied Captain Huang, clad in a smart black uniform, his bulging eyes sweeping over the jugs of wine and sumptuous dishes laid out on the tables.

With Sun Fu's help, Tao Jiuxiang brought the Captain a clean bowl and chopsticks, and set a series of dishes before him. Hurriedly, she poured him a glass of liquor, urging, "Please take a seat, Captain. All of us folk in the mountain wilds depend on your martial prowess for protection!"

Ward headman Qin Zhanyun chimed in, "Well said. Captain Huang is our local tutelary god! All of us here rely on your prestigious name."

Placated by flattery and wine, Captain Huang sat contentedly.

Lifting his leather satchel, Captain Huang informed Li Diezhu that he had come as soon as he had learned of the robbery, adding, "I heard that brigands ransacked your house and kidnapped Mawu, but you never reported it."

Li Diezhu said, "I wanted to, Captain, but I was afraid it would provoke the bandits to tear up their meal ticket and harm Mawu."

Captain Huang waved his chopsticks, and, exhaling a wine-saturated breath, said, "When those brigands kidnapped Lieutenant Li, none of you spoke up. If you let them get away with it, then in a few days, they'll come grab me, and the entire Huangshui Militia will collapse! If each household provided one man with a rifle, Corporal Wei and I would drive those bastards so far back that they'd be eating black-sesame filled rice balls in Nanjing!"

Deliberately, Qin Zhanyun said, "They'll harm Mawu if you attack. Even with two hundred guns, Mayor Xiang of Peartree Moor, a relation of mine by marriage, couldn't defeat those bandits."

"You wealthy landlords fear the bandits too much," snorted Captain Huang. "Marshal Yang Sen routed the brigands—killed more than ten thousand of them in Fengjie City. Even after working non-stop for three days, the vagrants and beggars could only bury half of them."

Ward chief Qin recalled that a few years back, not far from Huangshui, a dozen militiamen had fired at a brigand clad in a collarless purple gown girded with a wound grass sash. Amid the swirling snow flurries, the fellow, utterly devoid of expression, stood unscathed in a rain of bullets that splintered branches just above his head and kicked up mud around his feet. At his signal, bandits had swarmed forward with a collective howl. Captain Huang's equerry had been cut down, and the terrified militia fled in disarray.

Li Diezhu paled. Kneading his temples, he said decisively, "I would give up all my property for the safe return of my eldest son. But if one of those miscreant dogs harms a hair on his head, I swear I'll wreak a terrible vengeance."

IV

Xia Qifa took out a set of protective amulets, and asked each of the guarantors to sign them. With an air of regret, the *tima* pronounced, "As he was born under a lucky star, Mawu will make it home intact, with no martial action necessary; his safety, I fear, will come at great cost."

"If there is no martial action taken, I'll be regarded as a coward, a turtle who contracts into his shell!" Captain Huang frowned, reluctantly signing his name as a guarantor, glancing toward the curtain screening Xia Qifa.

Clutching his chest, Li Diezhu gnashed, "Once Mawu comes back, Captain,

I'll follow you to suppress those brigands. There'll be no place for them to hide!"

Resignedly, Captain Huang said, "Fine. I'll wait for the time being." With these words, he looked dubiously from Zhou Taiwang to the curtain screening Xia Qifa, adding, "*Tima*, don't confuse my name with his."

Emerging, Xia Qifa had become himself once more. Gravely, he answered, "I have already informed the King of Hell—there will be no mistake. But beware, Captain: the physiognomy of your forehead portends something ominous."

Captain Huang furrowed his brow, "So those brigands want a piece of me? I'll make ready, be wary in my comings and goings, and station sentinels in my courtyard." So saying, he hitched up his trousers, mounted his horse, and rode off.

Zhou Taiwang, who was illiterate, slowly drew a cross-shaped "ten" character to represent his name on the guarantee.

The following morning the rite concluded. Acrid black smoke clung to the ground. From his deerskin pouch, Xia Qifa removed a small portion of bezoar. He instructed Li Diezhu to take some, mixed in hot water, three times a day. After that, ancestors' staff in hand, he marshaled the rooster out the front gate in grand fashion.

Thoroughly besotted the previous evening, ward chief Qin had spent the night at the foot of the stove. By the time he awakened the fog had lifted. After breakfast, he took leave of Li Diezhu, expressing his sympathies. Qin Liexiong, however, sat lumpish at the threshold, his limbs still slack with hung-over torpor.

Ward chief Qin turned to Zhou Taiwang, "My kinsmen by marriage, share a horse with Qin Liexiong on the way back."

Tao Jiuxiang told Sun Fu to see off the ward headman; Sun Fu hurriedly readied a mount.

Just back from Peppercorn Bend, Masui greeted Qin father and son, "Those god-damned brigands ransacked our home and took everything. Thank you both for all you've done."

Ward chief Qin said sympathetically, "Don't stand on ceremony—we're all neighbors here. What's urgent now is to find a way to get Mawu back."

Suddenly, out of the corner of his eye, Liexiong spotted Jin entering the kitchen with her daughter on her back. Stupefied, he mumbled, "I don't want to leave yet. I need a drink of water before I go."

"I'll get you a glass," said Zhou Taiwang, pushing a straw cushion under Liexiong's buttock.

"I'll—I'll go myself." Liexiong abruptly struggled to his feet and hobbled toward the kitchen.

"Sit down, division leader Qin," sharp-eyed Tao Jiuxiang called. "Jin, bring in a wet towel." Placated, Liexiong settled back down.

The previous day, accompanied by Masui and her mother, Jin had hurriedly surveyed her and Mawu's land on Peppercorn Bend. After measuring out the land, she signed the deed over to her father, handing over a three-and-a-half acre swath, including half an acre where goldthread was ready for harvest. Face wet with tears, she had passed the night at Peppercorn Bend. At cockcrow, she had returned to Gengguping on horseback, following Masui. No sooner had she entered the kitchen did she hear her mother-in-law's summons. Sweeping a sweaty lock of hair from her forehead, Jin dipped a towel in the cold water and delivered it to Tao Jiuxiang.

Tao Jiuxiang took the towel from Jin and sponged off Liexiong's face, saying, "Thank you, division leader Qin." Liexiong sat silently on a hay mat, stealing glances at Jin as she retreated to the kitchen.

Zhou Taiwang passed him a cup, saying, "Have some tea . . . good cure for a hangover."

Liexiong gulped down several mouthfuls of water, then said, "Come on, give me a hand up."

Sun Fu led Liexiong's dark short horse. With Zhou Taiwang's help, he trundled Liexiong onto the back of the horse.

"I'm off," said Liexiong, once mounted.

Behind him, firmly grasping the reins in one hand and supporting the still-inebriated Liexiong with the other, Zhou Taiwang offering a curt parting, "We're off."

Chapter Eight

I

Accompanying Masui, militiamen Cui Four and Lidu, each toting a cumbersome load of silver dollars from the sale of the Li family lands, set out from Jin Shaosan's household in Peppercorn Bend and moved toward Azure Dragon Temple.

In this world, two kinds of burden grow heavier with each passing step: a corpse and a load of silver dollars. Both Cui Four and Lidu were saturated with perspiration, their shoulders so raw and abraded by friction that from time to time they passed their heavy bundles to Masui. Finally, following the brigands' request, they reached the huge sour fig tree behind the old monastery.

Suddenly, three men disguised as mountainfolk rushed out of the woods. Ferociously, they shouted, "Leave the silver. Now go back and wait for the hostage!"

Failing to see Mawu, Cui Four didn't budge. "That's no exchange," he answered. We won't go back until we've seen Mawu is safe."

Masui added, "Let us have a look at him."

The bandits pressed forward, drawing daggers from their leg wrappings. One snarled, "Another word and I'll slit your throats!"

Masui's knees went weak. Though the three of them carried swords, he doubted they could take the bandits. Reluctantly, Cui Four and Lidu set down the silver. Like a gust of wind, two bandits snatched up the loads and sped off.

For several minutes the third remained, glaring, dagger in hand. Then he, too, dashed off. The two militiamen wanted to pursue, but Masui stopped them, fearing more bandits were nearby.

In trepidation, the trio returned to Gengguping. From a distance, they saw Tao Jiuxiang stumping along the slope leading to the stone tower, waving and calling out, "Ransom money! The ransom money?"

"We delivered it," Masui answered uneasily.

At this, Tao Jiuxiang beat her bosom and cried, "Oh, *Tima* Xia! Why must your ominous predictions so unfailingly prove true! You said we'd lose our money and property. Sure enough, though Mawu escaped and made it home, we still delivered the ransom!"

"They told us to go home and await Mawu's arrival," Cui Four murmured timidly.

"He's already home!" Tao Jiuxiang shouted, thumping her bosom and stomping her feet.

Breathlessly following overwrought Tao Jiuxiang, the three emissaries entered the house. Shocked, they beheld Mawu sitting next to the stove, mud-stained from head to toe.

"Did you give them the ransom?" asked Mawu directly, before they had an instant to catch their breath or gulp down a drink of water.

"They tricked you," groaned Li Diezhu, sick at heart. "Mawu escaped!"

"So we paid all that silver for nothing!" Masui was stupefied. Despairing, Cui Four and Lidu wept.

"Fools! If you never even saw me—never saw the hostage—why did you hand over the silver?" asked Mawu, perturbed.

"There were a lot of them," sniveled Masui, "all armed with knives."

With a ragged beard and disheveled hair, Mawu recalled his captivity. He had been imprisoned in a cave, with his hands and feet trussed. The brigands fed him several ears of corn a day; when he was thirsty, he drank the run-off from mountain springs dribbling from the ceiling. "Last night," he indignantly recounted, "several bandits were gambling and boasting round a stone table covered with a yellow cloth. On the cloth were characters reading, 'Butcher Militia, Seize Tax Money, Plunder the Rich.' They were bragging about the robbery. I listened and learned that the attack was orchestrated by a chieftain nicknamed 'Black-tailed Snake.' He was sitting at the table with his back toward me."

They all listened, dumbfounded.

"Aiya!" howled Li Diezhu, ferociously clapping his palm to his face, "It is I who provoked Heaven's wrath!" He thought back to the day the tower was completed. Approvingly beholding the stalwart tower's stonemasonry, he had boasted that no one could breach the tower unless he transformed into a black-tailed snake and slipped in. Sure enough, his prideful words had proven prophetic: the tower had been successfully overcome by a "black-tailed snake"! Burning with fury, Li Diezhu wished he could tear his mouth off his face.

"'Black-Tailed Snake' was a dismal card player, always throwing his good cards," Mawu continued. "When he was about to discard his best card, I nudged him with my foot to signal him not to throw it. He discarded a different card, and as a result won a pile of silver dollars. Just before dawn, 'Black-tailed Snake' went out of the cave to take a shit. Asking me to hold a torch for him, he loosened my feet but left my hands tied . . ."

"It was dark and cold outside," Mawu seethed. "When I saw 'Black-tailed Snake' squatting over the edge of a big stone pit in the torchlight, I moved forward abruptly and kicked the bastard into the shit-hole. I grabbed his bag and rushed pell-mell through the woods, frantically scrambling up cliffs and down escarpments, until I made it home. Take a look at this . . ." With these words, Mawu opened a sheepskin rucksack, pouring out dozens of silver dollars the "Black-Tailed Snake" had won gambling. There was also a roster of the bandits' spies in Xiedong and Huangshui.

"God-damned bastards—the lot of them deserve to be chopped up by a thousand blades! Now they'll have no place to flee!" said Tao Jiuxiang.

"Aha!" chuckled Li Diezhu, recovering his spirits. Excitedly, he crowed, "I said the bloody sons-of-turtles wouldn't get off easy—now for every hair on Mawu's head they touched, they'll have a tuft of hair yanked out!"

After ten days as a hostage, Mawu was stained with filth and grime like a savage. Quickly, he washed, combed his hair, and threw on a short coat. He loaded his rifle, slung it over his shoulder, and rode toward Huangshui.

The woods were abloom with vibrant banks of wildflowers, filling the gorge with an array of colors. Halfway between Peppercorn Bend and Gengguping, Mawu encountered Jin, a fine woven bamboo hat perched on her head, riding home accompanied by her servant girl Ran. Gazing at her lovely full moon face and large, flashing dark eyes, he suppressed his desire for her, and said curtly, "Wait for me at home. I have to settle scores with those sons-of-bitches!"

As soon as he reached Huangshui, a militiaman called out, "You're free, Lieutenant Li! Something bad happened: Captain Huang's just been killed!"

"Who? Who's been killed?" Mawu asked, his eyes opening wide in surprise.

"Captain Huang was killed by one of his own men!"

The barracks were in utter turmoil.

Mawu had heard that Captain Huang had recently taken an alluring and lovely concubine. Rumors circulated that embracing the new and neglecting the old, he lavished all his attention on this new beauty. Seething with resentment, Captain Huang's scorned wife began flirting with his bodyguard and the pair of them engaged in an adulterous affair. Fearing the consequences, the bodyguard preemptively murdered Captain Huang, then absconded to join the bandit Liang, taking a handful of militiamen and guns with him.

In the isolation and gloom of these remote mountains, there were few entertainments and opportunities for boisterous merrymaking. Mountainfolk, eating the bounty that grew from the region's fecund earth and inhaling the pungent musk given off by venomous snakes and ferocious creatures in rut, were even crazier in matters of the heart than cityfolk.

Eager for revenge, Mawu disregarded the tumult among the militiamen and took the roster of bandit spies straight to the fretful Mayor of Huangshui at government headquarters. Without bothering to ask how Mawu had managed to escape, the mayor, preoccupied with Captain Huang's death, promptly dispatched Mawu to the Fengjie City office with notification detailing the unfortunate events in his jurisdiction. Mawu accepted the missive and hurriedly rode toward the county seat.

With the sudden and violent death of the most powerful and prestigious figure in the region, Huangshui was abuzz with rumors and gossip. Zhou Taiwang was petrified and with guilt and dread, fearing that as he had vainly used Captain Huang's name and birthdate before the King of Hell, the deceased's vengeful ghost would return to mete out punishment. Only after he visited Xia Qifa and the *tima* assured him that Captain Huang's ghost meant him no harm did the umbrageous clouds of horror begin to lift from his heart.

Another rumor circulated in Huangshui: hoping to replace Huang as Captain of the militia, Qin Liexiong had approached the Mayor with eight hundred silver dollars to spread around to local officials.

Amid this tumult, Mawu returned with an order issued by the Fengjie county government to "capture the bandits and restore local peace and security." Striding quickly and purposefully into an opium den, Mawu located the Mayor and delivered the handwritten order from the county governor, along with the roster of bandit spies. Struggling to emerge from his opium haze, the Mayor looked at the list with confusion, and then, tightening his belt, asked, "Where did you get this?"

"A brigand dropped it. I picked it up," Mawu answered.

"How can we track down Captain Huang's horse attendant? We need to capture that murderous rascal," the Mayor demanded impatiently.

"If we capture some spies from the roster who run messages for the bandits," Mawu answered, "we can find out his whereabouts."

Finding this reasoning sound, the Mayor ordered him to muster some militiamen, and arrest the spies on the roster.

Mawu coordinated an operation directing groups of militiamen to accompany local headmen from the wards in Huangshui to arrest the spies. Trekking up slopes and over crags, these groups reached their assigned households only to meet with the wilting glowers of surly and rugged housewives, cleavers in hand, fiercely continuing to chop vegetables on the their cutting blocks. Scared that the housewives were in cahoots with the bandits, the militiamen worried that if they insisted on further investigating they might expose themselves to an ambush. After several circuits around the mountains, they returned empty-handed.

Confounded, the ward chiefs approached Mawu, imploring, "Lieutenant Li, let's go arrest them together . . . it's awfully tough to enforce the law among our mountain neighbors."

"All right," cried Mawu furiously, "We'll go together!" However, he left the weak-kneed ward headmen behind, and took the vice-headmen in their stead.

This new approach proved effective. In one ward after another, they arrested the brigands' agents and messengers and dragged them to the Huangshui jail. To kill two falcons with a single arrow, after ten days of imprisonment, the county government sent a dozen former spies off to join the army under the escort of a troop of local militia beating drums and clanging gongs. All the bandits, however, remained at large, including Captain Huang's treacherous bodyguard. Before the bandits moved on, they exhumed the corpse of "Black-tailed Snake" from the pit of excrement and buried him in a hollow that locals still call "Bandit Gulch."

II

Huangshui was rampant with murder and plunder. Rumors mushroomed surrounding the attack on the stone tower at Gengguping. Some claimed that Jiang Ermao, having missed the chance to meet his lover near the big tree on Damei's wedding day and later learning of her death, had conceived a seething hatred of the Li family and asked Liang the bamboo-strip craftsman to help him exact revenge. Others maintained that Zhou Taiwang, familiar with the layout of the tower and bitter over his sister's maltreatment, had conspired with Liang. Still others said Qin Liexiong, burning with desire for Jin and unable to endure the humiliation of seeing her wed another, had hatched a plot with the notorious bamboo craftsman.

At Gengguping, oblivious to this gossip, Li Diezhu had recovered his spirits after his longstanding illness just in time to concern himself with the goldthread harvest and the ominous tidings of the encroaching war.

No one knew for how many eons the wondrous stalks of rhizome had grown and decayed in the mountains of Huangshui. Beginning in the Yuan dynasty, people transplanted goldthread nearer their homes on the forest margins. Classified as *ranunculaceae*, goldthread was included in Li Shizhen's Ming dynasty pharmacopeia, *The Compendium of Herbal Medicine*, where it is called the Goldthread Claw of the Divine Farmer's Rooster. Its leaves are long and thin, like those of coriander. Covered with root hairs, the taproot is shaped like an eagle's talon, only thicker. The underground rhizome is helpful in curing diarrhea, cooling overheated humors, quenching fever, and reducing inflammation. The rhizome both confers longevity and loosens taut muscles, making it indispensible to practitioners of martial arts. Goldthread grows in damp and shadowy environs, saturated in *yin* ethers, maturing very slowly, growing only several inches over seven years. When folk around Huangshui suffered headaches or fevers and when their livestock were stricken by disease, goldthread was a panacea; one merely needed to soak a few cut slices of the dried root in warm water and drink the concoction, and within a few hours they would be cured! It was better than opium!

In one of the many local legends swirling about the precious rhizome, a hunter dreamed that a white-bearded old man told him that in the forest grew a divine grass; if he dug it up and replanted it, he would become very wealthy.

When the hunter awakened, he followed the old man's instructions. Sure enough, at the foot of a venerable tallow tree, seemingly armored in shell and scale, he beheld a dark-green cluster of creeping grass the size of a washbasin. With care, the hunter dug up the luxuriant bush by the roots and transplanted it in the shade of the red fir tree beside his house. With each passing year its seeds dropped, the roots spread a bit farther, and the emerald-green patch slowly grew. He took a rhizome to the herbalist in Fengjie City to ask its price. Delighted beyond measure, the herbalist told him it was a rare wonder medicine capable of eliminating cold and damp ethers, drawing out toxins, and curing fevers and chills; he gave the hunter a long string of coppers. Only then did the hunter realize that the old white-bearded fellow was the incarnation of the Immortal White Tiger. He kept the mystical flora, this "money-shaking grass," secret from the outside world; each year when the seeds ripened, he collected them himself—never giving away a single one. However, his daughter knew the secret. On her wedding day, she concealed some seeds in one of her embroidered shoes to share with her husband. Soon, all the mountainfolk came to enjoy the benefits of this heaven-bestowed rhizome!

Li Diezhu was sure that, despite the present difficulties, as long as the family had goldthread they could manage.

One noontime near harvest time, Li Diezhu headed through the woods toward a prime patch of goldthread that promised to yield more than a full bushel-basket of rhizomes, even once they were dried and stripped of their hairy tendrils. Given the plummeting prices, he mulled whether or not he should dig up the rhizomes this year. As he weighed the matter, his ears picked up the back-and-forth giggling and cursing of lovers from a nearby grove. Listening carefully, he recognized Masui's voice, intermingled with the twittering of a woman. Pushing the branches aside and craning his neck, he saw the woman was Sun Fu's wife. His face ashen with rage, he retreated back toward the household.

When he reached the yard, he picked up a long-handled besom from beside the pigpen, plunged it into the manure pit, gave it a stir, then, like a falcon descending on a pair of doves, dashed back toward to adulterers, brandishing the filth-bedaubed broom in a towering rage.

"Filthy animals!" roared Li Diezhu. Although he had indulged his desire, coupling in the fields and rolling in the dirt, he had done so with his own wife. At this thought, he surged forward with redoubled fury, his stinking weapon held aloft. With all his schooling, the family had upheld Masui as a sage; now, bitterly disappointed, Li Diezhu raged out of control. Humiliated, Masui fled from his onrushing father, trailing at the heels of Sun Fu's wife.

Brandishing the stinking broom, Li Diezhu unleashed a stream of curses in their direction. When Masui finally returned well after supper, Tao Jiuxiang savagely tore into her ignoble son.

Oblivious to Masui kneeling penitently at the foot of the bed, Li Diezhu lay glassy-eyed on the cypress bed, smoking opium. Years before, master craftsman Zhu Shun had carved the bed, featuring exotic flora and ferocious tigers running up and down the bedposts, as if descending escarpments; the frame was lacquered red, flecked with gold. As he gazed into the main hall, where Sun Fu was meticulously painting two cypress coffins, Li Diezhu felt his own decrepitude and mortality. Suddenly, he keenly missed his youngest son, Mahe. No tidings of Mahe had reached Gengguping. He had no idea where Mahe was fighting, or how many Japanese devils he had killed. On the battlefield, a solder could be shot at any moment—bullets don't have eyes, after all. However, Mahe would be safe, he told himself: fate was good to the scions of the Li family. With these thoughts, he dazedly closed his eyes and drifted into a dream in which Mahe hid behind a massive outcropping of rock while Japanese planes emblazoned with the rising sun swarmed overhead before alighting on top of the rock like so many flies. In yellow Imperial Army uniforms, the Japanese soldiers surged forward. Mahe mowed down the front ranks, firing continuously, but the Japanese soldiers charged ahead as though they had imbibed Liang the bamboo craftsman's divine elixir. Ineluctably, amid the hail of bullets, always advancing and never retreating, the Japanese devils hemmed in Mahe and his comrades. Then, everything was enveloped in an awful quiet: the gunfire went silent and the battlefield was enveloped in an eerie obsolescence that shrouded the corpse-strewn grounds. Amid the suffocating nervousness, he saw Mahe and his comrades grappling hand-to-hand the devil soldiers. One Japanese devil, whose cap had fallen off revealing his disheveled hair, raised his bayonet to pierce Mahe's chest. Feeling as if the bayonet were thrust into his own chest, Li Diezhu twisted to one side. As the Japanese devil prepared to thrust a second time, he seized the bayonet and killed the bastard as though he were butchering a swine. Pulling out the bayonet, blood jetted forth. So, even devil soldiers were creatures of flesh-and-blood! He was jarred from this satisfying musing by Tao Jiuxiang's spooked cry, "O, spirit Tiger! Spirit Tiger! . . . You scared me with your devilish yowls."

"Teeming Japanese devil soldiers, fearless as the brigands—they kept coming. I wonder if Mahe is okay," Li Diezhu mumbled, clutching his chest.

"Who knows where that child is," Tao Jiuxiang's voice trembled, her eyes moistening.

"May our ancestors bless and protect my son—and make him an invincible soldier." Li Diezhu sighed helplessly. Through the window the night fog clinging to Gengguping heard his prayer; lifting, it began to drift eastward.

III

The first streaks of dawn pierced the darkness to reveal Li Mahe standing on the spine of a winding mountain ridge. Emerging from their caves in nearby dales and valleys, many soldiers like him ascended the crest.

Huangshui was out of sight, far to the west. From his vantage, Mahe could only see the meandering Yangzi flowing through the gorges, then abruptly turning, disappearing behind an imposing rectangular spire of basalt. According to legend, when Pangu had severed Earth from Heaven he had set the awesome tower of basalt on this spot, ordering the churning waters of the Yangzi to flow eastward.

Atop the highest peak, an officer, having just bathed and cleansed himself, stood before a flat stone, and arrayed an offering of wine and incense. He looked upward with piety as the incense smoke danced skyward, then knelt, prostrating himself before the tablet of his ancestors, intoning a prayer to heaven high above—*I, Hu Lian, Commander of the Eleventh Division, hereby with utmost sincerity announce to the tutelary divinities of these mountains and rivers:*

Today I lead my righteous army to defend our soil, to protect the land that our ancestors toiled bitterly to cultivate and bequeathed to us. Prostrating myself and offering wine to the ancestors and spirits, I swear, pledging my life, that we will steadfastly guard this sacred ground to the death. Heaven bless and protect us!

Fiery red, the morning sun floated in a sea of clouds. Gradually rising, it shed a golden radiance upon the mountains and valleys.

On both sides of this sharp bend in the Yangzi, steep cliffs overlooked the quick-moving waters. Any watercraft moving along the great river had to turn abruptly; it was reputed to be the most dangerous turn along the entire Yangzi. In his history class, Mahe had learned that time and again the ancient state of Ba, staunchly guarding this strategic natural defile, kept the kingdom of Chu out of the Three Gorges. Now, at the very moment the sun emerged in its full splendor, the soldiers, young men of Ba and Chu, knelt together before the basalt monolith and kowtowed to Heaven, swearing that they would keep the Japanese devils out of the Three Gorges.

The people of Huangshui identified themselves as descendants of Ba. Mahe found it curious that according to legend, from its very inception Ba—raiding to the east and launching campaigns to the west—was in a perpetual cycle of warfare, having neither fixed borders nor stable territory. From the moment the Immortal White Tiger, the Lord of the Granary, brandished his sword and led his kinsfolk by boat from their stone caverns and moved upstream along the waters of the Yangzi, theirs was a legacy of constant battle. Willingly forsaking the sensual delights of clouds and rain, they shot and killed the lovely Goddess of Salt Water, annexing her territory and seizing her salt mines. Ever seeking resources and territory, there were campaigns and conquests without surcease, until at last, defeated, they changed their clan name and fled along the watercourses of the great Yangzi. Nobody knew where they had disappeared to. This, too, occasioned further speculation and generated legends.

Impatiently, Mahe awaited the coming battle. He had hunted monkeys and wild boars, but had never killed a man. When the moment came, he wouldn't hesitate. Photographs of the bestial depredations of the Japanese devils ran through his mind. In one, a naked young woman was lashed to a chair, her legs, lifted high by the binding ropes, spread to clearly expose her genitals to the camera lens. She wore her hair short, and her round face was lowered. He had never seen a woman naked, and had been filled with curious yearning. Yet, now, summoning to mind the image—carefully looking at the woman's full breasts and her genitals, raw and mutilated from being gang-raped by countless Japanese devils—he was filled with keen sorrow and mounting wrath. No one knew how many times the devils had ravaged her. Silent tears of indignation coursed down his cheeks. He would kill those bastards! There was another picture of a smirking Japanese officer, sword in hand, triumphantly holding aloft a severed Chinese head. Mahe seethed with anticipation: only cutting off a Japanese devil's head could slake his burning fury!

His company was defending Empress Pass, the only overland route the Japanese devils could take from Yichang, to occupy the strategic stronghold at Xiling. Constructed overlooking the sharp bend in the Yangzi, cannon terraces had been carved into the rock face of the mountains. From this vantage, the rugged timeless topography was breathtaking. Any Japanese warship coming upstream would be cannonaded relentlessly, fore and aft.

After he joined the army, Mahe was sent to Yunyang for two months of intensive training, after which he was dispatched to the 94th company of the Nationalist Army, and stationed on a mountain fifteen miles from Xiling Peak. Proving a quick-witted crack shot, he was charged with manning a machine gun nest. Looking down on the V-turn in the Yangzi, absorbed in the panoramic grandeur, Mahe's mind wandered back to the emerald mountains and valleys of Gengguping. An electric agitation coursed through his body: He would mow down the Japanese devil soldiers as if he were scything down so many straw dummies. He would make his parents and brothers proud.

"What a picturesque land! You think Japan has such a beautiful place?" mused a soldier beside Mahe.

"Definitely not," answered Mahe. "That's why they came here to occupy China."

Shaking his fist, the soldier howled, "I want to bomb Tokyo to ruins!!!"

In seeming accord, the rock outcrop whistled with a fierce gust of wind.

Bundles of rice straw floated on the Yangzi, put there by the local folk; on the bottom of the river, mines were bound to stone blocks. Stationed in mountain caves, a mortar platoon and a heavy machine gun platoon waited in ambush. It was rumored that the oncoming Japanese troops were Imperial Army regulars, "steel monsters," attacking with relentless ferocity and unrestrained aggression. Mahe figured he didn't give a damn if the invaders were wild beasts or demon-soldiers: the Japanese would get through Empress Pass only over his dead body. He had accepted his fate of dying young and alone. Thinking of his parents and his home in Gengguping, he felt guilty. Fearing that his family wouldn't allow him to join the army, he had enlisted without their permission. Now on the cusp of battle, he recalled them fondly, comprehending at last the grief that his sacrifice would bring them. However, his sorrow would be even greater if he failed to kill a bunch of Japanese devils! At dusk, flocking birds returned to their forest perches and nests, trilling and chirping just like the birds in Gengguping. A drifting mountain mist kissed his forehead.

IV

In the fourth lunar month, the Gorges filled with what appeared to be an endless festival bursting with lively sound, with red and white smoke everywhere. But these were not cheerful firecrackers marking a wedding: this was intermittent gun and cannon fire shaking the heavens. Just after the last of the villagers in the area had fled, Japanese planes painted with the red rising sun arrived from Yichang.

In formations of three, the planes rained an incessant blinding hail of bombs, like meteorites or shooting stars, down onto the rugged peaks and jagged ridges. Along with the deafening explosions, the very mountains were aflame. Long-range mortar shells from the Japanese base camp exploded, shattering rock that had stood for countless eons. As the earth ruptured and the mountains quaked around him, Mahe waited in the cave in shock: the vicious savagery of these goddamned sons-of-bitches knew no bounds. It seemed like the apocalypse.

The thunderous explosions lasted for several hours before finally dying away. An uneasy calm settled over the battleground.

A murderous air of death and danger hung over the narrow and steep trail that led to Empress Pass; splintered wood, shattered rock, and clots of earth littered the winding path. Looking through his gun sites, Mahe watched a yellow-clad mass of Japanese devils, armed with bayonet-mounted submachine guns, methodically move into his line of fire. Fifty yards away . . . thirty . . . twenty . . . the machine guns opened fire from the defense works on the mountain, a torrential barrage of bullets showering the encroaching devils, riddling them full of holes. From ten yards away, Mahe could see the grim, demonic faces of the Japanese soldiers.

Despite the locust-like storm of bullets, the Japanese devils always charged forward and never retreated an inch. When the front line was mowed down, the next row surged forward, returning fire with savage howls, as fearless as the spirit brigands. Some in the foremost ranks did not collapse till they sprawled awkwardly at the very mouth of the cave, twitching and thrashing, bloody air bubbles burbling from the bullet holes piercing their bodies. So great was the number of dead clotting the battleground that, flustered by the endless bodies, the deity Wuchang, charged with shepherding souls to the netherworld, complained of his exhausting toil as he chained them together.

Gloom submerged the pale sun. Endless bullets rained on, scarring tree trunks like scales of a fish. At the mouth of one cave, a mortar had blown apart the broad trunk of an ancient tree; in the sulfur haze of gunpowder its splintered reddish pith was strewn like the spattered guts of an animal.

In the cave, Mahe's blood and adrenaline pumped furiously. He kept firing till the barrel of his gun was white hot. It seemed to him that he was mowing down demons rather than killing human beings. These pig-shit, son-of-a-bitch Japanese devils may have eaten the food of men, but Mahe could smell their bestial reek. As though possessed by the bellicose spirit of the White Tiger, Mahe fired unceasingly, intoxicated by the endless rat-a-tat of his machine gun. Wave after wave of Japanese devils were repelled, until finally the furious onslaught was halted.

The corpses of his comrades-in-arms were piled beside the splintered stump of the ancient tree, like so much kindling. This was the first time Mahe had seen such a large number of corpses. His heart was tormented with sorrow; his mind burned with outrage.

The message arrived from the division commander, "Every last man defend our position to the death! Fight to the death and shed your last drop of blood for our country!" The platoon leader checked the remaining weaponry, allocating each man a light machine gun, several grenades, a bayoneted rifle, and a dagger.

"Those Japanese are tough sons-of-bitches!" the platoon leader bellowed, breaking a long silence, "When they attack again, be ready for a bayonet fight. Hold your ground! Victory or death! No man gets taken alive!"

Just after they finished their breakfast rations, nine Japanese bombers from Yichang flew over dropping a precise and devastating bombardment on the remaining Guomindang troops, wiping out all of the remaining mortar and anti-aircraft gunners, and inflicting major casualties on the heavy machine-gunners. Their defensive cover was obliterated. In the onslaught, the platoon leader who had boldly rallied the men before breakfast was killed.

Then the Japanese devils, clad in khaki uniforms, launched yet another assault, cunningly hurling canisters of tear gas ahead to suppress enemy fire. Billows of white smoke, like the poisonous exhalations of demons, wreathed the ground. As Mahe and his comrades fought through blinding, burning tears, the Japanese devils charged, gleaming keen bayonets aimed forward.

Blindly, Mahe and the others hurled a round of grenades before emerging from cover to engage the Japanese devils.

One Japanese soldier, army cap fallen off and hair disheveled, howled as he thrust his bayonet at Mahe. Twisting swiftly to one side, Mahe bayoneted the enemy soldier twice in the back of the neck—jets of fresh blood spurted from the wounds. From the side, another Japanese devil lurched toward Mahe. As he retreated a step, the bayonet pierced Mahe's right side. Countering nimbly, Mahe thrust his bayonet into the bastard's midriff. The battlefield echoed with clattering bayonets, agonized cries of the dying, and murderous howls of life-and-death battle, a cacophonous symphony carried by the mountain winds.

Abruptly, the frenzy of killing stopped. For a moment the grounds fell silent. After this interval, the Dare-to-Die Corps of the Guomindang Army rushed to the forefront. They saw an unkempt seventeen or eighteen-year-old soldier astraddle a Japanese devil, eyes flashing with fury, hands wrapped around his adversary's throat. Dirty and ragged from the rough-and-tumble fight, the youth's uniform was torn and bloodstained, its buttons undone. Engaged in hand-to-hand combat, the youth had first been pressed to the ground, but had struggled to overturn and pin the Japanese devil. During the fracas, he had sustained a bayonet jab to the back. Eyes wide open in death like a savage tiger, he gave his life for his country. The corpse of a second Japanese devil—likely the one who had delivered the fatal bayonet thrust—leaned against the young soldier. Their three bodies were piled together; their bayonets scattered. The terrible carnage of battle spread around them: some like Mahe throttling the enemy even in death, others biting off enemy's ears or gouging out their eyes. A testament to grenade blasts and mortars, mangled arms and legs hung from trees. Jackstrawed corpses lay before the collapsed cave, Japanese devils and Nationalist soldiers commingled. Anguished moans came from the dying.

Before the Dare-to-die Corps could catch their breath, the Japanese devils launched another attack. Using the mounded dead as cover, the Dare-to-Die troops rested their machine guns on corpses, firing relentlessly, riddling the foremost Japanese ranks like a honeycomb. Only after the last of the Japanese devils had fallen did their machine guns fall silent.

Chapter Nine

I

Mawu finally returned to Gengguping. Anxious, he spurred his horse; since heading to Fengjie City with the roster of bandits, he had not gone back home, and had heard no tidings of his parents or wife.

Riddle-like hearsay and cryptic rumors circulated in Huangshui. However, there was no evidence that Jiang Ermao had joined the bandits, nor were the names of Qin Liexiong or Zhou Taiwang among the spies listed on the roster. Thus, no progress had been made on the mysterious attack on the tower. Furthermore, Qin Liexiong and ten of his underlings had opened a teahouse on a bustling street in Huangshui, which was doing brisk business. Lining palms with bribes, Liexiong was hand-in-glove with the local officials. The strain of this seemingly unending series of tribulations left Mawu vexed and grumpy.

Mawu lit his tobacco pipe, smoking slowly with Li Diezhu. Over the tumultuous past fortnight—a time too hectic for him to ungird his belt or savor his food—he had managed to capture several spies, but hadn't gleaned the least scrap of information about the attack on the tower. Agitated, Mawu said, "Dad, the townsfolk are all gossiping about the tower. Some say Jiang Ermao, seeking revenge, led Liang the bamboo weaver and the bandits to attack; others claim it was Zhou Taiwang; still others maintain that Qin

Liexiong colluded with Liang—lending him a dagger to kill an adversary."

"Follow Jiang Ermao's tracks closely," said Li Diezhu bitingly.

"The guy's never home, and his wife says she knows nothing about his whereabouts." Mawu answered.

"Without evidence, you can't accuse anybody." Li Diezhu said, staring hard at Mawu.

"I'll find proof," responded Mawu, furrowing his brows.

"Oh, and as the old saying goes," Li Diezhu sighed heavily, "'You can know a man's face, but you can't know his heart.' Though your brother Masui may look straightforward, he's dealing from the bottom of the deck—having an illicit affair with Sun Fu's wife. Third Auntie Zhang has set up an engagement for him with a girl from the He family. Her father chops kindling, tends fires, and cooks at Azure Dragon Temple; her elder brother joined the army last year; and her younger brother's still at home. Engagement gifts have already been sent." While Masui ought to have long since had a son or daughter, after Damei's grim death, it was necessary to lower the family's standards. Even though the He's girl was homely, it was better than seizing the wife of another.

Mawu mused, how could Masui go so far off kilter in love and marriage? Probably he was yearning for a wife.

"After discussing the matter with your mother, I sold three acres of the hilly fields and several goldthread-sheds that I purchased from the Xiangs to the Qins for eight hundred silver dollars. With the money, we can hold another wedding ceremony for Masui. With the leftover silver, I can hire geomancers to determine an auspicious site for my tomb. Then, once I'm dead and buried, I'll offer blessings and protection to all of you in every endeavor." So Li Diezhu spoke, gazing at his eldest son.

"Father, Qin Liexiong wants to be the new militia Captain and has bribed the Mayor with a large sum of money." Mawu said hesitantly, his cheeks blushing redder than the clusters of hot peppers hanging from the eaves. He continued, "I, too, want to be Captain. Otherwise, I'll join the army like Mahe. There's no way I'll work under Qin Liexiong."

"How could you leave home at a chaotic time like this?" asked Li Diezhu, his brows knotted in anger. "How many guns are under a Captain?"

Mawu replied, "One hundred and fifty men. And our family will be safe if I station a detachment of militiamen at our block tower."

Hearing these words, Li Diezhu's mien immediately softened. He asked,

"If I give you the silver from the land sale, can you win the captaincy over Liexiong?"

"It will double my chances . . . but at least set aside some silver for Masui's engagement feast," Mawu said guiltily.

"We'll push back the engagement feast till the fall and figure out other means to pay for it," replied Li Diezhu, tapping the bowl of his tobacco pipe.

"I'll find the best *yin* and *yang* masters to locate you an ideal grave plot, Pa!" Mawu swore passionately.

Mulling it over, Li Diezhu decided to throw his full support behind eldest son Mawu's bid for captaincy of the militia. He opened his safe, in which the silver dollars were neatly stacked. Father and son thus took a decisive step—breaking the cauldrons and sinking the boat—going all out to secure Mawu the post. Together, they loaded the clinking and clanking silver into two bamboo baskets.

Mawu didn't return to the tower till the dead of night. Availing themselves of the respite from the chain of frenetic events, he and Jin stole a night of blissful union. At daybreak, however, he headed straight to the courtyard to carry the silver dollars. Wearing a formal long gown and new straw sandals, a new white kerchief wrapped around his head, Li Diezhu was readying the horses.

"Your father will accompany you," Tao Jiuxiang said, lifting her head from her preoccupation with fastening Li Diezhu's long gown.

Li Diezhu rolled up his sleeves, carrying two baskets of red chili peppers and loading them into the cart. It took Mawu a moment to register that the silver dollars were hidden beneath the red peppers. "Dad, you might as well stay home," said Mawu anxiously.

"Back when you first joined the militia, this old man accompanied you," said Li Diezhu firmly, "and today, this old man's going with you again!" Though apprehensive, Mawu set off with his father, each of them on horseback.

Heading to Huangshui, the big black horse not only carried eight hundred silver dollars hidden under red chilis, but transported Mawu and his bold ambitions. For more than a decade, the Li family had lived in the primeval forest, earning the respect and admiration of the mountainfolk. Yet father and son harbored even greater aspirations: The Lis could become the lords of Huangshui, an ancient town with a lively history of a thousand years.

As they reached a steep cliff overlooking a deep gorge, the mountain path, carved into the sheer cliff face by arduous will and toil, narrowed to shoulder-width. Mawu dismounted, fearing the horse bearing their cargo of precious "chili peppers" might tumble down the cliff. Leading the way, he carried one of the baskets along the narrow terrace. Suddenly, turning a bend, a black wild boar appeared, its dense, white-tipped bristles rising like hackles, the late-morning sun glinting on its terrible long tusks. Rather than fleeing, the creature launched itself right at Mawu. Although Mawu was a crack shot, the boar was on him in a trice: he had no time to grab his rifle. His hands wet with nervous sweat, Mawu unconsciously braced his back against the cliff. Mawu twisted away, evading the initial charge and counterattacked, delivering an agile and powerful kick—the same sort of kick that had sent the dread "Black-tailed Snake" into the pit of excrement—that launched the two-hundred and fifty pound boar over the edge of the ravine and into the yawning abyss.

Li Diezhu set down his gun and laughed, "What an unexpected harvest! On our way back, we'll tote that meaty bastard home." He thought this an auspicious sign.

II

In the aftermath of Captain Huang's murder, the Mayor of Huangshui had been busy from dawn until late night with ten thousand matters, large and small. That very morning he was in the midst of paperwork to recommend a candidate to the county governor for the captaincy of the Huangshui Militia. As soon as Mawu arrived, he called on the Mayor.

Father and son entered the office, toting their "chili peppers." "Reporting to the Mayor," said Mawu, abashedly. "After selling his goldthread, my father has come especially to see you, sir."

"Dear elder," began the Mayor, addressing swarthy-faced, red-cheeked Li Diezhu in his long gown and new sandals, a white towel swaddling his head. The Mayor's gaze swept over the baskets of chilis, and then he stopped writing for a moment, continuing peevishly, "Don't make things difficult for me! Both Lieutenant Li Mawu and Qin Liexiong are from eminent local families: so whose gift should I accept?"

With a rustic's awkward reticence, Li Diezhu edged forward, and said ingratiatingly, "Mayor, sir, there's no trouble in this matter. Just accept presents from both parties, and recommend both candidates to the county.

It's both easy and fair."

"Hmmm, that's a great idea," the Mayor nodded, his face beaming with relief. "Like they say, wisdom truly comes from the elders."

Pleased, the Mayor recommended both candidates for the Captaincy of the Huangshui Militia. When the document reached the county governor in Fengjie City and he saw the names of Qin Liexiong and Li Mawu, he recognized the latter as the officer who had recently been recognized for "merit in suppressing bandits." Thus, he took up his writing brush and underlined the name "Li Mawu" in red ink, adding the four characters, "This candidate is approved."

Qin Liexiong's eight hundred silver dollars had been cast into the ocean.

The announcement of Mawu's appointment as Captain caused a stir in Huangshui. When Lidu—the militiaman who had been stationed in the tower—brought word to Gengguping, Li Diezhu was squatting against a tree outside the gate, pensively smoking a bowl of tobacco. Hearing the good news, he gazed at Tao Jiuxiang in a with a quirky half-smile, chanting a tune like a naughty boy,

"Nothin' to worry about, not a care in the world."

Tao Jiuxiang fiercely hurled an ear of corn at him, but Li Diezhu didn't care a whit, and went on chanting,

"Don't tire the young folk with your anxieties and sorrows."

After that, he stood up and roared exultantly, "Aoooo—oo—wey!" toward the mountains. Tao Jiuxiang bent over with laughter, her face beaming red as if drunk. Breathlessly, she chuckled, "How truly potent Xia Qifa's protective amulet is!"

"Tell Mawu to lead his men," said Sun Fu excitedly, "and take revenge on those bandits!"

"Someday, they'll take down that bamboo weaver masquerading as a tiger spirit." Li Diezhu vaunted, his eyebrows dancing, his face radiant.

After learning of his promotion, Mawu was too busy hosting banquets and being feted to return home. He had a message delivered to Gengguping asking his father and Masui to come and help him deal with the series of feasts. Pipe in hand, Li Diezhu urged Masui to ready the horses, leaving Jin at home to accompany little Yongyu and Tao Jiuxiang.

At Peppercorn Bend, Jin Shaosan, too, received an invitation. Delighted at the tidings, Jin's mother joyfully saddled a horse and rode to Gengguping, carrying a load of gifts to see Jin and her granddaughter. Even in her wildest dreams, she had never expected her son-in-law, Mawu, to rise to become militia captain. Beaming with pride and sheer delight, she mused that from now on, the Lis would be second only to the mayor in Huangshui.

Wearing a bright-colored embroidered tiger-head cap and a pair of delicate tiger-head shoes, Yongyu rushed to her grandmother crying "Granny, Granny!" Wreathed in smiles, Jin's mother clasped a silver necklace round Yongyu's neck, warmly holding her plump little hands, swaying as she chanted:

> *My little daughter will come back,*
> *All sugared dumplings and silken shoes;*
> *Trying pair after pair, never she'll lack,*
> *She'll be happy wherever she goes . . .*

Contented, Jin giggled along with Yongyu.

Turning to her daughter, Jin's mother whispered, "Is Mawu keeping another woman outside?"

Jin answered, "No."

"Oh, my daughter," said Jin's mother with a low sigh, "Do you know our Jin family's story? We were poor in the very beginning. When your grandfather was a young man, he walked a hundred miles to Huangshui, making a living peddling cloth. He'd eat just one meal a day, and was often so hungry that he'd beg a bowl of rice gruel at country inns. Before long, innkeepers were so fed up they'd just slosh some gruel on the ground at the sight of him. Yet in the end he built the tile-roofed houses of our Jin family. Though nowadays our family has accumulated a little fortune, your father is mild-mannered and has no real influence in Huangshui, so he still gets bullied. Now your husband has some clout and has made a name for himself. He has to attend to men's business, so you need to be a good wife and follow in his wake."

"I will," replied Jin, combing Yongyu's hair.

Several days later, Li Diezhu and Masui finally returned Gengguping on muleback. At the sight of Jin's mother, Li Diezhu began apologetically, "My dear in-law, Mawu is too busy attending to his new duties to deal with matters at home."

With a broad grin, Jin's mother answered, "A real man should conquer the world rather than nesting at home. Our Jin family is blessed to have Mawu as a son-in-law."

Jin looked resentful, as she had figured Mawu would return with them. Noticing his sister-in-law's unhappiness, Masui hastened to explain, "Mawu always has Gengguping in mind, but he just posted two new official notices. The first urgently requests laborers, horses, and mules from each district; the second offers a reward for information leading to the resolution of the brigands' attack on the tower."

Taking in hand the cup of tea offered by Tao Jiuxiang, Li Diezhu cheerfully instructed Sun Fu, "Tomorrow, take my big black horse and head straight to Qin Zhanyun's home. Then, go tell the *tima*, Xia Qifa, that we'll prepare an engagement banquet for Mahe and Yinmei!" He had inquired in Huangshui, and learned that Mahe's unit had been fighting along the Yangzi on the Hubei border for more than a month, killing tens of thousands of Japanese devils. Pleased, he mused that the Li men were destined for greatness, born under lucky zodiac signs.

Sun Fu nodded and said, "I'll take care of it right away—otherwise, Yinmei will be betrothed to another fellow."

Li Diezhu sprang up and pronounced proudly, "No danger of that: the *tima* promised Yinmei to Mahe with his golden mouth and jade words."

Elatedly, Tao Jiuxiang said, "Well, let's get busy. We have so many preparations for the next fortnight!"

III

Watching Mawu's meteoric ascent and hearing of Mahe's glory in battle agitated Masui, filling his heart with distress. Nostalgically, he recalled his school days in Fengjie City: if only Mawu had sent his letter rather than turning it over to his mother, his life and career might have taken a very different trajectory! But what, alas, is the use of dwelling on lost opportunities?

While Mawu awaited his formal appointment as Captain, the girl from the He family was hastily married to Masui. Once the He family received the betrothal gifts, unable to wait until autumn, they insisted that the wedding take place as soon as possible. After all, with goldthread selling so poorly, hardscrabble life in the mountains was tough—marrying out a daughter meant one fewer mouth to feed. Both Masui and the bride were content with a simple ceremony. Therefore, though Tao Jiuxiang bought incense and candles, and hired several musicians and a sedan to carry the bride, the wedding banquet was far less elaborate than the previous two.

Lying in bed with He, Mawu sometimes stared dumbly at the joist upon which Zhou Damei had hanged herself, mulling the nature of happiness. In the depth of one night, lost in just such ruminations, he suddenly heard a gentle leaf whistle outside, followed by a whisper, "Li Masui . . . open the door."

The voice could be none other than that of Zhou Damei, who had long since been buried at Lihaku. How could she have returned? "I will never open the door for you, ghost," muttered a shocked and trembling Masui.

From beyond the door, the voice continued, rising in volume, "Open the door. I'm a human, not a ghost."

"If you come back once you've been buried, you're a ghost!"

The voice menaced, "Whether you open the door or not, I'm coming in!"

Petrified, heart thumping uncontrollably, Masui awakened. So it was a dream. After weathering the enervating night, Masui rose at daybreak to the jarring discovery that their two pairs of shoes, placed neatly at the foot of the bed before they went to sleep, were scattered around the room. The same thing happened for three successive nights, leaving Masui a sleepless wreck.

When Tao Jiuxiang learned of these strange events, she had the joist sawed off at once. She still felt ill at ease: Xia Qifa had already performed an exorcism—how could this sort of thing happen?

Squatting at the gate of the main house, shiny and smooth bamboo pipe in hand, Li Diezhu snarled at Masui, "If you haven't done anything to be ashamed of, what're you afraid of? I can sleep peacefully with my front and back doors wide open without fear. If you want to dispel evil spirits, just remember the following chant: 'Heaven and earth are contained within me, a toxic curse upon the demonfolk to the northwest'—it's a potent spell to melt metal, splinter trees, make the waters dry up, extinguish fires, crumble mountains, sunder rocks, bind spirits, and drive ghosts back to the netherworld." He extended his left hand, his four fingers contorted in a strange fashion, the joints of his middle finger bumping upward. He explained, "Shape your hand like this—it's the Mudra of the Ancestors . . . Xia Qifa taught me. It can banish devils and expel ghosts. Get it?"

Awkwardly, Masui tried to form the mudra, but failed to do it right. In the end, his middle finger stuck straight up. Frustrated, Li Diezhu cuffed Masui, crying out, "Ai! What a friggin' oaf!" He then interlaced the fingers of his two hands, forming another mudra, saying, "Try this one—the Mudra of the Ancestress. Its power is even greater—like a shackle. If you hear the ghost in front of you, pull the mudra backward; if the ghost is to your right, move it to the left—in the opposite direction. Only in this manner can you capture and bind the ghost, making it groan with agony." Masui practiced until eventually his hands could form both more or less fluidly. He recited the spells until he could chant them by rote.

Gazing at the wintersweet tree in the yard, Li Diezhu sincerely warned, "Just remember, never recite that chant when you're hunkering down for a shit."

Masui dared not tell his wife about the ghost. Nightly, he engaged in a sleepless battle of wits with the ghost, constantly muttering the chant and forming the mudras, making moves and counter-moves to shackle and ward off the vengeful apparition. In this manner, his newlywed days were spent not in nuptial rapture but in a state of constant fear and vigil.

Having successfully completed his mission to deliver news of Mahe and Yinmei's forthcoming betrothal feast to the *tima*, Sun Fu returned from Dragon Decapitating Gorge. He brought back an important piece of news: Xia Qifa had decided to formally transmit his shamanic arts to Xia Liangxian, his only son. Red paper notices were pasted along the streets of Huangshui, inviting the townspeople to attend the gala ceremony in ten days.

For the mountainfolk, this was an event of great import. Li Diezhu set down his pipe—smoke from its bowl still wafting upward—and said excitedly, "So it's time for the little guy to succeed his old man and don the clothes of a shaman . . . he's been an assistant ever since he was a little kid."

For a *tima*, having no successor was far worse, far more lamentable and tragic, than being childless. Xia Qifa had to bequeath his shamanic knowledge to the next generation; otherwise, he would face the wrath of the gods and spirits, condemned to eternal torment without surcease. Though according to tradition a *tima* should not transmit the shamanic arts to his own son, Xia Qifa cleverly sidestepped this ancient rule by disregarding generational naming practices within the family genealogy: rather than calling his boy Yinxian, he named his son Liangxian. Technically, Xia Liangxian, then, could not be regarded as Xia Qifa's own son. Succession was equally important in Daoism. Years earlier, when the venerable master of Azure Dragon Temple conducted his succession ceremony, hundreds thronged from far and wide to bear witness. Such grand rites of passage only took place once a generation.

Animatedly, Tao Jiuxiang said, "We'll need to stagger these events . . . to better prepare."

Li Diezhu held aloft his pipe, announcing majestically, "We'll hold the betrothal feast after Xia Liangxian's succession."

Masui sat beside the stove, silently envying both Mawu and Mahe. Why was his fate alone so cumbersome? His life so lacking in vitality?

Bustling with excitement, Tao Jiuxiang prepared for the betrothal. She prepared a long, detailed shopping list for Mawu. Meanwhile, their sow was in heat. Their two boars were too young and too small, so she asked Sun Fu bring his adult boar to breed her. But it proved to be too late: during the night, the sow clambered over the fence and ran away. Combing the mountainslopes, they called for her everywhere, but it was in vain. Two days later, however, the sow came back down from the hills on her own, grunting and snorting. Overjoyed at unexpectedly recovering the creature, Tao Jiuxiang apologized to the sow, letting her back into the enclosure and feeding her. Surprisingly, while the sow was indifferent to Sun Fu's boar, she appeared interested when a wild boar emerged from a thicket and trotted around the pigpen. Li Diezhu went to the tower, asking three militiamen to hide in the bamboo grove and shoot any wild boars near the pen. Yet for each wild boar they killed, two more emerged from the forest! In the end, the sow was pregnant and Tao Jiuxiang guessed that she had been bred by one of the wild boars. Who knew what trouble this litter of piglets might cause? The slightest lapse could lead to trouble.

Mawu had been absent from Gengguping for quite a long stretch, Tao Jiuxiang thought uneasily.

Chapter Ten

I

After a sleepless night, Mawu entered the lonely teahouse followed by Cui Four, his grave, ashen countenance reflecting none of the pleasure one might expect to see in a newly appointed officer. An order had arrived from the county government instructing local officials to offer consolation and rewards to the families of local soldiers who had died as martyrs in the War of Resistance against Japan. According to several reports, seventeen brave young men from Huangshui had died on the battlefield: Li Mahe was one of them. Mawu couldn't believe his eyes; his heart beat frantically. How could Mahe be dead? The war report recorded that Mahe's regiment had taken part in the great triumph in west Hubei. In the fifth lunar month, one hundred thousand Japanese devils gathered in Yichang, swarming Xiling Gorge to occupy the upper Yangzi River Valley. Mahe and his comrades-in-arms had died in a fierce firefight defending the narrow pass winding up the steep cliffs overlooking the river.

The report of the martyrs included a terse account of Mahe's military career. He had trained in Yunyang before being sent to the front in Hubei as a machine-gunner. He had single-handedly taken more than a hundred enemy lives before he fell. While Mawu hadn't turned up a single clue related to the plundering of the tower, the evil tidings of his brother's death were plainly before him in black-and-white print. A sour numbness filled his mouth and nose as he read on: the martyrs also included Sun Fu's younger brother, who went down in a blaze of glory in a firefight in Henan against the Japanese; the younger son of the Zhou family, killed six months earlier on Dabie Mountain in Hubei; and one of Masui's new in-laws, He Wanwan, a sniper killed by Japanese bombers in faraway Hebei.

Motherfucking Japanese devils! Even if he flayed the lot of them alive, Mawu's rage could not be quenched. He wished he could head straight to the front to take revenge, but he couldn't: Huangshui, this ancient town, needed him. Several days earlier, an important official missive arrived ordering him to dispatch twenty-five strong laborers from Huangshui to Fengjie City.

After a morning of rainshowers, the skies had cleared. As it was not a market day, the usual thick lingering vapors of hot tea and tobacco were not hanging so heavily in the teahouse. Ignoring the welcome of the obsequious manager, Mawu sat down at an eight-seated table, filled with sorrow and indignation. To respond to the writ from the Fengjie City, the Mayor ordered that each of Huangshui's wards supply two laborers and, claiming to be on sick leave, charged Mawu with overseeing the draft. Unfortunately, several laborers recruited six months earlier had secretly absconded, telling fellow mountainfolk that they had been mistreated, beaten, and half-starved. Naturally, this made recruitment difficult. After canvassing all eleven wards in greater Huangshui, Mawu finally enrolled twenty-two laborers, including one of Jin's cousins; still, he was three short of fulfilling the county government's quota. As households were scattered about the vast mountains, it was impossible to visit them all. Mawu had just been appointed Captain: this new responsibility distracted him from his other duties. Fortunately, Ran Hongyou, headman of the Ninth Ward, found the three extra men, two from the Lis' tenant households. The population of the Ninth Ward, including the hamlet at Peppercorn Bend, was rather concentrated. Ran Hongyou succeeded in persuading the three through sheer intimidation, concocting a story that Captain Li had issued an order that those who refused to comply would be executed. So Ran Hongyou, too, had learned to wield authority—a cunning fox borrowing the fierce tiger's terrible might. Bitterly, Mawu wondered whether the man deserved commendation or punishment. Suddenly, he noticed two strangers enter the teahouse.

No resident of Huangshui was a stranger to Mawu; he knew them all at a glance. The two men—one tall, the other short—wearing old, tattered gowns and blue turbans of homespun cloth, both appeared roughly fifty years old. Their unkempt, dusty appearance showed them to be outsiders. Sitting on a bench, they ordered a pot of tea. The tall stranger said, "Look at these majestic, winding mountains—ridges and crags like a dragon's back—with veins and arteries of water coursing through them—this is truly a site worthy of a man of great fortune and honor. However, what would be the ideal location for a tomb? The base of the mountains or the peak?"

The short man answered, "Near the peak, reflecting the man's exalted status." The tall one said, "What about along a ridge?"

Startled, Mawu realized these men were "dragon-seekers," geomancers—experts in locating ideal sites for palaces, houses, or tombs by studying the position of mountains and rivers. Trying to shake his melancholy, he turned to them and asked, "What are you two arguing about? Can you tell me? I'm the militia captain here."

The shorter dragon-seeker rose, saying, "An honor to meet you, captain. We've been dragon-seekers for many years. We've come in fits and starts from Changyang, in western Hubei Province. It's taken us half a year to reach Huangshui."

Mawu asked indignantly, "The Japanese bombed the hell out of Yichang! How did you honorable elders ever make it here?"

Rolling up his sleeves, the shorter fellow answered, "When we can't follow roads, we wind our way along mountain trails. Traversing the ridges and crags of these majestic, draconian mountains, we seek the perfect site to expel demons and make evil spirits submit, a dragon's cave that might help sweep away the Japanese devils."

Staring at them, Mawu asked, "Have you found it?"

The taller man sipped his tea, and, emphatically tapping the table, replied, "Like the sinuous body of a dragon in motion these mountain ridges wind their way here from Yunzhong, past Changyang in western Hubei, and into this region as if reaching their destination."

Reseating himself, the shorter man added, "We've worn out ten pairs of sandals searching these mountains—from the Peak of the Supreme Ancestor, seeking the Mount of the Lesser Ancestor. After a few days rest, we'll continue our search."

Cui Four interrupted, "Dragon caves are rare in the human world and incredibly hard to find, but there are other kinds of underground caves.

There's a ditty around here that goes,

> *Of grotto neath Lihaku they speak,*
> *Little peak to the big peak,*
> *Horse-saddle mount of the oxhead mount,*
> *Two carp leap on the golden sand,*
> *Find this site and great fortune you'll command:*
> *Of ten sons, nine have rank and wealth beyond count.*

"Never heard that song," Mawu muttered skeptically, brows furrowed.

Cui Four said, "Just ask any of your older tenant farmers . . . they'll know."

The two dragon seekers looked at each other and decided immediately, "Tomorrow we'll search for the cave."

Mawu thought that if he fulfilled his promise to find an auspicious site for his parents' tomb, it might mitigate to some small degree their sorrow at learning of Mahe's death. "To tell the truth, good elders," he sighed, "I'm looking for a suitable residence in the netherworld for my aged father. If you can locate an ideal site, a cavern worthy of a noble, I have two hundred silver dollars to offer." So saying, he paid for their tea and dispatched Cui Four to tell his underlings to arrange a formal send-off for the laborers on the morrow with gongs and drums.

Dusk was settling in as they emerged from the teahouse. The tall dragon chaser asked Mawu for Li Diezhu's eight-character zodiac sign. He raised his head and exclaimed, "The rivers and mountains will reveal a long-hidden perfect spot for a fortunate man like that—it's predestined!"

His colleague patted Mawu on the shoulder, saying with satisfaction, "You are as lucky as your ancestors were virtuous."

Early the following morning after sending the laborers away with a stirring speech, Mawu led the two dragon seekers into the mountains. Cui Four and another militiaman followed, both clad in straw ponchos and bamboo hats.

The cliff rose to the left of the road, the valley fell to the right. A fresh accumulation of snow had fallen overnight. In the gray dawn, the five men rode along the horsetrack single-file. Year-round, the clear water in the Inkblack Creek wound its way through the valleys. Two pairs of penetrating eyes traced every contour of mountainscape, having following these mysterious and ancient ridges from their very origin, hundreds of miles away, to the endpoint, which they sensed was near.

"We're surrounded by mountains. How do you know where they start? After all, this 'dragon's cave' is extremely rare. Seems like we might well vainly wander for half a year without finding a thing," weary Mawu said skeptically.

The tall dragon seeker grinned, waxing poetic:

> *Foremost masters are guided by the constellations' course,*
> *Middling masters seek the rivers' source,*
> *Only those of the lowest rank wander the mountains on foot or horse.*

Fear not, we two are guided by the stars. If there's a fine grotto in these mountains, an auspicious site, we'll locate it."

His colleague added, "The mountain ridge, this dragon's spine, winds for a thousand miles, its majestic peaks crowned with clouds and fog. If we seek accumulations of clouds and mist, we can locate the grotto."

"Since such a location promises great fortune and eminence for future sons and grandsons, why not seek it for yourselves?" Mawu blurted, asking a question long weighing on him.

The tall man turned and replied bitterly, "Only one predestined can occupy the numinous ethers of such a locale. Otherwise, Heaven will punish the interloper."

His colleague chimed in, "How could tattered wanderers like us, men to whom paltry fate has allotted scant happiness, hope to occupy such a site? At least the spirits and divinities have blessed us with clear sight to pursue our vocation as dragon seekers."

II

Like a row of ants, Li Diezhu's tenants filed across Speargrass Plain, a cogongrass-clotted mountainslope with impoverished soil. Tan, one of the tenants, had just built a log cabin. A narrow path led to its gate.

"There's Lihaku," announced Mawu, pointing beyond the slope. Hungry and exhausted in the cold, steam rose from his mouth. Beyond the valley rose several picturesque crags. On the peak to the right, two massive boulders, one big and the other smaller, crouched like a pair of tigers. "This region— these valley plains and the ten-odd surrounding ridges—is called Lihaku. Means 'Land of the Tigers.' Let's warm up and get something to eat." Mawu dismounted, leading his horse toward the tenant's cabin, followed by his militiamen.

Speargrass Plain faced a bend in Inkblack Creek; the breathtaking panoramic vantage left the dragon seekers in an awestruck silence. For six arduous months, they had braved heat and cold, obstacles and dangers, vainly seeking the Peak of the Lesser Ancestor. Then a chance encounter in a teahouse had led them to the very mouth of the dragon's grotto! In amazement, the dragon seekers stood on the narrow plain looking up at the rugged, majestic ring of mountains. One said to Mawu, "Thank you for your hard work, Captain. Please go in and have some tea. We'll be in soon."

Mawu and the militiamen entered Tan's cabin, which still smelled of fragrant wood. Meanwhile, the geomancers—the two best known *fengshui* masters in Changyang—stood in the cold, eyes animated with fervent excitement, gasping in delight as their tattered robes flapped in the biting wind. At long last they had located the site where the Immortal Tiger Lord had descended from the White Tiger Star to the mortal world in the tiger hour, of the tiger day, of the tiger month, in the Year of the Tiger! In Changyang, people called the site White Tiger Tumulus. From the ancient misty ethers enveloping the Mountain of the Supreme Ancestor, the dragon seekers had followed the geomantic emanations over countless ridges, hunting for this mountain-engirded site. Now, having reached the site that radiated such powerful numinous energy, sensing its momentous importance, to confirm their hypothesis they took out their geomantic compass to measure its azimuth in respect to the constellations and the Five Elements. With their celestial and terrestrial compasses they tabulated the precise meridian of the location of this site that had been and would be so closely intertwined with the rise and fall of the Lis.

The mountain air was pregnant with the potent numinous ethers radiating from the subterranean cavern! If an unworthy corpse were buried on the site, the stone guardian tigers crouching on the mountainslope, protecting the grotto beneath for countless eons, would exhume it with their fearsome claws and cast it away.

"This location will bring about both great prosperity and crushing tragedy," said the tall geomancer, warm tears of excitement cascading down his cheek. "For the man interred on this site, among three generations of his children and grandchildren, one will be an indomitable conqueror, passing through a hail of bullets he will expand borders and open up new domains, suppressing ghosts and subduing demons, accumulating wealth beyond all reckoning, yet his checkered fate will bring him endless turbulence and wrenching tragedy."

His short colleague, too, muttered anxiously, "While this is burial site befitting an emperor, it emanates a murderous air. It may bring military success to the offspring of the man buried herein, but future generations of the family will be ravaged by war and suffer profoundly in a world awash in blood!"

Both lamented, "Why must it be so? Why must it be so?"

After his remarkable achievements in the mortal world, the Immortal Tiger Lord would return to his celestial palace on the White Tiger Star. But his descendants would be shadowed by an endless litany of bloody wars, migrations, and suffering. If they located the precise spot and buried the deceased in the hour, day, month, and year of the Tiger, it would have a tremendous impact not only upon the Li family but on the entire Tribe of the Tiger. On this point, the two foot-weary geomancers were perfectly clear. In the past, they mulled, perhaps other geomancers had been here, but had kept it secret. One could not casually publicize such a site of dragons and tigers, a grotto worthy of a magnificent sovereign: such secrets, long guarded by heaven and earth, must be treated with great discretion. A dragon seeker who foolishly divulged this pulsingly numinous location would be accursed by Heaven; the rarer the spot, the more severe Heaven's retribution.

"Disasters and blessings are unpredictable. Both depend on the will of the spirits." From his robes, the taller geomancer extracted a set of bamboo trigrams. Holding them before his chest for a moment, he murmured a prayer, then cast them on the ground. Three times he repeated this rite, throwing the divining sticks, each time exchanging an ominous look with his colleague. "What can I do?" So saying, he knelt down, wailing as he gathered the tallies like a child weeping for a lost toy.

"Is there no other alternative? Could this truly be the convoluted will of the gods?" howled the shorter man, joining in.

Unaware of these developments, Mawu and his men had been drying their clothes by the fire inside. Emerging, Mawu asked suspiciously, "Is someone crying?"

Hurriedly wiping tears from their cheeks and tucking away the bamboo tallies, the geomancers answered, "No one's crying."

Nonplussed by their queer expressions of mingled alarm and dismay,

Mawu queried, "So, did you find it? Is there a grotto here?"

"Yes," they solemnly answered.

"So where is this wondrous cavern?" Mawu asked.

The taller geomancer thought for a moment, rubbed his moist eyes, then, pointing at Mawu's very feet, said seriously, "Captain, you're standing directly above the heart of the grotto." Hoping to sidestep the murderous punishment foretold—even if it meant markedly diminishing the magnitude of the prophesied wealth and blessing—the geomancer deliberately pointed several yards away from the exact center. In this manner, he might avoid the wrath of the spirits while the Li family might avert utter massacre and extermination, and still accumulate sufficient wealth.

Mawu lowered his head in amazement, looking at the pebbles and grass. Dubiously, he asked, "This is the auspicious site of the cavern?"

"Mountains determine the fate of posterity, rivers influence the clan's fortune," continued the tall geomancer. "Look, the draconian mountain chain engirds us and the two branches of the winding river converge not far from here—this portends a bright future for the family and wealth like the ever-flowing waters of the Eastern Sea. If your father is buried here, it will bring great fortune for your family. It is an auspicious spot for his tomb."

"Encountering you two elders was truly a blessing for our family," said Mawu thoughtfully. Gazing forward at the cliffs rising from the mist-hidden vales, he cheerfully added, "The meal's ready. Please come in and eat."

In low spirits, the geomancers put away their tools and entered the cabin. Sitting around the stove, they drank a bit of corn liquor, eating the simple fare served by the tenant. Neither said a word about the site. Like so many free-floating stars far above these rugged mountains and these hard-bitten mountainfolk, their otherworldly eyes fixed on Mawu. These eyes betrayed unspeakable sorrow.

Outside, it was raining again. Having seen the two dragon seekers working and measuring for so long, Old Tan and the militiamen burned to ask about the grotto, but, seeing Mawu's grave countenance, they kept silent.

III

Blanketed by thick fog, the deep gorges and vales in the mountains rarely saw the light of the sun. After passing a night in Old Tan's cabin, Mawu led the militiamen and the geomancers through the mud and fog to Gengguping. As they zigzagged forward, the geomancers suddenly caught sight of a pack of hunting dogs standing on a rock outcropping, barking in their direction. With a curt command, Mawu silenced the dozen hounds, who promptly scattered, wagging their tails. In a clearing in the thick woods stood a lonely wooden building surrounded by a fence. Looking out at them from the gate was an old man wearing a white bandana and a black cotton gown.

Mawu dismounted, leading the guests up the rocky outcropping to the gate. "Dad, these two masters have come from Hubei Province. Yesterday, they located the ideal spot for a tomb in the valley."

Li Diezhu had long sought the right spot for a tomb. Delighted by this unexpected boon, he greeted them warmly, "Welcome, honored guests. Let's drink. Bring out some dishes!" After tying up his horse, Mawu returned carrying plates of dried fruit and sliced meat and set them on the ledge beside the firepit as his father chatted amiably with the guests. Supping a mouthful of liquor, he asked calmly, "Dad, had you heard of that folk ditty?

> *Of a grotto neath Lihaku they speak,*
> *Little peak to the big peak,*
> *Horse-saddle mount of the oxhead mount,*
> *Two carp leap on the golden sand,*
> *Find this site and great fortune you'll command:*
> *Of ten sons, nine have rank and wealth beyond count.*

The old tenants all knew it."

With unbridled pleasure Li Diezhu rejoined, "Ah, Mawu, my son, I know it well. Some of those old tenants know that us Lis are tiger-spawn. Looks like its heaven's will that I'm to be buried on the plains of Lihaku."

In the midst of cracking a walnut, the shorter geomancer stopped suddenly, and asked, "Did you just say, honorable uncle, that your family is the issue of a tiger?"

Li Diezhu laughed, the stubble of his short beard transparent in the firelight. "Us mountainfolk often talk nonsense . . . it is unbelievable. Please stay a few days in my home and relax, partaking of delicious foods and listening to our farfetched yarns."

With tongs, Masui gripped cured meat from the joist above and roasted it over the firepit. He asked, "Since you elders came through western Hubei, have you heard any news of the war?"

The short geomancer answered, "We set out from Qingjiang, and stumbled upon a battle at Xiling Pass. The soldiers pressed us to anchor mines in the Yangzi, and clot up the river with bundles of straw and kindling to entangle the Japanese warships. In the end, we won the battle, but the Yangzi was dyed red with blood."

The tall man added, "The Japanese devils withdrew so frantically that they had half their corpses thrown into the river."

"Those dog-fucked bastards—may they be forever imprisoned in their watery graves!" Mawu mumbled to himself.

Tao Jiuxiang and Masui's wife He returned from the fields. At the sight of the guests, they hurriedly boiled rice.

Masui called out cheerfully, "Ma, these two masters have come from western Hubei." He turned to the geomancers and added, "Masters, my younger brother fought there. His troops killed more than ten thousand Japanese devil soldiers."

The short geomancer responded, "The mountains are catacombed with niches for cannons and machine guns. Is your brother artillery, infantry, or navy?"

Gloomily, Mawu answered, "Infantry, in the front lines at Empress Pass."

Alarmed, the tall geomancer chimed in, "So, he's in the Eleventh Division! That scene was nightmarish, a bloodbath. After the battle, the mountains were covered with rotting corpses, sundered bodies, and limbs reeking in the midday sun. Soldiers were burying bodies in mass graves."

"If only we could locate a hidden grotto with a true hero's aura—a site that would help expel these demons and secure the country for posterity!" The short man sighed.

"The Japanese devils have come to our land killing and plundering. If this threat is not extinguished, there's truly no heavenly justice. Although locating a hero's grotto would portend the rise of a martial conqueror, one capable of subduing ghosts and vanquishing demons, it would herald the beginning of endless carnage, bloodshed measured in generations rather than years," pronounced the tall man ominously, gazing out the window.

"So if the perfect geomantic site were found, it would give rise to a martial lord, a conqueror and savior who would butcher the Japanese and drive them from our land? Damn the consequences! So what if it brings about generations of bloody chaos? It's worth it." Mawu countered, his face darkening.

"It's not so simple. Commingled with the site's extraordinary noble aura is a powerfully wicked, murderous air." Looking down at the fire, the tall man spoke softly but heavily.

"If we made known a site that led to oceans of blood, generations of suffering, and an endless litany of chaos and death, we would be guilty before both heaven and man of unforgivably heinous crimes." The short geomancer lowered his head.

"Is Lihaku the site?" asked Mawu, visibly agitated.

"Relax, Captain. We haven't located it. We're just speaking hypothetically. Such a wondrous grotto would likely be discovered in a more watery region. The burial site we located will bring happiness and fortune to your family." The tall geomancer answered Mawu with an anguished smile.

After a long silence, Mawu turned suddenly to his father, "Dad, the county authorities sent notice that seventeen soldiers from Huangshui were killed in battle."

Li Diezhu answered, "Killed in battle? Who?"

Fixedly staring at the fireplace, Mawu answered, "Sun Laosan, Zhou Erwa, He Wanwan, an older brother of Masui's wife . . . and Mahe, seventeen in all."

"Who?" Li Diezhu's eyes nearly burst out of his skull.

"Brother—Mahe, He Wanwan, and Sun Laosan are dead? . . ." burst forth from shocked Masui, but, seeing Mawu's hard stare, he didn't finish.

"Mahe is dead?" asked Li Diezhu, the muscles in his cheek twitching.

'What?" exclaimed Tao Jiuxiang. She had been cutting vegetables off to the side. Like a violent blow, Li Diezhu's words struck her.

Li Diezhu gazed at Mawu, doubt mingling with panic in his eyes, "So . . . your brother will never come back?"

Tremulously, Mawu murmured, "Bullets don't have eyes."

The chopper fell from Tao Jiuxiang's hand and she slumped to the ground, catatonic. Masui howled in anguish.

"How far is Huangshui from the battleground?" asked Li Diezhu.

"By water, going there and back would take a month. By land, two months," said the short dragon seeker, sympathetically.

"After I attend to official duties, I'll go by water," Mawu said sadly, helping Tao Jiuxiang to her feet and looking into his mother's creased, aged visage.

"Can you . . . bring him back to Lihaku?" asked Li Diezhu bitterly.

"Let his soul come back home!" sobbed Masui.

"Bringing home the dead may prove difficult. Our soldiers and the Japanese devils are tangled together in a chaotic mess. Limbs are ripped from torsos; heads are severed from bodies. A mass of decapitated heads filled one pit we saw—it was impossible to distinguish one from the other," the tall geomancer interrupted, shaking his head.

Tao Jiuxiang suddenly staggered to her feet, moving unsteadily toward the dark window. "My son," she slurred. "I want my son."

Alarmed, Masui leapt to his feat, calling out, "Ma, Ma ... Mother!"

Oblivious, she stared outward. Dense sorrow clouded the skies above Gengguping.

IV

The geomancers rested two days before humbly declining Li Diezhu's entreaties that they stay on. Cupping their hands before their chests, they bowed and departed.

Despite the family's shortage of money and wrenching sorrow at Mahe's death, Mawu made good on his promise to richly reward the dragon seekers. Men of principle who admired the family of a brave, loyal soldier, the geomancers insisted on accepting only part of the sum. As the strange pair departed, Mawu read something else, something profoundly chilling, in their expressions, and though this unsettled him, he had no chance to question them further. He ordered several militiamen to see them back to Huangshui. Thus, itinerant dragon seekers, having afforded the Lis a measure of consolation, left to wander the boundless mountains, using their esoteric arts to detect celestial essences and terrestrial ethers, to locate more precious sites. Once more, Gengguping was submerged in loneliness.

In shocked disbelief at Mahe's death, Masui remained speechless for days on end. Though Mahe was about his size and build, his brother was a crack shot with quick reflexes, easily excelling him in martial prowess. He was no match for his brother playing at staves or wielding a blade. Now, however, Mahe, his dear brother, was no more. Why couldn't he have died in Mahe's place? His timorous heart ached with sadness and loss. When alone, he wailed aloud—not only for the once spirited and lively Mahe, but for himself. Two deaths in the family within a year—a wife and a younger brother. How strange!

Mawu stayed for three days before quietly departing for Huangshui, where he hired a group of workers to go to Speargrass Plain. Shortly, they began to excavate and prepare ground for the tomb. They worked from dawn to dusk, living in the nearby tenant's cabin, and following Mawu's every direction.

A few days later, Li Diezhu went to check on their progress. From afar he heard the clangorous *"ding-dang"* of the craftsmen at work. Like small twinned hillocks, mounds of stone and earth were piled high on the site. Years before, he had purchased this plot from the Xiangs. All this time, marching to and fro across this land, cutting wood and hunting, he had failed to grasp its hidden geomantic potency. Furrowing his brow, he surveyed the small plain, its grass swaying in the breeze. So perhaps these plains—and the surrounding valleys and river—really were connected to his ancestors. The thought afforded Li Diezhu a certain solace. With a sigh of sorrow, he had asked the workers to build a separate vacant tomb as a memorial for Mahe. His departed son was only eighteen, a fresh-grown footstalk of a cucumber plant—yet he had left nothing behind. What an utter tragedy! If only he could butcher the lot of those Japanese devils! At the thought, Li Diezhu heart palpitated violently and he felt a dull ache. He wished he had taken better care of Mahe. He had dreamed that Mahe and his comrades were tussling with the Japanese devils. As the Japanese devil, disheveled and wild-eyed, desperately thrust his bayonet into Mahe's chest, Li Diezhu felt as if the blade were being driven into his own midriff. Ferociously, he drove his sword forward, gutting the bastard as if he were butchering a swine. But Mahe had been cut down in the end. His dear son! Mahe was so silk-skinned as a child that when Tao Jiuxiang bathed him he was like a little loach, ever slipping out of her grasp. Li Diezhu was sick with grief at the thought of Mahe's smooth skin riddled with the bloody perforations of bayonets. Whether standing or sitting, Li Diezhu was in agony. He took a measure of solace in the conviction that before he fell, Mahe must have driven his bayonet into a number of those Japanese bastards. His son had not died in vain. Suddenly filled with a deep love for his deceased son, he wanted to build a fitting memorial tomb for Mahe's clothing and effects, one that would forever stand beside his own, so that father and son might rejoin one another as companions in the netherworld. In death, he would embrace his son and listen to Mahe's war stories.

"Yesterday, I heard that the Guomindang had driven the Japanese devils back to Henan." Standing at the edge of the tomb pit, hoe in hand, Masui reported to his father in a soft voice.

"It's always a good thing to raise more sons," hissed Li Diezhu between his teeth.

Hearing the blame in his father's words, Masui dejectedly rebutted, "Years ago, I wanted to go to school in Chongqing to take part in the anti-Japanese campaign, but you didn't let me go."

Li Diezhu said scornfully, "If you were a man, you'd go straight to the front and kill a Japanese soldier to avenge your brother's death … but if you failed to come back in one piece, your mother and I would suffer even more."

Disspirited, Masui continued, "I could have served our country by schooling, but you didn't let me continue."

Li Diezhu said sadly, "That's not true. You're the most literate fellow in Lihaku, but you can't waste your life reading books. You need to think about career and family, like your eldest brother." He stopped. Mawu was the right sort of man for battle. His hardwon position as militia Captain had brought the Lis to unprecedented heights of glory. But, oh, how sorely he regretted having not having more children!

Masui paused for a moment, grimly watching a scudding cloud. "We'll need more wood and stone for materials. We also need to pay the workers and purchase foodstuffs."

Li Diezhu watched the men hard at work on the tombs, then, furrowing his brow, said, "Between securing Mawu's position and paying the dragon seekers, we only have two hundred silver dollars at best. You figure it out."

Masui answered heavily, "We can cut costs elsewhere, but we can't have a shabby graveyard. This is the site of our Li family ancestral tombs. Tomorrow, I'll go sell the remaining goldthread."

Li Diezhu countered, "Rhizome prices are low, you know?"

Masui sighed, "I know, Pa. I'll get what I can. It's better than having an unfinished burial site for want of money."

"Master and young master, please come into my cabin to warm up." Returning from gathering kindling, the mother of Tan, the tenant farmer, seeing father and son talking on the grassy slope, called out to invite them in.

Looking up, Li Diezhu answered, "In a little while. Can you make some dinner?"

Mother Tan said cheerfully, "Right away. We have a haunch of venison."

V

Foremost herb or root under the sun,
Matching cinnabar powder, goldthread's second to none.
Evil ethers and baleful spirits—it dispels these things,
Health and longevity the wondrous rhizome brings.

This verse was written on the old wall of Master Cui's rhizome shop on the market street in Huangshui, for all buyers and sellers to see.

Masui drove his mule past the shop's entrance.

"Li Masui, it's been a long time." Shi Eryang hailed his old gambling buddy loudly, his cotton coat unbuttoned. "Let's go get a drink."

Masui shook his head. "Call in any prospective buyers. I need to sell this goldthread today."

Shi Eryang asked in amazement, "How can you sell goldthread now? The market's bottomed out."

Despondent, Masui said, "Just help me find buyers. Money's tight."

Hunkered on his slippers in front of the doorway of a teahouse, a peddler called, "Li Masui . . . long time no see. Come smoke a pipeful of opium with me."

Showing him the lumpish dried rhizome, Masui said, "Come on, help me drum up some customers."

With surprise, the peddler asked, "You been sniffin' smoke from toxic winter gourd ash? How can you sell rhizome now?"

Masui replied, "Money's tight. Just help me sell it."

The peddler grinned, "For better or worse, your eldest brother's the militia Captain. How could you folks be wanting for money?"

People congregated to see what was happening. Partly out of sympathy and partly to ingratiate himself to the Lis, a grain dealer purchased the entire load of goldthread. While drinking afterward, however, Shi Eryang criticized Masui, telling him that he was too naïve for his own good: even given the rock-bottom prices, he had sold the rhizome at a great loss. Shi then regaled Masui with an array of guaranteed get-rich-quick schemes. Duly impressed, Masui felt he had gained greater insight into the ways of the world. Hearing that Master Wang of Azure Dragon Temple was conducting a mass in Peppercorn Bend for the mother of Peng Yuju, an unsuccessful candidate on the old imperial examination, Masui hurriedly led his mule to see the ceremony, without having so much as seen his brother Mawu.

Masui reached Peng's home at dusk. Seeing the remains of paper and incense, he knew the ceremony was over—Peng's mother had been buried and the family ancestors had returned to the shrine. He quickly asked Peng, who was hushing his barking dog, "Elder brother Yuju, is the Daoist priest still here?"

Peng Yuju was one of Mawu's tenants. Reading the anxiety on Masui's face, he responded, "What's the matter, young master? The Daoist master is drinking tea."

Daoist Master Wang was resting beside the fire. When he saw a young man clad in fine cotton-cloth enter, he greeted, "Ho, Masui. Have you eaten dinner?"

Masui said politely, "No . . . thanks. I have an urgent matter for the Daoist master."

Wang asked, "So what matter has brought you such a long way to seek me out?"

After chatting casually as he sipped tea, Masui broached the subject: "My room is haunted. By night, a spectral force scatters shoes and socks around my bedchamber. Help me, Master. You performed an exorcism, so why am I still haunted?"

Thoughtfully, Wang mused, "The rites of a Daoist priest are designed to enhance blessings and to lessen karmic retribution for sins. However, efficacy depends upon the specific circumstance."

Masui frowned, casting several glances toward Peng Yuju, who, promptly taking the hint, rose, saying, "You two go on chatting . . . I need to clean the outer hall." Several of Peng's sons and nephews were about to head in to join the conversation, but Peng shooed them away with an admonitory glare.

Cutting to his true motive, Masui leaned close and whispered, "Both in this world building houses and for the netherworld building tombs, my family's expenses are great and our funds are depleted. Will you teach me alchemy?"

Master Wang said seriously, "I have no knowledge of alchemical arts, but I do have some grasp of conjury."

In great amazement, Masui asked, "What is conjury?"

Wang explained, "A conjuror's arts . . . Xia Qifa has mastered them. For example, if we were tired from walking and thirsty, I might place a stick beside the road and ask if you wanted wine. If you did, you might drink wine from the stick; if you weren't thirsty or when you'd had enough, it would revert into an ordinary stick."

"Can one use this art to create silver dollars?" asked Masui.

"Yes, it's the same principle." Wang replied.

"Please, oh wise Daoist master, show me: conjure up some silver dollars," awestruck Masui requested eagerly.

"There are twenty-four mudras one must learn to master the psionic arts, and I have only grasped nineteen. I must first perfect the remaining five codes," explained Daoist Master Wang guiltily. He added, "A code must be practiced for forty-nine days. You need to rise early every morning, pour a bowl of rainwater, and repeatedly follow a series of mudras while facing eastward. Only after you have perfected all twenty-four can you transfer objects at will. However, you can't transfer too much—just enough for one's immediate need. If you get greedy, not only will the transfer fail, but worse, you'll have no offspring. Xia Qifa can teach you this art."

Disappointed, Masui asked, "So even if I learn it, I can't use it that much. Daoist master, do you have any better magical means to obtain money?"

Wang glanced at his disciples, coming in and out of the room carrying his gongs, drums, and other ritual instruments. He answered, "There is one other path, but I dare not speak of it casually."

Masui entreated, "No matter. Let's step outside and you can tell me at the gate."

Hesitantly, Wang supped a mouthful of tea before rising and walking slowly from the room. He had a narrow face. His forehead was bare. The tufts of hair on the back of his head were gathered in a small, tight braid. As he walked, he drew a melon-seed skullcap from his pouch and set it on his head. Masui followed on his heels.

Bringing in a platter of roasted peanuts, Peng Yuju saw them leaving and hurriedly inquired, "Daoist master, where are you headed?"

"Just out into your yard to enjoy the breeze," Master Wang answered. For a few moments, Masui and Wang stood under a pear tree, looking over the darkening fields in the faint moonlight.

Courteously, Masui began, "It's just the two of us. You can tell me now."

Remaining silent for a spell, Master Wang listened to the high-pitched chorus of frogs and insects. Finally, he whispered, "At high noon of the fifth day of the fifth lunar month, the day of the Dragon Boat Festival, wander the wilderlands, the mountains and gullies, until you encounter two snakes sporting around, one large and the other small. If you see the big snake swallow the smaller one, disgorge it, then swallow it again, just bide your time and don't interfere. But when the big snake swallows the smaller one for a third time, and the small snake's head is still projecting from its mouth, make your move: with a machete cut the big snake in two seven inches behind its head. That way you'll get both snakeheads; folk around here call it the "poisonous amphisbaena." Then take it home, dry it in the sun and wind, and soak it in jar of liquor. After you have steeped it for a long while, dry it in the sun again. When a family is holding a grand forty-nine-day funeral, leave the "poisonous amphisbaena" in a bowl of rice on the site the rite is being performed so that only the nose shows. Don't let the host find the bowl, otherwise he'll make you pay compensation. Once all of the Buddhist scriptures have been incanted, the potency of the magic will take effect. On the ninth day of each lunar month, burn incense in a bowl along with two silver dollars. The following morning the bowl will be brimming with silver! Remember, don't use too big a bowl. Follow this recipe, and you can amass a tremendous fortune."

"It must be noon on the day of the Dragon Boat Festival?" said Masui curiously.

"Exactly," answered Wang. "That is the moment when the venom of the hundred crawling creatures reaches its greatest potency."

Disappointed, Masui said, "It's wildly unlikely that anyone would come across the two snakes at precisely high noon on the Dragon Boat Festival. That's too much trouble. How about lending me a parcel of prime land beside Azure Dragon Temple, and letting me grow silver dollars there?"

Taken aback, Wang stared at Masui and asked, "And what will you plant?"

"Nowadays, the price of goldthread keeps plummeting," said Masui importantly. "But opium has become a big seller. Let me rent out several acres land from the temple to grow opium poppies. After the harvest, I'll sell them in Enshi secretly for ten times the price of goldthread!"

"Our temple owns a patch of woodland—but the disciples depend on that land to raise a few crops to provide money for incense, candles, and food," Wang answered, trying hard to maintain calm. Built during the early Qing dynasty, Azure Dragon Temple owned and superintended seven acres of woodland. Long-term laborers were hired to work and protect their land, while outsiders were forbidden by law from harvesting timber on temple property.

Masui persisted, presenting Shi Eryang's get-rich-quick scheme to Master Wang: "Once I turn a huge profit from the opium, I'll use the silver to buy the temple several cartloads of rice, five gallons of *tung* oil, and get all of the your disciples new robes for every season. Master, you and your disciples will be living the good life!"

"As Daoists, we cannot break government law," Wang said, looking downward as he stroked his chin.

"Outsiders can't enter temple grounds. Nobody will know as long as you keep it secret," Masui continued shamelessly. "The Mayor smokes opium. And even if the secret gets out, as militia Captain my elder brother Mawu will shelter us."

Wang raised his head, looking into the darkness beyond, and said, "This humble Daoist monk dares not agree with your proposal."

"Think it over. Stop by Gengguping anytime for a cup of tea," Masui responded glumly, defeated.

Chapter Eleven

I

From afar the flood dragon, protruding from the cliff, its tortured visage peering out from the stone prison where the creature had been long immured, gazed beyond the clustered bamboo groves, past the shimmering gold rice paddies, to the Xia homestead. Over the past decade, Xia Qifa had shaped the valley, taming its wildness. On this long-anticipated day, his home had become the site of the grand ceremony in which he would formally transmit the shamanic arts to his son Xia Liangxian, and initiate the youth as a *tima*.

Carrying a load of rice and *tung* oil, Mawu led several militiamen, Sun Fu, Masui, and his heavy-hearted father into Dragon Decapitating Gorge. Flanked by his two sons, astride a sturdy yellow horse, Li Diezhu rode deliberately. Several mountainfolk squatted at the gate to Xia household using hammer and knife to cut thick, coarse yellow rice straw paper into floral patterns. Everyone knew that this yellow paper was the only currency spirits accepted. As he tore the tiger-yellow straw paper to kindle the fire, Xia Qifa welcomed Li Diezhu.

Divided into three parts—upper, middle, and lower—a labyrinthine genealogical chart hung from the wall of the main hall, an elaborate diagram featuring images of various immortals and spirits. On the topmost echelon was Celestial Sovereign; in the middle, the Three Sovereign Ancestors, the holy ancestors of the clan; and on the bottom, the Five Furies marshaling soldiers to assist the superior immortals. Knowing the importance of this ceremony, on the previous day Xia Qifa had addressed prayers to the entire pantheon: "Respectfully, oh spirits and immortals, I pray you rouse yourselves and come forth, whether riding in your spirit carriages, trekking by fleet foot, or taking wing:

> *Your awe-inspiring might shaking heaven and earth,*
> *From great temples on mountaintops and lesser shrines on hillocks.*
> *O spirits of heaven and earth, wise ancestors and teachers,*
> *I pray you come to my assistance.*

After singsong chanting the whole night through, spirits and immortals from every quarter, from mountain eyries and underwater palaces, congregated in Xia Qifa's courtyard. Adhering to principle, the female divinities and spirits filled the inner quarters, while male deities and immortals gathered in the main hall; so crowded with spirits was the Xia household that one latecomer had to squat atop a woven bamboo basket, while another stood on a rice bucket. Their invisible bustle and soundless clamor filled the household.

Several assistants made their way through the on-lookers carrying a newly cut banana trunk, thick as a human head. As they set the seven-foot trunk upright on the millstone in the hall, they were spattered with jets of fresh, viscous liquid.

Xia Qifa strode toward the banana trunk, then, running his hands from bottom to top, chanted forcefully:

> *O tree let your sap run at the touch of my hand;*
> *Flow and cease at my command.*
> *One mouthful dries the Yangzi's eastward flow,*
> *Staunch your flow, tree; stop, don't go!*

With the chanting, the copious flow from the trunk stopped at once. A collective sigh escaped the marveling throngs.

The oxhorn thundered from Xia Qifa's yard. The shaman's disciples formed a human ladder and affixed a four-foot tall spirit tablet to the top of the banana trunk, which rose above the roofs, a totem to ward off demons and evil spirits.

One after another, mountainfolk arrived bearing wine, meat, money, and rice. Li Diezhu watched as ward headman Qin and his third son Qin Lieniu toted a crock of fermented corn liquor; Zhou Taiwang brought a basket of fresh artemisia leaves; Jin Shaosan presented tea and a sheaf of tobacco leaves. Elderly scholar-gentleman Wang Binquan, too, arrived on horseback, along with other neighbors.

"If only the *tima* had given Mahe a protective amulet, he would have survived the battle," bleary-eyed Sun Fu sat heavily on the ground.

Xie Chongmin, a mountain dweller from Shi Family Embankment, said, "That's right! My son just got drafted. I'm gonna to ask for an amulet."

Another fellow chimed in, "My second son just left to join the army. Who knows if I'll ever see him again?"

Masui stopped writing and said, "Uncle Xia, when a Japanese plane crashed on the outskirts of Fengjie City, the devil pilot was burned with blisters all over his face. He had a protective amulet with the same design as yours."

Xie Chongmin asked, "What did that Japanese devil look like?"

The other fellow questioned, "Did he have horns on his head with daggers mounted on them?"

Masui replied, "No, he looked similar to us except he was severely wounded. I couldn't understand a word he said."

Learning of Mahe's death, Xia Qifa sighed despondently, "Long ago, following the Qingjiang River and its labyrinthine tributaries our ancestors reached the edge of the world. As the ancient songs reveal,

> *Heavenly fire burns the sun,*
> *Earthly fire scorches forests and sand;*
> *Righteous lightning fire*
> *Immolates all of the wicked in the land.*
> *Into the river we launch dragon boats,*
> *Nowhere in the five lakes and four seas we can't float.*

When a dragon boat embarks upon the river it can reach the Five Lakes or the Four Seas—any point in the world."

"Is Japan at the edge of the world?" mused Xie Chongmin.

"The earth is a sphere. There are no edges," Qin Lieniu answered. Home on vacation from a modern school in Fengjie City, he was seventeen. Knowing the conscription law "one son for a family of three, two for a family of five," he planned to enlist in the army the next year when he came of age.

"The so-called 'edge' refers to the farthest extent of the world known to boatmen at the time. In ancient times, before the rivers were all dammed and dried up, even a little wooden scull could reach the farthest end of the world."

Wang Binquan, wearing a scholarly black skullcap, explained.

Swallowing a mouthful of saliva, eyes bulging, Li Diezhu seethed, "If our ancestors reached Japan, why didn't they butcher the bastards?"

"Heaven alone knows how to rid the world of such evil spirits!" Xia Qifa gave a deep sigh tinged with sorrow.

> *A thousand-year battle and our blades never rust,*
> *Fighting till the wicked demons turn to dust.*

Xie Chongmin recited two lines of an ancient song.

"Did *timas* go to the front and save our soldiers?" wondered Old He, Masui's father-in-law. When he had received the death gratuity for his fallen son He Wanwan, he had wept the whole night through.

"If a *tima* accompanied the troops, they'd be unbeatable—it'd be like King Wu of Zhou leading the righteous campaign against wicked last ruler of Shang!" Xie Chongmin cried.

"Soldiers could be grouped by village, with a shaman leading each brigade," ward chief Qin suggested to Li Diezhu. "No more officers bullying enlisted men out of their pay—or slapping, beating, and cursing them. Mawu could propose this to his superior officers."

Mawu told to him, "It wouldn't work. The troops don't believe in our gods."

"People think we're backward savages!" cried Xie Chongmin excitedly. "They don't know that our tiger ancestors were the vanguard of King Wu campaign against evil last ruler of Shang!"

Qin Lieniu interjected, "They were called tiger warriors!"

Jin Shaosan drifted to another topic. "*Tima*, even your grain is magic. Last summer, five of my goats were stricken with a pestilence and died. The rest of the herd was sick and I couldn't figure out why. When I saw you selling fava beans in the Huangshui market at a low price, I figured I'd feed them to my goats. So I bought thirty or forty pounds of beans; the next day when I fed them out, the goats had all recovered."

Squinting, Xia Qifa explained, "My fava beans were damp and getting moldy."

Gazing at Jin Shaosan disapprovingly, Wang Binquan opined, "The wet beans probably grew a kind of mildew that fortuitously cured your sick goats."

II

Deep into the night, tired mountainfolk chatted around a bonfire. When he had finished drawing amulets for the pair of newly enlisted soldiers, Xia Qifa lit his pipe from the flames. Moving aside to make room for the *tima* on a section of tree-trunk, a bleary-eyed militiaman suggested, "*Tima*, how about showing us a magic trick?"

"Come on!" the congregated mountainfolk urged, turning their attention to Xia Qifa. Though they had long heard tell of his mystical powers, they knew he rarely causally revealed his powers.

Desiring to dispel the sorrowful atmosphere, heavy with ominous rumors of war, Xia Qifa went into his house and shortly returned holding a steelyard in one hand and an earthenware urn of rice, sealed with a red piece of paper, in the other, a gift from Xie Chongmin. Though he had chanted the whole night through, he did not betray the slightest hint of fatigue. With every set of eyes fixed upon him, Xia Qifa thrust the arm of the steelyard through the red paper covering the urn's mouth, then lifted the heavy vessel off the ground by the steelyard's arm.

Recognizing the earthen urn that he had gifted the shaman, Xie Chongmin knew that it contained twenty pounds of rice. "Whoa ... let me have a try." But when he took the steelyard beam in hand and tried to lift the urn, it did not budge an inch.

"Hunh?" The mountain folk cried out in amazement. Crowding forward, they saw that the jar was filled to the brim with rice.

"*Tima*," asked Xie Chongmin, incredulous, "How did you do that?"

"Take care with the grip as you raise it up." So saying, Xia Qifa lifted the urn again in the same manner. Folk clustered round the *tima* like a colony of mice swarming a fresh-cut field of grain.

Grasping the beam of the steelyard with great care, Xie Chongmin tried to lift the urn once more. Failing yet again, he turned to the shaman, captivated, and asked, "*Tima*, teach us a few of your magical tricks."

Xia Qifa said, "If you lack wisdom, you cannot grasp the shamanic arts; if you lack practical knowledge, you cannot grasp shamanic arts; if you lack perseverance and commitment, you cannot grasp the shamanic arts. Unless you are the right sort of man, you'll injure yourself and others."

Using a burning twig to light his pipe of tobacco, Old Li Erdie, one of the

Xias neighbors from a nearby ridge, sighed, " 'while back, powerful as *Tima* Wu of Huangshui used to be, one of his lazy disciples failed to grasp his teachings. Once when this disciple performed a rite, he was unable to control the tutelary spirit. Then and there, a small snake the size of an earthworm emerged. Slithering up a tree, it grew into a grotesque serpent. He had summoned the creature, but had no idea how to make it go away. An ominous blue fire enveloped the entire building, though the flames caused no damage. Unable to deal with the crisis, he sent a sedan chair to fetch his master. Though *Tima* Wu was in his eighties and looked feeble, as soon as he arrived he blew his spiral horn several times and the fire went out. Looking at the snake wrapped round the tree, *Tima* Wu brandished his sword and railed, "Dog-fucked cur, why do you not heed my command? Bull-fucked wretch, why do you not follow my directions? Dog-fucked reprobate, why not become smaller? Bull-fucked degenerate, how can you return to your proper place without growing smaller?" No one knew whether *Tima* Wu's furious curses were directed at disciple or snake. In any case, the snake crawled down the tree, shrinking smaller and smaller so that by the time it reached the altar it was the size of an earthworm again. On his deathbed, *Tima* Wu told his disciple that if he ever encountered a spirit he couldn't dismiss, he merely needed to unleash a similar barrage of curses. Nevertheless the locals had lost faith in the dog-fucked disciple, and after Old Wu passed away nobody invited him to perform rites.' "

Xia Qifa mused, "Hard as the shamanic arts are to learn, they're far more difficult to transmit." For better than a decade, every time *Tima* Xia had gone to perform a rite, his son Liangxian had accompanied him, helping with all sorts of preparations: sifting and curing ritual ingredients in a bamboo-framed sieve and preparing libationary vessels, lighting incense sticks and burning paper, beating the gong and intoning background chants. At rest, he constantly instructed his son, explaining nuances of rites, subtle tricks of the trade. Like most shamans, Xia Qifa found the phrase *"Tima* of a Cold Altar"— meaning that a shaman had failed to pass down his arts and teachings to a successor—utterly unbearable and humiliating. This was an abhorrent crime against men and spirits alike. Fortunately, promising and clever—though lacking the gravitas of his father—Xia Liangxian had mastered most of the hundred arts, memorizing countless chants and ceremonial regulations.

Approaching Li Diezhu, Jin Shaosan, reeking of a heavy perfume of alcohol, solicitously said, "Old friend, you'd better take a nap."

As he huddled with the others ringing the bonfire awaiting the initiation the following afternoon, the flickering tongues of fire illumined Li Diezhu's haggard visage. Sadly, he answered, "I'm not tired."

"Listen to this," interrupted Erniang, Li Erdie's wife. "Earlier this summer I had an ache in my breast so I came to see the *tima*. In his courtyard, a horse-dragon in the form of a rainbow was drinking water, while he watched from under the eaves. As soon as I hailed him, the horse-dragon shot back up into the heavens."

Picking up the strand of conversation, motioning toward the yonder cliff face, her husband Old Li Erdie continued, "The fir tree growing on the forehead of the immured water dragon is turning greener. The rainbow must have been that water dragon; I doubt another dragon visited from heaven. Every day, the tender-hearted *tima* begs King Yu to have mercy on the imprisoned dragon, believing it can change its wicked ways and cultivate goodness."

Xia Qifa said thoughtfully, "When the creature first took the shape of a water dragon, he wrought such great calamity and havoc, causing mountains to crumble and great surging floods to inundate the lands, leaving a vast swath of destruction in his wake, that King Yu had to control him with lightning bolts, thunder claps, torrential rains, and gale-force winds. Even if the water dragon had fled to the Eastern Sea, King Yu would have had the huge golden-winged *peng* bird swallow him."

Old Li Erdie said, "Some years back on a thundering pitch black night, I saw King Yu's golden lightning hooks fix that trembling dragon to the cliff."

All of a sudden, Wang Binquan suggested, "Look how smooth the cliff face under the dragon is. There's hardly any trees or grass. As a reminder to posterity, we could carve a commemorative inscription of the names of the local soldiers, martyrs who have died in the War of Resistance."

"That's a great idea. I'll mention it to the Mayor!" Mawu cried, his eyes sparkling.

A chorus of mountainfolk clamored: "Absolutely!"

"Protected by our young heroes, we'll be safe from all monsters and devils."

At this juncture, a slim young girl arrived, clad in a short blue jacket trimmed in black and a pair of black trousers. She moved gracefully, a spring to her nimble step. Set beneath upturned lashes and delicately arched brows, her "vermilion phoenix" eyes were narrow and long, flashing a clear, piercing light. Mawu felt that she looked familiar. He found the indescribable charm of her poise as enthralling as the mysterious, mottled patterns of a peacock's plumage.

"Dad," said the little girl. Reaching Xia Qifa, she tugged at his sleeve, "Ma wants you." Xia Qifa rose and followed her back to the house. Transported, Mawu's gaze followed her every movement.

III

"Folks, fellow neighbors!" shouted Xia Qifa, "Thank you one and all for coming to witness the ordination of my new successor. In coming years, please offer him your support."

"Congratulations on finding a worthy disciple to carry on your enterprise," Wang Binquan pronounced solemnly.

"Congratulations! May you visit one thousand families, enjoy great popularity, and confer tremendous benefit upon us all." Mawu proposed the first toast to Xia Liangxian at the midday feast, cheerfully raising a cup of liquor in his honor.

To entertain his guests, Xia Qifa dug out a huge earthenware crock of liquor that he had buried three years earlier. And so it was, under the influence of the piquant liquor, that several score of his countrymen witnessed the ceremony in which the *tima* transmitted his shamanic arts to his son and disciple.

After dinner, Xia Liangxian hung a long string of firecrackers from a branch of a willow tree outside the gate. He asked several relatives of soldiers to shoot bamboo tubes filled with gunpowder skyward to ignite the firecrackers. The loud and festive crackling and popping would mark the formal start of the ceremony.

Eagerly, Old He seized and lit the thickest bamboo tube, firing a colorful spray of sparks toward the firecrackers. He failed to light the firecrackers: some sparks shot far above the string, while others died away too quickly. Next, Sun Fu came forward, chose a medium-sized bamboo tube, lit it, and fired, but he too failed. Well aware of the challenge of lighting firecrackers with such a bamboo cannon, Mawu selected a stubby tube, added powder, set it on the ground, and lit it. The thick spray of sparks shot upward, finally igniting the stubborn fuses of the firecrackers, and setting off a loud rat-a-tat-tat chain of sound.

Vaguely conscious of a vivacious, limpid gaze of admiration fixed upon his person, Mawu vainly scanned the crowd for its source. Sensing that lingering gaze once more, silent and close like an animate creature, a leopard stalking prey, Mawu turned in another direction and, for a moment, locked eyes with a young girl. Abashed, she turned away.

Mawu rose and strode over to her, asking gently, "Are you Yinmei? You've grown tall. Do you still remember me?"

"Yes, I remember my elder brother Mawu," said Yinmei, with her silvery, mellifluous voice, her cheeks blushing crimson as she met his stare.

"I hardly recognize you. You've grown into a beautiful young woman," said Mawu in surprise. But at that very moment, the image of Mahe overwhelmed him in bitter wave of sorrow.

From the bonfire outside the gate, Li Diezhu raised his head and looked toward the pair. He figured that the young woman did not know of Mahe's death. With a sigh, he said, "Yinmei, this is Mawu, your elder brother."

Brightly, she responded, "I know. Liangxian told me that that my two elder brothers, Mawu and Masui, and you, Uncle Li, were all coming."

Li Diezhu looked at Yinmei affectionately. Four years younger than Mahe, at fourteen she had grown tall and beautiful. As his thoughts naturally returned to his youngest son, he was wracked a heartrending sadness.

A sonorous drumbeat began. Donning his feathered headdress and clad in a long gown, deerskin pouch in hand, Xia Qifa ran out of the yard like a golden pheasant, moving toward the woods behind the house with Xia Liangxian trailing close behind, a frenzied expression on his handsome face. Lifting his red skirts as he frantically ran like a crazy witch, the *tima* sped on till he disappeared from the sight of the congregation. Turning abruptly, he breathlessly asked his son, "Is anyone behind us?"

Xia Liangxian, raising his blade-straight eyebrows, answered, "There is one far behind us!" His father had taught him this answer beforehand—for the ceremony of ordination and succession this was a pivotal moment. In the presence of gods, he could not answer "yes," or else his father would not choose him as successor; nor could he answer "no," for then the *tima* would have neither successor nor offspring.

Relieved, Xia Qifa stopped, hiked up the hem of his skirt, and sat cross-legged on a bed of pine needles. Craning his neck skyward, he focused on a distant, drifting cloud. Waving a hand toward the cloud, Xia Qifa captured it, and with a flourish fashioned a splendid nimbus above his head. Xia Liangxian knelt before his father, sweat beading, rivulets running down his cheeks. Surrounded by a mulberry trees and evergreen firs—trees that reached the heavens—father and son sat together. Hidden by the boughs of the sacrosanct grove, under the aegis of the cloud, Xia Qifa passed on to his son and disciple all the esoteric mantras and special techniques for using ritual vessels, the mudras and secret chants, of the river shamans.

Hours later, father and son emerged with brambles, pine needles, and straw clinging to their clothing. Silently Li Diezhu and the gathered guests gazed at father and son, seeing that Xia Liangxian now held the deerskin pouch, and that Xia Qifa's face radiated a new contentment.

Xia Qifa had cut down the banana tree in front of the house, and in its place put two black-lacquered square tables. After burning incense and casting the trigrams, he spread a ten-foot long blue cloth over the two tables. Then a disciple, acting as an assistant, held up a tray with ten cups of wine in preparation for the *tima*'s libation.

Among the onlookers were a handful of wives and girls, including the shaman's bright daughter, Yinmei. Before the ceremony, Xia Qifa repeatedly urged his assistants to concentrate single-mindedly upon their duties, not casting stray glances into the crowd: in performing the libation, not a single drop of liquor could be spilled! As a result, his disciples, nervous yet focused, conscientiously burned incense and paper for the gods. Riveted, the crowd dumbly beheld the rite as a growing cluster of supernatural beings gathered, hidden, both inside and the yard of the Xia household and beyond the gates.

Xia Liangxian appeared in his newly fashioned ritual robes and feathered headdress. His sharp-featured light brown face set against the festive red of his ceremonial garb, the young man cut a dashing figure. Coming out of the haze of incense, Xia Qifa solemnly hung an embroidered pouch around his son's neck. Six months earlier, at Xia Qifa's request, Old Li Erniang had instructed her ten-year-old granddaughter to embroider the pouch—it could only be stitched by a pre-pubescent girl. When it was finished, Xia Liangxian spent weeks carefully writing the names and ages of generations of past *timas*—finally coming to his father's name and his own—along with mantras and charms, onto a piece of paper which he folded and sewed into the lining like a memorial to the throne. For a newly ordained *tima*, this was a certificate of validation; once it was sewn into the embroidered "certification pouch," nobody would see it again. Shrouded in mystery and secrecy, the pouch conferred upon the young *tima* an air of legitimacy. It remained with a shaman until his death, when, in accord with ceremonial rules, it was burned to ashes.

Solemn and silent, like the stage of a drama, the audience hall had been arrayed with two square tables. Seated at one table, Xia Qifa, in his fifties, inwardly was profoundly moved to see his son Liangxian kneel before the other. Between the two tables was fixed a white length of cloth, a "bridge" connecting the *tima* to his chosen successor. "Behold," he began, instructing his son. "You must maintain perspective and humility, never making show of your ability or acting with malice, but abiding by the following rules. First, you must never curse Heaven and Earth, for they are my father and mother; second, you must never casually or capriciously summon the wind or rain, for they are my elder and younger brothers; third, you must never vainly call forth divine soldiers; and fourth, you must use mantras, charms, and spells with great care and responsibility."

Xia Liangxian knelt before the "bridge" and prostrated himself, then blew the oxhorn to signal his agreement.

After gravely enumerating the ten prohibitions, Xia Qifa bestowed the ten benedictions, conferring his most heartfelt good wishes upon his son.

"I will keep all of these in mind," said Xia Liangxian readily, his almond-shaped eyes flashing. Finally he had become a respected *tima* like his father, attaining the status and position he had yearned for since childhood.

As unending noisy chains of firecrackers exploded, firelight and the moon above illumined the space outside the gate. With chopsticks, a disciple tweezed a piece of raw meat from a platter set for the gods and held it before Xia Qifa's mouth. The *tima* brushed it with his lips. The disciple then presented the morsel to Xia Liangxian, who chewed and swallowed the ceremonial sliver. Once again, the powers and the arts of the old *tima* were symbolically transmitted to his son and successor.

Brandishing swords, father and son leapt off the tables, their red skirts opening wide like umbrellas as they danced and chanted:

> Lore handed down from the venerable master of old,
> To our grandmaster and master's master transmitted and told.
> Spirits batten themselves to me, make this body divine,
> Deities take possession, spirit perfected and body refined.

All you supernatural beings, among my disciples concealed,
When I summon you forth, you shall be revealed.
A hundred times, a thousand times, no matter where you're hidden,
When I call you forth, oh spirits do my bidding!

The succession rites of the river shamans were complicated. In the chant, without exception, Xia Qifa mentioned each of his predecessors. He danced so gracefully and vigorously that he seemed to depart the earthy world and enter a trance. Though Xia Liangxian had studied the choreographed steps of this dance from the age of five, the sprightly youth lacked his formidable father's skill.

On and on, father and son danced in concert, following the off-kilter paces of Yu the Great; like gracefully reeling drunkards they treaded the seven stars of the Dipper, entering a frenzied ecstasy. Every time Xia Qifa chanted two or three lines, Xia Liangxian turned a circle. Overall, the young man performed thirty-three vigorous circumambulations before fainting and falling to the ground: he had ascended to the thirty-third layer of Heaven in spirit, and finally had become a master *tima*!

IV

As the curtain of night began to rise revealing a faint light in the east, another burst of fireworks resounded. The fragrant smoke of burning cypress commingled with the sulfurous reek of gunpowder, a heady incense adding to the festal aura of the night. Beneath this cloud of incense, the congregated folks found themselves lost in an otherworldly trance. Enrapt, careworn Li Diezhu and his sons, Mawu and Masui, for the moment forgot their heartaches.

The narrow strip of dawning sky slowly broadened and brightened, though the surrounding mountains remained dark and silent. From dusk to dawn, the Yinmei and her mother tirelessly busied themselves preparing food and drink for mortals and spirits alike, leaving them smudged with ash and reeking of smoke. Xia Qifa's disciples not only assisted in lighting candles and burning incense, but also served buckwheat cakes, dofu, and tea. Only after respectfully offering food and drink to the spirits amid a clamor of cymbals and gongs did they turn their ministrations to serving breakfast to their mountain neighbors.

The horizon reddened anticipating sunrise. Men and spirits, both astir, followed their separate paths. Li Diezhu told Mawu that he wanted to stay on with Xia Qifa for a couple of days to chat with his old friend. Mawu asked Masui to stay with their father, giving him a rifle, before heading back to Huangshui with his militiamen.

Torches in hand, the mountainfolk said their goodbyes. On horseback and foot, a party of a dozen, including Sun Fu, Old He, and ward chief Qin and his son, embarked for Gengguping. Jin Shaosan and a group of fellow townsmen headed toward Peppercorn Bend Hamlet. Xie Chongmin and a fellow villager from Shi Family Embankment were among the most satisfied as they departed, both clasping the protective amulets the *tima* had drawn for their sons.

Worried that his father would collapse from exhaustion after two sleepless nights, Masui urged, "Dad, you'd better go take a nap."

Li Diezhu nodded his assent. Xia Qifa, having seen off the various spirits and immortals, set up a bed for his old friend.

What a sound sleep Li Diezhu enjoyed! Wicked spirits and baleful influences had been banished, swept away from every corner of the Xia homestead. For the first time since he had learned of Mahe's death, he slept soundly. After helping Xia Qifa put away his ritual implements, Masui, too, passed out on Xia Liangxian's bed. The *tima* distributed cash to his disciples, and sent them off. Only after an entire morning's toil did the Xia family finally settle in for a nap.

Hunger awakened Li Diezhu in the mid-afternoon. Slipping on his sandals, he shuffled to the stove and sat beside it. Rubbing his eyes, Xia Qifa emerged from his bedroom. Masui and Xia Liangxian were talking in the kitchen, helping Yinmei and her mother serve a late lunch on the square table. Over the hot meal, Masui hunted for topics to chat with Yinmei, while Li Diezhu sat silently in a trance-like malaise. Xia Qifa understood the nature of his old friend's anguish; he, too, was deeply saddened by the loss of Mahe. To alleviate Li Diezhu's sorrow, the shaman told him, "When the White Tiger Immortal led his people forth from the stone caves, after endless bloodshed and battle, they carved out a realm in these gorges. After they were defeated, they fled along the endless streams and tributaries of the ancient river to the edge of the world, taking with them the legendary River Chart of the Nine Provinces designed by flood-queller King Yu the Great. A prophecy tells that together they rose to become the White Tiger constellation, and that everywhere those stars shed their light would be ensanguined by countless massacres, bloody uprisings, and wanton destruction; but from this blood the people of the White Tiger would rise again. This prophecy has been passed on for centuries, from one *tima* to the next. Listen, my friend, Mahe was sent by the White Tiger Immortal to save our homeland from war and devastation. Now he's returned to the White Tiger's side, where he can enjoy the incense and offerings of his living kinsmen. Set your mind at ease. The wicked Japanese devils, guilty of endless murderous atrocities, cannot escape the retributive thunder of heaven and hellfire from below!"

Li Diezhu sighed, "Gladly I'd sacrifice these old bones for a chance to go with Mawu and get rid of those bastards!"

Masui flushed, feeling that his father was obliquely criticizing his uselessness. He grumbled discontentedly, "If the White Tiger Immortal has flown up to become a constellation, how could we be his offspring anyway?"

"Where a tiger treads, traces of fur are left behind; where wind blows, soughing is heard in its wake. Our ancestors have left their coffins along the steep cliffs. Let's go into the mountains and take a look." With a gesture of empathy, Xia Qifa invited father and son. Xia Liangxian scrambled to his feet and joined them.

From their vantage they could see, projecting from the cliff opposite, the head of the majestic dragon that King Yu the Great had captured and imprisoned. The boughs of fir tree growing on the dragon's brow looked fuller and greener.

> *Made from a chain of white mountain flowers,*
> *This rope binds immortals, a lasso of power;*
> *I deliver it to you, my successor,*
> *In order to capture the calamitous dragon.*

> *From a hundred woven stalks of grass forged,*
> *This blade decapitates immortals, divine sword;*
> *I deliver it to you, my successor,*
> *To decapitate the wicked dragon...*

Completing the chant, Xia Qifa went on, "Seeking to gain power by returning to the ocean, that wicked creature made a frenzied rush for the sea, causing havoc—spinning off tornadoes, prompting mountains to crumble and rivers to flood. In the end, however, it was captured, trussed up, and has been imprisoned in the cliff for thousands of years. The dragon has suffered, enduring horrible punishments: Its liver and lungs were cut out, sliced up, and minced into paste. To atone for its wicked conduct, the unfortunate creature swore to cultivate goodness. After seventy-seven transformations, it finally emerged from its prison of stone as an earthworm, wriggling in the muck, ever bitterly plowing earth in the fields, never gazing at the heavens above."

"If that's true, why do we burn incense for the dragon?" Xia Liangxian asked, puzzled.

"The calamity-bringing beast has been immured for many years. If the dragon sincerely repents, King Yu the Great may still decide to save it. I would like to witness its atonement and release." Xia Qifa told his son.

Deeply moved, Xia Liangxian asked, "Once its freed, will the dragon fly away?"

"Of course. At that moment, there will be a heavy thunderstorm and the cliff will collapse." Xia Qifa furrowed his brow, looking toward the protruding stone head.

"I want to see it transform into a true dragon and soar into the heavens," Xia Liangxian said.

"It depends. If he doesn't rectify his conduct, it might never happen."

"And if he misbehaves, or can't change?" asked wide-eyed Xia Liangxian.

"Then never again may he assume his form as a dragon."

"He will ever remain an earthworm," said Xia Liangxian, turning to Masui.

Xia Qifa added sympathetically, "Therefore, he must strive to cultivate virtue."

"Uncle Xia, what signs would reveal that the dragon has expiated its sins?" Masui asked skeptically.

Gazing fixedly at the stark cliff, Xia Qifa answered, "The fir on its brow will grow taller, its needles will become deeper green, and the stone lotus on the mountain will bloom."

"A stone can blossom?" Masui responded in shock.

Xia Qifa replied, "The bare stone lotus will grow a coat of moss so dense that it appears as a green efflorescence."

Listening to Masui and Xia Qifa, the image of a golden firebird, the gargantuan immortal avian the mountainfolk spoke of with hushed wonderment, winged suddenly into Li Diezhu's mind. If only, he cursed inwardly, giving voice to his boundless indignation, such a divine bird would soar across the Eastern Sea and swallow the lot of those Japanese demons, those odious jackals, leaving behind the crunched-up remnants of their bones for feral dogs to gnaw.

V

Li Diezhu's spirits had risen after his two days of recuperation at the Xia household. On the third day, taking leave of the *tima*, he and Masui departed. As the journey from the *tima*'s home to Gengguping spanned fifteen miles of rugged terrain, father and son ended up passing the night in a hunter's cabin along the route. Leaving early the following morning, by noon their horses reached Arrow Bamboo Gulch, an arcing five-mile bend in Inkblack Creek before its waters passed through Speargrass Plain and joined the Enshi River. From afar, Li Diezhu heard the clangorous sounds of laborers from Speargrass Plain and knew that the workers and craftsmen were toiling to build his tomb.

From the vantage of an embankment, father and son beheld the newly raised earthen mounds of the empty tombs; before one were scattered burned incense, paper, lit candles, and fragments of firecrackers. "Venerable master," a builder paused to say, "Yesterday, Captain Li delivered two pieces of Mahe's clothing. He instructed us to place the clothing in the coffin before burying it. Please take a look and see if we've done it right?"

Mahe's tomb mound was set next to Li Diezhu's own future tumulus. Offering the builder a cigarette rolled in a tobacco leaf, Li Diezhu said, "Well done. Thanks for the hard work!" He settled on a stool that Masui had taken from a nearby tenant's cabin, thoughtfully drawing on his pipe. After a moments, he ordered, "I'll have more incense and paper delivered. Remember to burn them for Mahe every day."

Just as Li Diezhu finished his pipe, Masui emerged from the tenant's home, summoning his father and the builders for lunch.

Refreshed after their midday repast, father and son set off once again. As the sun dipped below the western mountains, an orderly phalanx of several dozen dholes appeared on the opposite hill slope, advancing at a leisurely pace. Seemingly oblivious to the appearance of Li Diezhu and Masui, the pack never broke ranks. Li Diezhu was alarmed to discover that the dholes were arrayed in the very same formation as the divine brigands who haunted his dreams. Even a spirit tiger would steer clear of a pack of this size! Tensely, Li Diezhu clasped the rifle Mawu had left him. Masui rode before him on a white horse, his fear palpable.

Warily proceeding, each side gave the other a wide berth. When the dholes entered the forest, however, they, recognizing Li Diezhu as the very hunter who had fired at them as they attacked the wild ox, fled pell-mell. Though the evening was crisp, Masui, profoundly relieved, was soaked to the bone with perspiration.

By degrees, it grew dark. Holding torches, Masui rode in the lead; Li Diezhu followed on his roan horse. As they approached Zhou Damei's grave, the dense forest closed in on them. An icy, soughing wind moaned, a chilling sound like the exhalation of spirits whistled through the tangled branches. Neither could tell whether the unearthly groans issued from earth or mountain, man or animal, immortal or god.

"What's that noise?" gasped Li Diezhu, "What was that?" Something moved off to the side of the path; an ominous sibilant exhalation followed.

"It's her," cried Masui. "It's her!"

"Nonsense!" reproached Li Diezhu.

A moment later, Masui cried again, "Listen! That voice just now . . . speaking, maybe singing . . . a chorus of voices."

A sequence of singsong groans rolled through the air, rhythmic murmurs that made their flesh crawl.

"*Aiyo!*" cried Masui, holding the reins in one hand and his torch in the other, "I'm busting for a shit."

"Hurry up," said Li Diezhu hesitantly, "Give me your torch."

Leaping from his horse, Masui passed his father the torch. "I'll be quick with it," he rejoined, hunkering at the foot of a banyan tree. Brows furrowed, Li Diezhu also dismounted, striding forward a couple of paces and ungirding his belt for a piss.

"Don't throw it at me! Don't!" cried out Masui in quailing horror.

"Who are you talking to?" Li Diezhu skeptically turned toward his son.

"That creature," Masui quailed, cinching his pants, "It threw sand at my back."

Snorting as he rolled up his sleeves, Li Diezhu glowered at his son and said, "Let's go. Take the lead."

"I'll follow you, dad." Embarrassed, Masui struggled to screw up his courage as he mounted his horse and fell in behind his father.

A thick fog settled over the forest. As they proceeded, Li Diezhu heard indistinct murmurs from off in the woods from time to time. Sensing something unusual afoot, he roared furiously, "God-damned dogspawn, are you a person or a ghost? If you're a person, show yourself! If you're a ghost, begone!" Recalling Xia Qifa's instruction, he formed the mudras with his hands, moving them in every direction to expel any ghosts that might be present.

The murmurs gradually died away, and Li Diezhu relaxed. Momentarily, however, recognizing that none of the usual night sounds were present, not even the soughing wind, his sense of heightened unease returned. A nameless terror gripped father and son.

Cui Four was on duty in the tower that night. For a stretch, he slipped down to the kitchen to flirt with Ran, the cookwoman, before returning to watch, peering out the gun loop until he dozed off. He was jarred awake by a faint cry from below, "Come down and help me, man! The ghosts at Gangou Bridge are too ferocious! There was nothing we could do. Send militiamen to rescue my father!"

Hearing Masui, Cui Four clambered to his feet. Heading to Mawu and Jin's chamber, he pounded forcefully, "Captain Li! Captain Li!"

Thinking that the plunderers had returned, Mawu jumped to the ground, threw on his clothes, seized his gun, and burst through the door.

"Second Master said ghosts are teeming at Gangou Bridge. We need to go rescue your father," Cui Four told him.

Mawu put on his coat and rushed downstairs. In the dim light of the *tung* oil lamp, he beheld a bedraggled Masui, hair unkempt and clothing torn, looking much like he had after his narrow escape from "Black-tailed Snake" two years earlier.

"Quick! Go to Gangou Bridge. Father and his horse fell into the gully," wailed Masui. "It was horrible! Those ghosts made the bridge collapse . . . I tried to carry father out of the gully a couple times, but couldn't make it."

The rock-strewn gully beneath Gangou Bridge was ten or fifteen feet deep. Worse, the bridge was not far from the old ghostly hardwood and Zhou Damei's grave. Mawu snorted angrily, "Even if they're ghosts, I'll seize them by their short and curly hairs and show them what's what!" When he had crossed two days earlier, he mused, the beams underpinning the bridge were firm and sturdy. How could it collapse so suddenly? It didn't sound like the work of ghosts. Suspicions piqued, carrying torches and a sedan chair for Li Diezhu, he rode toward Gangou Bridge with five militiamen.

"Take a double-door leaf as a stretcher for the wounded horse!" cried out Masui from behind. Hurriedly, Cui Four strapped a door-leaf on the back of his horse.

All was enveloped in heavy fog. By the time the riders reached the bridge, they were soaked with dew. The bridge had collapsed, leaving only a single trunk, one of the joists of the bridge, connecting the two sides of the valley. On the far side, Masui's white horse stood alone, unable to cross. In the dense fog, the torchlight failed to illumine the gully-bottom. Mawu stared toward the old tree, its thick trunk and long branches faintly visible, then swiftly clambered down the gully wall, in his anxiety ignoring cuts and scratches from jagged stones and scrub brush.

In the torchlight, he saw Li Diezhu and his yellow roan splayed out among the boulders. Running over, Mawu exclaimed, "Dad!" Li Diezhu showed no response, not even an eye blink. Sick at heart, Mawu knelt by his side.

Clinging to sturdy vines, two militiamen edged down to the bottom of the gulch and joined their Captain.

In the torchlight, Mawu saw traces of blood, though he could not tell if they were from rider or horse. He ordered the militiamen to bind his father to his back with the vines and creepers clinging to the gully walls.

With Li Diezhu mounted on his back, the climb up the sheer gully walls proved difficult for Mawu, even with the militiamen assisting from behind. Halfway up, as he scrabbled for purchase in the loose earth, Mawu sent a shower of rocks and debris raining down on the unfortunate duo. The other two militiamen on the lip of the gully helped dig handholds and finally pulled him to the top, where they soon secured comatose Li Diezhu in the sedan chair.

The militiamen managed to maneuver the injured yellow roan atop the double-door, fastening it with vines. The creature's breathing was labored, its body blood-stained, its mouth frothing. As the men struggled and pushed, Mawu directed a team of four horses—using the stout creepers as ropes—to raise the cumbersome stretcher from the gully. Finally, the poor creature was saved!

"Look, Captain Li, the underpilings of the bridge seemed to have been dug out and sabotaged," called an alarmed militiaman, pointing as he held a torch aloft.

Grimly, Mawu surveyed the damaged stonework of the bridge: support stones had clearly been removed from the abutments. He ordered the militiamen to repair the bridge, then turned to his white horse, which was looking attentively at him, "Wait here until the bridge is fixed, then help carry your yellow roan partner back home." With these words, he and Cui Four lifted Li Diezhu in the sedan chair, and in the dense fog they wound homeward as quickly as they could along the narrow forest path.

When they reached home, Li Diezhu was still unconscious. Tao Jiuxiang undressed her husband, discovering that his undergarments were soaked with piss. His battered body was black and blue, but there were no open wounds. Hurriedly, she sponged his body with an herbal poultice that had been steeped in wine for two years, then spoon-fed him some water.

"Bewitched fog," Li Diezhu suddenly muttered, lips aquiver, "That thing . . . it dragged us down . . ."

Eyes wide with horror, Tao Jiuxiang hurriedly told Masui to go burn paper to placate Zhou Damei, while she busied herself preparing opium for her wounded husband.

Exhausted, Masui complained that he felt dizzy. Reluctantly, he carried a half-basket of paper to a nearby slope, emptied it, then set the small mountain of paper alight. Soon, butterflies of ash rose, flitting through the dense smoke and sparks, blending with the rising fog, and floating slowly toward Gangou Bridge.

Chapter Twelve

I

Mawu sent a group of stonemasons to Dragon Decapitating Gorge toting hammers and chisels and shouldering baskets and ropes to begin work. The Mayor had been so delighted with the suggestion that martyrs' names be inscribed on the cliff face that he had excitedly proclaimed the location a site for "promoting the moral education of the people." As the local government was covering costs for the project, Xia Qifa had agreed to provide room and board for the masons.

That autumn, crops grew extremely well in Peppercorn Bend. Few people cultivated goldthread, as there was no market. The rugged slopes were scattered with patches of corn; swaying with the weight of abundance, stalks grew a few inches with each rainfall.

Mawu, however, was in a foul mood. Its skull fractured and belly torn open from the fall into the gully, his yellow roan charger had died. For weeks, his white horse, too, had been spiritless. To manage the relentless pain, Li Diezhu smoked half a bag of opium and took medicinal alcohol twice a day. Who had done this, he wondered. Qin Liexiong? Zhou Taiwang? Some disgruntled tenants?

Another crisis was brewing. A young deserter from Peppercorn Bend who had fled home was seized and sentenced to die before a firing squad. The deserter, Jiang Shemi, was a cousin of Jiang Ermao. After long negotiations, the supervising officer agreed to allow Jiang's brother-in-law, Peng Yucheng, to enlist in his stead, but fined the Jiangs two hundred silver dollars. Rather than paying, the Jiangs colluded with other families that had enrolled sons and refused to pay taxes. As militia Captain, all of the aggrieved parties appealed to Mawu, who felt more anxious than he had when the brigands took him hostage. Perhaps there really was a wrathful ghost haunting the Lis! One foggy morning, he prepared to head to Azure Dragon Temple to ask Daoist Master Wang for a ghost-warding talisman. Irascibly, he muttered, "After all, Master Wang performed the exorcism on Zhou Damei. It's his responsibility!"

At that very moment, he saw a figure running up the narrow, bramble-locked path leading to the tower. Vigilantly, Cui Four cried out, "Who goes there?"

"Me." Zhou Taiwang emerged from the fog. "I want to talk to Captain Li."

"About what?" asked Mawu.

Zhou Taiwang advanced two paces, asking, "Are the terms of the reward notice you posted last year still valid?"

Taken aback, Mawu answered, "Of course."

Zhou Taiwang nodded, "Then I want to make an official report."

Mawu handed two silver dollars to Lidu, saying, "Go take care of things. I have business to attend to."

Following Mawu and Cui Four, Zhou Taiwang entered the tower. He whispered, "I know who backed the attack on the stone tower."

Brows atremble, Mawu eyes bored through Zhou. "Do you have evidence?"

"Yes," Zhou Taiwang replied. "After Damei's death, Qin Liexiong tried to incite me to take revenge by revealing the layout of the tower to the bamboo craftsman, Tiger Incarnate Bodhisattva Liang, but I didn't go along with him. Later, Jiang Ermao came to my home, asking me questions about Gengguping. I knew that he'd joined Liang, and told him go to see Qin Liexiong. A couple days later Jiang told me that Qin had proposed that goats would form the first wave of the assault. He sent two brigands to scout things out and buy them in Peppercorn Bend. I was there when Qin Liexiong lent them the money. They paid him back later. When everything was set, the brigands launched their attack under cover of darkness."

Glaring ferociously, Mawu asked, "Why didn't you report this earlier?"

Sniffling as he tried to stifle his tears, the aggrieved Zhou Taiwang told his tale. After Damei's death, he began working for the Qins, and gained Qin

Liexiong's deep trust. Every other month, Qin Liexiong sent him to Wanxian County with thirty silver dollars to buy morphine. One year earlier, when he heard the Qins were planning on buying the fields from the Lis, he invested all his savings to purchase an acre of land. However, Qin Liexiong suspected that Zhou Taiwang had embezzled money in the field bargain. He thought of a wicked scheme to entrap Zhou. One day, after Zhou Taiwang returned from Wanxian and delivered the morphine, Qin Liexiong put it in a wooden cabinet without even looking at it. The following day, Qin Liexiong took out the morphine in Zhou's presence and took a draw on his pipe. Suddenly, Qin rounded on him and roared, "This swill is fake! Zhou Taiwang, you must have eaten panther's gall to have the audacity to embezzle my money!" The accusation left Zhou Taiwang at a loss for words. Forced to pay compensation for the supposed theft, Zhou was bankrupted. Turning the matter over in his mind, Zhou could not swallow the indignity. Finally, he decided to exact revenge by revealing the entire plot to Mawu.

Gritting his teeth, Mawu asked coldly, "Do you have the nerve to confront the guilty parties and testify in county court?"

"May I be minced into pieces and my ancestral line be forever severed if I utter a lie!" Zhou Taiwang swallowed a mouthful of saliva, and went on, "I also know what happened at Gangou Bridge. Jiang Ermao always talked about getting even with Masui. When he heard that Masui was coming back from the Xias', he asked me to join him and waylay Masui at Inkblack Creek. Initially I agreed, but remembering that you had always treated me with respect, Captain Li, I changed my mind when I saw your father and Masui coming. So, Jiang Ermao went and sabotaged the bridge himself. Unexpectedly, instead of Masui your father took the lead; as a result he fell into the gully and was injured. I swear that every word I've said is the truth, and that I will testify." He added after a while, "I only ask that in addition to the rice you offered as a reward that you lend me some money to set up a business in Wanxian County. After I testify, there's no way I can go on living around here."

Though livid, Mawu maintained a semblance of calm and said, "After you testify, I'll lend you capital to start a business!" As if suffocating, he unbuttoned the cotton-padded jacket of his uniform.

The price of goldthread kept falling. The cumulative cost of ransoming Mawu, offering bribes to secure Mawu's appointment, and building the family tombs had left the Li family threadbare. Mawu wanted to build a new house for Jin in Huangshui, but it wasn't feasible in these dire circumstances. Mawu and his militiamen were encamped in the cramped barracks. Although he agreed to help Zhou Taiwang escape, he wouldn't have enough silver for the loan until after the fall harvest. His facial muscles tensing at the thought, Mawu instructed Zhou Taiwang to keep his secret until the trial.

Jin felt lonely. Mawu's rapacious lust and seemingly insatiable desire for her had cooled. Fearing that Mawu had fallen for one of the coquettish streetwalkers in Huangshui—like the bedeviled fog clinging to the riverbanks, these girls clustered around handsome young Mawu—when he returned to Gengguping, she paid close attention to his moods and actions. What if he brought back some lowborn hussy as a concubine! Knitting her brows, she went to confront her husband with a heavy heart. But as she approached, she overheard Zhou Taiwang's words and was shocked into silence. No wonder Xia Qifa had seemed puzzled when he called forth the ten guarantors to fashion the protective amulet for Mawu: two of them turned out to be vicious saboteurs!

"I'm off to Huangshui!" Mawu purposefully strode outside, calling to Cui Four, "We're heading to the militia station. Tomorrow we'll collect the grain levy."

II

The paddy rice in the valley had ripened, parcel after parcel of full-headed, arching golden stalks, like a sage's elegant, flowing calligraphic strokes rendered on silk. The villagers were busy with the rice harvest. Red chilis were spread out to sun dry in every household's yard; yellow sheafs of corn hung from the eaves.

With a squad of militiamen, Mawu rode into Peppercorn Bend. They set up sentinels and stationed themselves in the yard of Peng Yuju, the former failed scholar who had become a tenant of the Li family, preparing to seize his tax rice once the tenants had finished the harvest.

Respectfully, with a placid expression, Peng Yuju asked Mawu if he would care to play chess. As evening settled, under the guard of the militiamen the sun-browned tenant farmers formed a long line, all of them shouldering back-baskets and toting sacks filled with rice. Shortly, a militiaman entered the room where Peng Yuju and Mawu were seated, reporting that the tax rice had been gathered. Deliberately, Peng Yuju raised his head, and addressed Mawu calmly, "Captain, would you be willing to remit this year's grain tax?"

"Why?" Mawu asked, setting a chesspiece down heavily.

"Perhaps, because this year an inordinately high number of troops enlisted from Peppercorn Bend, you could cancel the rice levy?" Peng Yuju continued, his knowing tone insinuating he was a move or two ahead of Mawu.

"Peppercorn Bend women are as fertile as the soil. Why shouldn't we enroll a few more men in the army to fight the Japanese devils?" Mawu responded coldly.

Peng Yuju looked him in the eye, asking, "Since these young men are fighting for our country, why aren't they provided medical care when they're sick? Why are their rations paltry and their barracks ramshackle? And why are they cursed and beaten like criminals?"

Enunciating each word slowly and carefully, Mawu said, "Nor do I wish to see my neighbors ill-treated. According to regulations, deserters are to be shot. I intervened and persuaded the army to accept money in place of your in-law Jiang Shemi's life."

Peng Yuju raised his head, "My younger brother Peng Yucheng volunteered to take his place. So why is the army still fining the Jiangs?"

Irritated, Mawu answered, "If every soldier were a deserter like your brother-in-law, how could we win the war? Troops must maintain strict discipline."

With an air of reserve, Peng Yuju suggested, "Since you're such a good man, Captain, why not pay the two hundred silver dollars on Jiang Shemi's behalf?"

Holding his growing anger in check, Mawu answered, "In collecting the grain tax, I routinely go light on the tenants and on the Jiang family, too. Since my family was robbed and blackmailed last year, things have been tight—we're an eminent family in name only. The two hundred silver dollars will help the Jiangs avert disaster: it's restitution for Jiang Shemi's very life."

Mulling this over for a moment, Peng Yuju rejoined, "So, Captain, why do you think that your family's tower was attacked and ransacked?"

Mawu abruptly stood up—livid, pupils bulging—and spat, "Some treacherous thieving curs in cahoots with the bandits covet property and seek to lay hands on any riches they catch sight of!"

Hearing these words, Peng Yuju rose slowly and said, "Though this sincere advice may ring unpleasant in your ears, you would be wise to heed my words.

Avarice clouding his heart and mind, Li Masui tried to pressure Master Wang of Azure Dragon Temple to grow opium, in violation of the law. You, Li Mawu, bribed government officials to gain your position, forcibly seizing tenants' grain to pay the cost. A hundred stone of rice is nothing to you, but to us peasants it is the difference between subsistence and starvation. Why make new enemies over such a trivial matter? Haven't you heard the saying that 'one thing lost is another gained?' " His graying head swaying to and fro, the failed local examination candidate salted his speech with archaisms, twisting the tenants' refusal to pay taxes into a righteous stand.

"So you're blackmailing me with the threat of bandits!" Seething with rage, Mawu turned purplish-black, his lips trembling.

"It's not blackmail, it's wise counsel: the most prudent policy is peaceful resolution. In any event, we will not pay this year's levy rice!" Peng Yuju grew increasingly excited. Hearing the argument, Peng's family clustered around the two.

"There was no enmity between us, but your duplicity has forced my hand." Blood roiling with hatred for manipulative Peng Yuju and the deceitful tenants, Mawu yanked out his pistol.

Several of Peng Yuju's sons and nephews quickly seized Mawu and held him fast. Seeing this, the militiamen swarmed forward, joining the fracas.

"What should we do?" Peng Yuju cried. Shouldering forward to join his sons and nephews, he sought to wrest away Mawu's pistol.

With a violent jerk, Mawu freed himself and, with a loud howl, fired his pistol just as Peng Yuju sprang toward him. There was an earthshaking report, and Peng fell to the ground clutching his chest.

"Help! Captain Li killed my husband! Captain Li killed my husband!" Seeing Peng Yuju fall, his wife ran outside, wailing like a madwoman.

In all the bedlam, a pair of nephews carried Peng Yuju from the room. Several other sons and nephews remained, grappling and tussling with the militiamen. At that very moment, a dark mass of bandits, heads swathed in yellow turbans, strips of yellow ribbon binding their arms, appeared on the opposite slope. Collectively kneeling in prayer, they chanted ominously:

> *Warriors of shadow march ahead, with murderous spirit;*
> *Soldiers of light follow behind, an awe-inspiring force.*
> *The fangs of shadow warriors are sharp as sabers,*

Our claws like serrated bayonets.
Dauntless, we cut down dragons and serpents in combat,
Adamant, we advance left; brooking no opposition, we move right . . .
None can stand in our way.

After incanting the battle chant of the Immortal Tiger and drinking their blessed water, they unleashed a mighty collective roar, "Charge! Kill them!" Then, swarming forward so that the earth shook and the heavens quaked, they launched a sudden, frenzied charge toward the Pengs' yard. To protect their rice, the tenant farmers had sought the protection and support of Tiger Incarnate Bodhisattva Liang! As soon as the pistol sounded, the bandits swarmed forth from their concealment in a nearby bamboo grove, brandishing their demon-headed swords. Though they did no harm to the tenants, the terrified farmers, quailing before the onslaught, panicked and ran pell-mell.

A standard-bearer carrying a proud banner emblazoned with the large character "Divine" approached. Before him another brigand, a necklace of bullets bouncing off his chest, straw sandals on his feet, pantlegs scrolled up above his knees, dashed forward, yelling, "We're impervious to bullets and blades. Come on, bastards, shoot me!" Rags trailed behind this savage tatterdemalion as he ran, trailing him like so many streamers. This was none other than the notorious Tiger Incarnate Liang! Several dozen bandits charged on his heels. Mawu's detachment of militiamen shuddered, seeing that the bandits advanced without the slightest hesitation, their eyes ever riveted forward, never glancing sideward.

As alarmed as the militiamen, the sons and nephews of the Peng family disengaged and scurried away. As the bandits reached the Pengs' yard, the militiamen barraged them with gunfire, but even their crack shooting couldn't hit Liang. Frustrated, Mawu repeatedly fired at the standard-bearer. When he fell, another man took his place and raised the banner again. Inspirited, Mawu cried excitedly, "They're just flesh-and-blood men, not ghosts! Don't be afraid. Fire with me!" The death of the standard-bearer dispelled the belief that the bandits were impervious to bullets; the morale of the militiamen rose dramatically! Many bandits fell as the gorge echoed with gunfire.

Mawu continued firing at the new standard-bearer. After a shot grazed him, the flagman cast the banner aside, drew a sword from his back-sheath, and flung himself at Mawu. As Mawu sighted his rifle to deliver a fatal shot, the man slashed him with a desperate swipe. Seeing this, Liang sounded the rallying cry, "The divine Tiger has risen! Kill them all!" The brigands swarmed, chasing and killing the scattering militiamen, pursuing them for quite a distance before a trumpet blast signaled them to regroup.

Cui Four picked up Mawu, who had received several slashes in the throes of battle, and slung him over his back as the remaining troops beat a hasty retreat, clambering up escarpments and scampering over gulches. As darkness settled, the forest merged with the sky. By turns, the demoralized militiamen carried Mawu until they reached Jin Shaosan's gate. Exhausted, they thumped the gate so hard that it echoed off the mountains. Jin Shaosan was eating dinner when he heard the pounding. Throwing down his chopsticks, he headed out for a look. Stiff as a board, his wife stood at the gate, oil lamp in hand.

Chests heaving with exhaustion, several militiamen shouldered their way in, a bloody man limply sprawled on one's back. Someone called breathlessly, "Captain Li is dying!"

"Send for the *tima*. Hurry!" Jin Shaosan screamed, stamping in horror.

"Cui Four has already gone to find him," a militiaman answered.

Mawu's swarthy complexion had blanched, becoming waxen and sallow from blood loss. His eyes were closed tightly, like those of a dead man.

As she led the militiamen carrying Mawu to Jin's former room, Old Mother Jin wept bitterly, "Oh, son-in-law, please don't leave behind an orphan and a widow."

"Who . . . who did this?" Jin Shaosan asked in trembling voice.

"Peng Yuju—he was in cahoots with Liang the bamboo craftsman," responded a weary militiaman with a tattered uniform. "We lost many men. They took the rice levy, too." Several men were stained with Mawu's blood.

"May that odious bastard be minced into ten thousand pieces! Fifty years of classical learning straight up a cow's asshole!" cursed Jin Shaosan. Timidly, he ventured, "Would one of you go to Gengguping and tell the Lis to send someone?"

The ravenous militiamen were devouring the remaining rice and fried bread in the kitchen. Ricemeal bread in hand, one man rose, wiped away his tears, and volunteered, "I'll go."

"Aji, Aji," Old Mother Jin summoned Jin's sixteen year old brother. "Is that the *tima*? Go and see if it's Xia Qifa? Tell him to come quickly!" Aji took a long look at his mangled brother-in-law before shooting out of the house into the inky blackness.

Carrying his deerskin pouch, Xia Qifa, followed by Xia Liangxian and Cui Four, hobbled along the winding horse-path. Saturated with dew, he trudged through the dense night fog, listening to Cui Four's endless tearful imprecations. Before passing over a ridge or through a valley, the shaman sounded a stentorian note on his oxhorn, requesting that local evil spirits withdraw and make way.

After meandering for four hours along the path, a hazy figure suddenly appeared from the opposite direction. Breathless Aji panted, "Please hurry, *tima*. The path is bumpy and treacherous! Please hurry. Mawu, my brother-in-law, is severely wounded."

Xia Qifa chanted an ambling, rambling singsong chant as he walked,

> *No smooth road, lo, to walk.*
> *Just a slippery, rutted mud track, lo, to pace.*
> *Tangled wild brambles entwine*
> *Travelers on desolate mountain roads.*
> *A wanderer, I travel by water when I meet a river.*
> *When currents are swift, quickly I move.*
> *Nothing can hold this vessel back.*
> *When I meet with a tree, it splinters;*
> *When I collide with a hill, it collapses.*
> *We're moving fast, lo, through rapids ever faster,*
> *Sit down and firmly grip the gunwale, fellow travelers.*
> *For floating in the waters, ah, I see the spirits of the drowned.*

The four picked their way through the cold fog, taking turns carrying two large baskets. One was a pottery urn containing one hundred thousand ghost warriors.

III

Wracked with anxiety from the moment she awakened, Tao Jiuxiang tended to her husband. Bruised and battered, unable to swallow anything other than rice broth and milk, Li Diezhu lay abed breathing feebly. Who would have thought that the Daoist exorcism had failed and that Damei's vindictive ghost still haunted the old tree and Gangou Bridge? And Mawu still hadn't returned with the protective talisman from Azure Dragon Temple. She decided to send for Xia Qifa the next morning. Regardless of distance or weariness, the *tima* never refused a request. While she was loath to summon the *tima* to treat minor illnesses or small disasters, these past few years a series of misfortunes had befallen the Lis.

Something queer, too, happened to the family's sow. Bred by a wild boar, she birthed ten strapping, energetic piglets that grew at a shocking rate, putting on forty pounds in a single week. Looking for any weak point in the pigpen fence, they attacked the chickens and squealed with hostility at anyone in sight. Tao Jiuxiang asked Sun Fu to sell the crossbred piglets in Huangshui, but their wildness, protruding jaws, and pointed ears gave pause to any prospective buyers. Finally, he managed to sell nine of the ten to a hotel restaurant at a low price, leaving only the wildest and most rambunctious male unsold. Sun Fu could do nothing but carry it back. That very night, fashioning a makeshift shrine before the pigpen, Tao Jiuxiang burned incense and lit a pair of candles, offering paper money, wine, and meat, and praying to the deity of livestock and the earth god to help their creatures be fecund, obedient, and healthy. She even vowed to offer the half-breed piglet as a sacrifice to the Bodhisattva of the Sty, so that the creature might be a domesticated pig in its afterlife.

Tormented, Masui said, "Ma, it's all my fault. My offense to that madwoman has brought on this string of disasters."

Tao Jiuxiang fixed him with a hard look: "Did you mistreat her?"

"No, never! May I be stricken dead by lightning if I lie!" Masui stammered.

"If you didn't bully her, don't talk nonsense! A righteous man has nothing to fear: he can sleep soundly with his doors wide open!" Tao Jiuxiang declared.

However, wracked by guilt, Masui tossed and turned through the night. Toward daybreak, rising to piss, he heard a loud knock at the gate. "Open the gate, sir," hollered a bone-weary militiaman, his hoarse voice piercing the mountain stillness: "Brigands killed Captain Li..."

Out of her wits, Tao Jiuxiang burst into tears and unloosed a string of curses as she rose from Li Diezhu's side, dashing outside in bare feet.

Sun Fu opened the gate. As it swung open, the man staggered in, followed by a gust of cold wind. Addressing Tao Jiuxiang, who stood behind Sun Fu, he choked out: "Ambushed by bandits... most of us were killed... Captain Li was cut down."

Fastening his trousers as he emerged from the house, Masui gasped, "What?"

Letting out a sorrowful cry, Tao Jiuxiang swooned.

Gaining his bearings, the militiaman clarified, "Captain Li's still breathing. The men carried him to Jin Shaosan's place. Cui Four went to summon the *tima*."

Tao Jiuxiang recovered her wits, ceased crying, and ordered tearful Masui, "Go get Jin! Leave immediately with your sister-in-law to see Mawu. Bring some silver."

Though it was early autumn, the Li household seemed to be in the throes of winter. From the hazy depths of unconsciousness, Li Diezhu croaked, "Mawu, Mahe . . ." His eyelids twitched ever so slightly and his mouth fell agape, letting his tongue loll out.

"Don't get it backward! Mawu is still alive, old tiger. Listen close—he's alive." Forcefully, Tao Jiuxiang pushed Li Diezhu's jaw upward. Her strenuous efforts were to no avail: his mouth opened ever wider, his tongue stuck out further. Cradling her husband's head, Tao Jiuxiang grimaced, and amid a rain of tears she fiercely berated Damei's malicious spirit, "My family didn't mistreat you. Why are you stirring up trouble again? Go see your lover, Jiang Ermao. Didn't you want to marry him? Go. Go quickly!"

Li Diezhu's eyeballs rolled upward, showing only their terrible whites. His tongue stretched further, as though dragged by some invisible force. Li Diezhu wanted to call Mawu back home, but the path was cluttered with old friends milling about—some spirits, some ghosts, and others men. Hurriedly, he hailed them. With each greeting, his tongue stretched out and retracted again, causing him excruciating pain. Abruptly, with one final, violent movement, he wrenched his head to one side, leaving his bereft wife and youngest son weeping at his side. Anxious for his firstborn Mawu to the last, Li Diezhu passed on at the age of fifty-six, riding the wintry winds howling outside to join the Li ancestors. The sun set.

Tao Jiuxiang and Masui wept, calling out in anguish to the heavens and knocking their heads on the earth, hoping to recall Li Diezhu's soul before it fled beyond their reach. Suddenly, from the forest to the northwest came a blood-curdling tiger's roar, low and terrifying, causing the ten hounds to erupt in a frenzied chorus of barking. Falling leaves danced in the wind;

the mountains lay still in the encroaching darkness. Sobbing, Tao Jiuxiang covered her husband's face with three sheets of straw paper, placed a pair of chopsticks and a bowl of egg-fried rice at his feet, burned a stick of incense, then asked Masui to light a string of firecrackers outside the gate.

She sent Sun Fu to invite Xia Qifa. "When I return," asked Sun Fu, wiping his tear-stained cheeks, "shall I fetch Daoist Master Wang, too?"

"No!" Tao Jiuxiang answered emphatically, her watery eyes wide open. "The *tima* will preside over the funeral. He's seen off all the members of my family. With him in charge, they're all flourishing on the other side!"

However, in the wake of the terrible roar, Masui and Sun Fu were reluctant to set out. Tao Jiuxiang took the forked *beijue*-wood staff that the *tima* had given Li Diezhu years before, repeating the shaman's instructions as she handed it to Sun Fu, "Tigers fear this staff. When they see it, they can't raise their hackles. Take it and go."

Sun Fu dawdled for a few moments before drumming up his courage and heading off leading a horse. After a couple of steps, he turned and said, "Cui Four has probably brought Xia Qifa back to Peppercorn Bend by now . . ."

Tao Jiuxiang said, "Then set out for Jin Shaosan's home. After the *tima* saves Mawu, request him to come perform the funeral. Masui, stay home."

Hanging a string of firecrackers from a bamboo pole outside the front gate, Masui took out a match and directed a militiaman, "Go to the tower and get my sister-in-law." Raising his eyes at the very moment, he caught sight of a tiger stalking through the woods a stone's throw away. Clearly visible, as if it had just stepped out of a legend, the tiger emerged from the forest. Cruel ruffs of white fur stood out on its neck. The character for king 王 was prominently etched on the creature's powerful brow. Terrified, Masui dashed into the house. "Ma," he stammered, "A t-t-tiger . . . a spirit tiger has come!"

Her grieving interrupted by Masui's panicked cries, Tao Jiuxiang poked her head outside. However, she saw nothing at all. Alarmed, she asked, "Where's the tiger?"

Masui sniffled, "There . . . it swaggered into the forest . . . you can still smell him."

Tao Jiuxiang wandered over and looked around. Sure enough, the pungent odor of tiger urine hung in the air, stalks of grass were bent and crushed, and a string of plum-blossom-shaped paw prints were impressed in the earth. Tensing with fear, jaw set tight, she silently retreated to the gate and took out flint and steel to light the firecrackers.

"Ma! Are you trying to attract the tiger?" asked Masui in trepidation, clutching the bamboo pole.

"The tiger's just passing though. They don't like firecrackers: it won't come back," asserted Tao Jiuxiang. Exasperated, Masui lit the firecrackers. Popping and crackling, the firecrackers announced to the rugged wilderness the end of a man's life.

From the tower, Jin also heard the thunderous roar. A moment later, the militiaman burst through the gate, bearing bitter tidings, "Ai! Madam, the Old Lady wants you to come right away. Old Uncle—your father-in-law—just passed away."

"Hunh?" Jin set her daughter down. While she knew that the lingering injury from the gully and malignant sores on his legs tormented her father-in-law, she never thought that they would prove fatal. Hurriedly rising and striding from the room, ignoring Yongyu's question, "Ma, What does 'passed away' mean?" she demanded, "Where's Mawu? Is he back?"

"Ai! Captain Li was severely wounded by the bandits . . ." As he spoke, the ominous crackle of the firecrackers echoed: at that moment, Jin's entire world collapsed. Oh, her tears! A mountain woman's cruel lot is a river of tears. She had no memory of the grief-wracked walk from the tower to the house. Arriving, Tao Jiuxiang embraced her and the two wept inconsolably. Finally, with the help of Ran, the cookwoman, Jin mounted a horse and, following Sun Fu, headed for Peppercorn Bend.

IV

The morning fog had yet to lift as Jin and Sun Fu ventured along the mountain path. Hidden by mist, some creature shuffled through the forest. Nervously, Sun Fu held the forked staff. Jin followed, oblivious to danger, lost in a haze of grief, sobbing over her father-in-law's sudden death and deeply worried about her husband. At midday, they reached the Jin homestead.

Gone from its resting place between navel and backbone was Mawu's soul. All morning, like a dauntless general, Xia Qifa had commanded spirit warriors from the pottery urn to seek out the unmoored soul. He placed the urn at the Jin's front gate, and hung the curling ox horn on a wooden upright in the main hall. From the deerskin pouch, the *tima* took a pinch of herbal medicine and placed it in unmoving Mawu's mouth. On Mawu's wounds, the shaman plastered a poultice. He handed several other medicinal herbs to Old Mother Jin, instructing her to boil and decoct them. Old Mother Jin knew that these wondrous roots and miraculous herbs were no ordinary medicines. To gather these rare medicines, which only grew on steep cliffs, daring herb collectors rappelled down the scarps. Guardians of the precious fauna, immortal birds pecked the ropes until they frayed and snapped, causing herb collectors to plunge to their deaths at the gorge's bottom. Shamans and herb collectors who managed to gather these hardwon precious herbs stored them in tripodal pottery urns.

Father and son donned their ritual apparel. According to ancestral rules a *tima* could not pass control of spirit troops on to his successor, so while Xia Qifa marshaled the ghost generals and soldiers from the urn in the other world, Xia Liangxian busied himself burning paper and chanting protective incantations. Incense smoke gradually curled skyward.

"I summon forth a pair of wild boars. Go forth and seek the soul!" Xia Qifa commanded, going through a prescribed series of ritual paces and poses, forming mudras with his hands as he moved. "I summon a pair of domestic pigs. Go! I summon one hundred thousand fierce spirit warriors. Go! I summon the eight great Buddhist guardian warriors. Go! Scour the heavens! Scour the earth! If you can't find the soul, seek it in the underworld. Go, soldiers, seek out Li Mawu's soul! Fly!"

Though Jin Shaosan and his wife knew that Xia Qifa and his son were bone weary and famished from the long journey through the darkness, Mawu's life hung in the balance. Constantly fretting, they watched the old shaman direct invisible troops to every corner of heaven, earth, and the underworld in the desperate search for Mawu's soul. Like a full moon, an oil lamp to one side illumined these three realms. As dawn approached, the *tima*—drained to the point that his shoulders sagged and it seemed his skeleton had left his body—launched one final frantic search, exhausting his arts as he directed the spirits: finally, one of Mawu's eyelids fluttered ever so slightly.

"Bring me the herbal decoction," the shaman panted.

Just as Jin and Sun Fu tied the horses to a hitching post and bustled in, Old Mother Jin arrived with the remedy.

"Mawu!" Jin gasped, rushing to her bloodstained husband's side, "How did you get so badly hurt?"

Hearing the cries of his wife, Mawu raised his eyelids, and his pupils dazedly swept across Jin's face. His lips trembled, but no sound came forth.

"He's recovering," said Old Mother Jin, handing the bowl to Jin. "Feed him."

Wiping her tears, Jin took the bowl, and gently poured a spoonful of the warm, dark liquid into Mawu's half-open mouth. "Swallow . . . swallow it," she beseeched, her eyes glistening.

Everyone encircled Mawu, watching as, his lips and throat moving with great effort, he sipped several spoonfuls.

The father and son tandem of river shamans were greatly relieved. Xia Liangxian kept burning paper and chanting at the gate, while Xia Qifa recalled the ghost warriors to the urn with several blasts of the oxhorn.

"Old Tima," whispered Jin Shaosan, "You two must be famished. Come eat."

"All right," Xia Qifa agreed, deliberately moving toward the table.

"Come eat, brothers." Jin Shaosan addressed Sun Fu, the Li family's head laborer and the despondent remaining militiamen. Sun Fu headed into the kitchen, a strange expression etched on his face.

Jin Shaosan placed dishes on the table and joined them. "Thank you both for your hard work in saving my son-in-law's life." Worried, he added, "How long before my son-in-law can eat solid food?"

Calmly, the *tima* answered, "Two or three days. Give him something soft."

Graciously, Jin Shaosan gushed, "You're truly a god among men!"

Xia Qifa said thoughtfully, "Though Yama, the King of Hell, may have relinquished his hold on Mawu, I don't think the Peng family will let him go so easily. I'm afraid that there's nothing I can do to help him in the future."

"What?" Jin Shaosan's rice bowl trembled in his hands.

Gloomily, Xia Qifa asked, "An eye for an eye: shouldn't one who kills pay recompense with his life?"

Alarmed, Cui Four countered, "Didn't those goddamned brigands kill enough of our militiamen to slake any thirst for revenge?"

"But who killed Peng Yuju?" asked Xia Qifa.

"Captain Li. So you think they're hellbent on killing Captain Li?" Cui asked, setting down his chopsticks.

"The town government will definitely discipline Mawu!" Jin Shaosan said, perturbed.

Xia Qifa said, "Mmmm-hmmm, the government tends to punish faulty officials before meting out justice to wicked mobs."

"So whatever can we do for my poor son-in-law?" blubbered Jin Shaosan, tears rolling down his cheeks.

A dull, faraway look in his eyes, another militiaman offered, "These days, the government's only concerned with collecting taxes. They aren't gonna help."

"*Woo, woo,*" Sun Fu, silent since his arrival at the Jin household, suddenly wailed, "There's no right time to say this . . ."

Xia Qifa asked, "What's the matter?"

Sobbing, Sun Fu reported, "When he heard about Mawu, the Old Master passed away. *Tima,* the Old Mistress is waiting for you at Gengguping to come and see off his soul."

"Alas, my kinsfolk!" exclaimed Jin Shaosan, blanching.

For a moment, everyone stood dumbstruck. His face a pale mask of misery, Cui Four instructed, "Don't mention his death in Captain Li's presence!"

Xia Qifa fixed Sun Fu with a look of anxious surprise, then silently rose and left the room. Standing at Mawu's bedside, the old shaman's eyes—though he hadn't slept a wink in a full day—still shone with a vigorous clarity.

"Hold a rite . . . for my fallen comrades in the militia," rasped Mawu in a voice as thin and frail as a strand from a spider's web, his face bloodless and eyes tightly closed. In this season, the ten-odd militiamen killed in the battle with the bandits should have been enjoying newly harvested rice with friends and family around a fire. According to local custom, when a man died a sudden, unusual death, his corpse could not be transported home and buried in his clan's cemetery. Fearful that the wandering manes of the dead militiamen would run riot, haunting Peppercorn Bend and visiting further disasters upon his family, Mawu begged the *tima* to perform a ceremony to give solace to their souls and lay them to eternal rest.

Grasping Mawu's gist, Jin whispered to her husband, "We'll invite him to perform the rite as soon as possible. I'll speak to him and fix a time." She choked back tears of sorrow, her heart shattered in a thousand pieces: she couldn't tell Mawu that his father, Li Diezhu, lay cold and dead in the courtyard at home.

Approaching his father, Xia Liangxian whispered, "Dad, for now, we'd better tend to the severely wounded. We can head to Gengguping tomorrow."

The old shaman nodded almost imperceptibly. He departed early the following morning. Before taking leave, with careful instructions in soft undertones, Xia Qifa handed the deerskin pouch to his son. Then, followed by Sun Fu, who shouldered his ritual instruments, the *tima* silently went out through the gate.

"I'll be there in few days," Jin Shaosan sobbed in parting.

After a discussion, Jin and Xia Liangxian notified the families of the dozen deceased militiamen that they could bury the corpses on a slope between Peppercorn Bend and Gengguping. In this manner, they might burn incense and paper to honor the deceased without their ghosts haunting people and disturbing livestock.

Assisting Xia Liangxian, Jin stood on the slope as a howling wind arose, fitting company for the grief and indignation welling up in her bosom.

A single stone marked their huge collective earthen tomb mound.

"The local tutelary deity of the underworld claims souls, keeping the boundaries between life and death. The Azure Dragon is of the East stands guard in front of the mountain; the White Tiger of the West protects the rear. Spirits of those men killed in battle," dashing Xia Liangxian chanted with his sharp, resonant voice, a cock cradled in his arms, "whether your orphaned souls are in the netherworld or wandering the forests and mountains, may they ever enjoy generous offerings of paper money and rice bread. There are no taboos: I offer a rooster to your souls . . ." Accepting a knife from Jin, he slit the rooster's throat with a firm hand. Completing the rite to afford their violently wrested souls a measure of solace, the young *tima* pasted a mixture of blood and feathers on the tombstone erected for the militiamen.

V

Li Diezhu's corpse was laid out in the courtyard. Grief-stricken, Tao Jiuxiang wrapped a swath of white cloth around her head. Twisting a handkerchief in hand, she wept freely as she chanted:

> *Year after year, bamboo seeds produce new shoots,*
> *Fruits ripen in due season.*
> *Flowering bamboo is soon to die,*

Rotting fruit falls from the vine.
My old tiger ... can love me no more,
Ai, he's gone ... back whence he came!

With Sun Fu and Jin in Peppercorn Bend to attend to Mawu, only Tao Jiuxiang and Masui were left to sit in vigil beside Li Diezhu's bier. After a lifetime of relentless hard work, the "old tiger" was stretched out, stiff, lonely, and cold.

Lidu returned from Azure Dragon Monastery midday. He had failed in his charge: as the Daoist master had gone to the county seat, Lidu was unable to bring back a protective talisman. Seeing Li Diezhu dead, he dropped to his knees, guilt-stricken, and wailed aloud, his sobs joining Tao Jiuxiang's unrestrained cries.

"In the name of world fashioner Fuxi," called Xia Qifa, chanting as he strode into the courtyard fully attired in ritual garb, "Heaven possesses the eight trigrams, and earth has four quarters. A man has three ethereal spirits and seven corporeal souls, and ghosts issue forth twelve beams of faint light. Please tell me, madam, when did the deceased fall ill? What were his symptoms? Which doctor did you invite to treat him? What medicines did he take?"

"What about Mawu ... ?" Trembling at the sight of the *tima*, Tao Jiuxiang asked in a broken, hoarse voice.

"He'll be able to eat within a few days," sighed the old *tima*.

On hearing this, Tao Jiuxiang knelt before the *tima* and answered in a singsong chant,

Days one and two, a high fever day and night,
Days three and four, for food and drink he lost appetite,
Days five and six, potent medicines couldn't make him right.
After that, his soul took flight.

Her mourning lament was as bitter as the biting winter wind. Finishing, Tao Jiuxiang suddenly looked up with red, swollen eyes and asked, "*Tima*, where are you from?"

Xia Qifa intoned, "Great Shamanmount."

"What have you seen there?"

In response, Xia Qifa chanted,

> *"I've seen an eighty-year-old man shoulder a carrying pole,*
> *A seventy-year-old woman tote a heavy basket load.*
> *I've seen the four seasons' summer heat and winter snow,*
> *The solar crow and the lunar hare come and go,*
> *The three rivers from their sources eastward flow.*
> *I've seen the fate of man, its joy and woe:*
> *But even if to the North Star a man piles his gold,*
> *Under a desolate mound his white bones moulder and grow cold."*

Though it sounded melancholy, something about the primitive rhythm of their back-and-forth chants soothed Tao Jiuxiang.

After a spell, Xia Qifa directed Masui to beat the mourning drum, a thunderous instrument made with the hide of a brownish-yellow bullock that was the collective property of the wards. Usually kept at ward chief Qin's household, the previous evening the drum had been carried muleback to Gengguping.

Sun Fu cut a ten-foot bamboo pole and to its end tidily fastened three precious parcels—tea, rice, and powdered cinnabar—along with fifty-six bundles of paper money. To serve Li Diezhu in the afterlife, he set the bamboo pole at the head of the coffin, together with seven peachwood bows.

The beat of the mourning drum and its resonant echo filled the entire valley. Mountainfolk stopped work and followed the summoning sound to its source to attend the funeral.

Tao Jiuxiang distributed swaths of white cloth to the mourners, who wrapped their heads in turbans. Standing before the coffin, clad in feathered headdress with a bronze bell in hand, Xia Qifa began muttering incantations to commemorate the deceased and dispel evil spirits. He shook his bell with one hand, while, with the nimble fingers of the other hand—in a dizzyingly rapid succession of gestures—mimicked not only wind and rain, mountain and river, thunder and lightning, but every imaginable beast and bird, flower and plant, under the sun and moon.

After the mourning rite, Xia Qifa donned the majestic mask of the Immortal White Tiger, brandished his sword, and loudly beat the drum. Filled with awe, mountain folk began to dance "the granary dance"—a ritual dance some called "Dance of the White Tiger"—in groups of threes or fives. A lugubrious melody came from deep within the *tima*:

> *We were born of Heaven and Earth,*
> *Our ancestress the Goddess of Salt.*
> *Of the five offspring of Wuluo Mountain,*
> *Sky-king of Ba, White Tiger Lord of the Granary,*
> *Was progenitor of countless sons and grandsons,*
> *His issue proliferated in these mountains.*
> *Now like a river in time I sing chants to my ancestor,*
> *A flowing song binding remote antiquity to the present.*

Incense smoke curled around the rafters of the hall, well illumined by red candles. The light of the votive lamp's eternal flame set in the lower right hand corner of the coffin danced and flickered. Portraits of the White Tiger, the eight directional deities, and a bevy of other immortals and spirits kept a stern watch over the proceedings.

Where in the vast netherworld, with its endless labyrinth of forked paths, would Li Diezhu's soul and spirit wind up? Solemnly standing beside the leather drum, a machete balanced on a shoulder, with drumbeats and rhythmic chants, haggard Xia Qifa guided his old friend's soul. Following the Tima, the other mourners intoned. One of the mountainfolk took over the drumsticks and beat the drum with fluid, regular strokes, keeping perfect time with the chant. When he tired, another man seized them and beat the mourning drum powerfully until he was saturated with sweat.

Representing the Qins, Qin Liexiong bowed to Tao Jiuxiang at the gate to express his sorrow. Together with other mourners, he burned incense and entered the house. He staggered over to join the others dancing and stamping to the rhythm of the drumbeats, turning and twisting, stalking back and forth, howling and caterwauling, coiling and springing, imitating the movements of a tiger. He rubbed his face the way a tiger smooths its whiskers, then bent his knees and shook his rump to simulate a wave of the tail. Finally, he threw his head back and howled, "*Aoooo* . . . Kill!" Bathed with hot sweat, his swarthy face beamed.

After Xia Liangxian finished the ceremony at Peppercorn Bend, he hurried to join his father. He arrived at Gengguping, accompanied by Jin and her father.

Weathering his father's death and his elder brother's grievous injury in a single day had forced Masui to grow up. He silently stood behind Tao Jiuxiang, lending a hand whenever necessary. The mountainfolk continued to dance around the coffin with frenzied abandon. He watched for a long while before, unable to resist a moment longer, he took his place among the dancing mourners. Clever Masui proved a natural—stamping left and pouncing right, he followed the movements of the others, soon fluidly melting into their company. After all, he, too, was the spawn of the Tiger—a scion of the mighty creature capable of leaping gorges with its powerful legs and scrambling up steep scarps with its mighty claws.

Suddenly, the drum rhythm changed: Xia Qifa and Xia Liangxian replaced the dancers circumambulating the coffin. Father and son bent at the waist and locked eyes, then slapped palms and knocked elbows. Circling each other they sprang and jumped, uttering intermittent howls. As a finale, gracefully executing a move known as the "Tiger Leap," handsome Xia Liangxian did an aerial backward somersault, passing over his father's head and landing catlike before the coffin.

Afterward, Xia Qifa led his disciples in a tireless three-night, two-day performance. First came the drum music: three sets with small-scale battle drums and three thunderous sets of large-scale war drums. Next came six sets of six mounted archery dances. Finally, they staged seventy-two "breaking enemy ranks" martial dances, set to cymbals and drums. For three days in the packed main hall of the Li household, Xia Qifa passionately chanted in the old regional dialect, clutching the bronze bell in one hand and the machete in the other, re-telling and re-enacting the arduous rise of the Tribe of the Tiger, as they fought endless battles and cleared away briars and brambles to carve out a realm. Transported by the *tima*'s whirling paces, the sonorous clanging of the bell, and the endless chants, the mourners felt as though they had arrived in the kingdom of their proud ancestors.

All the mountainfolk exclaimed in admiration that only Xia Qifa could organize such a solemn and spectacular funeral, a ceremony worthy of a great warrior.

At dawn on the fourth morning, the old *tima* stood beside the coffin and resolutely shattered a tile, a symbol of the mundane, this-worldly life. In this manner, Li Diezhu might, for once and for all, sever his earthly attachments with his well-built, sturdy house and ascend to heaven as a white tiger.

Leading the funeral procession, several women accompanied Tao Jiuxiang to Li Diezhu's tomb.

Xia Qifa asked his helpers to burn two bundles of cornstalks in front of the tomb. After the ashes were swept, he entered the cavernous mouth of the tomb and drew an auspicious talisman, activating its numinous force by sifting cinnabar powder over it. Re-emerging, he took a rooster from Xia Liangxian, bit off its coxcomb, and consecrated the inner chamber by sprinkling the cock's blood. Finally, he asked the pallbearers to carry the coffin slowly into the tomb chamber.

Firecrackers exploded. Xia Qifa spritzed the burial site with realgar wine to expel baleful influences and evil spirits. Masui and Jin, representing Mawu, knelt together, and covered the coffin with three spadesful of earth. Soon, with the assistance of the mountainfolk, an impressive mound was erected over the tomb chamber for Li Diezhu.

Chapter Thirteen

I

A stream of incidents—robbery, kidnapping, Mawu's severe injury, and her husband's death—had left poor Tao Jiuxiang grief-stricken. Ever since the Li family had pulled up stakes and moved into the dense forest, their fate had gone through wild fluctuations—meteoric rises and abrupt plunges, like the mountains and gorges surrounding the Yangzi.

As darkness fell, Tao Jiuxiang took Li Diezhu's bamboo pipe down from the wall, her heart filled with sadness. Packing the bowl and lighting it, Tao Jiuxiang slowly took a draw from the long-stemmed pipe. Across the fireplace from his mother, Masui, mired in his addiction to opium, sat listlessly. Mother and son sat in silence: the once-proud Li family had gone to the dogs. Finally, exhausted by the weight of cumulative sorrow, each crawled off to bed.

In the fortnight that followed Li Diezhu's burial, the county governor received reports from Azure Dragon Temple and the mayor of Huangshui that Captain Li Mawu had opened fire on a group of tenant farmers, resulting in the deaths of a handful of farmers and a dozen militiamen. Worried that Mawu's appointment would reflect badly on him, he promptly discharged Captain Li. Seeing the post vacant, Qin Liexiong immediately bribed his way into the office at the cost of a leopard skin and five loads of goldthread. Riding a black horse on inspection, Qin Liexiong wore a black uniform, a rifle slung over his shoulder, a squad of rifle-toting militiamen at his heels. Seeing anyone suspicious in the roadway ahead, he would yell, "Out of the way!" Then, giving his horse a hard stroke to the flanks, he imperiously rode on through. Given this sudden turn of events, Zhou Taiwang kept mum about Liexiong's ties with the bandits, and continued running errands for the Qins as before.

Meanwhile, Peng Guang'ai, the eldest son of Peng Yuju, lost no time rallying kinsmen and friends to form a band of brigands. Burning incense, they took an oath of blood vengeance. Peng invited Liang the bamboo craftsman and his men to teach them martial skills and tricks. By this time, Liang's followers had grown into a veritable army. Claiming to "steal from the rich and give to the poor," his influence had expanded into neighboring Wanxian County. Inspired, Peng Guang'ai armed for rebellion, donned a crimson robe and, under the banner "Resist Tyranny, Protect Families," assumed the title "Great Tiger Bodhisattva." He seized all the rice from the Lis' fields and swore that he would cut off Mawu's head. Facing this crisis, Jin Shaosan spread the story that after badly wounded Mawu had arrived at his home, he had slipped in and out of consciousness. Shortly after learning he had been discharged as Captain, Mawu had lapsed into a coma and died. Afterward, he was buried in the mass grave with the other militiamen. He told Mawu to hide and sent word to Gengguping, telling his in-laws not to call on him, lest they expose his carefully constructed rumor as a blatant lie.

After several days in hiding, Mawu slipped back to Gengguping on a windy, moonless night. His old home had lost all of its former vitality: a miasmal gloom hung over the rhino's rump. He awakened Tao Jiuxiang, knelt in the darkness at the foot of her bed, and said tearfully, "I have failed our ancestors."

In the light of a lamp held by Sun Fu, Tao Jiuxiang tightly clutched her son's sweat-soaked body, and said, "You poor beast, child . . . everyone outside the family thinks you're dead!"

Hearing a familiar voice, Masui emerged from his room. Sure enough it was his brother Mawu, whom he had missed day and night. With mingled surprise, delight, and anguish, he asked, "How's your wound, brother? Ma's almost fretted herself to death."

"It's almost healed." Mawu said, casting a pained look at his mother. "Ma, I'm heading to Wanxian County to find Elder Brother Wang. Then I'll return to drown the Pengs in a sea of blood."

"Who?" Tao Jiuxiang asked.

"Wang Zhengming." Mawu said, looking fixedly toward the lamplight.

Tao Jiuxiang racked her brains to recollect a Wang Zhengming. Finally, she remembered Mawu telling her that Wang Zhengming was the eldest son of her sons' teacher, scholar-gentleman Wang Binquan. Wang Zhengming had gone to primary school in Huangshui, then to a modern school in Chongqing for a Western education. He made a name for himself: marrying the daughter of a Chongqing tycoon, going into business, and ending up in Wanxian as head of the local Paoge syndicate. As Captain, Mawu had met Wang Zhengming and his wife several times in Wang Binquan's home, when the couple returned to Huangshui for Spring Festival. Whenever Mawu spoke Wang Zhengming's name, his voice trembled with admiration. Tao Jiuxiang sighed, "As they say, 'every enmity has its origin, every debt has its creditor.' Since you killed Peng Yuju, his relatives naturally want to hunt you down and take revenge. Just lay low and keep hidden until the storm subsides: let them believe you are dead. Don't take rash action."

Nervously, from behind her husband, Masui's wife ventured, "If Eldest Brother leaves, what will become of the family?"

Tao Jiuxiang retorted, "It'd be much worse for us if the Pengs found him here and captured him."

After a meal, Mawu went to the tower with his mother. Since Qin Liexiong had assumed the post of Captain in Mawu's stead, the militia outpost had been moved to the Qins' homestead along Inkblack Creek. The remaining militiamen had vacated the tower, leaving only the cookwoman, Ran. Hearing Tao Jiuxiang's voice, faithful Ran bustled over, answering the door barefoot. Seeing Mawu, she placed a hand over her mouth in astonishment and gasped, "Is he a man or a ghost?"

Tao Jiuxiang said irritably, "A man back from the gates of hell."

Dawn began to break.

Mawu's familiar, forceful knock roused Jin from a sound sleep. She rose, opened the door, and found that it was Mawu in the flesh. Throwing her arms around him, she buried her face in her husband's chest and sobbed. With a gaze taking in his familiar wooden bed and his bleary-eyed daughter, Mawu swept Jin off her feet and sat down next to the stove, his wife in his lap.

Sitting on a wickerwork stool, Tao Jiuxiang took a few puffs on her pipe before addressing Jin, "Daughter-in-law, Mawu's going to have to leave

Huangshui: the Pengs are not going to let go of their vendetta."

Mawu told Jin his plan. She could only wring a handkerchief and weep.

Tao Jiuxiang said, "Mawu needs to get out as soon as possible—he should rest and take off tonight. Don't cling to him so he dilly-dallies."

Miserably, Jin sobbed, "I know. We can't let anyone find Mawu."

Gazing at his wife, Mawu gnashed, "After I come out of hiding, we'll make a fresh start!"

Tao Jiuxiang said, "I'll take Yongyu out to the yard when she wakes so she won't kick up a ruckus. That way, you can get some rest."

Jin shot a grateful look toward her mother-in-law. Yongyu was sure to cling to and pester Mawu: it had been nearly a month since she'd seen her father. Jin fetched a basin of water so her bone-weary husband could wash up, then Mawu slipped into a side-chamber to rest.

Ran boiled porridge for breakfast. Coaxing Yongyu with toys and treats, Tao Jiuxiang carried her granddaughter out to the yard after the meal.

After preparing a bundle of food for Mawu, Jin lay down beside her man. She looked her sleeping husband up and down. Mawu had aged. A crewcut had replaced his youthful jaunty, mid-length haircut. Though he still radiated heroic vitality, exhaustion had sculpted the contours of his handsome face, carving creases and furrows on his brow. In a deep sleep, his breathing was regular and peaceful, as though he were blissfully unaware of the surrounding danger. After he leaves today, she wondered, when will we be together again? At this thought, a fresh stream of tears ran down her cheeks.

Until mid-afternoon, Mawu lay in bed with Jin in his arms. As the sun set, Tao Jiuxiang led Yongyu back to the stone tower. Tao Jiuxiang whispered to her granddaughter, instructing her not to tell anyone that she had seen her papa; otherwise, she might endanger Mawu and the family. Accompanying these words, Tao Jiuxiang raised a hand and ran her finger across her neck, making a throat-slitting gesture. Eyes widening, Yongyu swallowed in alarm, nodding her head.

When his daughter returned, Mawu played with Yongyu for an hour or two.

"Dad, why did those bandits steal our family's rice?"

"The greedy tenant farmers went behind Baba's back—they were in cahoots with the bandits. That way they could keep all the rice for themselves."

"But why didn't the bandits rob the Qins?"

Mawu, tongue-tied, didn't know how to explain to his daughter the bandits' implacable hostility toward the Lis. Odious Jiang Ermao—a vile bastard deserving of beheading—should answer for it. And Qin Liexiong, that mean-spirited, vicious creature! He would get rid of them sooner or later. He hoisted his daughter up, replying, "I don't know, either. Don't ask so many questions, little Yongyu."

Masui returned at suppertime, his wife He trailing well behind him. The remnants of the Li family gathered that evening for a thankgiving feast.

Later, in the pitch-dark embrace of night, Jin watched her man don a bamboo hat, mount his horse, and disappear into the mists.

Matters quickly grew more complicated. As Captain, Qin Liexiong's primary duties were putting down uprisings, quelling banditry, and keeping the peace. Thus, unexpectedly, while both Qin Liexiong and the Peng family shared bitter enmity toward Mawu and the Lis, a savage, protracted feud broke out between the new Captain and Peng Yuju's lawless sons and nephews.

As Peng Guang'ai, the self-proclaimed "Great Tiger Bodhisattva," gathered more men to expand his forces, he sent for Xia Qifa several times, asking the *tima* to serve as his adviser. He had once seen the old *tima* perform a remarkable ceremony climbing a ladder of swords, treading on their blades barefoot until he reached the top of the tree to which the blades were fixed. After brandishing a string of tallies to exorcise evil spirits, he descended the ladder of swords, solemnly chanting:

> *Climbing up the sword ladder's easy, but its tough climbing down,*
> *Hard as carrying a bamboo basket of water to a high mount's crown;*
> *Fixed to the tree-trunk, the silver-white blades,*
> *Step by step, to the top I've made it.*
> *Each pace the sword edge seems to cut into my feet,*
> *As demons I expel and spirits I greet . . .*

Peng slavered at the thought of the power he would command once the Tima taught him to sword-walk. Xia Qifa, however, politely declined Peng's invitation. Instead, he sent Xia Liangxian to teach Peng a mnemonic chant:

> *When the oxhorn alarm thrice sounds out,*
> *Our troops ascend the sword ladder mount;*
> *I have been a stout man since my mother birthed me,*
> *Never fearing spear or blade would hurt me.*

This chant, the young shaman told Peng, would help protect his men from harm.

This led to one of the most violent and tragic days in the tortuous history of Peppercorn Bend. In his effort to fend off the strenuous "bandit extermination" campaigns launched by militia Captain Qin Liexiong, Great Tiger Bodhisattva Peng Guang'ai had established a military base of operations in Peppercorn Bend. He trained his farmer-bandits relentlessly, transforming them into formidable force of soldiers, fierce and die-hard, ever ready for battle. Wearing straw sandals, pant legs scrolled up to their knees, heads swathed in yellow turbans, the bandits cut imposing if tattered figures. By day, they set up yellow banners and a pair of tables draped in yellow cloth and held "court" to adjudicate disputes that flared among the mountainfolk within their territory. On the banners was written,

> **Farm without paying taxes. Slaughter hogs without a pork levy.**
> **Buy and sell rice without interference.**

A sentinel stood guard under the banners, blowing a trumpet to call court to order. It was not only the Lis: none of the landlords in greater Huangshui collected levy rice from their tenants that autumn.

Caught in the middle of the ferocious battles between two bitter enemies—Qin Liexiong on one side and Great Tiger Bodhisattva Peng on the other—Masui was at a loss. If Qin Liexiong were killed, Peng and his bandits would hold sway. If the Great Tiger Bodhisattva perished, Qin Liexiong would become insufferably arrogant. Still, he would relish the defeat and death of either one of these foes. Tao Jiuxiang's mind, too, was as tangled as a mass of palm fibers; she didn't know who to help and who to harm.

Unable to deal with the growing power of Great Tiger Bodhisattva Peng, Qin Liexiong reported to the county government office, requesting more troops. Finally, after considerable negotiations, he secured the support of Battalion Commander Wei and his men from neighboring Zhongxian County. With a combined might of more than one thousand soldiers, they encircled Peppercorn Bend. The bandits, however, adopted hit-and-run guerrilla tactics, refusing to be lured into any large-scale pitched battles with the government troops. Small groups launched a series of quick-hitting ambushes from dense forest groves and narrow passes, fleeing once they had inflicted damage. When gathered, they were armed bandits; when dispersed, they were farmers. Faced with these tactics, the frustrated government troops resorted to burning the huts and homesteads of the tenant farmers. Seeing their homes burning, the enraged mountainfolk massed, launching a desperate, bloody uprising. In a savage battle that left the recently harvested fields of Peppercorn Bend saturated in blood, the tattered farmer-bandits overcame the joint forces of Qin Liexiong and Commander Wei.

II

After mulling over the dilemma—which of the family's bitter enemies she wanted to see emerge triumphant—Tao Jiuxiang came to the conclusion that she would pray to the departed spirit of her husband Li Diezhu to defeat Peng the Great Tiger Bodhisattva and help government forces gain victory. That way, Mawu could return home sooner. Her prayers, however, went unanswered. For six months, Battalion Commander Wei and Qin Liexiong hunted the bandits. Not only were the Captain and the forces from Zhongxian thwarted at every turn, but the brigands swelled in number. They even had the temerity to kidnap Jin Shaosan.

Before dawn one day, as Old Mother Jin and Aji made rice bread by the light of an oil lamp, several hidden bandits poisoned the watchdogs. Then, pretending to be passersby asking for a light for their tobacco pipes, they swarmed in as soon as the kitchen door opened a crack. They silenced mother and son—telling them not to cry out, or else. The bandits then surged into the bedroom and seized sleepy Jin Shaosan without any resistance. They dragged off bags of rice, money, and Jin Shaosan himself, blubbering for mercy. To get enough silver to ransom Jin Shaosan, Old Mother Jin had to sell the family's goldthread slopes to the Qins—who passed the deed on to Liexiong.

When Qin Liexiong received the Jins' land deed, he sighed with emotion, feeling like a made man. His thoughts turned—as they often did—to the lovely woman that haunted his dreams and waking hours alike: Jin. On a warm afternoon, two militiamen in tow, he walked up the narrow stone stairs leading to the tower at Gengguping.

Cruel fate had addled the most intelligent child of the three Li sons. In the wake of the family's string of tragedies, Masui abandoned himself to opium. A single dose cost a bushel of rice. Just outside the courtyard gate, a score of opium poppies grew. In springtime, Tao Jiuxiang scraped away the milky latex tears seeping from the green seedpods, then boiled them to extract more opium. Mountainfolk knew all too well the seductive toxins of the opium poppy, its addiction that could wither a man's spirit and body. In the past, Tao Jiuxiang used the opium to treat illnesses in the family and ailments of their livestock. She would send Masui to Huangshui to sell leftover opium and buy grain seed. These days, however, the family's patch of poppies was no longer sufficient for Masui's constant use. Though He called her husband when she laid out a steaming breakfast on the table, the food would be long cold by the time Maui dragged himself out of bed. Annoyed, Jin chided her mother-in-law, "Unless we divvy up the property, my brother-in-law will reduce what's left of our household to opium ash!"

Masui's second wife, He, had birthed a weak, runty son, Yongzhi. Hearing Jin's words, He was so terrified that, holding Yongzhi in her arms, she knelt before Tao Jiuxiang and said, "Ma, I am a useless wife: it's my fault that I haven't persuaded Masui to give up opium. But without your presence, his addiction would get worse and worse. If you divide up the property and make the three of us live independently, what would become of the two of us— mother and son?" Tao Jiuxiang thus abandoned the idea of cutting off Masui. After all, she loved her grandson, and, what was more, she could not bear to refuse her daughter-in-law's pathetic appeal.

Jin, however, staunchly refused to leave the stone tower and move in with the rest of the family. She was determined to preserve Mawu's estate and property in his absence. Although bandits had robbed the tower, its spacious chambers and well-crafted furnishings had been left untouched. If she could only rent out their remaining acre or two of mountain fields to tenants, she could support her daughter, herself, and steadfast Ran the cookwoman.

She had never expected that Peng would prove so fierce and formidable, that months would stretch into a year, leaving Mawu in exile, unable to return home. When, she wondered despairingly, would this ever end?

With the stature of a large child, Qin Liexiong limped nearer and nearer, flanked by the two militiamen. Hearing the dogs bark, Jin looked down from the window. Watching stumpy Qin Liexiong pound at the door in his smart, new uniform, the ruddy glow of her lovely cheeks immediately became ashen gray.

"Open the door!" Liexiong barked, "I'm here on official business."

The thick doors opened. Liexiong ordered his men to wait outside, and entered the living room. Seeing that Jin was just as fragrant and sweet, as lovely and charming as ever, his beady eyes opened so wide that his eyeballs nearly bulged out of his skull. A green fire of lust blazed up in his heart. Mawu was dead: it was his turn to possess this woman.

Jin said, "What's the matter? Be quick."

Eyes riveted on her, Qin Liexiong, without evincing a hint of irritation, replied, "In my effort to reclaim Peppercorn Bend and to avenge your husband's death, I've almost been killed by Peng Guang'ai half a dozen times. Can't I even get a cup of water?"

"Bring some tea," called Jin to Ran, who was shucking corn in the next room.

Qin Liexiong said, "I come expressly to see you. You've been widowed for a full year, and have had time to duly mourn your husband. I want to join our two families together in marriage."

Jin retorted, "I'm going to file a lawsuit against you. You instigated Zhou Taiwang to report the design of this tower to Liang the bamboo craftsman. If you hadn't put him up to it, the bandits wouldn't have robbed us. If the bandits hadn't robbed us, Mawu wouldn't have had to take a grain levy from our tenants. If he hadn't been out collecting taxes, Mawu's gun wouldn't have gone off and killed Peng Yuju and the Peng family wouldn't have risen up in revenge. My family would still be flourishing and wealthy. You're the one who dragged my family down—and now you have the face to come here and propose marriage! Get away from me!" Jin wiped away her tears.

"That was Jiang Ermao, not me. Don't listen to the lies of other people trying to sow discord." Qin Liexiong gazed fixedly at Jin's face, sizing her up, as if uncertain whether she was a benefactress or an enemy. "The Lis have fallen from prosperity because Mawu stirred up trouble. He wived you by force, but my Qin family isn't to be trifled with. He tried to seize the levy rice by force, but the tenants at Peppercorn Bend aren't the sort of folk to be pushed around, either. Now he's dead, but I won't hold that against you." With these words, he suddenly grasped Jin and pulled her into his embrace. "We should have been husband and wife from the start..." Though short in stature, large-headed Qin

Liexiong possessed inordinate strength and huge hands.

"Help!" Jin screeched. Ran, the cook-woman, dashed into the living room.

"Get out! This is none of your business!" snarled Qin Liexiong.

Ran, however, said seriously, "Captain Qin, you're going about this all wrong. You're a man of position and standing in these parts. It's my mistress's good fortune to be courted by such a man. You just need to find a matchmaker to negotiate the marriage and formally ask for her hand. A man of your status can't simply cast aside decorum and propriety."

Relinquishing his grip on Jin, Qin Liexiong's prideful face darkened. "Fine . . . fine. I'll look for a matchmaker. But if you're playing games, I promise—things will end very badly for you." So saying, he stalked out the door.

As soon as he reached home, Qin Liexiong sent a militiaman to invite Third Auntie Zhang for tea.

"Third Auntie, when have I ever treated you shabbily?" Qin Liexiong asked the cunning matchmaker, "When have I ever done you wrong? Back when you helped match Mawu with Jin, how much did the Lis pay? This time, if you succeed in making Jin mine—in arranging a formal match—you can name your price in money and grain and it will be brought to your doorstep." With these words, he rose from his armchair, only head-and-shoulders taller than the red-lacquered table. "If you can release an evil spirit, you can catch one: you helped my rival—now help me! Otherwise . . . ," grinding his teeth, he glowered at the matchmaker. After a moment, he barked, "Now go to the Lis and make this match. Go!"

Slapping her thighs as she shed tears of indignation, Third Auntie wandered along the narrow roads in the darkness. Sobbing, she chanted,

> *Heaven and Earth are so unfair,*
> *It rains on me but shines over there.*
> *'Tis my bitter lot to cross mountains and peaks,*
> *Yet all revile the old matchmaker when they speak.*
> *If catkins hang from the chestnut tree flower,*
> *They say the greedy matchmaker wants noodles to devour.*
> *If the flowering chestnut bears a cupule instead,*
> *They say I just covet a meaty pig's head . . . ai!*

She sat ponderously on a stone, took out a handkerchief, covered her head, and went on singing,

> Red flowering pomegranates fill the whole wood,
> I'm the weaver-woman who stitched them together but good.
> Cloranthus flowers, roots deep in the soil of the ridge;
> The matchmaker's the one who built the bridge.
> For days on end these roads I wander binding many a couple,
> My bones may be weary, but my honeyed tongue's supple,
> Rambling to and fro, bearing others' worries and cares,
> But who thinks for a moment of my pain and despair? . . . Ai!

As she chanted sadly, a group of monkeys approached the old matchmaker, blinking their eyes and knitting their brows to mimic her gloomy expression. Several naughty monkeys pelted her with rotting fruit.

Upset, the downtrodden matchmaker tottered on for a distance when she was suddenly struck by an idea. Doubling back, she returned to the Qins. Silver-tongued though Third Auntie was, as she approached a frowning Qin Liexiong the old matchmaker quailed. "Captain Qin, I have an idea."

Surprised to see her again so soon, Qin Liexiong asked, "What?"

"You can't tell a soul that I came up with this plan," said Third Auntie, anxious, leaning toward Liexiong conspiratorially. "If you are determined to have Jin, you'd better just send your men to seize her. Say I go and propose this match to the Lis: Even if they agree, Jin's a widow and this is her second marriage—she'd have to be brought to your household in a black sedan. Think of how it would look for a man of your standing—you'd lose face. Therefore, the best course is to seize her by force."

Qin Liexiong looked approvingly at the old woman and nodded. Third Auntie Zhang, after half a lifetime of matchmaking, truly had a head on her shoulders.

Swearing an oath that he would make Jin his woman, Qin Liexiong sent a militiaman dressed as a woodcutter to hide in a dense cypress grove not far from Gengguping to keep a close watch on the tower.

On a mild spring day in the fifth lunar month, Jin headed out on horseback with Ran to visit her home at Peppercorn Bend. Before they had gone far, they were ringed by a group of masked men. In a trice, Jin was snatched from atop her horse and whisked away.

III

"Don't cry, sweetie, I've missed you like crazy. You're in my home now—much better than living as a widow with the Lis." Liexiong sought to soothe Jin, who, after crying and cursing the entire way, had been locked away in a side chamber of the Qin homestead. Liexiong gave strict orders that no one else was to enter.

"We're not compatible—our horoscopes don't match. You'd better just let me go home or you'll be trapped in bad luck." Jin sniffled, her hair disheveled, her face streaked with tears, her embroidered short-sleeved calico smock rumpled and frayed.

"My father told me that our signs are compatible. In any case, today we become husband and wife." With a leering grin, Liexiong placed powerful hands on her shoulders.

Forcefully, Jin pushed him away.

"This is my house. You're a pheasant locked in an iron cage. It doesn't matter if you're unwilling; you have to accept it. Even if you don't want to do it, it's going to happen. Now get over here!" With these words, Liexiong cornered Jin.

"Listen," a desperate Jin wiped her tears and said, "Mawu isn't dead. He's been hiding from the Pengs, but he's coming back."

Liexiong said in astonishment, "Everyone says he's dead and buried with the other militiamen on the slope near Peppercorn Bend, heading toward Gengguping. It's no use cheating me. And even if he really comes back, I'm not afraid of him—man or ghost. Now, sleep with me!"

And so it was that Qin Liexiong took Jin, Mawu's lovely wife, by brute force and made her his concubine. Liexiong's mother and wife, however, united against Jin, relentlessly bickering and picking quarrels at every opportunity. Liexiong had to move Jin to a new house at the end of the main thoroughfare of Huangshui.

Withered and wasted away, every day Masui drove the herd of goats up the slope, a copy of the *Seven Heroes and Five Gallants* in hand. As the goats grazed, he looked skyward, losing himself in thought, oblivious to the bitter mountain wind.

Tao Jiuxiang seethed. There was no word from Mawu; they should never have spread the rumor of his death. After all, kidnapping a bride was not against the law in Huangshui, and it was only natural for a widow to remarry. Telling her that the "wood had already become a boat," Masui persuaded her to accept the bitter fact. She tried to bite her lip and endure the loss, but seeing motherless five-year-old Yongyu, Tao Jiuxiang was plunged into a dark depression. Every sunrise, she knelt, hair loose and untidy, at the gate and, patting the ground with her palms, chanted,

> *Within Huangshui, in the home of accursed Qin Liexiong:*
> *May all his clothes be ruined by mold, and termites wreck his home.*
> *May his plum and peach orchards wither, his cured meat rot on the bone;*
> *May his salt be filled with maggots; drinking, may he choke on a stone.*

She even uttered a curse wishing death upon Qin Liexiong every time he climbed a rise or passed through a gully. Her imprecations finally brought about the beating of the funeral drums for the Qins. The deceased, however, was not Liexiong but his father, ward headman Qin Zhanyun.

The Qins met with a string of disasters. Jin, who could not bear her thrall to loathsome Liexiong, took revenge. She bathed her netherparts in an aromatic decoction of frankincense and myrtle from a nearby apothecary, an aphrodisiac that sent Qin Liexiong into a relentless rutting frenzy, one that left once rugged and stocky "Short-an-Inch" utterly exhausted and emaciated. To help him recover, his wife Zhou sent her brother Zhou Taiwang to bribe an executioner with three silver dollars for the freshly severed penis of an executed bandit. Though she fed it to Liexiong to help recover his masculine vitality, it proved vain! Captain Qin's militiamen got wind of this and soon word spread all over Huangshui. One wag coined a saying that caught on: "If you love a man, ply him your best pussy; if you hate a man, ply him your best pussy."

When he heard this saying from Zhou Taiwang, the already downcast ward chief Qin sunk into a deeper gloom. The keen-taloned hawk itches to sink its claws into the back of a hare; a savage tiger yearns to hone its teeth on prey: ever since the Li family had moved here, the Qins met with a series of difficulties and obstacles. Time and again, the two families had clashed, locking horns and crossing swords. He deeply regretted not nipping the wild ambitious and boundlessly covetous Lis in the bud: if he'd run them off from the start, none of these subsequent misfortunes would have befallen his family. Since the Qins had moved to Inkblack Creek forty years ago, not a single member of the family had been stricken down by illness or disease. But now, with greater Huangshui enveloped in internecine war and the country plunged in a life-and-death struggle with the Japanese devils, the benevolent and principled ward chief, careworn and troubled, felt the ponderous weight of these matters pressing on his chest. He was stricken with a severe, debilitating illness and soon breathed his last.

The Qins went all out to stage a grand funeral for Magistrate Qin. To prevent an ambush by the bandits, Liexiong sent Tima Xia Qifa and Daoist Master Wang to negotiate a ceasefire. Great Tiger Bodhisattva Peng, out of respect for prestige of these two luminaries, agreed to a one-month truce.

The magnificent funeral—lasting four days and four nights, with an endless flow of banquets—drew an even greater number of mourners than Lie Diezhu's death. It was a solemn affair: dolorous trumpets sounded and melancholy oxhorns groaned, echoing off the cliffs and through the valleys. Invited to jointly stage the ceremony to see the popular local headman off to the netherworld, Xia Qifa and Daoist Master Wang faced an unprecedented challenge. The two parties deliberated long over the division of labor: the Tima and his son, clad in red ceremonial garments, were responsible for the funeral dance, and would guide Qin Zhanyun before Yama, the King of Hell; for his part, black-robed Wang would expiate the sins of the deceased and clear the path, ensuring the ward chief's spirit safe passage. On the burial day, the funerary procession stretched half a mile, including drummers, gongmen, and trumpeters; musicians and lion-and-dragon dancers; porters bearing incense burners and platters; and a train of mountainfolk carrying floral wreaths, pennons with elegiac couplets, and funerary banners. The procession was so long that when the head reached the tomb, the tail could still see the Qins' lovely home on Inkblack Creek.

Great Tiger Bodhisattva Peng's rapidly ascending fortune took a sudden and unexpected turn for the worse. The wicked Japanese devils, who had long wrought savage atrocities in China, could not defeat the Chinese people and declared an unconditional surrender. In charge of the greater Yangzi River Valley, Nationalist General Yang Sen thought the mountainfolk—ever engaging in petty vendettas, dodging the draft, and resisting levies at a time their country desperately needed manpower—were short-sighted and foolish. Therefore he ordered Chen Houting, a brigade leader serving under Wang Lingji, a division commander of the Nationalist army stationed in Wanxian County, to personally lead troops to help the militia to subjugate the bandits in Huangshui.

The final battle between Great Tiger Bodhisattva Peng's men and the Nationalist forces was waged in Peppercorn Bend. After imbibing a magic elixir, Peng charged through a hail of bullets, leading his men into battle. Brandishing a long sword, he weaved left and danced right, slicing the heads cleanly off several government soldiers. Seeing the bandit leader unharmed, the baffled Brigade Commander Chen later wrote in his report: "Many bandits were shot to death on the battlefield, but their leader, riddled with hundreds of bullets, remained unhurt. His clothes are filled with scores of holes, but there was no evidence of wounds except for tiny pox-like dots on his body where the bullets struck. Ballistics experts will need to investigate."

The battlefield dissolved into bloody chaos. The bodies of beheaded government soldiers staggered about before collapsing down to the ground. Heaven and earth were filled with the cries of the dying. Amid the gunfire, Xia Qifa, clutching a banner reading, "Rescue the Dying and Heal the Wounded," hurried onto the battleground with several disciples and scores of villagers. Together, they buried the dead and tended to the injured.

Shot in the back, one bandit writhed on the ground. During the battle, a bullet had pierced his abdomen, allowing air to enter, before exiting through his stomach; as he continued fighting, his abdomen had inflated, growing larger and larger. Roaring "Hold your breath!" Xia Qifa knelt over the agonized fellow, inscribing a character in the air above the wound. The bandit fell limp to the ground, and was carried off by kindly villagers. Later, the wound was covered with a mud poultice three times and the man recovered, bearing telltale scars on both sides of his body. He lived for another ten years. Xia Qifa also tended and cured a number of Nationalist soldiers. Moved by the tireless ministrations of the shaman, men on both sides fervently said, "Even as we fight like cats for scraps on this plate of blood, let no one do the slightest harm to Xia Qifa or his family. To do otherwise would be utterly inhumane."

The battle raged from the break of dawn till mid-afternoon. Finally, Peng could no longer resist the onslaught of government forces, and, hemmed in, was forced to flee toward Dragon Decapitating Gorge with two dozen bodyguards. There was no escape from the gorge. The names of war martyrs were graven on the cliff beneath the immured dragon, set below a quatrain that read,

> *Cunning and cruel our neighbor to the east,*
> *Wantonly seeking to leave our China destroyed and fleeced,*
> *Though our brave martyred soldiers may be gone like flowing sands,*
> *Let our wild mountainfolk friends and neighbors ever together band.*

The solemn poem bore witness to the realization of the ancient prophecy that foretold rivers of blood and slaughter among these mountainfolk.

The sun had already sunken behind the mountains, leaving a blood-dyed western sky in its wake. Government troops swarmed through the mouth of the gorge, surrounding the bandits. A commander cried aloud, "Do not resist! We only want Peng Guang'ai! We'll let the rest of you leave in peace. Abandon Peng Guang'ai and flee for your lives!"

Cornered in the gorge, Great Tiger Bodhisattva Peng saw no way out. How he wished that, like his great Immortal White Tiger ancestor who once led the fierce people of Ba, he too might fly up into the firmament on the day of his doom and become one of the stars above! Sadly, he mused, "Even immortals are sometimes defeated: Why should we, too, not be killed in battle?" He urged his bodyguards to abandon him and save themselves; but to a man they refused, vowing to fight by his side to the end. The end came quickly: fighting by the side of the Great Tiger Bodhisattva in the fading light the lot of them were shot to death.

Seeing Peng fall, the Nationalist forces—having sustained tremendous losses in the course of the battle—surged forward to search for his corpse. The soldiers swore that they would carve off a hunk of that enchanted dog's flesh and eat it raw. But though they scoured the area where the bandits made their last stand, they could not find Peng's corpse anywhere in the quick-falling darkness. At last, deeply perturbed, they returned to their bivouac in a huff.

Busy tending to the wounded in Peppercorn Bend, Xia Qifa and Xia Liangxian did not return home that evening. After the government troops left, Old Mother Xia sent two neighbors to check whether Peng was truly dead. Afraid of the darkness, the two put the task off until the following morning. Shortly after dawn, they entered the shallow vale, whispering, "Great Tiger Bodhisattva, where are you? Come out, and we'll carry you back home."

Shortly, the pair located Peng's corpse in a dense clump of bushes. One dragged the corpse, while the other pushed aside the brush. His body proved almost wieghtless, so that even after they bore the body to all the way to Peng's homestead in Peppercorn Bend neither man had broken a sweat. That very night funeral drums resounded, summoning more than two hundred villagers from near and far. Rumor circulated at the funeral that government forces had bought off one bandit who, forgetting principle for profit, fed the Great Tiger Bodhisattva a rice cake soaked in dog blood, dispelling Peng's mystical powers. Otherwise, the bullets fired by the Nationalist troops never could have penetrated his flesh. Thus, the heroic bandit king was secretly interred among the mountain crags above Peppercorn Bend.

With Brigade Commander Chen's defeat of the Great Tiger Bodhisattva, the Lis, the Jins, and the other wealthy households in Peppercorn Bend were utterly delighted: long had they awaited the day when they could once again plant and harvest crops without the depredations and interference of the brigands. Exhaling a collective sigh of relief, Huangshui staged lion dances and dragon lantern dances, celebrating both the victory over the bandits and the defeat of the Japanese devils. The lively festival lasted a fortnight: the deafening clamor of drums and gongs bespoke the untrammeled joy of the mountainfolk. Honorary ribbons were presented to the soldiers. Captain Qin Liexiong personally beat the festal drum and sang, "The red banners wave and flutter . . ." With a flood of songs and a whirl of dances, Brigade Commander Chen and his men were sent away in triumph.

In the aftermath, weary and complacent Captain Qin Liexiong wanted to bring Jin, several months pregnant, back to Arrow Bamboo Gulch to give birth at his homestead. However, he was adamantly opposed by Old Mother Qin, who refused to allow Jin entry to the house on the grounds that she was born under an unlucky star and Liexiong's wife Zhou had already birthed two sons. Unable to oppose the joint resistance of his mother and wife, Liexiong reluctantly sent two militiamen back to Huangshui with the tidings.

Over the past year, unending anxieties about women in the inner quarters and brigands afield left the harried Captain in such low spirits he could scarcely recall the delectable fragrance of the crawfish from Inkblack Creek.

Part II

Chapter Fourteen

I

The dense clusters of corn stalks, scattered here and there, were already more than half a man's height; with abundant sunlight and fecund soil, their broad leaves arched, verdant and vital, like so many tapered silk ribbons. The cart road to the Li homestead on Gengguping remained. As one approached the crest of the hill, the undergrowth grew increasingly dense, encroaching on the path. The dense bloom of azaleas had come and gone, leaving visible the oily-bright leaves and the tangle of contorted trunks wrapped in sharp-thorned creeping vines.

> *My blade enters clean, comes out covered with blood,*
> *Oh, today I'm gonna slaughter me a good fat hog.*

Flushed crimson with drink after sharing some cups with a fellow hunter, Zeng Laomao, a plowshare maker, sang loudly as he staggered toward his home at the foot of the mountain. His upper torso was bared, his shirt casually tossed over a shoulder. As he lurched forward, his ditty burbled on:

> *I'll cut off a chunk, you slice off a piece,*
> *Let's dress this pig and eat some meat.*

"Laomao, you're drunk again. Careful of ghosts barring your way," Among several tenant farmers, their trouser legs and sleeves scrolled up, one fellow looked up from weeding corn and chuckled, interrupting Zeng's merry tune.

Zeng snorted, "Every ghost's afraid of me ... I ... ahh ... ahhh ... .ahhh." He raised his lips skyward, wolfishly exhaling a mighty cloud of alcoholic vapors.

Coming from the other direction, walking at the foot of an escarpment, came a porter shouldering a load of firewood and a timber trader in a long gown and a felt hat. The tenants watched the two curiously. Their gaze rested upon the trader as they whispered to each other, "Is that ... ?" "That's Captain Li!"

"It is ... but he's dead and buried."

The tenants spat and fled.

Wrapped in deep thought, Mawu returned from Wanxian County wearing a style of felt hat that was fashionable in the city. His eyes were grave, suffused with grief; but his posture and broad shoulders still reflected his unyielding vigor. Wang Zhengming had taught him quick-hitting guerrilla tactics and presented him with eight new imported rifles, so that he might do battle with Qin Liexiong and Battalion Commander Wei. Wang Zhengming's reputation and name card gave Mawu safe passage to Greenstone, where he disembarked before the gorge narrowed and the turbulent waters of the Yangzi became a whirlpool as they passed through Kuimen Gate. When he disembarked from the boat at Greenstone, he had hired a porter to carry his load of "firewood" concealing the rifles. Since then, day and night he had grimly trudged homeward.

Over the past two years, he had led a tempestuous, peripatetic life, following Wang Zhengming to Fengjie, Wushan, Yichang and Chongqing. But as he wandered, he couldn't help missing his mother, Jin, Yongyu, and Masui. During this interval, his complexion lightened, a short beard sprouted on his chin, and the expression of causal arrogance he sometimes wore as a young man became an ever-present wariness.

Before Mawu headed home, Wang Zhengming held a parting banquet. As soft music played on the gramophone, Wang revealed to his protégé with gentle words the truth that Qin Liexiong had seized Jin by force, a secret he had kept for a year-and-a-half fearing that knowledge of his wife's kidnapping would have distracted Mawu and made his exile unbearable. Shocked and infuriated, Mawu jerked one of Wang Zhengming's arms so violently that he tugged his benefactor to the ground. An unslakeable rage coursing through his veins, he burned to speed home like an arrow. He felt puzzled and humiliated: as he had waged a tireless life-and-death struggle for his motherland, that odious bastard had stolen his wife and destroyed his family. Why should a revolutionary pay such a bitter price?

"You back home, Cap'n Li?" drawled Zeng Laomao with an inebriated murmur, blithely unconcerned that he was standing face-to-face on the narrow mountain track with a man reputed to be dead.

"I'm back," replied Mawu.

Triggered by a sudden thought, Laomao staggered two paces then stopped stock-still. Gazing at Mawu with bloodshot eyes, he asked, "You a man or a ghost?"

It dawned on long absent Mawu that he was dead in the eyes of his fellow Huangshui countryfolk. Casting an annoyed glace at Laomao, he retorted, "You're the damned ghost! I'm alive."

"Ah . . . didn't think you looked like a ghost." Braced by alcohol, the plowshare-maker clasped Mawu in an amiable bearhug while secretly biting his left middle finger so that he drew blood. As he reeled back, Laomao smeared blood on Mawu's gown, shouting, "You afraid of that, ghost?"

Looking at the blood soaking into his gown, Mawu frowned, "If I'm a ghost, why do I have a shadow?" He pointed to a clay statue in a tree hollow, adding, "And would the earth god let me pass?"

With blood-red eyes, the plowshare-maker gazed at Mawu dubiously, "Let's go down to the river and see if you have a reflection."

After his long walk, Mawu was thirsty. He turned to the porter, "Hey mate, let's take a break and drink some water." Preoccupied by cumulative sorrows, he hunkered on the river's edge and removed his cap, gazing at his reflection. Two years ago he was the man. In the streets of Huangshui, even the beggars invited him for a drink. Back then, none dared scold him when he acted the derelict; or even when his horse cropped grain from a passing field. As he pondered the current state of affairs, he drank several scoopfuls of water from his cupped hands and wiped his dripping jaw. Turning to Zeng Laomao, he said gravely, "Before I was a ghost; now I'm a man."

His alcohol-addled mind clearing, the plowshare-maker saw Mawu's image in the water. He took out a bamboo tube he carried, dipped it in the river, and took a deep draught. He splashed a second tubeful on his overheated midriff, and asked skeptically, "You really alive?"

Fixing his gaze on the plowshare maker, Mawu said, "I've been in Wanxian and Chongqing for a spell. How's the goldthread market?"

Still reeking to high heaven of drunkenness, Zeng Laomao answered, "The price is rising. Couple days ago, the Zhous sold a load for 80,000 yuan. Ha! Aha! I get it . . ."

"Get what?" Mawu asked, puzzled as a string of giggles erupted from the drunk.

The bemused plowshare maker responded, "I'm laughing 'cause you were on the run from Great Tiger Peng. Now that he's dead, you've come back home."

Mawu passed a small patch of goldthread on the slope, then turned to Zeng Laomao with a somber expression and said, "It's true. The Captain Li you once knew is dead. I'm another man now. If you have time, stop by my stone tower for a cup of liquor and some tea." After that, he nodded his goodbye to the plowshare maker.

When the price of goldthread bottomed out, Tao Jiuxiang stopped collecting rhizomes for several years. When she heard that goldthread prices were rising again, she planted some precious stalks long hidden in a sandy cave hollow in a nearby cliff.

That afternoon, Tao Jiuxiang was sitting in the courtyard shucking corn when watchdog Black Leopard began to bark. As she raised her eyes, a man strode into the yard, a felt hat on his head. Betraying no hint of alarm, Black Leopard trotted over to greet him in a friendly manner. Crossing the threshold, the man removed his hat and called, "Mother!"

Her hair completely white, Tao Jiuxiang tottered as she struggled to her feet; Mawu hurried over and supported her with firm hands. Behind her stood Yongyu, who had grown much taller, blinking her eyes incredulously. A delighted and astonished Masui emerged with his new wife and puzzled young son, a nephew Mawu had never met.

Guiltily, Mawu tousled his daughter's hair.

"Your wife," said Tao Jiuxiang deliberately, "is in Huangshui."

II

Entering the stone tower, Mawu stared blankly. Once so full of life, love, and energy, its interior chambers were now tomb-like, covered in dust and spiderwebs. Stroking his beard, wracked by torment, Mawu collapsed on his bed.

Masui stood to one side, dejectedly smoking a homemade cigarette. Tao Jiuxiang followed them into the room, shaking her head. Her voice quavering as if her stout heart were broken, she uttered, "So bitter . . . my poor eldest son!"

Sitting up, Mawu hung his head and wept. Gradually composing himself, he calmed and raised his eyes. Changing the topic, he reported, "When I was in Yichang a fortnight ago I visited the battleground where Mahe fell. Because the battle was fought in the heat of summer, the remaining soldiers were so afraid of plague and pestilence that they just hurriedly buried the bodies in a mass grave and left. Since then a dreadful chorus of groans and howls, both in Chinese and Japanese, have echoed nightly in the mountains. The locals are petrified and have sought government help to summon *timas* from far and wide to perform an exorcism. When I told the mayor of Xiling Gorge Village that Uncle Xia Qifa was the perfect man for the task, he wrote a letter of invitation at once—said traveling expenses would be reimbursed. We need to send for Uncle Xia right away."

Tao Jiuxiang said sadly, "With Mahe buried there, it would be good if he took part in the rite. How can he get there?"

Mawu answered, "He needs to disembark from Wanxian County and head downstream by barge, then change to a smaller boat at Xiling Gorge. After a couple hours heading upstream, he needs to anchor at the bank and climb up into the mountains. The journey takes four or five days. Masui had better go with him."

Tao Jiuxiang wiped away her tears, "Tomorrow Masui will go to Dragon Decapitating Gorge and ask the old *tima* to set out."

Masui asked, "I still don't get it. Do we change boats at Yichang?"

Mawu said, "Yeah. A couple days before I arrived, locals captured two Japanese dressed in long gowns and talking Chinese."

Masui asked nervously, "What were they doing there?"

Mawu replied, "They were disguised as Chinese . . . they'd come by boat from Nanjing with steamed bread and wine to make offerings to deceased souls of Japanese devils sunken in that watery grave. After they got drunk, people recognized them as Japanese and grabbed 'em."

Tao Jiuxiang sneered, "How can devils pretend to be men?"

Mawu said, "An old man was gathering kindling by the riverside when he saw a stranger setting out incense sticks, pacing and murmuring, hands raised above his head. He also saw another stranger weeping. He thought they were a couple of *tima* some household had invited to perform a rite, but the longer he listened the more it seemed something wasn't right. Initially he thought the two were speaking in tongues, but then the old man, who had been captured by Japanese soldiers and forced to do hard labor, realized they were speaking Japanese. But it turned out they weren't soldiers; they were shamans who had accompanied the Japanese imperial army. At first folks didn't believe them: beat them half to death before they were taken into custody."

Tapping off a head of cigarette ash, Masui offered, "The Guomindang National Army should execute them."

Mawu said, "Ma, Masui my brother . . . from now on don't mention the Guomindang Nationalist Army. Chiang Kai-shek has started a civil war, but the Communist Party is going to overthrow him and found a new state."

Startled, Masui murmured, "A new state?"

Mawu warned, "Don't speak of this to anyone."

Tao Jiuxiang said, "The mountains are high and the emperor is far away. Dynasties come and go—doesn't make a bit of difference in this remote nook."

The shrill voice of Mawu's wife He pierced the darkness, "Ma, dinner's ready!"

Mawu looked around the desolate bedchamber once more before rising and following his mother and brother, trudging down the stone steps. With a clangorous echo, Tao Jiuxiang closed the heavy door to the tower behind him.

For three years, He had boiled rice for Masui and the Li family. Over the meal, when she heard her mother-in-law mention that her husband was to accompany the *tima* Xia Qifa to a huge shamanic rite on the battleground in Hubei to help usher Mahe's soul to Heaven, she recalled that her own eldest brother had fallen in battle in distant Hebei. Gazing without appetite at the dishes on the table, she sat cocooned in a reverie of woe.

Mawu held up his bowl of wine. "I'll write Wang Zhengming a letter, asking him to help buy Uncle Xia and Masui berths on a ship." He turned to Masui: "You can present it to him when you reach Wanxian."

Yongzhi, Masui's son, had just begun to sit up by himself at the table. With cheerful cries, he ate sloppily, strewing food all over the table. Masui fed him several spoonsful of meat and vegetables, instructing him, "Little fellow, your baba's off to Yichang. Try to get a little more food in your mouth. Don't make grannie chase you around to feed you."

Setting an example, Yongyu offered, "Look, little brother—eat like this."

Yongzhi slid down from the bench, mischievously toddling beneath the table. Grabbing her son by the arm, He roughly set him back to the bench, scolding, "Sit tight and eat! When you're done you can play with your cousin. If you don't behave, Mama will give your ears a good boxing!"

Flailing his arms and stomping, Yongzhi called out, "Boxin' Mama, boxin' Mama!" Masui and Tao Jiuxiang glared balefully at He. Tao Jiuxiang reached over and wiped his Yongzhi's snotty nose.

Mawu emptied his wine cup. Seeing that his mother had added meat and vegetables on top of the rice in his bowl, he tucked in, shoveling down one big mouthful after another. Setting down his chopsticks, he quietly announced, "I'm going to see Yongyu's mother."

Sun Fu, placing a tureen of soup on the table, responded, "Ever since his fight with Peng and the bandits, Liexiong's turned his place in Huangshui into a veritable fortress, with militiamen keeping sentinel. Nobody can enter without his permission."

A stifling silence settled over the room. Giggling and joking with Yongzhi a moment earlier, Yongyu fell quiet. As her face contracted into a mask of anguish, she sobbed, "I miss my Mum."

Hurriedly, He wiped away her niece's tears.

Gnashing his teeth, Mawu took a pack of foreign cigarettes from his pocket. Walking briskly to the fireplace, he lit one. Knotting his debonair brow, grim determination etched on his face, he took several long draws in succession.

III

At the crack of dawn Masui set off, wending his way to Dragon Decapitating Gorge, Mawu's letter to Wang Zhengming and the invitation from the mayor of Xiling Gorge carefully tucked away. Tao Jiuxiang had asked him to bring back a small bag of earth from the stronghold where Mahe had fallen.

After Masui departed, without the slightest mention of Jin, Mawu roamed the gorges and valleys inviting a small group of rugged mountain men—men, including the plowshare-maker, Zeng Laomao, known far and wide for their swordplay and marksmanship with a rifle—to the stone tower for a cup of tea. Rather than giving vent to petty personal grievances and enmities, he launched into a discussion of larger issues of state, warning his fellow countryfolk, "Though the Japanese devils have surrendered, Chang Kai-shek is apt to launch a civil war, dragging us all into a quagmire far more bitter than the most acrid tendril of goldthread."

Apprehensive, the plowshare maker warned, "Don't talk crazy. I'm neighbors with a ward chief."

Mawu said to the seven bold worthies assembled, "Listen, Gengguping is so closed-off and remote that all you folks know is the little patch of sky above us—you can't see the big picture . . . the larger situation in the country—in China. Cityfolk all know that the Japanese devils have raped, violated, burned, and murdered our fellow countrymen. Luckily the Communists' Eighth Route Army and New Fourth Army fought back, sacrificing their lives in their bloody fight against the evil invaders. Meanwhile craven Chiang Kai-shek and his government fled to Chongqing to hide, abandoning our fellow Chinese to wanton death and destruction, so that even those fortunate enough to survive had to leave their native homes and fields in desperate flight as hunted refugees."

The plowshare maker grinned, "In Huangshui, the mountains are high and the emperor is faraway. Who's king don't matter none to me!"

Mawu recalled swearing an oath at Wang Zhengming's behest before an impressive portrait of Mao Zedong on his patron's wall. "Look," he said thoughtfully. "A man should live and die with purpose. Who among you has the nerve to follow me and take a man's life?"

"Whose?" asked Zhao Changyou, a bamboo craftsman from Peppercorn Bend.

"First, I'll give each of you a gun!" said Mawu resolutely, opening a cabinet. Taking out an armload of modern rifles, he declared, "A rifle for every man who follows me!"

The unused bayonets glinted in the afternoon sun. Zhao Changyou ran his rough hands admiringly over the smooth butt of a rifle, his eyes staring toward the endless forest. "A semi-automatic rifle! I could do anything I want with that! So tell me, who do you want to get rid of?" he asked, lovingly sliding the bolt back and forth.

Mawu looked him in the eye, "Qin Liexiong. He's crushed an uprising of the people—of the peasants—and seized my wife by force. He's not just a bloody foe of my Li family, he's part of a clique of warlords that oppresses the masses. Let's form a guerrilla unit and eradicate him. Huangshui is remote and on the borders of three different counties—beyond the reach of the longest whip. It's like Jinggangshan for Mao Zedong—the ideal place for guerrillas to operate."

Zeng Laomao, at a loss, asked, "You do realize the Huangshui militia is no pushover. How do you plan to get the upper hand?"

"We'll triumph with strategy and cunning." Mawu answered.

"Qin Liexiong has kin ties with Xiang Jintang, the mayor of Peartree Moor in Enshi County. Won't Xiang Jintang want revenge?" one fellow timidly mused.

"Right now Xiang Jintang, the wicked local tyrant of Enshi, is besieged by bandits. We'll beat drums in the mountains to alarm the tiger: when we eliminate Qin Liexiong, it will serve as a warning." As Mawu spoke, he caught hold of a cat, pierced it with the point of a knife and let several drops of blood fall into bowls of wine on the table. "Now take up your rifles, lads, and drink up!"

The cat's blood represented the blood of a tiger. Mawu and the seven men raised their bowls and emptied them.

As Mawu dragged the pig from the pen and laid it out on the flagstones, ready for slaughter, Tao Jiuxiang gasped, "What are you doing?"

"These good folks say that as I've been lucky enough to come through these disasters alive, I ought to invite them over and slaughter a hog to celebrate." He divided the men into two groups. One butchered the hog, scalding it, scraping off the bristles, and dressing it; the other learned the "Three Rules of Discipline and the Eight Points of Attention," the military regulations for the People's Liberation Army soldiers that Mawu had copied from Wang Zhengming's notebook.

"Look, as revolutionary soldiers," Mawu began, in a low, serious voice, "you need to keep the Three Rules and Eight Points fixed in your minds. Rule Number One: Obey the orders of your commanding officer; only when we march in cadence can victory be gained. Rule Number Two: Do not take a single needle or piece of thread from the masses; in turn, the masses will offer their support and love. Rule Number Three: Any property and goods captured in battle must be turned over to the authorities for the public good; in that manner, the burden on the masses will be diminished . . ."

The two groups of men listened, in turn, learning the rules and points by heart, and when they had finished the study session, adjourned to enjoy a feast of pork dishes. After they finished, Mawu led his guerrilla detachment out the gate.

As scout, Zeng Laomao discovered that Qin Liexiong had left his compound and returned to the Qin family home in Arrow Bamboo Gulch. Under the moonlight, the guerrillas clutched their rifles, moving down the slopes until they reached Inkblack Creek. In the very heart of the night, at the rear of the file the plowshare-maker saw a huge snake—seven feet long and thick as a man's leg—slithering across the creek in the moonlight, like a small boat leaving a wake, its prow cutting through the water. Hearing a gasp of astonished horror, Zhao Changyou turned to see Zeng Laomao step into the stream. Rushing back, he dragged the plowshare-maker to the bank, as Zeng Laomao wordlessly motioned toward the creek waters. Following the trajectory of his comrade's tremulous raised arm, Zhao Changyou saw the long serpent, its head and tail invisible, the large white splotches on its black skin glistening in the moonlight. The snake swam to and fro, whooshing through the water. Alarmed, Zhao Changyou rushed up to Mawu and seized his wrist, saying anxiously, "There's a giant cauliflower rat snake back there, churning up waves three feet high!" When Mawu and the others went back to look, they couldn't see anything, but heard a splashing sound, as if something was cutting through the water.

"It's a huge snake . . . so long I couldn't see its head or its tail," Zeng Laomao explained. He went on to say that just before he saw the snake, he'd seen a female figure beside a spectral fire in the distance, crouched close as if to keep warm. In the firelight she looked like Zhou Damei.

Could she have returned as a mane from the netherworld to visit her sister Ermei? Mawu wondered. Not wanting to show that his resolve had faltered, he rounded on Zeng Laomao, glaring daggers, and said coldly, "No one's making you come. If you don't have the nerve, then leave."

"I saw her," said Zeng Laomao, "I swear."

Zhao Changyou added, "Me, too."

Feeling the snake and Damei's ghost portended something ominous, Mawu decided to return home and chose another time for action.

Two days later, Mawu asked his mother for two bushels of buckwheat. Two of his men spent the whole night grinding it into flour. Tao Jiuxiang passed the following day baking it into cakes. Before embarking from Mawu's home for a second time, the men fortified themselves with several plates of buckwheat cakes.

Upon reaching Inkblack Creek, Mawu asked Zeng Laomao to burn a stick of incense. A pale, gibbous moon hung in the night sky; a chill night wind soughed through the trees. Yet the wispy column of incense smoke rose skyward unbroken, without swirling and dispersing. Mawu was pleased.

Though the mountain wind was raw, by the time they had reached the creek Mawu and his men were sweating. As dawn broke, they arrived at the Qin homestead on the alluvial plain at the foot of a steep scarp. Shortly, when a bleary-eyed porter opened the gate to fetch water from the creek, his mouth was gagged and a cold bayonet was pressed against his throat. Guessing what the masked guerillas wanted, the terrified porter, his legs gone soft, inclined his jaw towards the inner chambers. Knowing that most of the militiamen had been sent to burn incense, Mawu and his men stormed into the chamber. The doors were unbolted. Oblivious, his eyes closed in dazed contentment, Qin Liexiong lay back smoking his opium pipe, a stray lock of his disheveled hair—cut in Huangshui's latest fashion with a center part—pasted to his forehead. Qin Liexiong's first wife Zhou slept by his side; a servant girl stood beside the bed. With a bayonet thrust toward the familiar face of his foe, Mawu opened a huge gash, cutting off a piece of Qin's scalp. Liexiong opened his eyes, and, through the blood running down his face, saw, to his great astonishment and horror, the murderous bearing of his erstwhile neighbor! As Qin desperately reached for the pistol he kept hidden under his pillow, Mawu plunged the bayonet deep into his chest. "Short-an-inch" crumpled, slumping to the floor.

The servant girl screamed. Qin's wife was so terrified that her pee flooded the bed. Repeatedly kowtowing, she begged, "Mercy! Have mercy! Spare my life!"

IV

After Mawu killed Captain Qin Liexiong, he stuffed the mouths of Qin's wife and maid with cloth, leaving the women bound and gagged, face-up, on the bed. Although his men had learned the "Three Rules of Discipline and the Eight Points of Attention," one fellow named Luo Jiaji stripped off his rags and replaced them with Liexiong's new coat; Zhao Changyou slipped into the kitchen, opened the oven, grabbed a hunk of cured pork and stuffed it into his mouth, before quickly fastening a bundle of loose silver dollars, packets of opium, and a pair of rifles to a carrying pole. By the time Liexiong's militiamen finally noticed the incursion, the guerrillas were already halfway up a nearby ridge. Though the shocked militiamen gave half-hearted pursuit and fired a few shots in their direction, they were few in number and, fearing ambush, quickly retreated.

Arriving on Speargrass Plain, Mawu called for a halt. Searching his men thoroughly, Mawu confiscated all the stolen property and ordered Luo Jiaji to remove the silken coat. Reluctantly taking off the coat, Luo Jiaji stood holding his rifle, his upper torso naked. After hiding in a copse all day, they moved under cover of darkness back to Gengguping. As Tao Jiuxiang watched silently, he allocated a several dozen cartridges to each man. Excitedly they left, returning to their homes.

Mawu peeled off his blood-sodden coat, handing it to his mother. "I've killed Qin Liexiong!"

Tao Jiuxiang dropped the bloody coat in a basin. Worried, she said, "Sooner or later the Qins will find out, and the government will back them. Go hide out with Wang Zhengming again." So saying, she dumped a bucket of water into the basin to scrub the coat.

Mawu said, "Now that I'm back, I'm not planning to leave again."

Tao Jiuxiang shot a sorrowful glance at her eldest son: "I've birthed and raised three sons; I don't want to grow old alone."

Mawu said, "I'm going to stay in the tower for a couple of days and see how things unfold." Then he took the guns, silver, and opium from Liexiong's home and hid them in the cave behind the tower. He secreted himself in the stone tower, warily observing every flutter of grass in the wind.

In two short years, three militia captains had been cut down or killed. This chaos greatly alarmed the provincial government, marring the victorious afterglow of the War of Resistance against Japan.

Lying in bed in the pre-dawn of his fifth day immured in the tower, Mawu heard the half-dozen hunting dogs in the yard erupt into a furious chorus of barks. Following suit, the hound he kept in the tower bayed furiously. Through the loopholes, he saw four or five militiamen rushing the tower. Seizing the loaded pistol from under his pillow, he moved through a hidden exit to the densely thicketed copse. Warily, he slid into the old cave in the cliff-face, where the family had taken refuge the first time the tower came under siege.

Tan Ruideng, vice mayor of Huangshui, led a group of militiamen to the

Li family's nearby homestead. In a well-coordinated attack, seven men simultaneously forced their way in through windows, throwing bleary-eyed Tao Jiuxiang into a panic and terrifying Masui and He out of their wits. "Li Mawu, where are you? Come out!" Tan Ruideng growled harshly.

"Mawu died two and half years ago." Tao Jiuxiang said.

"Hurry up and search! He's not dead." Tan Ruideng ordered.

"Mayor Tan," said Tao Jiuxiang anxiously, "Couple years back my Mawu served as a militia Captain, grabbing bad guys for the local authorities. We're a law-abiding family. What the problem?"

"Madam, we are no strangers to you," replied Tan Ruideng. "To tell the truth, I'm glad Mawu is alive . . . but he shouldn't have killed Captain Qin. We found a discarded worn coat in Qin Liexiong's house. One of Qin's bloodhounds followed the scent to Luo Jiaji's place. Now we know everything."

"Sir," reported a militiaman, entering the room coat in hand. "No sign of Mawu, but I found a bloody coat."

Regretfully, Tao Jiuxiang gazed at the imported cotton coat. Dried blood was almost impossible to wash out. Her carelessness had imperiled her eldest son.

Tan Ruideng said seriously, "One playing with a sword should keep the blade pointed away from himself; one raising a tiger should keep the cage tightly locked. Am I right, Madam?"

Looking beyond the courtyard, Tao Jiuxiang responded with steely resolve, "In this family, sword and tiger are well kept. But anyone who messes with the blade or places his head in the tiger's mouth will meet with grievous harm!"

Another militiaman entered, reporting, "Sir, someone's slept in the tower; the quilt is still warm."

Tan Ruideng barked, "Tell Li Mawu that if he does not surrender himself within five days, all his properties will be confiscated. I would prefer not to do that." He mounted his horse, turned, and added, "My old lady, please think it over." After that, he departed, followed by the detachment of a dozen militiamen.

Once the militiamen were long gone, Tao Jiuxiang went to the cave opening and called softly, "Come on out, they're gone."

Crawling out, Mawu joined his mother, cautiously moving along the steps to the tower. Suddenly, a woodcutter appeared, axe in hand; he wore a conical bamboo hat and patched short pants, toting a woven basket full of kindling on his back. Mawu recognized the fellow as Ma San, who had stayed at their place on Gengguping years before while gathering medicinal herbs. Now, Ma San worked as a messenger for Wang Zhengming. After flashing signals to each other, the pair of them warily entered the tower.

It was hard to place Li Mawu in the turbulent undulations of Huangshui's annals: he was one of those rare larger-than-life figures who transcend conventional moral standards of praise and blame. Ma San presented Mawu a confidential letter from Wang Zhengming. From this missive, Mawu learned that one of Liang the bamboo craftsman's underlings, captured in Wanxian County, had confessed that Liang and Qin Liexiong had been in cahoots and plotted to rob the tower. Wang Zhengming told him that he had taken care of things, and instructed Mawu to promptly surrender himself to the county government; he had lined palms with opium and silver.

Tao Jiuxiang was puzzled, "What is this Wang Zhengming thinking . . . having you walk right into the wolf's open maw?"

Through a sleepless night, Mawu grappled with the dilemma. Rising before dawn, finding Tao Jiuxiang sitting in front of the fireplace smoking, he felt a keen pang of regret. Across the fireplace from one another, mother and son sat in heavy silence.

Finally, Mawu rose slowly and said resolutely, "Elder brother Wang has a lot of friends in the army and the government. He won't let harm befall me." So saying, he lit a torch and departed without a backward glance.

V

Jin Shaosan had heard that Mawu was back. But as Mawu hadn't come to pay respects, he couldn't really go to Gengguping to visit his son-in-law. After all, his daughter was with the Qins now. Several days passed before Cui Four revealed to him the news of Liexiong's death. He gasped, sitting for a spell with mouth agape and eyes dilated until, shaking off the shock, he mounted his horse and headed to Huangshui. Though he was by nature timid, his charming daughter, with her flower-like loveliness and moon-like voluptuousness, had brought him half a lifetime of turbulence.

When he reached Qin Liexiong's house in Huangshui, for the first time nobody stopped or question him. As he crossed the threshold and entered the splendid three-gated interior courtyard, a quartet of women emerged from the interior hall, bamboo baskets mounted on their backs. Among them was Qin Liexiong's wife Zhou, a petit and delicate, neat and trim woman with a thin face and pared-down cheeks; a pair of elegant bracelets adorned her wrists and her hair was pinned up in a bun. Her eyes were swollen and red. At the sight of Jin Shaosan, she calmly greeted him, rasping, "My mother-in-law sent me to gather up a few of *our* things!"

Well aware of this woman's envy and hatred for his daughter, Jin Shaosan only responded with a polite bow. A maid led him to the bedroom where Jin lay. He hadn't seen his daughter for six months. Her face was pale, her belly swollen like a round ox-hide drum. He said, "Oh, Daughter! Your mother asked me to come visit you."

"Baba," said the distraught Jin. "What can I do?" On the eve of childbirth, she had lost another husband.

Holding back tears, Jin Shaosan approached his daughter and whispered, "I've heard that Mawu is back."

"Who told you?" Jin asked, incredulous, raising her tear-streaked face.

"Cai Bangzi, one of the tenant farmers," Jin Shaosan answered. "Just now I bumped into another person... I think it was Wang Zhengming."

"Are you sure it was him, Baba?" asked Jin in surprise.

"He's the kind of man who stands out in the street," said Jin Shaosan.

The Wangs' private academy was just down the street from Qin Liexiong's teahouse. Each time Wang Zhengming, the eldest Wang son, a figure of influence and notoriety, returned to Huangshui, it occasioned a lasting murmur of speculation. This was the first time since Jin's kidnapping that he had come home. Often, Jin had wanted to ask Old Wang to ask Wang Zhengming about Mawu's whereabouts, but Liexiong kept a close tether on her and she'd had no opportunity. Every time she left the compound—even on the pretext of a quick trip to the apothecary—several militiamen followed. Now that both Mawu and the legendary Wang Zhengming had reappeared, she sensed that something important was afoot. Nervously, she asked, "Liexiong, is he..." She suddenly stopped speaking, staring wide-eyed at her father.

Startled, Jin Shaosan stammered, "Mawu's just returned. Could it be that ...? Could he...?"

Jin sobbed, "If Mawu killed Liexiong, won't he be sentenced to death?"

Alarm danced in Jin Shaosan's eyes. He sighed, "Oh! Your mother and I have discussed it: we want you to come back to Peppercorn Bend. You can't upset yourself about everything else; first, you need to birth the baby."

"When he sees me like this, there's no way Mawu will take me back." Jin wiped her tear-swollen face with a handkerchief. "I'm not leaving this house. I'm not going to let the Qins reclaim it. They were just here, taking all the valuables they could lay their hands on." Recalling the abusive shit that Liexiong's wife Zhou had rained down on her while she lay helpless on her parturition bed, Jin felt an overwhelming despair for the pitiful fetus inside of her and a pervasive sense of pessimism for her future.

Jin Shaosan remained silent. She was right. His daughter Jin had a sound mind and her words carried the force of reason: At this pivotal moment, she couldn't abandon the house. It would be easy enough for Jin to return to Peppercorn Bend, but she couldn't live there for the rest of her life! Wiping his tears away with a sleeve, the careworn father left and returned home alone.

Even in the gloom and driving rain, people recognized mastermind Wang Zhengming as soon as he returned to Huangshui. Though nobody knew for sure precisely who this prodigy's contacts were or what strategies and pressures he had brought to bear, what was certain is that a month later a crowd of people gathered outside the township yamen to read an official proclamation:

> It is hereby announced that Li Mawu of Gengguping shall be fined 800 yuan. Though according to law, Li Mawu's murder of Huangshui defensive militia Captain Qin Liexiong is a capital offense, a crime of the most serious magnitude, there are extenuating circumstances. One villager has come forward and testified, supplying evidence that six years earlier, in league with bandits headed by Liang Xijiu, Qin Liexiong conspired to attack Li Mawu's home and seize his property. Given these mitigating circumstances, and given that Mawu has penitently submitted himself to the Law and confessed to the crime, the Court, in its mercy, has meted out this reduced sentence.

For the family it was like the end to a wonderful fairy tale: Mawu had returned to Gengguping unscathed! Intermittently howling with joy and weeping, Tao Jiuxiang cradled Mawu in her arms for a long while. Finally, cupping her eldest son's face, she scrutinized him with a mother's keen eye under the sunlight. Crow's feet creased the corners of Mawu's eyes;

new folds and wrinkles furrowed his face, which had taken on an aspect of wolfish cruelty, changes wrought by time and the turbulent, wandering life of an outlaw. Thank the gods and spirits, she mused, that the dignity and reputation of the Li family had been restored! Since her son's return from Wanxian, Mawu had become taciturn, either remaining silent or uttering words beyond her comprehension. He burned hot and cold. Instead of calling locals "countryfolk" or "villagers," he now referred to them as "the people." Whenever he uttered these two simple words, a zealous conflagration lit up his eyes, as though he were swearing an oath by fire. After he murdered Qin Liexiong, locals nicknamed Mawu "Tiger." Scrutinizing the face of her son, at once so familiar and so strange, Tao Jiuxiang could not help feeling the stir of vague misgivings.

Quickly, another surprising official missive was handed down: the mayor had recommended that Mawu be restored to his former post as militia Captain. However, the Fengjie County governor dismissed the recommendation on the grounds the backwoods folk of Gengguping were a bunch of outlaws. Instead, Tan Ruideng, vice mayor of Huangshui, was concurrently appointed Captain. After Liexiong's death, the family summoned Lieniu, the third son of the Qin family, back home, requesting that he quit schooling. Fond of silver, Tan Ruideng, accepted the bribes from both the Qins and the Lis and appointed intractable foes Lieniu and Mawu as militia lieutenants. Mawu was placed in charge of the seventh, eighth, and ninth wards; Lieniu was charged with supervising the tenth and eleventh.

Gloomily, Tao Jiuxiang mulled that the Qins and the Lis were destined to be bitter enemies until the end of time.

VI

Qin Liexiong's teahouse and incense hall were passed onto his younger brother Lieniu. Paying little heed to public safety or his administrative duties, Lieniu moved into the teahouse, gathering his elder brother's cronies and disciples to plot revenge.

Goldthread prices spiked, reaching 150,000 *yuan* per bushel, which prompted goldthread speculators to swarm into Huangshui for the first time in nearly a decade. One merchant named Zhang Daxin noticed a "for rent" sign pasted in front of a fashionable, well-constructed courtyard in a prime location on Huangshui's main thoroughfare. He rented the front yard of the house for his business, gathering rhizome while selling imported lighters and cloth from Chongqing.

A local scribe had written the notice at Jin's behest. She had given birth to Liexiong's child, a baby girl she named Baoyu, Embracing Jade. To make enough money to get by, Jin had decided to rent the front courtyard. After Qin Liexiong's murder, his mother and wife, living in the Qin homestead beside Inkblack Creek, hoped that Jin would remarry so that the Qins might reclaim the house. However, Jin, at twenty-six, had resolved, in the face of misfortune, not to relinquish the house; without it, she would have nothing. Ever since Qin Liexiong kidnapped her and installed her in the house, Qin's underlings had kept her under close surveillance. But now, after her month of parturition lying-in, she was free to come and go as she pleased. However, fearing the wagging tongues of gossipy neighbors, she remained inside, lonely and gloomy, sitting in the yard with tiny Baoyu in her lap. She often wore wide-legged pants and a white, short-sleeved shirt, along with a black-collared blue coat embroidered in blue and white patterns along the sleeves and fringes. Despite her melancholy, Jin had retained her charm and become even more voluptuous.

One sunny and clear morning, a trio of strangers suddenly appeared in the Jin's front courtyard—apparently to do business with Zhang Daxin. Looking to be a goldthread dealer of status and means, one wore a traditional scholars' cap and a long silk gown; he was accompanied with a pair of coarse-looking servants, one tall and the other short. The gentleman said that he would like to speak with the owner of the compound. Fearing they were fellow goldthread dealers, Zhang Daxin retreated to his storehouse while his men sought vainly to stall them. The three brushed past Zhang's assistants, entering the rear courtyard through a side gate.

Jin's maidservant Wan, washing clothes in the court, immediately saw through Mawu's disguise, and exclaimed, "Just a minute. I'll let her know you're here." In a dither, she scurried into the inner chambers.

Though Mawu waited for quite some time, Jin did not emerge. Finally, losing patience, he asked Zeng Laomao and Zhao Changyou, both dressed in new coats, to keep watch, and he burst into the inner chamber.

He was assailed by a swirl of scents, both familiar and strange. A bamboo hamper beside the bed was half-filled with soiled cloth diapers. Through the parted curtains of a mahogany canopy bed, Mawu spied—on the opposite side—a woman seated in a high-backed armchair, nursing her baby. Seeing a man charging in, she pushed up the front fold of her moon-white jacket, protectively embracing her child.

Mawu fixed his gaze, one of astonishment and sadness, on Jin's face. Neither spoke. Their eyes locked, expressing compassion and resentment. Hurriedly, Wan swept up little Baoyu in her swaddling quilt and shuffled into the next room.

Wind whipped the rice paper covering the lattice windows, soughing its timeless song of the miseries and raptures, the separations and partings, of husbands and wives. A strand of regret threaded its way into Mawu's heart: this was his fault—he shouldn't have left home. His departure had sundered his family and placed Jin in this circumstance. Removing his cap penitently, he said with anguish, "I've hurt you. My sorrow knows no bounds."

"I haven't heard a single word from you since you left." Jin looked straight into his eyes, tears brooking down her cheeks, her voice trembling. "You've already killed him. What do I do now?" She covered her face with a handkerchief and wept.

Mawu cast a glance through a doorway, toward the baby in the other room. With a sense of otherworldly detachment, he sized up the child born of Jin and Liexiong. When Jin calmed, he offered, in a low sibilant whistle between clenched teeth, "Give the baby to the Qins and come home with me to Gengguping."

A sharp gasp punctuated Jin's weeping. She weighed the torment little Baoyu would suffer if she sent the girl to the Qin homestead on Inkblack Creek. After all, Zhou, Liexiong's wife, had already borne him two sons.

"Don't cry. Tell me what you think?" Mawu persisted nervously.

"I don't have the face to return home . . . it's too shameful." Jin stared at him, wiping tears away.

A crestfallen Mawu slipped her a silver hairpin fished from a pocket, softly saying, "Here, I bought this last year in Wanxian when I was thinking of you."

Jin remained silent, her eyebrows arching in bewilderment. Mawu sat serenely for a moment, hand extended, before rising, standing before Jin, and clumsily fastening the pin in her hair. Sobbing disconsolately, Jin removed the hairpin and clutched it tightly.

Profoundly moved, Mawu slipped his scholars' cap back on and rapidly departed Qin Liexiong's residence, Zeng Laomao and Zhang Changyou in tow.

Back at Gengguping, he told his mother that he had visited Jin in Huangshui.

"What do you plan to do next?" asked Tao Jiuxiang, fixing a trenchant glare upon her eldest son. An ugly rumor had flitted from the streets of Huangshui into the outlying hills over the past year: to invigorate Qin Liexiong's limp, tiny member, Jin had bought a cocktail of aphrodisiacs and stimulants from the herbalist. With such disgraceful gossip floating around, how could the Lis show their faces?

Mawu lit a rolled cigarette he had brought from Wanxian County, and answered, "Bring her back to Gengguping."

With a long sigh, Tao Jiuxiang spat, "Then our Li family will have no honor, no face at all!"

Early the next morning, she asked Mawu to take a pair of pups born to Black Leopard, their best hunting bitch, into the woods to see if the whelps proved capable hunters. Of the dozen-odd hounds they had raised, Black Leopard had the keenest sense of smell. Before Mawu had followed them half a mile, Black Leopard caught scent of some creature and set off, the two young hounds close at her heels.

Shortly, they came across a wild sow and a pair of piglets. One of the whelps intrepidly bolted forward, grabbing the haunch of a piglet with his sharp teeth. When she heard her piglet's squeals of pain, the sow furiously rounded on the young dog, seizing a shoulder in her powerful jaws. Black Leopard leapt to her pup's defense, sinking her teeth into the sow's rear leg. The agonized sow relinquished her grip on the whelp, twisting toward Black Leopard and savagely ripping the hound's flank asunder with her sharp canines. Black Leopard slumped to the ground, as sow and piglets madly plunged into the bosky undergrowth.

Rather than pursuing the wild pigs, Mawu ministered to poor Black Leopard, tucking her intestines carefully into the cavity of her stomach and doing his best to cover and stanch her gaping wound with banana leaves. Tenderly, he scooped her up in his arms and headed home.

Seeing how grievously Black Leopard was wounded, Tao Jiuxiang was chagrined. She bustled about, fashioning a poultice from her turban, which she swaddled tightly around the injured dog. "All Black Leopard's offspring are hunting dogs through and through," she sighed. "In dogs, crossbreeding can lead to better stock, but it's different for people. I'm not having that adulterous whore live with this family!" She made up her mind and her eye blazed with firmness.

"Ma!" retorted Mawu bitterly, "Jin's no whore!"

"I suppose we could allow her back for Yongyu's sake, but—" Tao Jiuxiang declared firmly, her face contorting into a stern mask, "only if you take another wife!"

Wolfishly taking draw after draw from his cigarette, Mawu flushed red.

Chapter Fifteen

I

A massive basalt cliff rose from the river. Ships passing its foot, where the mass of rock ended abruptly, rounded a turbulent corner as the waters veered sharply. Arrayed atop the cliff were twenty-four "soul summoning" banners. A scattered village of farmhouses was set along the far bank, where the waters bent.

The water was clear, looking from the vantage of the cliff like a V-shaped green silken ribbon at one's feet. When the Japanese Imperial Army sought to push inland along the Yangzi to reach the soft, rich plains of the Sichuan basin, they had to move through these mountains and pass this stretch of river. But the mountains served as a natural bulwark, and several well-placed grenades or a single cannon could halt boat traffic, making the river impassable.

After the raging battle at the stronghold at Xiling that year, an ominous change had taken place in the lives of the villagers. Wild dogs dragged out bodies of dead soldiers haphazardly buried in shallow mass graves; bones littered the mountains. Though the villagers re-interred the bones, by night eerie greenish spectral figures haunted the hills. It was impossible to distinguish whether these undead were Nationalist soldiers or Japanese devils. After a series of torrential storms, piles of white bones were revealed once again, cluttering the crags and slopes. Mischievous herders would brandish a thighbone to spook fellow shepherds. Gamboling lambs limped along, after getting their tender hooves caught in the mouths of skulls. One goat got his pair of horns caught in the eye sockets of a skull and walked around wearing a mask of bone for weeks, looking like a horrific mountain demon emerged from legend.

To placate the dead, the petrified villagers set up the white paper flags everywhere. At a loss, the hapless mayor called on the villagers to collect the bones and inter them yet again, this time in deep pits. He also appealed to the villagers, rich and poor alike, to contribute money for a large-scale ceremony to calm the spirits and escort the undead souls to the netherworld.

From near and far nine celebrated shamans arrived to perform the rite. The mayor welcomed them with pomp and circumstance, presenting each a brand-new red ceremonial garment. However, there was only a single five-colored feathered headdress. The mayor and his representatives asked the shamans to choose the one among them most worthy of donning the cap. The nine shamans vied for an entire night, their nine pairs of straw sandals competing in an aerial dance to display magical prowess. By dawn the shamans unanimously acknowledged Xia Qifa the victor, electing him chief *tima*, and presenting him the avian headdress.

They demarcated and arranged a huge ritual ground atop the cliff. A new homespun cloth streamer rose above the turbid Yangzi River. The nine resounding oxhorns traversed the waters, echoing off the cliffs opposite, moving through the village on the far shore.

Villagers had tied and bundled trees from the western slope to construct a makeshift teepee-shaped ritual hall with an altar for spirit tablets. Masui helped Xia Liangxian grind ink and then displayed his graceful calligraphy. After writing "Commemorating the lost souls of fallen Chinese soldiers," Xia Liangxian directed him to write "Commemorating the lost souls of fallen Japanese soldiers." Masui raised his head and looked at the young *tima* in amazement.

Xia Liangxian explained, "My old man wants to exorcise all of the ghosts. If we don't send all the spirits back to the netherworld, the *feng-shui* will still be out of kilter and restless ghosts will continue to haunt this place."

From behind Masui came the sigh of another shaman. "Just write: 'All of them are victims of war, men who perished fighting for their lords.'" Still bewildered, Masui raised his brush again and set to his task.

Gongs and drums thundered. As the nine *tima* tirelessly chanted singsong incantations, two dozen disciples held triangular flags, dancing to the rhythmic drumbeat that did homage to the gods. Two nights passed, and the fog on the river finally lifted. Attired in his eight-fold skirts and wearing the new headdress, Xia Qifa flourished his ceremonial blade in one hand and formed a series of mudras with the other, exhausting his arts to reverence a succession of spirits, from the highest divinities of the firmament—the sun, the moon, and the constellations above to the local tutelary god and the myriad creatures below—the birds and beasts, the insects and fish. Xia Qifa acted as the lead chanter and the others as his chorus. Arrayed behind him, they chanted in accompaniment, over and over, a mysterious and ancient rhythmic hymn.

For yet another night, Xia Qifa offered respects to all the celestial gods and terrestrial spirits. Finally, he strode out the gate of the ritual precinct they had fashioned and blew his oxhorn again and again; the other shamans sounded their horns in response. The world was enveloped in darkness. Then, the villagers lit a hundred torches and began burning paper for the dead, money for the netherworld.

Masui wrote out a memorial tablet for Mahe, then burned endless sheets of paper for his deceased brother. On that final night as he chatted with villagers, he heard tales of the savagery of the war. He was convulsed in fear and horror by these tales, which had left him trembling tearfully for half the night as he remembered his brother. The dog-fucked Japanese bastards had sought to invade and occupy the rivers and mountains that world creator Pangu had left behind. How utterly loathsome!

He also heard tell of an amazing incident that had taken place in Xiling Village three years earlier. A little boy born into the family of a villager named Wang Youcai liked playing with the bullet shells and helmets that his parents had gathered, even during meals and at bedtime. If his parents took them away, he burst into tears. When he had just begun to speak, his breath smelling of mother's milk, the toddler uttered, "I'm a Japanese person." Angrily, his father Wang Youcai retorted, "If you're Japanese, why are you in my house?" The boy said, "You promised me a cake, and now I've come for it." Wang Youcai gasped, "Who the hell are you?" The boy said, "I'm the ghost of Kojima." Wang Youcai broke into a cold sweat, recalling that in the throes of battle between the Nationalists and the Japanese, a desperate Japanese soldier had taken refuge in his farm. On the pretext he was heading out to get the man a cake, Wang Youcai informed Nationalist troops of the man's presence. As a result, six or seven soldiers shot the Japanese soldier to death in a watery ditch and buried him in a shallow grave beside his tobacco field. Panic-stricken, Wang Youcai offered, "I'll give you the flour pancake—just get a berth on a warship back to Japan and take it with you. Go away!" The boy appeared unhappy upon hearing this, and grew silent.

As the little boy grew, the Wangs discovered that little guy was partial to uncooked fish and vegetables rather than cooked fatty meat and organs. Moreover, as he learned to write, he was particularly afraid of the characters "Nationalist" and "army." When he was naughty, family members would threaten, "If you don't behave yourself, the Nationalist army is going to get you!" Hearing this, he would immediately sit paralytically still, not daring to move a muscle. When a villager saw him standing on a wall and peering down at the Yangzi River below, he teased the boy by saying, "Hey, little Japanese doggy, you waiting for the Japanese warship to come spirit you away?" The boy quickly grew weary of such jokes.

Masui did not believe the preposterous story. He figured that if the soul of a Japanese soldier had really transmigrated into the child, the villagers would have beaten him to death. Reportedly, representatives of the village had asked the boy to hold the mourning tablet for the dead Japanese soldiers, promising a lamb to the Wangs for his service. However, Wang Youcai proved unwilling, prompting a lengthy negotiation with the mayor.

Masui snapped, "If that kid is truly a Japanese soldier reincarnate, the Wangs should have been beaten the little bastard eight times a day."

The fellow responded sadly, "Wang Youcai tried to starve him, saying, 'I've long since paid you back the flour pancake I owed, so why don't you just go away?' So the unhappy boy, pissed off at his father, battened himself to his mother. We all called him "lil' Japanese Puppy,' which angered his mother so much that she stamped and cursed. Besides their three pock-faced daughters, she felt fortunate to have a handsome son, who politely offered her food at dinner. Imagine having a child who was a reincarnated Japanese soldier—what a nightmare! The poor Wangs! "

Masui felt his scalp tingle and his hair stand on end.

Thundering gongs resumed. Torches danced wildly and oxhorns sounded. On the ceremonial grounds, the nine shamans waved their ritual blades. Holding aloft the wooden plaque bearing the characters, "Commemorating the lost souls of fallen Chinese soldiers," the mayor followed in their wake.

Masui craned his neck and watched a child marching behind them, tightly clutching the tablet reading, "Commemorating the lost souls of fallen Japanese soldiers." Wearing a confused expression, the boy—the millstone around the neck of the Wang family—walked deliberately. It was apparent that the little guy had no idea what was going on. Nonetheless, inwardly Masui remained bitterly indignant that they were lamenting the deceased Japanese soldiers.

At the end of the procession came young Xia Liangxian, cradling a rooster in his arms, and the village representatives, carrying meat, food, and wine for the fallen soldiers; finally, the rest of the villagers followed, torches in hand. The parade marched westward, arriving at the teepee-shaped ritual hall.

II

The spirit banners and bonfires dotting the mountain slopes created an otherworldly air. Xia Qifa ascended to the high altar and lit incense and firecrackers with a flaming branch. Resonantly, he chanted:

> *Sough sough sough sough whistling winds*
> *Howling like a tiger sweeping past mountains——*
> *Expanding your borders, conquering wherever you go;*
> *Who can resist your gale and blow?*
> *Where you pass, the triumphant trumpet sounds,*
> *The clarion oxhorn blasts, the war drums pound.*
> *Slaying your foes without spear or knife,*
> *Taking their lives, devouring flesh raw,*
> *Guzzling fresh blood that drips from your maw . . .*
> *In the Azure Dragon's lair, dragons abound*
> *In the White Tiger's cave, tigers are found.*
> *On the battlefield beneath sun and sky,*
> *Flesh-and-blood men fight and die . . .*

Caught up in Xia Qifa's rhythmic and sonic momentum, crickets, nightbirds, and frogs chorused, trilling, warbling, and croaking with abandon. Bonfire flames danced and tree branches swayed in the breeze, so that it seemed that heaven, earth, and man were in concert. Led by Xia Liangxian, the village representatives burned incense and paper, then lit firecrackers for the fallen soldiers. A dense aromatic haze drifted from the ritual grounds to settle over the Yangzi.

> *Xia Qifa hurled rice in all directions, calling out with ardent sincerity:*
> *O souls, come home, for the enemy is dead and gone.*
> *Chill wind, thunder, and battering rains wrack the wilderness:*
> *Poor souls, huddling at the river's margin or cliff's foot,*
> *Don't curl up sadly in your lonely grottoes or weep on the desolate*
>   *riverbank,*
> *Heed the heartfelt calls of your kinfolk and dear ones, oh souls.*
> *Old and young, large and small—come back!*
> *O souls—beloved of your fathers and mothers,*
> *Return to your family plots, your ancestral halls.*
> *Come by sky, transported by scudding clouds;*
> *Come by earth, borne on the backs of myriad ants.*
> *With the long strides of the crane, on the powerful wings of the eagle;*
> *Come running, come flying—*
> *O souls, fallen Chinese and Japanese soldiers,*
> *Heed the calls of family and relatives—*
> *And return home!*

On and on, Xia Qifa chanted verses more multitudinous than the blades of grass dotting the mountainslopes. Masui knelt, burning bundles of paper for Mahe. He watched rising ash and embers mingle with the fireflies, then fade and disappear. Looking beyond to the stars, he wondered which firefly contained Mahe's spirit. Ardently, he wished that his intrepid brother's lonely spirit might rise from its unmarked burial to enjoy the offerings of paper money, incense, and delectable foods before soaring back home through clouds and fog, finding eternal rest and solace in the tomb the family had prepared for him at Lihaku.

With fervent piety, Xia Qifa continued unabated, his incantations so moving and elemental that the fire danced ever more furiously, the night birds sang ever more piercingly, and the branches shook ever more wildly, reaching a crescendo as he called forth:

> *O spirits holding your punt-poles, grip them firmly;*
> *O ghosts rowing your sampans, guide your vessel carefully.*
> *The waters quicken, the rapids churn;*
> *Grasp firmly your punt, steady as the boat turns.*

Don't recklessly steer into the teeth of the storm:
Avoid the turbulent course, keep straight, safe from harm.
Clamber up the slopes, down the slopes,
Like a rushing ox or leaping deer.
Climb the steep cliffs, the path to heaven, dauntless:
Fear not the crow of the cock,
Fear not the baying of hounds.
Among the burning incense smoke and fragrant tea,
Let us entertain you with endless liquor.
Pouring one cup after another.
O soldiers of both sides who died serving in battle,
O souls and spirits, go, go home, return to your families!

The humid night air seemed saturated with blood, sweat, and tears. The dense smoke and fog made it seem as though the hamlets and mountain peaks were islands adrift in the billows.

Facing an unseen host of spirits, Xia Qifa solemnly bowed, then descended from the altar and headed toward the makeshift ritual hall, burning incense and paper along the path. The village representatives followed, carrying the memorial tablets and leading the three sacrificial animals—ox, sheep, and pig. Led by Xia Liangxian, the other villagers burned incense and paper, and lit firecrackers. A small mountain of yellow paper sheets burned slowly into ashes.

Outside the teepee, a huge flag had been erected. Two *timas* lit firecrackers to welcome Xia Qifa. The two commemorative tablets were set in the hall. Aromatic smoke from an incense burner rose, coiling round the roaming spirits of the fallen.

"Sweet dew from the peach-flower well, pure cleansing waters from the apricot flower well," Xia Qifa began a singsong chant, his keen eyes focused on the spirits, his expressive hands in constant motion as he washed dust-covered and wind-burned ethereal bodies—thoroughly cleaning the faces, the necks, the backs, the hands and feet—of the departed souls. Finally, to conclude the rite he emptied the basins of dirty water outside the ritual hall, placing the foot-basin and the larger bathing tub upside-down to symbolically settle entanglements and resolve lingering disputes.

"Because the calamitous dragon has run riot, you have lost your lives, making resentment well in your bellies, hatred fill your hearts," Xia Qifa lowered his voice, amiably and intimately addressing the two tablets as though he were sharing a whispered confidence with a pair of old friends:

> *Set out and return home,*
> *Rid yourselves of the rankling bitterness in your bosoms;*
> *Return to human world,*
> *Cast the seething anger from your hearts.*
> *Rise without hatred,*
> *Embark without weapons.*
> *Find indwelling happiness,*
> *Let cheer permeate your hearts.*
> *Only then can you become good spirits*
> *And truly enjoy the incense smoke and offerings.*

Dawn marked the end of a long night that witnessed sacrificial offerings of sheep and ox, endless burning of incense and paper, and ritual incantations, all to usher the fallen ghost soldiers home, to guide them from rootless torment to solace. Though the horizon had changed from gray to yellow-pink, Xia Qifa cast an invocation, so that in the surrounding mountains the cocks did not crow and the dogs did not bark. He burned incense, bowed, left the ritual hall, and headed to the grave-site where they planned bury all the bones once and for all, burning and scattering paper as he walked. The other shamans burned the two mourning tablets, which gave off a thick smoke that joined the rising smoke of the incense and paper.

The soughing winds of the dying night whistled. Birds kept to their nests. Unending strings of firecrackers popped and crackled. Lingering moonlight leaking from the clouds silvered the surface of the ever-flowing Yangzi. More than a hundred torches flickered on the slopes. Finally, the fallen souls began their separate sojourns from the battlefield, crossing a thousand mountains and myriad watercourses as they returned home at long last.

III

As ships moved to and fro along the river, the explosive price of goldthread finally dropped to a more normal level. Though merchant Zhang Daxin's shop was in the front courtyard of the compound in Huangshui, his heart and mind often dwelled on the voluptuous and charming beauty in the spacious inner courtyard. One husband had abandoned her and a second husband had been murdered. He felt commingled desire and pity—more the former than the latter—for his lovely landlady. One day, when business was flowing freely and he saw Jin and her daughter sauntering out in the street to catch some afternoon sun, he offered little Baoyu a necklace.

That night, Jin asked her servant girl to cook several dishes to thank Mr. Zhang for his generosity. After his one visit, Mawu had not re-appeared. She didn't expect to hear from Gengguping again, and knew what the men of Huangshui were like. She sat at the pearwood table, her soft, glossy hair unbound, settling like a cloud over her shoulders, subtly bobbing and shimmering with her every movement. Moonlight filtered into the room, miraculous ethereal white moonlight—insubstantial as gossamer, yet more powerful than lead and iron; a ghostly light that blanched the courtyard, promising to change fates, to bring at once happiness and misery. Jin's moonlit complexion was pale, her long hair dancing in the otherworldly light. When she spoke, her teeth showed alluringly like pearls half-hidden in a treasure box.

After several toasts, Zhang Daxin felt a pleasant languor settle over him, as if the two of them were afloat on clouds and mist with the moon hanging above, drenching them both in its intoxicating pale light. One moment, he felt that the moon was in the sky, and Jin was in front of him; the next, he felt Jin was in the heavens, and the moon before him. The goldthread dealer's heart leapt excitedly, lingering, suspended between heaven and earth. Goaded by sweet inebriation, he asked Jin, "Madam, you're a beauty raised in a wealthy family, but now you're a widow living here alone with your poor little daughter—with no one to rely on. If you don't find it distasteful, perhaps you'd be willing to come to Chongqing and live with me?"

Jin was taken aback, ill at ease speaking to a stranger. An anxious sorrow ablaze in her eyes, she sighed, "I'm afraid my lot is a bitter one!"

Zhang Daxin laughed, candidly, continuing, "What bitterness? My two wives lead a contented, happy life. And if you joined us, what's another person? The more, the merrier . . . and you're prettier than either one of them!"

Jin studied Zhang's eyes carefully, feeling that he spoke the truth. Though he was a bit old, the man was rich, good-natured, and possessed a generosity of spirit. She didn't know how he had come by such a large sum of money. Could men from big cities all be wealthy men of means like him?

"If you don't object," said Zhang, "I'll inform the Qins, and make them a present of several bolts of foreign-style cloth." With these words, he clasped Jin's fragrant, fair hands in his own.

Jin's cheeks crimsoned. "The Qins would be ecstatic if I left. You needn't waste your resources."

"It's no problem," said Zhang, "I own a cloth factory."

"Do you really want to marry me?" asked Jin, eyes downcast, her large earrings swaying gently. Over the months and years, she had often envisioned her future, imagining the misery she would endure under the cold glare of Tao Jiuxiang if she returned to Gengguping. The image of ill-fated Zhou Damei flitted into her mind, frightening her out of her wits. A proud woman, she could never return to the stone tower and show her face with dignity in this lifetime! Better to live humbly as the third wife of a stranger!

"Of course!" Zhang brushed her cheek with his fingers, adding, "Do you think the Lis will have any problem?"

"I haven't been part of the Li family for a long time," Jin answered meekly. "They won't interfere."

Zhang reached out and took Jin in his embrace.

Thus Jin, having married two successive captains of the Huangshui militia and an affluent goldthread dealer from Chongqing who had once been her tenant, became a local legend. That night in bed, Jin artfully displayed her gratitude to her generous husband-to-be, the man who had extricated her from a grim, untenable circumstance. The following morning, still entwined in the warm embrace of the goldthread merchant, she found the silver hairpin Mawu had gifted her and resolutely snapped it in two. She sent her maidservant to Gengguping to hand the broken troth to Tao Jiuxiang, her erstwhile mother-in-law, the stalwart woman who had loved and despised her for so many years, together with a message that she was soon to be married.

Mawu heard the news from his mother. Immediately, he headed to Huangshui with Yongyu. As they passed through the woods, sweet-tempered and pretty Yongyu gathered a bouquet of wildflowers for her mother.

Tending her baby girl in the rear courtyard, Jin was astonished to look up and see father and daughter, Mawu and Yongyu, enter. "Mum!" called out Yongyu cheerfully, offering the colorful spray of flowers to her mother, excitedly smiling from ear to ear.

"Yongyu!" cried Jin. Hurriedly, she set the baby girl into the cradle and clasped Yongyu in a tight embrace.

"So what's this I hear?" Mawu hissed.

With a heart-piercing quaver, Jin said, "I had to get married some time. Please . . . don't block my escape route. For the sake of our former love!"

"Ma will come around and accept you," said Mawu, his strained face pale. With a tremulous hand, he lit a rolled cigarette and added, "Just give her a while—she'll change. Come back to Gengguping with me, for Yongyu's sake."

"Mum," Yongyu, still in Jin's arms, craned her neck and pensively gazed back at her mother. "Why are there more men and fewer women in the world?"

Taken aback, Jin stammered, "I don't know."

"I'll tell you," giggled Yongyu. "Back in ancient times, Fuxi and his younger sister began to create humans. Fuxi created men, and his younger sister made women. Fuxi was so strong and efficient that that he created four men in the time it took his sister to make three women." Guilelessly, Yongyu slipped one of the wildflowers into a fold in the front of Jin's garment, then clapped her hands and continued, "Fuxi said, 'It's time for lunch.' His sister answered, 'Wait a minute, I've only made three women.' Fuxi said, 'Forget about it. Let them all live together. If one of the men dies, the widow will marry the leftover man—it'll be like plowing a field that's been plowed before, like raking a furrow that's been raked before.'"

Jin's pretty face contorted in shock; she looked down at her daughter, dumbfounded.

"Who taught you that?" Mawu snapped reproachfully.

"My auntie told me that." Stung by the rebuke, wide-eyed Yongyu sadly looked up at her mother. "She asked me to tell Mum!"

Mawu slapped Yongyu on the cheek, prompting her to commence a loud wailing. Quickly, the maidservant bustled in and spirited Yongyu away.

"It's my fault!" Mawu murmured angrily, taking another draw on his cigarette.

Tears brooking down her cheeks, Jin sobbed, "I can't show my face at Gengguping. There's no place for me there. And there's no place for me at Peppercorn Bend."

"You can come back!" said Mawu in an undertone, "It'll be just like before."

"If I went back to Gengguping, how could things be like they were before?" asked Jin woodenly.

"And what will things be like if you marry a goldthread merchant?" retorted Mawu excitedly.

"You should hunt for a stepmother for Yongyu." Jin gazed at him tearfully. "I'm going to Chongqing, where nobody knows what's happened in Huangshui. What's more, the Qins will make trouble if I go back to Gengguping, but there won't be any problems with my marriage to Mr. Zhang. He's already proposed the marriage. The Qins approved."

"I need their approval?" Mawu flared, his eyes suddenly animated with a dangerous light.

"You killed Liexiong as soon as you returned." Jin tasted the violent acrimony in his words, and dejected, added, "If you act the outlaw again, the government's not going to let you get away with it. Yongyu's grandmother wouldn't want you to break the law."

Mawu realized that Jin's words were half true. More importantly, Wang Zhengming had stuck out his neck for him—and he couldn't let his sworn elder brother down. "I . . . ," He stammered in anguish. Suddenly, he threw down his cigarette butt, swept up Jin in his arms, and strode purposefully toward the bedroom.

To Mawu's surprise Jin, usually so docile and gentle, resisted fiercely, fighting like a wildcat. As he tried to pin her down and pawed at her clothing, she rolled right and twisted left on bed. Wary that Yongyu might come in at any moment, Mawu rose from the disheveled bed, furious and breathing heavily. While he could see that his former wife was truly resolved to marry Zhang, he mused that if Jin weren't Yongyu's mother he would have taken her by force. Glowering at little Baoyu in the cradle, he sorrowfully departed.

On the bed, enervated and flustered, Jin nearly cried her eyes out.

IV

Since he had learned of Jin's impending marriage, an aching hatred constricted Mawu's heart. News spread quickly in Gengguping that Zhang Daxin, the goldthread dealer, was going to hold a gala, big city-style wedding banquet in Huangshui to marry Jin and make her his third concubine.

After the feast, he returned to Chongqing, with his newlywed concubine and little Baoyu—whom the Qins rejected—in tow. As the Qins were unwilling to sell Zhang the house he had been renting, he purchased an acre plot of prime rhizome growing land on a mountain-slope, and placed his new father-in-law, Jin Shaosan, in charge of collecting the goldthread, giving the Jins a cut of the profit once the goldthread was sold.

His will sapped and his heart ashen, Mawu plunged into a dark abyss. To jar him from his despondency, Tao Jiuxiang considered finding him another wife. So Third Auntie Zhang returned to Gengguping yet again, but the wily old matchmaker failed to find a single prospect. Trusty old laborer Sun Fu suggested, "Ask Mawu what he thinks about Xia Qifa's daughter. See if he'd agree to marry Yinmei?"

Tao Jiuxiang was taken aback. The Xias and Lis had been close for generations. Before Li Diezhu's death, he had planned to marry Yinmei to Mahe. But Mahe had died young, and Li Diezhu was no more. While the Lis had fallen on hard times, Xia Qifa's reputation as a powerful *tima* had spread far and wide, so that everywhere in the mountains his eight-fold shamanic robes were known. Feeling unworthy and ashamed, Tao Jiuxiang recalled the humiliating lesson of Third Auntie's failed mission to Peartree Moor so many years ago. Haltingly, she answered, "Yinmei is all grown up now. Why would she want to marry Mawu?"

Languidly smoking her pipe beside the stove, Third Auntie asked Mawu with a faint smile, "You want me talk to the Xias about a possible match with Yinmei?"

Sitting woodenly with his brows knit, Mawu made no answer. Tao Jiuxiang thought that he had steeled his heart and determined to remain a bare stick for the rest of his days. But just as the matchmaker was about to depart, he wistfully sighed, "Why would Yinmei fancy me?"

Third Auntie Zhang tapped the ash from the bowl of her pipe. After half a lifetime of matchmaking, she could read young men and women, and— beyond interpreting the hour, day, month, and year signs of the zodiac—she had a nigh unerring sense of compatibility. Still, she made mistakes: Third Auntie wanted to make it up to the Lis for brokering the disastrously ill-suited union between Masui and Zhou Damei. Raising her thin brows, she looked at bedraggled, heartbroken Mawu, and decided to give it a shot.

Soon, on a morning cloaked in mist, the matchmaker set off, carrying a ham with the tail still attached. Four or five days later, on an afternoon shrouded in fog, the matchmaker returned victoriously with an empty wicker back-basket. Tao Jiuxiang had feared Xia Qifa would refuse the offer; Third Auntie's successful negotiation prompted her to thank heaven and the magnanimity of the Xias. After all, Tao Jiuxiang mused, the Xias and the Lis were longstanding friends and fellow countryfolk. The two families knew each other outside-in: trunk and roots, branches and knots.

As Yinmei and Mahe had not been formally betrothed, over the past two years many families had made marriage offers and several young men had courted her, but Yinmei, now having eaten eighteen years of meals at her parents' table, showed no interest in any of them. As the years passed, her mother grew increasingly anxious. Yinmei had often heard her parents talk about the Li family over the years; she had seen Mawu before, and felt a certain affinity for the notorious fellow. When Third Auntie visited to ask for her hand on Mawu's behalf, Yinmei inquired in some detail about Jin before bashfully assenting, which created a stir in the Xia household.

Finding a marriage prospect for his handsome son Xia Liangxian was also a source of headaches for Xia Qifa. When handsome Xia Liangxian followed his father to various towns and villages to exorcise ghosts or propitiate spirits, the dashing young man left countless titillated hearts of nubile maidens and young wives in his wake. Requests for Xia Liangxian's horoscope came from every quarter. For his part, Xia Liangxian proved unable to resist the wild-eyed flirtations of a village head's charmingly sensual daughter Wang Yu'e. After an initial heated bout of lovemaking, Yu'e passionately swore to Xia Liangxian that she would never marry another. Xia Liangxian, for his part, was similarly smitten, and the pair met to couple clandestinely wherever and whenever opportunity afforded. The Wangs—who had engaged their daughter to the second son of a district head before either child was born—felt shocked and humiliated: As the saying goes, once an honor-bound gentleman gives his word, even a team of chargers can't chase it down. Feeling he had lost face before his friends, the village head locked lovely Yu'e in her chambers. The scandal left the Xias, too, a family of principle and honor, in a dispirited state. They had long planned to marry Liangxian to the granddaughter of old Li Erniang of Dragon Decapitating Gorge. Several years before, the pretty young girl had embroidered a belt for their son during the transmission ceremony. However, haughty Xia Liangxian hadn't shown the slightest interest in her. From childhood, he had shown himself to be bright, good-natured, and tractable, so no one had expected that he would prove so infuriatingly capricious and bull-headed on the matter of his engagement.

And now Xia Yinmei showed a similar willful resolve to marry Mawu! Although the Xias and the Lis were old friends, Mawu, known far and wide as "The Tiger," was an outlaw who had murdered Qin Liexiong in cold blood. Moreover, Mawu already had a previous marriage. His former wife Jin had taken another husband, which would leave their daughter in the unenviable role of stepmother to Yongyu if she married Mawu. Simply put, it was an undesirable match . . . a bad match! Though Mother Xia talked herself hoarse trying to dissuade Yinmei for half a night, her efforts were in vain. With a series of frustrated sighs, she continued the discussion first with her husband in bed, and then with the kitchen god before the stove. Only then did she at last resignedly consent to marry their daughter to frightening Mawu. Now, the Xias could devote all of their energy to dealing with their wayward son. After all, the future of their family hinged on their son, not on their daughter.

And so Tao Jiuxiang held a fourth wedding ceremony at Gengguping. She wanted the ceremony to be just as festive and lively as Mawu's marriage to Jin.

The unanticipated consent of the Xias raised Mawu from his wallow of anguish. In order to prevent Qin Lieniu from launching a sudden retaliatory attack, he garrisoned a fully armed complement of militiamen in the tower. He also invited the vice mayor and militia captain of Huangshui, Tan Ruideng, to his wedding feast.

Seven days before he wedding, Yinmei began a heart-rending and tearful chant to lament her departure from Dragon Decapitating Gorge:

> *O my father and mother,*
> *Your humble and lowly daughter*
> *'Tis like paper ash at the foot of the stove,*
> *Swept up by the swirling winds to drift away;*
> *Like a little mountain sparrow,*
> *Leaving its mother when grown.*
> *With no branch to perch upon, no nest to shelter,*
> *Off I fly this morn, who knows when I'll come back?*
> *Mother—three years I wriggled in your warm embrace,*
> *Now I leave you with whitening hair, careworn creases on your face.*
> *As I grew, my long cloth skirt becoming a tattered smock,*
> *Still you carried me from mountain to mountain, from rock to rock.*

Ever worried that hungry I might grow,
Or that I'd catch a chill when the cold winds blow;
O Ma, leaving you is like an arrow piercing my heart,
O Pa, parting from you is like having my liver cut from my body!

Old Mother Xia firmly clasped her daughter's hands in her own wrinkled hands, tears cascading down: "Your chant has teeth like a fierce yellow-furred hound. I can feel it rending my heart and liver apart!" Old Li Erniang and her granddaughter came to accompany them in the parting lament. Seeing Yinmei in her red wedding dress, the girl dabbed her own moist eyes with a silk kerchief, all the while rapaciously watching Xia Liangxian carry a scuttle of hot coals into the house. Covering her face with a handkerchief, Yinmei sang forth her sadness in separating from her brother:

When I see you, oh my brother,
Tears rain down on my chest.
You, who has lavished so much attention on this little sister,
Will send me off to his family.
And when we come to the edge of the high cliff,
You won't turn back.
And when we arrive at the brink of the abyss,
You won't turn and leave.
And if we pass through the gates of the palace of Yama, King of Hell,
You'll accompany me to the innermost chamber.
When you return home, burn paper for me,
And even in the netherworld I'll be content.

V

Although Yinmei's song for her elder brother was tinged with sarcasm, she felt for Xia Liangxian. Once she departed, she would no longer be able to share in his troubles; nor in the future could she help her family face their struggles. Rather, she was off to Gengguping, where that mysterious man awaited her. Reluctant to climb into the wedding sedan and leave home, she wailed for seven days and seven nights, sinking into ever deeper misery, wailing even when she combed her hair or ate—wailing to the ancestors, to her parents, to her brother, and to the family hounds. Yinmei was not truly comparing her husband's home to Yama's underworld palace—there was a timeless, rehearsed quality to her protestations: to show she was a dutiful and virtuous daughter, most every soon-to-be bride would carry on and weep piteously before leaving her parents' home. In the mountains, most felt this was an important criterion in judging a bride's character. A daughter who left her family to marry without tears and heartfelt chanting—or one who made an empty show with half-hearted weeping and insincere chanting—was considered a young woman of low character, possessing neither virtue nor talent. Learning that Yinmei had wailed for a full week, Mawu was overwhelmed with pride.

As she left, Yinmei wept, bowing repeatedly to her parents. Her sleek, dark hair had been combed into a bun and fastened with a silver pin. Her brother carried her to the sedan chair. The large red swath of silk covering her face concealed her inner excitement. Having just learned several days earlier that his lover Wang Yu'e had been hastily married to the second son of the district head, and had left home with a sorrowful, ululating lament trailing behind her, longer than her dowry procession, distraught Xia Liangxian absently watched his sister's wedding sedan move off toward Gengguping. Porters hauling Yinmei's dowry, including a brand new loom and a bedspread made from colorful, crimson-trimmed silk that she had woven prior to her engagement with Mawu, accompanied the sedan. Over the years, she had gathered cotton leaves and stems, madder, indigo, plum flower, and begonia, then dyed a basket of cotton thread in crimson, before weaving these materials into all sorts of elegant images: lotus flowers, lotus leaves, osmanthus, lilies, swastikas, peach pits, writing brushes, and an interlaced pair of shoes, all symbols of a happy life and ideal marriage.[1] In this bittersweet state, Xia Yinmei, a girl born and bred in these mountains, was carried off to become part of the Li family.

The wedding sedan bumped and jolted over Gangou Bridge past the eerie old hardwood on the rocky ridge. But the *tima* Xia Qifa had fastened a bronze bell, handed on through generations of Xia ancestors, to one of the sedan poles. Its loud clanging issued a sonorous warning to ghosts and spirits alike: Beware, spirits, for this is a *tima*'s daughter, and if you behave with the slightest impertinence or indecorousness you will find yourself a powerful foe for generations. Above, the sun shone down on the mountain path as several

---

1. Taken collectively, these symbols are a series of homophones explaining how a well-matched couple can have a succession (lotus) of distinguished (osmanthus) sons and will exist in harmony (shoes) until old age.

clouds scudded across the azure sky. Alarmed by the bell, a pair of yellow Siberian weasels dozing in a nearby rock hollow fled into the depths of a stony niche. The flirtatious twittering of birds sounded from the topmost branches of the tree and the crags above. A beautiful patterned butterfly circled the birds before gracefully drifting off in pursuit of the wedding sedan.

Though the wedding was less extravagant than Mawu's first, the occasion was at once livelier and more solemn. A large number of guests congregated.

The trees that Li Diezhu had planted behind the house were already thicker than a water bucket, and even in the strongest gale one could hang a tung-oil lamp under their sheltering canopy. On the stone courtyard and embankment in front of the Lis homestead, the site of so many sufferings and triumphs, Xia Qifa and his disciples performed a series of rites and plays for three days running, the backbeat of the remarkable deafening drum drawing an ever-growing number of well-wishers and onlookers. It was said that only this sort of thunderous drumbeat could connect heaven, earth, and the netherworld so that it might be heard not only by men but by spirits above and ghosts below. Some guests sat on benches, chairs, and grass mats, while others squatted or stood watching the festal ceremony.

As the drums shook the heavens, everybody awaited the burning of incense to commence the wedding. Waxen tears slid down the pair of cheerful red dragon-and-phoenix wedding candles. Prostrate on the ground, through the gauze of her veil Yinmei looked at the rugged outline Mawu's shadow cast. Something about this man's ethers—his aura, his scent—appealed to her. She watched Mawu perform the timeless tradition of the three kneelings and the nine knockings to the ancestors, prostrating himself then rising again. She anticipated that soon, ever so soon, her shadow would mingle and merge with Mawu's. Lost for a moment in voluptuous reverie, Yinmei's cheeks blushed redder than a ripe wild strawberry.

"Let the groom go to the hall and the bride to the wedding chamber," the master of ceremonies shouted. Ever wary, Mawu motioned his militiamen over with a sleeve.

"Captain Li," called out jocular Zeng Laomao. "Let's make a bet. If you can get your new bride to speak tonight, you win: one yuan per sentence. But if you can't get a word out of her, three yuan for me! How about it?"

"Easy money!" Mawu grinned, nodding in agreement.

"Then hurry off to the wedding chamber," Third Auntie urged.

Mawu turned, hustling off through the covered gate and into the nuptial chamber, where his bride was approaching the wedding bed. When she had made the bed, master craftsman Zhu Shun's wife murmured incantations,

> Lay the quilt, spread the sheets,
> Blessings and happiness, ever complete.

Mawu charged forward, perching himself steadily on the side of the bed. Much to his surprise, Xia Yinmei came right over and sat down on the bed as well. According to Huangshui lore, the one of the newlyweds who sat closest to the middle would be the dominant partner down the road. Taking advantage of Yinmei's nervousness, Mawu clasped his new bride firmly round her waist and coarsely shunted her to one side. Watching from afar, Tao Jiuxiang beamed with satisfaction.

Stealthily, Zeng Laomao and other militiamen concealed themselves outside the wedding chamber, peeking through the paper-paneled windows. After the guests had left, Mawu called twice, "Yinmei, Yinmei." Not answering, the bride simply gazed at him with limpid eyes.

Again, Mawu called softly, "Yinmei, Yinmei."

Sensing prying ears outside their wedding chamber, Yinmei remained silent.

Thinking quickly, Mawu pulled the quilt she had embroidered up to his chin, then said, with a series of short and long sighs, "Clever and capable as my new bride is, this wedding quilt is a little too short. If I pull it up to cover my shoulders, my feet are exposed; and if I cover my feet, my shoulders get cold."

Xia couldn't help crying scornfully, "You're holding the quilt width-wise."

"One yuan!" Mawu said, rising quickly.

"What?"

"Two yuan!" said Mawu.

"Are you crazy?"

"Three yuan!" cried Mawu, triumphant.

"You are crazy!" huffed Yinmei.

"Four yuan," Mawu went on.

Outside the window, a chagrined Zeng Laomao couldn't help crying out: "Now I've lost three . . . no, four yuan!" Mawu laughed, "They bet me that I couldn't get you to speak: I won a yuan every time you opened your mouth." With an expression somewhere between bemusement and anger, Yinmei looked at her husband.

"Yinmei, I'm so thankful you're willing to marry me. You don't despise me?"

Yinmei shook her head.

"And you're not afraid of me?"

Once more, Yinmei shook her head.

Deeply moved, Mawu said, "Yinmei, you've grown up . . ."

Clouds obscured the gibbous moon. The militiamen departed, leaving only Sun Fu and his wife remaining—though Yinmei was blissfully unaware of their presence. Forgetting herself, the bride hummed a sentimental ditty, "Oh dearest, O sweet brother . . . come and dive into my river. Aya-ya-ya."

Taken aback by Yinmei's forwardness, Sun Fu abruptly dragged his wife away from the chamber. Sun Fu's wife, for her part, was such an unabashed gossip that the very next day she eagerly bustled over to Tao Jiuxiang, gleefully replaying Yinmei's every sensual croon and moan. Pointing at the mulberry and blaming the locust tree—as folks in Huangshui say—Tao Jiuxiang reproached her shameless daughter-in-law as she drove away a cacophonous flock of birds in the yard that morning. Mawu pretended he didn't understand his mother's ill-humored grumbling, while Yinmei lowered her head, maintaining a humble silence.

Shamelessness aside, the new bride proved remarkably diligent. Every spare moment she sat at her loom plying the treadles with her feet, nimbly working warp and weft with her hands, an oxhorn thimble on each index finger as she tirelessly wove patterned cloth. Yinmei wove everything imaginable—flowers and grasses, birds and insects, not even Xia Qifa's favorite lighter could escape becoming part of one of her colorful creations—into quilts, coverlets, curtains, and pillowcases that filled every corner of her new family's home with color and life. Seeing how assiduous her new daughter-in-law was, Tao Jiuxiang stopped grumbling and reflected happily how fortunate is was that Yinmei had finally married into the Li family.

Chapter Sixteen

I

With the advent of spring, the myriad creatures awakened from hibernation and the mountains once more teemed with the living thrum of yearning and mating. Snakes found a patch of sunlight to warm their bodies. Insects trilled. Tao Jiuxiang mashed wormwood leaves into pulp, added rice, and cooked steamed buns. Burning incense, she placed the bitter-tasting buns in the votive niche, a vernal offering to spirits that helped block up the holes of venomous snakes and insects.

Afterward, she seated herself in an armchair in the living room, called together the family, and solemnly announced her decision to divide up the family property. She parsed the family holdings into three lots. To Mawu she gave the remaining land at Peppercorn Bend, feeling that its miasmal alluvial terrain somehow fit her eldest son's prickly character. She split the acreage of mountain land on Gengguping and near the family tombs at Lihaku between herself and Masui's family.

Irked by the division, Masui's wife He grumbled that her mother-in-law had more affection for newly arrived Yinmei than for her. Heedless, under He's watchful and disapproving nose, Tao Jiuxiang had a four-room, tile-roofed house built at Peppercorn Bend for Mawu and Yinmei, hoping that they would soon bear her more grandchildren.

The morning the family moved to Peppercorn Bend, slender, bright-eyed

Yinmei and her stepdaughter Yongyu climbed into a sedan; gallant Mawu strode beside them. A lengthy train of porters followed them through the forest, carrying furniture and household goods. In the distance, a flock of white cranes soared overhead. From the sedan chair issued a charming melody:

> *Aya, Climbing up the slope in the early morn,*
> *Rifle on your shoulder and a powder horn;*
> *Aya, see the golden pheasant flush, rising from the glen,*
> *Fire your rifle, watch it fall down again.*

As Yinmei chanted, her pearly face shone with youthful radiance in the brilliant morning sun. Mawu raised his rifle and fired; two white cranes fell. One of the porters leapt to retrieve the quarry. Then the procession moved on jauntily through the spring verdure, passing through forests and cultivated fields on the way to Peppercorn Bend.

Yinmei had a melodious voice. Though she might go a full day without speaking, she could never pass a single day without breaking into song. On she chanted, singing day and night, night and day, whether at Gengguping or Peppercorn Bend. But when Mawu took her in his strong arms and put his lips to hers, or pressed them to her cheek or her neck—when those powerful, chapped lips sucked on her tongue—Yinmei felt her limbs slacken and her knees grow weak, breathing quickening and heart racing, pattering like a rabbit's, as she collapsed, semi-conscious, into Mawu's embrace. The first time Yinmei lapsed into this coma of desire, Mawu was at a loss—anxiously poking and prodding her, rubbing her limbs and cheeks to help her revive. Mildly alarmed, he considered seeking help from others but was too embarrassed. Mawu soon discovered, however, that all it took was a forceful kiss and a rolling bear hug to resuscitate her. From then on, night in and night out, the two were twined in the smothering and intoxicating toils of sensuality.

Peppercorn Bend was part of Fuling County, tucked in among the mountains and crags, the valleys and glens, to the northeast of Fengjie. Along with Wanxian County to the east and Enshi County to the west, this mountainous belt of three counties—scored by gorges and crisscrossed by fast-running rivers and creeks—had a long-standing reputation as a lawless borderland inhabited by outlaws, opium runners, rebels, and smugglers. After Mawu settled at Peppercorn Bend, he held a series of raucous feasts, inviting mountainfolk from far and wide—boisterous revels that drew carousers from as far away as Chongqing and West Hubei, descending on his homestead like water flowing downhill, like a pack of wolves to carrion. Every imaginable manner of booming drinking song, uproarious shout, and joyful noise issued from Mawu's home except one—the cry of a new baby. Learning of the goings-on at Peppercorn Bend, Tao Jiuxiang was shocked and saddened.

As summer approached, Tao Jiuxiang neatly swathed her hair in a kerchief, donned a wide-brimmed bamboo hat, mounted a mare, and headed to Peppercorn Bend to pay her first visit since the partitioning of the property. Masui, his wife, and their two-year-old son Yongzhi followed; Sun Fu brought up the rear.

Mawu had not anticipated the family visit. He and Yinmei kept busy killing chickens and boiling meat for the guests. Nine-year-old Yongyu was delighted, dashing in and out to show her grandmother around the place.

Outside, Tao Jiuxiang saw several men practicing the assembling and firing of rifles. They didn't look like militiamen. Guessing that they were Mawu's private armed corps, she asked bluntly, "Where does the money to support them come from?"

"Power grows from the barrel of a gun," Mawu explained. "Elder Brother Wang supports me and funds this force, but keeps himself behind the curtain." In addition to his militia brigade of twenty, Mawu had a private army of two dozen.

Why was Wang Zhengming keeping himself in the dark and using Mawu as his teeth? What kind of medicine was he keeping in his gourd—in short, what was he up to? Uneasily, Tao Jiuxiang mused that nothing came without a price: she felt certain that ulterior motives lay behind his generous assistance. The Wangs were Huangshui nobility. Wang Zhengming controlled a riverport in Wanxian County. His younger brother Wang Zhengxiong, also closely affiliated with Mawu, became a teacher in Huangshui after graduating from Chongqing University.

The tidings of the death of Tiger Incarnate Bodhisattva Liang the bamboo craftsman spread through Huangshui. It was rumored that bandits had invited him to attack troops stationed in Enshi, where even several heavy machine guns failed to rebuff Liang and his men. In desperation, the soldiers stripped off their uniforms and tied on yellow armbands, disguising themselves as bandits. In the surrounding mountains, there were several different groups of brigands who often collaborated to coordinate attacks on local militias.

Mistaking the Enshi militia for one of these bands, Liang welcomed them into his stronghold. Taking advantage of the usually cautious bandit king's lapse, the troops launched a sudden attack from within and without. Liang was shot to death on the spot. The bloody grounds of his stronghold were littered with bullet shells and corpses: some of his followers died, others fled. Liang's head was hung on the city gate of Enshi. Hearing the news, Mawu exhaled, silently gazing up the mountain path.

"Every enmity has its origin, every debt its creditor," mused Tao Jiuxiang. Most all the bitter foes of the Lis were dead, so what else did he want?

"How are you, Auntie?" Four rugged men in short-sleeved shirts greeted her smilingly. Carefully sizing them up, Tao Jiuxiang felt that they weren't ordinary mountainfolk. She had heard that Lieniu, the third son of the Qins, hellbent on taking down lawless Mawu, had pressed the lawsuit and, that failing, had gone to Enshi three times to recruit additional troops. But Mawu had gathered so many friends that he no longer feared reprisal. However, she found something about this savage-looking quartet disquieting—they seemed to as fierce looking as the four Buddhist heavenly kings. Through the unbuttoned shirt of one thickset fellow with a heavy beard, she could see a chest of thick, matted hair. Yinmei told her that the four had arrived just after the Pure Brightness Festival, when tombs were swept, and had stayed for more than a month. Tao Jiuxiang frowned.

II

"Ten coppers for a family portrait. Ten coppers. How 'bout it, landlord?" The photographer from Huangshui clamored outside the gate, camera in hand. Oblivious to the new arrival, Tao Jiuxiang fixed a baleful glare at the stalwart bearded fellow.

Mawu took a sample picture and showed it to his mother, saying, "I've seen pictures like this at the Wangs. Photography has caught on in Wanxian County." He recalled a picture of Wang Zhengming in which his mentor posed in suavely in a fur-trimmed overcoat and a fur cap, with his wife seated beside him, dressed in a Manchu-style body-hugging *qipao*, with pert bangs and long, wavy hair flowing down to her waist. Such breathtaking modernity sent the mountainfolk into paroxysms of envy!

"How can a person fit into a picture?" Masui's wife squinted, in an agony of curiosity.

"Just sit there and you'll appear on the picture with the push of a button," Masui said. When he had gone to school, he had accompanied classmates to a photographer's studio.

"Ten coppers? For how many people?" asked Yinmei.

"As many you like it," the photographer offered.

"Take a picture for us," called Mawu, guiding his mother to the bench.

"All right," said the photographer, "Let the old lady sit in the middle of the long bench . . . your two sons sit on either side, with your young wives standing behind."

Yinmei tugged on Mawu's sleeve, indicating that he should change into his new long gown.

Furrowing her brow and peering dubiously at the device hanging from the photographer's chest, Tao Jiuxiang asked, "Can that thing suck out my soul?"

"No, Ma," replied a bemused Masui. "Photography's been popular in the cities for a while. I would have set up a family portrait, but I wanted to save us money."

Tao Jiuxiang bound her hair with a ribbon while the others tidied up their clothes in preparation. Mawu cheerfully hoisted Yongzhi up, perching him on his knee.

The photographer counted aloud, "One . . . two . . . three!" then pushed the button.

After the flash, everyone clustered around the camera, discussing the mysterious and marvelous device. Tao Jiuxiang pulled Mawu aside, and surreptitiously asked if the bearded fellow might be a convict escaped from the execution grounds? Mawu answered with a laugh, "Shall we invite the convict to join us in a family portrait?"

Tao Jiuxiang asked about the four newcomers. Mawu told her that they were acquaintances of the Wangs from Wanxian County. Though she didn't pursue the matter, Tao Jiuxiang planned to visit Old Wang in Huangshui the following day.

In the presence of strangers, the family was a bit reserved at dinner. Tao Jiuxiang felt ill at ease, fearing that the plans and ambitions of her firstborn would bring further dangers down upon the family. Why couldn't he just keep out of trouble and work on growing a new family, birthing a few more sons? And why couldn't a talented and principled wife like Yinmei, a daughter-in-law with a good head on her shoulders, keep him on the straight and narrow and start growing a family?

"Live a simple life as wife and husband," urged Tao Jiuxiang, finding Yinmei during a quiet moment before bedtime, her piercing eyes riveted on her daughter-in-law's flat stomach and hips. "Do I need to invite your brother to perform some sort of ceremony?"

"Ma!" said Xia, blushing crimson. "Soon . . . just wait a little longer."

"Birthing a child," Tao Jiuxiang sharply reminded her eldest son before her departure, "is what truly makes a family prosper."

The following day, Sun Fu set off first for Gengguping. Mawu helped his mother mount up and saw her off. She rode to Huangshui, followed by Masui and his family.

Though it had been years since Tao Jiuxiang last visited the streets and markets of Huangshui, she had not come for sightseeing or pleasure. Fearing headstrong Mawu—having gathered scores of guns and a growing force of rough-and-ready men—might become ever more untrammeled and lawless, she resolutely entered the grounds of the Wang family's private school.

That afternoon, having assigned homework to his disciples, Wang Binquan changed into his short coat and began practicing a series of military spear drills—like "Jiang Ziya goes fishing"—in the courtyard. With ease and fluidity, the well-muscled master parried, spun, and thrust, wielding the heavy eighty-pound metal spear as though it were a mere toothpick. Suddenly, he stopped short, taken aback at the sight of his former student Li Masui and his mother, Tao Jiuxiang.

"Sir," said Masui respectfully, "my mother and I have come to pay a visit."

"Mr. Wang, I offer thanks for your kindness in teaching my sons to read and write." With these words, Tao Jiuxiang removed a packet of tea and a haunch of cured meat from Masui's basket.

Though he had long since retired from his government post, Wang Binquan was greatly admired by mountainfolk far and wide for his broad learning. He had married five wives in succession, each dying young and childless. Finally, at the age of fifty, his sixth wife bore him two sons and a daughter. Master Wang lavished attention on these sons, this late-arriving pair of precious pearls, teaching them the Four Books and the Five Classics, to help them to a successful future. The brothers were the first young men from the region to attend Chongqing University. Certainly, they must be principled, righteous men, thought Tao Jiuxiang.

"Welcome! How's your family?" greeted Master Wang warmly, putting down his spear and asking an assistant to serve tea.

"Faring well enough, thanks to the blessings of our ancestors," Tao Jiuxiang answered. For some time, she had been trying to figure out how to broach the purpose of her visit. "Mr. Wang, have you seen our Mawu recently?"

"Not for some time." Wang Binquan replied, stroking his beard, "Is something wrong?"

"He's made a lot of new friends—its hard to read the deep and shallow of them," Tao Jiuxiang began cautiously. "I just hope he keeps the family in mind ... and in his reckless audacity doesn't lose sight of face and appearances."

"A man can never have too many friends," mused Wang Binquan, savoring a sip of tea. "The same seeds will grow differently when planted in different soil. Some grow upward toward the sun," he added. "Others grow downward."

Tao Jiuxiang said seriously, "Master Wang, could you offer him some direction?"

"Mawu has a good sense of up and down . . . he will find out the right direction," Wang Binquan continued thoughtfully. "Like a plant, man has an innate feel for light and darkness. Even a stalk of grass will shrink in darkness and reach skyward to the sun, unfurling its blades. This is what my son has told me," Wang finished, a smile creasing his eyes.

Failing to grasp the gist of his response, Tao Jiuxiang knit her brows. This elusive old fellow was far too erudite for her liking.

III

As Mawu left to see off his friends, Yinmei sat at the window, seemingly hunched over a drawing. When Mawu returned, she was still drawing. Curiously, he stole up behind her, figuring she was designing a new floral quilt. To his surprise, he discovered that she had rendered a savage and an unkempt wildwoman sitting on a rock, her breasts exposed, her fingers interlaced, forming a mudra so that her index fingers pointed forward and her thumbs pointed skyward.

Mawu was breathless with amazement. As a key member of the local yamen, he was constantly asked to mediate disputes, so that his home had become a "courthouse with rough-hewn benches," teeming with all manner of guests and friends. Emulating Wang Zhengming's gift of gab, silver-tongued Mawu preached "Land to the tiller!"—fiery "take-from-the-rich-and-give-to-the-poor" bombast that was music to the ears of the sundry impoverished mountainfolk and outlaws. Mawu would sit on his stool holding forth for hours on end. Drawn from the rhetoric of Zhai Rang and the Wagang agrarian rebels who helped overthrow the Sui, the brotherhood of bandits from Liangshan Marsh during the Song dynasty, and Sun Yatsen and the syndicate that had overthrown the Manchu Qing dynasty, his slogans carried almost the same persuasive force as his father-in-law Xia Qifa's chants.

"Yinmei," he asked, "what is it that you're drawing?"

"A diviner-queen," she answered.

"A diviner-queen?" asked Mawu, puzzled, "What can she do?"

"She's the witch-goddess of conception," whispered Yinmei, dressed in a blue shirt.

Mawu's sunburned face beamed. He sat beside his wife, asking, "So . . . we have a baby?"

"Her fingers possess magic . . . she can bring us a son," responded Yinmei.

"So you don't need a man—she can give you a child?" Mawu teased.

Next to the raggedy witch-woman, Yinmei had sketched a bow-legged, hirsute wildman clutching a gnarled spiral staff before his chest.

Looking at the staff, Mawu furrowed his brows, "And what's this. Looks like a rattan-bound walking stick."

"My father's walking stick is called the Ancestors' Staff," said Yinmei, cheeks blushing red. "It is also called a birthing staff or a sons-and-grandsons staff."

Damn, her sketch was sexier than an erotic "spring palace" print! Playing dumb, Mawu asked, "So is there an assassin coming? Is the hairy guy getting ready use his powers to fight?"

"No," Yinmei answered, looking up at him, "the goddess is bestowing her blessing upon him."

Holding back laughter, Mawu caught his wife in a bear hug and said, "Can you show me how she bestows blessings?"

Nimbly extricating herself, Yinmei moved to the edge of the bed. "It should be done like this." With these words, she gently clasped her palms together. Moving them apart, she then began deliberately interlacing her fingers one by one: first her pinkies, then her ring fingers, her middle fingers, and finally her index fingers. Pushing the heels of her hands together, she pointed her thumbs inward, thrusting them into the narrow cavity between her palm. Mawu noticed that Yinmei's hands were in the same position as those of the witch-spirit in her sketch. Swaying, Yinmei inverted her hands, forming another mudra, her fingers in the shape of a lotus, pulsing and contracting as her thumbs pushed into the heart of the flower.

Titillated and amazed, Mawu took his wife in his arms, saying, "How did you learn that?"

"From my brother . . . I've watched him perform a fertility rite for people seeking children. The sons-and-grandsons stick is hung from the back," Yinmei answered shyly.

"Can the staff produce a child?" Mawu asked, smiling fondly at his wife.

"Just as hardy stalks of grain yield fine kernels, so the staff of sons-and-grandsons produces strong, healthy sons," said Yinmei shyly, her cheeks blushing again.

Fire erupted from Mawu's eyes. He folded Yinmei's picture, then stripped off his shirt and loosened his trousers. However, Yinmei, worried, ducked away again and said, "To have a son we can't just go at it pell-mell . . . there are techniques."

"Tonight everyone else is out! So let's conceive a good, stout son!" shouted Mawu decisively, giving an angry thump to the bed frame. Busy with his nightly audiences, banquets that lasted to the wee hours of the night—as folks in Huangshui said, "the hog's just back from the butcher shop, but its already half gone"—Mawu had nearly forgotten his mother's admonition.

That night, kneeling beside Mawu, Yinmei lit three sticks of incense in the main chamber. Amid the smoke of incense, the *tima*'s daughter staged a fertility rite, solemnly going through the sensual mudras as she piously chanted:

> *Incense smoke, gold and silver,*
> *Yellow wax, precious incense river.*
> *Grandfather Heaven, Grandmother Earth,*
> *Bless us with a child's birth.*
> *To the gate of our family Li,*
> *Bring a healthy child for husband and me*
> *Well-shaped buttocks, eyes keen and bright,*
> *Healthy lips and tongue just right.*

Hearing her fluid chant and eloquence, Mawu was filled with admiration. Once they were in bed, he fondled Yinmei's breasts, musing proudly, "All Huangshui knows that your Xia family and Wangs are the most learned."

Removing her final article of clothing, Yinmei threw herself into Mawu's ardent embrace. Since her mother-in-law had uttered those ominous words, she had felt a sense of trepidation. Knotted with Mawu in the vertiginous throes of love, she exerted all her vitality to goad her man to plunge deeper and deeper into her. In the midst of their lovemaking, she chanted a birthing song she had learned from her father:

> *Chosen partners horizontal embrace,*
> *Woman and man clasped together face to face!*
> *Come into me. Fuck, ah!*
> *Plow a furrow in my fecund soil, climb my slope good.*
> *Lift me up high, inundate me with your flood.*
> *And when the planting's done, may it be found,*
> *New life growing inside the womb's rising mound!*

Mawu panted, relentlessly driving deeper as she chanted in gasping fits and starts:

> *I de-sire land . . . O, I de-sire fields,*
> *I de-sire mountains . . . the river's fertile yield.*
> *I de-sire clouds . . . O, de-sire rain,*
> *De-sire earth below, sky above the fruitful grain.*
> *I de-sire a boy . . . Oh, I de-sire a girl,*
> *De-sire all the spirits and ghosts . . . of the world.*

Under the newly tiled roof, that sultry night witnessed one of the most protracted and intense bouts of intercourse in the turbulent history of Huangshui. Her breath tickling Mawu's ear, Yinmei dreamily exhaled a final, goading hoarse whisper:

> *Plunge your shaft into my swamp,*
> *Sinking deeper every pounding thump.*
> *Cock's crest swelling, turgid lust,*
> *Bolder, harder every thrust.*
> *Grind like a millstone, bear a son.*
> *Pound like a hulling hammer til we're done.*

Consumed body and soul, bewitched by Yinmei's incantatory spell, Mawu burned incandescent with passion through the entire night.

Alas, bliss is always ephemeral. Xiang Jintang, entangled with no end of harassment from surrounding bandits, politely declined Qin Lieniu's request for military support, but delivered two-dozen guns. He urged Lieniu to head straight to the county seat to report Mawu's suspicious activities.

So one summer day, Qin Lieniu, ever plotting, seeking any opening to take down his hated rival, went to the Guomintang Party Committee of Fengjie County and, with a belly full of wrath, reported, "I have ironclad evidence that Li Mawu of Peppercorn Bend, with artful cunning and deceitful rhetoric, has gathered a band of wicked followers and is instigating them to engage in illegal activities." The Guomintang County Committee took Lieniu's report seriously and issued a secret order to the mayor of Huangshui to "exterminate the threat as expediently as possible." Fortunately for Mawu, Wang Zhengming got wind of the order and alerted Mawu, ordering him to gather his guerrillas and retreat into hiding deep in the mountains to await further instructions.

Chapter Seventeen

I

Even half a century later, the passage of time and countless downpours could not scour the lingering redolence of gunpowder and blood from that fateful summer. With the slightest stirring of time and space, the fell reek of murder still rose from the soil.

Having received orders from Wang Zhengming, Mawu sent Yinmei and Yongyu off to Dragon Decapitating Gorge, out of harm's way. He asked ward chief Ran Hongyou to feed his two pigs. After that, he informed all his militia and guerrilla troops to temporarily disband, seeking shelter with relatives or friends.

It was not long before the first rifle salvos echoed in the valleys. Vice mayor Tan Ruideng ordered an attack on the nest of brigands in Peppercorn Bend and appointed militia Captain Qin Lieniu to lead the campaign. However, time and again the elusive and rootless bandits outmaneuvered the troops. First, a bunch of bandits encircled the Xiedong government offices, killed the mayor, captured several militiamen, and plundered the armory, carrying off rifles and gunpowder. Next, they launched a raid against the town headquarters in West Leping, leaving the wealthy scrambling to conceal their gold and silks. Fortunately, Battalion Commander Wei—serving under his general Chen Houting—arrived with his troops, forcing the bandits to retreat across Speargrass Plain toward Hubei.

All told, a dozen attacks, large and small, struck government yamens in the region, prompting the infuriated Battalion Commander Wei to launch a large-scale hamlet-by-hamlet search-and-destroy campaign. However, this bandit extermination campaign proved utterly fruitless, for the brigands concealed themselves in remote mountain caves and densely forested valleys, making it impossible for a battalion of soldiers to encircle them. By night, the bandits haunted the forests and mountains preying on troops straying from the battalion, launching guerrilla attacks and sniping sentries, fleeing the moment they were chased. Then, shocking tidings arrived from Enshi City: Xiang Jintang, governor of Peartree District, had been assassinated in the deep of the night, and the bandits had escaped with General Yang Sen's recently arrived store of ammunition and gunpowder from the armory!

Kuomintang civil defense forces in Fengjie and Enshi counties received a confidential telegram from Wanxian and several days later launched a sudden attack. Coordinating with Battalion Comander Wei, the joint civil defense forces from Fengjie, Wanxian, and Enshi fanned out in a fifteen-mile semi-circle hemming in the bandits and sweeping forward.

At the same time, a company of Nationalist troops was sent to Gengguping. Soldiers encircled the old Li homestead, then, roughly shunting the family with rifle stocks, corralled Tao Jiuxiang, Masui, and his wife He, little Yongzhi in her arms, into the kitchen shed beside a stack of firewood. On the pretext that Mawu had already confessed his guilt, they demanded that the family turn over all their weapons.

"Mawu has been gone for six months," cried Tao Jiuxiang dubiously, her face contorted with anxiety. "We don't have any weapons."

Though the soldiers searched for hours, breaking down walls and digging up the floors, they didn't find a thing. Frustrated, they smashed the kitchen utensils. Before leaving they rummaged around, claiming sundry hairpins and bracelets, and carrying off all the cured hams hanging from the rafters.

In Peppercorn Bend, everybody—men and women, young and old—were marched to the top of a slope where several machineguns were set up. When they arrived, Battalion Commander Wei launched into a speech: "Good folks, elders, brothers and sisters, listen to me. Wang Zhengming, Wang Zhengxiong, and Li Mawu have rebelled and become bandits. They are enemies of the government and the people. Anyone with any information about these bandits should come forward immediately. If anybody is found to be involved with the bandits in any way, don't imagine you'll escape alive. I swear to you that anyone "colluding with the bandits," "concealing the bandits," or hiding weapons without reporting to the government will perish in a hail of machinegun fire..."

But his speech made no impact: from morning to late afternoon, not a single person came forward. Finally, on Wei's order, they burned Mawu's house to the ground and arrested Tian Degui, a fellow with ties to the guerrillas. Wei announced on the spot a reward of one hundred and fifty stone of rice for the capture of bandit chieftain Wang Zhengming and a hundred stone for bandit leader Li Mawu. Just as the reward was being posted, word circulated that Mawu and a band of Communist party guerrillas had carried out all three of the recent assassinations of Kuomintang officials on Wang Zhengming's command.

"Mawu must have eaten the gall of a panther!" ward chief Ran Hongyou exclaimed, stamping his feet. "Why would he go after Xiang Jintang way over in Peartree Moor, a good fifty miles from Peppercorn Bend? Even if as district head Xiang was a ruthless local despot, he's never harmed Mawu's hometown. And Xiang comes from a notable family in which two generations of his forefathers had passed the military examination. Plus, Xiang's son-in-law is a commanding officer in General Yang Sen's army. Li Mawu must be stark raving mad!"

Tao Jiuxiang gasped at the news. She had known the peaceful days wouldn't last, but she had never expected her eldest son to stir up such great trouble. Dark days had descended upon Gengguping once again.

One of Battalion Commander Wei's squads captured one of Mawu's guerrillas, Jiang Chunyun, who was reconnoitering in the mountains on the marge of Peppercorn Bend. He was imprisoned along with Tian Degui in township headquarters. To force them to reveal the whereabouts of Wang Zhengming and Li Mawu, the two were cruelly tortured using an array of techniques like "splints under ten fingernails" and "waterboarding the inverted duck." But despite the relentless torment that left every inch of their bodies pocked with cuts and scars, both men steadfastly denied any knowledge of "treacherous bandits."

Battalion Commander Wei killed Tian Degui at first. Then he bound an empty gas can full of live coals to Jiang Chunyun's back with metal wire. As Jiang's flesh sizzled, the pain grew so intense that he lapsed into unconsciousness. He revived briefly, only to faint again. When they dragged him from prison, hearing the bolt-action rifle cock and knowing death was imminent, he cried out "Long live the Communist Party!" In the field before the Wangs' homestead where he had once worked as a laborer, where the radishes he had planted grew rampant and green, Jiang Chunyun was shot twice in the back of his head. Fresh blood, together with his ebbing life, gurgled forth from the bullet holes, oozing into the rich earth.

At Wang Zhengming's dire warning, Old Wang Binquan had fled to Fengjie City ahead of the Kuomintang's arrival at Peppercorn Bend. Unfortunately, the Communist leader's younger brother Wang Zhengxiong, chairman of the People's Representative Committee in Huangshui, failed to escape the net. In desperation, he disguised himself as a wandering cotton quilt-maker and fled toward Zhongxian County. However, sentries stopped him at a checkpoint, suspicious to see that his teeth were brushed. Battalion Commander Wei tried to compel him to reveal the whereabouts of Wang Zhengming and his men, but Wang Zhengxiong refused. Wang was beaten to a bloody pulp with a heavy strap so relentlessly that the leather broke into three pieces. Shortly, on the fifth day of the eighth lunar month, Wang Zhengxiong was turned over to the Wanxian County authorities and executed on the charges that he had "colluded with and sheltered bandits" and "conspired with bandits to harm the people." Before his execution on that starry night, Wang Zhengxiong silently prayed that he might miraculously ascend to the White Tiger Star in the heavens, like his ancestors. Just before the fatal rifle shot rang out, he shouted, "Long live the Communist Party!"

At daybreak, Battalion Commander Wei ordered troops to light tung-oil bamboo torches from the firepit in a nearby farmhouse to burn the Wang homestead to the ground. Three times the troops returned from the neighboring farm with torches before they finally succeeded in setting the house ablaze. Dense smoke erupted heavenward; the compound burned for four days and four nights, illumining the path for Wang Zhengxiong's ethereal soul to rise skyward and his corporeal soul to descend to the netherworld. During the bandit suppression campaign, Qin Lieniu rose to become a member of the Kuomintang's Steel Resistance Squad. The squad refused to allow Wang Zhengxiong's corpse to be carried through the streets, forcing Wang's brother-in-law and several others to carry the corpse along a circuitous path through the jungly overgrowth of the sharp-ridged mountains.

"So far its just been killing," cried Battalion Commander Wei, his dilated, bloodshot eyes sweeping the surrounding forests and mountains, "Now it's time to burn this lawless backwater to the ground!" When an order arrived from Wanxian County to suppress the bandits as quickly as possible, he furiously commanded his men to set the mountains aflame. Wei howled, "Even if you avoid capture, I'll burn the lot of you bastards to death!" He blockaded roads to Peppercorn Bend and Cold Wind Gulch. The next day saw a fifteen-mile serpent writhing in agony: the mountain ridges burned, wreathed in dense, choking smoke as tongues of flame snaked skyward. Pregnant mountain apes were incinerated, their babies burned to a crisp, greeted by a world of fire as they burst forth from amniotic sacs. Gripped by unutterable horror, scaly and furred tribes burst from grottoes and groves, running, crawling, and slithering for their lives. The conflagration encompassed a hundred square miles; even as night fell the mountains were lit bright as day. Above, the sky was baked red; below, the scorched earth seemed to tell the story of a new world, a volcanic orb spewed out, entropic ejaculate of a newborn universe. Standing on a high peak and bearing witness, Wang Zhengming was gripped by smoldering rage and misery.

The conflagration burned for a full month before dying out in the heart of the primeval forest. Countless wild creatures were burned to death, though not a single member of the Communist guerrillas was harmed. Eternal Heaven bore witness to the carnage, yet remained silent.

After the departure of Battalion Commander Wei and his troops, Old Wang Binquan returned to find his house—in the family for three generations—burned to the ground. Nearby stood the new grave mound of his youngest son, not far from the cluster of the six graves of his wives. Keenly aggrieved, the old man fell to his knees, pounding his chest with his fists as he wailed. Once all had been happy and harmonious. Now, everything was gone!

When Wang Binquan had learned that his sons were in peril, he offered substantial bribes to the Nationalist County Committee officers. But his efforts proved vain, for both his sons were labeled "principal leaders among the wicked bandits." He could do nothing but fret, gasping with deep sighs. Ever since his dismissal from office, he had understood the corruption and ruthlessness of the surrounding warlords. At home, he had devoted his days to educating his sons. He had never expected that these two proud, principled sons would drive the Wangs to ruin.

In the rubble and ashes he discovered an intact plaque with five graven characters: Heaven 天, Earth 地, Ruler 君, Parent 親, Teacher 師. The tablet, painted black with the characters graven in gold, had been set in a votive niche. Miraculously, although the altar below had been reduced to ashes, the tablet had remained unscathed. Wang Binquan, though a full seventy-years old, hoisted from the rubble a granite basin with floral reliefs, weighing more than a hundred pounds, and set it before the grave of his youngest son. Then, taking the tablet, he returned to the family ancestral hall, and lived there.

While the dead were gone, the survivors lived on. One day, Wang Binquan's son-in-law took his spade and dug up some radishes to feed the remnants of the family, old and young, women and children. When he turned over the soil, he was amazed to discover that, beneath lush overgrowth of greens were tubers as large as a human head! Consecrated with human blood, the radishes were swollen to prodigious size. Anxiously, Wang Binquan instructed his son-in-law to re-plant all of the radishes. Eventually, the Wangs harvested and sold the radishes on the market. However, no one in the family ever ate a single bite.

A month after moving into the ancestral hall, Wang Binquan passed away.

II

The curtain of night settled over the mountains and valleys. The deep indigo darkness swallowed all sound so that not the slightest trill of frog or murmur of a beast could be heard. In the cooling night, the silent forests blanketing the mountains felt more like a desolate haunt for demons.

Eight or nine days later, Masui heard a rumor that Mawu's head had been hung from the city gate of Fengjie; his notorious elder brother had met with the same fate as Liang the bamboo craftsman, the scourge of Huangshui. Overwhelmed with sorrow, Masui tearfully reported to Tao Jiuxiang, "Mum, Mawu's been captured . . . they say he's already . . . already . . ." He dared not go on speaking.

"Don't talk nonsense. Your eldest brother is fine! He's just fine," Tao Jiuxiang interrupted, resolutely asserting. "They haven't captured him!"

Years ago Mahe, her second son, so filled with mischief and verve, was killed on the battlefield. Now would heroic and audacious Mawu be taken from her as well? Recalling little Mawu's dirt-smudged face as he marched with the wandering Tribe of the Tiger through the forests, Tao Jiuxiang sat outside the courtyard gate, tears coursing down her cheeks and flooding her heart. She recalled Li Diezhu and Mawu, father and son, cutting a swath through thorns and vines with machetes; her eldest son with a braided straw rope binding his waist, recklessly driving several goats up a ridge; Mawu mounting a horse, his face contracted into a faraway steely gaze, a loaded rifle slung over his shoulder; his grim aspect upon returning home from Wanxian County with the bundle of guns; the zealous man at Peppercorn Bend delivering rousing speeches railing against tyranny and injustice. Looking at stray patches of withered grass on the slope, her eyes burned hot and red, drying her tears. Tigers loved stretching and rolling luxuriantly in such patches of speargrass; boys herding cattle would bed down and rest in the tall grass. Truly, there was something divine about this speargrass: cattle grazed on it; mountainfolk use it to thatch roofs; girls wove it into baskets; folk girded their waists with belts plaited with it. There was even something soothing and hypnotic about the way it swayed in the breeze. Confronting hardships and disasters, her ancestors over the centuries had used fermented speargrass and rice to make a filtered wine, then offered libations to the gods to secure their blessings. And they bundled speargrass to perform divination, to foretell the inauspicious and the auspicious. Some subtle intimation of the undulating speargrass told Tao Jiuxiang that Mawu lived, that her first born was alive!

She thought once again of the old myth: At the very moment of the clan's imminent extinction, the White Tiger transformed into a handsome young man who married a herder girl. Their progeny became the Li family. The young couple were grazing their sheep when a thunderbolt exploded, metamorphing the White Tiger into a shining white star that flew up to the heavens.

Starlight from on high, distant and ancient, faintly illumined the valley. Firmly grasping a stalk of speargrass in her hands, Tao Jiuxiang looked up into the night sky. Seven stars above took the shape of a tiger, its head in the west and tail in the east. The star that formed the tiger's head blazed so bright that it burned its way indelibly into the mind of any who gazed upon it! Oh, ancient Immortal Tiger, you who led the tribes forth from the underground grotto, waging countless bloody wars and battles in the world of men, are you a curse or a blessing, our savior or our bane? Why do you keep descending from on high to lead our people to salvation, to damnation, if it is predestined that we—your descendants—will be plunged, time and again, into this endless litany of bloodshed and slaughter?

Masui said, "Mum, please come back into the house, Mum. Please!" He swallowed his tears and murmured humbly, "Although in your eyes I'm not the son Mawu is, I swear I'll take good care of you. Your old age will be peaceful, safe and sound." Tao Jiuxiang wanted to weep but no tears came. Together, Masui and his wife supported Tao Jiuxiang, leading her back into the house.

Impetuous Mawu was capable of anything. How could such a man meet with a normal end? Masui mused gloomily. Better to lead a bland, mundane life. His wife He—possessing neither Jin's voluptuous beauty nor Yinmei's clever ingenuity—suited him perfectly. If his mother lived with them, she could pass the years in peace and quiet. What more could one hope for than shelter from the waves and wind of life? Lost in these reflections, he only then noticed that a mountain man donning a mangled straw hat had followed them through the gate. Tao Jiuxiang recognized Zeng Laomao, the plowshare craftsman. Tao Jiuxiang caught hold of his sleeve, asking with an anxious rasp, "Where's Mawu? Where's Mawu? Mawu?"

Zeng Laomao told her that Mawu was still alive. The head dangling from atop the city gate was not Mawu's. Hearing these words, Tao Jiuxiang's lips moved ever so slightly, curling into a queer smile that creased her grim face.

In filing a report to his superior officer, Battalion Commander Wei had lied: to show that he had not been derelict in fulfilling his duty and to send a message that would cow the rebellious folk of Huangshui he claimed that Wang Zhengming and Li Mawu had been executed. He ordered his men to decapitate Jiang Chunyun and Tian Degui, and to display their bloody and unrecognizable heads from the top of Fengjie's city wall. A public announcement proclaimed that these were the heads of Wang Zhengming and Li Mawu.

As Zeng Laomao had claimed, Li Mawu and Wang Zhengming were still alive, hiding beyond the long reach of Battalion Commander Wei. After the mountains had burned, they concealed themselves in the dense primeval forests by day and sheltered in cliff-face caves at night. Not wanting to alert the Nationalist troops of their position with a gunshot, they fashioned bows with mulberry limbs and made arrow shafts with straight *lei*-tree branches to shoot monkeys and small game. When a monkey was hit, it would break the arrow and cast it away, then stanch its wound with leaves and climb to the treetops. The nimble monkeys shuttled among the trees with remarkable speed, swinging from branch to branch, from vine to vine. Only if they dropped to the ground were the men able to capture them. Mateless monkeys howled in protest outside the cave each night. The cave where the guerrillas were sheltered, recently the lair of a great, shambling black bear, penetrated deep into the cliff. Nearby, the nocturnal snuffles and growls of the dispossessed bear filled the men with dread.

Mawu dispatched Zeng Laomao to sneak back to Peppercorn Bend and drive his hogs—that Ran Hongyou had been tending—back to their forest hideout. After Zeng Laomao left the cave, the black bear trailed him at a distance—ambling through the forest just beyond arrowshot, cloaked in the dense fog. Unnerved, Zeng Laomao made his way back, only to learn that Ran Hongyou had already sold both hogs. Worse, Ran threatened to turn Zeng Laomao in. Fortunately, Ran's wife stopped him, warning, "Oh, no. If you do, Master Tiger Mawu will wreak vengeance. You'll bring down misfortune on the whole family!" After mulling it over, Ran Hongyou let Zeng Laomao go. Empty-handed, the plowshare maker made his way back to the cliff cave, threading his way around the persistent black bear.

It was still a month until the autumn harvest. The thirty guerrillas struggled to subsist on wild persimmons. It was at this juncture that Zeng Laomao headed to Gengguping carrying a message written by Mawu, asking Tao Jiuxiang for help.

Clutching Mawu's note in her hands, Tao Jiuxiang offered a heavy sack of rice to Zeng Laomao. Seeing him disappear into the haunted mists of the night, she returned to the family shrine, burned incense, and, going out the gate of the homestead, made three bows in the direction of the White Tiger Star. After that, she knelt and prayed for her eldest son. Rising at last, she turned to Masui and said, "Now your eldest brother's fate is in the hands the bodhisattvas and the demons."

Incredulous, Masui asked, "How could Battalion Commander Wei possibly find them amid the vastness of these mountains?"

"Battalion Commander Wei isn't the problem," said Tao Jiuxiang. "Hunger is. What happens when a pack of rugged carnivores are driven to the brink of madness by hunger and thirst? One day soon they'll mutiny and someone'll take my Mawu's head."

Masui was struck dumb.

Knowing that her eldest son was teetering on the keen edge of a sword, Tao

Jiuxiang dared not ignore his crisis. Having given careful instructions to Zeng Laomao, a couple of days later—and every two or three days after that—she sent Masui and Sun Fu to place a large sack of rice and some vegetables in a hollowed out dead tree where Mawu's men could get them at night.

Although Masui was scared, he knew that his elder brother's life might hinge on these shipments, so he delivered them faithfully. Whatever they brought, the ravenous guerrillas ate! In a fortnight, the thirty starved men consumed a staggering amount: peck upon peck of rice, hog after hog—until not a single one was left in the pigpen, potatoes and corn beyond reckoning. Masui's wife bitterly complained that this rapacious gang of eaters would bankrupt the Li family!

And so, the guerrillas weathered the crisis. Their liaison, herb gatherer Ma San, finally sent a confidential letter telling them that the vanguard of People's Liberation Army troops would skirt the Three Gorges of the Yangzi River, and, following the cliff path along Inkblack Creek, would arrive from Enshi.

Meanwhile, on Chen Houting's order, Battalion Commander Wei had relocated his men to the far shore of the Yangzi River. The Nationalist troops were plotting to take advantage of the elevation of the terrain to stop the People's Liberation Army from crossing the Yangzi River at Greenstone Dock.

III

Ringed by a deep brown-yellow penumbra, looking as though it were covered in hair, the gibbous moon hung, silent and tranquil, in the vast, cloudless sky. Mountainfolk knew that such a murky aureole marked the coming of a fierce wind. Mawu was sleepless. His guerrillas had followed him back to Gengguping. Suddenly, out of the darkness the deafening roar of a tiger sounded. He shuddered. All the pigs and sheep at Gengguping had been slaughtered to feed his men. At the bloodcurdling sound, the four remaining hunting dogs erupted in a fierce, frantic barking.

From another direction, he heard a second tiger's roar. Folks around Huangshui often said that one mountain isn't big enough for two tigers. Mawu figured that this second tiger was hightailing it faster than a gust of wild wind.

"Waa-oooh, Aaooo-woooh!" Another roar reverberated; it was difficult to distinguish the roar from echo. The sound made one's flesh crawl. He smelled it lingering in the night breeze: an acrid, fishy taint, the mating scent of tigers.

So, Mawu thought, perhaps it's mating season: one tiger was sounding a lusty mating call, and the other was roaring in response. What a mighty coupling that would be! Only when there was such a dark lunar halo would these divine creatures copulate. The male would jump on to the female's back, biting the furry folds of skin at the back of her neck, at once gaining purchase and expressing his ardor. After mating ten or twenty times in succession, the male would loose a loud concluding roar and leave.

Mostly, Mawu had learned tiger lore from his father. Li Diezhu had told him that no matter how lowly or primitive, coupling creatures engaged in intercourse never look a mate in the face. Animals have an instinctive fear of gazing at the contorted face of a mate in the orgasmic throes of climax, for to do so would be to glimpse in the same instant the divine and the daemonic, to confront death. The mountain wind whistled, scattering dead leaves from ancient trees. From the gorge below emanated a chill air of decay and death.

Apparently, the tigers were not only interested in mating. The following morning, Tao Jiuxiang found that four hunting dogs had been mauled to death. The spirit creature must have concealed itself on the leeward side of the house to hide its pungent reek from the keen-nosed hounds. No one had heard a sound.

The mountains and valleys around Huangshui were rife with tigers, especially the crags and alluvial plains of Lihaku. Surprisingly, the creatures seldom carried off children and rarely assailed the flocks and livestock of the villagers. Tigers were ancestors. Mountainfolk and villagers along the alluvial banks alike treated the creatures with reverence and fear. Tao Jiuxiang and the others were disturbed by the uncharacteristic tiger attack. Only years later recalling the event did Tao Jiuxiang realize with wonderment what had occurred in that autumn of 1949: "No wonder that tiger flew about the mountains and plains, rampaging and killing—it marked the end of a dynasty, the dawning of a new era!"

In the morning, mist enveloped the ridges, drawing sky and earth together. Choosing five guerrillas, Mawu followed the plank road along the cliff face and animal trails covered with decaying leaves, winding through the gorge along Inkblack Creek. As the gorge narrowed to a bottleneck, a canopy of interlacing vegetation encroaching from both sides formed a lush canopy of green. Gazing up, he followed the cliff, stone hewn by strokes of a great axe, rising upward;

below, a tangle of vines, creepers, and brush covered the ground. They cut their way forward, hoping to rendezvous with the People's Liberation Army men coming from Enshi.

By midday, the ground mists had risen, and sky and earth became separate spheres again. Birds glided freely on the currents of a noontime breeze.

The vanguard of the PLA soldiers marching from Enshi bivouacked in Tea Mountain Hamlet, a village on a narrow plain nestled in the mountains between Peartree Moor and Huangshui. After bedding for a night in a cave, the guerrillas reached the edge of in the primeval forest opposite Tea Mountain Hamlet. At the edge of the forest, Mawu kept watch from beneath a jutting rock, propped precariously on the roots of a fallen tree and pushed skyward. The hamlet was guarded on both sides and from the cliff behind the village. Looking down silently at his PLA comrades below, he thought of his days in Wanxian County three years earlier. The recollection of his good fortune at having gained the patronage and friendship of a true, hard-boiled revolutionary like Wang Zhengming suffused his bloodstained heart with pleasure.

"Who is it? Hands up!" a sentry suddenly shouted from an overhanging escarpment above, a PLA officer's star visible in on his cap. Mawu was too excited and nervous to reply.

"Hands up or I'll shoot!" The sentry yelled, cocking his rifle bolt emphatically.

Struck by a sudden inspiration, quick-witted Zeng Laomao stripped off his clothes, and clambered out onto a rock, and announced, "I am . . . we are the guerrillas. We're here to welcome you PLA men." Twigs and other detritus clung to his dirty, matted hair.

The entrance of the stockaded village opened and several PLA soldiers emerged, covering stark naked Zeng Laomao with an army uniform.

When the PLA men learned that this was the ragtag band of guerrillas that had decimated the military forces of Xiang Jintang, the mayor of Peartree District, a PLA officer clasped Mawu's hands warmly and said, "Thank you for clearing the obstacles from our path! We took an overland shortcut to avoid engaging key Kuomintang defenses. Chiang Kai-shek thought our troops would enter Sichuan either through Swordgate to the north or through Kuimen in Fengjie. He was wrong." So saying, he cheerfully ordered two soldiers to present three crates of bullets to Mawu and the guerrillas.

Mawu swelled with pride.

After staying the night at Tea Mountain Hamlet, Mawu asked Zhao Changyou to act as a guide for the PLA soldiers. Then, following the PLA officer's directive, he returned home to muster troops, reconnoiter, and block any advance by mobile Nationalist troops.

Chapter Eighteen

I

Several years later, for a number of reasons recorded in the annals of the Three Gorges region, the People's Liberation Army suppressed Mawu and the guerrillas. But that autumn it was Mawu's guerrillas, along with the monkeys and hawks, who guided the PLA soldiers through the valleys and canyons.

As the guerrillas made their triumphant return to Gengguping after receiving the PLA's orders, a colorful array of yellow leaves floated and danced on the breeze, swirling around them. Autumn was the most beautiful season. The mountainscape was painted with the yellowed stalks of paddy rice, the green of cornstalks, the vivid reds of azaleas and poppies.

Defeated Kuomintang officials in Huangshui were busy selling off their goods and property. Scattered groups of defeated Nationalist soldiers flooded into town, requisitioning pigs and chickens on sight. They surged into Ran Hongyou's home, ordering him to guide them out of the region.

Ran Hongyou complained, "But, officer, I'm your ward chief."

Impatiently, the company commander snapped, "And once you get back home, you'll still be ward chief."

The guerrillas stopped the retreating Kuomintang soldiers at Changkou. During a lull in the firefight, Mawu called out, "Surrender and you won't be harmed." The Kuomintang soldiers lay down their arms and knelt, begging for mercy. But as Zeng Laomao approached to gather up their discarded weapons, one Kuomintang soldier suddenly seized a rifle and tried to fire—only to have his gun jam. The veteran soldier then leapt up, drawing a pair of pistols from his boots, firing blindly over his shoulders as he fled. Braving the hail of bullets, Zeng Laomao chased the enemy soldier for several miles before killing him. Though bullets ripped holes in his pantlegs, Zeng Laomao was unscathed. Searching the man, Zeng Laomao found two silver dollars, which he pocketed rather than placing them in the communal kitty. Years later he was sentenced to two years in prison for appropriating public funds.

When Mawu bumped into a nervous Ran Hongyou, he ordered the ward chief to be bound and punished. Meanwhile, a new People's Government office was established in Fengjie County. Wang Zhengming was appointed Vice Chairman of the Political Consultative Conference of the Communist Party in Fengjie. When the Huangshui office of the Political Consultative Conference was established, Mawu was made Mayor. Zeng Laomao, Zhao Changyou, and other guerrillas were designated as officers in the civil defense force.

As they stood outside Huangshui's government headquarters, proudly changing government plaques, they heard a group of women wearing bamboo hats gossiping: "How bizarre it all is! To get revenge on Li Mawu, Qin Liexiong fought for years against the Great Tiger Bodhisattva and his bandits, but in the end Old Mawu still murdered him." Overhearing the gossipy women as he rounded a corner, Masui leapt to his brother's defense, "Qin Liexiong got what he deserved. He conspired with bandits to rob my family's stone tower and kidnapped my sister-in-law. Watch your wagging tongues, ladies!" Taken aback, the women pinched their shriveled lips together and retreated.

A bamboo basket slung on his back, Masui had come to Huangshui to purchase a new plowshare. Just a few weeks of tilling the rugged, rocky topsoil in the mountains was enough to blunt, bend, or break even the best-wrought plowshare. Mountainfolk would return their plowshares to the Huangshui market, exchanging them for new ones.

Masui swapped his old plowshare for a new one, then headed to a familiar shopfront to buy opium. However, at the shop's gate he caught sight of Mawu approaching from the township government headquarters. Flanked by two young attendant militiamen, Mawu sported a smart, collared four-pocketed cadre uniform; two pistols hung from his belt. Startled, Masui turned and said, "Elder Brother, I came to get a new plowshare, and to visit you and my sister-in-law."

With a serious look, Mawu warned in a low drawl, "No more opium. The new government is cracking down on opium smoking and opium-trading. Stop by my house and have your sister-in-law bake you a couple of ricecakes for the road. Then head home. There are lots of bandits around."

No wonder the price of opium was rising, thought Masui, disappointed. He fiddled with his money, pretending to be mulling over buying pancakes, then left, not daring to purchase opium right under Mawu's nose. His brother—Mawu the outlaw, Mawu the militia Captain, now Mawu the Mayor—was the pride of the Li family. He fought to quell the rising wells of vinegary jealousy and resentment.

Masui headed to the cadre dormitory, where Xia Yinmei, his sister-in-law, gave him a couple of ricecakes. Wandering homeward along the paths back to Gengguping, Masui forgot his annoyance about the opium and chanted a merry ditty:

> *Came across some pretty flowers in full spring bloom, ma-ya!*
> *A-ya, ga-la, ya-sha, hey!*
> *A host of fine tippling officers gather to drink in the room, ma-ya!*
> *A-ya, ga-la, ya-sha, hey!*
> *Entering the quarters, the new officer . . .*

Walking, he thought of his eldest brother, ever the bold and reckless man of action; but now, on top of that, Mawu seemed to have developed a clever, calculating mind, enabling him to plot to kill Xiang Jintang and enable the People's Liberation Army soldiers to freely enter the Gorges. What a remarkable sequence of events! Before the PLA soldiers had reached Huangshui following the gorge through which Inkblack Creek ran, they had arrived at Greenstone Dock after crossing countless mountains and rivers. Not only had they driven off Battalion Commander Wei, but they had crossed the Yangzi River and launched an attack on the Nationalist capital, Chongqing. How else could the PLA soldiers have found the narrow paths through the rugged mountains and steep escarpments known only to heaven, earth, and the scions of the immortal White Tiger? What a queer matter it was!

In the dim firelight, Tao Jiuxiang sat before the stove drawing on her pipe. Masui entered and sat beside his mother, opening a parcel and saying cryptically, "Sister-in-law Yinmei gave this to me . . . a portrait of Chairman

Mao. He is the highest official in the new dynasty. He asks us not to buy land, but to sell our fields!"

Tao Jiuxiang, having braved countless chill winds and frosts over the decades, scrutinized the benign, avuncular expression on the man's well-proportioned face in the portrait. "Put it aside," she warned. "Don't show it to others."

Excitedly, Masui countered, "What are you afraid of? Mawu has two pistols hanging off his butt and a pair of soldiers following him. He's even more powerful now than when he was militia Captain!"

Tao Jiuxiang cupped her face in her palms and murmured, "If Battalion Commander Wei and his men return, it will mean trouble."

Masui knew his mother spoke the truth. He thought of the soldiers he had met in Huangshui: the lot of them looked more like students, not even old enough to grow a mustache. He hastily hid the portrait in a cabinet.

Cannonfire echoed through the distant hills.

The PLA soldiers camped in the region needed grain. Mawu's primary duty involved collecting a rice levy. The Kuomintang Special Committee of Fengjie dispatched Xie Erjin, a Nationalist officer native to Fengjie, to Huangshui to collaborate with Tan Ruideng, the former militia Captain, to form an "Anti-Communist National Defense League" to seize grain and guns. Xie Erjin was the son of Xie Chongmin, who years earlier had asked Xia Qifa for an amulet to protect his son against the Japanese invaders. The *tima*'s amulet had kept Xie Chongmin safe and sound on the battlefield—both against the Japanese and the People's Liberation Army. In recent months Xie Erjin had hidden in the dense forest, gathering a band of brigands, and appointing them to various military posts and ranks. His company commander was none other than Qin Lieniu.

A spate of rebellions erupted in the volatile borderland. Emboldened by the turmoil, groups of bandits mushroomed. A "tiger spirit" would gather a force of men and horses, and other lesser "tigers," lacking sufficient men and resources to rival him, would join his band. Xie Erjin, protective amulet on his chest, incorporated a group of bandits from Enshi as his vanguard, and marched fiercely on Huangshui's headquarters and grain depot.

Armed with pistols and rifles, swords and sticks, spears and axes, bandits of every description, old and young, poured down the slopes, converging on Huangshui from all directions. Under the guard of Zeng Laomao, Zhao Changyou, and other local officers, the government headquarters in Huangshui were tightly secured, the main entrance defended with a machine gun. Rather than passively awaiting the onslaught, they flung open the back gate strafing the bandits with automatic rifles. At that very moment, gunfire exploded from the nearby mountainside, riddling the machine gunner and killing him. Guns blazed from the front and rear gates of the headquarters as Zeng Laomao, Zhao Changyou, and others strove to fight their way out. Soldiers fired on the bandits from another position in the mountains. Alarmed, Qin Lieniu, thinking a detachment of PLA soldiers had arrived, called for a retreat; he and the bandits quickly scattered. In fact, the source of gunfire from the mountains was Mawu, who had hurried back to Huangshui from a meeting in the county seat. From the elevated vantage of the ruins of the Palace of King Yu, Yu the Great, he saw the bandits besieging Huangshui.

The military power of the new government was fragile. In short order, bandits killed more than a dozen PLA soldiers and grain levy collectors. The brigands then ransacked the township headquarters in Xiedong, taking guns and grain. In retaliation, the PLA brought out the artillery: overnight, they mobilized a company under the leadership of Vice-director Zhao, a man from Wanxian County, arming them with two small cannons and an 82-millimeter mortar. Shortly after daybreak, having identified the bandits' position, Vice-director Zhao launched a relentless barrage of mortars and cannon fire. With precise execution, choreographed by a flagman brandishing a red banner, the land shuddered as a series of deafening explosions resounded in the mountain passes.

For the entire morning, cannons and mortars fired without cease, causing billowing clouds of black smoke and red lightning to rise. Trees splintered and debris flew, heavens darkened and earth sundered, as terrified bandits hiding in the undergrowth wailed bitterly. Beaten, recognizing that they were no longer invincible, they removed their spearheads—turning spears into carrying poles—and scurried away in desperation.

The folks of Huangshui were scared half to death by the cannonfire. Heart thumping like a rabbit's, Zhao Changyou murmured to himself, "The PLA is powerful! Oh, how lucky I am to have joined the guerrillas!"

Mawu saw tall, thin Old Mother Qin standing on the hill path, a woven bamboo hat on her head and a basket strapped on her back, gazing tearfully toward the mountain pass. He knew that she was imagining her son's tragic death, his intestines and inner organs festooning the tree branches. "Madam," said he, "tell your son to come back and be rehabilitated. China is liberated now. Tell Lieniu not to fight the people's government. I'll forget about past grudges and grievances."

"My son Liexiong fought against the bandits for years to get revenge for you, but in the end you killed him," Old Mother Qin muttered.

Mawu said, "It's not my fault that he was killed. He chose to stand with reactionary rulers. If I sided with the exploiting classes, I, too, would be killed."

Old Mother Qin sighed, "Mawu the Tiger, you can do anything you want. Why bother to bury the enmity between our families now?"

"Madam, don't worry. We Communists follow public duty; we do not countenance petty vendettas and private hatred," Mawu said seriously.

"I see. You don't dwell on past enmity . . . nor do you care about past ties and obligations." With these words, Old Mother Qin limped away. As soon as the gunfire stopped, she clambered up into the mountains to seek her son. Qin Lieniu was hiding in a cave with a few close followers. When they slept at night, one watchman held a burning incense stick. When the incense burned down and singed his fingers, he awakened the others and they moved to another cave. Sooner or later, he knew, they would be hunted down.

Finding her son, Old Mother Qin convinced him and his men to surrender. After the bandits lay down their arms, Mawu explained the new Communist policies to them. However, Qin Lieniu still cried out in annoyance, "Eldest Li, you've won. Why go on with all these principles? If you want to cut our flesh away from our bones, carve away. If you want to kill us, then kill us."

Swallowing his anger, Mawu retorted, "If I wanted to kill you, we wouldn't be having this conversation."

Another longstanding enemy of the Lis, tall and swarthy Jiang Ermao, stood defiantly beside Qin Lieniu and glowered, "Do whatever you want. You've beaten us. If you want to kill us, kill us; if you want to mince us to pieces, just mince away."

Mawu glared at him and said severely, "If you reform your conduct, you will be considered a good citizen of Huangshui. If not . . ."

II

Gaining momentum in a series of twenty-odd battles and skirmishes, the powerful People's Liberation Army had captured more than five hundred bandits, including Jiang Ermao and Qin Lieniu; many of the surrendered brigands were bound and imprisoned in an old granary in Huangshui.

Grinding his teeth, Vice Director Zhao looked at the lot of them. "Mayor Li," he said to Mawu, "I need to talk to you."

Mawu said, "What's the matter, Commander?"

Zhao hissed angrily, "I want to kill the lot of them!"

"Commander," Mawu, feeling his heart leap wildly, asked in surprise, "Do you want the blood of innocent men on our hands?"

"In dealing with the mountainfolk, our soldiers have consistently shown kindness and mercy. Even firing the heavy machinegun, we shoot only intermittent bursts. These cutthroat bandits, however, die clutching their rifle barrels in a rigor-mortise grip. We've fought them for years," Vice Director Zhao continued. "Even after Liberation, our soldiers have perished by their keen bayonets and spearpoints . . . You folk of these gorges are true savages— vicious and cruel! I've heard you regard the carnivorous and bloodthirsty White Tiger as your ancestor. Is that true?"

Mawu remained silent. He felt fortunate that Wang Zhengming had taken him under his wing and led him to the gateway of a new, magnificent world. Now, having matured and standing at that entrance, his perception had changed and he saw clearly that his fellow mountainfolk were shortsighted and narrow-minded, stubborn and conservative. They knew relentless struggle, fighting fiercely to the death. They knew little more than the land and the swatch of sky above these mountains and valleys. But they knew nothing of class struggle and the interests of new China. Under these circumstances, it was difficult ask Zhao to spare their lives. However, he was shaken by the thought of five hundred aggrieved ghosts complaining to the Immortal White Tiger, demanding a bloody and terrible vengeance. In Mawu's troubled dreams, his fellow mountainfolk cursed at and spat upon him. That very night he wrote a detailed report and, through Wang Zhengming, submitted it to the superior authorities.

As they awaited a final decision, the situation grew increasingly tense. A platoon of PLA soldiers was stationed next to the granary where the bandits were imprisoned, but the doors and windows of their temporary prison were dilapidated and damaged. Were the bandits to rebel and charge out *en masse*, the PLA troops would be hard-pressed to regain control. Zeng Laomao, Zhao Changyou, and other officers were sent into the mountains to collect grain. Meanwhile, armed to the teeth, Mawu manned a sentry post with two communications officers.

Two days later, in the afternoon, the rotary-dial telephone in the township headquarters kept ringing. An urgent message arrived from the county government ordering them to send a messenger immediately to fetch a top-secret missive. Nobody knew its contents. Nervous and agitated, Mawu, sleepless for two days and nights, dispatched one of the communications officers. He set a submachine gun on a wooden table in the sentry post, its muzzle peeking out the watch hole, pointing directly at the main gate of the granary.

Long after midnight but well before the following dawn the crackling of gunfire suddenly resounded nearby. Some men emerged from the barracks and reconnoitered the area but, finding nothing out of the ordinary, soon returned.

A while later, the night silence was broken by a sharp knock on the wooden door of the sentry post. "Who goes there?" called Mawu.

The only reply was a louder, more urgent series of knocks.

"Who goes there?" Mawu repeated, riveting his tense gaze on the wooden door.

Outside, a desperate voice answered, "Me."

Discerning the voice of the communications officer, Mawu hurriedly unbolted the door. The man staggered in, propped against the doorjamb, face pale as a sheet and chest heaving. He held a torch in one hand and a pistol in the other. Struggling to gain his breath, the man panted, "Tiger!"

The tremulous communications officer explained that a massive tiger had barred the mountain path, its eyes shining like two red lanterns, more terrifying than seeing the soulless fire in the eyes of a ghost one encounters in a deserted tomb at midnight. Terrified, he had unloaded an entire clip of ammunition at the creature. A gurgling, guttural explosion had issued from the tiger's throat, like a loud and horrible cough, as it crashed thunderously down the cliffside. He did not know whether it was dead.

"It's a tiger," Mawu exhaled, relieved. "There are lots of local legends about the spirit tigers. We dare not kill them for fear of heaven's retribution. There is a vibrissa whisker on a tiger's chin that enables it to discern a man's true original form. If it senses that the man is a pig or goat, it attacks; if it sees the shape of a person, it won't." He looked at the wide-eyed communicator, passing on the folksy wisdom of his father, "If you meet a tiger again, step aside and give it space—move toward the cliff's edge. Don't look straight at it or stare it in the eyes."

"G-g-g-give w-w-way t-t-to a t-t-tiger?" the communicator's teeth still chattered uncontrollably.

"Or you can point a fresh-cut forked branch of a *beijue* tree at a tiger. It has to be a *beijue* branch. A tiger will cringe and move away when he smells it."

Still gripped with horror, the man stammered, "I–I–I was af-f–fraid of it."

"I'm afraid, too, but my father met tigers twice and wasn't attacked." Uneasy passing on family lore to the PLA officer, Mawu switched topics, saying, "Let's have a look at the missive."

With trembling hands, the man offered Mawu a document with a red seal. The notification read: "The provincial government will make the final determination whether or not to execute the bandits of the so-called Anti-Communist National Defense League." Not daring to delay, Mawu promptly sought out Zhao.

The following day, when the imprisoned bandits, who knew that their fate hung in the balance, got wind that the PLA officer had encountered a tiger, they rejoiced, convinced the creature was a manifestation of the White Tiger come to bless and protect them.

Wearing his bamboo hat, Xia Qifa happened to come to market that afternoon. When he heard rumors of the incident batted about the streets of Huangshui, he hurried to township headquarters and asked Mawu where the officer had met the tiger. Mawu sent the young communications officer to guide the shaman.

Together, the two returned to the site of the encounter. Basket on his back, Xia Qifa wore a patched blue gown, his pantlegs rolled up to his knees. Along the route, the *tima* broke a forked branch from a young tree, its trunk only as thick as a ricebowl.

Astonished, the communications officer asked, "Is that a *bei . . . bei . . .*'

"A *beijue branch*," finished Xia Qifa.

"Does a tiger really fear it?"

"Not at all," said Xia Qifa irascibly. "With its keen nose, it can't stand the scent. Only a tiger can smell it."

Half-convinced but still skeptical, the young officer broke off a branch of his own. He knew the locals revered tigers as their ancestors. Not only was it forbidden to attack or kill tigers, but every household worshiped the beasts!

He wondered if the locals saw Wu Song, the famous tiger-killer, as a hero or a villain? "Old man," he began, "Have you heard the tale of Wu Song killing the tiger?"

"Yes."

They continued picking their way along the trail. "Can you tell it to me?"

III

Xia Qifa had high cheekbones and thick eyebrows perched above his recessed, yellow-tinged orbs. Over the past year he had begun to grow a beard, which made him resemble an owl. Stroking his beard, the shaman said, "I s'pose I'll tell the tale to this young comrade, then." So saying, he began to pick his way down a narrow, precarious trail to the bottom of the valley. "Wu Song came to an inn and called for a drink. The tavernkeeper's wife asked, 'How much? If you drink more than three cups, you won't make it over the ridge.' Wu Song answered, 'Bring me everything you've got!'"

The officer followed Xia Qifa, using the *beijue* branch as a walking stick. Worriedly, he called to Xia Qifa, "Careful, old man!"

Heedless, Xia Qifa continued: "So the inkeeper's wife says, 'There's a tiger on the ridge!' Wu Song shrugged, 'So, I'm not afraid!' He finished the three cups of wine and left, carrying a pole over his shoulder. Along the ridge road, he heard snorting and snuffling in the woods. Then and there, out leapt a tiger. He raised his carrying pole and knocked it tumbling over the precipice to the bottom of the cliff."

Seeing the old *tima* recount the story in such animated fashion, the communications officer once again cautioned, "Watch your feet, good elder!"

"Just take care of yourself," said Xia Qifa. "A moment later, a snuffling and a gnarring came from the woods again. As Wu Song turned, a second tiger burst from the undergrowth. But he parried its charge and sent that tiger tumbling down the cliff as well. Waiting a while longer, he heard a growling and a snorting coming from the woods yet again. Sure enough, a third tiger emerged. Wu Song beat it to death with his carrying pole, then trundled its corpse off the edge of the cliff."

After a pause, the shaman continued, "Wu Song stood waiting for a spell to see if any other tigers would come. When none appeared, he clambered down to the bottom of the cliff and found three men draped in tiger skins, clutching iron hooks in their hands, sprawled out dead. There were a number of other bodies were scattered at the foot of the cliff. Wu Song returned to the inn and asked the tavernkeeper's wife for a room. She said, 'I told you there were tigers barring the ridge-road!' Wu Song answered, 'I killed them all.'"

"Why is your version so different from the old story?"

Taking a deep breath, Xia Qifa glanced back at the young man and, not deigning to answer, continued, "The innkeeper's wife asks, 'How many tigers did you kill?' Wu Song answered, 'Three.' At these words, the woman burst into tears, for the tigers Wu Song had killed were her three sons in disguise. The other dead bodies at the base of the cliff were victims that the tiger-sons had assailed—seizing their money, property, and lives."

"So ever since then, people crossed the ridge freely, without meeting any harm . . . your version is unique," said the young man, exhaling from exertion as they neared the bottom. "When I get back, I'll tell the others!"

Beside a dense clump of brush they found tiger tracks. Finally they located a wounded tiger beside a huge boulder hidden in the copse. It was a massive male, weighing around four hundred pounds. Patches of coagulated and dried blood matted its white chest fur. It leaned peacefully against an outcropping of rock, sheltered from the wind. Its forepaws supported its upper body, as though it were resting.

Unnerved, the communications officer firmly grasped his pistol. Lying in hiding in the underbrush, the two watched the tiger for a long while. The creature remained motionless. Gently, Xia Qifa took two bundles of a wild herb used to cure gunshot wounds and a wild hare from his basket, both presented to him by local folks in the Huangshui market earlier that morning. He tossed the wild hare; it rolled to a stop right beside the tiger's forepaws. The tiger sat stock-still with its eyes open.

Uncertainly, Xia Qifa edged forward, lobbing the bundles of herbs in the direction of the tiger. Still, there was no response. Emboldened, the communications officer threw a stone at the tiger. Then he launched a second stone, and a third that caromed off the beast's shoulder. The tiger, however, remained seated in the same position, not budging an inch.

The young officer's wildly beating heart finally settled back in his chest. He finally understood: the tiger was dead. Knowing it was dying, the tiger had found a secluded niche and propped himself up, so that he might gaze straight into the forest, majestic and fiercely proud, like an indomitable warrior. The officer rose from their hiding place in the brush and asked cautiously, "Will other tigers come to bury it?"

"No," answered the shaman.

"Will panthers and wolves come to devour him?" asked the communicator.

"No, they fear him."

Curiosity piqued, the young man asked, "So will it stay sitting that way forever?"

Xia Qifa said, "When its skin and flesh rot, ants and other insects will descend upon the corpse and divvy up the remnants."

"Mayor Li told me that one of the tiger's chin whiskers let it see the invisible and show a man's true form. Good elder, will you find that vibrissa and give it to me?"

Xia Qifa responded, "Impossible. When a tiger dies, those whiskers fall to the ground and disappear into the earth."

"What a pity!" the young fellow sighed, disappointed. "Old man," he went on nervously, "let's hurry back. It'll be dark soon and it's dangerous out here at night."

As twilight darkened, they fashioned a torch, climbed back up to the road, and headed back to Huangshui. Darkness had long settled by the time they arrived at town headquarters.

Chapter Nineteen

I

Just before the New Year, the verdict from the provincial court was delivered to Huangshui: only the seven most egregious perpetrators—Tan Ruideng, the former militia commander; Xie Erjin, the Nationalist officer; and five other notorious bandit chiefs—were sentenced to death by firing squad. These seven were promptly led out and shot to death, collapsing like so many bamboo poles before a firing squad's hail of machine gun bullets. The amulet will only protect the virtuous: Xie Erjin, who thought he was deathless, fell like the others before the machinegun muzzles. Though Qin Lieniu was a company commander, he was spared after repenting of his crimes and swearing allegiance to the new government. Jiang Ermao, too, was spared.

However, just after the New Year, the telephone rang: a message came from the Public Security Bureau of Fengjie County informing the headquarters at Huangshui that Qin Lieniu had firmly maintained his counterrevolutionary stance and a refractory attitude during rehabilitation. As a result, he was executed.

Before long, the "Oppose America, Aid Korea" team came to Huangshui to draft young men into the army to fight abroad. Mawu, armed with a revolver, went from meeting to meeting. One day, as he emerged from the main entrance of the government offices, a figure howled, "Tiger!" launching a stone and rushing him. He ducked the stone, but found himself face to face with unkempt and irate Old Mother Qin. Cursing angrily, she pummeled her chest, then peeled off a shoe and stormed toward Mawu. The communications officer ran over and grabbed her, getting her under control. The gate sentries wanted to imprison her, but Mawu stopped them. Uneasily, he headed off to another meeting.

Despite the high-sounding propaganda and the festive beating of drums and banging of gongs, very few young men in Huangshui volunteered to enlist in the army. Of a parochial mindset, the local women, unwilling to see their mainstays for working the land depart for some faraway war, staunchly forbade their husbands to leave home. Even once a man was drafted and wearing a large red flower to mark his enrollment in the People's Liberation Army, the womenfolk would hand him a suckling infant and take off in protest. Mawu felt greatly pressed. At the very moment, however, Qin Longping, the Qins' youngest son, came forward to volunteer. Mawu asked in surprise, "Does your mother support your enrollment?"

Qin Longping said, "Yes. And I come to enlist accompanied by my mother." The little fellow staff-fighting with his older brothers on the flat rock in front of the Qin homestead so many years back had grown into a strapping man, though he was still fatter than a bulbous wax gourd.

Of the four Qin sons, only Longping remained alive. Thinking of all that had transpired, Old Mother Qin's willingness to let him enlist puzzled Mawu. He asked, "You're aware that your brother Lieniu was executed by the people's government?"

Longping said quietly, "My third brother stepped out of line. He got what he deserved."

Without another follow-up, and despite the negative evaluation of the family's political background, Mawu promptly helped Longping enroll; the corpulent fellow was welcomed into the People's Liberation Army, a red flower pinned to his chest. Because volunteers were hard to come by, the authorities lowered standards for draft enrollment.

Slogans were pasted along the streets of Huangshui reading, "Land to the tillers!" When villagers—clad in their old, tattered clothing—were organized to take part in parades, their faces beamed with joy.

When the authorities classified all of the local wealthy households, Tao Jiuxiang was labeled as a landlord. As a result, the stone tower and the family homestead were confiscated. The Poor Peasants' Association allocated her only three rooms at Gengguping, leaving three more for Mawu. Because of Masui's opium addiction, he had smoked away most of his property; as a result he was classified as a middle peasant. Learning of this decision, his wife was delighted. The Peasant Association allotted them three decent rooms and encouraged her to join their ranks. Zhou Taiwang, Sun Fu, Shi Eryang, and Wang Donghe drew lots for the remaining rooms on the Li estate. Though once a wealthy landowner himself, Shi Eryang's inveterate gambling and opium smoking had bankrupted the family. He had been forced to sell his house, and his wife had run off with a salt merchant. Subsequently, he had married Sun Fu's niece, Sun Xiaoxiao. Now, together with their two sons, they settled down in the Lis' former courtyard.

The Li family's former tenants occupied the goldthread fields. All of their confiscated property was piled in a huge heap in the yard—down to the smallest hairpin and bracelet. The entire house was emptied, as if plundered by brigands.

Sun Fu, his family, and the other families moving into the Li compound formed a queue stretching out the front gate. An official took their fingerprints and apportioned them a share of the confiscated goods. Though Sun Fu had never dreamed he would meet with such good fortune, he grumbled to his wife, "I've worked for the Lis as a hired hand for years. Why should the others, who have never worked this land at all, get the same share as me? The Poor Peasants' Group is unfair."

When they carried out the wooden cypress bed engraved with flower patterns, Tao Jiuxiang protested vigorously. Mawu was forced to hustle home and urge his mother to be an enlightened landlord and not conceal or cling to her possessions.

Tao Jiuxiang retorted angrily, "Mawu, you and the guerillas already stripped us bare of all our livestock and grain—so what are you playing at now?"

With the charred end of a half-burnt branch Mawu executed a series of hooks and curls, drawing a pair of huge characters on the stove: "*Geming* 革命: Revolution." Clapping his hands, he added, "That means wiping out the exploiting classes."

Seething with indignation, Tao Jiuxiang cried, "Your father bought that finely carved bed with the gold nuggets he discovered. He didn't exploit anyone!"

Mawu removed from his pocket a pamphlet titled "The State Council's decision concerning the classification of class statuses in the countryside," and left it with Masui, prodding him to read it with their mother. Then he hurried off to Peppercorn Bend.

"Go to hell!" cursed Tao Jiuxiang, furious. She felt that her eldest son had changed, turning into the same sort of crusty old pedant as the first man he had killed, the failed examination candidate Peng Yuju.

Masui sized up Mawu's handwriting on the stove, then picked up the branch and wrote several characters next to them. Gazing at the charcoal characters, Tao Jiuxiang asked Masui, "What did he write?"

"The characters for *revolution*. See how inferior his handwriting is to mine," Masui said scornfully.

II

Mawu went to Peppercorn Bend to attend a mass meeting in which the poor villagers told about their suffering and struggles in the old days, before Liberation. All the rich farmers were tied up and displayed on stage. Proactively professing his guilt, Jin Shaosan had voluntarily handed in a small parcel of silver dollars, explaining that he had been plundered by the bandits and was nearly bankrupt.

While Mawu was inclined to believe him, other members of the Poor Peasants' Group—figuring the Jins were hiding something—were not convinced in the least. "They don't shed tears till they see the coffin! They don't start retching till ya rub their noses in dogshit!" someone called out, egging on the masses. As their burgeoning indignation took on a life of its own, they burned a large bunch of incense, mixing in chili powder and cooking oil. They bound Jin Shaosan and his wife on a tall bench above the acrid smolder of burning incense, roasting and smoking the Jins until blood dripped from their mouths and noses.

Mawu suggested, "Isn't that enough for her? Let's spare the woman."

The head of the Poor Peasants' Group said, "Naw, the she-tiger is the more savage of the two."

Mawu said, "She's shackled. What harm can she do?"

With an air of irritation, the head of the Poor Peasants' Group shot back, "So, feeling sympathy for your mother-in-law?"

This retort silenced Mawu.

Unable to bear the excruciating torture of being roasted alive, Jin Shaosan hoarsely pleaded, "Enough . . . I . . . I confess." Broken, he told them where his silver was buried. Then and there, the members of the Poor Peasants' Group dug up several hundred shining silver dollars. Mawu was dumbstruck.

Emboldened, the peasants in the struggle session grew ever more daring. A woman suddenly jumped up on stage and—in a voice quavering with emotion—pointed a shaking accusatory finger at Mawu: "I want to bring to light the crimes of Li Mawu! He is a murderer and a plunderer of goods! He bullies and oppresses others in this town! He ordered people to tie up and beat my husband, Ran Hongyou. When they went to market, my husband was so afraid that he bent down and pretended to tie his shoes just so Mawu wouldn't come up behind him and kick him off a cliff. Speak up, Tiger Li, you striped monster! Isn't that the truth?"

Before the meeting, Ran Hongyou's wife had greeted him and said hello, but now she had leapt up on stage to accuse him. Disconcerted, his cheeks flushed crimson. Another former tenant strode onto the stage, yelling, "I accuse Li Mawu of unfairly coercing labor and imposing grain levies by force; of bribing government officials and of bullying and oppressing tenants. I also accuse him of murdering Peng Guang'ai and charge his family for causing the death of Zhou Damei. The Li family must answer for these heinous crimes." It was Jiang Shemi, the cousin of Jiang Ermao. Several other villagers clamored to voice further grievances. If not for the strenuous efforts of members of the Land Reform Work Team, Mawu, the Mayor of Huangshui, would have been dragged up on stage and subjected to further abuse.

Sensing the changing winds, Zhang Daxin arrived in Huangshui almost as soon as Battalion Commander Wei had departed. People thought that he had come to purchase goldthread and grain, but he was in Huangshui to return rent money to his former tenants and to divide his land among them. Within a single day, he had re-apportioned all of his fields, even the cherished alluvial fields in Peppercorn Bend, to his tenants. Wild with joy, they stripped off their clothes and stamped half-naked through their fields. One fellow, like an exultant and drunken earth god, grabbed a fistful of mud and smeared it on his limbs and cheeks.

One tenant dug up the goldthread rhizomes in his fields and sold them for thirty silver dollars. With this windfall, he built a new house and bought an ox. Still having half the prodigious sum left over, the fellow had no idea how to spend the remainder of his fortune. The man's wife wept with anxiety.

Before leaving Huangshui, Zhang Daxin divvied up all of his and Jin's property. The Huangshui government gave him a receipt of acknowledgment and a travel permit. At his departure, he told his gloomy parents-in-law that, as the new government had banned concubinage and polygamy, he had decided that he would live with Jin as his only wife, as she had birthed him a son. Jin Shaosan and his wife were greatly moved.

Before long, Mawu received a directive to arrest thirty-odd prisoners, including the former Huangshui district officials and corrupt gentry. Some were freed after a brief period of incarceration. The final fifteen, whose number included several captured Nationalist agents, were imprisoned in a granary to await inquisition. A fortnight later, the granary door opened; Mawu stood under the eaves and sternly commanded, "Out. All of you can go home."

In desultory fashion, the fifteen men rolled up their quilts and moved slowly out the gate. A group of six militiamen including Zeng Laomao and Zhao Changyou, both low-level military administrators in the new local government, followed them.

"Are you really going set us free?" asked a former Nationalist ward chief.

"We're lettin' you go home. Let's go!" Zeng Laomao cried, motioning at the man with the muzzle of his gun.

"Well . . . then just free us here?" another branded reactionary cautiously ventured.

Zhao Changyou said, "You'll be freed up ahead. All of you."

"I'm afraid we're going to see our ancestors!" Tang Zhengmo, a former district head accused of colluding with the bandits, muttered skeptically.

The others grew restless. "Either kill us or free us," grumbled a corrupt ward chief. "Just tell us the truth so we can pick a good place to die." An uneasy silence followed. Zeng Laomao and Zhao Changyou stared at him blankly.

After the released prisoners and guards had marched a short distance, Tang Zhengmo stopped and suddenly said, "Do as you like. We won't take another step."

"You're just going to kill us. We're not going any farther!"

"Here's just the spot," sighed a Nationalist spy, taking his bundle down from his shoulders and unrolling his quilt, spreading it on a sunny bank of stone. "The perfect place to die." A bloom of wildflowers and plush patches of grass grew amid the scattered deposits of rock. Beyond lay the primeval forest.

"Right . . . just the spot," another ward headman despaired.

"If you really aren't going walk any farther," responded Zhao Changyou in a huff, "we'll meet your demands."

Hemmed in on the slope, the prisoners milled about angrily. They caught his drift: the rocky slope was to be the site of their execution. "You brainless beasts—festering dregs in the hog trough!" said Zeng Laomao, "Chiang Kai-shek's millions of troops have all gone to the dogs, yet you still oppose the Communist Party. You must be looking to die!"

With one last glance at Zeng Laomao, the Nationalist spy called for the other prisoners to sit quietly on their quilt bundles and await the deadly gunfire. Years ago, he had enrolled in the Nationalist army with Xie Erjin. For years, he fought against the Communists and the Japanese, rising to become a company commander. The Nationalists sent him along with Xie Erjin to stir up resistance to the Communists, but in the end the People's Liberation Army soldiers had captured him.

Zeng Laomao and the others hastily opened fire, as though worried the collective silent prayers of these men in their last mortal moment might enable their aggrieved ghosts to lodge complaints and accusations before the White Tiger on high.

Contorting and twisting in a macabre dance beneath the shower of bullets, the fifteen prisoners tumbled backward. One man who remained erect, teetering in agony, called forth, "Give me another shot!" The tireless rapidfire strafing left the guns vibrating in the hands of the newly recruited militiamen. With sweat brooking down their foreheads, veterans Zeng Laomao and Zhao Changyou ran busily about to make sure that none of the prisoners was alive.

III

Soon after the mass execution, a lotus blossomed near Li Diezhu's tumulus.

In the triangular shanties, the stilt-columned multi-storied *diaojiao* houses, and the wooden-sheathed homesteads dotting the primeval forests around Huangshui, legends—often invented on evenings around the dusty firelight of the hearth—were plentiful as the forlorn howls of wolves. Though none could attest to their veracity, this lore lent a vivid air of mystery to the forests and vales.

One such story tells of Mother Tan, who married at eighteen and moved to Speargrass Plain before Liberation where she worked as a tenant farmer for the Lis with her family. Her husband had long since died, leaving her three stout children, strong as bull calves, and a ramshackle hovel, only twenty yards from Li Diezhu's tomb mound. When Li Diezhu was newly buried, Tao Jiuxiang frequently went there to mourn. Old Mother Tan would always accompany her, wailing in solidarity.

One summer night Old Mother Tan was shucking corn at home when she suddenly noticed a light outside her house. When she stepped outside, she saw a faint globe of shimmering light rising next to Li Diezhu's tomb, growing larger, sometimes separating and sometimes coalescing, sometimes remaining stationary and sometimes flitting about like a flock of golden chickens. Astonished, Old Mother Tan rubbed her eyes with her sleeves. Then, she rose and crept over, throwing her winnowing pan over the will o' the wisp. When she lifted it, however, nothing was there.

The following day, Mother Tan told her sons. The lads agreed that the golden lotus growing on the site where she had seen the will o' the wisp contained the numinous air of heaven and earth, the concentrated essence of the sun and moon. Everyone marveled that the Li family had chosen such an auspicious site. However, Mother Tan and her sons felt it peculiar that the lotus had blossomed beside the tumulus rather than on the mound.

Tao Jiuxiang felt the dragon chasers had bamboozled them! If the tomb mound were truly set above the dragon cave, the portentous golden lotus should have bloomed right on the tumulus! Now the prophecy, "Of ten sons, nine shall have rank and wealth beyond count," would never come true!

Probably the dragon chasers had deliberately chosen the wrong spot for Li Diezhu's grave! Some said that heaven would have smitten them dead or blind had they revealed the true spot. In a dither, Tao Jiuxiang wrung her hands and stamped, cursing endlessly, "Murderous heaven! Those accursed dragon chasers have brought ruin upon us!"

Not long thereafter, ill fortune befell Mawu.

As the years of Tao Jiuxiang's middle age waned and her senescence dawned, Mawu had won his widowed mother's full confidence. After her houses and property were confiscated, however, her temper grew ever more eccentric. She worked doggedly day and night on a ridge behind the house—incessantly cultivating, planting, and weeding her tiny half-acre plot to scratch out some crops to support herself. She stubbornly refused the help of Masui and He. One of her new housemates and neighbors, Wang Donghe, asked, "Your eldest son is Mayor. Why work so hard?"

Tao Jiuxiang scowled, "If I only eat what I grow, then I'm only exploiting myself!"

As Xia Yinmei grew heavy with child, she was too embarrassed to toddle back to Dragon Decapitating Gorge to visit her parents. The old *tima*, Xia Qifa, had been branded a "disguised landlord." All of the Xias' fields and property were confiscated, and half of his holdings had been divided among the poor mountainfolk. Naturally, the Xias were unhappy with Mawu.

Relentlessly busy with official duties, Mawu hired sedan chairs to carry his swollen-bellied wife and Yongyu back to Gengguping, asking his annoyed mother to take care of them. One afternoon, just days before Yinmei went into labor, Mawu suddenly returned. He was thinner, his face haggard and his hair longer. No guards attended him, nor was he armed with his pistol. With a melancholy look, he told Tao Jiuxiang that he had been stricken with arthritis, owing to his stay in the caves a few years back; herbal poultices from the pharmacy did not work. "I've asked for sick leave. In the future, I'm going to come back here and graze sheep at Gengguping." He added a couple of logs to the stove, and said quietly, "Mum, I'll turn the two sheep in your enclosure into a flock of one hundred."

Puffing on her pipe, Tao Jiuxiang shook her head. The Peasant Association had confiscated the long-handled, splendid pipe that Li Diezhu left her; Masui had fashioned a makeshift short pipe with a bowl. Gazing at her firstborn, she instructed, "Go to Dragon Decapitating Gorge and burn paper. Ask the old *tima* to cauterize you with iron!" The wildfire in Mawu's eyes had cooled. She wondered what had befallen him.

"Cauterizing with iron is related to a ceremony that calls on the spirits of heaven, earth and the underworld. It's too powerful," said Yinmei, her massive belly protruding. "The government now forbids the burning of paper. My father wouldn't dare. Don't we have a left over vat of father-in-law's snake-steeped goldthread liquor? That will help cure it." From watching her father treat others as a girl, she knew a little something of the treatment of arthritis.

Tao Jiuxiang let out a puff of blue smoke. Looking at her eldest son, she asked, "Have they agreed to let you step down as Mayor?"

Knitting his dense brows, Mawu put the head of his pipe to that of his mother's, drawing hard on the stem to light the tobacco. Grimly, he said, "The Poor Peasants' Group held a meeting and accused me of seizing crops by force. They've fanned the flames, and now all the former tenants and poor peasants are trying to take me down."

"Mayor Li!" a furious cry erupted from outside the gate, "Did you think that I wouldn't find you hiding out in your old nest? I demand that you explain why you had me thrown in prison for ten days!" In stormed Third Auntie Zhang, who, rather than being fastidiously dressed as usual, appeared unkempt and ragged, her hair uncombed, her face dirt-stained. She went straight for the water jar, held it up and gulped down several huge mouthfuls.

"What's wrong?" asked Tao Jiuxiang in amazement.

"They say I married a landlord's daughter to a poor peasant's son. Look! Look!" wailed Third Auntie Zhang, wiping her tear-scarred cheeks then rolling up her sleeves to show them rope impressions on her frail arms. She then hiked up her smock, revealing dark welts on her back.

"You need to be more politically aware!" said Mawu.

Utterly baffled, aggrieved Third Auntie protested, "I didn't marry any peasant's daughter to a landlord's son. Don't I know the families around here?"

"In the future, don't worry yourself about making matches for young folk," advised Mawu. "They can figure out how to keep the family line going on their own."

"So I'm just sticking my nose in other people's business?" Third Auntie smacked her thigh emphatically. Bitterly, she proclaimed, "I don't care if bachelors and young maids sing mating songs and copulate like a bunch of rutting beasts: henceforth I swear that I'll never bother with making matches again!"

"I'm tired," said Mawu. He turned and strode out, tension and restraint etched on his troubled brow.

IV

On the eastern slope behind the house, the trunks of luxuriant walnut trees stretched skyward, their dense canopies of branches spreading out like a pair of huge umbrellas. Each day the rising sun first peeked out from behind the trees, before shedding its full light on Gengguping. And each year the surrounding pear and peach trees bore several baskets of sweet and sour fruits. In the breeze, undulating waves of green-white speargrass surged and ebbed invitingly, awakening in Masui a pleasant boyish wonderment, a desire to roll wildly to and fro in the embrace of the tall grass.

Masui trudged back from the slope, shouldering a heavy manure bucket. "Let me get that," said Mawu. Masui headed back into the house and gulped down a bowl of sweet wine, hoping its flavor would mute the stink of the manure as he loaded it into the bucket. He looked on wide-eyed as Mawu donned a woven straw poncho and carried a bucket of manure to Tao Jiuxiang's fields. With a long-handled wooden ladle, he drizzled the night soil onto the growing plants. Halfway through the bucket, however, shooting pain from his arthritic knees forced Mawu to rise. He dropped the ladle, struck a match, and lit a hand-rolled cigarette, greedily inhaling and exhaling. He lay down in the tall speargrass to rest, thinking about what to name his future child. Caught up in his reverie, Mawu nearly forgot to finish fertilizing the field.

Now that four households of poor peasants had moved into the Li homestead, there were too many people to use the well. Therefore, at Mawu's suggestion, the two brothers dug a second well behind the house. Digging with spades, sending up sprays of earth behind them, the two worked relentlessly, breathing heavily and dripping with sweat. After half a day's labor, though, fighting through the rocky, hard mountain earth, the hole was only a bit deeper than a washbasin. But the two kept on, and after three days of work, muddy water seeped into the bottom of the well. Overnight the water became clean and clear. Mawu had just enjoyed the first refreshing sip from a gourd ladle when several armed militiamen arrived. In front of Tao Jiuxiang, they politely yet insistently told Mawu that he needed to come back with them to township headquarters for a "bandit extermination" meeting.

"Come home right after the meeting," Yinmei plead anxiously, the quilt rising like a hillock over her pregnant belly. She would give birth any day now.

The militiamen stayed the night at Gengguping, then, under the wary and distressed gaze of Tao Jiuxiang, departed with Mawu the following morning.

Though the morning sun had not emerged from behind the clouds, a dark crimson light showed in the eastern sky. Wind swept through the mountains, and ground fog swirled, roaming under the feet of the men. Together with the hunting dog Black Leopard, Yongyu followed, running and jumping along the footpath.

"You'd better head home, Yongyu," said Mawu. His daughter was riding a *beijue* branch hobbyhorse; he was certain Tao Jiuxiang had given it to her.

"In a few minutes," said Yongyu cheerfully.

"I'm afraid you'll meet a tiger," said Mawu.

"The tiger's asleep. Besides, Grandma told me tigers are afraid of this." She brandished the branch mischievously. Then she stopped, and said, "Okay, Pa, I'll go back."

Mawu looked at his daughter standing under a blooming azalea, small and lovely. Silently, he turned and marched forward. After a stint he glanced back saw that Yongyu was still trailing him. Seeing that she had been caught again, she giggled, "Papa, I'm really heading back this time."

"Go on back. Just wait—Mum's going to birth a little brother for you," said Mawu, winking at his daughter.

The surrounding primeval forest covering the mountains watched them, silent. Oh ancient ridges, how many eons have you gazed up at the stars? O golden sun on high, how have you borne the weight of countless dawns? O familiar moon, how much hardship and joy, how much dearth and bounty, have you witnessed? And now, before this timeless earth and sky, a new life would be born into the Li family. Though my life has been a bitter struggle, Mawu mulled, haunted by misgivings, how different the world that my child will be born into than the world into which I was born! As he moved toward Huangshui, he knit his thick brows, gravely staring forward.

That night, Yinmei gave birth to a baby boy without any complications. They named him Yonggang, a name they had chosen beforehand.

The shadowy mountains, ancient forests, and starry sky were tranquil. On a refreshing zephyr floated a scent redolent of the distant past. Tao Jiuxiang nimbly stitched the baby's umbilical cord with white thread, which locals took as a symbol of tiger's hair. Though she wished the blessings of the spirits and ancestors upon her new grandson, ominous forebodings clouded Tao Jiuxiang's heart. Ignoring Yonggang's lusty wails, Masui's wife He tucked a bitter spoonful of goldthread extract into the baby's mouth. As she wiped down the infant's body, Tao Jiuxiang whispered tenderly, "May the bitterness now prevent you from enduring future hardship, sweet child." She mixed the remaining goldthread extract with Yinmei's milk, and touched it to the corners of her eyes, saying, "If you dab a mixture of breast milk and rhizome extract on the corners of your eyes, you won't tear up in the wind—it works wonderfully." After tidying up, she picked up and dandled Yonggang, gently caressing her grandson's red, tender head, carefully scrutinizing the tiny wailing creature's every movement. Recollecting Mawu's birth so many years back, she recalled holding him in this same manner. The expressions and cries of father and son were so similar that for an instant she didn't know whether she was holding Mawu or Yonggang.

For the first two days of his life, Yonggang bawled incessantly. Perhaps he cried for his father's absence. No one knew for sure. Masui headed to Huangshui to make inquiries, and was horrified to learn that at the meeting Mawu had been stripped of his position as Mayor; afterward, he had been taken into custody and imprisoned for crimes against the people. His replacement was Vice Mayor Ma, who wore a military uniform and spoke a northern dialect.

Tao Jiuxiang instructed the other family members to lie to Yinmei, telling her simply that Mawu had to deal with an urgent matter. Less than surprised, she figured that her eldest son—whose callousness had left a number of minor functionaries and ward chiefs dead, creating countless enemies—had probably been trapped in a plot by the county authorities.

The afternoon sun drifted above the mountains, like a boy herding a flock of goats. Mountainfolk started working at dawn and didn't rest until dusk. At noon, they burned a brush pile on the margin of their fields and roasted freshly dug potatoes in the dirt and ash beneath the flames. After a short while, a sweet aroma rose from the fire. As folk gathered round the fire, cupping roasted potatoes in their hands and eating them, they saw Li Mawu, their former militia Captain and Mayor of Huangshui, escorted away by his own men. They were surprised . . . but not all that surprised.

After all, from the start, Mawu's tortuous life had never followed an ordinary track.

Chapter Twenty

I

Around the time when Yonggang turned a month old, Yinmei finally got wind of the truth. Walking back to the house from the newly dug well, she dripped some water from a cupped hand into her infant's mouth. Inside, she took the dried fragments of snake—removed earlier from the lees of the goldthread liquor in the earthernware urn—then ground the pieces into powder and mixed them with food. Completing this task, she traced the character for king (王) on her infant son's tender forehead, and placed a rooster at the bottom of her bamboo back-basket, along with some clothes and food. In doing so, she let her baby symbolically "ride" on the back of a "divine phoenix," protected from evil spirits or demons as she embarked on her trip to government headquarters in Huangshui.

Zhao Changyou and Zeng Laomao, former military adjutants of Huangshui, had been transferred to a goldthread plantation. The new military secretary was a nephew of Zhu Shun, the master builder. Secretary Zhu told Yinmei that Mawu had been arrested and several days earlier had been escorted to the county seat. Zhu assured her that Mawu would not be permitted to meet with family or relatives.

Yinmei slung the back-basket over her shoulders, fastened Yonggang to her chest with a swaddling cloth, unfastened the bridle tether, and mounted her horse.

Secretary Zhu reassured her, "Don't worry, Ma'am. The county government's already sent notice that he's not to be bound, hanged, beaten, or shot."

Without the slightest acknowledgment, Yinmei rode toward the county city.

A strong wind soughed through the mountains, prompting branches to snap and the trunks of ancient trees to groan. Darkening clouds gathered. In a cliff cave, a tigress quietly tended her pair of cubs.

After another half-day's trial, Mawu was led back to the jail and placed in a detention cell. His eyes were weary, his limbs exhausted. The two wardens tucked into their lunch, but Mawu had not eaten for three days and three nights; he'd only had a few cups of water. An ethereal, melancholy voice drifted into his mind, leaving Mawu to wonder if he were so overwrought by hunger that he could no longer tell illusion from reality:

O my darling, let me see you off to Five-mile Slope.
O cruel heaven, Duke of Thunder, will you thwart my hope?
O cruel heaven, Duke of Thunder, raining down your ire,
You shan't keep me from my darling, from the one that I desire.

Yinmei's haunting chant sounded like a banshee's wail, its inimitable timbre as ancient as the sibilant winds snaking through the gullies and crags. Battened to his mother's chest, Yonggang wakened with a lusty cry. The combined force of his son's resonant wail and Yinmei's witchsong jarred the cobwebs of despondency from Mawu; he gasped, then burst into tears.

"Quit singing!" thundered a warden rudely. "What is that infernal racket? Do you know where you are? Keep quiet!" The eerie, mysterious tune floated somewhere between the festal red of a wedding and the mourning white of a funeral.

Mouth agape, dumbfounded Mawu remained silent for a moment, before suddenly snaking his hand out between bars toward the guard's rifle.

"What you wanna take my gun for?" exclaimed the man, shunting his arm aside.

Mawu said, "To shoot somebody!"

The guard cursed, "Who? Tiger, mind your manners! You keep stirring up trouble and we'll starve you for another couple days!" So saying, he walked away.

Like a crestfallen beggar, Mawu bit his lip and humbly said, "I'm sorry." He gripped the bars of his cell window and asked, "Could you please deliver this to the woman outside?"

The guard turned round. Mawu had a black handkerchief in hand, the sort the mountainfolk often used. Hesitantly, the warden took the kerchief, striding off toward the main entrance of the government headquarters. Outside it was overcast and sultry, on the verge of rain. The warden stood in the doorway, barring Yinmei's entry. "Thank you, Elder Brother," she said, accepting the kerchief. She handed him a parcel, adding, "Please give this to Mawu."

Distant thunder rumbled. A furious pother kicked up, wind wildly gusted and whistled, shaking doors and rattling windows, snapping branches and blowing down small trees. The guard glowered, snapping, "Now go away. I'm eating lunch. It was your damn chanting that brought on the thunder!"

"Hurry up and go home!" The other warden appeared, adding, "Storm's coming!" He pawed thorough Yinmei's parcel, and found it contained only clothing and food. Exchanging several murmured words with his colleague, the two headed back into the compound. Yinmei's gaze, dark as the brooding sky, followed them until they disappeared around a corner.

"You still want to shoot somebody?" asked the guard, a fellow brusque in temper but kind in heart. He tossed the parcel into the cell. "Here's some food. Won't do to have you starve to death on our watch."

Opening the parcel, Mawu stuffed a potato cake into his mouth.

The heavy noontime sky was murky like dusk. Claps of thunder exploded. Large drops of rain fell, first slowly, then all at once in a downpour that swept over the earth. Though Yinmei sheltered under the eaves of a shop, cocooning Yonggang with her body, she was caught in the wind and rain and soaked to the marrow.

"What are you doing there huddled with a little baby in the midst of a storm like this? Where are you from?" asked the shopkeeper, seeing Yinmei removing her back-basket and starting to nurse Yonggang as he peeked out to close a window.

"We're from Huangshui," Yinmei looked up and answered dispiritedly. "Uncle, I've brought a rooster. Can I kill it and use your pot to make soup? You can have half." Bedraggled, looking as though her soul had lost its mooring, Yinmei's drenched hair was pasted to her forehead.

"Okay," agreed the man. "I heard you chanting that forlorn song. Do you have a family member in jail? Huangshui is so far away; you can't go home tonight. You can stay in the shop next door—it's mine."

When Yonggang fell asleep, Yinmei bundled him in a homespun swaddling cloth and tied him on her back. She pulled the rooster from the lower section of her basket and carried it into the shopowner's kitchen.

At dusk the thunderstorm stopped and the sky brightened.

Carrying a big tureen of chicken soup, Yinmei anxiously returned to the main entrance of the county headquarters. The offices were closed for the day and the main gate was locked. However, an old man was on duty in a small gatehouse. "Dear Old Uncle," Yinmei beseeched, "Could you open the gate and let me in?"

"It's past hours—offices are closed. What's your business?" asked the old man.

"I want to deliver food to someone inside."

"Who?"

"Li Mawu ... he's in jail."

"It's past hours. I'm just a gatekeeper. I can't let you in."

Disappointed, she entreated, "Please, Old Uncle, do me a favor and deliver this soup?"

The old man passed the soup to one of the prison guards working the evening shift. The guard, in turn, carried the tureen to the cell window, calling, "Li Mawu!"

Smelling the fragrance wafting up from the rich, golden broth as the jailer handed him the chicken soup, tormenting thoughts of the hardship facing his wife and tiny son wracked Mawu.

II

Eyes downcast, a haggard and sullen Yinmei returned from Fengjie City several days later in witheringly low spirits. She carried with her grim tidings from the trial: accused of ambiguous political standing and having a "chequered history," Mawu was going to be transferred to the Wanxian gulag, sentenced to five years of rehabilitation through labor.

Mawu seemed fated to a turbulent succession of dizzying ascents to the heights of steep precipices, followed by breathless plunges to the bottoms of dark abysses. It seemed as though the Lis were in the toils of some inauspicious portent. Hunchbacked and bent, Tao Jiuxiang grew ever more eccentric. Each morning found her hobbling to and fro outside the courtyard gate, mumbling as she picked her way along with her cane. She loosed a guttural roar toward anyone who looked askance at her, alarming and puzzling gawkers, and occasionally prompting them to spit out "wicked old bitch of a landlady" as they retreated.

Yinmei cried day and night, endless tears that dried up her breast milk. She fed Yonggang goat milk instead, and though the swaddling infant furrowed his brow he did not refuse it. What a splendid baby boy! And so life went on. Some days later, Old Mother Jin timidly ventured to Gengguping. As she started to wander up the slope, she saw from afar a disheveled old woman standing alone, furiously jerking a staff aloft to the heavens, then violently planting it in the ground. Approaching, Old Mother Jin found that it was Tao Jiuxiang. Old Mother Jin gasped in astonishment, crying out, "What on earth are you doing?"

"I've seen the Eight Kings," Tao Jiuxiang leered at Old Mother Jin. "They say the wicked have wronged Mawu, but not to worry: they will right the injustice."

Weary from her journey, Old Mother Jin halted, her chest rising and falling.

"The Eight Kings" were chieftains of the Tribe of the Tiger, transcendent masters of martial arts; their images were rendered vividly on the eight feathered crests of a *tima*'s headdress. From birth, they were suckled on tiger's milk. They grew up strapping men, titans capable of eating more than a peck of rice at a sitting. In the Tang dynasty, Emperor Minghuang, the Illustrious August Xuanzong, distressed by repeated uprisings along the western frontier, sent out the Eight Kings, each at the head of twelve thousand men, to lead a punitive campaign to suppress the rebels. After a series of battles, they returned victorious. Minghuang, fearing that the Eight Kings would usurp his throne and seize the mountains and rivers of the Great Tang as their own, poisoned the lot of them with wine at a celebratory banquet. But when the Eight Kings were encoffined, their corpses rose up silently one after another, and, standing firm, knit their tiger-brows and stared balefully, eyes protruding and expressions obdurate, at the assembled court. A furious peal of thunder sounded and plunged the imperial palace into darkness. Horrified, Minghuang crawled under his throne in Golden Terrace Basilica and hid, swearing a quailing oath, "If only the lot of you will keep quiet, I'll invest you as the Kings of Eight Regions, and you shall preside over the territories around

Shamanmount. Commemorative temples and shrines will be built in your name; we will forever offer sacrifices and burn incense in your honor." Hearing these words, the corpses of the Eight Kings finally slumped back into their coffins. True to his word, Minghuang held a grand funeral and pronounced that henceforth annually incense would be burned and sacrificial offerings made on the third, fourth, and fifth days of the new lunar year to pay homage to the Kings of the Eight Regions. The mountainfolk held these apotheosized heroes in the highest reverence, so much that whenever they felt wronged or suffered a grievance they appealed to Eight Kings for help.

Old Mother Jin sighed, "Oh, my old sister-in-law, even the highest mountain can't block out the sun; and even the heaviest ox can't crush a louse. Just burn more incense for Mawu!"

Tao Jiuxiang made no reply. Rather, she thrust her walking stick into the earth once more. Seeing Old Mother Jin entering the courtyard, Yongyu took a break from shucking corn beside the stove and dashed out, shyly calling, "Grandma!"

"Good girl," said Old Mother Jin, fishing out an egg-sized incense pouch from inside her shawl and hanging it around her granddaughter's neck. She knew that Yongyu now had a little brother. She thought bitterly of the bleak future that awaited motherless and fatherless Yongyu, of the hardships she would endure. At the thought, she sat down on a bench beside Tao Jiuxiang and whispered, "Yongyu's mother sent me a letter. She wants Yongyu to go to school in Chongqing."

Tao Jiuxiang glanced up in alarm, "Does she know about Mawu?"

"Aji wrote Jin to tell her," answered Old Mother Jin. "Zhang Daxin is so wealthy and kind; he gave this to me last time he visited." She rummaged through her pockets again before locating a small photograph of a beautiful lady holding a little girl. The lady's long, wavy hair flowed down her back; the little girl was dressed in a skirt. "This is ...," wondered Tao Jiuxiang doubtfully, gazing at the picture.

"It's Yongyu's mother, and that's Baoyu. She's five now." Old Mother Jin's face crimsoned slightly, as she added, "Her letter says that little girls in the city go to school at seven or eight. Because they're more worldly and educated, they aren't as naïve us country girls here. Let Yongyu go to Chongqing for schooling. If she stays here in Huangshui, she'll just get hauled off and manhandled by these savages."

Knowing the truth in Old Mother Jin's painful words, Tao Jiuxiang felt a keen pang of pity for Yongyu. Her granddaughter was twelve; when she wasn't stricken by misery or sadness, her large, limpid eyes made her as beautiful as her mother. But fate has not been kind so far. Who knew what bleak future awaited her in Huangshui?

Absently, Yinmei stirred soup on the stove. Though she had never seen her husband's first wife, she had heard of Jin's beauty. She couldn't help casting a sorrowful glance at the picture. The elegant, modern lady in the picture bore no resemblance to the rustic, sun-browned women in these mountains. Unconsciously, her mouth gaped and her eyes danced, betraying a complicated tumult of feelings.

"We're no longer as well off as we used to be," said Old Mother Jin, holding Yongyu affectionately. "Elder sister, if Yongyu goes to live with her mother, it will free you of a burden."

Tao Jiuxiang knit her brows and remained stubbornly silent.

"Mum," said Yinmei sadly, "though we need a helping hand here and Yongyu cooks and looks after her little brother, it would better for her to go to Chongqing."

Nudged by the winds, a cloudhead surged over the mountains. "Yongyu," asked Tao Jiuxiang, taking her granddaughter in her arms, "Do you want to stay in Huangshui or go to Chongqing?"

Yongyu grinned, "Grandma, I want to go to a modern school and wear fashionable clothes. I'll come home to visit during vacation." The photo of her mother with the pretty little girl in the pert dress had aroused in her envy and curiosity.

Tao Jiuxiang mulled that over the years she had been second to none at Gengguping; Jin alone had gained the upper hand. That woman, like a scintillating sun, possessed a glamorous sway that made every man weak in the knees. Couldn't Yongyu, if she were educated and literate, become even more powerful? Exhaling a mouthful of tobacco smoke, she asked Old Mother Jin, "How is she going to get there? Will her mother come pick her up here?"

"She can come with me," said Old Mother Jin through the fragrant tobacco smoke. "Aji will escort her to Chongqing."

"Fine," said Tao Jiuxiang, "Her mother can bring her up and marry her off to a good husband in the future."

Yongyu leaned against Old Mother Jin. The latter put an arm around her, sighing, "Our house has been confiscated by the Peasant Association. They're using it as a warehouse. We three are crowded into one wing. Ever since the men in the Peasant Association roughed up my old husband and dug up our silver, he's taken to bed more dead than alive. He doesn't eat or drink. This morning he said he wanted some morphine. I hear that the Cuis are secretly selling it. But a parcel costs five bushels of rice. I turned our stores upside-down but we've only got three. Can I borrow a couple bushels from you to send that unfortunate soul off to the next world in peace?"

The rice harvest was coming. There would be a good yield from Tao Jiuxiang's plot. For the sake of their former relationship, Tao Jiuxiang gave her two bushels of last year's rice.

Yongyu made three kowtows to Tao Jiuxiang before departing Gengguping with a grateful Old Mother Jin.

III

Waiting until midnight, Tao Jiuxiang stealthily burnt incense, praying to the Eight Tiger Kings. In the inky darkness, the three sticks of incense smouldered faintly, like ghost fire. Believing the ethereal souls of those immortals dwelled in the contortions of the dancing incense, Tao Jiuxiang flung herself on the ground, prostrating herself and repeatedly knocking her forehead against the floor, kowtowing, so that her brow was stained with dust. In the predawn she lay wide-awake, wondering how her daughter-in-law Yinmei and grandson Yonggang would get on with Mawu gone.

The rain began early in the morning. A dreary veil, a gloomy chill, settled over the mountain forest: above the sky was overcast and below a cloak of mist covered everything. An involuntary shudder shook Tao Jiuxiang. To better care for tiny Yonggang, who was still suckling at the breast, she humbled herself and invited Yinmei to come live at Gengguping. "Yinmei," said she. "Come live with me. I'll try my best to help you and your son live better."

Deeply moved, tears brooking down her cheeks, Yinmei sighed, "Thank you, Ma, for taking care of us. After all, we, mother and son, are like spiders without a web, scattered leaves separated from the branch."

The ears of corn had begun to swell on their stalks and the field needed weeding. At dawn, Tao Jiuxiang and Yinmei rose to eat breakfast. Before the stars set, they emerged from the gate: Tao Jiuxiang carried the bamboo tube filled with water and a basket of food; Yinmei trailing behind her, Yonggang slung on her back. Arriving at the fields, they hung the food and the baby's back-basket from a tree limb, and, leaning the bamboo tube against a rock, bent down to weed. Only at noon, when she heard Yonggang wailing, did Yinmei take a break. Heading into the shade of the tree, she wiped the sweat from her brow and started to nurse Yonggang. Tao Jiuxiang took some food from the basket and the bamboo water-tube to her daughter-in-law, who had finished nursing. Sated, little Yonggang drifted off to sleep, one of his mother's nipples still cupped in his mouth. The cool, comfortable breeze lulled drowsy Yinmei and Tao Jiuxiang into a nap against the tree trunk. Awakened by the twittering of sparrows and cawing of crows, they hung Yonggang up in the tree again, and went on working in the afternoon sunshine.

When they finished weeding the field, Tao Jiuxiang felt slack with exhaustion. Unexpectedly, she saw that Yinmei seemed unfazed. Beneath her daughter-in-law's delicate exterior, she discovered, there was an obdurate strength and will. Yinmei was as hardy and resilient as the speargrass on the slope. Within six months, Yinmei became the main laborer in the family. Even the stubborn ox obeyed her. Black Leopard and the other dogs helped her graze the sheep. Watching her on the slopes, neighbors murmured in amazement, "Aiyo! Check out that tireless ghost woman!"

In the blink of an eye, Yonggang turned two years old. One day, Yinmei returned shouldering a bundle of kindling. Tao Jiuxiang helped her unload and stack the kindling. Then, she broached the bad news: "Haven't you heard about your parents? They confiscated the old *tima*'s ritual instruments."

Yinmei gaped in horror.

Unless she first burned incense and ritual paper, Yinmei was not allowed to touch the instruments her father Xia Qifa used to expel demons. Passed down through six generations of *tima*s, her father's ritual sword, a powerful ghost-dispelling blade, possessed tremendous power. There were also several grotesque masks. The shaman would don them, chanting and sprinkling the blood of a rooster, to drive away ants and other insects. With a particularly keen pang, she felt the loss of the waist-sash embroidered with the names of generations of *tima*, her first piece of weaving created at the age ten under her mother's direction. Although the handiwork was rough and childish, her father said that such embroidery must be done by a girl younger than twelve. That year, her grandfather formally passed on the shamanic arts to her father, and Xia Qifa had become a true disciple. Later, Old Li Erniang's granddaughter embroidered one for her brother, Liangxian. When a *tima* plied these instruments, the blessings or misfortunes of family and community hung in the balance.

Urgently, Yinmei asked, "Where did you hear that, Mum?"

"It being bandied from yard to yard," answered Tao Jiuxiang, offering Yinmei a bowl of potatoes and rice. Worriedly, she went on, "I wonder what's become of all the ghosts and demons the old *tima*'s captured? I hope he's okay."

Yinmei hurried back to Dragon Decapitating Gorge with Yonggang on her back. She spent the night at a huntsman's house in Lajia Gully and arrived at her parents' homestead the following noon.

During land reform, three families had moved in with the Xias. Arriving to find the courtyard empty, Yinmei entered the house and set down her basket. Seeing her parents and elder brother glumly gathered around at the cookstove, Yinmei instructed her son, "Say hello to your grandpa!"

Clambering out of the back-basket, Yonggang hailed, "Hi, grandpa!"

Xia Qifa gave his grandson a bearhug. "Ho," he cried, affectionately tousling Yonggang's hair. "What a fine young fellow!"

"What's brought you over here?" Old Mother Xia asked. Rising from a straw mat, she passed Yonggang a potato cake, asking, "So, do you piss your bed at night?"

"He doesn't pee in bed anymore," answered Yinmei. "Mum, is everything all right?"

"They took the sword," sighed Old Mother Xia. Glancing at Xia Qifa, she continued, "Now, we're worried about the embroidered tablets and the masks."

Yinmei felt her entire being go slack. How many demons, evil spirits, and monsters had quailed before that blade? All but the boldest fled in alarm at the mere sight of the sword; the most ferocious devils would obediently squat in a corner of the house, not daring to move without the shaman's permission. Now that the sword had been confiscated, who knew when or if it would be returned?

IV

Xia Qifa looked haggard and old. His long hair, flecked with white, flowed past his bare shoulders. His unclothed chest was crimson in the firelight.

Deeply saddened at the sight of her careworn father, Yinmei asked, "Dad, where are your spirit generals and troops? Were they confiscated, too?"

She remembered how her grandfather, on his deathbed, had bequeathed a spirit army of ten thousand soldiers to her father. These righteous and dutiful warriors were kept in a sealed earthenware urn, summoned forth with mudras and incantations on rare occasions to expel ghosts and demons haunting and possessing the sick, so that their corporeal and ethereal souls might be recalled to their bodies; as soon as the spirit warriors fulfilled their mission, they returned to the urn. According to the shamanic code, this nether army would be passed on to Liangxian, her brother. Then there was the sheep leather pouch containing all the ghosts and demons her father had captured over half a lifetime. Some looked like stones, others like a spider, and still others resembled a tree root. Before his death, the old Tima would hold a ceremony to release the sprits.

"These creatures," said Old Mother Xia, "will make trouble if they are loosed haphazardly. But so far no one's taken the pouch or the crock."

Yinmei breathed a sigh of relief.

"Nobody's asked for them yet," Xia Liangxian chimed in. "The People's Army have searched us a couple of times. They demanded the masks—said that next time if we don't cooperate and hand them over they'd burn hot chilis to torture us."

"That kind of torture is unbearable. The acrid smoke makes you bleed from every orifice," Old Mother Xia shook her head fretfully.

"Things will be all right with Mawu. By the time this little critter clambers around for a few more years, he'll be home. But your brother . . . he's rather troublesome." Xia Qifa spoke, holding Yonggang in his arms.

Yinmei knew that her father was still anxious about her brother's prospects for marriage. She murmured, "Dad, too many girls are smitten with him and he's too proud." Handsome young Xia Liangxian was an eloquent speaker and good singer. Every time he headed out to aid the mountainfolk and help his father avert a catastrophe, some lovely young woman would cast amorous eyes in his direction. Though he faced more temptations than other men, all of his many love affairs proved fruitless. His first torrid love affair with Wang Yu'e, the daughter of a village headman, ended when she was expeditiously married off to the son of a district head to whom Yu'e had been engaged before either of them were born. His second love affair was with Old Li Erniang's granddaughter, a good-natured young girl who hoped to starch his clothing and wash his robes forever after as his wife. But Liangxian's ardor cooled, and he merely treated her as a sister rather than a lover. The third time, he became enraptured with Miss Tian, the alluring concubine of deceased military commander Huang Tianliang. But facing his father's strident opposition, he had ended that amorous escapade. The fourth time, he fell in love with a girl named Ma Si. But just after the matchmaker formalized the engagement by exchanging horoscopes, Liangxian met lovely Tian Xiaoxiao and staunchly refused to honor his betrothal. Xia Qifa, who had long endured his profligate son's proclivity to flit from flower to flower, had to deliver a load of gifts to the Ma family in compensation. Initially, Xia Qifa sought to quash his wayward son's ardor after the youth threw himself headlong into a fifth love affair with Tian Xiaoxiao, the sister of Captain Huang's concubine, fearing that such a union was taboo. But in the end, as Liangxian was beyond twenty—a little old for taking a wife—the *tima* reluctantly offered his approval. After all, the pair seemed to be a good match. However, on the eve of the marriage, the Tians had a sudden change of heart. They returned the betrothal gifts and within three days married Tian Xiaoxiao to a man from Fengjie City. Perhaps, they speculated, the Tian sisters were exacting revenge on Liangxian. No one knew. Now well into his twenties, Xia Liangxian remained a bachelor.

Xia Qifa grumbled, "I didn't mind so much when he was younger, but this is growing irksome." He did not understand why his son—in most cases such a good, obedient young man—was so intransigent when it came to dealing with women.

Now that the Xias faced hardship, Yinmei sensed her father's growing vexation. Consolingly, she offered, "Dad, with so many men and women in the world, there's bound to be a good girl who will end up my sister-in-law."

A bitter grin flitting across his elegant features, Xia Liangxian sat aside, bitterly remarking, "How could it be that no one wants to marry me? Let's drop it." Then, suddenly stricken by an inspiration, he promptly switched topics, "The matter of the masks is urgent. How about moving them away . . . why not hide them at Gengguping?"

Old Mother Xia added, "That's a good idea. We should have thought of it earlier." Yinmei was taken aback. In her present situation, under her mother-in-law's roof, how could she take such a risk? And yet, how could she refuse her family, her flesh-and-blood? Lost in this quandary, she studied the fire.

With one sweep of his striking eyes, quick-grasping Xia Liangxian read his sister's thoughts. "They won't look for the masks at Gengguping. Don't hide them in the house; just bury them in a secure place nearby and mark the spot. We can dig them up in a few years."

"Right, right," Old Mother Xia agreed.

Her eyes reddening, Yinmei pleaded, "Ma, let me think on it."

Looking at his daughter with mingled guilt and resignation, Xia Qifa declared, "Carry the Celestial Sovereign White Emperor and the woven genealogical tablet back to Gengguping and bury them safely. We'll keep the other instruments here."

Xia Liangxian fetched a basket from the inner chambers. When he returned, Xia Qifa reached in and fished out an age-old crudely carved mask. Running his fingers gently over its surface, he held it in front of him so that he and the White Emperor were face-to-face, eye-to-eye. It seemed as though the two held a brief, soundless conversation. The White Emperor's eyes were open wide, his pitted cheeks bumpy, his coarse aspect fierce, imposing, and proud. A human warmth seemed to emanate from his wild visage.

Long ago the son of shamaness Mengyi, the Lord of the Granary, transformed into a white tiger and led his fellow tribesmen to a series of victories in battle. Though his martial prowess contributed greatly to solidifying the dynasty on the central plains of China, his resounding successes alarmed the court. The emperor welcomed him to court with a festal banquet, then poisoned him with wine. Before the throne in the Hall of the Golden Bells, the ferocious white tiger, writhing in rage and agony, stretched out his fearsome claws, eyes bulging and terrible brow furrowed, reducing the Emperor to a tremulous mass. Only when the Emperor designated the tiger "Celestial Sovereign, White Emperor" and formally set up shrines and regular sacrifices did the tiger nod his maw and depart, soaring into the firmament. A tribal deity invested by the earthly emperor himself, the mountainfolk esteemed the White Emperor above all other divinities. His splendid temples put the shrines erected for other local deities to shame. For two centuries, the mask of the White Emperor had been passed from generation to generation of Xias and used in ceremonial dances. The mask was stored in a sandalwood box with other ritual masks. When a person invited the shaman to perform a ceremony involving the White Emperor, the night before the scheduled rite sounds of knocking and shuffling could be heard from within the box. When Xia Qifa opened the box in the morning, the White Emperor's mask invariably had found its way to the top.

Xia Liangxian bundled the tablets and the mask together in a sheet of plastic and hid them at the bottom of Yinmei's basket. They placed Yonggang on top to make sure he could fit in comfortably. Old Mother Xia prepared corn porridge and sour stewed mustard greens for her daughter and grandson. Early next morning, accompanied by Xia Liangxian, Yinmei departed, carrying Yonggang and the White Emperor on her lithe, sinewy shoulders.

Xia Qifa fastened his long gown and strode up to his mountain field, a hoe on his shoulders. As Yinmei and Liangxian walked along the mountainslope path, the wandering strains of his song embraced them from behind:

> *Shouldering a well-woven basket,*
> *A handsome young boy riding in it;*
> *The girl has become a mother,*
> *Her face radiant like no other.*
> *The boy's face scrubbed white and clean,*
> *'Little rooster' peeks out the slit in his pants to be seen,*
> *All fleshy bumps and lumps and folds;*
> *O what a fine sight to behold!*

When Yinmei looked back she saw no one, but recognized the familiar chanting of her beloved father.

Chapter Twenty-One

I

Encumbered with the ritual instruments and her father's weighty expectations, Yinmei returned to Gengguping with a heavy heart. Entering the gateway, she felt something was amiss: instead of greeting her as usual, the pair of hunting dogs barked and growled nervously.

"What is it, Black Leopard? Fiercy?" Tao Jiuxiang glanced up at Yinmei, asking, "Did anything happen along the way?"

Yinmei dared not keep her mother-in-law in the dark. Promptly, she set down the basket and told her mother-in-law the secret it contained. Without even daring to eat or drink, she waited until dusk, then snuck out and buried the White Emperor and the tablet on the margin of their cornfield.

The pair of hunting dogs entered the house ahead of her, wagging their tails.

When Longping, the youngest son of the Qins, came back from the "War of Resistance against America and Support for Korea," he was appointed leader of the production team. Longping frequently held struggle sessions, mass gatherings attacking the Xia family for their feudal customs and backward superstitions. Therefore, from the moment they buried the White Emperor, the two strong-willed women, Tao Jiuxiang and Yinmei, were on tenterhooks. They became tractable and lamb-like, ready to obey anybody. Yinmei in particular would never protest her innocence, no matter how vicious the invective rained and accusations hurled became.

"So, the two tigresses have learned to submit," production team leader Qin Longping crowed after one gathering.

The following spring saw the establishment of the people's communes. Except for a tiny parcel of land left to each household, all private fields became communal property. Recalling the legend of the lotus that had bloomed next to Li Diezhu's tomb, Old Mother Qin told her son, production team leader Longping, to allocate that choice parcel to her grandson Qin Ji'an, the son of Qin Liexiong and his first wife, Zhou. Receiving authorization, a delighted Old Mother Qin commanded her sons and nephews to build a wooden cabin for Ji'an and his new wife on the site where Old Mother Tan had seen the lotus bloom. When the house was completed, Old Mother Qin wanted to invite Xia Liangxian secretly to perform a geomantic rite, to confirm it had been erected on an auspicious site and to dispel baleful influences. Initially, Qin Longping did not agree. But Old Mother Qin rounded on him angrily, "This is a matter involving the future of our entire family . . . not just you. The hell with your disapproval! Ask Xia Liangxian to come for the ritual ceremony at night. As long as we keep our mouths shut, not another soul will know."

After Longping reluctantly acceded to her wishes, Old Mother Xia stealthily headed to Dragon Decapitating Gorge with paper and incense. However, no matter how urgently or sincerely she pressed him, Xia Liangxian staunchly refused. He recalled all too well that during the "reduction of rent and interest" movement and "anti-bandit, anti-landlord" campaigns, the Peasant Association had stripped the Xias of their property. And now Qin Longping had launched his campaign against the "feudal" and "backward" Xias! He loathed the cadres from the commune and the production team. Besides, if the militia caught him performing the rite, he would be severely punished!

Old Mother Qin then sent Longping to persuade Xia Liangxian. Unable to deny his strident mother's request, the production team leader reluctantly went to the Xias in person to seek the help of a man he utterly despised. With forced cheer, he smilingly sought to persuade Xia Liangxian, "Just do it this once. Nobody will find out. Even if they do, just say I asked you to do it. I'll take care of the militiamen!"

Initially, ill-disposed toward the government and Qin Longping, and anxious about the consequences, Xia Liangxian had been deadset in his refusal. However, the visage of the White Emperor floated into his mind; in the end, worried about the instruments buried at Gengguping, he grudgingly agreed. Picking a lucky day, he left Dragon Decapitating Gorge and headed to Speargrass Plain.

Marking early spring, clusters of pink flowers dotted the fields like jewels. To the morning twittering and "whoo-hoo" of cuckoos, a train of mountainfolk moved out to begin work in the fields. Without asking others for help, Tao Jiuxiang and Yinmei borrowed Zhou Taiwang's ox to plow the cornfield where the White Emperor's mask was buried. Yinmei led the ox ahead, while Tao Jiuxiang, having passed more than half a century of winters and springs, walked behind, spreading the corn seeds. She held a basket in her right hand and a wickerwork winnowing pan in her left which she moved side to side, seeding the earth. Her hands moved in harmonious rhythm, as though she were performing a simple, timeless dance.

The ox trudged forward pulling the plow. Suddenly, however, as they approached the edge of the field, the beast stopped and refused to budge an inch, no matter how vigorously Yinmei whipped it. Breathless with alarm, Yinmei realized that the mask and tablet were right below them. Straining with all her might and beginning to panic, she vainly tried to lead the ox away. The stubborn ox bent its neck, tossed its huge head to one side, and drove a large, curved horn into the earth; when the contrary creature raised its head, a muddy plastic bundle dangled from its horn. At that very moment, Shi Eryang—now a member of the People's Army—appeared, a .38 bolt-action rifle jauntily perched on one shoulder. Alertly, he saw the unusual bundle and guessed it was some sort of hidden property. Hustling over into the field, he snatched the bundle and thundered, "Ghost-spawn wenches!"

Eagerly, Eryang tore open the bundle. When he discovered its contents he exclaimed in shock, "What the . . . ? You two ghost-spawn wenches play at being obedient, but you're more audacious than men!" Eryang dashed up the ridge, calling cheerfully to Zhou Taiwang, who, hearing the uproar, had wandered over, "Call production team leader Longping."

"No, Eryang, no!" entreated Tao Jiuxiang, stumbling as she rushed forward, and falling headlong into the newly plowed and planted field.

"Mum!" called out Yinmei sharply, hurrying to help Tao Jiuxiang up.

With a quick glance at the bundle, Zhou Taiwang figured out at once what had transpired. In tandem, he and Eryang bellowed: "Production team leader! Production team leader!"

Again and again, their shouts echoed off the mountains and resonated in the valleys. After a while, the stentorian voice of Qin Longping bellowed from afar: "What's the matter? . . . What's the matter? . . . What's the matter?"

For the folks of Gengguping, it was an unforgettable afternoon. The mask of the White Emperor and the tablet woven with the names and zodiacs of thirty-eight Xia master *timas*, beginning when the first *tima* established his altar centuries ago and culminating with Xia Qifa and Xia Liangxian, were unceremoniously burned into ashes by Shi Eryang. Bearing witness, Zhou Taiwang stood at his side, watching a strand of blue smoke wind its way skyward toward the setting sun. Dizzy and sick at heart, Yinmei fainted and slumped to the ground.

Old Mother Qin scolded Longping for his role in the incident. However, he argued, "The two militiamen who found those things were right there. What could I do but burn them into ashes. Besides, Li Mawu killed my brothers Liexiong and Lieniu. The mere sight of those two ghost-spawn witches makes me sick with rage."

At these words, Old Mother Qin fell silent.

Xia Liangxian had set out at dawn on the previous day. He passed the night in a deserted hunting shanty. The following day he arrived at Gengguping. Walking quickly in long strides, he listened to the twittering and trilling of hundreds of birds in the trees. Curious, he slowed his pace. Sadly, unlike his father, he could not understand the language of birds. It was still well before sunset on the spring afternoon, so he decided to visit his sister and ask where the mask was buried.

The trees were budding and the wildflowers were in first bloom. Suddenly, he saw a dried corpse of a lizard thrust on the spiky branch of a horse mulberry. He spat, giving the shrub a wide berth. He knew this was the wicked mischief of an ill-omened shrike, a "butcher bird." These birds impaled insects, frogs, and lizards on thorns or branches, then forgot to eat them. The budding shrub decorated with the corpses of small creatures prompted a shudder of revulsion; feeling a premonition of evil, Liangxian grew wary. With his heartbeat quickening, he approached the old Li homestead, a compound that now housed three or four families. He saw Masui clamber out of the pigsty after hunkering down for a shit.

"Why are you here?" Masui asked, hiking up and fastening his pants.

Xia Liangxian said, "I've come to see my nephew. Where is he?"

Masui spared a hand to point to the room, a queer expression creasing his face.

II

In the course of his brief conversation with sister Yinmei, Xia Liangxian's countenance underwent a dramatic change. His blade-straight brows drooped; his neck contracted. Expressionless as a zombie, he trudged slowly toward Inkblack Creek. As he reached the plains of Lihaku, he saw a shadowy figure on the path. Old Mother Qin was waiting for him.

"I came to meet you. I was afraid you'd get lost," greeted Old Mother Qin, relaxing as the young shaman came into sight. "The house is right down below ... when you hear running water, we'll be there."

On the moonless night, it was too dark to see the surroundings clearly. Xia Liangxian, jaw set and brows knitted, followed Old Mother Qin up and down several ridges before hearing the sound of flowing water.

"Here we are. Go on in and have a rest," welcomed Old Mother Qin.

The house had only been finished a few days earlier, and the fresh scent of wood and mud-plaster pervaded both inside and out. Qin Ji'an and his newlywed wife emerged to greet Liangxian. Ji'an was as tall and strapping as his father, Qin Liexiong, was short and lame. Production team leader Longping was nowhere to be seen.

Shyly, Qin Ji'an said, "Uncle Xia, please have a bowl of fried egg porridge. Dinner will be ready any minute now."

Xia Liangxian remained silent, a granite expression frozen on his handsome visage. Old Mother Qin felt vaguely unsettled, but took comfort in the thought that there was no way the young *tima* could have found out so quickly what had happened that afternoon. "Thank you for all your trouble," she smiled. "Look, your knees are mud-stained. We've prepared the incense, candles, and paper."

Ji'an took out a wicker basket half-filled with yellowish rice straw paper, saying, "Look, Uncle Xia, is this enough?"

Xia Liangxian seemed to hear nothing. He pushed his bowl aside and sat in front of an oil lamp, his face contorted as though he had been stricken with a severe disease. Lowering his head, he took out his curved scimitar and hammer and, one after another, cut the sheets of paper, currency in the netherworld of spirits and ghosts.

The rite to bless the newly built house began at midnight and ended shortly before dawn.

A faint light filtered through the windows as Liangxian finished. Graciously, Qin Ji'an offered, "Uncle Xia, please have a bite to eat before you leave?"

Xia Liangxian collected his utensils, unbolted the door, and strode out in silence. In the pre-dawn, he looked out over the embankment. Old Mother Qin and Qin Ji'an accompanied him as he circled the house. Rounding the corner, the young *tima* stopped, startled: immediately rising from the back wall was a large, long moss-covered tumulus. A small doorway on the rear wall led to a low, log kitchen shed with a slanted roof that was built into the side of the mound, right next to the tomb's stele. No wonder he had sensed a ghastly presence! He realized this must be Li Diezhu's tomb. He had been here on the burial day. Years had elapsed, and in the past night's darkness he failed to recognize it. Stock still, he surveyed the terrain.

"Uncle Xia, what are you looking at?" Qin Ji'an asked. "The place where we set the foundation was flat, but cramped. There was no way around it—we had to build right next to the tomb."

Xia Liangxian said nothing. He caught a hold of Ji'an's pantleg, then, wiping the mud and dew off his hands, departed, winding his way along the path behind the grave. Old Mother Qin and Ji'an watched the retreating figure recede, feeling their flesh crawl.

As he supped on his evening meal, Qin Ji'an felt like something was wrong with his legs. His wife Zhang, a fair-complexioned woman from Peartree Moor, was a good cook. She poured her new husband a half-bowl of corn liquor and served him stewed greens with tofu and a plate of fried slices of cured ham. In a good humor, Qin Ji'an ate his fill, preparing to retire for the night and go to bed with his wife. When he tried to rise, however, he found himself paralyzed. His buttocks were fixed to the bench; his legs had taken root.

Zhang was alarmed. She figured her husband was overwrought. Each day he had labored from dawn to dusk with his kinfolk building the new house, and every night he intertwined with her for a couple of bouts of lovemaking. The previous night, he hadn't slept at all because of the geomantic rite; and he had worked all day on the house and in the fields. She figured he was simply exhausted. She wrapped a quilt around her husband, hoping that he could rest right there on the bench. Far into the night, however, Qin Ji'an could not budge. Zhang could do nothing but solicitously cover him with a second quilt. Anxiously, she said, "Just try to get a little sleep. I'll send for a doctor at daybreak."

"I need to piss," said Qin Ji'an. With a great exertion, he twisted to one side, trying to lift himself off the bench, but his thighs and buttocks seemed heavy as a hillock and he could not move an inch.

Zhang brought a chamber pot. She tried to help her husband unfasten his pants, but as Qin Ji'an couldn't raise his buttocks, she couldn't remove his longjohns.

"I've pissed my pants," groaned a disheartened Qin Ji'an.

III

Zhang weathered an agonizingly fretful night. At daybreak, without combing her hair or washing her face, she ran to Old Mother Qin for help.

Qin Ji'an, who had sat upright at the stove all night, was snoring loudly with his head drooped on his chest. Old Mother Qin bustled over and shook her grandson awake. "Try standing up," she ordered.

Drowsily, Qin Ji'an strained to raise his legs and move his buttocks, then resignedly exhaled, "I can't."

Pacing the room, Old Mother Qin extended a hand to lean on one of the uprights in the new house. She exclaimed, "Why is this post soaking wet?"

Zhang came forward, saying in amazement, "Where is the water coming from?"

Droplets of water oozed from the upright. A rivulet flowed down to the floor, forming a tiny pool.

Wide-eyed with consternation, Zhang cried, "There's no seam, no crevice—where's it coming from?"

Nervously, Old Mother Qin mused, "Probably the young *tima* got wind that the mask of the White Emperor was burned."

Zhang said, "I'll run for a doctor."

Old Mother Qin said hopelessly, "There's no point. That underhanded Liangxian has him under an evil spell. Bull-headed, intractable Longping brought on this disaster. He's brought harm down on my grandson!"

"Grandma, my feet . . . they're paralyzed," Qin Ji'an moaned.

Old Mother Qin tearfully ordered, "Get Longping. He's the one who caused this!"

As Zhang dashed off, a terrified Qin Ji'an asked, "Grandma, will I be paralyzed for the rest of my life?"

Guiltily, Old Mother Qin said, "I'll cook you a meal. Then we'll ask the old *tima* to help."

Longping entered the house, stamping and roaring, "Goddamn it! That wretched cur has the audacity to play these tricks! I'll send soldiers to deal with him!"

Like the droplets of water trickling down the wooden upright, tears rolled down Old Mother Qin's cheeks. She sighed, "You don't know their terrible power. Merely spraying a mouthful of water, they can banish a malevolent ghost to the corner of the house. Do you think they fear the likes of you?"

Longping asked, "Then tell me, Ma, what should we do?"

Old Mother Qin ran her index finger along the rivulet of water flowing down the post, saying, "A wise man will not fight when the odds are stacked against him. I'm going to Dragon Decapitating Gorge to humbly seek their help."

Longping blurted, "Let me take care of it."

Old Mother Qin barked in retort, "You! You want to go! You—who are dumb enough to burn their sacred instruments passed down from their ancestors to cinders—want to go ask for their help? You want to die? I'm going." Feeling she'd spoken a bit too caustically, the old woman bit her tongue.

Old Mother Qin doted on her strapping young grandson. Eager to help him out of the trouble, she wolfed down a meal before scurrying off toward Dragon Decapitating Gorge, toting a packet of tea and straw-paper sheets. As she started rather late, she arrived at Lajia Gully at sunset. Not daring to walk farther, she spent the night at an acquaintance's home. At daybreak, she rose and pressed on.

Father and son were weeding in the Xia plot. Xia Liangxian caught sight of Old Mother Qin first. Desiring to avoid the old woman, he said to his father, "I'm going into the woods to get kindling."

Huffing and puffing, Old Mother Qin clambered up the slope. Before she spoke, the old *tima* looked at her and said, "I knew you would come."

"How?"

"The birds . . . they told me," answered Xia Qifa in a melancholy tone.

"You understand the birds?" Old Mother Qin blinked in disbelief.

"Once I saw two snakes twined in a mating dance on a road and separated them by flogging them with a branch. That same night, a woman visited me in a dream, asking why I'd beaten her husband. I said, 'Your husband was entangled in an adulterous union with another; I took it upon myself to break up their intercourse. Instead of being angry, you should thank me.' Placated, the woman answered, 'I can see you speak the truth. I really should thank you.' Then, she blew a mouthful of air into my right ear. When I awakened the following morning, I understood every chirp and twitter, every caw and call, of the birds."

Old Mother Qin's hair stood on end. Wracked by a shudder, sweat brooking down her forehead, she pleaded, "Old *tima*, my grandson is paralyzed. Water is flowing down the pillars of his new house. Please save him."

Xia Qifa returned home, his hoe balanced on his shoulder. The shaman was in his sixties. His salt-and-pepper hair hung below his shoulders. Sitting at the stove, he puffed restlessly at his yard-long tobacco pipe. Though tea and rice-straw paper were two of his favorite things, he did not accept Old Mother Qin's proffered gifts.

Wracked by guilt that Longping had wronged the *tima* and deeply worried about her grandson, Old Mother Qin wept, a pained singsong chant welling up from deep within: "Do be generous of spirit, oh *tima*, show mercy . . . Woo . . . my son Longping did what one in his office had to do . . . Ai! But Shi Eryang and Zhou Taiwang, those two grandsons of cuckolded turtles, too bold! The pair of them glaring at him like jackals, like hounds . . . he did the only thing he could do as production team leader."

"Go home. Your problem is solved," Xia Qifa answered. His careworn eyes flashed from within the dense haze of tobacco smoke, at once world-weary and opaque.

Filled with doubt and on the verge of tears, Old Mother Qin scuttled back to Speargrass Plain. When she returned, Zhang called out excitedly, "Grandma!

Ji'an can walk again! He's out behind the house washing—he beshat himself." So the old shaman was true to his word. Her grandson could walk. Water no longer streamed down the pillar. Seeing the evil spell was broken, a greatly relieved Old Mother Qin, her back soaked from the arduous journey, collapsed on the stove-bed.

Xia Liangxian did not return home until sunset. When he entered the gate on cats' paws, he saw his father sitting at the stove. The old man's face was crimson; the room was permeated with sweet reek of tobacco smoke and the pungent tang of liquor. The *tima* never drank or smoked—to chant with spirits and gods, one's mind had to be lucid and one's throat pure. Heart sinking with fear, Liangxian started to skulk away.

"Stop," Xia Qifa commanded. Though his voice was not loud, it made Liangxian tremble inwardly. "Why did you cast the body-fixing spell and throw the five elements off kilter so that water dripped from wood in the Qins' new house?"

"I loathe them . . ." Xia Liangxian dared not lift his head. The ceremonial sash adorned with the genealogy of thirty-eight generations of Xia shamans and the mask of the White Emperor had been burned. The entire line of ancestors had been shamed, utterly humiliated! And what was a shaman to do without the ceremonial sash that validated his status as a *tima* and his position within the longer lineage?

"Henceforth, you shall eat from this ricebowl no longer: You're a *tima* no more," Xia Qifa pronounced, his grim voice echoing. Drawing again and again on the tobacco pipe, he felt as though he was in the grasp of a powerful inauspicious force, a force that left the old *tima* lonely and bereft of hope.

Xia Liangxian understood that his father had dismissed him. After all, the codes and principles of the *timas* that his father had solemnly passed on to him were crystal clear. He had violated a basic tenet—but the old *tima* knew why he'd done it. Opening his almond-shaped eyes wide, the aggrieved young man protested piteously, "Father, I know I've done wrong. I can change!" His legs went slack as though unable to bear the weight of his torso. He staggered.

"One of our forefathers violated the shamanic code. Infatuated with a beauty, he cast a spell so that she stripped off all her clothes before him. In the end, the woman, humiliated, pitched herself off a cliff. Soon, he too met a bad end." Xia Qifa cast a vexed glare at his son.

Tears glistening, Liangxian wailed, "I'll change. Never again..."

A deep sigh erupted from Xia Qifa's chest. With an expression of cumbersome sadness, he said, "No, you'll make trouble..."

So it was that Xia Qifa, the thirty-seventh *tima* in the Xia lineage, a man many revered as a living god, sat awake for the duration of this singular night and made a most painful decision. One by one, sinking ever deeper in a consuming malaise, he recalled the codes of the ancestors. Finally, shortly before sunrise, unable to listen to his aggrieved son's pleadings and protests any longer, he banished Xia Liangxian, the thirty-eighth, once and for all. The line of succession was severed forever.

Chapter Twenty-Two

I

Fish and shrimp darted about the waterweeds and reeds, the pools and eddies, the niches and grottos of Inkblack Creek. Production team leader Qin Longping, who had lived along the creek since birth, had eaten his share of fish and shrimp over the years. Since the communal kitchen and canteen were set up at Lihaku, the mountainfolk, afraid of arriving late for lunch and dinner, arrayed makeshift A-frame teepees around the canteen, and vied like wolves to claim their three meals a day. As the simple fare of porridge had failed to win over the people, Longping reluctantly incorporated the tasty fish and shrimp from the nearby creek into the cafeteria's repertoire.

The stringent opium prohibition had forced Masui to overcome his addiction. As a result, in good health and high spirits, a black cotton shirt cinched round his waist, a hoe resting on his shoulder and a basket mounted on his back, he led the three women of the family—mother Tao Jiuxiang, wife He, and sister-in-law Xia Yinmei—out to break sod for new fields. At dinnertime they went to the cafeteria together, joining the queue to await their meal. Like suckling pigs, the trio of little children—Yongzhi, Yongguang, and Yonggang—swarmed around them, pushing and nuzzling, running back and forth in anticipation of the meal. Scrawny Yongzhi, Masui's firstborn, at six, shoved aside his little brother Yongguang and cousin Yonggang, three and two respectively, to get the fullest bowl.

By the time they had finished the tasty fish and shrimp, it was completely dark. Men and women, old and young, rose to head home. Qin Longping approached Yinmei and said, "Today, you sang very well. Tonight, the team is going to Arrow Bamboo Gulch to net shrimp. If you help out, tomorrow you'll get half-a-day's rest from labor."

Yinmei agreed and sent Yonggang back with Tao Jiuxiang.

After the mask was burned, goldthread, once so rampant in the mountains around Huangshui, grew more and more scarce. It was forbidden to grow goldthread privately. The local government ordered every household to open up new fields to grow more rice. Instead of ordering Yinmei to labor with the masses, production team leader Longping had given her a gong and a striking hammer, assigning her to compose and sing planting and weeding songs to boost morale and productivity.

When Yinmei expressed initial reluctance, Longping snorted, "We both know who you are, mask-hider."

"Just sing as you're told," timid He urged.

Knowing she could not refuse, Yinmei stood on a ridge for several moments gathering herself, before beginning to strike the gong in a regular cadence: "*Dang! Dang! Dang! Dang! Dang! Dang!*" Then she began to sing:

> *Heavy fog settles on the dawning morn,*
> *Covering houses of men and fields of corn.*
> *A red cloudhead rising in the east,*
> *Purple clouds gather in the west.*
> *On high, clouds of gathering purple and surging red,*
> *Descend to leave a proud red banner waving in their stead.*

In the beginning her voice had been low and uncertain. However, as she found her rhythm and cadence, her voice grew louder, stronger, and more melodic. Her hands swung, keeping time, moving in synchronicity with her powerful chant.

"*Dang! Dang! Dang! Dang! Dang!*" chimed the gong. On Yinmei chanted:

> *Red flag planted on the field's marge,*
> *My voice is pure, my song echoes afar.*
> *If you want cured ham, better raise your hogs right;*
> *If you want a full ricebowl, better plant day and night.*

Careful! Don't let the blue sodworms devour the leaves,
And don't let yellow ones gnaw sprouts and seeds;
Don't let the old crows peck away at your yields,
And don't let the wild hogs root up your fields!

Production team leader Longping was dumbfounded. No doubt, the woman was a gifted singer. "Keep singing," he ordered, seeing that Yinmei had stopped and was standing dazedly on the embankment overlooking the field. "Keep singing!"

Yinmei took a drink from her bamboo water tube, then continued singing and striking the gong until sunset. Listening to the young woman clad in a blue coat, a white handkerchief wrapped round her head, the laborers spirits were buoyed. One stout fellow guffawed, "She sings as well as the old *tima!*"

"Keep working hard, and just as sure as this thing hanging 'tween my legs is long an' strong we'll be designated a model vanguard production team," a satisfied Longping exulted, grasping his crotch.

After dinner, only Yinmei, Longping, and four cooks remained in the canteen. When the cooks left to wash dishes and cooking utensils, Longping grabbed a machete and said to Yinmei, "Let's cut some bamboo poles for the shrimp trenches."

Yinmei nodded, her throat hoarse after a full day of singing.

The gibbous moon hung in the sky, but the bamboo grove was dim. Even at high noon, one passing through the mottled bamboos would shudder in fear.

The ears of corn stand erect like an ox's horn,
The tufted stalks of rice stick up straight like the blade of a knife,

Brash Longping sang this ribald song as he cut down a pair of bamboo poles. Hearing Yinmei pass close by, without lifting his head he snaked a strong arm out and caught the silver-tongued woman by the waist. Dropping his machete, he reached out with his other hand, roughly shucking off her pants and throwing her to the ground. Merrily moving to straddle her, he finished the lyrics of his ditty:

The leaves of the green beans are large as tureens,
And the shafts of sorghum could hold a huge drum.

Shocked by the sudden attack, Yinmei let out a sharp yelp, but clasped in Longping's strong embrace and pinned, her struggles were vain. Only her head could move. She lay on her back, feeling the damp, cold fallen leaves of the mottled bamboos beneath her. She wanted to call for help, but the thought of the humiliation and shame this would bring down upon her stifled the cry in her throat. On the verge of slipping into complete resignation, she heard Longping shout: "Hey, don't throw shit at me!"

Yinmei, too, sensed that something was being cast down from above.

"Who has the balls to pelt me with sand?" Longping called out, momentarily distracted from his ravaging.

Yinmei struggled to move her limbs, but was unable to. Calming herself in the brief respite, she cried hoarsely, "It's that thing, the creature!"

"Whatever you are, I've done nothing to offend you, so you'd better not mess with me," Longping growled skeptically, holding her fast. Steeling himself, he loosened his belt and shed his pants, revealing his large navel, which stared Yinmei eye-to-eye like a firing button; and then out of his shed trousers sprang his ramrod-hard, trembling cock.

A handful of icy cold droplets pelted Longping's neck, prompting him to look off into the darkness. Yinmei, too, felt the icy shower. Relaxing her breathing, she rasped, "Hand me my pants . . . that creature's afraid of them."

Longping was terrified, fearing the haunting of some evil spirit. He had heard many queer legends, and knew that ghosts and forest sprites feared unclean, polluted things like womens' undergarments. As he passed Yinmei her pants, the hidden creature rained down another icy spray of needles.

Yinmei put her pants on her head. Discombobulated, Longping muttered a steady bluestreak of curses, rising and staggering back as he pulled up his own pants from around his ankles.

Seeing this, Yinmei quickly pulled on her pants.

Longping cursed, "Cunning witch woman—you tricked me!" Just as he spoke, though, a sudden pitchy blackness fell over the bamboo forest. His flesh crawling with "chicken-skin bumps," Longping was nearly scared to death. An incantation for exorcising demons that his mother had learned from Daoist Master Wang and taught him as a child came to mind:

> *Oh red, red sun, arising in the east;*
> *Three times I call: dispel ghost, devil, beast.*

No, that wasn't quite right . . . he stumbled over the words. Then, stricken by an inspiration, Longping sang aloud:

The east is red, and the sun rises high,
Mao Zedong ascends into China's sky.
He strives for the people's happiness, hu-er-hey!
A savior shooting star, he lights the night like day!

As he sang these lyrics over and over, the bamboo grove gradually brightened. Looking back, he saw Yinmei ten or fifteen feet away, silently glaring.

The kitchen staff at the canteen had just finished the endless buckets, pans, bowls, and chopsticks, when they saw Yinmei trailing Longping coming from afar, bamboo poles on their shoulders. They walked in the moonlight, casting long shadows on the ground that trailed them like a pair of spectral haunts. Even queerer was the tremulous way they carried the poles: No doubt they had met some sort of wicked forest spirit!

"Get machetes," barked Longping. "Hurry up! Cut these bamboos into strips and weave shrimp traps!"

His order banished the speculations of the kitchen staff, and immediately the three men and three women set to work weaving shrimp traps. It was not until after midnight that the six headed to Inkblack Creek, encumbered with a hundred-odd quickly woven bamboo traps.

They bound cypress branches inside bundles of rivergrass and placed them in the shrimp traps. Attracted by the fragrant cypress and the dark leaves of the rivergrass, shrimp would swarm, thick and fast, seeking food. The next morning they could pull the traps and, if they were lucky, gather two or three buckets full of shrimp.

After setting the traps in the creek, Yinmei and the cooks returned with Longping to the Qin homestead and slept on the *kang* stove-bed. With a savage yawn, Longping stormed off and huffily flung himself down in bed with his wife.

At dawn, after a few short hours of rest, they would return to pull the traps.

II

Despite the bumper harvest that fall the leaders of the commune still complained, claiming crop production per acre was too low. After turning the problem over in his mind, production team leader Qin Longping resolved the problem by adding a pair of zeroes to the original figure, thereby not only satisfying but far exceeding the quota. He ordered the workers in the Inkblack Creek production team to carry all the harvested grain to Peppercorn Bend, where it was stored in the barn of the Jin family's former courtyard, now re-purposed as the granary of the production brigade. Because not a single grain was left at Inkblack Creek, the cafeteria ceased operation. Mandatory labor was shortened to four hours a day. People moved out of the teepees surrounding the canteen and headed home, foraging for food to subsist. Several men banded together to hunt wild hogs. Zhou Taiwang was a superb hunter. At night, he could tell the species of animal from the light glinting off his quarry's eyes. Shimmering eyelight meant a deer; intermittent eyelight close to the earth told of the presence of wild hare; and there could be no mistaking the steady, unblinking gaze of the tiger. No matter how confused and messy the sets of claw or hoofprints, he could gauge at a glance the movements of wild hogs, knowing how long it had been since they passed through, and the number of boars, sows, and piglets. He planned a hunt with Shi Eryang, bringing a couple of good mountain dogs. Their strategy was to drive the hogs toward a narrow defile where Masui and Sun Fu waited with rifles.

At one juncture, a sizable wild boar plunged into the undergrowth, then not a sound was heard for a long spell. The hunting dogs circled the copse, barking fiercely. Finally, Zhou Taiwang fired into the dense brush. With an ear-splitting squeal, the boar erupted from the creepers, gashing open Zhou Taiwang's buttock with a tusk, then madly dashing toward the forest. Nipping at its flanks, the hounds followed in close pursuit. Moving from their station, Masui and Sun Fu intercepted the boar and, firing their rifles in unison, dropped it on the very margin of the forest.

Zhou Taiwang's injuries were severe: even after seeing a local doctor and using plasters, the two-inch gash on his buttock and puncture wound from the bite took a month to heal. In the end, the costs of treatment and lost labor far outweighed his share of the meat. For a long while Zhou retreated at the mere sight of a wild hog. It simply wasn't worth it, he mused. Then, he changed tactics: instead of hunting with dogs and a rifle, he began using steel-jaw traps, setting them under leaves and dirt along the forest paths that hogs wandered. Trapper Zhou Taiwang worked alone.

All the mountainfolk struggled to survive. In his spare time, Masui walked the woods, a hunting rifle on his back, hunger making him bolder by the day. One afternoon, he came across a slack-bellied black bear standing like a man on its hindquarters and reaching with its forepaws to get at the honeycomb inside a huge papery wasps' nest on a low-hanging branch of a pine tree. When the bear scored the gray nest with his claws, the frenzied wasps counterattacked. Roaring in pain, the bear flailed at the wasps with its left paw; with its right, it scratched at the painful welts rising on its tender nose and face. Then, in a fit of rage, the bear violently pushed the large, half-rotted pine tree to the ground. Pouncing on the nest, the starving creature scooped gob upon gob of honey into its swollen maw. Slavering at the thought of delicious honey, Masui was seized by a fit of greed and fired at the bear. But just as he shot, the bear flung itself on the ground to avoid the relentless wasps, rolling this way and that in an utter frenzy. As the rifle's report echoed off the mountains, the black bear clambered to its feet, and, rearing up, clapsed Masui in a tight embrace; the creature cuffed him, first on one cheek and then on the other. As Masui staggered back in a daze, the bear caught him with a ferocious backhand, sending him sprawling onto a mossy boulder. Petrified, Masui didn't move a muscle, pretending to be dead. After snorting and snuffling, the bear ambled off. Then, as the battered and bruised Masui rose, the agitated mass of crazed wasps swarmed him, relentlessly stinging left and right. In misery, Masui threw himself back down on the boulder, his cheeks puffed up larger than buttocks. By the time several members of the production team arrived, alerted by the rifle shot, they found Masui lying still, his face buried deep in the moss. When he painfully raised his head, he looked like a grotesque clown with a lumpy face and mossy beard. And yet the moss, which drew out poison from the wasp stings, had saved his life.

Though Masui recovered, he bore four or five scars that forever reminded him of that unfortunate outing. Still, as soon as he could walk again he haunted the primeval forest and mountain groves, hunting for his starving family. Alas, with so many folks desperate for food, creatures grew scarcer by the month, so that even wandering for half a night he rarely saw so much as a shadow of a wild chicken or hare, let alone bigger game.

One early summer night, Masui meandered through the woods, torch in hand. Weary and frustrated, he stopped to rest. All of a sudden, he heard a distant, stifled sound of a gunshot hitting home. Not wanting to go home empty-handed again, he ran toward the sound like the wind.

"Peng!" resounded a second shot. This time there could be no doubt. Masui recognized the muffled thunk of a bullet hitting a massive animal . . . probably a wild hog. Who could be lucky enough to track down a huge creature these days? Puzzled, he crashed breathlessly along, scrambling up ridges and scarps, hopping over rocks and ditches. Finally, cresting a rise he beheld a horrible sight in front of a tree: under the brambles lay a great golden-orange tiger striped with black, its still body aglow in the moonlight. Clad in ox-leather from head to toe, a man hid behind a boulder, clutching a homemade rifle in one hand and a rock in the other. One after another, he fired stones at the tiger. Hearing Masui emerge from the primeval forest, the man turned toward him, his eyes beaming a green light like twin lanterns, like ghost-fire emanating from a corpse. It was Zhou Taiwang! Terrified, Masui gaped; his eyes bugged. He retreated, scurrying up into the branches of an ancient tree.

"It's dead," called Zhou Taiwang. "Good thing you're here. Go get others to help!"

Masui was frightened out of his wits. Clinging to a tree branch, he gabbled, "I don't . . . don't know . . . don't dare."

Panicked, Zhou Taiwang explained, "It was caught in my steel jaw clamp. What was I supposed to do? I put it down with two shots. Besides, what are we supposed to do when there's nothing to eat?" As he spoke, he picked up a few more stones and lobbed them at the tiger.

There was an old witchsong in the mountains:

> *A-hunting in the mountains,*
> *Mountain-cleaving ax in hand I go;*
> *Split a thousand cliffs open,*
> *Cut a path down to hell below.*
> *Striding across peaks like walking on a plain,*
> *Wandering through valleys where rivers of cloud flow.*
>
> *Wild goats trail me as I trek over every crag;*
> *Pheasants at my beck and call crawl into my game bag.*
> *River deer I catch at will, as I walk the woods around me:*
> *Hail to the mountain god who bestows this endless bounty!*

But audacious Zhou Taiwang had trapped, shot, and killed the most sacred creature in these forested mountains! Masui shuddered at the sight of the black-and-yellow stripes in the moonlight, a nameless fear gnawing at his mind. Suddenly, a second living tiger emerged next to the fallen tiger's limp body. Its tail thrust skyward, the creature sprang and capered, leapt and rolled about with tremendous speed. Right in front of an awestruck Zhou Taiwang, the creature danced, its gorgeous, striped body at once flexible and powerful, undulating like a thick, colorful homespun quilt. Of all the movements of the birds in the sky and the beasts on the ground, the mountainfolk most admired this dance. When they wanted to describe a certain impetuous panache, a reckless flair, they would admiringly say, "Ai! He's dancin' with his tail upright." The tiger was fearless, seemingly oblivious to the presence of the tiger-killer and the corpse of its dead mate. Frisking about like a cat, it capered and cavorted time and again, and then disappeared without any warning, leaving not a trace. Hyperventilating, Masui held a branch with one hand and slapped himself in the face with the other. He realized it was not a second tiger, but the ghost of the dead tiger bidding one last joyous farewell to the world of the living before departing for the realm of the ancestors. Sweet Mother! When the ancestors came to settle scores with the living, what then? The dead tiger lay still, its left foreleg caught in the steel clamp, stained with blood; but its eyes stared forward, as though it were poised to spring. Bloody paw-prints marred the trampled grass and tamped-down leaves where the tiger had thrashed about and breathed its last. Banzi, Zhou's usually ferocious hunting dog, lay whimpering, pressed to the earth, her head lowered and tail between her rear legs.

Masui was caught in the grips of an inner struggle. True, the tiger was his ancestor, his kin. But this dead tigress was as long as a large table. Her meat would be fatty and delicious.

"Quick! Get the others," urged Zhou Taiwang, unwrapping his white turban and using it to cover the eyes of the tigress. He, too, feared the wrath of the ancestors. Alive or dead, he didn't want the tigress to get a clear look at him. It was said that after a tiger died, beneath the earth where its eyes last fell was a treasure called the "tiger's prowess." On a moonless night, if one dug two feet deep beneath that precise spot, they might find one or two nuggets of obdurate "tiger's prowess." Possessing tremendous manna, it looked like amber and had the capacity to dispel all sorts of demons and evil spirits. Zhou Taiwang so feared the tiger's gaze, however, that he dared not look for it.

Filled with misgivings, Masui calmed his wild heartbeat. However, he mused, Zhou Taiwang would bear the brunt of the ancestors' wrath; he, after all, had killed the tigress. Masui scrambled down the tree and rushed homeward, covering more than two miles before he breathlessly arrived in the courtyard at Gengguping. Chest heaving, he knocked at the door, "Zhou Taiwang shot a big cat. Help us carry it back!" he roused Sun Fu and Shi Eryang. Soon, they were hurrying back to the site.

"With a steel clamp?" asked Sun Fu, jogging forward.

"Yeah, Zhou Taiwang caught the tigress in the clamp, then shot her," Masui explained nervously.

"Ah?" the two others slowed their pace, taken aback. When the mountainfolk say "big cat," they generally are referring to a tiger or a leopard. They also called the tiger a "striped cat," and the leopard a "spotted cat." Believing that hunting a tiger brought catastrophe down upon one's family, both Eryang and Sun Fu had figured "big cat" meant a leopard. Even in the yarns spun by the elders, neither had ever heard of hunting tigers in these mountains.

"That audacious motherfucker Zhou Taiwang must want his head severed from his shoulders!" said Sun Fu, eyes protruding.

"Goddamnit! Chop yer own head off... the creature's dead!" retorted Masui.

Grinding his teeth, Shi Eryang said, "It's damned if ya do, damned if ya don't: We'll be cursed to death if we eat it, and we'll starve to death if we don't. Might as well tote it back as food."

The three quickened their pace.

III

The head and eyes of the tigress were swathed in Zhou Taiwang's white turban, so that lying on a bloodstained mat of grass she looked a bit like a massive mountainman clad in a tigerskin. The four men fashioned two rings of rattan creepers, placing one just behind the forepaws of the tigress, engirding her chest, and a second in front of her rear legs, encircling her waist. They pushed a long, stout tree branch through the two rings, then hoisted the tigress in unison. All at once as they lifted, the four legs dropped, and for a moment it looked as though the tiger was standing; and as they moved forward it seemed as though her four legs were treading along. Masui shivered inwardly, a cold shudder wracking his tired body. The other three saw it too. Alarmed, they hesitated, myriad horrors creeping into their unsettled minds.

"Are we g-g-going or not?" Shi Eryang asked meekly.

"Ai! Let's go . . ." said Zhou Taiwang, drumming up his courage.

Finally the four, not wanting to return home empty-handed, began to pick their way up and down the slopes. It was not until some time in the nether hours between midnight and dawn that they finally carried the tigress through the gate.

Zhou Taiwang removed the front door to his house, and, together with Masui, Sun Fu, and Eryang, carried the tigress inside. They removed the rattan hoops, then took out a comb, and respectfully, tenderly, combed the matted fur. As he combed, Zhou Taiwang mumbled a remorseful singsong chant, "Oh, striped tiger, so blind you were caught in my trap, in my iron clamp, so that we had to carry you here: May you soon ascend to heaven. Please don't blame us for this wrong." With that, he picked a sharp knife and cut a seven-foot long, two-inch wide seam in the skin of the tigress running from the thumbs of her huge padded forepaws down the length of her chest. He opened the cavity and gutted the tiger, dressing it as he would a hog. Meanwhile, the others lit fires under cooking pots in the courtyard. By the time the new day dawned, the stewed meat of the tigress was ready.

"Mum," Masui's wife He called, approaching Tao Jiuxiang's bedside with a bowl of piping hot, rich broth, "Are you up? Hurry . . . have some of this. Masui and some other guys from the courtyard hunted it last night."

Tao Jiuxiang peeled back her quilt and slowly propped herself up on an elbow.

"Eat it while it's hot. There's enough for seconds if you want. I'm going over to wake up my sister-in-law." Placing bowl and chopsticks on the table, He left abruptly. Shortly, she carried two bowls of hot soup into Yinmei's bedchamber, presenting them to her sister-in-law with a hint of pride, "Your brother-in-law hunted down some prey. Come on, it's morning . . . get up and eat. Let Yonggang eat, too. I'm going to get Yongzhi and Yongguang."

Recently, the production team had assigned Yinmei to carry charcoal, a strenuous task that left her dead tired after a day's work. Each night she slept like a log. Now, to her surprise, she opened her heavy eyes to see a bowl of soup set beside her. She shook sleepy Yonggang awake, pulling him to his feet and quickly dressing him. Yonggang slurped a mouthful of soup, but tasted nothing special. He tweezed a piece of meat with his chopsticks and shoveled it into his mouth, working it around. He scrunched up his nose, feeling that the meat was tender but oddly redolent of incense ash. The little fellow was famished, however; so, with a shrug, he wolfed down the meat and drained the soup in short order. Yinmei, too, ravenously downed her bowl. When they finished, mother and son were perspiring uncontrollably.

Greedily eating as she walked, He peeked into Tao Jiuxiang's room, asking, "Ma, you finished? You can have more. So can my sister-in-law and Yonggang."

Overhearing her, Yonggang bolted from the adjacent room, bowl in hand.

Though she was starving, Tao Jiuxiang worked her way deliberately through the bowl of soup, without relish. As He passed by, she tipped the bowl and took a final swallow, drinking the soup to the lees. "It's not wild hog," she said matter-of-factly.

Licking her lips, He said, "It's more savory than hog—it's tigress. Zhou Taiwang caught it in a steel-jawed trap."

Tao Jiuxiang gasped, murmuring, "No wonder it tastes like incense ash: people burn incense and paper for tigers." Seized by a sudden fit of illness, she doubled over and retched mouthful upon mouthful of watery and stringy gobbets of meat.

"Ma," He set down her bowl and supported her, saying, "You ate too fast. Slow down! There's plenty in the pot."

But Tao Jiuxiang kept vomiting—after regurging the meat and soup, came bile; after the bile, convulsive dry-heaves. For a moment, Yinmei stood dumbstruck, then her muscles violently spasmed, and she, too, squatted and started to disgorging jets of soup and meat everywhere. Disconcerted, He cried out, "Masui, quick! Come help!"

Pale as a sheet, Tao Jiuxiang pointed at the bed. He helped her lay down. Masui rushed in to find the floor an inch deep in vomit. "Ma," he cried, "What's wrong?"

Yongguang and Yonggang entered, bellies distended, crying for their grandmother. Tao Jiuxiang merely curled up in bed, pulling up the quilt to cover herself.

"Ma said the meat tastes like incense ash," He explained to Masui. "People give burnt offerings to tigers. But now we've eaten her flesh!'

The couple exchanged uneasy glances. But just at that moment, piercing lamentations erupted from several women in the courtyard.

"Oh, my dear grandson . . ."

"My son, ahhhh... ahhh."

Masui and He saw Zhou Taiwang's wife and mother weeping bitterly. The youngest Zhou son, a twelve-year-old boy, had met a tragic fate. Though no one knew how much meat the boy had eaten, after swilling down three or four bowls, sweaty and parched, he had gulped down several quarts of cold water. Then, suddenly, he keeled over and dropped, stone dead. Amid a chaotic milling ruck of wailing Zhou kinsmen, Zhou Taiwang squatted in the doorway weeping.

Consuming the meat of a tiger generates tremendous internal heat, a fiery energy compounded in the dead heat of summer. In a single morning, the hungry denizens of the former Li homestead had consumed more a ninety pounds of tiger meat! Now glutted, every man, woman, and child was sweating profusely and burning with thirst. And yet after the Zhou boy's sudden death, no one, no matter how keen-edged his or her thirst, dared touch a single drop of water!

IV

Near the steel-jaw trap, people found tiger tracks. The grass around the trap was tamped down and stained with blood. Early the following morning, someone was sent to alert Longping; the production team leader was not surprised, for he knew Zhou Taiwang to be an intrepid hunter and trapper. Promptly mounting up, he rode the production team's black charger to Gengguping.

All morning Zhou Taiwang's wife wailed without cease as she began preparing for her youngest son's funeral. The skin and skeleton of the tigress were set in two piles outside the gate. Ears perked, several hunting dogs warily looked on, but dared not approach the heaps of skin and bones. In the afternoon, Zhou Taiwang's wife flayed off some of the fat; as the Zhous did not have an ounce of oil, she intended to render some for a mourning lamp to place at her son's feet. But when Old Mother Zhou saw what she had planned, she was horrified and curtly chastised her daughter: "We dare not do such things," she warned. "Oil can be offered as a sacrifice to Lord Tiger, but tiger oil can not be used to honor deceased men. It will bring no good to the child in the netherworld, and may bring harm down upon our whole family." Her tearful scolding was interrupted by a loud shout from outside, "Zhou Taiwang, where's the tiger you killed?" Longping stormed through the gate in a towering fury, having learned that the dwellers of Gengguping had already divvied up and consumed the meat.

Zhou Taiwang said, "Gone. It's all eaten."

The production team leader abruptly shouldered his way into the kitchen, lifted the lid of the cooking pot, and found the dregs of soup that still remained. Tipping the pot at an angle, he swallowed down eight or ten ladlesful. Wiping his lips with his sleeve, Longping snorted, "The tiger is a precious animal and should not be hunted. Do you want to be labeled a reactionary?"

Zhou Taiwang argued, "I set the trap for wild hogs or deer—I never thought I'd find a tiger. My poor son was starving . . . hadn't eaten for several days, but now . . ." Too choked up to continue, Zhou raised a hand to wipe away his welling tears.

Qin Longping, himself visibly thinner, merely gloated at Zhou's misfortune, responding, "Who told you lot of gluttons to hoard the meat and wolf it all down yourselves! If you'd brought the tiger to the cooks at the cafeteria, everyone would have been allocated a few spoonfuls. And one thing's for sure: your kid would still be alive!" At the sight of the skin and skeleton of the tigress piled outside the gate, he waved his hand in what was intended as a gesture of magnanimity and said, "Well, I'm a kindhearted fellow and won't punish your wrongdoing. Take the remains to the purchasing station in Huangshui and sell them for herbal medicine. Whatever you get belongs to the production team! Li Masui, get a couple back-baskets. Now! Tomorrow morning the commune will be holding a meeting."

Masui shuffled off to find two baskets. He arranged the bones in one, and folded the tigress's skin in the other.

Beholding the splendid tigerskin, Longping pronounced, "This skin should be dedicated to Chairman Mao Zedong as an expression of the loyalty of the people of Lihaku. Come on!" He and Masui picked up the baskets, mounting one on each flank of the black horse. Unexpectedly, the horse took fright, wildly bucking and rearing, pissing and shitting uncontrollably, and flung the baskets to the ground. Though they tried to mount the baskets several times, their efforts were in vain. The horse grew increasingly skittish. Thrown from the baskets and caked with dirt, the tigerskin and skeleton reeked of horse piss and filth.

Longping grunted, "Guess I'll have to carry the damn thing myself!" He squatted down and hoisted a basket onto his back, then barked toward Masui, "C'mon, grab the other one ..."

Breathlessly clambering up ridges and across vales, the two toted the skeleton and the skin; each basket weighing more than a hundred pounds. Even as the day cooled and the sun sank toward the western horizon, the two looked as though they had been caught in a torrential rainstorm: sweat coursed down their shoulders and overheated backs, for they had eaten the tigress's meat and drank the rich, fatty broth. Both reeked with the sour and fishy stink of blood, flesh, wet fur, bone, and filth.

They finally arrived in Huangshui deep into the night. Fortunately, the guesthouse was still open. They booked a room for a half-night. The next morning, Longping sent Masui to have the skin tanned, while he sold the bones, claws, and gallbladder to the purchasing station. Then he headed to the commune meeting, where he proudly announced his intent to send the pelt to Beijing to honor Chairman Mao.

Emerging from the tanner's shop, Masui heard the telltale clang of a handheld gong. Then he heard a familiar voice vigorously chant, "I've stirred the winds of hell ..." After a moment, a younger, pure voice followed, "And I've lit the ghostfires!" Intrigued, Masui followed the mellifluous and rhythmic chants to their source: on the opposite side of the road, two men approached, their faces inked black; one held a torch, the other a gong and a palm-leaf fan. The latter alternatingly struck the gong and waved the fan. In turn, with perfect cadence and rhythm, the two incanted their repetitive chant. Encountering several acquaintances along the street, they came to a hesitant stop: it was the old *tima*, Xia Qifa, and his son, Liangxian. Several party member cadres trailing behind them shunted the father-and-son pair on, signaling them to keep marching and not dilly-dally. Striking the gong again, Xia Qifa chanted, "I've stirred the winds of hell ..." Then Xia Liangxian waved his fan and sang, "And I've lit the ghost-fires!" As he chanted, he raised his torch—made of soft paper mulberry bark—high above his head. This sort of torch could not be extinguished by wind, no matter how strong the gust.

As father and son chanted the length of the main street of Huangshui, a growing crowd of onlookers watched. Time and again, Xia Qifa answered the resonant "Tang!" of the gong with his sonorous, "I've stirred the winds of hell!" Another gong beat, "Tang!" followed by Liangxian's shrill and charming, "And I've lit the ghost-fires." As they passed, a group of naughty teenagers giggled, spat, and cast clods of earth at the Xias.

"Masui," wizened Third Auntie Zhang muttered, looking up from her task of sweeping the street with a besom. She bustled over after furtively looking left and right, and whispered, "Long time, no see. Is your mother okay?"

"She's all right," Masui answered. Afraid of being seen by the Xias, he slipped into a supply shop.

Third Auntie followed him in, and murmured, "The Xias are in serious trouble! I heard that when production team leader Tian sent them to a Mao Zedong study group, a snake trailed them into the classroom and scared the living daylights out of the party organizers! Everyone steers clear of them, especially of your brother-in-law. Girls and wives are petrified, and flee on sight as though chased by wolves; rumor has it that if a woman, old or young, carelessly steps on one of the *timas'* taboo symbols, she'll be compelled to cling to him like a rattan creeper to a tree trunk, and follow him to the ends of the earth."

Pock-faced Masui felt sorry for ill-fated handsome Liangxian. He sighed, "You know, Old Xia repudiated his son as a *tima*."

Third Auntie Zhang arched her thin brows and said excitedly, "Folks are still wary of the young one. Right after the cadre finished construction on the new administrative building, he passed by and the stout new wall started falling apart, chunks of plaster and earth dropping all over the place." Gaining traction, gossipy Third Auntie's lips picked up speed, "When the wall collapsed, the director was so pissed that he cussed out the builders. As the masons were moving loose earth away, they saw a mouse pushing against the collapsed wall. The masons claimed that this was proof that they'd been wrongly accused and that someone had cast some sort of hex on the house. So they dragged Xia Liangxian to the authorities. Damn, what a mess! When they interrogated him, he swore that he had never used dark magic to hex the house. But after he made water drip from the new wall at the Qins' house, nobody believed him. They even gave the old *tima* a pummeling or two."

Masui shot a cautious glance down the street, then, after a terse parting, lowered his head and bolted out the side door. Late that night he reached Gengguping, completely spent. The following day, he dared not mention to Yinmei her brother's interrogation or her father's beating. He simply told her that he had brought tanned tigerskin to commune headquarters for transport to the county offices.

Chapter Twenty-Three

I

An iron cauldron was set on the street like some gross implement of torture. Scrolling up pantlegs and shirtsleeves, the instructing cadres put sweet potato vines, wild greens, and rice husks into the pot. When the cauldron boiled, they called for those parading the gonging Xia father and his son up and down the streets of Huangshui to stop. The director addressed Xia Qifa, saying, "I've heard you possess magic swallowing powers. Let's see it: eat all of it . . . drink the soup to the lees!"

More and more gawkers gathered, drawn by the spectacle. A sour aroma wafted in the hot, dense air over the cauldron; residuum of greens and rice hulls floated on surface. Xia Qifa frowned. At this struggle session to expose his deceptions, his arcane tricks, the director pushed a big ladle into the *tima*'s hands, brusquely saying, "Okay. Eat it all!" Xia Qifa accepted the ladle; bending forward and reaching into the cauldron he scooped out ladleful after ladleful of boiled wild greens and vines. Lowering his head, he shoveled them into his mouth with chopsticks. Before long, he had slurped down two-dozen ladlesful, never biting or chewing, and the entire cauldron was empty. Nothing special happened. The *tima* did not show the slightest discomfort. Embarrassed, the director rasped, "Repair the wall that Xia Liangxian destroyed within a day. If you finish rebuilding it, it will make up for your crimes against the people; if not, it will compound the offense!"

It took a team of six or seven laborers a fortnight to erect the earthen brick walls of the house and to tile the roof. Xia Qifa recalled the severe drought four decades earlier when the county governor, Pockmarked Zhang, wearing straw sandals, had held a pistol to his head and forced him to perform a rain-bringing ceremony. One could propitiate disasters wrought by heaven, but what could be done about catastrophes brought on by man? The old shaman sighed wearily, "I've eaten too much to practice my arts. Let me go home and prepare for two days. Then I'll return to fix the wall."

The cadre leader, figuring the old man was frightened, said curtly, "Fine, as you will. I'll take you at your word, but two days from now you must return and rebuild the house in front of everyone."

At last, father and son were released and allowed to return to Dragon Decapitating Gorge. When they reached home, Xia Liangxian devoured a dozen of his mother's maidenhair fern root rice cakes like a ravenous wolf, bathed, and promptly fell asleep. During the month that the "study group" had held him prisoner they had dressed him up as a scaramouch in blackface and paraded him up and down the streets seven or eight times. Befouled, ink and dirt-stained, he had not washed his face or rinsed his mouth once during that time. Now he scrubbed and scrubbed, as if trying to wash away the clinging layers of shame and humiliation.

Xia Qifa neither ate nor slept. Rather, he sought out several sticks. Then, sitting on a straw mat, he gloomily set to work, fashioning a man-sized effigy out of rice straw. As he worked, he chanted in a faint, dolorous voice:

> *Hidden in forests of tufted maidengrass,*
> *From all the world concealed,*
> *When the wind parts the tall grass sways,*
> *Still my whereabouts are not revealed.*

"Time to make myself scarce," thought the old *tima* to himself. "Otherwise, danger will be upon me." He cut the long stalks of pliant, tough rice straw into lengths, then with a skillful, familiar hand, bound bundles of straw around the armature of sticks to create a straw man. As the effigy took shape, he chanted:

Hidden in an abyss countless miles deep,
In a cave of dark clouds concealed;
When winds buffet the clouds this way and that,
Still my whereabouts are not revealed.

"Yes, time to disappear. Otherwise, I'm sure to meet a bad fate," mulled Xia Qifa, knitting his white, feathery brows. Deep into the night, he hummed and bundled, bundled and hummed. When finally he finished the straw man, he placed a straw hat on the effigy's head. Only then did he stop chanting and trundle off to rest.

The following day at noon, a pair of soldiers came to Dragon Decapitating Gorge to detain Xia Qifa and bring him in to Huangshui.

The previous evening, after the crowds around the soup cauldron had dispersed, the commune kitchen's black sow suddenly dropped dead. The pig-keeper's frantic cries summoned a growing crowd to the pigpen: what they beheld struck the lot of them dumb! The sow's belly was bloated to grotesque proportion; the poor creature had ruptured and burst asunder, issuing from the gaping split was a stinking, pulpy mass of wild greens and sweet potato vines. The director's face grew taut; he knew that the wily old shaman had pulled one over on him. Returning to headquarters, he dispatched the soldiers to seize Xia Qifa.

When the PLA soldiers entered the yard, they saw Xia Qifa emerge wearing a straw hat. With no further ado, they grabbed the shaman, trussed him up, and dragged him back to Huangshui. Xia Liangxian watched from a hidden vantage behind the house as the two apprehended and carried off the straw effigy.

On a dim, moonless night, the old *tima*, overwhelmed with indignant sorrow yet ever vigilant, walked rapidly along a footpath tracing the gorge, carrying slung over his shoulder a leather sack containing all the ghosts and spirits he had captured over the decades. It seemed as though his movements controlled the night sky: with each passing step, a few more stars dotted the firmament, lighting his path. From time to time, Xia Qifa heard the nightsounds of birds and beasts, shrieks and groans issuing from the ridges. A lone figure, he moved through the night, first scrambling through brambles that ripped his long gown, then picking his way along a slope covered with jagged stones. Finally he arrived at a halcyon spot that he chosen long ago, a sheltered niche hidden in the crags between Huangshui and Greenstone.

As he walked through this vale, he murmured farewells to the ghosts and spirits in the sack. Finally, he stopped at the top of a hillock. He took the leather sack from his shoulder and opened it, releasing the various ghosts, spirits, and demons back into the wider world.

As the stars faded, the waxing moon emerged, bathing the exposed mountainsides in a cold, silvery light. Xia Qifa, joined by his shadow, piously inclined his head toward the burning joss sticks and paper. Then, from the leather bag he removed a sealed jar, placing it gingerly in a crevice in the rock. The jar, handed down to him through generations of Xia *timas*, contained one hundred thousand spirit warriors from the netherworld, ready to fight at the shaman's summons.

Not every shaman possessed so many spirit warriors and horses. As soon as he placed the jar in the crevice, the old man wept, thinking of a story passed down from his forefathers: one day long ago one of his remote ancestors, a shaman whose arcane arts were powerful indeed, was picking medicinal herbs in the mountains; to avoid a rainstorm he ran into a cave. An eerie red light emanated from within, issuing from strange red crystals, polyhedral and half-translucent, studding the cavern walls. He recognized it at once as cinnabar, the mystical panacea of the heavenly deities, a drug far more precious than gold. Pulverized and made into a decoction, these crystals could transform one into an immortal. Future generations hired dozens of workers and a team of mules, continuing to mine the rich vein; one caravan even crossed the Yangzi and the Han River, delivering endless cartloads of cinnabar to the First Emperor of Qin in Xianyang for the ruler's grand mausoleum that included a vast subterranean deathless world with rivers or mercury and oceans of quicksilver.

But in recent centuries, his family had come down in the world. Xia Qifa had failed to transmit the spells, the mantras, and the codes of the *tima* to his son. The line was irrevocably severed. As the phrase "Shaman of a Cold Altar" floated into his mind, shame and despondency gripped Xia Qifa.

Under a flood of white silken moonlight, he trembled. Unconsciously, the tremble turned into a series of hops and stomps, a bird-like dance. As though the wind god were presiding over some nocturnal rite, the shaman's long gown swooshed in the air as he danced on and on, so single-mindedly rapt in his dreamwalking that the surrounding tree branches began to sway and move with him. On the ground, his shadow and the shadowy limbs danced and whirled. Finally spent, the old *tima* lay on his back atop a ridge, motionless in the predawn chill. At a loss, he gazed up at the constellations above, his heart descending into a frenzied turmoil.

Standing by the *tima*'s side, a strange, tattered mountain man sighed gently. The old *tima* felt the man's hand caress his face. Dizzy and disoriented, he asked, "Who are you? Why aren't you home at this late hour?"

The eccentric fellow answered, "I'm trapped in a cliff. I can't go home."

The old *tima* was taken aback. When he saw the scales and shells covering the man's exposed wrists, he understood with whom he was speaking. Gently, he urged, "If you rectify your conduct and your actions are good, you'll be set free in due time."

The dragon entreated, "Please tell the gods and buddhas that while I may have run amok and caused a calamitous flood, it is nothing compared to the cruelty routinely wrought by mortal men."

Xia Qifa answered, "But your disastrous flood created a swath of destruction that reached the ocean. To make amends, you would have to succor all of mankind."

"Succor mankind? . . . behold the savagery they inflict upon each other."

"The gods and buddhas shall likewise mete out punishments for their wrongs."

The dragon said, "You're a good man. Thank you for caring for me all these years. When I'm liberated, I shall repay you."

Sighing, the old *tima* mulled, "Paradise and hell are wrapped together in a single bundle." With a vigorous effort he struggled to his feet, as through nudged by some invisible force. This same force somehow sustained him as he staggered a full ten miles; reaching the Xia homestead, he collapsed.

The shaman lay in bed, unable to eat a mouthful of rice or to let water pass his lips. Fretful Old Mother Xia wiped away tears and climbed the slopes gathering turtledove vernonia. She ground the downy leaves into pulp, making a half pot of medicinal greenish-brown immortal tofu, mixing in incense ash. But Xia Qifa failed to eat a single bite. Ever since being forced to eat the cauldron of pig slops, his stomach seemed spoiled. He had no appetite for anything.

As the sun sunk behind the mountains, several silver-tailed bushtits roosted, twittering on the horse mulberry shrub outside the window. The old shaman listened as they flitted toward him, nodding their heads, bobbing their tails, and waving their wings. "Heaven and earth grow dark, but they are not fully dark yet; we want to chatter, chatter, chatter ... Here is a man who can go anywhere as he wants, yet why has he not yet left for the land of his ancestors? Why?"

Another bushtit flew back and forth in front of his window, chirping, "*Ji-ji* ... so it ends. *Gua-gua* ... it's time!"

Startled, Xia Qifa listlessly looked out of the window, knowing that his day had come. He told Xia Liangxian, whose handsome face was bruised and swollen beyond recognition, to send a message to Yinmei.

Production team leader Qin Longping had been directing the folks to build clay furnaces at Lihaku to smelt iron. Yinmei was part of a group of laborers assigned to carry the leftover charcoal from Lihaku to the big blast furnaces at Peppercorn Bend. Laborers received work points based on the weight of the charcoal. Every day, Yinmei transported two or three loads. Famished and exhausted, her hands black with coal, Yinmei wore a pair of ragged commune-issue blue work clothes. Learning from the messenger that her father was severely ill, she gave her basket of coal to Sun Fu (who, returning empty-handed, promptly doubled back to Peppercorn Bend), and hurried back to Lihaku to request leave.

"Tell your father," adopting what he took to be a consolatory tone, the production team leader instructed Yinmei, "that if he's sick he should go see the medics in the commune clinic and get them to prescribe medicine. Tell him not to get up to his old tricks. If he gets caught again, he won't get off so easy ..." For a ghost-spawn witch, he mused, she talked and behaved in a decent manner. Her tear-smeared, charcoal-and-soot blackened face looked truly otherworldly, ghastly and horrible.

With a string of "yeses," Yinmei sped off to Dragon Decapitating Gorge. Many of the thick-trunked, rattan-wrapped ancient trees in the forest had been cut to feed the furnaces. A soft moss carpeted the road home, making the route smoother and easier. Still, she had to pass a night in Lajia Gully before she reached home.

II

Haggard Xia Qifa had not expected his daughter arrive so quickly. With effort he raised his head, telling his son, "Support me . . . hold me up."

Seeing her sallow father, Yinmei unfolded a kerchief and carefully tweezed something that looked like a pair of needles and said, "Dad, Zhou Taiwang trapped a tiger; Yonggang cut off two of its vibrissa whiskers . . . they can cure you."

Alarm danced in Xia Qifa's faintly lit eyes. Grasping the edge of the bed, he gasped,

"Even if your aim's true, you can't shoot it;

"even if you shoot it, you can't kill it;

"even if you kill it, you can't dress it;

"even if you dress it, you can't cook it;

"even if you cook it, you can't eat it . . ."

Clasping his father's feverish body to his chest, Xia Liangxian finished the cautionary verse:

> *Punishment from above, food gone, pots broken,*
> *Teeth fall, tongue sundered, words unspoken.*

Xia Qifa struggled to rise, but failed. Heartbroken, he murmured, "Put them in the shrine . . . the votive niche."

"Do it," Old Mother Xia directed her daughter, "Listen to your father."

Yinmei delicately placed the tiger's vibrissa in the niche and lit a stick of incense.

From his sunken eyes Xia Qifa piercingly gazed at his daughter. Forcefully, he said, "One day a man came across several others skinning and dressing a tiger. Hungry, he cut off half a catty of meat for himself . . ."

"Let me tell it." Xia Liangxian broke in, afraid his father was getting overwrought. The young man continued: "The man's son was a promising student, and each day passed through a forest on his way to the village school. A spirit tiger turned into a white-bearded man and stepped out from behind a tree to address the boy, "Your father borrowed half a catty of meat from me. Tell him to repay me."

Holding his father's shoulders and cradling the old *tima*'s head, he went on: "When the son returned home, he said to his father, 'Dad, you borrowed a slab of meat from some fellow. He wants you to pay for it.' Annoyed, the man huffed, 'Who did I borrow meat from? Tell him to come get it himself.'" When the son passed through the forest again, the old man emerged and queried, 'Did you ask your father about the meat?' The son said, "I did. He said that you'd better come get it yourself."

Xia Qifa stared at his daughter with bloodshot eyes. Caressing his father's hair, Xia Liangxian continued: "Learning of the father's response, the tiger crept up soundlessly behind the man as he was hunkering down for a shit, and bit off a hunk of flesh from his buttocks. The following morning the son encountered the old man yet again, and told him, 'My dad was bitten in the ass while he was shitting; he's been up all night howling in pain.' The old man sighed and answered, 'Your father owed me half a catty of meat. I asked him to pay. He refused. What else could I do? I had to come take it myself. Bring this medicine back to your father."

Casting a glance toward his sister, Xia Liangxian went on: "When he arrived at home, the son gave the medicine to his father. The father asked, 'Where do you get this wonder-medicine? As soon as I applied a poultice to the wound, the pain was gone!' The son replied, 'First the old white-beard tore into your buttock; then he gave you medicine to cure the pain.' Only then did the father recall the tiger meat he'd eaten and realize what had happened."

"If you eat the meat of a tiger, sooner or later you'll pay," Xia Qifa added, when his son had finished. The old man's cheeks flushed crimson; his breathing grew ever more labored. Staring in a queer manner off into space, he panted, "If you meet with some urgent matter, cast my bamboo trigrams to divine a path." Anxiety creased his weary face.

Feeling a rush of panic, Xia Liangxian looked down at his father. In these days, families were no longer allowed to perform the traditional funeral rite to see off the soul of the departed. Nor did the family have any white cloth prepared. Tears of agitation streamed down his cheeks.

Long ago, his father had told him a tale of a dragon prince, who, having met with bitter defeat at the hands of a great *tima*, took the guise of an ordinary man and presented himself to the shaman as a pupil. He planned to master all of the *tima*'s arcane tricks and mystical arts then use them to take revenge. For three years, the shaman taught his pupil; only six months remained until the hidden dragon's training was complete. The dragon prince said, "Master, I've been your disciple for years, yet you've never visited my home. Please come pay a visit." Feeling this to be a reasonable request, the shaman followed the disguised dragon prince back to his lair. Discovering his student's home was a majestic grotto in the heart of a mountain containing a grand palace with upturned eaves and tall ramparts, the shaman was taken aback. Whenever the *tima* passed through a gate, the dragon prince shut the doors behind him. Altogether, they crossed twelve thresholds, entering the very heart of the complex. Inwardly, the *tima* grew ever more wary. The dragon prince paid respects to his master, toasting him with a glass of wine. He then offered a second toast. When the dragon prince offered a third toast, the shaman politely refused. The *tima* addressed his disciple, "Let's see how well you recall your lessons." So saying, he flourished his arms, and his fingers adroitly formed the mudra of the Tiger Ancestor. Deftly, the dragon prince responded, torqueing his hands into the mudra of the Ancestress. The *tima* then flashed the General mudra, with one upthrust finger, but the dragon prince nimbly parried with a two-fingered Sun-and-Moon mudra of his own. The *tima* said, "Disciple, you have truly grasped the Way!" The dragon prince smugly answered, "Master, for three years I've lived in the terrestrial realm; today is the day you perish here in the netherworld!" With a deep sigh, the *tima* said, "Before I die, just let me glimpse the sky one final time." The dragon prince said, "Fine!" Then he bored a bowl-sized hole in the roof of his cavern and asked, "Master, can you see the sky?" The *tima* squinted, "No." The dragon prince made the hole larger, asking, "Master, how about now?" The *tima* replied, "Not yet." Then the dragon made a massive hole the size of two basins, asking, "Now?" The *tima* said, "Yes, I see the sky!" As he spoke, the *tima* knocked the dragon prince down with a demon-binding pellet, and, gathering all his strength, leapt out of the hole.

Because of this story, mountainfolk always said, "When a *tima* teaches a disciple, he always needs to keep a few extra tricks up his sleeve; when you show someone a path, make sure to leave yourself a way to retreat." And when a *tima* is dying, his family removes three tiles from the roof, one for each time the wily *tima* asked the dragon prince to widen the hole. By custom, the opening is covered in white to welcome the spirits. As the family had no white cloth, Old Mother Xia tore a bedsheet. Sadly, soldiers had confiscated Xia Qifa's eight-pleated ritual skirt and headdress. Without these, how could the old *tima* reach paradise and pay his respects to the celestial spirits?

Overwhelmed with sorrow, Xia Qifa seized his son's hands, a single tear leaking from his eye. In a melancholy voice, the shaman rasped, "What's today?"

"The fifteenth of the eighth lunar month."

A strange, soft light shone from the dried-out face and recessed eyes of this "Shaman of the Cold Altar." With a sense of reverence, he muttered, "The gates of heaven are opening."

Liangxian felt his father's grip tighten.

"It's rather dark when there's an opening in the roof, so I've hidden some moonlight for you to use later."

Xia Liangxian asked, "Where is it?"

"In the bamboo basket at the foot of the bed. Take as much as you need."

Sorrowfully, Xia Liangxian whispered, "I'll be okay, Dad. Don't worry." Xia Qifa gazed affectionately up at his son, running his gnarled hands over his son's fingers one by one. Yinmei's sleeves were wet with tears. Kneeling next to her father and brother, she gently massaged the dying man's chest.

Wracked by an internal fire, the skinny chest of the old *tima* heaved up and down. Though his fingers grew ice cold as he gazed up at his son, Xia Qifa's eyes burned hotter than an iron plowshare heated to expel evil spirits. His fingers intertwined with his son's, forcing Liangxian's forefinger to cross his ring finger, then pressing these conjoined fingers up to the third joint of the middle finger. When he finished, the shaman closed his eyes, his light of seventy-three years forever gone. Xia Liangxian looked down at his hand and, lo and behold, his father had forced his fingers into the mudra of the Tiger. Recalling that his father had told him that one was not to shed tears at the death of the *tima*, Liangxian swallowed the great sorrow he felt and worked to extricate his hand from his dead father's.

III

As evening turned to night, laborers returned to their homes. Suddenly, they heard crackling reports of firecrackers echoing in the distance. One ruggedly handsome fellow who had worked for the Xias for several years, a man known for turning the heads of women and for his steady hand, wondered aloud, "Think the old *tima*'s passed on?"

His workmate speculated, "Probably."

Yinmei and Old Mother Xia dressed the thirty-seventh Xia *tima* in his shroud. Only with great pains was Xia Liangxian able to extricate himself from his father's death grip. Freed, he drew an image of hell on the floor with a charred stick from the stove. Then, straining with exertion, he lifted half a millstone and placed it on the image, blocking the path to hell. He carried his father to a chair and sat the corpse upright, placing two earthenware bowls beneath his feet. Then, Xia Liangxian climbed up on the roof and removed three moss-covered tiles. However, inside it was still pitch dark. He jumped down through the hole and pulled the bamboo basket out from under the bed. With a wooden ladle, he spooned the contents of the basket skyward. Sure enough, as his father had promised, a column of moonlight found its way through the hole and began to fill the house.

Xia Qifa's face and memorial tablet shone brightly in the moonlight.

Xia Liangxian, though excommunicated as a *tima*, was still versed in the magical arts. He watched his father's ethereal soul pass through the particles of dust dancing in the moonlight and ascend through the opening in the roof, rising into the heavens to become a celestial master.

It began as the most paltry funeral ever witnessed for a *tima* of the Xia family. There was no ritual procession. A neighbor who had served Xia Qifa as an acolyte for a few years in the past came, incense in hand, and mourned the *tima* by making twenty-four kowtows. Two groups of neighbors came and offered incense with bowed heads. Yinmei knelt to thank their kindness. The reverence they paid her deceased husband so moved Old Mother Xia that she offered them wild vegetable pancakes and gifted them tobacco leaves to take home.

Just as they were about to depart, Xia Liangxian took the oxhide drum from beside the votive niche and began to rhythmically beat a tattoo on it with a pair of batons, first forcefully thumping the center, then striking the edge with a light, staccato trill. Hearing the infectious alternating beats, the neighbors could not help dancing around the deceased *tima* in his chair.

The Xia homestead came alive. Hearing the lively drumbeat and the fireworks, Old Li Erniang and her family came down from atop the ridge to mourn Xia Qifa. Nimble Xia Liangxian danced with abandon, his head soaked in sweat. As he and two of his father's former disciples beat the drum in turn, he seemed to have forgotten the succession of beatings he had suffered at commune headquarters. Amid the clamor, the drum-strikers let the batons rise and fall. Whenever Xia Liangxian chanted a line, the neighbors sang out in response. When people tired, they took a break to have a smoke and eat a vegetable pancake, then went on dancing. The din grew louder and louder, so vastly different than the monotony of their daily lives.

On beat the mourning drum, intermittent weak trills and powerful thumps that reverberated in the mountains, rumbling afar in the night sky. Through the night, Yinmei tremulously knelt on the ground. Only when she saw the branches take shape in the light of dawn did she relax her vigil, knowing that her father's spirit, blessed by gods and spirits, had made it safely through the night.

Her relief was short-lived, however, for just as she rose, she saw a uniformed official come storming through the gate—it was Tian, the production team leader from Dragon Decapitating Gorge.

For several nights, the cadre organizers dragged the straw man through the streets of Huangshui in a series of struggle sessions. When the "old *tima*" failed to respond to the director's order to rebuild the house, they tirelessly interrogated him. Yet even when the barrage of questions turned to shouting, and the shouting became violent shaking and beating, the stubborn old man remained silent. Finally, frustrated and tired, the cadre members hurled him back into a cell. When production team leader Qin Longping returned to headquarters to file a political report and saw the shaman in jail, he thought it mighty queer and muttered, "I thought Xia Qifa was in bed more dead than alive . . . what's he doing here?"

Arriving at headquarters from the *tima*'s home, Tian overheard him and felt his heart sink into his stomach. So the wily old *tima* had pulled off one final trick! First, Xia Qifa had made them play the fool by having the swine swallow the tureen of vile stew in his stead; now to find out the prisoner they'd interrogated for days was a straw effigy! With sweat coursing down his face, the antsy production team leader paced back and forth. After the meeting he hurried back to Dragon Decapitating Gorge.

Still far from the Xia's courtyard, he heard the thunderous mourning drum. Entering the gate, he was dumbfounded at the sight of the festal mourning ceremony for the old *tima*. Sternly, he railed toward the people, living and dead, "So even half-dead, you've still got the nerve to trifle with the cadre leaders, eh! Think you can send a straw man to take your punishment? And now, before we've even resolved your last offense, I come here and find your family engaged in superstitious feudal practices!"

In dismay, Yinmei knelt trembling, biting her lip until it bled.

"Please listen, good elder brother," Old Mother Xia approached the official and said, "Think of all the good deeds my old husband did for others throughout his life . . ." Choking on a thousand reminiscences, she began sobbing.

"Madam, I won't be too hard on you," production team leader Tian began, "but based on the accusations of informers, your family has been designated a primary target for observation. If I don't crack down on you, I'll be politically degraded!"

"This is the only kind of mourning we know. We don't know the modern songs, only the old chants," said Old Mother Xia heavily.

Gruffly, production team leader Tian retorted, "Whoever doesn't know the new revolutionary songs must report to the commune study group to learn them!"

Anxiety danced in Xia Liangxian's eyes. He held a baton in either hand, looking like an ox thief caught leading the stolen creature away by the halter.

The production team leader sized up the sweaty mountainfolk for a moment, then, adopting a conciliatory and encouraging tone, said, "You all ought to sing, 'Sailing the Seas Depends on the Great Helmsman.' Together now . . . sing!"

The mountainfolk looked quizzically at each other; nobody uttered a sound. Tian seized the batons from Xia Liangxian, and, attempting to emulate the alternating strong and weak drumbeats, urged, "Sing with me. Sing! Sing!"

So it was that Xia Qifa's funeral was forcibly interrupted. Haltingly and arhythmically, the neighbors sang,

> Sailing the seas depends on the Great Helmsman,
> Like the myriad things depend on the sun . . .

Noticing that Xia Liangxian wasn't singing, Tian fixed him with an imperious glare. Xia Liangxian had no choice but to reluctantly join the others and break into song:

> Just as fish can't leave the water,
> Nor melons leave the vine,
> The revolutionary masses can't live without the Communist Party,
> The sun of Mao Zedong Thought forever shines!

Tears flowed as he sang. Yinmei wiped away her silent tears.

"Look, people sing revolutionary songs even for an old *tima*," Tian remarked. At daybreak, he instructed the mountainfolk, "From now on at funerals, sing revolutionary songs! Understand?" He set down the batons, rubbing his eyes, and, giving a satisfied chuckle, addressed the deceased, "Old *tima*, you'd better bring these revolutionary songs down to the underworld and teach them to Yama."

Xia Liangxian nearly choked on sobs of indignation.

Humbly, Old Mother Xia offered, "But Yama doesn't like the sun . . ."

Tian concluded, yawning, "I'll give you a one-day leave for mourning. Xia Liangxian report tomorrow to the commune to attend a study group!"

Only then, after swallowing a couple of mouthfuls of water, did the weary neighbors return to their homes. Having worked to educate and rectify the backward, stubborn Xias, the dutiful production team leader washed his face and departed, swinging his heavy arms back and forth as he marched back toward Huangshui.

Xia Liangxian dared not fire the bamboo cannon; he merely lit off a few strings of firecrackers before carrying his father out of the house. Yinmei followed her brother; Old Mother Xia wailed loudly, remaining at the gate.

Tranquility enveloped the boundless mountains and endless sky. Many years earlier, Xia Qifa had selected the perfect geomantic site for a tomb on the steep hillock that rose behind the Xia homestead. Liangxian carried his father on his back, thinking all the while about the endless stories his father had told. The old shaman's corpse felt almost weightless.

Since the Poor Peasant Association confiscated the camphorwood coffin from the Xias, Xia Qifa and his son had been digging out a tomb chamber on the mound in their spare hours. After two years of work, they had excavated an impressive chamber inside the mound, with wooden boards paneling the interior. From the mound, they could see the inscription honoring the martyrs from the War of Resistance Against Japan and the head of the dragon immured in the cliff. Time and again, Xia Qifa had appealed on behalf of the dragon to Yu the Great, urging him to give the creature a chance to correct his faults. Over the decades, the fir trees growing on the dragon's forehead had become more luxuriant. In recent years, however, the trees had withered. Now, no one knew whether the wretched water dragon would ever be freed.

When they arrived at the mound, Xia Liangxian set his father down. Brother and sister scattered pulverized ruby sulphur and cinnabar powder inside the tomb. Then they carefully ensconced their father in the chamber, and then covered the entry with planks and earth. Along with the *tima* Xia Qifa, the last of the mountainfolk who understood the language of the feathered tribes, they buried a treasure trove of local lore, legends, and arcana that would never again be exhumed.

Chapter Twenty-Four

I

Old Mother Xia sat in the yard, the deep creases in her face contorted in grief. Elbow propped on her knee, her right hand supported her face as she worried about the path by which her husband might ascend to the heavens.

Somber Xia Liangxian entered the large family room of the house, looking up at the hole in the roof where he had removed three tiles. He had no idea how to comfort his mother. If only damned production team leader Tian had come an hour later they could have properly ushered Xia Qifa off to heaven! Surely, Tian was some demon incarnate bent on interrupting his father's safe passage.

With a leaden heart, feeling that she was drowning in a sea of bitterness, Yinmei cleaned the house. Her thoughts were not only occupied by her father's death and her husband's absence: recently, ten-year-old Yongzhi's feet had become so swollen that her nephew could no longer walk. Masui asked her to bring herbal medicine back when she returned. For all knew, the old *tima*, in addition to performing ablutions and using mudras to exorcise demons and capture spirits, treated the sick with massage and herbs. Everyone knew that the Xias grew all varieties of roots and herbs; unfortunately, people had long since dug them up. Yinmei sought them in vain, finding only bare plots where her father's herb gardens had once been. After looking dumbly at the fallow earth, she quietly asked her brother what to do. Xia Liangxian absently muttered, "Try some dog meat—it's moist and has curative properties."

The mountainfolk did not eat dog meat. Yinmei thought she had heard wrong. She looked at her brother dubiously.

"Since these days we dare consume a tiger's flesh, is any meat off limits? The flesh of a yellow hound is best; next best would be the meat of a black or white dog. But don't cook it on the stove or the *kang*, lest you offend the Kitchen God!" Xia Liangxian said, his face ghostly pale.

Yinmei remained silent, leaning heavily on the doorframe to prevent herself from collapsing. The once happy and lively Xia family was no more. Looking at her pitiful mother, Yinmei felt overwhelmed with guilt. The generous moonlight flooded down the slope, peeking through the windows, offering the broken family some consolation. Hanging his head, Xia Liangxian, assigned to report to the study group the following day, kept his mother and sister company far into the night, before dragging himself off to bed.

Worried about Yongzhi, Yinmei parted from her grieving mother the next morning, returning with heavy footsteps to Gengguping. When she entered the house, Tao Jiuxiang said, "Sun Fu brought a letter from Mawu in Wanxian County."

To supplement his commune subsidy, Sun Fu carried letters and parcels to the Huangshui post station twice a month. Every month Yinmei—who could read but not write—sent a letter to Mawu in prison, penned by her brother-in-law. At the end of each letter, she instructed Masui to write, "Everything is okay with Ma and the family. I miss you."

Half a year earlier, when Mawu wrote to his family, telling them that the prison labor team had been opening up new farmland and reclaiming wasteland, some odd new expressions had crept in. He wrote about "changing the objective world" and "reforming my thought," claiming that he was working to "slough off his old self to remold a new man."

But this time, the letter had a different tenor. Masui struggled to control his quavering voice as he read: "Dear mother and Yinmei, my wife, recently I have been tortured by arthritis. How I long to eat the wild herbs—the purslane, the bracken fern roots, and the woodear fungus—of Gengguping! Please send grain coupons and dog meat. The prison medic has told me that dogmeat is vital for my treatment . . ."

Yinmei opened her eyes wide in alarm.

Worried, Tao Jiuxiang mumbled, "He's sick . . ."

Feeling as though she were melting, hungry and tired from the journey, Yinmei took the letter in trembling hands. She held it close to her face, poring over every character, every stroke. On countless dismal and lonely nights beneath the quilt she had recalled Mawu's caress, his breathing, the way he cradled her right breast in his hand as she slept, locked tightly in his embrace. Each time Mawu sent a letter from Wanxian County, she fondled and read the letter over and over until the sheet of paper grew soft and wrinkled. Looking at the familiar handwriting, imagining the pain that racked Mawu's body, tears clouded her eyes. She stammered, "Dog meat . . ."

Chagrined, Tao Jiuxiang recalled the old *tima* and asked, "How's your father?"

"Dead . . . buried yesterday . . . ," stammered Yinmei.

Mouth agape and eyes listless, Tao Jiuxiang's low spirits plunged further into the abyss at the thought that Xia Qifa, the most powerful man she had ever known, was no more!

Glancing at the date of the letter, Yinmei noticed it was two months old. She gasped, wiping away tears. Mawu's long imprisonment was coming to an end, and the family eagerly anticipated his return. Yonggang had never seen his father. What if, like Yongzhi, Mawu was overcome by sickness and hunger and couldn't even rise? The thought was too horrible to bear. But, after all, there was nothing to eat.

Of the many hunting dogs that used to be around, only two remained: Black Leopard and Zhou Taiwang's Banzi. When Black Leopard was younger, she was a superb hunter, sporting a magnificent glossy coat and long, powerful jaws, with three stiff whiskers under her chin. Whenever a yearling ram ventured too far up the slope, the loyal hound circled behind it, barked, and drove it back. When Yonggang was an infant and slept in the cradle, she faithfully guarded the cradle. The moment Yonggang pissed, she would bark to alert Yinmei. Now, there were no more sheep; and they didn't need her to watch Yonggang. Black Leopard had become old and thin, her coat dusky and bedraggled. Each day she curled up and dozed in the yard.

With Yongzhi and Mawu's illnesses, eyes naturally turned toward poor Black Leopard. Masui and Yinmei gazed at the raggedy old hound for quite some time, a grim light emanating from their eyes.

"Black Leopard! Black Leopard, come on," Masui walked toward the corner of the courtyard. Ever at her master's beck and call, Black Leopard slowly struggled to her feet, wagging her tail as she trotted to Masui. Hardening her heart, Yinmei brought over a basin and washed the hound. Yonggang, having no inkling what his mother and his uncle had planned, helped them bathe Black Leopard.

Sorrowfully, Tao Jiuxiang gazed at Black Leopard, extending a dried, wizened hand; slowly, she ran her hand the length of its back three times, then led Yonggang back into the house. Masui called the dog over to a tree in the courtyard and slipped a rope around her neck. The guileless hound simply wagged its tail cheerfully, woofing as she shook her shoulders. Panting, she bent down and licked Masui's feet. Only when tortured Masui recalled his ailing child Yongzhi—weak and pale with a grotesquely distended stomach— did he steel his resolve and string up the hound from a branch. Hanging in midair, forepaws flailing, Black Leopard struggled to breathe, a raspy whimper issuing from her throat as the noose tightened. Soon the miserable hound's feet stopped scrabbling in the air.

II

When dressing the dog, Masui felt sick at heart. Yet he toiled on, for what else could he do? He began by making an incision from the corners of the hound's mouth with a small blade, cutting a seam down the underside of the mandible, along the sternum, then the length of his belly. Then he opened the chest and belly and scooped out the inner organs, so that stomach and intestines spilled out and blood and juices stained the earth; their foul exhalation hung in the air. Yonggang broke away from Tao Jiuxiang and burst from the house. Seeing Black Leopard had been transformed into a pile of skin, bones, organs, and red meat, he wailed, accusingly asking his mother Yinmei, "Black Leopard's done so much for our family. Why did you kill her?"

Tears glistening, Yinmei responded, "We need Black Leopard's flesh to cure your father and Yongzhi. They're sick and will die if they don't get meat. Only Black Leopard can save them . . . and, after all, she's getting old."

Not placated, Yonggang—who felt a deep affection for the hound— continued crying and shouting. Through anguished tears he retorted, "So, are we going to mix Grandma with herbal medicine and eat her too?"

"Quit talking nonsense!" snapped Masui. "There's no other way. You want your father and cousin to die?"

Yonggang's eyes widened in horror. Yinmei, tormented, paid her son no heed; instead, she bent her mind to getting food coupons. She cut off a small strip of dog flesh, and brought it to Sun Fu, surreptitiously seeking his advice. Recalling his role in old times as a well-treated henchman of the Lis, Sun Fu told her that a goldthread plantation had been established in Dafengbao. Most workers there were rightists or disgraced officers; word had it that some of them had grain and food tickets hoarded from their former positions that they traded for eggs or homespun cloth.

Though she had neither chicken nor eggs, Yinmei was a nimble weaver. She bought some cotton thread with the pittance of money she had set aside to buy salt, then sat at the loom night after night weaving sashes, knowing that Mawu was waiting, desperate for her aid. The oil lamp cast a flickering, dim light, projecting her wraith-like, ethereal shadow against both earth and wall. For a moment Yinmei stopped work, staring blankly at her shadows. She turned to Yonggang, who was lying in bed, "Let Ma teach you a character."

"What is it, Ma?" asked Yonggang, rubbing his eyes.

"It has four strokes," said Yinmei, "though no single one is upright. Anyone encountering it, young or old, will pay respect and bow with clasped hands. Can you guess what it is?"

Yonggang thought for a long while, his jaw cupped in his hands. What character could be so fierce that even his grandmother would pay homage? Finally, puzzled, he gave up, "I don't know … what is it?"

"The character is *fu* '父'… the *fu* in father." Yinmei beamed. "Remember it well. I'll have your uncle to teach you to write it, and then I'll test you." The six-year-old boy felt pleased that he had learned something new. And Yinmei, too, felt a surge of happiness, glad that she had taught her son this most important of characters.

Curiosity piqued, Yonggang asked earnestly, "Mum, what's my father like?"

"Tall, handsome, and good at shooting," Yinmei smiled cheerfully. "Much better looking than your Uncle." She set down her shuttle and staggered to her feet. From beneath the bed, she extracted a faded family portrait in which a dozen people—Li family members and wives, laborers and guests—clustered around Tao Jiuxiang.

"Is that my father?" asked Yonggang, pointing out a long-gowned man with a stern expression next to Tao Jiuxiang.

"That's him!" Yinmei exclaimed, delighted. "How did you know?"

Yonggang didn't reply. He gazed at Mawu for a spell, then pointed at a toddler in Tao Jiuxiang's arms and asked, "Is that me, Mum?"

"No," Yinmei replied, "That's your cousin Yongzhi . . . he was only two. You weren't born. That was our old house at Peppercorn Bend. Your Grandma built it for your father and me. Not long after the house was done, your father had that picture taken when Grandma and Uncle came to visit. Your Grandma was so nervous . . . she'd never had her picture taken before."

"When is my father coming back?" asked Yonggang for the ten-thousandth time. The boy had never seen Mawu, and with each passing day the ponderous confusion pressing down on his heart weighed more heavily.

Looking at the picture, Yinmei reassured, "Soon, very soon. Now go to bed."

"You come to bed, too, Mum," urged Yonggang. "I want you to sleep with me . . . I'm hungry."

"I need to weave for a while longer," Yinmei said, tucking the photo back under the bed. "Go to sleep right now: you won't feel hungry once you're asleep."

For three nights running, using a warped piece of oxhorn as a shuttle, Yinmei sat bent before the loom weaving a homemade cloth in traditional colors with a cat's-paw pattern, fashioning a beautiful cloth that could serve as a quilt or a curtain. She departed before dawn, taking the cloth. Yonggang waited anxiously. Well after sunset, she finally returned with a slab of pork and a handful of food and grain coupons.

A peculiar story surrounded this particular haunch of cured meat, one that stretched the bounds of credulity. The case of the cured meat—involving the two most disgraced, irredeemable reactionaries in all of Huangshui, men who had been paraded before the masses, struggled against, beaten, and imprisoned so often that most felt that the pair had become hopelessly addled and off kilter—was never solved.

III

The bizarre case of the cured meat began when the cadre re-education study group at the commune in Huangshui ended. The handful of counterrevolutionaries, reactionaries, rightists, and others among the "five black categories" were allowed to return to their homes on the mountainslopes and riverbanks. Only production team leader Tian of Dragon Decapitating Gorge was detained. Xia Liangxian had reported Tian to the commune Director, telling him that the Tian had forced people to sing "Sailing the Seas Depends on the Great Helmsman Mao" during Xia Qifa's funeral. The commune director was outraged and ordered Tian escorted to Wanxian County, where he was imprisoned alongside Mawu. "But I'm Chairman Mao's faithful and dedicated servant . . . ," the aggrieved Tian protested, stammering and gazing skyward as though praying for intervention as he was led away.

"Got what he deserved—damned headless bastard who doesn't know *yin* from *yang*," Xia Liangxian vindictively mused.

A cold wind sliced through the gorges. Filing out from the commune headquarters, their dirty quilts and sleeping mats bundled on their backs, the various "black elements" passed the canteen. Glancing in the doorway, Xia Liangxian spied three pieces of cured meat hanging from the rafters. He slowed down, purposefully clearing his throat. Daoist Master Wang responded and the two of them sidled off, ducking into the doorway unnoticed.

Later, the pair trekked along a ridge, clad in gray, cotton-padded coats, their faces tucked low in their collars. When they met an elderly cattle herder along the track, Wang wearily instructed, "Old man, if three kids pass don't spook them, okay?"

Annoyed, the old man brandished his whip toward the cattle, responding with a surly rasp, "Why the hell am I gonna scare a couple of kids?"

Not long thereafter, a trio of pig-tailed little boys in cotton-padded coats came running along the path, their lovely, bright faces covered with an oily sheen of sweat. When the old herdsman asked, "Where are you off to?" they didn't reply. The old man's curiosity was piqued. He suddenly recalled the faces he had seen half-concealed in the cotton-padded jackets: the two men were the former master of Azure Dragon Temple and the son of the *tima*! What kind of hellish trouble would a pair of notorious snake spirits and ox demons like them be making? Sensing something unusual, he called out, "Hey, where are you going?" But the three boys kept trotting into the teeth of the icy wind, not paying a whit of attention.

The old man wheeled his ox around, irascibly giving the creature's rear haunch a few sharp whips as he croaked hoarsely, "So you whipper-snappers won't answer an old man? I'll find out where you're off to!" Spurred by the pain, the ox lowed and trudged after the old fellow.

Famished and bone tired, Daoist Master Wang slumped down at the foot of a huge boulder, sheltering from the biting wind. Looking skyward, he sighed, "Lo! To seek the machinations of immortals in the primordial mysterious yellow above, one realizes that the myriad things are born of that primordial chaos . . . Ah, perhaps we shan't starve to death today, after all . . ."

"Indeed!" Xia Liangxian said grimly, huddled beside him on the ground.

After a while, like cheerful young students unburdened by schoolbags, the three lovely little boys came skipping along. With three swishes of a supple branch, Master Wang knocked them down, one after another; then and there, they transformed into three pieces of greasy, dark cured pork. Their braided pigtails were but palm fronds.

Xia Liangxian understood that Wang had used his arcane powers to animate and transmogrify, turning the pieces of cured pork into little boys who had followed them. Excitedly blowing on his palms, the young man exclaimed, "Your powers are truly great!" Revitalized, his handsome eyes flashed; Xia Liangxian gathered horse mulberry branches and kindled a fire.

> *With a pearl of bewilderment in my mouth,*
> *I turn Heaven and Earth upside-down.*

Chanting as he smelled the savory crackling pork, Wang sighed contentedly, "Sometimes a wolf needs to show his fangs to get a meal!" The sorrow creasing his face was gone, replaced by an anticipatory relish. The two sat around the fire.

"Someone's coming!" Xia Liangxian said abruptly, hearing approaching footsteps. Hurriedly, they covered the cooking slab of pork with branches and hid the remaining two into their clothing. Leaves rustled in the soughing wind as the old oxherd bustled over breathlessly.

"Where are they?" the old man asked doubtfully, his chest heaving. "Have those three kids come by?"

Wang was tongue-tied. Given the nature of the spell, if he denied the existence of the boys the cured pork would disappear once and for all! Therefore, changing tack, he asked gently, "Good old fellow, where's your ox?"

"On the slope grazing." The old man inhaled, then sniffed again. With his toe, he nudged aside the ashes revealing a seared haunch of meat dripping grease, giving off a most delectable aroma. Overwhelmed with mingled amazement, suspicion, and wide-eyed excitement, he gazed at the meat and rebuked, "You can fool my eyes, but not my nose! Where'd you steal this from?"

Seeing the Daoist master hesitate, Xia Liangxian cut in, "It's not stolen."

With a wary and hostile sideward glance, the old oxherd asked, "Well, where's it from then? That's a mighty fine piece of meat!"

Wang said, "My family preserved this remarkable piece of meat for so long that it became a spirit. One evening, it escaped and wrought havoc, laughing and kicking up a ruckus, eating all the rice cakes in the pot, setting fires and causing harm. But we lured it out of the house and now we're incinerating it in this "five thunder" fire. Once it's burned to ashes the spirit will cause no more harm."

"What kind of fool do you take me for?" the old man snorted. "Nobody believes your drivel!"

Screwing up his courage, Xia Liangxian fanned the flames and pushed the slab of pork further into the fire so it hissed and crackled: "Listen, old man! Can you hear the cries of the children? Better not eat this meat, or they'll be incarnated inside of you and take possession of your body."

Hearing the crackling of the fire, the old man said, "Yeah, it sounds like the cries of children, but I've got gall. If you aren't gonna eat, I will. When I'm through, I won't tell a soul."

"Let's eat together then!" Wang smiled bitterly. "Since you're not afraid, we'll just tuck in, too."

Sitting fireside under the sheltered overhang of the boulder, the three tore the cured meat into strips that they devoured with gusto. The old man ate his fill; beads of fat dripped down from the corners of his mouth. Then, hearing his plow ox low in the distance, he reluctantly rose, shooting a yearning glance back at the remaining pork. Fearing that dholes or jackals might get to the creature, he sped off; still greedily chewing a gobbet of meat, he stuffed the rind of his cured meat in a pocket.

Xia Liangxian and Wang waited for a spell. Relieved that the old man didn't return, they parted, heading their separate ways, the rest of the cured meat carefully concealed in their clothes.

After hurrying along the uneven paths, up ridges and down into gorges, Xia Liangxian finally arrived at the crossroads leading to Peppercorn Bend. Ahead of him he saw a familiar figure and recognized his sister, Yinmei. Affectionately, he hailed, "Yinmei, what are doing in these parts?"

Halting and looking back at her brother, Yinmei sighed, "I'm off to the

Huangshui Post Office to send Mawu food and grain coupons."

Xia Liangxian grunted in response. Lowering his head, he found a remote, unpeopled bamboo grove. Hidden momentarily, he used a bamboo strip to cut a hunk off the cured meat, which he hid in a sleeve. As Yinmei approached, he took it out quickly and handed it to her.

Yinmei was stunned, "Where do you get that pork?"

Nervously, Xia Liangxian explained, "It's not stolen."

"Where is it from?"

Xia Liangxian whispered, "Just cook it, okay?" Petrified of prying eyes, he dared not linger. Hands atremble, he bolted off toward Dragon Decapitating Gorge.

Yinmei knew her brother had just endured a month's indoctrination and punishment at the study group and must have obtained the meat through crooked means. Still, in her present straits, she had no intention of giving it back. She hid it in her sleeve and hurried back to Gengguping. At dusk, just before she reached home, she collapsed. Her legs felt soft as cotton; her clothes were soaked with cold sweat.

Chapter Twenty-Five

I

Night fell without the return of his mother. Yonggang grew ever more hungry and fearful. Masui and his wife returned from the fields to discover Yongzhi dead, his stomach horribly swollen, shining with the grotesque glow of dropsy. Black Leopard's flesh had not saved the boy. Tearfully, Masui and He rolled his corpse in a bamboo sleeping mat. Tao Jiuxiang, plunged in bottomless sorrow, watched. Yonggang felt for his cousin, but he was even more concerned for his mother. He lit a torch and, step by step, headed along the path toward Huangshui. Before long, he found an unmoving figure crumpled on the mountain trail.

Seeing the torchlight, Yinmei struggled to her feet. In surprise, Yonggang cried, "Mum?!"

"I'm dizzy. My heart is racing and my limbs have gone slack," Yinmei panted. Though only six, tiny but stout-hearted Yonggang supported his mother back to the compound at a snail's pace, bearing most of her weight.

Yinmei was skinny and weak, with an empty basket on her back. She whispered to her son, "I exchanged my weaving for food and grain coupons at the farm."

"How much did you get?"

"Five pounds," Yinmei answered with satisfaction. "I've sent it to your father."

"Yes. Your father was sick when he wrote two months ago. I don't know what kind of shape he's in now."

Yonggang blurted, "Mum, Yongzhi's dead."

Yinmei, already pale as a ghost, grew silent. Stumbling into the house, she collapsed into bed. "I need water."

Yonggang brought her a gourd ladle half-filled with cold water.

After drinking, Yinmei raised her head. From the greenish tint in Yonggang's eyes, she knew that the pitiful child hadn't eaten all day. Slowly, she extracted a long, black slab from her sleeve.

"Oh, cured meat! Where's it from?" cried Yonggang, his jaw dropping in amazement.

"Hush! It's not stolen. Your Uncle gave it to me. Now, boil and eat it right away . . . Have they buried Yongzhi?" Yinmei asked, slumping back into the bed.

Yonggang answered, "Yes." He put the slab of cured pork into the pot, added water, placed a lid on the three-legged clay pot and put it on the fire. As he added kindling, he shuddered, recalling his dead cousin Yonggang wrapped up tight in a bamboo mat on his father's shoulder. Tao Jiuxiang had instructed Masui to bury her grandson well out of sight of the homestead.

Faintly, Yinmei advised, "Overcook it, make sure it's done. Otherwise it will be hard to chew and that would be an awful waste." Her eyelids drooped. "When it's done, tear off a piece for Grandma."

Yonggang said, "What about Uncle and Auntie? They're crying over my cousin's death."

Closing her eyes, Yinmei said, "There's so little to divide. Just bring it to Grandma. She'll know how to parse it up."

Wandering over to the pot, Yonggang peeked in and said, "Let me see if it's well-done yet."

Yinmei glanced at her son and said, "Just a minute. Don't tell anyone where the meat's from—otherwise your uncle will be in big trouble."

"Okay," said Yonggang. Then he asked eagerly, "How 'bout now? Is it ready yet?"

"Almost. Just smell that fragrance."

"It smells delicious," said Yonggang, inhaling deeply.

"It's almost done," said Yinmei. "Just close your eyes. Remember that four-stroke character we were talking about the other night. First say it, then write it in the air . . . then the meat will be well done."

"The character is *fu* . . . father." Yonggang closed his eyes. With his index finger dancing through air, he traced the strokes. Then abruptly he opened his eyes, walked to the pot, and, licking his lips, said, "Now, it's done for sure."

"Careful," Yinmei warned from behind. "It's hot. Can you ladle it out yourself?"

"Don't worry, Mum," returned Yonggang. He stood on a woven-grass stool and fished out the meat with a gourd ladle, carefully carrying it over to his mother. Mother and son eagerly breathed in the delectable fragrance wafting from the cured pork.

"Oh, it smells so good!" Yonggang reached out and grabbed the slab of meat, but, scalded, quickly withdrew his little hand with a sharp yelp.

Yinmei, revitalized by the delicious aroma, cautioned, "Wait a few minutes for it to cool." Yonggang set the meat on the table and went over to tug his mother upright.

Mouth watering, unable to restrain himself a moment longer, Yonggang hustled back to the table. "I'm sure it's okay now." But all that was on the table was an empty calabash ladle. There was no trace of the meat.

"Where's the meat?" he cried, his eyes almost falling out of his head as he desperately circled the table, searching. "The meat? Where's the meat?"

How bizarre! Yinmei asked, "Did you misplace it?"

"No!" replied Yonggang, increasingly alarmed.

Yinmei staggered out of bed, rising panic driving her to her feet. Mother and son looked around the room for the missing pork. Keen-eyed Yonggang saw Zhou Taiwang's dog Banzi gnawing on something behind the door. "The cured pork!" he screamed, seizing a piece of kindling and flailing it wildly as he rushed the hound. Wagging its tail, the hound leapt to one side and avoided the attack, the hunk of meat firmly between its teeth. Yinmei, too, grabbed a log and went after Banzi, but the dog fled through the door, disappearing into the darkness outside. Yonggang gave chase, but the beast was lost in the night. Outside the doorjamb, Yonggang fell to his knees and burst into tears of anguish, choking, "Banzi! Banzi!"

II

Faint with hunger, Tao Jiuxiang had slept intermittently throughout the day. Now, in the pitch dark of night, she finally emerged, woozy and disoriented. She vaguely recalled that Yinmei had gone to Huangshui that morning, and didn't know if her daughter-in-law had returned. Clutching Yonggang's little hands, she asked gently, "Why are you crying, my grandson?"

"Banzi stole my thing," Yonggang wailed, contracting into a fetal ball.

Zhou Taiwang came out of his room and saw the howling child folded up in a corner of the courtyard amid the spiderwebs and refuse. Curious, he asked, "What did Banzi take?"

"You'd know if I told you," Yonggang blubbered.

"Banzi! C'mon, Banzi!"

Hearing his master's voice, Banzi trotted out of the darkness wagging its tail. Freshly sated with the cured pork that he had bolted down under cover of the night, Banzi contentedly sauntered toward Zhou Taiwang. At the sight of the hound, Yonggang's agonized cries redoubled.

"What did Banzi take?" Zhou Taiwang demanded angrily.

"He stole my . . ." Yonggang agonized.

"Your what?" pressed Zhou Taiwang.

"He stole my . . . precious little meat bauble," Yonggang sniveled miserably.

"What? Where did you get meat?" Zhou asked dubiously.

"I just had some . . ." said Yonggang.

Eyes widening, Zhou Taiwang called the dog over. He dropped to a knee, and, placing his nose right beside the dog's maw, inhaled deeply several times. "Yup, sure smells like he's just eaten some meat." He cuffed Banzi in the side of the head, snarling, "Odious cur! So you come across a windfall and don't share with your master!" Twisting her head to one side, Banzi yelped and retreated.

"Since when do you have meat?" Zhou Taiwang snapped, stalking toward Yinmei's room.

"Is your Mother back?" Masui asked blankly, bereft at his son's death.

"She's back . . ." Frightened Yonggang flung himself into his grandma's arms. They all followed Zhou Taiwang into the room.

Staring blankly, Yinmei sat on the ground. When they entered, she merely shook her head, sighed, and muttered incoherently. Yonggang and Masui picked her up and helped her back to the bed.

"Did you exchange the weaving for coupons?" whispered Tao Jiuxiang as she sat down on the edge of the bed, her wrinkles quivering.

"Yes," answered Yinmei feebly. She looked at Yonggang's dirt-smudged face and said softly, "I traded for a baked potato, too—roasted in the ashes. I could smell it from a long ways off . . ." Though he wasn't sure if his mother was telling truth or just hallucinating, Yonggang's mouth watered. As Yinmei cast a final piteous glance at her son, she closed her eyes and fell faint.

Seeing the lid off three-legged clay pot on the stove, Zhou Taiwang leaned forward for a noseful and then greedily swallowed one big ladleful after another. The fragrance of cured meat filled the room. "Just right—not too hot, not too cold," he said, smacking his lips with satisfaction before firing an accusatory question at Yonggang: "So whose cured pork did your mom steal?"

Yonggang snorted, "It wasn't stolen."

"Damn it! " Zhou Taiwang murmured to himself. "I'll just ask others at work tomorrow and solve this case."

The following day Yinmei did not rise and go to work. Rather, she lay in bed all morning. Around noon, she finally stirred, deliberately moving her limbs and opening her eyes. She watched the particles of dust in the sunlight slanting through the window. With an effort, she stammered, "There's a . . . four-stroke character. Though no single stroke is upright . . . anyone . . . young or old, will pay respect and bow with clasped hands. Can you guess?"

Promptly, Yonggang answered, "I've got it, Mum. It's 'father'." Heedless of the consequences, faithful Yonggang dashed out to the fields and dug up several seed potatoes. He boiled them and took a bowl to his mother.

Yinmei held the bowl and ate a single tiny potato. She raised her hands, and, with a sigh of deep satisfaction issuing from deep within, exclaimed "Ahhh!" Then her breath stopped. Yonggang looked on in horror as his mother's face paled. Sitting upright beside the bed, he nearly cried his eyes out.

At dusk, the mountainfolk returned from the fields, hoes and rakes over their shoulders. Strange rumors had circulated that day, talk that the old *tima*'s daughter, Yinmei, had conjured a slab of cured pork from thin air. If not, then where had it come from? Nobody had meat these days. Production team leader Qin Longping instructed Zhou Taiwang, "Publically interrogate her when you get back tonight. We'll get to the bottom of this." Along with the others, Zhou Taiwang, inwardly mulling how to conduct the investigation, hurried back to Gengguping.

Yinmei's room was silent. Several neighbors barged in; through the half-opened bedcurtains they spied a supine figure. When Zhou Taiwang's wife came forward for a closer look, she recoiled in fear: A corpse lay in bed, its face covered with rice-straw paper. "Dear gods!" She loosed a piercing scream, as cold sweat began to course down her brow. Unnerved, the neighbors departed and headed to Tao Jiuxiang's room, where they found the "old ghost-spawn witch" sitting at the stove, her head nodding down to her chest, little Yonggang clasped in her arms.

"Li Yonggang," Zhou Taiwang addressed the child with formal authority. He dragged Yonggang from his Grandma's arms. "Since your mother's dead, you need to confess: where was that slab of cured pork from?"

Terrified, Yonggang bawled, "My Mum brought it home."

Zhou Taiwang interrogated, "Who did she steal it from?"

Yonggang answered, "The meat's not stolen. She just brought it back with her." Recalling his mother's warning, he swallowed the word "Uncle."

A cunning light danced in the bulging eyes of Sun Xiaoxiao, Shi Eryang's wife. She asked, "So from what homestead's tree branch was the cured pork hanging?"

Shaking his head, Yonggang sobbed, "I don't know."

"Nonsense!" Eryang spat, turning to Tao Jiuxiang, "And you? Do you know where the meat's from?"

"I don't know." Though her eyelid drooped with weary sadness, Tao Jiuxiang held her gray-haired head high.

"She's dead now. You didn't get the details last night. How are we going to clear things up now?" Sun Fu sighed.

Zhou Taiwang regretted that he hadn't got to the bottom of the mystery the previous night. Hoping to follow the vine and get to the melon, Zhou had never expected that Yinmei would die so soon, taking with her the secret of the cured pork. All of the wretched starvelings in the fields expected some resolution, but it seemed none was forthcoming. He searched Tao Jiuxiang's room thoroughly, but found nothing. The inquisitors then ransacked Yinmei's chill room, vainly turning pots and bowls upside-down. Finally, empty-handed and frustrated, they dispersed.

III

Like a dark spirit, Xia Liangxian appeared at Gengguping. He had returned to Dragon Decapitating Gorge with the cured pork and told the story to his mother. Both mother and son were so anxious that the old oxherd would turn informer and tattle on him. Feeling forebodings of further disaster, after a single night Old Mother Xia urged her son to hide out at Gengguping.

As Masui nailed together several wooden slats to fashion a simple, makeshift coffin, he was a surprised to see Xia Liangxian slip into the yard in the moonlight.

"Brother-in-law, who's that for?" whispered Xia Liangxian.

"Yonggang's mother—she died this morning," Masui replied bitterly, overwhelmed with sorrow and guilt.

Xia Liangxian stood dumbstruck in the courtyard. His threadbare, rumpled trousers were caked with dust. His addled mind was already askew, but now he felt even more puzzled: Just yesterday his sister had seemed fine when he'd met her along the road! Hearing Yonggang piteously call, "Uncle," then, seeing Yinmei's stiff corpse laid out on the bed, the finality of it all became clear. A spasm violently contracted his angular, handsome face.

Wracked by sorrow, he thought of his sister's grim plight since she left Dragon Decapitating Gorge to marry Mawu. So little happiness, so much torment! How quickly the luster in her beautiful long dark hair had faded, her bright eyes grown dull, her healthy cheeks become sunken and sallow! So fleeting her grim life!

Sweeping down from the surrounding ridges, the mountain winds fiercely howled and groaned.

Tao Jiuxiang, clinging to the wisdom of the ancestors, believed that a properly chosen site for a man's grave could benefit his household and his ancestors; the location of woman's grave could bring prosperity to her in-laws' family and descendants. Sorrowfully, she asked Xia Liangxian to determine an auspicious location for Yinmei's grave, one that might bring future good fortune to the Lis. Amid tears and sighs, Xia Liangxian wandered the hills, finally selecting a site for Yinmei's grave not far from the stone tower. Regretting that he had failed to bring incense, candles, or sacrificial straw paper—all basic necessities for a funeral rite—he showed Tao Jiuxiang the spot.

It was a hidden, recessed patch of land tucked between several hillocks and mounds. No matter which direction the people approached from, they could only reach it by heading downhill to the floor of the basin. The following morning, Masui humbly went to production team leader Longping, entreating him for permission to bury Xia Yinmei on the chosen site. For a sunless fortnight, the mountains had been enveloped in clouds and gloom. Uncharacteristically magnanimous, Qin Longping promptly took out his seal and stamped the Li family's application for the burial plot.

When Masui returned to Gengguping, he found Tao Jiuxiang holding a bowl half-filled of water, gently dribbling droplets of water into Yinmei's mouth, and softly encouraging, "Daughter-in-law, drink some water. In the next life, you'll be reborn in a happy and blessed place . . ."

Since Yinmei had married Mawu at eighteen, she had endured no end of suffering, yet never had a single complaint passed her lips. What a splendid, virtuous woman! Tears brooked down the creased corners of Tao Jiuxiang's eyes. Beholding her daughter-in-law's frail, skinny limbs, Tao Jiuxiang placed a hand on the coffin and said achingly, "Your husband's coming . . . why not let him have a last look at you?"

Afraid of being seen, Xia Liangxian urged Masui to commence the digging and ceremony at once, while the others housed in the Lis' former home were toiling in the fields. According to tradition, the coffin's procession could neither change direction nor stop along the route; otherwise, the deceased would be visited with great torment in the netherworld. Xia Liangxian and Masui wrapped Yinmei in a sheet and laid her in the coffin. They were about to close the lid when, all of a sudden, Tao Jiuxiang gave a distressed cry, "Wait . . ." She rushed over and slipped something into one of Yinmei's hands. In old times, people placed silver coins in the hands of the dead when they were buried. But who had silver these days? Curious, Masui looked closer and found that it was just Yinmei's favorite black handkerchief. His eyes reddened.

There was not a soul outside. Xia Liangxian and Masui lifted the rough coffin and carried it out the gate.

They passed through a copse that gave off a fresh, sourish bosky scent.

Still anxious about the cured meat, Xia Liangxian kept a vigilant watch on the path. Ahead, emerging from the woods and trudging along the stony ridge he saw a bareheaded man in a raggedy cotton-padded coat. There was something familiar about the figure. Restlessly, he asked, "Isn't that my brother-in-law?"

Masui looked up and gasped. For a moment he seemed paralyzed. Then he exclaimed, "Mawu! Heavens! Mawu is back!"

Yonggang had been trailing the two pallbearers, dragging two spades and sobbing. When he heard the name "Mawu," however, he let the tools fall to the ground. He stopped crying and stared fixedly at the stranger. The stranger adjusted a shabby bedroll on his shoulders. Raising his wrinkled face, he gazed toward the burial procession, bewilderment and horror in his eyes.

Following tradition, Masui could neither set down the coffin nor stop walking. Slowly advancing, with a flustered quaver he called out, "Brother?..." Tears cascaded from his eyes.

In this tragic fashion, after five years in prison, Mawu was finally reunited with his wife. Dropping his bedroll, he rushed forward, placing his gnarled hands on the coffin, and asked dazedly, "Masui, who is...?"

"Yinmei. She starved to death." Masui's voice quivered.

"My sister died bitterly, but we cannot stop on the way to the grave. Yonggang, greet your father," Xia Liangxian said sourly. "Quick!"

Yonggang's dilated eyes were locked on his father. "Pa," he spoke tentatively, tears spilling out. Mawu scanned Yonggang's small face.

"Liangxian found an auspicious site to bury my sister-in-law—a recessed spot he says is like a natural lotus throne. For once, Longping didn't try to cause trouble and gave approval for us to bury Yinmei," Masui explained piteously.

A film of despair covered Mawu's eyes. Disconsolate, he picked up a spade and took his son's little hand. Ambling behind the moving coffin, he cried hoarsely, "Yinmei, I've failed you..."

IV

A chill wind swept over the grave. Silent against the gray sky, the tower watched its old inhabitants, its unbreachable aura long gone.

Tearfully, Xia Liangxian opened the flimsy lid of the coffin and said, "You've come back just in time for a last look." Mawu set down the spades, knelt before the coffin, and carefully unrolled the mat to reveal his wife's rigid corpse. Wracked with anguish, he saw from Yinmei's tightly sealed eyes that his wife had changed a great deal in both spirit and form. Masui stood at his brother's side looking at his sister-in-law. From Yinmei's tightly closed eyes two droplets of water rolled down her cheeks. Thinking he must be imagining things, Masui rubbed his bleary eyes. But it was true: this wasn't the well-water Tao Jiuxiang had dripped into Yinmei's mouth, the dead woman's eyes were moist with tears! Xia Liangxian saw them, too. He sobbed, "Yinmei, your husband is back. Sister, depart in peace..."

Mawu placed his forehead against the coffin. Woefully, he asked, "What . . . what did she say in the end?"

Masui whispered, "Ask Yonggang."

Yonggang murmured, "Mum taught me to write a character."

"What character?" asked Mawu gloomily.

"A four-stroke character. Though no single stroke is vertical or horizontal, anyone encountering it, young or old, will pay their respects and bow with clasped hands," Yonggang recited.

Bewildered, Mawu looked at Yonggang and asked, "How is it pronounced?"

Tears streaming down his cheeks, Yonggang sobbed, "Mum said it's pronounced . . . 'Father'."

Mawu rewrapped Yinmei in the bamboo sleeping mat and clutched his son tightly, asking, "Where's Yongyu?"

"In Chongqing with her mother. Eating food from the stores in Chongqing—least she didn't die of hunger like the poor kids here. Just look at Yongzhi, my little son . . . he left this world just before Yinmei." Masui raised a sleeve to wipe his tears.

"What happened?" Mawu asked.

"He starved to death, too. We buried him the day before yesterday," Masui choked out a few painful words of explanation.

"What about our mother?" asked Mawu, trembling.

"She's alive," Masui said bitterly.

"Listen, brothers. Let's hurry. If folks get back from the fields and see us here tongues will start wagging and there'll be trouble," Xia Liangxian urged, worried about being spotted. He shot a guilty glance at Mawu, then nailed the coffin shut.

The sun was setting. Above the horizon spread a yellowish blush tinged with slate blue. A black eagle circled the recessed grave twice, then soared toward the clouds, bearing Yinmei's spirit into the firmament.

Time seemed to halt.

Calmly, Mawu, eyes cold as late autumn frost, looked from the coffin to listless and sallow Masui, then to the ashen and fearful Liangxian, finally resting on his solitary son—all skin, sinew, and bone. Masui handed him a hoe. Soon, the ridges echoed with the sounds the three men digging into the hard, rocky earth.

Darkness seeped into, then overwhelmed, the dusk. Shadowy figures emerged from the direction of the tower. Xia Liangxian ducked into a clump of bushes. Returning from work, the laborers pointed and muttered. As they passed close, Sun Fu broke the silence, hailing, "You're back?" Having long worked so long for the Lis as a hired hand, he recognized the bald fellow for who he was.

"I'm back," replied Mawu coldly, gripping his hoe.

"Good, good to see you're back," Sun Fu said, with a melancholy sigh.

The neighbors from Gengguping silently looked down at Mawu, their expressions betraying a variety of emotions—contempt, curiosity, and bewilderment. Nobody else spoke. After a few moments, they scattered, returning home, each with their own thoughts.

Full darkness now encompassed the mountains and valleys. With the efforts of the three men a mound of earth rose, covering Yinmei's coffin. Scrawny and dirty, Mawu stood beside his wife's tomb like a skeletal, dried out tree. Wearily, he nudged Yonggang, saying, "The rest of you better head home."

Xia Liangxian wiped away sweat and tears, but did not leave.

Masui added some earth to the tumulus, then whispered, "Yonggang, stay with your father." Rubbing dirt off with a sleeve, he left with Xia Liangxian.

Emerging from behind a cloudhead, the moon cast down its clean, cold light. In the moonlight Yonggang discovered several clusters of wildflowers; he picked them and set them at the foot of the mound. Mawu lifted Yonggang up in an embrace, touching his son's little face with a gnarled hand. Sobbing, he gasped, "Your Mum is gone . . . she's left us . . ." Resting his head on his father's shoulder, Yonggang finally relaxed his tight-wound little body and wailed, crying as though his heart would break. From this perch, Yonggang saw through his tears two figures emerging from the direction of the homestead, stumbling up a nearby slope. Yonggang recognized his neighbors, Wang Donghe and his wife.

Wang Donghe carried a rolled-up quilt. His wife followed, weeping, a hoe in her hands. Though just a child, Yonggang was no stranger to death: he had seen a number of folks buried. Yet still he felt afraid, understanding that in the bundle was the corpse of the Wang's second son, a rascal who used to shoot at him with a slingshot. In recent days, however, all the boy would do was lay splayed out on the ground, trying to warm his limbs in the sunlight. Grimly, Yonggang asked, "Dad, I'm starving. Am I going to die?"

Hugging his son, Mawu reassured him, "Yonggang, you won't die. Is there anything to eat at home?"

"Nothing. Nothing at all," Yonggang sighed like an adult. More and more tombs mushroomed around Gengguping. In the darkness and shadow, phosphorescent lights appeared here and there. Yonggang raised his emaciated face and told Mawu: "Grandma said, the red lights are the earthly gods and goddesses, and the bluish-green lights are ghost fires. Try to steer clear of them. The light of dead children is faint green. Dad, if I die, I'll miss you and grandma. If you see my ghost swinging from a tree branch, you shouldn't be afraid."

V

With a frosty expression etched on his face, Mawu entered Yinmei's room in a wing of his former homestead and looked down at the bed they had once shared. Dejectedly, he flung himself down. Only then did he notice his mother, Tao Jiuxiang, whitened and timeworn, sitting in a corner. "My son has returned," she murmured, wiping tears from her wizened face.

Rising to embrace her, Mawu called, "Ma!" The two held each other and wept.

"How you've aged!" Tao Jiuxiang exclaimed, her squint fixed on Mawu's gaunt visage. Keenly aware that both times Mawu had departed from home the family had failed to take good care of his wives, she was assailed by guilt. Looking at her firstborn, she said in a quivering voice, "I'm weak and useless. I've let you down."

"Brother-in-law, go to Masui's rooms and have some potatoes." Xia Liangxian, haggard to the point of faintness, whispered as he entered. Afraid of being found, he had kept hidden in Masui's rooms. At Tao Jiuxiang's behest, they had dug up a few dozen seed potatoes under cover of darkness, then cleaned and boiled them.

Mawu supported Tao Jiuxiang to Masui's house, where Masui's wife He offered her tottering mother-in-law a potato. Tao Jiuxiang accepted the hot potato. Wagging her head to and fro as she ate, the old woman struggled to choke down the potato. Addled with hunger, weary with sorrow, they had lost all sense of taste and any relish for food. After bolting down some potatoes, Xia Liangxian wrapped straw and rags around a branch to fashion a torch, then softly told Yonggang, "I'm leaving and going someplace far away."

"Where are you going, Uncle?"

"I'll wander the country," downcast Xia Liangxian muttered. Tall and thin, with high cheekbones and deep-set eyes, over the years he had come to resemble his father.

Shrunken belly half-full of potatoes, Masui raised his head and said with concern, "Though you've been burdened with bad fortune and might run into trouble here, you're sure to meet a worse fate if you flee. You might as well stay."

Xia Liangxian said, "Anyplace is better than here." Yinmei was dead. He couldn't hide in Gengguping for long. He had made up is mind to leave Huangshui altogether. This place was a living hell. As long he didn't starve to death, he cared little what he did or where he wandered.

Furrowing his brow, Mawu asked, "Will Yonggang's grandfather-in-law be okay with that?"

The room grew quiet. Masui's wife said, "The old *tima* has been laid to rest."

A frosty light radiated from Mawu's eyes.

Tao Jiuxiang asked, "What did your mother say?"

Xia Liangxian said in a low voice, "My old mother just told me to hide." Ever since he'd taken revenge on the Qins, folks in Huangshui treated him like an evil spirit. Whenever he passed a household's gate, the family hurriedly hung a ghost-repelling sword on the door. At present, however, he was more worried that the old oxherd would snitch on him to the commune authorities, causing him to be punished again.

The moon hid behind the clouds. The courtyard was enveloped in the shadow of the surrounding mountains. With a parting glance, Xia Liangxian lit the torch. He bent down and hugged Yonggang, saying, "I'll come see you." Then he opened the door and left the house, swallowed by the night.

Yonggang silently trailed his uncle out of the gate, but he could see nothing beyond the tall shadows of the swaying trees.

Inside, Mawu broke the painful silence, announcing, "Now that I've come back, I'm never going to leave again. In the future, we live and die together."

The mountain path snaked into the forest. The faint torchlight only extended a few steps into the dense ground fog. Ahead it was pitch dark. After leaving Gengguping, Xia Liangxian walked till daybreak. He passed through the valley of Inkblack Creek intending to follow those mysterious waters and see where they led.

Though mountainfolk spoke in hushed tones of the fell spirits and evil creatures dwelling in the grottoes and niches of the slopes and vales, Xia Liangxian walked unafraid, not sparing these demons a single thought. He had made his peace with ghosts and spirits, demons and gods; it was among the living that he felt ill at ease. He yearned for the cries of devils and the halloos of deities—for he belonged in their company. Soon, he hoped to attend a banquet of the spirits and eat his fill. The moon emerged and then hid; the sun rose and set. For two miserable and lonely days, Xia Liangxian walked without encountering another human.

The air was tacky with fog and rain. The waterfall cascading down into the gorge sprayed water in all directions. Lost in thought, Xia Liangxian stood on the lip of the gorge. Through misty eyes, he gazed at green slopes and terraced fields as the elevation fell in the distance. He sighed. As a young boy, his father had changed his middle name in order to mark him as his successor, to keep the Xia family's incense burning and the ritual instruments in good fettle. But as a headstrong young man he had recklessly used his powers, prompting his father to excommunicate him. He was no longer a *tima*. He was no longer anything. He had no place in this world.

Islands of green-clad mountain peaks jutted from the seas of clouds and mist. Hesitating, kneeling tearfully, Xia Liangxian gazed in the direction of Dragon Decapitating Gorge. Within the past month, his father and sister had died, one after another. If he left these mountains, he didn't know when or if he would return. And if he failed to come back, who would take care for his old mother? He cast himself on the ground, wailing, as if hoping to unburden himself of the cumbersome despair that weighed down his heart. The crabgrass beside him was soaked with tears.

Finally, he rose and retraced his steps, heading homeward.

Two soldiers sat at the stove in the Xia homestead, discussing what to do next. The township government had solved the case of the cured pork and sent them to arrest Xia Liangxian. Old Mother Xia, however, adamantly refused to tell them where her son had gone. After waiting a full day, the two were on the verge of leaving when the suspected criminal walked through the door.

Seeing the soldiers, dirty and disheveled Xia Liangxian bolted into the briar patch where his father had first taught him shamanic mudras and chants, peeling off his clothes as he ran. Amid the brambles in the horse mulberry copse, he began to dance like a madman, flailing his limbs as he incanted in a raspy voice:

> *Black gods of heaven, black spirits of earth,*
> *Come forth in these black months of black death and black birth.*
> *Black soldiers and black horses,*
> *Black generals marshal your forces.*
> *Bind these demons, bar their devilish path;*
> *With the five thunders mete out your wrath.*
> *Black five miles east and black five miles west,*
> *Black five miles north and black five miles south.*
> *Black in the center, Black are these days,*
> *Protect me and keep these wicked demons away!*

Seeing Xia Liangxian's gaunt but well-proportioned limbs shuddering violently in his seizure-like dance, they dared not advance to arrest him. They simply stood there gawking, watching the stark-naked man gyrate. On and on Xia Liangxian danced until he collapsed on his back. The wind howled down from the ridge. Still, the soldiers hesitated. Guardedly, one of them finally grabbed the discarded tattered shirt and placed it over the Xia Liangxian's stiff arcing penis, which proudly stood erect like a bull's horn. Then, they arrested him and dragged him away. As he was led back to the Huangshui commune, every time one of Xia Liangxian's limbs twitched or trembled, one of the soldiers drove a rifle butt into his ribs.

Chapter Twenty-Six

I

When Mawu returned home, the other mountainfolk watched him secretly and found that though he was barely forty he already had patchy, sparse gray hair, and looked stooped and aged. Folk began to say that Mawu's spirit had been broken: the sharp-toothed tiger had finally become a sheep. Yet there was still something unsettling about the man. When he went out to cut firewood for the cookstove, he wore a blank, icy expression and spoke to nobody. When he brought the kindling home, the other families living in the Lis former home on Gengguping heard the whetstone grinding away for hours. When they peeked in his doorway, they found the labor-reformed criminal sitting before a fire, hunched over the whetstone sharpening axes, knives, sickles, and machetes, one after another. In the firelight, reflections of the rust-colored blades flickered on his brow. Once again, the hearts of the onlookers began to quake.

Before long production team leader Qin Longping informed the folk at Gengguping that ten men must report to Huangshui for heavy labor, carrying grain. The Huangshui commune was unhappy with Longping's report that a number of people had died of hunger, and ordered him to work harder to compensate for his irresponsibility. Longping was forced to attend a struggle session and sent to collect manure from the commune's oxen. Although Longping felt ill used, he put aside old enmities and set out to undertake the task with other production team members, including Mawu and Masui.

Each day found them toiling for more than ten hours, using wheelbarrows to transport rice from the granaries in Huangshui to Fengjie City; then, they refilled the Huangshui granary with rice husks and straw, which they covered with a layer of rice for the upper-level cadres to inspect. They worked from early morning till night, leaving them bone weary with hunger and exhaustion.

The cadre held a county-level "exchanging collective experiences" conference in Huangshui. The Director of the commune strode up to the stage, tearing his overcoat open to reveal bold characters in red, reading, "We swear to become number one in productivity!" A glutton by nature, Longping could not endure hunger. When he loaded the wheelbarrows, he surreptitiously stuffed rice into his tall rubber boots along the way. Once, however, as Longping emerged from the granary gate he stumbled over the high threshold and the rice spilled from his boots, prompting the clerk to scream out in alarm. Longping's blood-shot eyes bugged out as though he wanted to murder somebody. Frantic, he cursed, "So I'm a goddamned thief, eh? Your fucking rice fell into my boot as I was working. How can you blame me?"

For his part, Mawu kept his head down and worked at a deliberate cadence, maintaining a well-trained silence. But by the time the grain transport work was complete, all of Huangshui knew that Li Mawu was back, occasioning no end of curious speculation.

One misty afternoon a group of people suddenly swarmed into the courtyard at Gengguping. In a familiar manner, they went directly to the room where Mawu and Yonggang lived. A thin fellow came forward, beads of sweat running down his forehead, his raggedy cotton coat unbuttoned to reveal a sun-browned chest. Seeing Tao Jiuxiang at the stove, he folded his hands together in respect and said, "Madam, do you remember me? I hear that Mawu is back."

Tao Jiuxiang fretted over her wifeless son Mawu and her motherless grandson Yonggang from morning till night. Though she seemed an addled old woman, whenever the fire was about to die out she added kindling and whenever the crock of drinking water was nearly empty she filled it with the gourd ladle. She raised her eyelids without offering a greeting, vigilantly squinting at the visitors.

Mawu entered from the back door. The speaker looked like one of the Pengs from Peppercorn Bend. Astonished, he whispered, "What's going on?"

"Mawu," came a warm greeting from behind the fellow. Gaunt Zeng Laomao, gray-haired and sun-browned, wearing a dirty blue collared tunic, stepped forward and offered Mawu a cigarette. In the past, Laomao, the oft-drunk plowshare maker, had addressed Mawu as "Captain Li" or "Mayor Li"; today he called Mawu by his given name for the first time.

"Oh, Laomao," Mawu grinned, accepting the cigarette and returning his greeting.

"You're finally back," sighed Zeng Laomao. He then added, "Tomorrow we're storming the granary at Peppercorn Bend to take the rice. You in?" When Mawu was arrested, Zeng Laomao, too, had done two years in prison for unlawful seizure of property after taking two silver dollars off the body of a dead Nationalist soldier. After his release, as he had experience smelting iron, he was permitted to settle down in Peppercorn Bend.

"Uncle," the leader of the group gazed fixedly at Mawu and said, "Back in 1937, for the sake of two hundred silver dollars my Grand-uncle Peng Yuju allied with brigands to seize your tax rice. Remember? I'm Peng Guanglin."

Mawu looked at him closely. Peng Guanglin was roughly thirty. His eyes were similar to Peng Yuju's. Mawu recalled that afternoon twenty years ago. Back when he was militia captain, Peng Yuju had invited him to drink wine and play chess; in the meantime, the crafty old scholar had allied with Liang the bamboo craftsman and induced a peasant uprising to resist the grain tax. To avoid death, Mawu had fled to Wanxian County, where, for the first time, he learned from Wang Zhengming about exploitation and revolution. Calmly, using the unlit cigarette for emphasis, he corrected, "They carried off Captain Li's rice. That Captain Li is dead."

Peng Guanglin said, "Anyhow, now I'm a bankrupt landlord and you're a released labor-reform prisoner. I have a matter to discuss with you. Would you like to join our company and go to Peppercorn Bend to seize some rice? Our slogan is 'Two Overthrows': We're going to overthrow the grain-hoarding commune and the stingy village canteen. We're going to take back what's ours! We're going to take back our rice!"

Ever since Longping had undertaken to follow the order to transport Huangshui's grain to Fengjie City, local barns and granaries had been emptied one by one, setting people's frayed nerves on edge. One of the few remaining fully stocked granaries was the old Jin family barn at Peppercorn Bend. Just the thought of the granary full of rice set people's stomachs grumbling. At

Peng Guanglin's bold request, the room grew silent. Nervously, Tao Jiuxiang looked from face to face.

Passing the door, Masui perked up his ears in alarm upon hearing strange voices clamoring to seize crops by force. Timidly sidling in, he was further startled to find a group of men ringing his elder brother, including a few familiar faces like Zeng Laomao and Peng Guanglin, the nephew of Great Tiger Bodhisattva Peng, the man who had spearheaded the rice riots against Mawu.

In one of the defeats that the Great Tiger Bodhisattva suffered, back when Peng Guanglin was a ten year-old boy in 1937, his elder brother Guangheng had been burned alive in a kerosene fire while attacking a granary in Xiedong. That evening when young Guanglin returned home, his mother, crying bitterly, informed him, "Your brother's burned to death." Kindly neighbors carried Guangheng's remains—an unrecognizable, rock-hard charred mass of bone—back to Peppercorn Bend. From that point on, Peng Guanglin had become as obdurate as his brother's remains. In these times, only such a man could become an outlaw capable of staging a rice riot to forcefully seize the government's grain!

Frowning, Peng Guanglin deliberately announced, "The production team has posted rules. Anyone opening a granary without permission will be summarily dismissed from the Communist Party; anyone stealing stored crops will be executed by a firing squad."

"Well, fuck their mothers!" Zeng Laomao lit his cigarette, then used it to light Mawu's. "Every day after working in the fields to fill these damn granaries, all of us emaciated, scrawny-assed fools scrounge for wild greens and dig up inedible roots while the unlocked granary is chock full of rice! Only thing's guardin' it is a goddamned piece of red paper with some idiotic regulations. Back in the old days, we would have long since busted that damn place open and stripped it bare!"

Grimly, Peng Guanglin said, "Elder brother, that year that my great-uncle rebelled to reclaim the levy grain from you, not a single person starved to death. This year, just in my household, three family members have died of hunger. In the past three days, I've buried two sons and a daughter."

Mawu squatted at the stove, smoking. A decade ago, inspired by Wang Zhengming, he had returned to Gengguping from Wanxian County to sound the clarion call of revolution. Suddenly, he turned his sunburnt face toward the group and asked, "Who's in charge of the granary?"

"Zhao Changyou," answered Zeng Laomao. "He's willing, but he doesn't dare—he's afraid of compromising his class status, ending up on the wrong side of the line." Seeing Yonggang pressed up against the wall, he chuckled, "Ho, Yonggang, you good little tyke. You know who I am?"

Curiously raising his narrow face and looking at the man, Yonggang shook his head.

"So, little guy, d'you want to eat rice or not?"

"Yes," whispered Yonggang.

Taking a long draw on his cigarette, Mawu looked at Yonggang.

Peng Guanglin said, "I'm a simple, rough-hewn creature. I only grasp straightforward things. Seems clear to me that it would be better to die with a full belly than to perish of hunger!"

Zeng Laomao was nearly sixty, but looked even older. Coldly, he rasped, "Mawu, back in the days when we had food, you armed us, turned us into guerrillas, and led a revolution. Nowadays, in every family hereabouts folk have starved to death. How can they call us counterrevolutionary if we take a little bit of grain to stay alive?"

Mawu smoked in silence, his head down in thought.

"Elder brother," Peng Guanglin thundered. "There was enmity between us in the past. Now, only you can lead us in this life-or-death struggle! Are you willing?"

Mawu flicked aside the cigarette butt, stood up, and said resolutely, "Tell every household to come to Peppercorn Bend tomorrow afternoon to collect rice. We're going to distribute it fairly: Families of up to five people can send one person to fetch three bushels; households of more than five can send two people and take six bushels!"

II

At dawn the next day, Mawu rose and dressed, then deliberately slid his feet into a pair of old straw sandals. Watching anxiously, Tao Jiuxiang quietly cautioned, "Why not have Masui and his wife go—too many people know you."

Mawu ignored her. Puffing on a hand-rolled cigarette, he silently slipped a back-basket over his shoulders and headed out the gate.

In the indistinct early dawn, Zhou Taiwang, Wang Donghe, Sun Fu, the

Suns' eldest son, Shi Eryang's wife and son, and others hurriedly followed Mawu out the main gate, baskets mounted on their shoulders. A year earlier, Shi Eryang had severely burned his hand and half his face at the stove when he was roaring drunk. Fortunately, his rugged wife, strong as most men, could carry the three bushels—better than a hundred and twenty pounds—of rice on her shoulders. After hemming and hawing, Masui, too, picked up a basket and followed in big strides until he caught up with the end of the line.

Along the route to Peppercorn Bend, Masui watched as groups of three and four joined their company, all carrying hemp sacks or back-baskets. The hungry throng grew as they neared their destination. He saw many familiar faces among them, including Ran Hongyou and Third Auntie Zhang. The man beside Ran Hongyou carried a homemade gun, which made him stand out. Masui recognized his old enemy Jiang Ermao, the man who long ago had sung amorous songs to and flirted with Zhou Damei, who had plotted with the bandits to attack the stone tower and kidnap Mawu, who had sabotaged the underpinnings to Gangou Bridge leading to Li Diezhu's death, and who had joined Qin Lieniu's gang of bandits. This rascal should have been imprisoned and punished long ago, but the county government's policy of amnesty and lenience had enabled him survive. Why should this kind of scoundrel join them and carry off a full basket of grain? Inwardly seething, Masui shouldered his way forward to find his brother. At one point, he spied Mawu with Zeng Laomao and Peng Guanglin among the crowd, but shortly he lost track of him. Arriving at the Jins' homestead in Peppercorn Bend, he saw thin, haggard Old Mother Jin cowering in a corner; her scarecrow of a son, Aji, squatted beside her. A big-character slogan was written on the wall in red paint: "Long live Chairman Mao."

"Elder madam, all the grain we've harvested is stored in your old barn," Masui said, embarrassed.

Lifelessly, Old Mother Jin said, "Every night I sleep in a room right beside the barn, yet I'm dying of hunger . . ."

Masui was taken aback. The thought of starving Old Mother Jin and emaciated Aji living in the very shadow of the barn piled high with rice but never so much as touching a grain was utterly insufferable. He whispered to Aji, "Go get something to hold rice. Be quick."

Old Mother Jin rolled her eyes slowly, murmuring, "It's a crime punishable by death!"

Not budging from his squat, Aji added, "Just yesterday, Lil' Rabbit, Jiang Ermao's twelve-year-old boy, stole something to eat from the field of the production brigade, but the brigade leader caught him and decided to shoot him as an example. With the rifle pointed at his head, Rabbit whined piteously, just beggin' for mercy. The brigade leader's gun jammed three times; he kept reloading, changing bullets. Finally, he just unloaded a clip into Lil' Rabbit. When Jiang Ermao arrived, Rabbit was a bloody mess. He carried his son home, but Rabbit died last night."

Masui gasped. No wonder Jiang Ermao was carrying a rifle! Looking around, he whispered, "Jiang's one of the five bad classes.[2] Most of the folks here today are poor and middle peasants. Don't be afraid. Just get yourselves some rice."

Hungry mountainfolk from every household swarmed the granary at Peppercorn Bend. All carried sacks or back-baskets; several men and women were armed with cleavers. The granary supervisor Zhao Changyou, pared down and thin as a skeleton himself, beheld the burgeoning crowd with astonishment. Standing in front of the announcement posted on the front gate, he asked restlessly, "What do you want?"

"We've come to claim our crops!" said Jiang Ermao.

"Open up the barn so we can take the rice. You can register whatever we take in your account ledger. We'll repay it later!" shouted Peng Guanglin.

Fretfully, Zhao Changyou said, "I don't have a grain of rice in my house. If I could borrow rice whenever I needed it, I would have taken some home long ago." He left the township government years before to work on a goldthread farm. Later, he had been reassigned as this granary's supervisor. At this critical juncture, he felt something stiff jab him in the lower back. Jiang Ermao was prodding him with the barrel of the homemade rifle. Mawu forcefully pushed Jiang's barrel upward, then fixed his erstwhile friend and militiaman Zhao Changyou with a stern gaze. Bewildered to see Mawu, fresh out of prison, flustered Zhao Changyou stammered, "This is state property. I need permission from the leader before I distribute . . ."

"Stand down. Look at all these starving, good people gathered here. We're going to take tens of thousands of pounds of rice," Mawu stated, lightning

---

2. The "five bad classes" refers to landlords, rich peasants, counterrevolutionaries, evildoers and Rightists, all of whom were the target of punishment before and during the so-called Great Proletarian Cultural Revolution.

flashing in his eyes. "If you stand in the way of the masses, you'll be trampled to death. Just stand aside and when there's an inquiry report the facts."

All Zhao Changyou could do was smile bitterly. Seeing more and more people crowding forward with cleavers and cudgels, he reluctantly abandoned his post. The villagers swarmed forward in a wave. Sundered, the wooden gate split open and the posted warning was torn to the ground and trampled. Desperate starvelings stuffed their sacks and baskets with rice and carried them home.

Masui failed to shove his way in. Fortunately, Third Auntie Zhang, who had pushed her way inside, hurriedly shoveled his basket full of rice. Starvation even got the better of production team leader Qin Longping, who, abandoning his government role and political consciousness, arrived with his wife and Qin Liexiong's first wife, carrying baskets and torches, to claim a share of the precious grain.

As darkness settled, Mawu was nowhere to be found. Masui lit a torch, returning with the others living at Gengguping. With each step, his excitement and agitation grew. With so many folks involved, he reasoned, Mawu should be safe. Peng Guanglin was very clever: even though they were all dying of hunger, no one else had thought of plundering the granary! Despite these worrying thoughts and the heavy load on his shoulders, buoyed by the thought of rice in his belly, Masui walked homeward with a spring in his step.

How long it had been since the Lis had inhaled the savory fragrance of fresh-steamed rice! That very night, Masui's wife He cooked a pot of rice, which the family devoured in no time. Crimson-faced, Yonggang and Yongguang choked down mouthful after mouthful, barely bothering to chew. Masui bolted down rice like a hungry wolf. Finally, contentedly leaning back, he exhaled, "Now that's worth dying for!"

How sad that Yinmei and Yongzhi had failed to live to enjoy this day! Filling two bowls of rice, He respectfully placed them, along with chopsticks, before their respective tomb mounds.

Mawu did not return until the next day. In addition to carrying a basket of rice, he brought a letter from Chongqing written by Yongyu, who had asked her uncle, Aji, to pass it along to Tao Jiuxiang. Feeling that her father might be out of prison, Yongyu asked if Mawu had come home yet. Her uncle had told her how bleak conditions were in Huangshui. She was fine: studying at school, where each month she was provided with certain ration of rice. Mostly, she was worried about her grandmother and father. Tao Jiuxiang was relieved to hear from her granddaughter. How clever of Jin, she thought, to remove Yongyu from this privation and suffering! Mawu wrote back to his daughter, telling her to work hard and be a good student, and not to worry about the family.

More than ten thousand pounds of rice were taken from the granary—enough so that the surrounding mountainfolk could survive for weeks. Nobody reported the case to the superior authorities. Implicated, production team leader Longping kept silent.

Though Mawu remained taciturn as ever, the courtyard bustled with life. After folks had eaten their fill, they looked upon him in a kinder light. By the time a fortnight had passed, however, the rice wrested from the granary was gone. One noontime, Peng Guanglin and Zeng Laomao paid another visit to Mawu. The three of them warily adjourned to a mountainslope and held a brief, yet animated, conference. Before long, they went their separate ways.

III

Several days later, a hard rain fell. At dusk, with thick clouds and dense mist gathered outside and rain pattering on the roof, Mawu sat in front of the stove sharpening an axe on the grindstone, spinning off mud and grit. Yonggang carried a small gourd ladle of water to clean the blade. Mawu said, "Don't bother cleaning it. The grit hones the ax keener. Couple of years and you'll be chopping wood. You need to grind it like this, nice and even."

Stoking the fire to prepare supper, Tao Jiuxiang affectionately watched her eldest son and grandson. Her pleasant musings were cut short, however, when Peng Guanglin pushed through the back gate, followed by a group of men dressed in straw rain capes, carrying baskets and armed with swords and spears.

Clasping his hands together in a bow to Tao Jiuxiang, Peng Guanglin said, "Elder Madam, please lay a few more places for supper."

Finished sharpening his axe, Mawu wiped the blade clean and dried it with a cloth. Turning to his mother, he said, "Ma, boil enough rice for us to eat."

Glancing at the group, Tao Jiuxiang asked, "How many of you are there?"

"More than thirty," said Peng, passing Tao Jiuxiang a hand-rolled cigarette. "We're going to Huangshui to seize grain. We'll stay in Azure Dragon Temple for the night. Several other men will rendezvous with us there."

Silently, Tao Jiuxiang added rice into the cooking pot. Outside, the driving rain continued to fall. Poking his head in to grab a couple pieces of dry kindling, Masui was surprised to see the gathered crowd and hear murmurs of conversation. Perking up, he asked excitedly, "We going to get more grain?"

"Are you coming?" Peng Guanglin asked, turning toward Masui.

With a bitter smile, Masui responded, "Uh, my wife's not feeling good—she's sick." Having eaten his fill for a couple of weeks, Masui's vitality had returned. He'd been a bit overzealous in taking out his ardor on his homely wife He, and after a couple of vigorous bouts in the bedroom, the frail woman had collapsed. Now, waiting on her day and night, he was boiling azalea water to help her recover.

"Let's eat first," advised Mawu. Lighting the bowl of his pipe, he was cooking a second pot of rice at the stove.

"Uncle Mawu, Elder Madam," Peng Guanglin said solicitously, "Let's eat together."

"Please go ahead and eat first," said Tao Jiuxiang, "The second pot of rice is almost ready."

"I'll get more bowls." Masui volunteered.

"All right, then we won't stand on ceremony," said Peng Guanglin, tucking into the rice. "After dinner, we've got a long way to go."

In a twinkling, the thirty-odd men had devoured all the rice from both pots. Mawu had wolfed down a bowl as well.

Tao Jiuxiang cast a sorrowful gaze at her firstborn son.

Mawu casually set his empty bowl on the stove, then deliberately draped his straw rain cape over his shoulders and pulled on his straw sandals. Then, grabbing his axe and a back-basket, he followed the others out the door without a single word of parting. Outside was pitch black; Masui's straw rain cape was soaked at once. Oil lamp in hand, Masui saw them off. When he returned to the kitchen, he told Tao Jiuxiang, "That gun-toting man beside Zeng Laomao . . . that was Jiang Ermao!"

Tao Jiuxiang was sitting on a stool, rubbing tender, dry argy wormwood leaves into tiny pellet-sized bits to help kindle fires. Hearing these tidings, she stopped short. She knew he had been one of Qin Lieniu's brigands then had settled at Peppercorn Bend. She spat and cursed, "That wretched headless bastard is a true bandit!"

For years, Masui had banished the odious fellow from his mind. He had reasoned, even if the bandits—and Jiang Ermao among them—hadn't stripped the stone tower bare, they would have lost their property during land reform a decade or so later. This he could forgive: Only his father's death at Gangou Bridge still roused his indignation. Ruminating on the past left Masui feeling muddle-headed, an inner turmoil matching the chaos of the room, cluttered with a mess of used bowls and chopsticks. With a sigh, he started to tidy up.

"Grandma," cried Yonggang from the inner chamber. Tao Jiuxiang rose to check on him. Lighting the lamp, she saw Yonggang perched on his wooden bed, his big eyes dilated. Excitedly, he clamored, "Grandma, I want to eat rice tomorrow, too!"

"Oh, dear grandson," said Tao Jiuxiang, "No one eats sumptuous meals every day." Covering him with a quilt, she chanted an old ditty,

> The firefly's soaring high, deceiving children with its lies;
> The firefly's flying low, tricking children with its glow.

As she droned on, she patted the boy, keeping rhythm. Yonggang extended his hands from the quilt to embrace his grandma. Tao Jiuxiang's chant grew louder:

> Fall in the stove, what a dreadful blunder!
> Climb to the sky, struck down by thunder!
> Crawl in a ground hole, by a serpent bitten,
> Listen to old grandma, good little kitten!

A lightning bug flew through the crevice in the window; its faint ghost light came and went above the bed. Tao Jiuxiang extinguished the light and said softly, "Now Grandma will tell you a story."

"Tell me, Grandma! Tell the story," pleaded Yonggang excitedly, yawning as he spoke.

"Long ago there lived a boy," she began. "Each day before daybreak he rose to cut firewood and graze his ox to help support his blind grandma. As he was a kind boy, the gods sent an immortal white tiger down from the stars above to help him."

Delighted at this rare treat, Yonggang giggled in the darkness.

Tao Jiuxiang continued, "One day, as the boy ranged through the mountain forests cutting kindling, a tiger suddenly rushed out of the woods. As the terrified boy scurried up a tree, the tiger, trailing behind him, got tightly lodged in the crotch of the tree. "Tiger, tiger," called the boy above, 'If you don't plan on eating me, just shake your head; but if you're going to eat me, nod your head.'"

Except for the intermittent faint glow of the firefly that revealed the wonderment in Yonggang's eyes, grandmother and grandson were enveloped in inky darkness.

"The tiger shook its head. Trusting the creature, the boy took his axe, hewed off the branch, and freed the tiger. The two became fast friends, like an elder brother and younger brother. When the boy needed firewood, the tiger headed up the mountain slope and into the forest to fetch it. The tiger was wonderful at gathering kindling: with a single flick of his mighty tail, he could collect a bundle! When the boy and his grandmother lacked rice, the tiger accompanied him to the rice-merchant's storehouse. Trembling with fright at the sight of the tiger, the fretful rice dealer would cry out, "Tiger . . . Oh, a tiger!" Then, in such a dither that he forgot to ask them to pay, the trembling rice-merchant would fasten a sack of rice on the tiger's back. The boy had no wife. One day, the tiger went to the home of the mayor and kidnapped his lovely daughter, running away with the girl on his back. That very night, the tiger built a house for the boy . . ."

So absorbed in the tale of the tiger and consumed by his envy for the lucky boy, Yonggang was blissfully oblivious to the murmurs of strangers coming from the kitchen; Tao Jiuxiang, however, heard them.

IV

As Masui cleaned the bowls, a man in a straw raincape suddenly burst into the house. Startled, Masui asked, "Did you lose track of the group? Come on in and warm yourself at the stove."

"It's pouring out there!" the man took a close look at Masui and queried, "You have anything to eat here?"

"Sure, sure," said Masui hurriedly. "It's all thanks to you."

The man followed up, "So you have rice left over?"

Masui said, "Sure, I'll boil some for you."

The man asked, "You have enough for around a dozen men?"

Masui replied, "Yes . . . yes. We do."

Meanwhile, more men swarmed in, all wearing straw raincapes, carrying submachine guns. "You're . . ." Masui stammered, struck dumb with puzzlement, "You're the People's Liberation Army?"

The man said, "We are People's Liberation Army soldiers!"

"Ah?" exclaimed Masui. Backpedaling, he frantically babbled, "I'm just a doddering fiftyish idiot blathering on. Don't take a word I say seriously. Oh, just don't smash me down." Though gray-haired, Masui was still a year shy of forty.

"Just serve us rice," said the man, "No one's going to smash you down. The People's Liberation Army is here to serve the people."

"Yes, yes," agreed Masui, so shocked that he nearly fell faint.

The man asked, "Were there some others here just a little while ago?"

Still rattled, Masui blurted, "Peng Guanglin and the others were here."

"Where did they go?"

Finally controlling his nerves, Masui grumbled, "I've no idea."

The man said resolutely, "Okay, let's move out and follow them."

Alarmed, Masui urged, "Um . . . just stay here tonight and have something to eat. You can head out tomorrow."

"Old man, just tell the truth!" The man said sternly.

"Okay . . . okay," Masui quickly capitulated, his limbs going slack with terror. "Tonight, they're . . . they're staying at Azure Dragon Temple . . ."

At a signal from the leader, the detachment of ten PLA soldiers gathered round the stove to eat. From their conversation, Masui gathered that the leader, whose name was Ma, Captain of the county's battle squadron, had gained intelligence that Mawu, Peng Guanglin, and others intended to seize the rice from the Huangshui granary, and was planning to stop them.

Halfway through her story to Yonggang, voices in the kitchen distracted Tao Jiuxiang from her narrative thread. She threw on her overcoat and went out for a look. She was shocked to discover ten machine gun-armed men in straw raincapes sitting at the stove as Masui cooked rice.

"Madam," called Captain Ma, "We are People's Liberation Army soldiers. We'd like to have a meal in your home. All right?"

"Ummm . . . ," ill-at-ease Tao Jiuxiang's gaze played from the sub-machine guns in their hands to Masui's sick-at-heart expression. Nonplussed, she mumbled, "Yes, yes, help yourselves."

"Grandma," called Yonggang.

Hesitantly, Tao Jiuxiang returned to the bedroom, blowing out the oil lamp and lying down beside Yonggang. Outside, the wind whistled, cumbersome clouds filled the sky, thunder rumbled, and a drenching rain cascaded down. She gave her leg a forceful pinch to make sure it was not a dream.

"Keep telling the story. What happened next?" Tired Yonggang rubbed his eyes.

Restlessly, Tao Jiuxiang settled in, nestling down and taking her grandson in her arms. She continued, "Later, the county governor learned that the oxherd boy had taken grain from the rice-dealer and kidnapped the mayor's daughter. He had the boy thrown into prison and fined him three thousand ounces of silver. When the county governor asked him if he pleaded guilty, the boy answered, 'No, my elder brother Tiger did it.'" In the darkness, Yonggang's eyes shone like a pair of fireflies. "The tiger had followed him to the county offices and roared ferociously outside the hall. Nearly pissing his pants in terror, the county governor sat paralyzed in his chair. In desperation, he released the boy, pleading, "Take the silver back to support your grandma . . . but just keep your tiger brother away from me!'"

In a veritable rapture, Yonggang lapsed into sleep, his eyes curved like two crescent moons.

The thunderstorm stopped. Seeing that his men had eaten their fill and were at the ready, Captain Ma, leaving no room for discussion, ordered Masui to guide them to Azure Dragon Temple. From the inner room, Tao Jiuxiang lay awake listening in agitation, feeling that she was caught in a repeating nightmare. The fate of her eldest son seemed to be fastened to the end of a whip-thong, which, whether brandished or brought down to lash, promised heartrending agony.

Masui dared not resist; he led the troops out the door. He was so frightened and tired that he stumbled countless times, then rose spattered and smeared with mud. Fortunately, he had eaten his fill; otherwise, he thought, he never could have navigated the steep, slippery mountain paths. How ugly and ignoble his role! And how grievous the wrong suffered by Mawu! Here he was guiding the People's Liberation Army soldiers to arrest the very men who had put rice on his table. And yet he felt that the PLA soldiers, too, were ignoble, fortifying themselves with the very same grain to seize the rice rioters. Pressing forward, a pathetic groan escaped from deep within Masui, sounding like some suppressed wail of the mountain wind.

V

Shortly before daybreak, the People's Liberation Army soldiers reached Azure Dragon Temple and set up an ambush, dividing up and laying in wait at the front and back of the compound.

"All you rice rioters who plan on seizing grain by force, listen!" Captain Ma called toward the temple, torch in hand. "Our policy is to punish the ringleaders. Those who have been forced to participate will not be punished!"

A homemade gun barrel protruded from a window, with its muzzle pointing straight at Captain Ma. Just as the report sounded, a sentinel threw Captain Ma to the ground and the bullet hit the tree behind him.

Leaping to his feet, Captain Ma strafed the temple, unloading a full thirty round magazine. Sternly, he bellowed, "All those hoodwinked into participation or involved against their will, come out immediately! The rest of you stubborn reactionaries will be killed!"

The forest in the early dawn remained dark and calm.

"Keep in mind," warned the anxious sentinel, "by law, those guilty of plundering state granaries will be put to death by firing squad. Surrender now and you can still survive. Otherwise, you'll meet with a terrible end!"

Masui lay prone, teeth chattering with fear, at the foot of a fir tree. Shedding tears, worried about the fate of his elder brother, he nervously raised his head and looked toward the ancient temple. Meanwhile, gunfire erupted from the rear gate—the four PLA soldiers there had opened fire with their tommy guns! Masui pissed his pants. Closing his eyes tightly, he buried his face in the moss. Masui considered that his dauntless elder brother had been fighting for half his life, engaging in dozens of skirmishes and battles. Could every battle be this savage, this violent? It was horrific! Better to die of hunger than to meet such a bloody fate!

"So, you want to see your elder brother and those men shot to death?" Captain Ma suddenly asked, hunkering down next to Masui.

Wretchedly, Masui looked up head and mumbled, "No . . . no . . . no. I don't want to see that!"

"Then go into the temple and convince your brother not to be an enemy of the people," Captain Ma said. Two PLA soldiers hoisted Masui to his feet and led him to the back gate. Two others followed, tommy guns at the ready.

Masui whimpered, "I'm afraid of being shot."

"Just talk to Li Mawu. No one will shoot you," a PLA soldier said, dragging him forward and shoving him in front of the gate.

"Mawu, please listen to me . . ." Masui gasped, sobbing as he spoke. A horrible silence followed. The smell of slaughter hung heavy in the morning air. "Oh, Mawu . . . ," Masui faltered, his brother's name caught in his throat.

Slowly, the rear gate opened, and, one after another, thirty-odd mountain folk, led by Ran Hongyou and Zeng Laomao, filed out, their hands raised over their heads. In the dim morning light, three men suddenly broke rank and ran, skidding down a steep escarpment and fleeing pell-mell. However, several PLA soldiers lying in wait at the base of the cliff charged toward them, tommy guns blazing fiercely. Lapsing into catatonia, Masui squatted on his haunches, rocking back and forth like an idiot.

With a couple of nimble leaps, barefoot Jiang Ermao plunged into a bamboo copse. Unable to catch him, and seeing that he was on the verge of escaping into the dense canopy of the primeval forest, the soldiers opened fire, mowing him down just yards away from the embrace of the woods.

The other two fugitives, Mawu and Peng Guanglin, lacked Jiang Ermao's agility and were soon cornered and captured alive by the PLA soldiers. No longer a fleet-footed young man with callused soles, Zeng Laomao, too, was quickly corralled.

A PLA soldier handed Masui a raincape, telling him to cover the corpse. Masui absent-mindedly picked his way down the ridge. Honeycombed with bullet holes, Jiang Ermao bled profusely; black-purple rivulets flowed down to the ground and congealed in pools. Masui shuddered, surprised that so much blood could drain out of Jiang Ermao's sinewy frame. This Jiang Ermao was an intractable enemy, a man who had, time and again—whether in cahoots with bandits bent on destroying the Lis or as a rival for Zhou Damei's affection—pitted his energies against the his family. However, now he lay dead, riddled with bullets, obliterated by the gunfire of PLA soldiers. Nauseous at the sweet reek of blood and death, Masui quickly covered his corpse.

The PLA soldiers bound Mawu and Peng Guanglin in chains, then escorted them toward Peppercorn Bend together with other villagers.

Masui dared not look Mawu in the eye. Awash in self-recrimination, he followed the procession of prisoners at a distance; shortly he slowed his pace and collapsed, sliding down a tree trunk and remaining motionless at its foot, like a dead man.

Shortly before they reached Peppercorn Bend, Captain Ma saw a familiar frail and disheveled old woman sitting beside the road, a carrying pole in the muck at her side. "Ma," he heard Mawu call. Ah, Captain Ma nodded, recalling the old woman from Gengguping the previous night.

"Mawu," Tao Jiuxiang called. Seeing so many guns the night before, she had known beyond a doubt that her firstborn would be cornered. Thus, long before dawn she bustled along to find out whether her eldest son was alive or dead.

"Ma, go home. You didn't need to come so far," Mawu muttered wearily.

Tao Jiuxiang held a bamboo cylinder full of water. After a hesitant glance at Captain Ma, she took a ricecake from her pocket and moved it toward Mawu's mouth. Recognizing the old wildwoman, the PLA men did not stop her. Mawu bent down and took a bite of ricecake, chasing it down with two swallows of water from the bamboo tube. Sidestepping his mother's embrace, he said grimly, "Hurry up and leave, Ma." He turned away and marched off with the prisoners, never looking back.

Tao Jiuxiang felt as though a knife were carving up her heart. Her recessed eyes were moist, her heart broken, like a moss-covered millstone. Something cold fell from the skies above, damping her cheeks and hair. She knew she was watching her firstborn heading to join his generations of ancestors, marching to his death. As she pursed her lips, she could not suppress a guttural eruption of sound from escaping the depths of her bosom. No one could say whether she was sobbing, growling, or groaning.

Chapter Twenty-Seven

I

On a morning a fortnight later, a crowd gathered on the vacant grounds outside the goldthread storehouse. Machine-gun-armed PLA sentinels formed a perimeter. Tables draped in red cloth atop a makeshift terrace marked the site of the tribunal; the placard featuring the trial announcement had been written in flawless strokes by venerable Doctor Cui, who long ago in the final years of the Qing dynasty had passed the imperial examination. Formal and upright behind the tables sat the county governor and local mayors.

Locked in cangues, fifteen men accused of plundering state grain stood facing the crowd. Their hands hung above their necks, forcing their heads to droop forward; the men looked a bit like the wicked water dragon locked in the cliff. Though more than thirty had initially been captured outside the Daoist temple, a number of "reluctant" and "coerced" participants had been set free, leaving fifteen to stand trial.

Through a blaring loudspeaker, the cadre members at various levels of government gave speeches, one after another, accusing the tightly bound, pilloried criminals standing before them of robbing grain. With a stern countenance, the county governor of the Communist Party thundered on, directing his wrath at the accused ringleader of the crop-robbing bandits: "Li Mawu, tell us how you gathered this reactionary gang from the five bad categories to plunder rice from state granaries?"

His graying head forced into a bow by the wooden rack, Mawu answered coldly, "Many folks were dying of hunger. The crops were sitting in the granary. I don't think that's a sound policy."

The grounds grew quiet. The commune director railed, "Li Mawu, in the past as a harsh official you forced tenants to hand over levy rice, inciting a peasant rebellion. History brands you a counterrevolutionary. How could you of all people have the audacity to criticize Party management of grain distribution and seek to undermine the Three Red Flags of Socialism! Then and now, you are a counterrevolutionary to your very marrow. Don't pretend to be righteous!"

Mawu paled. Enduring the excruciating pain of the cangue and the tight bindings, he enunciated, coolly and clearly, "Any revolutionary first needs to survive. I'm not pretending anything."

The tribunal grounds buzzed with chatter and loud whispers. The director retorted, "So, you think you're worthy of mentioning revolution? Death, as well as life, is common: Why make such a fuss about starvation? Quit talking nonsense. So, do you fear death?"

Mawu said nothing.

"Li Mawu, do you fear death by firing squad?"

Mawu remained silent.

Furious, the director strode in front of Mawu, roaring, "Tiger Li, are you afraid of being shot to death?"

Mawu looked at the loaded pistol tucked into the man's waist belt and said quietly, "I've done nothing to betray my conscience. I just want the people, young and old, to eat their fill of rice."

In a caustic tone, the director rebutted, "So the ringleader of the grain thieves has a conscience and says that he's done nothing wrong? What utter bullshit! You're notorious around Huangshui! The county government knows you've been plotting armed rebellion. And who needs the stolen grain that you've seized by force: relief rice is coming in a few days."

"Li Mawu, you are a criminal, recently released from five years of labor reform," the secretary continued. "You have committed unpardonable crimes against the Party and the people! I'm now going to solicit the opinion of the masses, excepting your relatives and family. If a single person comes forward and agrees that your forceful seizure of state grain was necessary and a good thing, then you will be brought back to prison and granted a re-trial. Folks, you have three minutes to come forward."

In a formal manner, he raised his left hand, looking at his watch. He began to count off the time, "One second, two seconds, three seconds... Two minutes left..." The audience gasped, hardly daring to breathe. Nobody said a word.

The secretary raised his left hand high and read loudly, "One second, two seconds, three seconds... We have one minute left..."

The crowd gazed with a paralytic sympathy upon their fifteen fellow mountainfolk, pilloried before them and put on public trial. Scenes from their shared lives floated through the minds of every man and woman. One superstitious thought circulated among the crowd: they recalled the fifteen ward headmen and landlords who had been executed, wondering if their ghosts had come to exact vengeance?

When Mawu's time expired, a fatal silence reigned: nobody raised a hand.

The commune director stood triumphant before the terrace, loudly declaring, "Our policy is to punish the ringleaders. Those forced to participate will not be punished! Li Mawu, the criminal, was released after five years in prison labor camp. Before Liberation, he was a bandit. When he returned home from prison, in his hatred for the people's government he plotted a counterrevolutionary rebellion, inciting his neighbors to break into state granaries and seize rice by force. Therefore, he is sentenced to death. The execution shall take place here and now."

The meeting ground grew silent as a tomb.

Soaked with sweat, frail Peng Guanglin was bound so tightly that his limbs trembled.

The director went on, proclaiming, "Prior to Liberation, Peng Guanglin's family possessed significant land and property; these holdings were redistributed during land reform. Because of the disenfranchisement and downfall of the Pengs, he was labeled a 'bankrupted landlord' after Liberation. He, too, harbors a deep hatred for the Party and our government; and he, too, plotted counterrevolutionary rebellion, inciting his neighbors to break into state granaries and seize rice by force. Therefore, he is sentenced to death. The execution shall take place immediately. Jiang Ermao, another ringleader, used martial force to resist capture by the PLA, and was shot to death at the site of the conflict. Zeng Laomao, another primary criminal, is hereby sentenced to fifteen years of imprisonment. Others involved were merely ignorant followers. Because they have shown a good and remorseful attitude and have confessed to their crimes, they will be escorted back to their hometowns for supervised education."

The onlookers breathed a collective sigh of relief.

The fifteen criminals were escorted to the west side of the slope, where they were arrayed behind a white line.

Moments before he departed for the Yellow Springs in the netherworld, the Li family tombs on the plains of Lihaku floated through Mawu's mind. How hollow now the bold prognostications of the dragon-chasing geomancers, the dreamy folklore that echoed in the lines of that ditty:

> *Of grotto 'neath Lihaku they speak,*
> *Little peak to the big peak,*
> *Horse-saddle mount of the oxhead mount,*
> *Two carp leap on the golden sand,*
> *Find this site and great fortune you'll command:*
> *Of ten sons, nine have rank and wealth beyond count.*

Mulling the yawning gap between the augured grandeur of yesteryear and the grim reality of the present, Mawu felt a cumbersome sadness. Everything was so quiet that he could hear the pounding of his own heart. He thought once more of skinny Yonggang, of his aged mother Tao Jiuxiang, and of Gengguping. Then it occurred to him how improbable it was that he was to die beside Peng Guanglin, a lifelong foe. Years ago, when he had locked horns with the sons and nephews of the Peng family, he had fled into hiding, leaving his hometown to join the revolution. Then, he thought of cutting down stumpy Qin Liexiong; of joining Wang Zhengming and swearing an oath to join the Communist Party in front of the sickle-and-hammer flag drawn on red paper; of killing Xiang Jintang at night; of his attack on Nationalist headquarters; and of the decision to execute the fifteen ward heads and landlords. A pervasive sorrow set his nerves aquiver, like taut strands of a spider's web. In his final moments, Mawu silently prayed that he, too, might miraculously ascend to the White-Tiger Star as his legendary ancestor had long ago.

The executioner pulled the trigger. "Peng! Peng!" two reports resounded in rapid succession. Mawu pitched forward, tumbling into his own growing pool of the commingled blood of man, god, and beast. The fishy reek of death filled the killing grounds of the makeshift tribunal. Gasping, face down, Mawu struggled to open his mouth to breathe. How he yearned to kneel before to the source of a mountain stream and drink deeply, but his tongue failed to touch a single drop of water. He heard the fierce howl of the mountain wind rushing through the forest like a tsunami. He felt waves of grass submerge his body. A queer noise, like the lilting twitter of birds, bored into his ears. Before him, the nebulous figure of Yinmei beckoned, urging him to come home along the mountain path to Gengguping. With one last affectionate glance at his spectral wife, he leapt up and ascended into the clouds and fog.

The two outlaws Li Mawu and Peng Guanglin were executed. Where the fatal shots had been delivered the bloody pith of their brains flowed forth.

Li Mawu had lived a life of legend—a reckless life of passion and violence, of suffering and loss, of excess and privation, a life as full of deep gorges and lofty pinnacles as the landscape around Huangshui that had shaped him! Yet what a desolate and lonely death! In 1968 the People's government executed Li Mawu, the "evil ringleader" of the rice riots that had emptied a state granary in the former courtyard of his first wife's family.

Though thirteen others had expected that they, too, would be executed, they had been set free. Zeng Laomao, the plowshare-maker, stood stock still. The executioner approached him and gave the old man a rough shove. Zeng could smell death on the man's hands and recoiled as if assailed by a ghost. For good measure, the executioner drove the butt of his gun into the ploughshare-maker's solar plexus.

"Ho, Zeng Laomao! Since you've avoided execution, you should become a law-abiding citizen and follow the straight and narrow," mocked a PLA soldier. Zeng recalled the last glares of the former ward chiefs and landlords that day when he, as a revolutionary officer, had marched them off and given the order to shoot them on a mountain slope. His face was pale, his limbs rigid: Zeng had never imagined that he, now branded a "counterrevolutionary," would survive this day. Surely this was due to some ancestor's blessing! In bewilderment he followed the soldiers away from the scene of the tribunal. After several steps, two sedan chairs appeared, emerging from the sugarcane fields. Seemingly, the Lis and Pengs had been informed of the executions and had sent men to carry off the corpses.

Peng Guanglin's sons and nephews rushed to his corpse. One took the dead man's hands, and another the feet. More overcome with horror than sorrow, they tearlessly placed the corpse on the sedan chair, lifted it, and left.

Xia Liangxian and Masui soon arrived. A verdict had been reached in the cured meat case: Xia Liangxian, as an accomplice but not the primary perpetrator, had been imprisoned for a month of re-education and indoctrination. On his way back to Dragon Decapitating Gorge, he received the bad news from Masui. As Yonggang was too young and weak, Masui asked Xia Liangxian to help fetch Mawu's corpse.

Arriving at the execution grounds, Masui knelt beside his brother's body and wailed. Bold, uncompromising Mawu was truly dead. Blood stained his once vital and handsome face; dried blood was caked on his temples.

They lifted Mawu's corpse onto the sedan.

II

Though distraught, Tao Jiuxiang shed no tears. She buried Mawu together with Xia Yinmei. The couple had met extraordinary deaths: As the oldsters might say, "one was a wicked spirit, and the other a hungry ghost." Folksy wisdom foretold that serious problems would arise if one buried two such entities together. Nor should they have been interred so close to the family's homestead. However, Tao Jiuxiang could not accept her eldest son's execution. Growing ever more eccentric, she came to believe that only if Mawu was buried together with his wife Yinmei in the same grave in the recessed vale close to the tower might all baleful influences be expelled. What a peculiar and bold decision!

Chanting to her ancestors and invoking tutelary spirits near and far, calling for their salubrious intercession through the vastness of time and space, Tao Jiuxiang, with her salt-and-pepper hair, prayed, "Oh ancestors and ancestresses, while alive you were mighty; now as spirits in the nether realm you are mightier still, ever present and all-seeing from low-lying dales to sky-piercing crags. Oh, you've seen all! Time and again, in every season, you've witnessed the disasters and calamities that have befallen your poor offspring. No matter how difficult the path my son walks in the netherworld, smooth his road with rollers; no matter how rugged and deep the caverns he must pass through, carve out the way with picks. Scythe down the tufted swordgrass above and below, mow down the tufted swordgrass to the left and right. Clear the way with powerful winds and heavy, cleansing rains. Let the God of Thunder cleave open a path, and let the Goddess of Lightning illumine his way. Oh, my ancestors and ancestresses, please let him pass unhindered by wicked spirits!" Her prayers were borne on the mountain winds to their remote destination. A tiger-striped butterfly, its wings lined with golden and black, slipped in through a crevice, flitting up and down before perching on dirty gauze mosquito-netting curtains, looking like one of Xia Yinmei's beautiful embroidered patterns come to life. Yonggang watched the wrinkles on his grandmother's face twitch and contract. Only when he saw the light in her bright recessed eyes grow dull did the young boy's stout heart quail.

At dusk one day not long thereafter, Shi Eryang stomped into the courtyard with a basket on his shoulders, breathlessly calling, "Grab yer baskets—be quick about it. Let's go get some rice and crops! Ho! Sun Fu! Zhou Taiwang! Wang Donghe!" Who would be brazen and stupid enough to go down that road again? Folks poked their heads out their doors, looking quizzically at Shi Eryang, then stared at each other, perplexed.

"C'mon! Let's go get some grain and vegetables!" Excitedly, he set his basket down, plunged in his hand and held aloft a handful of rice.

Skeptical, Sun Xiaoxiao gazed at her husband, and chirped in horror, "Two men were just executed for taking grain . . . are you . . . ?"

"The county government just sent relief grain and crops to Huangshui— six pounds of rice a person, along with six pounds of potatoes and corn. The commune has set up a claims office at Peppercorn Bend to distribute the grain and crops. May I be a god-damned cuckolded turtle's son if I'm talkin' shit!" Eryang swore.

Folk gathered round, sifting the rice through their fingers. Seeing Masui hanging back, apprehensive and despondent, Eryang stamped and said, "Li Masui, go to Peppercorn Bend and claim your rice and crops!"

Masui, sitting motionless, groused, "Who cares about people like us?"

Reproachfully, Eryang insisted, "Do as you're told and go get the grain. Our production team has got to claim our share by tomorrow. Every household has to go. I'll check the list. Wang Donghe, go tell the people down by Inkblack Creek. Now!"

"Okay, okay. I'm a' goin'." Wang Donghe did not hesitate any longer. Hiking up his trousers and tightening his belt, he headed out. "Does production team leader Longping know?" he yelled back dubiously from the gate.

"The commune dismissed him—they're gonna formally announce it later,"

Eryang explained, calming down.

"All right. We'll claim our share first thing tomorrow!" said Zhou Taiwang.

Masui did not sleep all night. As dawn filtered through the branches, he heard a shuffling in the yard, and, rubbing his eyes, he rose and slung on a basket. Outside, he fell in behind Eryang and the other neighbors.

Arriving at Peppercorn Bend, it became apparent that Eryang had not lied: the commune was distributing relief grain and crops. A table covered with red cloth sported a sign written in yellow characters reading:

RELIEF GRAIN AND CROP DISTRIBUTION SITE

To one side, Captain Ma sat silently, a pistol visibly holstered on his belt. At dusk, one after another the men returned to Gengguping laden with grain and crops. Soon, cooking smoke rose from each household's kitchen.

Word was out that production team leader Qin Longping, chastised for mishandling the plundering of the granary, had been dismissed. Shi Eryang—a man who, in a drunken stupor had fallen asleep on a stove, burning half his face beyond recognition and crippling one of his hands—replaced him. Though his mouth had been deformed in the accident, Shi remained the most garrulous fellow around.

Hunchbacked Tao Jiuxiang sent Masui to talk with Qin Ji'an. That the Qins had built a house on the "auspicious site" next to Li Diezhu's tomb left her feeling like a poison thorn was lodged in her eye.

At a production team meeting, Masui happened to end up sitting beside Qin Ji'an, a good-natured and affable fellow. Testing the waters, Masui asked, "So, brother, how's life in Inkblack Creek?"

"It's inconvenient—soon as you set foot out the front door, it's a bunch of mudholes and marshy dells." Qin Ji'an knew that the Lis were unhappy about the location of their new house. Giving his head a rub, he said, "We only built there because its level. Otherwise, I wouldn't live there. As soon as my son was born, he kept coughing. Half a year ago when he had a high fever, his mother carried him all the way to Enshi on her back to get medicine. It was bitter cold, but on the way back she stumbled and dropped the poor thing in the creek. Oh, my poor child!"

"It's hard to raise a child here," offered Masui in sympathy. He had heard that Qin Ji'an's child had died.

"I'm a strong guy, sturdy as a workhorse, but since moving there I've had to go see a doctor several times," Qin Ji'an said, a puzzled expression creasing his face.

The fellow did look different. Masui scanned his frail and weak limbs, and said frankly, "My family chose that site cause the dragon chasers said its watery *yin* ethers made it perfect for a tomb; but your family's built a house there. It's a good site for the dead, not the living. And during rainstorms, runoff from the roof drains on the tomb—and that's no good for the living or the dead. Might be better to move."

Sighing deeply, Qin Ji'an replied, "It's not so easy to pull up stakes and build a new house these days." Shortly after their fateful conversation, Qin Ji'an died suddenly of a stomach ailment while on the road.

Whether or not the deaths of her grandson and great-grandson were a coincidence, Old Mother Qin was terrified. One afternoon, she finally had the out-kitchen that abutted the tomb mound dismantled. However, she left the main house, built on the site where the lotus-blossom had miraculously appeared, standing. She was certain that the geomancers had played a trick on the Lis and that with her house built on the auspicious site, future generations of Qins would enjoy wealth, status, good fortune, and prosperity.

All iron-willed Tao Jiuxiang could do was silently accepted the Qins enduring presence on Speargrass Plain.

III

In Masui's tormented mind, the image of Mawu's bloodstained face gradually grew fainter over the months. Each day, accompanied by his wife, he went to work with his production team in the forest, basket over his shoulders and hoe in hand, digging, chopping, and grading earth, cutting down trees, and leveling the land. He was not as strong as he used to be; no matter how hard he toiled, he never could earn full work points. However, one day Shi Eryang announced a stunning piece of news: on the overseas market, a ton of goldthread could be exchanged for four hundred tons of steel! Zealously, the new team leader urged everybody to work with the tenacity of a wildcat dragging an ox. Nobody could slack off on production; rather, everyone should be energetic as a monkey howling excitedly from atop the highest slope.

Goldthread grew best manured heavily on the shady, forested northern slopes. Using straight, sturdy poles, the production team erected sheds on the goldthread fields.

As the new production team leader, Eryang sported a brimmed olive cap and under a black cotton-padded coat wore a formal collared shirt; his feet were shod with an impressive regulation pair of leather PLA army boots. His pantlegs were scrolled up above his knees. Goldthread was only one of the team's responsibilities. Shi Eryang also led the team to cut trees on the mountain slopes; today they were felling the trees on the slope above Gangou Bridge, including the notorious hardwood that had spirited away Zhou Damei all those years ago, the girth of its gnarled trunk so immense that two grown men could not reach their arms around it. Folks said it was haunted. Eryang claimed that if its splintered wooden bits were buried underground and dug up in five years, the edges and tips would be keener than a sword's blade. Standing beside the trunk, Shi Eryang hailed Masui, urging him to get the job started: "So this is the damned tree that took your first wife. Today, the first axe blow is yours!"

The episode from decades earlier drifted back into Masui's mind. Recalling the man in white, the incarnation of the tree spirit, that his wife Zhou Damei had mentioned, he briskly shook his head in horror and declined: "Oh, no, the production team leader should have the first go. Don't make me go first . . . I don't have the experience."

Sizing up the creeper-twined, moss-covered trunk, Shi Eryang insisted, "We're just getting started here—nobody has experience. I told ya to chop, so chop!"

Unable to delay things any longer, Masui looked in the direction of the other members of the team and, his facial muscles tensing in resolve, replied, "Okay, I'll do it." Closing his eyes he brandished the axe and, with trembling hands, struck the massive trunk a resounding blow that sunk the blade deep into the old tree. Masui paled, a single bead of sweat rolling down his forehead. Opening his eyes, he was relieved to discover that no blood was dripping from the gash.

Flourishing his hand, Eryang summoned one of the more rugged men; the fellow delivered a flurry of a dozen strokes in rapid succession. With a cacophony of hoarse croaks, a murder of crows erupted from the branches, flying far off in search of a new roost. Eryang ordered Masui and the man to stand on opposite sides of the tree, and cut it down with a two-man saw. Droplets of water fell from the branches like rain.

Atop the ridge, three groups of workers from the team marked trees to saw. Soon, the air echoed with the serrations of saw blades and yells of the workers. Alarmed birds flushed from branches and thickets; chirping and twittering, they soared in circles round the ancient tree. From early morning until dusk, Masui and his robust partner kept sawing. In the light of the gloaming, something extraordinary occurred: Two yellow weasels appeared from nowhere and began to circumambulate the old tree; from time to time the creatures stood up on their hind legs and groaned sadly. Yellow weasels were highly sought after: their precious little bodies were an apothecaries' dream— every part could be used in traditional medicine. In any other situation, the members of the team would have pounced on the weasels, attacking with poles or axes. But at this pivotal moment only the tiniest bit of pith still held the tree upright. The evening was windless. No one could read which way the great tree would fall. The two-man saw was lodged in the heart of the tree. Masui and his partner were nervous. Following local custom, they stripped down, throwing off one item of clothing after another—first caps, then coats, then shirts—to coax the tree to fall. But the stubborn old tree refused to be swayed and kept standing.

Suddenly, Masui's face grew mauve with horror. From the opposite side of the tree, his partner called out, "Look! Up there!" Masui looked up, glancing a wisp of a golden shadow move the branches, then disappear. The trunk shifted, then pitched, and lo! The hundred-foot old tree—its branches tickling the heavens and its roots anchored deep in the earth—fell straight toward him! Mouths agape, the other members called out in horror! Horrified, Masui dashed toward a cave opening in the cliff, his hands on his head. Hearing a crashing sound like an explosion, he flung himself to the ground like a dead man.

After a spell, when the dust had cleared and the leaves had settled, Shi Eryang hunkered down beside him, calling, "Li Masui, Li Masui."

Masui recovered his bearings. Looking up, he saw the crown of the falling tree propped atop a huge outcropping of stone overhanging the opening of the cave, at an oblique angle, while the trunk rested precariously just above his head. Trembling, he clambered out, trembling, feeling as though his body weighed 1,000 pounds. His two-man saw partner sat, jaw agape, off to one side. Seeing that Masui had somehow escaped unscathed, he said fearfully, "If it weren't for that stone, we'd both be d-dead!"

Masui's face was earthen-colored; his mind was totally blank.

There was a gaping hole in the forest canopy. Branches, snapped off as the mighty tree fell, were scattered about the forest floor. Here and there broken eggs, dying fledglings, and the debris of nests littered the ground. Some birds flew overhead, singing lugubrious songs like dirges in the darkening skies. Pocketing intact eggs, Shi Eryang said to Masui, "Lucky you took the first swing, brother. Anyone else would have been mashed into a flesh pie."

At the mention of "flesh pie," Masui shuddered. How many sheets of joss paper had he burned over the years to placate ill-fated and miserable Zhou Damei. Perhaps, in the end, it had worked: after all, he had survived the disaster.

"Pity those yellow weasels are gone," Eryang muttered, squinting and scanning the grounds.

The towering, lecherous old tree had fallen at last. Members of the production team began cutting off its remaining branches. As he looked in awe at the thick trunk, Masui's heart pounded in his chest. He couldn't shake a sense of foreboding and horror. If he were asked to answer for this act in the netherworld, he reasoned, it wasn't really his fault. After all, Shi Eryang had ordered him and the others to cut down the tree and kill its spirit; fault lay with the production team leader. Otherwise, the mountainfolk would never have done it. Gradually, relief replaced Masui's lingering dread: in the end the wicked sylvan spirit that had long haunted the forest was no more.

IV

Though dusk had nearly passed, the western horizon remained a drunken crimson. The arrival of the night wind, however, rapidly dyed the world black. The primeval forest still possessed an unutterable, stark beauty. The day's work was done; the following day another team would cut the felled trees into lengths and haul them away. Squinting in the darkness, the members of the production team continued to search for eggs. Gaining his bearings, Masui scrambled to his feet and picked up several large whole eggs from the fallen nests. Just as he started home, however, he suddenly saw Zhou Damei sitting behind a curtain of creepers in the mouth of the cave. Whistling a haunting melody on a leaf, she wore her tattered and shabby wedding dress.

Dizzy and breathless, Masui staggered backward. His heart quickened; his legs seemed to be as soft as boiled noodles. Recalling the ghost-expelling mudra his father had taught him so many years before, he moved his fingers and hands to banish the apparition of his first wife. The mudra did not work. Sitting with a chilling blank expression, Zhou Damei watched him fumblingly shape the mudra. In a tone of menace, she asked, "Why don't you remove that badge?"

Soaked in cold sweat, Masui looked down at the badge of Chairman Mao pinned on his chest. Summoning his courage, he answered, "No, I'm not going to take it off."

Zhou Damei said, "You don't dare."

After a moment of hesitation, Masui worked out the riddle. Featuring Chairman Mao surrounded by a radiant halo of sunshine, the badge had helped dispel ghostly Zhou Damei. No wonder he had survived the dying tree spirit's wrath! A warmth rising from his chest, he remembered that when she was alive his sister-in-law Yinmei had told him that ghosts couldn't stand hearing "The East Is Red." So, he belted out,

> *The east is red, and the sun rises high,*
> *Mao Zedong ascends into China's sky.*

Sure enough, Zhou Damei disappeared. With balled fists, Masui rubbed his bloodshot eyes. Bewildered and exhausted, he sank down on the forest floor.

"A-ho! A-ha!" Shi Eryang exulted. "Li Masui's singing 'The East Is Red.' That's the spirit! Sing it loud, brother! We chopped down that ol' ghostly tree. We're done for the day. Grab a few more eggs and head on home."

Masui's face blanched. Dumbly, axe in hand, he followed the other team members back to Gengguping. Back home, in a state of shock, he shoveled down several mouthfuls of rice, then shuffled off to bed. Later that evening, after lying silently for a good while, he related the queer incident to his wife.

Listening to the strange tale as she washed his work clothes, He was overwhelmed with astonishment. With reverence, she unpinned the badge and delicately set it atop a pile of his clean clothing. Seriously, she cautioned, "Chairman Mao is a man of great fortune. Remember to wear that badge every day! That ghostly witch-woman fears light."

Though the production team had overcome the tree spirit and Masui had solved the persistent haunting of Zhou Damei, in the following weeks the mountainfolk encountered yet a new problem. As Shi Eryang led the team in setting up a series of new goldthread lean-tos here and there in the mountains, a growing flock of black birds—the kind of birds locals called "iron vise" after their sharp beaks—circled and dive-bombed them, unleashing an arsenal of missiles—pelting them with shit and casting down an incessant rain of stones and bugs. If the mountainfolk ignored them, they abruptly swooped down, squawking as they grabbed people by the hair and savagely pecked at their backs. Folks had to stop working and brandish branches at the relentless birds to shoo them away. In the ferocious ongoing conflict waged between this warlike avian tribe and the mountainfolk, neither side escaped unscathed.

Around this time, another queer incident took place. A tigress with faded stripes launched a series of attacks on the farms and communes around Huangshui. First, the tigress ripped out the throat of an ox. Next, she mauled Cai Jianzhen, one of the villagers, to death. According to witnesses, after looking at him with a desperate hunger, the tigress devoured the upper half of Cai's body. Rumor circulated that the tigress was a reincarnation of Xia Yinmei wreaking vengeance. When the starvelings hungered for rice, everyone warmed to and welcomed Mawu; but when the commune director gave the folks three minutes to intercede on "Tiger" Mawu's behalf, nobody raised a hand to save him from death.

Captain Ma immediately returned to Huangshui, bringing a twenty-man crack tiger-hunting team. They didn't have to wait long. As the Ma's men approached Peppercorn Bend, a tiger darted from the undergrowth and threw itself headlong toward the lot of them. Hurriedly, Captain Ma ordered, "Open fire! Now!" He pulled the trigger, catching the tiger in the haunch. Abruptly, the furious tiger rounded on him, delivering a lightning fast cuff with a mighty paw that sent Captain Ma sprawling fifteen feet to the foot of a cliff. Though four or five guns fired in unison, the tiger seemed unfazed and sounded an earth-shattering howl; the ungodly sound summoned a powerful wind that shook the ancient trees, spraying broken branches in all directions. Furious gusts hurled sand and stone, kicking up a sour and pungent pother reeking of tigress that blew down several PLA soldiers. Though the barrage of gunfire was thick and fast, the wounded tigress disappeared into the swirling chaos.

Revenge-minded Cai Bangzi, the younger brother of Cai Jianzhen, volunteered to accompany the men on the tiger hunt. Strapped to his side was a keen machete that he had sharpened on his whetstone. He moved well in front of the team, tracking the tiger. Some four hours later, he found the tigress hiding in a dense clump of horse mulberry bushes. Fixed on him, the creature's round gleaming eyes beamed a furious light.

"Here!" cried Cai Bangzi excitedly, "It's here!"

With a guttural growl, the tiger sprang from its cover and pinned Cai Bangzi down. As he tried to fend it off, the tiger tore into his neck and shoulders with its pale fangs. The tiger-hunting team arrived, pistols and tommy guns in hand, but seeing man and tiger tussling together, they dared not fire. Anxiously, one soldier called, "Hack it with your machete!"

"Where's my machete?" yelled poor Cai Bangzi.

"Fastened on your ass," Captain Ma answered nervously from the other side of the underbrush, brandishing his pistol.

"Where's my ass?" screeched panicked and pale-faced Cai Bangzi, the tiger's hook-like claws anchored in the side of his neck.

One soldier fired, and the tiger rolled to one side. Seizing the opening, the other members of the team opened fire. Hot blood stained the layers of fallen leaves, and the powerful musk of the big cat permeated the air.

Shortly, Cai Bangzi died of the bite wounds. The tigress died too, her body riddled with scores of bullets.

But the scourge had not ended: over the next six months, another tiger went on an unprecedented rampage, devouring twenty draft oxen and fourteen pigs. When Shi Eryang attended the meeting at government headquarters in Huangshui, he was alarmed at the statistics. Rampant gossip floated around the streets and into the hills and valleys, murmurs that "Tiger" Mawu was visiting blood vengeance upon the ingrates who had gladly taken rice from the granary he had opened, but had stood idly by and watched his execution.

Skeptical, Shi Eryang returned to Gengguping, approaching experienced Zhou Taiwang for advice. "Folk are saying that Mawu's spirit from the netherworld has whipped tigers into a frenzy. You're an old hunter. What do you think? It's hard and dangerous work for the PLA soldiers to hunt tigers. Besides, after all he's done for us—bringing relief crops out here—we don't want to see kindly Captain Ma wounded."

Swayed by his argument, Zhou Taiwang offered a strategy: "First track the tiger and figure out where he makes his rounds. Then, hang a dog from a tree with a bag of lime tied to its tail. Have hunters up in a tree waiting downwind . . ."

Scornfully, Eryang retorted, "You call that a strategy? Everyone in Gengguping knows that."

"If it's so easy, why are we still getting attacked?" asked Zhou Taiwang.

Good point, mused Shi Eryang. "You tell me."

"Old brother," Zhou Taiwang raised his head, turning to ask Sun Fu, who had just arrived with two buckets of water and caught their conversation. "Have you heard of this strategy?"

Setting down the buckets, Sun Fu answered, "Nope."

"The way that the claws of a tiger glutted on food expand and contract differs from that of a hungry tiger on the prowl," Zhou Taiwang said. "I know tracking. We need to find a ravenous tiger that's just emerged from its cave. Then it will go after the hanging bait dog." Truly, only a seasoned hunter would propose such a wonderful tiger-hunting technique!

Overjoyed, Shi Eryang dragged Zhou Taiwang to Azure Dragon Temple to pitch the idea to Captain Ma and the PLA soldiers stationed there.

V

Everyone was shocked when Zhou Taiwang volunteered his trusty Banzi to the PLA men as bait for the tiger hunt. Of course, it was due to Shi Eryang's ideological persuasion. Early next morning, Captain Ma led the tiger-hunting team into the forest, along with Zhou Taiwang and Banzi. Zhou Taiwang carried a sack of baked potatoes. Banzi's acute nose quickly picked up the tiger's scent and the team found its paw prints. Kneeling and looking closely at some tamped down speargrass, Zhou Taiwang observed, "The tiger passed here during the first half of last night; the broken blades have already withered and darkened. If the tiger had passed more recently, the broken blades would still be fresh and green."

They tracked the tiger all day long, crossing ridges and valleys. After spending the night in a cave, they finally located their quarry not far from Dragon Decapitating Gorge. According to plan, Zhou Taiwang hardened his heart and killed Banzi, suspending the dog upside-down from a tree branch. A pitiable fate for the faithful hunting dog!

The splendid tiger meandered purposefully through the dense forest, its golden-black stripes reflecting mysterious light like a brilliant sunset. As the creature moved, its two ears suddenly perked up and it raised its nose, sensing something unusual. More hesitantly, in fits and starts, it gently padded forward, stopping behind a coverage of a clump of brush ten or fifteen feet from Banzi, sizing up the dead dog with its lightning eyes. Powerful and clever from long years in the mountains, the tiger did not impulsively jump out and seize the dog; rather, it patiently bided its time, watching with its piercing gaze from the underbrush. After a long while, ascertaining there was no danger, it gathered itself, then, in a single leap, seized Banzi between its powerful jaws, snapped the rope, and bounded into the depths of the forest.

It was early autumn; the tiger, Banzi hanging limply from his jaws, glided soundlessly over the fallen leaves blanketing the forest floor. Its vigilant translucent eyes scanned the route ahead.

Holding his pistol aloft, Captain Ma wanted to pursue immediately, but Zhou Taiwang held up a hand, signaling him to remain still. He whispered, "Keep calm, he's still too wild."

The tiger reached a slope rampant with tall, tufted speargrass and stopped to rest. Set above a river, the place was familiar and safe, with no strange scents. Lying in the deep coverage of the tall grass at ease, it tore into its prey with relish.

The tiger finally ate its fill. It wanted to wander around the mountains, but was unwilling to leave the haunch of the dog behind. In the past, the tiger ate only prey it had killed itself and left the moment it felt sated, never returning to finish the remains. But now prey was ever more scarce, so the tiger covered the haunch with branches and grass. Then, belly full and spirits high, the tiger playfully cavorted in the speargrass for a few moments, moved down to the river to lap at the waters, then loped off.

From a perch on a distant tree branch, Zhou Taiwang watched. He knew that the tiger would return for the meat sooner or later. He had led Captain Ma's team to the tiger's hiding place, easily following the trail of lime from the bag affixed to Banzi's forepaw. Once the tiger had left, Zhou stealthily moved to the swath of speargrass, cleared away the branches, cut an incision in the meaty part of the haunch with his hunting knife, and filled it with colorless potassium cyanide. Then he joined the others in the dense undergrowth along the riverbank to wait.

Returning from its jaunt along the forested ridges, the tiger wandered down to the river, immersing its powerful body in the green waters. Its black-striped golden fur shone in the afternoon sunlight that filtered through the canopy of branches. Fallen leaves floated about the mighty cat as it paddled and romped about. From their hiding place, Captain Ma and his men watched in awe. Only as the sun set in the west, did the tiger—refreshed and relaxed—return to his hidden cache. Not finding anything unusual, it bolted down the cyanide-laced haunch in several mouthfuls. Almost at once, it felt as though its inner organs were afire and dashed back to the river to quench its terrible thirst. By the time it reached the river's edge, the poor creature felt as if the heavens were spinning and the earth was whirling.

The tiger's innocent eyes filled with rage and pain. Crouching beside the waters, it rapidly extended its tongue time and again, drinking for dear life; it raised its head for a moment, then lowered it to drink again. Looking at its reflection, the tiger saw its splendid golden and black flame-like stripes gradually fade and begin to disappear. The creature loosed an agonized, "*A-woooo.*" Reeling to one side, it tumbled into the shallows, sending waves across the river that lapped the far bank.

The tiger raised its head for one final powerful roar; for a long time the sound reverberated in the surrounding mountains, making the forest tremble.

Half an hour later, the tiger-hunting team, still horror-stricken, emerged gingerly from their concealment. Several men tossed stones at the tiger's body to ascertain that it was truly dead. They cut arm-thick poles and strung thumb-thick creepers and vines back and forth to fashion a makeshift pallet to carry the tiger. However, the tiger proved too heavy for four men, and the narrow path would not allow more to take part. In the end, they cut the tiger into pieces; Zhou Taiwang and the soldiers each carried a separate part.

And so it was recorded in the local annals: with the aid of Zhou Taiwang, the PLA had succeeded in killing the monster-tiger for the people. To reward Zhou for his merit, the township governor had the tiger's tongue cut off and presented to him. Zhou Taiwang, in turn, offered the tongue to Captain Ma, greasing the skids so that his son Zhou Chuang could join the People's Liberation Army. Captain Ma accepted the memento proudly. As a tiger dislikes eating the fur of its prey, its tongue is covered with thorny, ridged serrations, bristly papillae each almost an inch long that help strip fur from meat as it eats. Captain Ma dried the tiger's tongue and gifted it to his wife, who used it to comb her lustrous, black hair every day.

Everybody knew that Zhou Taiwang had poisoned the last tiger in

Huangshui. He became a local celebrity of sorts. His demise, too, became known to all:

Shortly after Captain Ma departed, Zhou Taiwang was making gunpowder for his homemade rifle, mixing sulphur, charcoal, and saltpeter, when a rogue spark from the fireplace ignited a loud explosion. Masui was repairing the handle of his hoe at the gate when he suddenly heard a booming "Peng!" followed by a series of piercing screams from the Zhou wing of the courtyard. Masui rushed over to find Zhou Taiwang bloody and severely burned.

Masui and Zhou Chuang carefully put Zhou Taiwang on a litter and carried him to the clinic in the Huangshui. Zhou's monkey-like wife followed, tearfully trailing along. After several days of treatment in Huangshui, they carried Zhou Taiwang back to Gengguping. He was never again able to stand.

Chapter Twenty-Eight

I

Careworn Tao Jiuxiang sat on an exposed tree root and gazed skyward. From behind, Shi Eryang bellowed, "Get to work! If were gonna make these god-damned earthen blast furnaces work, we need at least a thousand big trees to start off. With five blast furnaces burning two tons of charcoal a day, in six months we can forge tons and tons of crude iron. We'll set up hundreds of sheds to grow goldthread in the fifty acres of razed forest. Then the tens of thousands of tons of goldthread rhizome we produce can be exchanged for tens of millions of tons of iron and steel! Goddamn it, let's go!" Oblivious, weary Tao Jiuxiang stared into space. Everyday, she worked with the production team making compost, hoping to cobble together enough labor points to cover Yonggang's school tuition.

"What're you looking at?" asked Shi Eryang.

Watching Yonggang tend an ox on a distant slope, Tao Jiuxiang's lips quivered and she muttered, "Poor child, your father is so cruel. Back and gone again so soon!"

Eryang grumbled, "Goddamned ghostspawn witch-woman!"

Lihaku had once been a prime habitat for tigers. After Zhou Taiwang poisoned the last tiger in Huangshui, however, tigers' tracks altogether disappeared from the mountains and valleys. More goldthread sheds now cluttered the ridges than in the past three hundred years combined. Nothing is inexhaustible and nothing lasts forever: wryly, Tao Jiuxiang watched people put up innumerable sheds, raze the primeval forest, cut endless bamboo groves, terrace the ridges, make blast furnaces, and quarry earth for tiles.

During the war against the birds, the mountainfolk had leveled the goldthread fields. With other members of the team, Masui wandered the forest seeking wild young goldthread rhizomes. For years, the mountainfolk had only grown crops, and now rhizomes were in dire shortage. Fortunately, among the deserted lean-tos and sheds they discovered a number of rhizomes. Clever Shi Eryang ordered them to search by torchlight, an effort that yielded an impressive initial batch of goldthread, which they transported to the purchasing station. As a result, each household received a generous share of the money. Tao Jiuxiang sent Yonggang and Yongguang to the new school in Huangshui. It was a half-day school; each day they spent four hours walking to school and back. When they returned, afternoon chores like fetching water and chopping kindling awaited.

One day after the brothers were dismissed from school, they met Xia Liangxian in Huangshui, who had come to purchase salt. Yonggang found his Uncle's face had become a dropsical mask. Solicitously, he asked, "Uncle, how are you?"

Turning to Yonggang, he sighed, "The hunter, Zhou Taiwang, is dying."

Yonggang retorted, "You're talking nonsense. He got scorched by gunpowder, but the clinic saved him."

Xia Liangxian said, "I've come to take his soul. "

Yongguang interrupted, "If the Yama wants his soul, he'll send a ghost minion. Why does he need your help?"

Xia Liangxian said, "Zhou Taiwang's home has several portraits of Chairman Mao; their radiant *yang* energy is so potent that ghosts are afraid to approach Zhou's body. Therefore, Yama has taken me into his employ as a taker of souls."

Seeing his taciturn Uncle's droopy eyebrows and half-closed eyelids, Yonggang felt ill at ease: this macabre incarnation of his mercurial Uncle was unlike the man he had known. Curious, he asked, "Are you really going to do that?"

Xia Liangxian said, "I'm reluctant to drag away his soul, as he has a family to support. But I have to. The Superintendent of Taking Souls is watching from the netherworld. Zhou Taiwang's lifespan in the world of men is at an end. I've already given him a nudge, though not a fatal one; he lives still, but will die two days hence."

Listening to this ominous prediction, the two brothers shuddered.

Sure enough, two days later Zhou Taiwang committed suicide. Following his injury, Zhou Taiwang had been bedridden for three years, tortured by a range of painful ailments and maladies. In the days leading up to his death, the suffering had become so intense that he had howled in agony. Finally, clutching his precious homemade rifle, the barrel pointing to the underside of his jaw, he pulled the trigger with a toe and shot himself to death.

Shocked by Xia Liangxian's words, the two brothers had told Tao Jiuxiang and Masui secretly when they reached home. Aghast, Tao Jiuxiang made the brothers swear not to tell anyone else. She told Masui that early on morning of the suicide she had heard booming outside the front door as she fastened on her basket. Yet when she opened the door, she saw nothing unusual.

Masui—though he dared not tell others for fear he would be mocked as superstitious and made to kneel on kernels of corn in punishment—knew that before a man dies his ethereal spirit wanders through all of the places he has known. This is called "collecting the footprints." For the average person, the spirit completes the journey to "collect the footprints" in a twinkling. But for a far-ranging hunter like Zhou Taiwang the peregrinations of the spirit would take far longer.

After his unusual and violent end, Zhou Taiwang was buried nearby; no *tima* helped exorcise evil spirits or ushered him to the netherworld. Tao Jiuxiang felt uneasy. Masui reassured, "Think of all the people around Huangshui in recent years who have jumped off cliffs, drowned, hanged themselves with hemp-braided ropes, and died of hunger and disease. None of the families invited a *tima* to exorcise evil spirits. Yongguang and Yonggang are grown up now. I don't think we should worry about it."

Still, he was concerned. He exchanged some of Xia Yinmei's old clothing for two new Chairman Mao badges that he pinned on the chests of Yonggang and Yongguang. Around Gengguping, people often saw phosphorescent lights at night. Even during daytime, someone claimed they had seen a ghost swinging in the trees. To get to school, the cousins left the courtyard along with the children of the other families at four o'clock in the morning. Trembling, they walked through the remnants of the forest in the darkness, bravely holding torches as they passed through the interstices of the worlds of spirits and men on their way to Huangshui Middle School.

II

Years passed, the solar crow and the lunar hare tirelessly tracing their celestial careers. When the schools closed down, Yongguang and Yonggang returned to Gengguping to help in the fields. The boys had grown up like young bamboos.

They harvested goldthread with iron hand rakes, deftly using knives to cut off thin, threadlike runners, putting the rhizomes in a bamboo strip basket to dry, then shaking the basket to winnow away the hairs and dirt before carrying their yield to Huangshui purchasing station. As they passed through Peppercorn Bend, they met up with a dozen Red Guards, among them Zhou Taiwang's second son. Yongguang stopped and greeted, "Zhou Er, glad to see you."

Zhou Er and other classmates had just returned from Fengjie City, where they had linked up with other Red Guard groups. For several months, his family had not heard from him. Old Mother Zhou grumbled constantly, "Who knows if that wild creature is dead or alive? Never so much as a word from him!" Wearing a yellow PLA uniform, Zhou Er said imperiously, "You Lis hounded my aunt Zhou Damei to death and harmed my father. Now you're going to pay!"

Daunted by the sudden attack, Yongguang looked to Yonggang, who merely shrugged timidly. Puzzled, Yongguang reproached, "Your aunt is my aunt. She didn't want to marry a normal man. Don't you get it? That tree demon seduced her and led her spirit away. And your father was so dim-witted that he killed himself. How can you blame us?"

Zhou Er glared at Yongguang and shouted, "Bullshit!" He bent down, picked up a stone, and hurled it at Yongguang.

"Make the Li family pay!" howled the Red Guards, showering Yongguang and Yonggang with stones.

The cousins took to their heels and fled back to Gengguping, downtrodden. Arriving home, they saw the old ox in the courtyard, alternately nodding and shaking its head as though it were speaking with someone. Lo and behold, as they turned the corner, Tao Jiuxiang was sitting on the stone steps in front of the house, a home-thrown clay pot in her hands, feeding the ox cornmeal as she chanted a melancholy tune:

> *Spring torrents down from the heavens pour,*
> *Yet you trudge through the fields, torch fastened to your horn.*
> *Your lead rope chafes till it snaps in half,*
> *The yoke leaves sores on your tired back.*
> *Flesh worn to callus by toil, work till the light is faint,*
> *Yet, you, good beast, never utter a single low of complaint.*

On hearing these lines, the eyes of the old ox grew moist.

> *Good ox, finest creature under the solar wheel,*
> *Even though your bitter lot is toiling in the fields.*

With these lines, Tao Jiuxiang shed tears together with the ox.

"Grandma, what's that you're singing?" asked Yonggang. He and Yongguang could not understand their grandmother's coarse, rustic brogue.

Raising her sleeve to wipe her eyes, Tao Jiuxiang answered, "Today is the Ox King's birthday. This old ox works all year long, so I'm offering it some grain."

It was said that long ago men depended on their own muscle, sinew, and sweat to plow the fields; they struggled to eke out a living from meager harvests. Then the Jade Emperor sent the Ox King-bodhisattva down to the mortal world, decreeing that as crops were scarce the Ox would eat but one meal every third day. The Ox King plowed the fields together with the people. Tired and hungry from his labor, the Ox King altered the Jade Emperor's decree so that it read 'three meals a day' rather than 'one meal every third day.' Infuriated, the Jade Emperor sentenced the Ox King to work in the human world forever. To show their gratitude for the Ox King's labor and help, the people designated the first day of the tenth lunar month as his birthday.

With the story of the Ox King in mind, the cousins entered the house and ate several roasted potatoes. Then, taking rice buns with them, they drove the work-weary old ox to the slope to graze. When it was sated, they led the ox down to Inkblack Creek, washed and scrubbed it with branches, and hung the rice buns from its horns.

When the old ox opened its eyes wide and saw its handsomely festooned reflection in the creek, it lowed contentedly. This day, its mistress had fed it delicious cornmeal mush and the young masters had offered it rice buns. The creature felt the accumulated bitterness, tension, and fatigue in its muscles melt away.

In more cheerful spirits, the two brothers had started driving the ox homeward when they saw a large crowd gathering. Tying the ox to a tree, the two shoved forward for a look. They saw a pile of fresh-dug earth and stone. A huge stone gate had been thrown open and a black lacquered coffin dragged outside! They were stunned: their grandfather's tomb was being desecrated!

Wearing their signature red armbands, the Red Guards swarmed like bandits, zealous eyes flashing against the sunset orange sky. Several worked to pry open the coffin. Then Li Diezhu's tomb was ripped opened! After the long exhumation, their triumphant moment of discovery threw them into a frenzy of excitement: though Li Diezhu had been underground for more than three decades, he had not decomposed at all; his face was pale and his blue silken funerary garment was perfectly preserved. Beads of quicksilver rolled around the bottom of the coffin.

Utterly rapt, Shi Eryang stared at the droplets of mercury, thinking it must be his imagination. Unable to help himself, he abruptly extended his right hand and rummaged beneath the body, hoping to find Li Diezhu's legendary gold nuggets; he ended up, however, with a handful of embalming fluid, mercury, and rotted flesh.

Li Diezhu's mossy tomb on Rivergrass Plain had become a target for Zhou Er's revenge; his fellow Red Guards served as his instruments. They dragged out Li Diezhu's corpse, smashed the coffin, and plundered the valuables. Not satisfied with this desecration, the Red Guards ransacked Mahe's empty tomb, throwing open the gate, smashing the coffin to smithereens, and fishing out the symbolic funerary clothes and tearing them to ribbons. Yongguang and Yonggang had heard about their youngest uncle, who had died on the battlefield in the War of Resistance Against Japan when he was their age. What a pity that he had fought for the Nationalists instead of the People's Liberation Army!

Once the crowds dispersed and night fell, they lit a torch, gathered up Li Diezhu's remains, placed them back inside the tomb, sealed their youngest uncle's empty tumulus, and set to repairing the tomb mounds.

The boys knew that their grandma was profoundly superstitious. Along Inkblack Creek there stood a number of jagged, queer-shaped stones that looked like various creatures—some hawks and others monkeys; Tao Jiuxiang believed these rocks to be divine beasts. A colorful array of wildflowers, red and white, blossomed in the valleys and on the mountainslopes; she believed they were flower spirits. In the aftermath of the desecration, the cousins feared that their grandma would die of rage. Profoundly alarmed, they hid in a copse until darkness, fretting and shedding tears. Once the crowds dispersed and night fell, they lit a torch, gathered up Li Diezhu's remains and placed them back inside the mound, then set to repairing the tomb.

Over and over again, a queer birdcall echoed through the mountains. The torch flickered in the night wind, first bright and then dim. In the shuddering light, the desecrated tombs had a desolate air. After Qin Ji'an's death, his wife Zhang remarried and moved to Enshi. Seeing the house built on the auspicious site empty, Old Mother Qin quietly moved in, ignoring the strenuous protestations of her son and grandson. After Qin Liexiong's death, his wife Zhou had remained in his home as a widow. When Old Mother Qin moved to Inkblack Creek, Zhou agreed to accompany her. The two widows determined to spend the rest of their years there grappling with the evil spirits that insisted on clashing with the Qins. Together the two stood at the gate of the timber-framed homestead, watching the two Lis work.

Yongguang and Yonggang returned home to find their grandmother sitting before the stove, her tear-scarred face a mask of seething hatred.

"Grandma!" cried Yongguang, kneeling beside her. "We reburied our grandfather."

At sunrise the following day, Tao Jiuxiang, regardless of her landlord status, knelt in front of the courtyard gate, incanting and cursing in her earthy brogue:

> *O, heaven high and earth below,*
> *Look at my poor man in his endless woe.*
> *Let all who have trampled him underfoot,*
> *Be stricken down by five lightning bolts.*
> *Whoever casts him down on the sloping rise;*
> *May a thousand devils gouge out their eyes.*

> *Ones who threw his remains in the meadow by the river:*
> *May they die without child, bloodline forever severed.*

Overnight, her gray hair had turned silvery-white. Disheveled, she faced east, looking toward the crimson morning clouds in the distance. Like some wicked venerable ancestress, she emanated an aura of malice.

Masui and Yonggang dragged her back into the house.

Before long, Shi Eryang was stricken by a severe illness. Amid his anguished screams, his wife Sun Xiaoxiao, her heart palpitating wildly in fear, took out the upper fang from the tiger Zhou Taiwang had poisoned. She boiled rapeseed oil in a pan, then seared the fang, planning to use it to perform a *guasha* scraping treatment to bring out bruises. Folk believed that because a tiger's fang was a sanguine and fierce tool for killing, it could ward off evil and insalubrious influences. Therefore, when a powdered fang was scraped on the site of an injury, a person would be restored to health within a day or two. On this occasion, though, as soon as Sun Xiaoxiao placed the fang in the red-hot pan, it exploded into thousands of fragments with a terrible *"Peng!"* Not knowing what to do, she gathered up the fragments and ground them into a powder that she fed to her husband. The treatment failed to help him in the least. She rushed to ask her son to help carry Eryang to the clinic in Huangshui. Before they could get out the door, however, Shi Eryang died.

Another strange rumor circulated.

On that very day, Xia Liangxian was weeding in the goldthread fields with the rest of the production team. While working, he suddenly closed his eyes and slumped to the earth, unconscious. Another member of the production team, a distant nephew of Wang Donghe, prodded him for a good fifteen minutes before he came to his senses. When the fellow asked what was wrong, Xia Liangxian merely cryptically murmured, "Just now, I took Shi Eryang's soul."

Eryang was supposed to live a few more hours, Xia Liangxian explained, but out of consideration for the family he had cut the man's lifespan short to save them the trouble of putting him on a pallet and carrying him all the way to the clinic only to then have to transport the body back home. Therefore, after discussing the matter with supervising ghost officials, he had simply claimed Eryang's soul a little earlier.

The man happened to be headed to Gengguping. As soon as he reached the courtyard, he heard bitter lamentations and saw Eryang's corpse laid out on the stove-bed.

Learning of Eryang's death, Tao Jiuxiang merely spat, "Got what he deserved!"

Word circulated that the incorrigible madman Xia Liangxian worked for Yama, the King of Hell. Though he ate the food of the living, he conducted affairs in the realm of ghosts. Despite prison and repeated punishments, nobody could make him mend his ways!

Chapter Twenty-Nine

I

The colorful panoply of local characters like Li Mawu, Zhou Taiwang, and Shi Eryang were gone. The remains of the pioneer and earliest settler at Gengguping, Li Diezhu, had been dragged from his coffin and strewn about. The dwellers of the courtyard at Gengguping, seemingly caught in the enigmatic toils of some daemonic curse, looked for answers: they concluded that the unabated fury of the two aggrieved spirits buried in the recessed vale lay at the heart of their unstinting woes. Some scolded Tao Jiuxiang for allowing the star-crossed couple to be buried so close to the Li homestead. The old matriarch sent Masui to build a bamboo fence enclosing the tombs, turning the graveyard into a garden and an orchard: inside the fence, she planted beans, pumpkins, and corn; around the perimeter she replanted pines and cypresses, and peach and plum trees. Chanting as she worked, she urged the spirits of her eldest son and her daughter-in-law to wreak murderous vengeance on any who might intrude.

Denizens of Gengguping shuddered at the whistles and whispers carried in the wind from the leafy trees and rank grass surrounding the enclosure, the nightly hauntings of the aggrieved rebel soul and his hungry ghost of a wife.

Tao Jiuxiang's remaining son and two grandsons grew accustomed to her eccentricity, to the existence of the graveyard garden, and to the constant presence of Mawu and Xia Yinmei's apparitions. The fruits and vegetable from the tomb enclosure became part of their daily meals.

Tormented by memories and fears, Masui's hair whitened. Recently, another fear had gripped him: the foundation of the main house at Gengguping that the Peasant Association had allocated to him was set higher than the ancestral graves on Speargrass Plain. Sooner or later, this off-kilter geomantic alignment would bring down further catastrophes upon future generations of Lis. If only the Peasant Association had allocated the main house to someone else, they might have averted future disasters. He shuddered at the thought, and, with Yongguang's help, moved all the furniture out of the main house, leaving it empty except for farming tools and sundry odd and ends.

Dressed in a gray shawl, frail and stone-faced, Tao Jiuxiang watched Masui and Yongguang bustling back and forth, covered in dust and spiderwebs. In the days that followed, the Li family shunned the main house except to take or put back a spade or hoe.

For the first time in many years, Yongyu sent Tao Jiuxiang a letter, reporting that Aji had told her and her mother of her father's death, and now that she had grown up she planned to get married in Chongqing. The letter also urged her grandma not to worry and said that she had no intention of returning to Huangshui, as she didn't want be a burden. Her mother Jin, Yongyu wrote, was in full agreement.

"So, then don't come back . . . don't come back. After all, sooner or later a girl wives another and becomes part of another family," Tao Jiuxiang sighed, rolling her eyes as she recalled Yongyu as a pert, young girl. She regretted that she had been unable to protect her granddaughter; Yongyu was probably best off depending on her mother Jin's arrangements.

Seeing his grandmother's forlorn aspect, Yongguang comforted, "Don't worry, Grandma. I'm young and strong, and one of these days soon I'm going to take a wife. You can treat her just like a true granddaughter." Fortunately, the smooth-cheeked youth had not inherited his father's pocks. While lending a hand to help out the Yaos in Peppercorn Bend, he had fallen in love with their daughter, Yao Xiuzhen. Sparks had ignited, and the two had secretly started a relationship.

Tao Jiuxiang looked skeptical.

Late that same evening, sixty-year-old Masui was digging goldthread rhizomes in his new plot on the slopes not far from Speargrass Plain. The

Huangshui government had just divided and apportioned rhizome plots to individual families. After digging up the rhizomes, Masui planned to dry them that very night, then haul them to Huangshui to sell.

Out of the gloaming suddenly echoed a familiar, bloodcurdling "*Waaa-ooough*," causing Masui to shudder. For years, no one had heard or seen a tiger. Startled, he dropped his iron hand rake and shimmied up a fir tree. Glancing in the direction of the roar, he saw a huge beast shoulder its way out of the underbrush at the foot of the jagged cliff. The tiger wandered over to the creek's edge, ate some speargrass, lapped up some water, and rested on an outcropping of stone before rising and heading off.

It was too dark for Masui to clearly discern the pattern of the massive creature's stripes. However, its eyes flashed like lightning, emanating not the usual lantern's light, but a piercing electric blue. Wondering if he was seeing straight, Masui climbed down and cautiously shuffled over to the slanted rock where the big cat had rested. The tiger's heat still clung to the rock, prompting Masui to recoil as though jolted by a shock. Masui returned to Gengguping, but when he sat down to dinner he was too agitated to eat a single mouthful. "Could that tiger have broken free from the netherworld? Its eyes were lit with ghostfire," he said, trembling.

"It's just a tiger!" Tao Jiuxiang sat beside the lamp, puffing on her pipe with a cold, scornful expression. "Everyone says there are no more tigers in Lihaku. They're wrong. They've always been here, hidden in remote and desolate places."

Yonggang asked, "Why did it come back?"

Emptying the bowl of her pipe, Tao Jiuxiang answered, "It wandered over a couple of ridges and came back to eat the speargrass alongside Inkblack Creek."

Masui disagreed. "No, it was a nightmare of a tiger, with blue eyes, like ghostfire."

Tao Jiuxiang said ominously, "Only a white tiger's eyes are blue!"

Local legends told that a tiger turned snow white when it reached an age of five hundred years. A tiger that lived a thousand years became an immortal king, a tutelary god of the mountainfolk, possessing the power to expel ghosts and subdue evil spirits. Having borne witness to the ghost tiger, Masui was too unnerved to sleep; the two beams of blue light haunted him like a waking nightmare. By the time he rose the following morn, he was convinced that heaven had sent the White Tiger King down to earth on a sacred mission; after arriving in a remote, unpopulated region near Seven Illuminations Mountain, the regal creature had crossed a series of ridges and concealed itself in the caves of Dragon Decapitating Gorge. Its peregrinations led the tiger to the fragrant creekside speargrass along the margin of Speargrass Plain.

News of the advent of the White Tiger spread like wildfire. A reporter from the county newspaper eagerly made his way to Huangshui to take pictures. With some background in zoology, he knew that the tiger in Lihaku was likely a South China tiger, and figured that the white tiger was a genetic anomaly. The South China tiger was the ancestor of all ten subspecies of tigers on earth. There was only a handful left in the wild. Unfortunately, after several days of trekking through the mountains, he could not find any trace of its existence and returned to Fengjie City, disappointed.

Soon, the white tiger receded into the clouds and mists of Huangshui, taking its place as one of the legends of the Three Gorges.

II

After Shi Eryang's death, Qin Shaocheng—a grandnephew from the Qin family—became the new production team leader at Gengguping. While other goldthread fields yielded a thousand pounds of goldthread rhizome per acre, his fields averaged 1500 pounds. Rather than instructing people in new techniques for cultivating rhizomes, however, he directed a campaign to plant new trees. Trees, he contended, could provide stakes and poles for goldthread sheds and for marking fields, and could help provide shade for growing goldthread. If folks kept cutting down trees, he reasoned, the forest would be gone, and that would destroy the most profitable basis of their livelihood, the goldthread.

Big trees from the primeval forest were scarce around Gengguping. Only five remained in the proximity of the old Li homestead. Qin Shaocheng hung a wooden placard on each with an official registration number and notification that these trees were now the property of the township government.

Day after day, together with the folks in the courtyard, Masui planted new trees on the mountain slopes. As the transplanted trees greened and came to life, Yongguang married Yao Xiuzhen, the girl from Peppercorn Bend. As folks in Huangshui had been urged to break with old customs and practices, a simple wedding took place with no matchmaker, no betrothal gifts, no sedan chair, and no extravagant ceremony.

Yonggang envied his cousin's happy marriage. Sighing deeply, Tao Jiuxiang said sorrowfully, "You should find a girl and get married, too."

"Only a pockmarked horse mulberry shrub would get hitched to me!" Yonggang groaned. Though he was a handsome, well-proportioned young man with good features, he was very conscious and ashamed that all of Huangshui looked at him as the son of a rebel and a criminal.

As Yonggang stoked the fire, Tao Jiuxiang bitterly shot back, "Don't let me hear you speak like that again!" Though she had grown thin as an empty hemp sack, a wind-dried eggplant, her mind was still razor sharp.

Yonggang grew silent.

Tao Jiuxiang began to chant a queer ditty,

> *Yo-ho, horse mulberry on the mountain high,*
> *Nobody could cut you down in ancient times;*
> *But if you ever meet a bold man like me,*
> *I'll take my ax and hack down your tree.*

"What kind of song is that, Granny?" asked Yonggang.

"A goddess cursed the horse mulberry and turned it into a twisted tree, lowly and worthless." Leaning toward her grandson in a conspiratorial manner, Tao Jiuxiang continued, "But long, long ago, the horse mulberry used to be the tallest, fastest-growing tree in the world; rooted in the earth, it could reach the heavens. Our ancestors could get to the Celestial Palace by climbing horse mulberry trees, and the gods descended to rendezvous secretly with beautiful mountain girls. The horse mulberry served as a bridge between heaven and earth."

Yonggang could not believe that horse mulberry shrubs, good only for kindling and cooking wood, were once so grand and powerful. Curiosity piqued, he ventured, "If horse mulberry trees used to reach heaven, how did they become the twisted, runty shrubs that they are today?"

"The taproots of horse mulberry trees are sunken deep in mountain soil, but their crowns used to pierce the clouds," Tao Jiuxiang ruminated, searching her memories as she puffed on her pipe. "A group of monkeys clambered up the trees eating the fruit, climbing all the way into the sky, nimbly hurdling the walls and entering the Celestial Palace. The palace was chock full of gold, silver, and jade. Overwhelmed by the splendor, one of them dizzily staggered back, upsetting a jade platter that shattered with a loud crash. Terrified, the monkeys fled, scurrying back down the horse mulberries, and hiding in caves. Investigating, the Celestial Queen Mother of the West discovered that the monkeys had ascended to heaven by climbing the horse mulberry trees. In a towering rage, she placed a curse: 'Henceforth horse mulberry trees will never grow tall. They shall take root the first year, grow crooked the second year, and be cut down for firewood the third year.' From that time on, the horse mulberry became a scrub, no taller than a man."

"What a pity!" exclaimed Yonggang, lost for the moment in reverie, transported to that strange world where men and spirits lived together. He added, regretfully, "Wouldn't it be awesome if we could climb a horse mulberry up to the moon, wander around for a while, then come back!" How bland the world has become, he mused, like a colorless and flavorless dream.

"The coffins hanging from the cliffs of Inkblack Creek were made with mulberry boards. The wood had a straight grain and it didn't rot. That helped the dead find their way to heaven. Of course, you can't use a horse mulberry for a coffin any more . . . they only grow to be five feet tall. But on the Pure and Bright Festival before people sweep their ancestors' graves, folk still pray in front of horse mulberry trees . . . I tell you, it works!" Tao Jiuxiang exclaimed.

"Grandma," asked Yonggang, "How could anyone mill a tree that tall into boards?" He blinked his eyes, asking, "Did they use a two-man saw with one person up in heaven and the other down on earth?"

Tao Jiuxiang had no answer. Downcast, she muttered, "Maybe the ancestors, too, weave their tall tales?"

Yonggang looked at the branch in his hand and hesitated, wondering if he should throw it into the fire. Grandmother and grandson looked at each other. Finally, Tao Jiuxiang grumbled, "Burn it. The curse of a goddess cannot be undone. Throw it in the fire . . . it's what she ordained."

The horse mulberries shed their leaves in winter; new branches and leaves grew in spring, and the tree bore yellow-green, caterpillar-like flowers; in summer, the flowers became fruit, at first green, gradually turning black-purple, hanging in clusters from the branches. Its branches were so brittle that even dullest machete could lop them off. In winter, when all the dry firewood was picked clean from the slopes, the mountainfolk would dig out mulberry roots, bundle them, and carry them home in baskets. But even when folk thought they had spaded out all the horse mulberry roots, the fresh red seedlings would still spring out of the earth the following year, and yield purple-black fruits in summer. Then the cycle would begin yet again; the horse mulberries being cut down and uprooted, but stubbornly growing back.

After that, every time Yonggang headed into the forest with his machete, Tao Jiuxiang's story of the monkeys and the celestial palace would come to mind. As he cut kindling, he would echo her chant:

> *Yo-ho, horse mulberry on the mountain high,*
> *Nobody could cut you down in ancient times;*
> *But if you ever meet a bold man like me,*
> *I'll take my ax and hack down your tree.*

Invariably, these lines made him giggle and infused him with cheer. He also hoped that, as he wandered through the woods, an immortal fairy maiden would descend and take a fancy to him.

One afternoon Yonggang called on one of his old classmates, Zhao Changyou's son, who lived at Peppercorn Bend. It happened that Ran Yulian, the wife of master builder Zhu Shun's second son, had stopped in. Seeing Yonggang, she whispered to Zhao Changyou, "What a good-mannered young man! Whose family is he from?"

Knowingly, Zhao Changyou answered, "He's Li Mawu's son."

Ran Yulian burst out, "Li Mawu's son? Why, he's grown up now. What a good-looking young man!"

Zhao Changyou joked, "Handsome, maybe . . . good luck playing matchmaker."

Ran Yulian remained silent, continuing to appraise the boy from afar. Seeing this, Zhao Changyou added, "The kid's a hard worker and excels at farming the land . . . it's just that he's the child of a landlord family."

Nodding, the woman shrugged, "I'm going to marry my daughter to him."

Taken aback, Zhao Changyou countered, "But his grandmother's labeled a landlord, you know."

The woman said, "My family are landlords, too. If she marries into a family with "poor peasant" status, she'll get bullied. This way I won't have to worry."

III

As prowling wildcats mated in the niches of the mountains and the flowering forests, a timeless vernal rite, Ran Yulian backed up her statement: the Zhus betrothed their daughter Mingxiu, the granddaughter of celebrated master craftsman Zhu Shun, to Li Yonggang.

Traditional wedding ceremonies had been banned as a vestige of the feudal past. No longer did a bride put on elaborate make-up and sing a heartbreaking lament when she left her natal family, nor was she transported in a sedan to the groom's homestead. Zhu Mingxiu walked to Gengguping, talking and laughing with her two sisters. At Tao Jiuxiang's behest, Masui slaughtered a pig for the nuptial feast. Having learned the new lingo espoused by the local Party leaders, Masui wrote a pair of couplets:

Wreathed in joyous smiles, the bride departs her parents' home;
With ambitious dreams for a bright future, she crosses her in-laws' threshold.

The production team leader, Qin Shaocheng, praised his verses.

Saddened by the lack of traditional pageantry, Tao Jiuxiang sent Masui to Peppercorn Bend to invite the drama troupe to perform. After the ban on traditional dance and dramas had been lifted, an amateur troupe had formed; as long as the host provided food and drink, they happily performed all over greater Huangshui.

Arriving in Peppercorn Bend in high spirits, he found several members of the troupe carving masks from silver poplar. Their woodworking skills were rough, and the characters they rendered in wood bore little resemblance to the figures from myth and legend. The old *tima*'s masks had burned, and Xia Qifa had never passed on the art of mask carving. All the villagers of Peppercorn Bend could do was smile bitterly and wistfully as they whittled their rough-hewn masks.

"What a likeness!" Masui flattered.

"If only that were true!" remarked a villager called Xiang Zhong, raising a half-painted mask of the Celestial White Tiger Emperor, and taking a long, critical look at this handiwork.

Masui took a breath and broached, "I have something to ask you."

"What is it?" asked Xiang Zhong, setting the mask on a table.

"My nephew's getting married tomorrow," said Masui, "Can the troupe come and perform?"

"Sure, sure," several others chimed in, "As we mountainfolk are all kith and kin, we ask no payment but a meal."

But the following morning, when Xiang Zhong put on the mask of the Celestial White Tiger, making ready to play the part, he was stricken by a blinding headache. The troupe had no choice but to change their repertoire.

After the wedding, Xiang Zhong fell ill for a month. It was said that only if a *tima* or drama-master who had played the role of the White Tiger and donned the mask ceremonially bequeathed it to a successor, might the disciple play the role of the storied ancestor. Any who violated this ritual protocol passed down from the ancestors through countless generations would be stricken with sickness or death.

Without the White Tiger, the dance lost all semblance of meaning. The dispirited players were unsure how to proceed. When Masui bumped into Xiang Zhong in the Huangshui market and listened to him vent his vexations, he suddenly thought of Xia Liangxian, and offered to invite the son of the last *tima* to join the troupe.

Upon returning home, Masui asked Yonggang to accompany him to Dragon Decapitating Gorge. Feeling guilty over Xiang Zhong's long illness following his wedding, Yonggang readily agreed. The next day, uncle and nephew, joined by Yonggang's new wife, Zhu Mingxiu, headed off together to call on Xia Liangxian, carrying joss paper, incense, candles, two bottles of wine, a pound of white sugar, and a pound of brown sugar.

As they neared their destination, the mountainslopes, once a colorful belt of horse mulberry shrubs and speargrass, now featured only drab patches of sere grass peeking from between the scree. On the far side the ugly head of the pilloried dragon jutted out of the sheer cliff, a single, thick fir tree growing from its brow like a great horn. A commemorative quatrain was inscribed at the foot of the cliff:

> *Our neighbors to the east, devious of heart and treacherous of design,*
> *Sought to annihilate our China, this splendid land of mine.*
> *But our valiant soldiers shed their blood on these shifting sands,*
> *Never shall we forget their sacrifice for this land!*

The poem—splendidly rendered in bold graven red characters that ran halfway up the cliff's face—had been written by Dong Biwu, a famous Communist Party leader. Beneath the poem were carved the names of the heroes who had given their life in the War of Resistance Against Japan. There was another commemorative inscription composed by Wang Binquan: "After the fateful day of July 7, 1937, with each passing day, bit by bit, the odious dwarf raiders from Japan encroached upon our divine land of China, wantonly robbing and killing as they went. To defend our beloved country, our homes and villages, loyal and heroic young men of Huangshui made their way to the front, standing tall to engage the wicked foe on the battlefield. Many fought to the last drop of blood. And though these valiant soldiers died in the War of Resistance Against Japan, they shall live forever in the hearts and minds of the Chinese people, remembered reverently as shining heroes, honored as exemplars forever worthy of our highest praise and admiration. If every Chinese possessed their valor and courage, no force could ever defeat our China!"

Seeing the ancient valley for the first time, Zhu Mingxiu gawked. With Xia Qifa's nurture and solicitude, the fir tree on the dragon's brow had gradually turned from yellow to green, coming back to life. But now, the tree's needles had turned a brittle yellowish-red. The surrounding mountainslopes, once a verdant swath of wildflowers, grass, and trees, teeming with raucous tribes of birds and beasts, had become desolate, pocked gray banks of boulders and scree. There was no sign of life on the lonely slopes; the stones no longer gathered even moss.

The faint chant of the old *tima* Xia Qifa from almost four decades earlier echoed in the wind:

> 'Neath the earth hidden a thousand years, a suit of armor cast of gold;
> To fight the calamitous dragon, to you I present it, my disciple bold.
> 'Neath the ground concealed a thousand years, a spear of alloyed gold;
> To fight the calamitous dragon, to you I present it, my disciple bold.

With the distant reports of firecrackers and the clanging of gongs, the old man's incantation to bequeath to his son the arts of communing with ghosts and exorcising baleful spirits from the world of men lingered. Befuddled, Masui gazed toward the Cliff of the Immured Dragon.

"That song . . . is that Uncle Liangxian?" asked Yonggang.

Taken aback, pock-faced Masui blinked sadly, as though emerging from a dream. With a bitter smile, he remarked, "I'm so old and muddle-headed for a minute there I thought it was . . . but no, you're right, it's your Uncle."

Chapter Thirty

I

When a debilitating illness felled his mother, Xia Liangxian opened the tomb of the old *tima* and laid Old Mother Xia beside her husband. Ensconced in the tumulus on the ridge the couple watched, waiting for the stone lotuses to flower and for the wicked dragon, captured so long ago by Yu the Great with his golden lightning hook, to be set free at last. In his spare time, Xia Liangxian—with neither father nor mother, neither wife nor offspring, neither brother nor sister—began digging his own tomb not far from his parents', a cavern for his eternal inhumation. Giving his spade a flamboyant brandish as he faced the harmonious interstices of light and shadow playing over the valley, he chanted:

> *To cut down an immortal, a vorpal blade,*
> *Forged for a thousand years in flame,*
> *Now, my disciple, to you I bequeath it,*
> *The head of the wicked dragon to claim.*

The trio from Gengguping picked their way up the slope, following the sound of his voice until they reached the shared tumulus of Xia Qifa and Old Mother Xia. There they found Xia Liangxian, his head canted to one side, lying supine in front of the small stele set before the tomb. On the stele he had recently engraved a new couplet:

"With mercury, world-shaking feats can be accomplished!
The dao can lead man to flight, astounding the heavens!

Standing at the foot of his grandparents' tomb, Yonggang called, "Uncle, we've come to see you."

"How are you?" cried Xia Liangxian cheerfully, casting a smile toward the wine bottles in Masui's hands. Slowly, he rose, standing next to the stele. "Let's head back to the house. I'm about to warm up dinner." He lived alone. Since Yama had appointed him a taker of souls, his once bright eyes had gradually grown dull, and his once handsome features grew ever more distorted. Each passing day saw him drinking, singing, and dozing off; sometimes he was lucid, but more often he was addled. For this reason, they had not dared invite him to Yonggang's wedding.

"Uncle, how are you?" greeted Zhu Mingxiu.

"This is my wife," Yonggang added respectfully.

Turning to Mingxiu, Xia Liangxian murmured, "How happy my sister Yinmei would be to see Yonggang married!"

"My poor sister-in-law's lot was a bitter one. Pity she didn't live to see that day. So what are you working on?" asked Masui, pointing to the newly excavated earth and stones.

"My last resting place . . . when the day comes that my two legs are stretched stiff and I am no more, my nephew can lay me to rest." Sighing, Xia Liangxian picked up his shovel and held it toward Yonggang, his eyes beaming with a hopeful light.

"Uncle, that's too far away to worry about now," Yonggang replied, in a wounded voice. Hurriedly, he and Mingxiu took out the joss paper, incense, and candles, and burned them in front of the tomb of Xia Qifa and Old Mother Xia.

Masui turned toward the dragon, observing, "Pretty shocking those characters carved in the cliff so many years ago are still there!"

In response, Xia Liangxian guffawed and began unraveling a yarn: "Once ol' Li Erdie was digging brake fern roots up on the slope when he heard a clanging. When he checked it out, production team leader Tian was directing a group of stonemasons to chip away those characters. He dropped his basket and screamed, 'You can't destroy those characters!' Tian retorted, 'We sure the hell can break and deface the reactionary writing of the Nationalists!' Li Erdie said, 'But those characters are connected to the soldiers who died in the War of Resistance Against Japan, young men in their late teens and early twenties. Their aggrieved ghosts are all seething with indignation. This's why the *tima* cast a spell to seal them in the cliff and make them keep watch over the dragon. If you smash off the characters, that wicked dragon will break loose from the cliff and wreak havoc—it'll bring down catastrophe on all our heads! Last year, I wanted to chisel off some flakes of stone for my pigpen, but after a few hits and knocks I felt uncomfortable and headed home.' Tian snorted, 'Seeing as that's the case, let's just let those pissed-off ghosts keep the wicked dragon in check.' So he ordered the masons to gather up their tools, and they went away."

Watching the drifting islands of rising mist and sinking cloud above the dragon's head, Masui smiled. He could not tell what they were doing, challenging or playing. This valley where the Xias lived and died was no ordinary place.

Suddenly recalling some recent news, Yonggang said, "Uncle, have you heard that China and Japan are going to re-establish diplomatic relations?"

Smile disappearing from his face, Xia Liangxian asked, "We're going to make friends with them?"

Yonggang looked up at the graven characters on the opposite cliff, saying, "I guess if the dragon can turn from the path of evil to good, so can the Japanese devils."

Slowing, Masui demurred, "The Japanese devils will never change. They're the most savage creatures under the sun."

Xia Liangxian ruminated, "What would your brother Mahe and his comrades-in-arms think of all this?" He lit the stove and boiled rice, then chopped up two bowls of preserved vegetables, baking them with chili peppers, soy, and vinegar.

Over the years, Masui had got drunk with Xia Liangxian five times: the first, at Mawu's wedding; the second, at his own wedding; the third, when Xia Qifa formally named Liangxian his successor; the fourth, at Li Diezhu's funeral; and the fifth, when Yinmei and Mawu were married. Each time had marked a significant event. On these previous occasions, Xia Liangxian drank sparingly to protect his throat and voice. But this time, he kept pace with Masui as they talked animatedly, their faces and necks hot red with the flush of alcohol.

Finally recalling the purpose of his visit, Masui leaned toward Liangxian and said, "Brother, I have a matter to discuss with you. A drama troupe has formed in Peppercorn Bend. Since you're such a good singer and dancer, they want you to join."

Raising his bloodshot eyes, Xia Liangxian said, "I don't have time for that. They gave me a quarter-acre goldthread field. I've been using horse mulberry branches for stakes. The mulberry takes root right above the growing rhizome, giving it natural shade. That way, I don't need to build a shed."

Looking at the pitted face of his once-handsome friend, a wave of pity swept over Masui. He urged, "You don't need to tend that little plot all the time. The troupe needs someone to play the White Tiger. You're the only one capable. If you're willing, I'm sure they'd be happy to come and help weed your goldthread field."

"The Celestial White Tiger? That's a role that can only be played and passed on by a *tima*. I'm an outcast. I can't take on that part," Xia Liangxian answered morosely, his wine-flushed face drooping into a mask of anguish. Regretting that he had broached the topic, Masui dared not bring it up again.

Seeing the change in his Uncle's expression, Yonggang took the dried, black mushrooms from his basket, and, squatting in front of Xia Liangxian, changed the topic, "Look, I brought you something. You know what these are?"

Xia Liangxian set aside his chopsticks, and, taking the mushrooms in cupped hands, scrutinized them closely in the lamplight beside the window. Finally, his eyes beaming, he said, "These are called human-headed mushrooms. Folks say these only grow on a coffin lid in the *yin* aura of a cold, damp grave before the vital energy flowing in a corpse is wholly extinguished. On rare occasions, over the months and years, the concentrated ethers of the corpse's breath, exhaled toward the inner lid of the coffin, cause these mushrooms to grow on the outer lid. They can be used to decoct a herbal remedy to enhance male potency."

Xia Liangxian broke off a piece and held it up to Yonggang, saying, "Try some." He put it in an empty bowl, and then placed the bowl in a cauldron hanging over the fire. Shortly, he removed the bowl and to the surprise of the visitors the mushroom had melted into a viscous, blood-colored liquid in the bottom of the bowl. Putting his lips to the bowl, he sipped a bit then passed it to Yonggang and Masui to taste.

Yonggang recoiled, waving his hands: "No, no . . . no way I'm gonna drink that. You're asking me to drink my grandpa's blood. No way I'm gonna drink that!"

The following day, Masui, Yonggang, and Mingxiu parted from Xia Liangxian and headed back toward Peppercorn Bend. Yonggang went with his wife to visit his parents-in-law. Having nothing else pressing to do, Masui tagged along, intending to tell the drama troupe the bad news.

As they left the ramshackle Xia homestead and Dragon Decapitating Gorge behind, the air was moist and heavy. The huge head of the immured dragon, locked for so many centuries in the cliff as punishment for its crimes, poked out of a rolling bank of mist as though breaking free from its cruel restraint of its cangue. How many centuries of torment had this creature silently endured? Looking from the ground fog up into the swirling mists as they left the wild valley, Masui suddenly bellowed, "Will the Celestial White Tiger Emperor dance again?"

The valley walls echoed, "Will the Celestial White Tiger Emperor dance again?"

Masui asked, "No dancing?"

The valley answered, "No dancing!"

Bemused, Yonggang joined in, hollering, "Will the White Tiger sing?"

The echo repeated, "Will the White Tiger sing?"

Yonggang asked, "No singing?"

The valley replied, "No singing!"

Silently, Masui strode onward, his face taking on a melancholy aspect.

Yonggang comforted him, saying, "It's just an echo."

When they learned that Xia Liangxian was not going to join them, the other players felt disappointed. Several actors cut down a bamboo pole. Then, donning conical broad-brimmed straw hats, they burned a ten-foot stick of incense on the top of the pole and, as they watched the smoke spiral skyward, prayed to the Celestial White Tiger, entreating him to give his blessings and permission to allow one of their company to wear his mask.

Half a moon later, Xia Liangxian headed to the market in Huangshui with a basket mounted on his back. In a nearby stall, Masui picked up a fistful of peppercorns, held them under his nose, and inhaled deeply. He looked up at the vendor and grinned, "We're just alike, aren't we?" Like Masui, the peppercorn merchant had a pockmarked face.

The peppercorn merchant guffawed, "Can't tell you from me!"

As Masui paid, a cheerful Xia Liangxian grabbed Masui's patched sleeve, saying, "I want to play the Celestial White Tiger."

Puzzled, he turned to Xia Liangxian, "I thought you said you couldn't."

Xia Liangxian exhaled, then, in a low, mysterious drawl, explained, "Every night since you left my father has paid me a visit, teaching me how to play the Celestial White Tiger Emperor. Initially, I refused. Each morning I woke up with a blinding headache. Last night, he came again and asked if I would play the White Tiger. Finally, I relented. He taught me all night long, but this morning I awakened refreshed, without the slightest trace of a headache." Dancing empty-handed, brandishing an imaginary sword, he began chanting the lines of the drama.

In his dreams Xia Liangxian had mastered the part of the White Tiger. "Ah!" exclaimed an astonished Masui. "Sweet mother! Did the spirit of the old *tima* truly come from the netherworld to visit you? So the old *tima* passed on his arts one last time!"

II

Still, the dilapidated old Li homestead and stone tower stood in the embrace of the mountains. On the slopes, the pear trees were in full blossom; heavy with grain, the rice panicles drooped. Around the house grew ormosia trees bearing red love beans, fir trees, and several thick ginkgos.

As the sun rose one morning, Mingxiu birthed little Fanwen.

The grass on the slopes swayed in the wind. Several twittering sparrows flitted about, bobbing up and down as they perched on stalks of grass. Holding his grandnephew, Fanwen, Masui wound his way past the overgrowth at the foot of the stone tower, opened the hedge-gate to the graveyard garden in the recessed vale, and called, "Ma, we've got guests."

The leaves of the vines and creepers covering the low tomb mounds of Mawu and Yinmei rustled in the breeze, sounding as though they were whispering secrets. Her hair snow white, Tao Jiuxiang extended a withered, skinny hand and picked two small pumpkins from a fine-haired vine. Turning toward the gate, she saw Yonggang enter leading two strangers, one old and the other young. From behind Masui, the older gregariously hailed, "How are you, good elder? Do you know who I am?"

Sunlight leaked through the branches and leaves, dancing in the corner of the graveyard. The young man approached Tao Jiuxiang and said respectfully, "Elder, I am Wang Tong, the eldest grandson of Wang Binquan, and this is my father. He has come to visit you."

Hobbling toward them, Tao Jiuxiang strained her gray-yellow eyes, exclaiming, "Wang Zhengming?" The Wangs had long been regarded as the most outstanding family in Huangshui, but they had paid a price during the revolution: Wang Zhengming had spent long years in prison. But now, looking trim and vital, he smilingly surveyed the vale and the tombs enclosed within the hedges. Deeply moved, he said, "What a beautiful, well-tended garden!"

Contentment swelling within, Tao Jiuxiang looked fondly at the pumpkins in her hands, then set them in her woven bamboo basket. Gazing at the two generations of Wangs, she said, "Earth swallows man, yet man depends upon the earth for his livelihood. Buried under the ground, man's death is eternal, yet eating the fruits of the earth men have subsisted for countless centuries."

Wang Zhengming beamed with delight. He took out a cigarette, lit it, and offered it to Tao Jiuxiang. Tao Jiuxiang shook her head. She drew a pipe from her waistband and tamped down some tobacco in the bowl. Then she extracted a flint from a cloth pouch, and, pinching some dry moxa tinder between the flint and her fingers, rubbed up a spark and lit her pipe. She took a long draw.

"The case of Mawu was mishandled. It will be redressed," Wang Zhengming began, exhaling cigarette smoke. Though small in stature, he was sturdily built. Over his sweater, he wore a gray, collared cadre shirt, unbuttoned; the untucked shirt fluttered in the mountain wind. Though he was hoary-headed, it seemed that that the years had not crushed his spirit. Like his father Wang Binquan back in the day, he sported an impressive goatee.

Sticking out her jaw, Tao Jiuxiang looked at him gravely, saying through gritted teeth, "If my firstborn suffered a grievance at the hands of the government, he will prosper in the afterlife; if my Li family has wronged the government, may I be cut down in nine ways now and here!" Her senescence made the towering fury burning in her eyes all the more terrible.

Wang Tong explained that Wang Zhengming and the commander of another guerrilla force in the mountains on the border of Chongqing and Hubei from back in the 1940s had ended up on the same provincial Communist Party Leadership Committee. The two had locked horns repeatedly. The other man ended up in a higher position and when the revolutionary history of the region was compiled, lots of worthy men from Huangshui were omitted. To redress their unfortunate exclusion, Wang Zhengming had penned a 50,000-character article titled "Blood, Sweat, and Tears: The Revolution in Huangshui," with the intention of submitting it for the tenth anniversary celebration of the establishment of the autonomous county government.

Hunchbacked and frail, Tao Jiuxiang was more than eighty years old, but unlike other doddering, garrulous octogenarians who might prattle on about trivia, her mind remained sharp and flexible. Leading her guests back to the house, she poked around with her bird-like, skeletal hands until she found a dark, bronze-colored key. With trembling hands, she used it to open a lock on a dust-covered, faded black lacquered cabinet and removed a blue bag that Xia Yinmei had placed there many years ago. In the bag was a yellowed photograph, a membership card of the Chinese Communist Party printed with golden sickle-and-hammer on a blue background, and a book titled *A History of the Bolshevik Party in the Soviet Union*.

Wang Zhengming looked at the photograph: it was Kang Dahuai, one of the important Communist leaders in the armed struggle at Huaying Mountain near Chongqing. Kang had died in a skirmish against bandits just before Liberation. Next, he opened the worn cover of the book, smelling the commingled sour scents of tobacco, gunpowder, cooking smoke, sweat, and blood. Underlined in pencil on the dog-eared first leaf was a passage written by Mawu:

Before the Russian Revolution of 1917 (for instance, in 1905), where the old tsarist system presided, conditions were ripe for the formation of a capitalist-democratic republic—indeed this was correct and revolutionary, because, at that time, the formation of a bourgeois-capitalist republic represented progress. Given the current state of the USSR, however, instituting bourgeois-capitalist measures would be both wrong-headed and counterrevolutionary, a serious step backward.

Tao Jiuxiang pointed a wizened finger at the two characters 革命 and said, "Revolution!"

Surprised, Wang Zhengming asked, "Can you read?"

"Mawu taught me those!" Tao Jiuxiang opened her toothless mouth and said proudly, the wrinkles on her face smoothing.

The first character Yonggang had learned was "father"; his mother had taught him. Seeing his father's handwriting, tears coursed down his cheeks. At dinner, they ate melon and fruit from the graveyard garden. That night, sharing liquor with his father's mentor, Wang Zhengming, he got drunk for the first time.

Soughing through the pine trees, the cold night winds blew fiercely down the ridges and shook the tumbledown house on the hump of Gengguping. A chorus of cicadas trilled incessantly. Suddenly, the night sky lit up, becoming ever brighter, with stars and constellations multiplying at exponential speed, a dazzling aurora like the Big Bang at the beginning of the universe. Wide-eyed, watching the night sky lit up brighter than day, Wang Zhengming and his son felt that they had stumbled on a celestial paradise. If only Xia Qifa—capable as the old *tima* was of reading heavenly phenomena and earthly patterns—were still alive, he most certainly would have been inspired, then and there, to improvise a shamanic chant to recall the momentous event.

Wang Zhengming recalled a story that his wise father, Wang Binquan, had often told him as a child. For countless generations, the untrammeled, wild-hearted martial sons and grandsons and great-grandsons of the White Tiger had walked these lands. A vital energy infused these big-hearted valleys and broad-sweeping ridges, the stomping grounds of these bold warriors of the Tribe of the Tiger. When the cruel governance of the despotic last king of Shang brought about a historic revolution, a heartfelt speech by King Wu of Zhou stirred the bold men of Shamanmount and Ba Mountain to action. So galvanized, one ancient starry night the men of the Three Gorges, led by the White Tiger, formed the vanguard and marched forward like an indomitable wind, with ghost warriors at the fore and men behind, throwing themselves headlong into a decisive battle against the powerful armies of the tyrannical Shang king on the wildlands of Muye. Ever surging forward and carving out a swath of blood, the warriors of the Tribe of the Tiger chanted their fearsome battle hymns amid the beating of drums and flashing of swords as monsters, men, and ghosts waged a furious battle. On the stroke of midnight, their enemies' morale cracked and the Shang king's armies surrendered, giving way to the advent of a new Zhou dynasty. At that singular earthshaking moment, a bard accompanying the troops turned his head and beheld a majestic celestial vision: on the stroke of midnight, the sun, the moon, and the stars all illumined the firmament. The gods on high, the bard recognized, were paying homage to King Wu of Zhou.

The night stars, old Wang Binquan had told his son some half a century ago, were more ancient than the earth; the earth, more ancient than the ancestors; the ancestors, more ancient than the myths; and the myths, more ancient than human history. A professional revolutionary educated at Chongqing University, a humbled Wang Zhengming now silently gazed up at the luminous starry night from Gengguping, overwhelmed by the undeniable truth reverberating in his father's words.

Chapter Thirty-One

I

One midday five months later, old Zeng Laomao, fresh out of prison, was holding court at Zhao Changyou's son's teahouse: "So Ev'ry mornin' I had to carry twenty loads of water on a yoke; ev'ry afternoon I hauled six armloads of grass to feed out to the hogs. Thought about throwin' myself into the river to drown, but I'm 'fraid o' water. So I decided to hang myself, but there weren't no rope. Finally, I figured I'd just cut my throat, but turn'd out the knife's blade was too dull . . ." Like caruncles on a turkey, skin drooped down the elderly fellow's neck. While Zeng had been sentenced to fifteen years, a good portion of his sentence had been commuted.

His old comrade, Zhao Changyou, now in his sixties, lived along the main thoroughfare in Huangshui, and helped his son run the small teahouse. Hearing a sudden eruption of firecrackers outside, his hand, holding a tumbler of rice liquor, trembled and the old fellow stammered, "Who died?"

Yonggang and Mingxiu entered, the former carrying a bamboo pole and the latter trailing, carrying a string of firecrackers, its tail rat-a-tat-tating a continuous staccato of explosions: "*Pa-pa-pa-pa—pa-pa-pa-pa—pa-pa-pa-pa—.*" When the firecrackers were spent, Yonggang exulted, "The court just redressed my father's mishandled case! Justice is served! The government finally corrected their mistake: my dad's been rehabilitated! He's a revolutionary . . . the verdict's been reversed!"

"So Li Mawu's case has been redressed?" asked Zeng Laomao, a dim light illumining his eyes.

The Zhao's eldest son waved his hands in the air and stamped in delight, crying out, "Li Yonggang! Li Yonggang! Have a cup of tea! It's on me!"

A new string of firecrackers was mounted on the bamboo pole and lit; acrid smoke rose amid the fresh outburst of crackling, making Yonggang and Mingxiu tear up. Wiping away tears, the young couple entered the teahouse.

When production team leader Qin Shaocheng brought formal notice of the court's reversed verdict and Li Mawu's rehabilitation to Gengguping, Yonggang loosed a wild shout of jubilation. Hearing the tidings, Tao Jiuxiang hobbled over from digging up potatoes in the field, her lips trembling with emotion. She wore a broad-brimmed bamboo hat to shade her from the blazing sun. Breathlessly, she cried out, "Buy firecrackers! Go! Light them up and shout the news from the streets!" So Yonggang and Mingxiu had headed into Huangshui and bought firecrackers, fastening them to the bamboo pole and cheerfully bruited about news of Mawu's redemption.

Eagerly turning to his father, Zhao Changyou's eldest son burbled, "I'm going to Fengjie City, too! If Li Mawu's been rehabilitated, maybe you can be, too!"

Zeng Laomao shook his head, "Don't make no difference to me!" He lived in Peppercorn Bend and had resumed smithing plowshares. He had no aspirations other than continuing to work the bellows, feed the furnace, and pull plowshares from the fire with his tongs.

For several days following Li Yonggang's triumphant announcement of his father's redemption, the sun hung above like a merciless seal impressed into the azure sky. One midday shortly thereafter, the young couple, Yonggang and Mingxiu, after brushing by the undergrowth at the foot of the tower, opened the gate in the hedge surrounding the tomb garden and lit firecrackers before the mounds in the recessed vale to honor their legendary parents, Li Mawu and Xia Yinmei.

The firecrackers startled the flock of sheep resting in the shade of bushes around the garden. Carrying bamboo baskets as they frolicked, Fanwen and the Shi family's little monkey of a grandson came from nowhere, singing a ditty:

The rattan vines of Bashan with leaves long oh so long
Crawling up cliffs and down gullies, they call for their mum.
Mum's so far away, the road is long oh so long,
So poor little rattan hugs a stone and cries for mum.

A luxuriant growth of rattan blanketed the tombs. Watching the breeze play over the rank grass and the rattan creepers stretching from the tomb mounds to climb the hedges, Yonggang smiled, feeling that the funerary park where his parents were buried possessed a mysterious power. Feeling another presence, he turned to find Tao Jiuxiang standing behind the hedge, wiping away tears.

The following dawn, Yonggang and Mingxiu accompanied Tao Jiuxiang to Lihaku, carrying incense, paper, candles, and dry offerings of food for Li Diezhu.

The spring orchids were in full bloom, with long purple stems and lush green leaves. The trio wound their way to Speargrass Plain along the footpath. A chorus of croaking sounded from an overgrown copse. Yonggang approached Li Diezhu's tomb, which he had rebuilt several years ago. For him, stories of the glorious ascendancy of the Lis were but remote legends, far from the penury, starvation, and humiliation that had been his lot.

Rank grass encircled the moss-covered tomb. The stele had been destroyed. After the deaths of her grandson and great-grandson, Old Mother Qin had ordered the out-kitchen dismantled (the cookstove within was left abutting the tomb), but had left the wooden post-and-beam house—which stood on the site that the luminous lotus had flowered—intact.

Hearing a commotion, a tall, rail-thin old woman with a shock of snow-white hair fastened with a blue ribbon stumbled out of the cabin, her face wrinkled and her back crooked. Tao Jiuxiang stepped forward and the two fierce old ladies stared at one another, each sizing up the other.

Neither moving nor betraying the least hint of surprise, Old Mother Qin called out, "So you've come!" as though she had been expecting Tao Jiuxiang all day.

"Yes . . . I'm here," said Tao Jiuxiang, unwaveringly staring at the Qins' house. She turned and tromped toward the tomb.

Old Mother Qin croaked, "I'm here with Liexiong's wife. No ghost or man is gonna chase us off!" With these words, she picked her way along up a slope and squatted beside aging Zhou Ermei, then slowly started breaking apart manure balls to fertilize the rows of vegetables in their garden.

"What a green thumb you have, good elder!" Yonggang praised her, impressed that this hale eighty-one-year-old matriarch of the Qin family, whose sons and grandsons had dropped one after another, now lived with ghosts for neighbors, in the shadow of the coffins hanging from the cliffs.

Tao Jiuxiang looked at the bent figure of Old Mother Qin, sighing, "Time is cruel, but that woman will never give in!" She knelt before her husband's tomb.

In the decades since the two geomancers—men long since perished, their souls drifting back to the ancestral mountains—had dowsed on this little parcel the presence of a precious underground grotto of dragons and tigers that augured a glorious fortune, the Lis had encountered a nigh unbroken string of catastrophes.

II

A staunch woman, toothless and slack-jowled, Tao Jiuxiang sat on the stoop, basking in the sun. Her face—creased by time, sorrow, and anxiety—had grown smooth. As she chanted, as she peeled off her worn short gown looking for fleas, exposing her wrinkled, sagging upper torso.

Mingxiu asked Yonggang, "What's grandma chanting? She seems asleep, but she's half-groaning, half-weeping."

Yonggang pressed an ear close to Tao Jiuxiang's mouth, and said, "She's singing:

> *Comin' from the shoal in the valley at the cliff's foot where the carp are gathering ...*

One day Yonggang's seven-year-old son Fanwen saw Tao Jiuxiang chanting like this and sealed a bamboo bee in a segment of bamboo. The moment the bee began buzzing he set the vibrating bamboo in his great-grandmother's lap, awakening the old woman with a start. Thinking he was merely being naughty, she crossly snapped, "Why don't you just go out and play?"

Fanwen replied matter-of-factly, "I'm afraid you're going die."

Tao Jiuxiang's lonely eyes blazed. Addressing her great-grandson in a purr, she said, "I won't die. When a tiger turns five hundred years old, its fur turns white. They can live a thousand years."

The little fellow turned to Tao Jiuxiang and said excitedly, "Mom told me that if an elder crawls into one of those hanging coffins on the cliffs—the 'caves of the immortals'—for seven days and seven nights they can shed their old skin and turn young. Great-grandma, why don't you go sleep in the 'cave of the immortals' and get young again?"

Softly, skinny and unkempt Tao Jiuxiang answered, "Yes, it's time for me to sleep in a cave of the immortals."

Suddenly, Fanwen asked, "Grandma, What does revolution mean?"

Tao Jiuxiang growled, "Revolution means killing—slaughtering people . . . why?"

Fanwen said, "Dad says my grandpa was an old revolutionary."

Tao Jiuxiang said, "He was."

Curious, Fanwen pursued, "So did Grandpa kill anybody?"

Hesitating, Tao Jiuxiang answered, "Yes, he did."

Blinking his spirited eyes, Fanwen asked, "What kind of men did he kill?"

The apparition of long-deceased Qin Liexiong appeared before her, raising his bloody stump of a leg to strap on armor. Behind him other nebulous spirit soldiers clad themselves in armor, readying themselves for battle. With a coarse rasp of a laugh, Liexiong gargled, "I've sent your husband to the netherworld and I'm coming for you next . . ." Outside the sky blackened. Gusts of wind whistled through the branches and leaves. Untranquil deaths ruptured the fabric of the mortal world. Uneasily, Tao Jiuxiang recalled all the bloodcurdling imprecations she had uttered over the years—cursing those who had robbed the stone tower, damning those who had desecrated the family graves, casting maledictions against those who had burned the *tima's* ritual instruments. Now her days were numbered, and their vengeful spirits were massing. Who would set up a ghost-expelling banner for her, clearing for her spirit the path to paradise and dispelling these baleful influences?

And after all these years spattered in blood and stained in sweat, she thought once more of her firstborn. No one was left to raise the soul banners and placate the anguished spirits of Mawu and Yinmei. The gifted Xia Qifa was no more. His son Xia Liangxian had been cast from the lineage of *timas*. Daoist Master Wang had died in poverty and obscurity. The piteous couple was left to haunt the gorges and crags of Huangshui with other aggrieved spirits.

Gloomily, she turned to Fanwen and sighed, "Your Grandfather . . . killed counterrevolutionaries . . ."

Fanwen's face clouded with doubt.

After a rainshower, the sun reemerged. In the little paddock near the compound, new life had entered the world. Masui's cow had calved. The wet newborn calf quivered, struggling to stand, its flanks breaded in red clay. Moving in a circle, the calf staggered, unable to keep its balance. It plopped back on its rear haunches for a moment, then scrabbled to its feet again. Old folks in Huangshui sometimes say that a newborn calf bows in every direction to pray for the protection of the gods.

With hoe and a spade, Yonggang prepared Tao Jiuxiang's tomb in the funerary park. He lined the burial chamber with bricks and stone slabs and mounded dirt over the grave chamber. On top of the mound he planted trees, flowers, and grass as a buffer from the wind and sun. Fanwen skipped and jumped around the fruit trees, watching Yonggang work.

Above, the warm sun shone down on the cursed horse mulberries on the slopes, transformed from towering trees into stubbly bushes, and on the hard-toiling descendants of the Ox King. Setting down his hoe, Yonggang called to Mingxiu, who was doing some washing nearby, "You'd better go and pick up some mushrooms for supper."

Shadow and light played over the dark mountains. After the rains, an array of mushrooms emerged, carpeting the ground and upholstering the trunks of trees—the caps of some larger than inverted ricebowls, others looking like colorful embroidered skirts, and still others like pale jackstrawed grass. Mingxiu blew on the gills of the mushrooms: edible ones gave a clear, sharp whistle, while poisonous ones gave off a full, sonorous sound.

Returning home with a basketful, she saw the pointed tip of Tao Jiuxiang's bamboo hat peeking from the ocean of corn on the slope. Sheathed by luxuriant broad leaves and budding ears, the chest-high cornstalks stretched toward the sun. Standing motionless, Tao Jiuxiang rested, propped on her hoe, crooked body bathing in the eternal sunshine, flyaway white hair undulating gently in the wind like the silky tassels of corn.

"Granny," Mingxiu knew that Tao Jiuxiang was a bit deaf. She approached the old woman and called aloud, "Granny! Granny! . . ."

As she approached, Mingxiu saw that Tao Jiuxiang's pupils were as white as her eyeballs. Mingxiu had heard that one who ground a crow's eyeballs into powder and rubbed it into their eyes might see the events in the earthly world from the other side. Perhaps Tao Jiuxiang had done this. The thought frightened her.

At eighty-five, Tao Jiuxiang, the most stubborn, iron-willed figure in the annals of Huangshui, had passed into the netherworld to meet Yama with her eyes wide open, like a tigress.

Epilogue

I

The meandering Yangzi River churned furiously between the lofty escarpments of Kuimen, howling and rushing as it surged through the narrow gorge, a violent succession of turbulent rapids and whirlpools. As the imposing walls of rock emerged from the morning mist, one of the offspring of Gengguping, who had over the years scattered across China like wind-borne seeds, single-mindedly typed on her computer:

> *Across a thousand miles of rugged mountains the Tribe of the Tiger built their dwellings. Though now these once-fierce people are withering like dried leaves, their remarkable, sanguine history, yet unknown to the outside world, played out for centuries in the cloud-and-mist enveloped primeval forests of the mountain slopes and along the countless tributaries—the capillaries and arteries of water cutting through gorges. Coffins of their ancestors dangle from sheer cliffs. With the new dam, soon almost every vestige—even the verdure of the valleys and the precipitous walls of rock—will be submerged under the rising Yangzi.*

The mountainfolk called standing, vertical waters "rain," and lying, horizontal water "river," a difference just as significant as that between mountain ridges and underground grottoes. She rose and poured some bottled water into a glass, then stared fixedly at it. Raising her head from the computer the woman recalled reading that a quantum physicist, having observed water crystals with high-speed photography, had concluded that water had the capacity to replicate and recall information. Does science, then, help explain how a *tima*'s blessings can tranquilize water, while his angry curse can make water turbid? In Dr. Emoto's experiment, which shocked the world, water crystals, hearing tango music, would dance in pairs. Perhaps Emoto's experiment explained the mystery behind a puzzling story her mother Yongyu told her on a moonless summer night in Chongqing. Once when her grandmother Jin was a little girl, she had an infected sore and a fever. The shaman Xia Qifa pasted a piece of straw paper on the wall, then stood two arms-lengths away from the paper holding a bowl of water. After incanting sutras, he shaped his free hand into a mudra. Then and there, a pattern of water similar to the mudra appeared on the paper. Jin drank the water from the bowl; the following day her sore was cured.

Most of the convoluted history of the Tribe of the Tiger, the most ancient people in all of Asia, is lost; their labyrinthine genealogies are unknown. Set precisely at 30 degrees latitude, Lihaku remains a mystery, defying human science and knowledge. Recently, in the region, a team of geologists discovered a complicated, interconnected system of underground caves and waterways stretching thirty miles, a vast network of karst formations that reached Dragon Decapitating Gorge, the valley where the *tima* Xia Qifa was buried. For billions of years, because of the geological leakage, water had flowed from the underground river through the dragon cave beneath Lihaku.

How did the forefathers of the Tribe of the Tiger, on mere canoes and punts, succeed in passing through treacherous, turbulent Kuimen, Gate of the Thunderous One-Footed Dragon, and continue eastward along the Yangzi River? The answer was that their clever ancestors had never passed through Kuimen! Availing themselves of the hidden, underground waterways, they had circumvented it! When Jin was alive, she told Yongyu many stories about the wicked dragon that had devoured the river waters and about Xia Qifa's storied battles against the creature. Truly, the legendary shaman had met a worthy adversary.

Since graduating from a university in Beijing, she had spent more than a decade utilizing mythology to try to unravel the history of her people. Recently, she had been selected as the Chinese representative to a massive international research project titled *A Comparative Study of Asian Folklore*.

Soon, she would head back to the project's research center in Hiroshima. Before she left, however, she needed to return to Huangshui to seek her roots.

While the gods enjoyed themselves, wandering the lands and roaming the skies, the mountains simply stood rooted in the earth. In the *Classic of Mountains and Seas*, a geographical treatise more than 2,000 years old, it is recorded that in ancient times famous shamans gathered on Danshan—or as some called it Shamanmount—a mountain of mercury filled with cinnabar that could grant a man immortality. The chief shaman there was Wu Xian, son of Fuxi, the earliest progenitor of the Chinese people; in the old folk songs he was called "Bird Xian." It was said that in his final hours, an impoverished and diseased Xia Qifa, peering forth from his sunken eyes, had delineated a clear genealogy of the Tribe of the Tiger: Bird Xian begot Cheng Li, Cheng Li begot Hou Zao, and Hou Zao begot the Tiger people. Their bloodline, then, was a glorious lineage stretching back to Fuxi, the progenitor of mankind and one of the legendary Three Sovereigns.

On she wrote:

> It was said that they were the offspring of the White Tiger. Based on advanced studies in ancient etymology and phonology, some scholars contend that "Fuxi" and "White Tiger" are two names for the same figure. As tigers were called "dukes of Ba" at that time, the descendants of the tiger became known as the people of Ba. According to a legend, one early morn as a blood sun rose in the east, the Immortal White Tiger, sword in hand, led the Tribe of the Tiger forth from the stone caves. After endless campaigns and battles, they carved out an empire in the gorges along the Yangzi. When they were defeated, they simply disappeared. One legend claims that on the verge of their doom the tribe soared up to the White Tiger Star, leaving behind a horrible prophecy foretelling that all future dwellers in the land upon which that star shed light would meet with repeated scourges and exterminations until the Tribe of the Tiger were reborn from this litany of blood. One legend says that they scattered and fled far away along the streams and tributaries of the ancient Yangzi, taking with them the legendary River Chart designed by flood-queller Yu the Great, first emperor of the Xia dynasty of old. As they departed, they left behind a sorrowful song:

Heavenly fire burns the sun,
Earthly fire scorches forests and sand;
Righteous lightning fire
Immolates all the wicked in this land.
Into the river we launch dragon boats,
There's nowhere in the five lakes and four seas we can't float.

Over the millennia, the migrations of the Immortal White Tiger and his offspring, their defeats and victories, left stories scored into the land itself, encoded on the rugged gorges and valleys where they battled and tilled, loved and struggled.

Inspired by the strange and wonderful legends of her hometown, she went on tapping on her keyboard:

Far, far away, to the east of the Bohai Sea there is a bottomless gully.
In this deep, deep gulch all of the waters from earth, the sky, and the sea
converge . . ." According to the ancient sage Liezi, the Milky Way above
and earth below were both connected to the sea. Hence, no matter where
the generations of the Tribe of the Tiger went—whether into the grottoes
beneath the earth, up to the stars, or out to the vast sea—they ended up in
the same place.

II

One arriving from the civilized world, from Chongqing or Beijing, to confront the sheer gorges and lofty mountains, cannot but be stricken breathless. While over the past half-century her mother Yongyu had recounted tales of Huangshui countless times, only now, a decade after her mother's death, had she finally resolved to seek her roots and return to her ancestral home.

Yonggang arrived in the depot at Fengjie City on a motorcycle to pick her up. After passing through Huangshui, there was no road marking the home stretch to the rhino's rump of Gengguping. An ill-defined trail threaded over ridges and through vales. Looking down from the azure sky like a huge tiger's head, a lone swelling, pearly cloud glowed.

Compared to the dilapidated stone tower covered in creepers and rattan, hidden among dense clumps of brush, the Li family's homestead on

Gengguping—while it had not recovered its previous magnificence—was not in bad repair. Hearing the puttering of Yonggang's motorcycle, several cousins, nephews, and nieces swarmed out to greet her. They gawped at her, studying her face and features, bluntly searching for some trait that made manifest their shared blood.

"Aaah…you're Yongyu's child?" Masui emerged from a doorway, supported by Yongguang. He had become an old man with white hair and a wispy white beard.

Touched, she called out, "Great Uncle," for the first time. However, at that very moment a sonic trilling, "*Aaao-wooo,*" emanated from her body. The howl came again, and again.

Startled and bewildered, Masui leaned heavily against Yongguang.

"*Aaaoo-wooo.*" As the howls continued, her cousins, nephews, and nieces stared dumbly. All of her grandmother Jin's stories came flooding back; recognizing the incongruity of her tiger ringtone in these mountains, she felt an acute pang of embarrassment.

"Sorry." She took out her cell phone and hurriedly excused herself to take an international call from a Japanese colleague at Hiroshima University seeking her assistance in coordinating a conference where people involved in the comparative folklore project might share fieldwork. They were puzzling over the overlapping permutations of the same legends that were told and the curious variations of the same rituals that were performed in many parts of East and Southeast Asia.

Seemingly oblivious to the fact that China and Japan had engaged in a fierce battle where the gorge walls rose and the river bent, her Japanese colleague was engaged in a comprehensive study of ancient and historical migrations from the Yangzi River Valley. According to human leucocyte antigen testing, a portion of the population from his archipelagic nation, which legends told was formed by coagulating brine dripping off a spear, shared a common genetic profile with men and women in southern China. Acting as the culture consultant for the Japanese government, he had put together a well-received documentary titled *Life Goes On: Ancestry, Migration, and Genetics in Greater East Asia.*

"You need to come to Lihaku to investigate," she replied. "And soon…before they put in the dam. If you can, bring me more materials on primitive rites in Japan, and anything you have on *yin-yang* talismans." Quickly changing her ringtone to a pop song, she entered the house.

Hands moist with perspiration, she offered incense at a small altar set in a votive niche beneath a vivid painted face of a tiger. In the local dialect, "tiger" was pronounced "*li*"—the same as the *li* in Lihaku . . . the Li passed down as their family name. Mountainfolk still worshiped this tutelary god in every household, reverently calling him Lord Tiger or Lord of the Granary. When performing a sacrifice, the *tima* of these people who seemed to exist in a world outside of time would pierce his forehead to offer a blood libation to this carnivorous ancestor.

Gradually calming, Masui gazed at the stranger, his grandniece.

Beneath an oily yellow sheen, mushrooms and chicken simmered over the fire. While the cauldron looked ancient, the food smelled fresh and savory. Yonggang sautéed mushrooms together with cured meat and dried chili peppers in a wok.

Over dinner, wizened Masui, overwrought with drink, posed a question: "So, there's a pair of tigers up on a slope—same color, pattern, and size. How do you tell the tiger and the tigress apart?"

Looking back and forth at each other, the family members answered, "We don't know."

Pleased, Masui asked, "Well, grandniece from the big city, what do you think?"

Looking at the kinsmen who had lived all their lives on these grass-covered slopes, she sincerely inquired, "How do you tell them apart, Grand Uncle?"

"Well, the quiet, motionless one is the tigress," said Masui, holding back a smile, "and the pacing, active one is the tiger."

Sitting outside later in the dim, flickering light of the oil lamp, she dragged her fingers through the tall speargrass—this grass capable of sheltering tigers and binding flood dragons. In the heavy mists and moist air, spirits still lingered. The lives of her grandparents and great-grandparents, their happiness and suffering, were bound up in this grass; her very existence in this wonderful and cruel world was connected to these blades of speargrass. Within months, or maybe a few years, almost every trace of these swaths of speargrass, these wild lands, would be submerged by the construction of the massive new dam, the greatest hydro-engineering project in human history, an endeavor that promised to scour virtually every vestige of the Tribe of the Tiger from the scarred and pocked face of the earth. Such is the way of the world: the past is irretrievably lost, leaving behind all that has gone; and time ineluctably marches forward, bringing what it will.

Not a soul was around. She climbed the original horse mulberry tree—tall and straight—up to the heavens, roaming, wandering in the direction of the White Tiger, toward the seven constellations of the west. Though no fields were visible, the incessant croaking of frogs and warbling of birds sounded in the mists. Nearly tripping over the winding rattan, she stumbled through the gates of a celestial palace. Clouds and fog drifted to and fro, coalescing then dispersing.

As the rising sun outlined the clouds with a fringe of gold, she saw through the mists the vague contours of the forest in distance. Perhaps finally the scions of the White Tiger had finally bid farewell to their sanguine past, their endless cycle of carnage and bloodshed.

At Gengguping, she was unable to tell heaven from earth, dream from reality; in the dense clouds and fog there was no trace of man, no history, and no memory. The past and future of these mountains and gorges were hidden. Amid these towering mountains, her presence seemed transitory, a mere illusion.

From the mists, echoing off the mountains, came a faint, singsong chant:

> *A hundred battles, eh, endless battlefields, eh-way-yah*
> *The jackals and wolves, eh, have been driven away, eh-way-yah.*
> *We've moved mountains, way-yah, zuo-way.*
> *Through ten thousand hardships, way-yo, and bitter suffering, eh,*
> *Way-yay-ya-way-zuo-yo, we've never lost heart, eh.*
> *We've moved mountains, way-yah, our spirit unbroken, zuo-way, eh.*
> *Way-ya, zuo-eh...*

About the Author

Fang Qi, a celebrated author and anthropological researcher, has devoted more than a decade to unearthing and archiving the rich mythology and shamanic lore of the Yangzi region. The original Chinese *Elegy of a River Shaman* has gone through four printings. The government has designated her collected materials on oral folklore a "Masterpiece of the Cultural Heritage."

More information can be found at her website: www.shamansong.org.

About the Translators

Norman Harry Rothschild, from a hill farm in western Maine, graduated from Harvard University with a B.A. in East Asian Languages and Civilizations and earned a doctorate from Brown University in Chinese history. He is currently a Professor of Chinese History at the University of North Florida. He has written several books on Wu Zhao, China's first and only female emperor and published articles exploring dimensions of religion, politics, ethnicity, gender, and environmental history in medieval China.

Meng Fanjun, a native of Shandong Province, China, is a graduate of Peking University with a doctorate in Translation Studies. After several post-doctoral years at Beijing Normal University, he took a position at the College of International Studies in Chongqing's Southwest University. He has translated or co-translated Spenser's *Hymne of Heavenly Beauty* and the *Complete Works of Shakespeare*; other translations include the canonical *Three-Character Classic, A Yankee on the Yangtze River, Chinese Stone Carvings*, and *Heritage of the Chinese Culture*.